ISLAND IN THE ATLANTIC

ISLAND
in the
ATLANTIC

A Novel by

WALDO FRANK, David 1889 ~ 1967

GREENWOOD PRESS, PUBLISHERS
WESTPORT, CONNECTICUT

Copyright 1946 by Waldo Frank

Reprinted by permission
of Duell, Sloane & Pearce

First Greenwood Reprinting 1970

Library of Congress Catalogue Card Number 73-104243

SBN 8371-3925-2

Printed in United States of America

To my father and mother

Turn you to the Stronghold,
ye prisoners of hope.

— *Zechariah*

In the eye of the Eternal, each man's life is a day.

— *Mayan rubric*

CONTENTS

PART ONE: MORNING

I

HOPE

THE BOY PLACED LIEBER'S *CIVIL LIBERTY AND SELF Government* with his notes in the slant-top desk that opened upward, and went into the hall. He had heard right: it was his father, home this early Monday afternoon; his father and mother were downstairs in the front hall! Jonathan could not make out what they were saying, but their excited murmur joined his impression of the sky, fevered and sullen, that he had watched while he worked. His weight on the banister to keep the stair from creaking, he stole down to the second floor; ashamed, not that he wanted to hear (he had the right to hear what was said in his house), but that he studied with so little concentration as to have heard at all. Perhaps New York was burning, but —When I work, I should hear nothing.

He heard: ". . . Brooks Brothers . . . flames . . . broken the windows in Mayor Opdyke's house on the Fifth Avenue." His father, still talking, followed the silent mother up the stairs.

"Jonathan!" she rebuked her son.

The boy glanced guiltily at his mother, and as usual when his father returned from business kissed the soft cheek under the black beard.

"Haven't you your work?" said Sarah Hartt, her eyes beneath the pure gray hair hard in the light from the opened bedroom. She was one height with both her man and her fifteen-year-old son.

"Tell him," said Joseph Hartt. "He's got a right to know." When the mother said nothing: "It's terrible, Jonathan; they're hanging the

3

poor Negroes. They say the Colored Orphan Asylum on Forty-second Street is gone."

Jonathan thought of General Lee perhaps outflanking Meade from Gettysburg in Pennsylvania: "Not the Rebels?"

"The scum," said his mother. "Our own Irish scum."

Joseph Hartt, his pale blue eyes upward, swayed as when he prayed in synagogue; his bare upper lip trembled.

"It's the draft!" Jonathan pondered aloud. "It's that three-hundred-dollar bounty, excusing the rich."

"It's an excuse for low-lives to plunder and drink," said Mrs. Hartt.

"They're forgetting the draft." The father spoke gently. "They're forgetting the strike of the longshoremen and the poor ignorant darkies they put to work on the ships. They're after the whole city."

"Like the French Revolution!" the boy exclaimed.

"Our troops will settle their 'French Revolution'! . . . Joseph, they won't touch *your* place?"

"They're not troubling with us little fellows."

Reassured, she turned to her son: "Go back to your work; *learn* about your 'French Revolution'!"

From the shadowed hall the boy saw the July sun in his parents' room pierce the bay window and inflame the broad mahogany bed where his father and mother (so different!) slept together. He went back upstairs to his own domain, the room he shared with his two brothers. The smoldering world outside the windows made the room suddenly unreal. Unreal was Reuben, nineteen and already a full-fledged businessman; no fear had driven *him* home, doubtless he'd make a good thing of the trouble. And unreal, too, was Philip, the family 'baby,' whom their mother let sleep mornings when there was no school (he had an uncommon love of sleep) and loaf all day through the summer. At this moment, while *he* was supposed to study, Philip and Lucia were enjoying the hot afternoon at the Sleip farm, 'way out on the Bloomingdale Road near Sixty-second Street. Philip was probably catching butterflies, perhaps they were drinking ice-cold lemonade. "Study!" he heard his mother's voice. "Do you want to have to go into *business* like your poor father? like Reuben? no doubt like little Philip?" (His twelve-year-old brother's talent was with animals: he could catch butterflies and frogs with his bare hands, as if the

4

creatures knew he would let them go unhurt; and all the neighborhood cats and dogs adored him.) Only his poor father who did not
know much was somehow part of what was happening; because he
thought *he* had a right to know.

Jonathan kept his eyes from his desk and climbed the seat at the
dormer window. This, by treaty with his brothers, was his territory.
On its one wall, General McClellan in a slouch hat reviewed his Army
of the Potomac (cut from Frank Leslie's weekly magazine); on the
other reigned Thomas Jefferson, Jonathan's god of righteousness and
reason. And between, through the window, the brick and brownstone city seethed in summer and smoke. Mother, noblest of women,
did not know everything. Even in Jefferson's America, democracy
was not yet perfect: look at Tammany and the Rebels. Even in free
America, even with the slaves all free, there might still remain *some*
unfinished business from the American and French Revolutions.
"Study and learn": his mother's voice. But it wasn't all in books. The
boy scarcely sensed that he was answering his mother, as he shut
the window (there were bound to be thunder showers in this sultry
air), and without a glance at his desk closed the door of his room
behind him. In the bedroom below, their door shut, his mother gave
a quiet command or judgment to her husband. He snatched his cap
from the twisted oak peg of the rack in the front hall, and stood
free on the street.

The change in his world struck him. To the west, as always, Stuyvesant Square: the same trees, the same lofty brownstone church and
squat red House of Friends; but no child romped on the grass, no
cart rumbled on the cobbles, and the old blue haze of his city was
reddened into fever. As if in search of bearings, he turned north in the
Second Avenue. Windows were down, awnings reefed, despite the
heat; Lancy's provision store was locked; the wooden Indian before
the tobacco shop, where his father bought his evening cigar, lay on its
face, the tomahawk smiting the pavement. A cab careened into view,
terror in the flogged horses, hoof and iron-rimmed wheel lesioning
the city's silence. Far ahead, smoke purpled on the buildings; the sun
over his left shoulder was a disc of blood-hot metal. Jonathan knew of
conflict and war; all his life he had read of them remote in books;
still remote, although nearer, in newspapers and table-talk. The real

5

was the peace in his home, the reasonableness of teachers. Now he was less sure. A woman and three men came close, the grime of their clothes and faces familiar from what he had seen in the slums of the Five Points, of Rotten Row near Grand Street, of Ragpicker's Row off Second Street where last winter he had found himself ambushed by toughs who put stones and bits of brick in their snowballs. As the four lurched past, he saw their eyes, and there was hate in them and a still more frightening exultance. He walked on a few steps, stopped, and looked back—toward the desk he had left and his mother's commandments he had broken. The woman and men had stopped, and turned too. They were drunk. He saw their mouths, cursing him. Gun-fire hammered uptown.

"Dude!" cried the woman, and raised the handle of a burnt broom; the men—a poker, a shovel, an axe in their hands—followed the woman toward him. Jonathan stood between the gunshots uptown, silent but still loud in his mind, and the curses. From behind the iron railing of an areaway, a woman's voice: "Leave the lad be! he ain't no nigger." The broom laughed and swept off the second woman's hat. Jonathan saw the red cheeks of his defender; he knew what *she* was. He walked quickly away, ashamed of what he owed a 'painted woman.' —I won't run! A block farther uptown, more and more stragglers; torn clothes and blood. A tall girl half dragged her hurt father; his filthy hand clasping her blouse for support bared her breast. No one now noticed the boy; from where they came, hurry was blowing like a wind and in the thickening smoke he felt the throb of anger.

He stopped at Twenty-third Street, where the cars on their long trot to Harlem crossed from the First Avenue to the Second. Along the rails' curve, one lay on its side, its windows shattered, and in a pool of viscid blood that caught the sun a woman's straw bonnet. Beneath the awning of a feed store stood the two unhitched horses and quietly feasted at a bale of hay. Men and women, in directions seemingly aimless, were blobs of dark heat in the bright heat of the square, and the boy thought of last summer at Cape May: the long beach, the sun's gold strokes as on a drum, the ladies with wet skirts clinging to their thighs. A block north, the loose avenue of brick and wood grimly tightened with a milling mass of bodies and Jona-

6

than saw flames in a long gray building. Suddenly, as the mob gathered him in, he was no longer afraid. In the gaunt roiled street, he felt the beach and the sea; in this anger, he felt a tenderness. A man in an old frock coat and battered stovepipe hat wielded a pitchfork; a man in mechanic's rig brandished a hammer; a woman, her blue skirt swishing, held a small pot with one geranium, while her voice like a cracked bell pealed *Only a Faded Flower;* an old soldier in the rusted fatigue uniform of the Mexican War stood marking time with his feet. . . . And it was to the boy the city summering—Cape May. A cut telegraph pole barred the street before the burning structure; the mob leaped it, became thick beneath the smoke of the gray structure. The tenderness was the anger.

"Thot ain't no arsenal; 'tis a laundry." The mob paused and with a new eye turned around (what had been its rear now its head) to the five-story flat-roof building across the street with soldiers in blue at some of the upper windows. "Don't fire it! We want the muskets." . . . At last: "Storm it!" But the mob in its forward limits did not budge; its energies swirled within itself, an amorphous creature that could grow fangs and eyes on all its surfaces. Now, from its center, a huge man with a red beard raveled it, pushing through. Free at its edge under the arsenal, he raised a blacksmith's hammer and strode to the door. A great blow rang; the next splintered fragments of wood; then the door burst, the crowd ejaculated forward, and as suddenly stopped again as shots spat from the soldiers at the upper windows. A man writhed in his blood toward Jonathan, women shrieked; again the dozen muskets of the corporal's guard licked at the body of the mob. Jonathan heard it heave like a hurt and winded beast. At the farthest edge where he stood was an iron fence that shut a green lawn, a private house, in incongruous peace. He saw a young man in overalls with bare blond head mount the stone base of the fence, whose spearhead points were above the height of his shoulders.

"Men!" His voice turned a hundred nearest to him. "Brothers and sisters!" The second round of shots—not repeated—had hollowed a concave silence. "This is your city, those are your guns. They belong to you. The city belongs to you. You've a right to take it over. But orderly, men! Don't use the kind of weapon that can be used against you." Forward—a repercussion of the now silent guns—the mob was

7

suddenly cataracted through the arsenal's smashed door, but at this farther edge the gold-haired young man drew a counter movement. Voices muddied his words: ". . . but don't—but don't. . . ." The murmur against him mounted. His bare throat tensed, he touched it with his hand to ease it, and the crowd with exquisite speed saw it was a fine hand and beneath the workman's shirt saw a delicate undergarment. "Silk-stocking!" someone shouted. The edge of the crowd thickened and rose to him . . . lifted the man. Jonathan saw as the head tilted upward his eyelids soft like a child's. Jonathan heard a groan, a visceral dark joy; the crowd lurched back toward the arsenal, leaving the·man who had cried "brothers . . . sisters" speared on the grill, his body crumpled and shrunken, sagging from the iron spearpoint through his neck and throat like a rag doll downward, except his face—white above blood—which rose from the iron like a flower on its stem.

A new vast silence spread from the tortured body, pushing back the pandemonium of the street. The rioters were overrunning the first floor of the arsenal. Some hurled muskets and pistols to the street; some forgot their purpose and set fires that now tongued the windows. Soldiers, suddenly framed in glare, vanished; rioters stood on the sills staring after the guns they had flung down; the flames licked the roof, men with frantic feet vaulted its parapet and leaped. The thudding bodies sobered the mob in the street; the red disc of the sun behind them paled as the huge bonfire burgeoned.

All was one instant for Jonathan; in the next he must die or get away. He ran blindly, and collided with a boy—a boy before him, who, he knew in the same instant of knowing he would not die, was not of the mob.

"Sorry, I—"

"Sorry—"

They spoke, and stopped, at the same moment; each knowing it was he who had run into the other, each feeling far beneath consciousness how the instant annealed them together.

"I guess I was scared," said the boy.

"I guess *I* was," said Jonathan.

The mob—men in blood, women in tears—broke past them; the arsenal behind retched and heaved flame; the boys walked in their own one silence. Jonathan felt his body whole like a song. Swimming

8

in the sea or afloat on his back with last summer's sun in his face, drinking cold milk at a farmhouse after a tramp through the body-warm meadows, marking *Q.E.D.* at the foot of a stiff geometry problem, agreeing with a page of Daniel Webster on the Indissoluble Union, lying in his bed ready for sleep: it was all here in this joy, it was all nothing beside this. He had never before seen this youth beside him, who had come with his own life returning—sweet and close as his life returning after the storm. The boy was fair as he was dark, taller, perhaps a little older, his hemp-pale hair rumpled and his handsome blue suit soiled. He had the same strangeness of his life returning. They walked more slowly when the mob had gone, and not a word was spoken.

At Gramercy Park the blond boy led to a gray stone house high on its own lawn. He took the gravel path past iron figures of a deer, a dog, a little Negro in painted jockey colors, to the stable with ivied walls and a quaint thatch roof. The boy opened the door; Jonathan in the cool shadow suddenly felt faint.

"Have a chair. Paddy!"

Heavy harness dropped next door with a clatter, and a stable boy showed his round face. "Young guv'nor, where've yez been!"

"Where's your old man?"

"The Blessed Virgin who knows keep him! He says to me, 'Water the hosses and polish the tandem harness. There'll be no drivin' this day.' And out he goes."

"Got any beer? Bring three bottles."

Jonathan in the dizzy shade saw the framed trotters and pacers on the walls, smelled the sweet emulsion of leather and manure. There was a cave in his stomach. He gulped the bitter beer; his head was a kite in a fresh wind, the kite's tail was his body.

The Irish lad drank his beer, visibly embarrassed and honored. —He's a servant. *I* must not feel honored.

"What are they afther doin'?"

His young gentleman wiped foam from his lips and trilled the fingers of his left hand like fiddling. "God, it was wonderful!"

"What was it, now?"

"It was a glory."

"Is it all over, then?"

9

"I hope not. It's just beginning."

"For the love o' the Saints, what is it just beginnin'?"

"Who cares? They're burning. They're looting."

Paddy's quick blue eyes went out the window up the walk to the gray mansion that stood a thousand miles from trouble. "Ain't you scairt?"

"Sure I was—for my skin. Oh, you mean for *this?*" His eyes had followed Paddy's. "Let them burn this for all I care." He put his drained glass on the floor, jumped up, still trilling the fingers of his left hand, and to Jonathan: "I never knew, the city's got a soul! Oh, beautiful." He felt Paddy skeptical, and turned to him again. "They killed a man; spitted him on the iron fence. Men bounced out of the burning windows like rubber balls. When they hit the pavement, they kept on bouncing." His feet traced a quiet jig.

"D'yez think they may be afther comin' here?"

"Why not?"

"Mebbe ye'll not be knowin', Master Evan, the Missus, yer lady mother, is up in her bed sick."

Evan's dancing fingers withered into a fist. "We've got to rescue her. Where will we rescue her *to?*"

Paddy stared; Jonathan needed to reassure his friend: "What they're burning, it's only big places."

"My father's Grosvenor Cleeve. My house is a big place."

The three lads stood close in the danger, which diverging reasons made a joy for them. "My house would be safer!" exclaimed Jonathan before he knew it. "It's not a big place. I live on Fifteenth Street near the First Avenue. My mother would be happy to hide your mother."

"Come on, then!" cried Evan and ran to the door: stopped short by a tall gentleman who opened it and stepped in.

Grosvenor Cleeve was a man in the portly middle forties. On his head was a sleek beaver hat, and he carried a gold-knobbed cane. The linen of his shirt and stock, despite the heat, was flawless. "Where are you going in such a hurry?" his deep voice rumbled; the only part of him, it seemed, that sweated.

Evan, silent and sulky, turned back and sat down, staring at the floor. Paddy slid toward the door leading to the stalls, from which he had come.

"You've been in the streets, I see. No place for gentlemen today, I venture to suggest." His eyes graciously swept Jonathan into the compliment. "Yet maybe it's just as well. You'll get an inkling, you young electors of tomorrow, what problems we face in our Republic. But it's no use losing your heads, that's just what we must never do. Who is your friend, Evan? Why don't you introduce him?"

"My name is Hartt."

"Hart," repeated Mr. Cleeve. "Not the Peabody Harts?"

"No, sir. My father—"

Mr. Cleeve waved his free hand. "No need, sir; and no difference." He had estimated the boy's black unruly hair, the full lips, the heavy eyes that brooded in a language alien to the Anglo-Saxon. "This is a land of opportunity, not pedigrees. You're an American citizen, that's enough for me. A future sovereign of our country, may God save it!" He held out his hand, and Jonathan, taking it, felt the gold seal ring. "I'm glad my son thought of the beer. These are thirsty days, sir. You're welcome, sir, in my home; but why the stables?" He turned back to Evan and let his glance slide on. "Paddy," he added sharply, "what do you mean by drinking with your masters?"

Paddy clutched his bottle and glass.

"I invited him to join us." Evan kept his eyes on the floor.

"All over the city, certain sections of the population have gotten temporarily out of hand. Among other things, they're breaking into the saloons and filling themselves with liquor. So fear makes *you invite* them—"

"Who's afraid?"

"Well, get over it and remember your place, sir. You're not a child any more. Boys no older than you are fighting in both armies. War brings squalls like this. Some of our victorious troops from Pennsylvania will ferry across the river tomorrow. But we're not waiting for them. No doubt, when they get here, we'll not need them. I'm on my way now to a small meeting at the Mayor's; the Governor will be there." He looked piercingly at Paddy. "Archbishop Hughes has addressed a message to his flock from his sickbed. The poor great man is crippled with rheumatism; otherwise he'd have been down before this to the Five Points, telling the Irish their duty to their betters and to Property."

"Yes, sir," said Paddy.

Mr. Cleeve turned again to his son. "We're forming a guard of businessmen and other decent elements to help the police, till the troops take over. You're nearly sixteen; you could shoulder a musket. May I name you for a volunteer?"

"No," said Evan, looking at his hands.

"And you still say you're not afraid?"

Evan looked up slowly from the floor to the fawn-colored trousers and the gold chain on the white batiste waistcoat: "I'm not afraid to tell you. No."

"May I ask why?"

"I'm not sure why," Evan whispered, his eyes again on the floor.

Mr. Cleeve chuckled and tilted his hat from his high brow. "Well, I won't name you. For your mother's sake."

Evan's lips moved in silent muttering.

"I'd like to ask you a question. Is it possible, since you say you're not afraid, your reluctance to do your small share in putting down this miserable rising of hooligans, has in it some element of—sympathy, for desperadoes who loot stores and burn public buildings?"

Evan raised his head— "I guess so"— and met his father's eyes.

Grosvenor Cleeve smiled. "Youth loves romance. Firing Weehawken Ferry and Spuyten Duyvil Bridge, stringing helpless darkies up on lamp posts, wrecking the newspaper presses of Mr. Greeley, pre-eminent friend of the common man, cutting down telegraph poles so New York cannot communicate with the rest of the country in this crisis of Republicanism—yes, a fair name for it is romance."

"We're not a jury," Evan spoke scarcely above a whisper. "You needn't make a speech."

Mr. Cleeve swallowed his anger. "To return to your mother: she's in bed with one of her migraines. She has no idea of the disturbance; if you don't wish her to worry herself to death, better not let her see you; she'd know in a flash you've been in the streets and that something was wrong." He turned to Jonathan. "Good-by, sir. . . . Paddy, get back to your work." He left them.

Evan jumped up. "Come on, men."

"Young guv'nor," Paddy said from his door, "the Mistress is safe. This house is safe. Didn't my old man just say it?"

"What did he say?"

"It was at breakfast this mornin': 'So they're fixin',' says he, 'to burn the city that give 'em food and lodgin', afther the famines and the landlords of Erin.' 'Tis a hard thing fer a man has the love o' Ireland in his heart and he livin' betwixt the loikes of such folly callin' itself Irish and destroyin' the hand that feeds it. Lucky,' says he, ' 'tis the Boss and the Mistress be livin' in the house shelters Christopher McGovern, and no Irish fool so much the fool for to touch a shingle o' the roof *I* lives in.' "

"He said that?" Evan was feverishly eager.

"He did say that."

"Bring three more bottles."

"Young guv'nor,—"

"Do like I tell you!"

When Paddy returned, Evan made him sit with him on the leather horsehair sofa beneath the portrait of *Clara Bell III.* "Your pop may be right about the house, but he's wrong about the city. The common classes *are* taking over, and the governor can't face it. That's why he talks so high. *He's* the scared one."

"Who'll be after polishin' the harnesses?" Paddy was puzzled.

"Maybe the old vultures in Mayor Opdyke's house."

"Geeze! Dey wouldn't know how!" Paddy was proud.

"You'll teach them."

"But they're killing Negroes," Jonathan ventured.

"Revolutions always make these little mistakes."

"What's a nigger more or less?" Paddy drank deep of the cool brew. "Me friend, Lorry Keegan, he was tellin' me when a nigger woman drops a baby, she has a whole litter, like the cats and dogs."

"It's not true," said Jonathan.

"Have you men finished your beer? This is no time for scientific arguments. Let's go."

Jonathan clung to his seat. "Where?"

"If mother's safe—to see the fun." Evan's left hand again began to trill. "Come along, Paddy."

"Geeze! Me, too?"

"Your days of taking orders are numbered."

Jonathan was in conflict; he had seen enough, he could see still the white face flower on the iron spearhead. But he could not abandon his new friend, his brother born of this day . . . born with him. Evan was already on the gravel path; Jonathan and Paddy followed.

Emma Corthuis Cleeve lay in her bed; it was too dark to read, her eyes winced with the glare of the sun in the bars of the drawn blinds; she felt the day's heat besiege and gradually conquer her room's precarious coolness. Her hand on the coverlet touched the two books she had not opened: *Beulah* by Augusta Evans, George Eliot's recent *Romola*. She knew what she would find in them: the glories of self-sacrifice, which was the main right of woman! Her finger laden with the heavy wedding band, the arrogant diamond solitaire, tapped nervously on the volumes. By men's money, by men's machines, by men's ambitions that drained them of their manhood, women were trapped. Women were desperate; and some of them wrote novels to fool the rest of them. But the truth was here in her room with the rose carpet that must be protected from the sun, the teak and mahogany furniture that kept the poor maid's feather-duster busy, the bed of headache, heartache. —I'm dead already. No, I'm the widow; my husband is the dead one. I'm alive, I am Evan's mother. She tried to remember when she gave him birth: this same room, sheet-swathed—the steaming basins, the white nurses, the black-bearded doctor—revolving round the red pain of her body. She could not recall the pain, Evan had not hurt her. When she cleft in two, hope healed her. *This* was the pain! how to give birth again to Evan. Infinitely harder was this birth against the world of his father.

—There are no men. Evan must be a man.

She had been a girl, alive; never a woman alive. The girl was still somewhere far within her, far away as her boy. That girl was this boy struggling to be a man, as once she to be a woman. Her mind could describe Emma Corthuis, daughter of Jacob Corthuis, the rich merchant. Her body had changed little: breasts still firm, black hair that still could fall down the lithe flanks to her waist. Only her body's flavor was no more. —I'm dead now, I no longer love my husband. Life can say, I am dead? Then death and life are not so different. Too puzzling for an ailing woman, middle-aged, on a hot afternoon. Too puzzling for a well young woman it had been, on cool days, on all

14

days. When she came to the bridegroom, she had everything to give him, and he had taken nothing.

Worlds in her for him! She could still hear them singing in her breast and womb. For a long time she did not admit, did not *allow* it was all nothing because the man took nothing, never came close enough to touch, to take, to make alive, although he too went through the motions of living: "Dearest . . . my wife . . ." and his arms held her, and his flesh came in to her. Until the day when she was forced to face the desperate lie of her home, of her bed, of her name. She remembered the incident—how absurdly trivial now, after ten years! A man, of course. Why must it always be by a man that woman knows life and death? Pierre Lubin, the stylish artist from Paris, whom Grosvenor commissioned to paint her portrait and Evan's; he talked like a man, and when at last she let him touch her, it was because her heart was full of desperate hunger for her husband; it was to learn some secret to help her win her husband. It had all been for Grosvenor, the fool! And for a little while, it seemed to work! It was a kind of play whose deep daring gave her confidence and pride with which, beyond her helpless love, to kindle Grosvenor; and he came alive in their home; in her new wisdom, he came alive in her arms. Until suddenly he suspected. He never knew, the damned fool; the cowardly fool, he never dared let himself ask a question that might force him to know and to divorce her. How clear she saw the process of his mind! The hands of the public-spirited great lawyer were not clean. She even knew the deal of the moment: the merger of three Broadway coach companies and their sale in false bankruptcy to the street railroad (after the Mayor and Aldermen got their share of the boodle, he pocketed a hundred thousand dollars). He could afford no public scandal like divorce. Simply—my God, how simply!—he set his wife aside. From then on, doubtless, he paid for his physical needs elsewhere. The needs of his soul he kept on satisfying in his deals, his law, his rotund speeches. It never occurred to the good man that in putting his young wife away, in denying her even the dangerous freedom of a separation, he was less good than Good. She had learned soon enough that Pierre was not more man than her husband. If he had wanted her, she would have stolen her child and somehow come to him. But he wanted his pleasure at no such price as responsibility for a woman.

15

His mouth reeked words of love; there was nothing he feared more than love. He was a businessman, too.

Evan was all; her second baby had died at birth, and there could be no other. Now she learned that for Grosvenor too, Evan was all; the battle for Evan began. Grosvenor had his son's life planned before he was born. Harvard, like his father; the law like his father; the same deals, the same politics; some day, the same remnant of a man, drained by the pursuit of power, taking some girl to wife. Emma lay in her helpless bed in this travail without blood, without birth. To bear her son to manhood! Evan was sensitive, intelligent, he had great talent for his violin. Why not take him to Europe where he could study music? He loved his mother, he hated his father; his heart had told him, without a word from her. Why then hopeless? —If only I had my money! The dowry of the rich girl she had been was, of course, her husband's. She could love her son, encourage his music and reading, she could pray for his confidence. But although Evan was distant from his father, he was not close to her. He loved her, but even love does not bring closeness? Emma's eyes filled with tears; she was praying, but God too was far away. God was cruel. "Give Evan grace. Give me grace for Evan." Emma knew the prayer was not acceptable to the true God, who gave grace where He listed, and to whom even a woman's love for her son was of the flesh and sinful. Women were alone in a world given by God to men. Even Jesus had denied his mother. When God came to earth, was it not by a woman who was no woman at all—the impossible Virgin? Emma raised herself on her bed and looked about her. The room crowded with luxuries stifled: the chaise longue, the gold-framed pier glass between the damasked windows, the rosewood boudoir table with silver candlesticks and the carved silver toilet set, touched the exposed nerve of her aloneness and made her know it. God, too, touched her only to make her know she was alone. She was bound to Evan by every nerve; and Evan was pulling away . . . alone, as she was! "If he goes to college, if he studies law, he is lost!" She spoke aloud, as if only the articulate words could fight for her. "He is fifteen; there's no time to lose. But I have no plan. Grosvenor has the plan." Even if she could make a musician of her son, that would not save him. Pierre too had been an "artist." She sat up in her bed, the tall woman in a nightgown of cool blue, and hid the room, where she had borne her son, from her face with her hands. . . .

Mayor Opdyke's residence had been attacked a second time; for safety's sake, the meeting was transferred to Mr. Livingstone's house on Jones Street near Lafayette Place.

Grosvenor Cleeve walked; it was more prudent than to ride in his carriage, and common cabs were not to be found . . . if found, were not to be trusted. This thought pierced the great man as no list of the dead on the fields of Chancellorsville or Antietam. Men must die; when public security demanded, men must die young; but that Grosvenor Cleeve whose father had been a trusted disciple of Alexander Hamilton, whose grandfather had gone with John Jay to England, whose maternal grandfather had signed the Declaration of Independence, had to walk the streets of his own city because his brougham might be stoned, and cabbies might be enemies—this was . . . Mr. Cleeve's vocabulary failed him. The fountain played; the awnings of the Gramercy Park House fended the sun from its stately rooms. It was hard to believe. Mr. Cleeve's weighty gold watch told him he had plenty of time; he'd drop by at Delmonico's, perhaps one or two of the gentlemen were there and they could go on together. But the doors under Delmonico's balcony were bolted; the square brownstone building had retired until a better day. Westward on Fourteenth Street, only the trees were normal; the wide street was hushed, a shutter on the north side blazed, clouds of smoke barred the view of the Palisades across the Hudson. Mr. Cleeve turned east. In Union Park, a squad of Metropolitan police bivouacked (their coats on the iron fence) near the spacious sparrow house built by public subscription. Under it, a howitzer on wheels; but the birds were gone. The church and the Springler Institute thrust their spire and square tower into the sultry air; the Springler House, finest of hotels, was shuttered tight; T. J. Coe and Company, Miller's Emporium for Ladies' and Children's Shoes, were boarded up. Mr. Cleeve's face sharpened as he went south on Broadway. His nose, a little too prominent, brought out the meditation of his brow, the shrewd pressure of his lips. The war was practically won; the constructive forces of business had won it, but if it was over before they could consolidate their hold, particularly on the tremendous promise of the West, the war could still be fumbled. **Mr. Morgan**, who had done so well with gold in the foreign markets, was right; so was General Meade not to press Lee too hard. Mr. Lincoln, of course, the impatient humanitarian, wanted the war ended in a hurry. He was wrong. The country was making money; but money must be firmer in the saddle before it could cope with the chaotic popular demands that immigration and peace would raise. These riots cleared the right course for commercial progress: a strong hand for money. Money wasn't strong enough, by gad, when hoodlums could burn ferries! Mr. Lincoln was no enemy to business; certainly not Messrs. Chase, Seward, Stanton. But if the Rebels suddenly collapsed, Mr. Lincoln could not be trusted. Look at New York. Mr. Cleeve contemplated the twisted car rails on Clinton Place. The Republican Party, yes!, the hope of the conservative business interests of the country—the hope, therefore, of the country. But it had already outgrown its first elected President. Honest Abe Lincoln, doubtless; he had served. Winning the heart of the sentimental public. Doubtless, he had served. . . . Thank the Lord: the Opera House still stood chaste as a Grecian temple; the church to the west, fine as the one like it by Sir Christopher Wren in London; although the vandals had ripped up the cartracks and toward the Bowery Mr. Cleeve saw an uprooted lamppost. The violence in our country! And no wonder, with the floodgates open to all the poor of Europe. He recalled the Macready riots at this very Opera House when he was a young man, some fourteen years ago it must be. Blood had already defiled those classic columns. And why? Because a great English actor, having won the love of New York, earned the hate of the Irish Bowery boys with their idiotic slogan: *Will you turn the city over to the British?* That night, *Macbeth* had not been played; but in a week all was well; and the Opera House still stood. A symbol, this stately square where Astor, Clinton, Lafayette Places merged: a little twisted iron, but permanent stone. He and his colleagues were the stone—marble and granite; were the architects of the nation. They'd give the final turn to the iron girders.

The three boys saw the smoke and sun in the southwest, and went toward them. Evan led; Jonathan clung close, his impulse to protect his newborn friend vaguely yet strongly justifying his disobedience to his mother; Paddy, a dog loosed from his leash, ran ahead, lingered, sniffing the signs of destruction, yet ever following the other two—who did not know where they were going. In Charlton Street, before a cabin with hollyhocks crowding the unpainted boards, the body of a Negro hung upon a tree. Evan muttered curses, Jonathan's heart stopped beating, Paddy crossed himself: "Blessed Virgin Mother, Blessed Virgin Mary." Inside the door that hung crazily from its broken hinge, crouched the figure of a woman dark as the room. Smoke thickened, closer to the river. Jonathan's eyes smarted; in Evan's there were tears, and the fingers of his left hand were again wildly trilling.

"Do you play violin?" Jonathan's question was an attempt to naturalize the fantastic afternoon.

"How'd you know?"

Jonathan did not tell him.

This was Greenwich Village; the boy felt the still green island and the Hudson pouring toward the sea, the town here was more rustic than to the east where he lived. They passed whole blocks of scattered squatters' shanties suddenly stopped by the regular mass of warehouse and mill. It was almost as much "country" as far uptown where the Albany post road skirted the new-planned Central Park at whose pretentious name Jonathan's father smiled: "Why central? A park for goats!" But here, unlike uptown, Jonathan felt the sea; the city floating in the sea! The crude force of industry tore at the fenced-in cottages, at the lanes, raising manufactories, pressing the poor dwellers into dust and disorder. It was the forward jagged edge of a life, cutting as it grew; cutting the town out from both the sea and the land. The boys stopped; the confusion of the city's will upon Manhattan's still verdant body and upon the waters beyond unconsciously held them. The smoke and the sun were dangerously fertile; the streets brooded, the silence was a warning.

"Perhaps we'd better go back." Jonathan's voice was weak, drained by a fear, and he hated himself for it. Paddy ran up, as if afraid to lose his guides.

Evan shouted: "Let's find the Hudson River Railroad Depot. Let's take the train to Buffalo. Let's live on a canal boat."

"And 'tis yer mother will be weepin' for ye!"

"The cars aren't running. Look!" Jonathan pointed to a twisted track.

A cart raced past. The driver stood, his arm clinging to the post (there was no seat) and, his reins lashed to it, flogged his horses. On the flat open floor that tilted back, three men lay between the high wheels, and as the cart jounced over the torn rails, one of them was tossed out. The cart flew on; the boys stood over the man on the cobbles. Blood from his brow mixed with the grime of his cheek, the saliva of his mouth. He looked up with sharp eyes at the lads.

"God blast Brogan, lavin' me like this."

"He probably doesn't know you've left him," said Evan calmly.

"Are you badly hurt?" asked Jonathan.

"I'm badly athirst." The man raised his head. "Where be I?"

"Franklin Street," said Jonathan.

"And the sojers?"

"What soldiers?" asked Evan.

"By God, 'tis peace descended on the city."

"You're bleeding," Jonathan protested.

"An' no disgrace, when the guv'ment, damn its black heart, sends all its armies agin the citizens. There's yer Republicans fer yez; yer Lincums and yer Opdykes. If only bully Fernando Wood was mayor."

"What soldiers?" insisted Evan.

The man raised himself on his arms, swung his head from side to side, and then fixed his gaze on the saloon at the uptown corner. "Saved," he sang, "by Jesus and Saint Patrick. All ye need do fer me, lads, is give me a lift to yon oasis in this bloody desert. What sojers? I'll be tellin' yez, and then ye can convey me to the bar o' me friend, Terence Palmer. I seen the whole battle. We wuz ten thousand strong, armed with everything from guns to th' broomsticks of our sweethearts. We wuz marchin' down the Broadway, our flags and No Draft signs flutterin' in the breeze o' summer, aimin' for City Hall in th' Park. Onct we wuz there, tidy and snug, the black Republicans can go shoot theirselves. And to think 'twas Sergeant Daniel Carpenter, whose brother many a time I've passed the pleasant word with in Mozart Hall—wasn't it meself got his nacherlization papers six days from his landin' green as an Erin field in Castle Garden? And 'twas his brother, himself, led the troops against us. 'Twill need more than one mug of ale to take the bad taste o' *that* out o' me mouth. What'd he do, the traitor, bad 'cess to his soul? I'll confess it was done pretty; not more than two hundred he had agin our five thousand."

"You said ten thousand," said Jonathan.

"Did I, now? I maybe was countin' the broomsticks. Two squads the Sergeant sends east and west from Broadway on Fourth Street; himself marches on us from Bleecker, so we wuz got at on t'ree sides 't onct. Such a racket o' musketry yez never did hear, not at Vicksburg, I'll lay me soul. Pete Drummond at me side fell wid a hole in his leg. We didn't know which way to turn, savin' uptown where we come from. I ran, wit'out sayin' good-by. Along comes Brogan's cart. I got no need o' him, now the Army's gone back to its palaces. Give me a lift, boys."

"What palaces?" asked Jonathan.

"The lad's fuller'v questions than a stuck pig with blood. Where the rich live is the palaces, young feller. Bond Street, Lafayette Place, the Fifth Avenoo clear up to Murray Hill." He groaned as the boys helped him to his feet. "That toss wuzn't too gentle. We'll gather again, and meet 'em. We got ten times ten thousand in the Sixth Ward alone."

They escorted the hurt man to the saloon, propped him up within the reek of beer, along with the other bodies, at the bar. "Come on," said Evan. "The man's right. This fight is just beginning."

As they turned south again, the sun-seethed harbor, the far hills of Staten Island and the sinking sun, gave a motion to the foreground of the city as if it were the prow of a ship.

Grosvenor Cleeve laid his stick and his hat, stroking it with his sleeve, on the marble-top table, approved himself in the Empire mirror, and followed the colored butler between the Livingstone portraits down the hall to the library where a half-dozen men sat with glasses—tall ones garlanded with mint leaves, small ones of cool sherry—in the shadowed room. On mahogany bookshelves the busts of Julius Caesar, Minerva, Washington, and Burke stared without recognition. Through the open window Mr. Cleeve saw a tree—an ailanthus (he reproved his irrelevant thought); a fence, a barn where a cock, baffled by the smoky afternoon, was crowing.

"The Mayor's been delayed," said the host.

"He'll be here with the Governor," said a little man with fox-red side whiskers and sharp eyes.

"We've had a message from the President." The young man who spoke had a nose like a red barge.

Mr. Cleeve settled in his chair, tasted his glass, smacked his lips. "What does Mr. Lincoln have to say?"

"He says, 'If you please, gentlemen, one Rebellion at a time.'"

The fox-whiskers gave a high-pitched giggle which, his knowing enemies declared, was worth a million dollars; it made most who heard it think the man a fool.

"He washes his hands?" concluded Mr. Cleeve.

"He leaves it to us," boomed the red barge.

"It's just as well," observed a handsome gentleman taking his stand in the corner of the bookcase, where his resemblance to Minerva's features was in evidence. "We have to admit the President knows when to look the other way. He's leaving the matter in hands . . . equipped . . ."

"That's part of *his* equipment," said Mr. Cleeve. "While he runs the War—none too expeditiously—he's giving others time to run the country."

"I think it's a cue," spoke the side-whiskers, who had made five million dollars selling shoddy woolens to the Union Army and *good* medicines to the Confederates (whose confidence as future customers must be kept).

"What do you mean?" boomed the man with the great nose.

The red sideburns began: "Mayor Opdyke and Governor Seymour will be here in a half hour. The Governor hasn't always the discretion of the President; too frequently, I mean, he forgets where *governing* must stop. Well, what I mean—" he paused, as if hoping someone else would say it.

The gentleman under Minerva, whose vision embraced transcontinental railroads and transoceanic cables, obliged: "You mean, we have just half an hour to agree on a plan of action. If it's definite, Seymour and Opdyke will be grateful; they'll support it."

"Precisely," said Mr. Cleeve, as if he had made the proposal; and the red whiskers whose idea had been vicariously voiced and approved chuckled to himself. It was said of him that he showed such humility in giving precedence to the egotisms of others that they repaid him by giving him their money.

"I was reading," he said, with diffidence, "—ah—in a memoir of Napoleon, where he says a battle can be won too early. That is, if the enemy retreats before its main force is engaged, it may not stand to be destroyed."

"Hm," Mr. Cleeve audibly nodded; the red sideburns glanced timidly about him, pulled a gold toothpick from his waistcoat, and began to explore his teeth; the big-nosed man lighted a huge cigar which gave the effect, as he puffed mightily, of a red-boilered barge full steam ahead.

The host of the house unfolded his contribution to the conclave; and as he spoke, a look of love moistened the sharp eyes of the man with the red sideburns. "The Seventh Regiment is on its way from Pennsylvania; it should be here by Wednesday, and when it comes, it can put out whatever disorder is still afoot like a heel on a match. On the other hand, much property can be destroyed between now and day after tomorrow. The Governor of Connecticut has expressed his willingness —privately, to an absolutely discreet, reliable party—to send us ten thousand troops training in Greenwich. They could come down, of course, without the trouble of crossing the Hudson. On the other hand, they're not so good as the battle-trained troops. But they could be here by morning. The Governor of Connecticut assumes his offer has reached the Governor of New York. It has been delayed, discreetly. What I say is: It would be an error to accept. Let the refractory forces come to a head. They're all Democrats, and if we give 'em rope enough, they'll hang their party, by gad!, for a generation. I say, give 'em rope. Let the Metropolitan police handle the situation. No one knows of the Connecticut troops. Keep it out of the papers. The Metropolitans, and the few soldiers we do have, can protect the large buildings; the new Guard of businessmen can hold *our* houses—"

"Let the mob have Greeley's *Tribune*," growled the red nose.

"Let them burn tenements and shanties. That'll fix Wood's people: to see their own homes destroyed. They'll turn against him."

"If it comes out—about the Connecticut troops—"

"It needn't," whispered the red sideburns, and fell again to picking his teeth.

23

"What if the Metropolitans can't hold their own?"

"Our Defense Guard will have a thousand under arms tonight."

"The Insurance Companies—"

"If no more insured buildings are harmed, they're solvent. The Guard has a full list."

"The shanties and the slums need a cleanup anyway."

"It's worth the risk," said the magnate who resembled Minerva.

"Risk," spoke Mr. Cleeve, "is the courage of constructive enterprise." A quiet exultation made the men solid with the mahogany bookshelves. The host said, "I surmise we're ready for the Governor and Mayor?" and pulled the scarlet scarf-cord of a bell. When the butler appeared, he pointed with his eyes to the bottles on the lowboy, and said, "Gentlemen, let's fill up."

"To the United States of America," Grosvenor Cleeve toasted; and every man, raising his fresh glass, was sure of his honorable share of the republic.

The Five Points was empty. In its triangular plaza, called Paradise Park, two rachitic trees dozed on the dust. The streets at its apex, Park and Worth; Little Water Street at the base; on its sides, southwest and east, Baxter, Leonard, Roosevelt Streets, and the Bowery down to Front Street, were a hive of tenements, slaughteryards, rat-baiting halls and cellars where lone old women and the blind found their level. From morning, the grog shops had been crowded. When news came of the rout on Broadway, the last men and the strong women clutched butchering knife, hammer, broken hoop, lath, brick-laying trowel, random musket, and drew west, as if in the smoldering sky the sun—symbol of hope that never touched their festered slums—were a red-hot iron magnet. The mob bore signs:

TELL OLD ABE TO COME TO NEW YORK
$300 OR YOUR BLOOD
WE'LL HANG OLD ABE ON A SOUR APPLE TREE

The mob had tender eyes worn down to fierceness. The mob had no plan. It avoided the Park, where the police camped before the brass and bells of City Hall. It had got wind that the troops marching from Gettysburg would cross the river (with ferries burned) at Tarrytown or Yonkers. As it moved west, its aim shaped: to destroy the Harlem River Railroad above Spuyten Duyvil—tracks and engines.

Stragglers from earlier battle joined it; women from shanties screamed at it or cheered; dogs barked, cats and pigs scurried, warehouses stood aloof in its hot wake. Near Chambers Street, the three boys heard it. They raced through an alley; a big dog gnawed the foot of a dead policeman. Jonathan chased the beast away, and stood trembling at his unconscious courage. A woman emerged from a cabin, waving a spindle; and her beauty, within the filth of her blouse and skirt, pinioned them.

"Move yerselves on," she cried, "lave the dog his feast. Are yez Jews or nigger-lovers, begrudgin' Champ the one square meal he's had since God give him a poor woman fer a mistress?" The boys' silence silenced her. "Who are yez? Whut's yer names?"

"Jonathan Hartt. This is my friend, Mr. Cleeve; and this is Paddy McGovern."

She dropped her spindle. "Can I be offerin' the young gentlemen a dish o' tay? 'Tis a nice afternoon fer a tay party."

"We'd love to accept," said Evan, "but we're drinking beer today."

"Beer, is it!" she laughed. Sullen again: "Who's got the price fer a can o' beer? My man's drafted; blood's cheaper."

"You be *our* guest." Evan took a silver dollar from his pocket. He held out the coin; the woman clutched it, tested it with her perfect teeth, slipped it in her stocking; then, sudden like a cat's leap, she spat in Evan's face. Evan wiped his cheek with his kerchief, and bowed.

Now, they saw the mob. In the open space between West Broadway and Chambers Street, with the depot shed toward the river, its rolling vibrance, freed of barriers, burst into voice and action. Carts, barrows, mortar-mixers, débris of planks and bricks, grew swiftly into a barricade. A young man and an old man with gray-streaked beard gave orders. A large group rushed forward to an abandoned car—the long Dolly Varden that six horses drew to the steam trains on Thirtieth Street—pushed it sidewise from its track, and dragged it through smashed glass to the barricade. The boys came close; Jonathan felt the eyes of the old man red and evil; the eyes of the youth lovable. And now they could see, although the mob was a single body, fierce-fanged at its edges, the sprawling ease within it: women squatted and gossiped,

25

men boasted and drank from bottles, puffing their clays. Across the empty cobbles, close to the depot, another group was forming.

Jonathan asked, "Who are they?"

"Look at their collars. *Gentlemen,*" sneered Evan.

Two Metropolitan policemen joined this group, looked across the barricade, and nodded. It was as if Jonathan had heard: "Let them go ahead. When the time comes, we'll fix them." And he was part of "them"! Suddenly, fear took him. There would be a battle: Evan and he and Paddy would be in it! —*Which is our side?* Will we die? Jonathan's hand touched Evan's, his fear vanished. He saw his new brother: the blond hair matted with sweat, the grimed cheek, the clear wild blue eyes! He felt himself dark beside this light, he loved him. That Evan Cleeve, son of the Revolutionary fathers, was taller, smarter, stronger, richer, he knew; and he was going to protect him! A drum out of sight wove with its tattoo the crass noises all about him; for the first time he sensed the mob in which he stood behind the barricade: lush, sprawling, dangerous, and tender. He saw the group opposite grow tense; then he saw the soldiers.

The pace of their feet brought silence to the mob who watched them swing single-file along the front of the depot. The commanding officer cried, *"Halt!";* the muskets struck in unison on the cobbles; all the square was silence. The city breathed and sweated silence; the sun stood on the rim of silence, baking it down.

Jonathan saw, between the depot shed and a taller building, a gray three-story house with a pale blue awning; on its façade: RIDLEY AND COMPANY. STEAM REFINED CANDY. Underneath, in equally large letters: SUGAR PLUMS. His heart yearned, tears were in his mouth. A stir seethed the silence, as steam murmurously seethes the nearly boiling water. They saw the officer come out from his little squad of soldiers and step forward into the tense vacuum of the square. Halfway, he stopped; he was carrying a sword, and his blue cap's vizor gave a gleam to his eyes.

"Disperse, now," he said. "Go home, now. We wish you no harm."

He was young and gallant, standing there alone before the mob's hate; Jonathan loved him.

"Hold, men!" shouted the young leader within the barricade; Jonathan loved him. "This is our city."

The officer spoke: "We don't want to use our fire. If you don't move at once, we'll have to."

On the candy factory's slate roof, there was a little dormer window. A man stepped out . . . all in an instant Jonathan saw the lithe mechanic's body, poised on the edge, flex like a drawn bow; the arm arrowed forward and a brick glanced from the officer's shoulder.

The officer did not turn, did not raise an arm; his mouth convulsively mastered his pain. He began to speak again; from the taller red brick building, heads showed at the parapet, stones came hurtling on the soldiers, a shot rang. The officer walked backward to his squad; with his left hand clumsily he unscabbarded his sword and raised it. The soldiers' muskets went from the perpendicular to the horizontal. A knot of disorder raveled through the crowd toward the front, a boy leaped free and sped across the square into the haven of the soldiers holding their guns at aim. Evan's and Jonathan's eyes met; they knew it was Paddy who had deserted. A howl of derision rose around them.

"This is our city," the young leader cried again. Stones crashed the shed in thicker volume, gunfire sputtered, a soldier collapsed slowly on his musket. The officer's sword went down, the squad's volley sparked; Jonathan heard no shot, but a man dropped in front of him, women screamed; he felt bodies crumple and then, a deep abdominal mutter as if the mob were wounded in its stomach. Suddenly, it broke into shrieking footfall of catapulted bodies. As he reached for Evan, a hand smote his face, he was blinded and went down, sensing without ears or eyes the solid squad of soldiers, muskets straight and piercing, board the carts and barrows of the barricade, while the mob exploded away.

The dining room where Sarah Hartt was setting the table had the atmosphere of an oven in which bread—good wholesome bread, of course—had recently been baked. The oak sideboard, the table with circuitous legs that got in the way of one's knees, the leather-back uncomfortable chairs, the lonely little window, even the Japanese screen in front of the doorless pantry with black angular cranes in a dun sky, were part of the room's heat. Sarah Hartt had no eye for domestic decoration; coziness in her cosmology was nonsense. Each piece of furniture in her home served its purpose and was kept clean; that was enough for a woman who knew the secrets of plain living and high

27

thinking and who often said, "My home is my temple." When Lucia and Philip were brought home by the servant, Frieda, from the Sleip farm, Mrs. Hartt went upstairs with her youngest boy and found that Jonathan was out. Jonathan was Sarah's favorite for no illicit reason and with no unethical results; she was as good a mother, she was sure, to Reuben, the mere businessman, to Lucia, the mere daughter, to Philip, who was not very bright. But her world had hierarchies; and now the son chosen to rise in the world—which meant to serve it as lawyer, great judge, perhaps statesman—had wilfully disobeyed her. God knew where he was in the dangerous city; God, who appreciated competence, would leave punishment to her. With compressed lips, Sarah Hartt returned to her bedroom, changed the cold compress for her husband's headache—by her orders he lay on the bed, and went down to set the table. (Mrs. Hartt did not believe in loading too much work on the one servant they could afford; that was why, contrary to all usage, she gave the weekly heavy wash to poor Mrs. Hanzel.) Then, the steep spiral pantry stair led her to Frieda's kitchen.

Although, like the dining room directly above, it faced north and its windows had iron bars ("like a jail," said Frieda), the kitchen was the most cheerful chamber in the house. On the window ledges were a few pale petunias, in boxes contributed by Frieda's suitor, Martin Schmitt, the carpenter who longed to be a farmer; the air through the open door from the yard stirred the aroma of pot roast on the range; and, principally, there was Frieda herself, humming as she cut cookies with a tin stamp from the sheet of dough flat on the table.

"Frieda," said Mrs. Hartt.

"Yes, mum." Frieda kept on humming and cutting cookies.

"We will have dinner promptly. Even though Master Reuben and Master Jonathan may be late."

"Master Jonathan!" The girl swung round. She was a buxom German, brought to New York as a baby; her broad face with high cheekbones, wide mouth, sky-blue eyes, suggested that some of her blood was Slavic. "Where is Master Jonathan?"

Sarah, without answering, walked back toward the pantry stair.

"He ain't gone out in them dreadful *streets?* Oh, Mrs. Hartt!"

Her mistress placed a foot on the first step, paused, and turned round. "You exaggerate, don't you, Frieda? It can't be so bad."

28

"Gott im Himmel!" Although Frieda spoke Manhattanese, strong emotion threw her back on the language of her fathers. "You had ought to been wid us. If Mr. Sleip hadn't come, sittin' on the box wid the coachman, and tellin' dose roughs he was as good an Irish as dey was—"

"Nonsense, Frieda!"

"Cross my heart." She touched the crucifix over her luxuriant breast. "We come straight down Broadway. At about Twenty-nine Street, you know, where the Samler farmhouse is, the fence was all smashed and dey'd tore out dose pretty little trees that was all boarded up. A bunch of *terrible* men stopped us. Did Mr. Sleip string 'em along!"

"But he's no more Irish than you are."

"He talked like the furnace man. He said he'd come all de way from Albany to join 'em; an' did they expect him to walk?" Frieda's laugh, a gay plumaged bird swinging high, fell. "But Master Jonathan—!"

"He'll be all right. Yes, he went out. And I forbade it."

"Gott im Himmel!" The girl went to her stove and began basting the roast, as if each vehement spoonful of sizzling fat was to bring the boy a step homeward.

When, fifteen minutes later, she set the soup tureen before her mistress at the pantry end of the table, the chairs of Reuben and Jonathan were empty. Lucia, all in gray except for the white muslin guimpe under her bodice, ate in silence. Philip, at his mother's left, gulped his soup noisily; Sarah had decided there was nothing to do about his manners; he was a good boy, but by some trick of fate he took after the rustics in his father's family. Joseph, too, ate in silence, wiping his black beard with a huge napkin, his gentle eyes searching his wife's face. He too was worried; but none dared to mention what they knew to be the cause of Sarah's compressed lips.

"Well, Lucia," she said to sustain the normal, "how was your day? Tell us all about it."

"Lucy Sleip's too fresh. She kept asking about Reuben." Lucia thought: —Praising my straw bonnet with the blue ribbon and broad rim! As if I didn't know why! Because it hides my horrid hair and bad complexion.

"She admires Reuben," said the mother. "More, I'm sure, than he admires her."

29

"She'd accept him in a minute, if he proposed."

Joseph Hartt frowned. "No Hartt marries a Sleip."

"Reuben soon will be making more money than you," retorted Lucia. "He'll marry whom he pleases."

The father's bare upper lip trembled; his eyes remained gentle. "Why," he asked his wife, "do you let our children go with such people?"

"Mrs. Sleip is a good woman. And they do like us. And it's healthy for Lucia and Philip to spend a hot day in the country, when we can't afford the seashore this year."

"Darby Sleip," Joseph ignored the rebuke. "We don't know how he made his money."

—If only he had a son, thought Sarah sadly, looking at homely Lucia. The girl's heavy features were like Jonathan's. If she had been a boy: the skimpy braids coiled on the back of her large head, the front hair crimped and parted in the middle, the two side ringlets, made her almost a caricature of the fine boy she would have been. Then her wilfulness would have been will; her bad temper fire, her restive mind power of intellect.

Reuben, who had his own house key, slipped in, kissed his mother and his father, winked at Frieda, and said, "No soup, please. The day's soupy enough. Mama, why don't you ever change the bill o' fare with the weather?" He attacked the roast as greedily as Philip, but more deftly; all his motions had a slick rhythm that offset the rhythmic clumsiness of Philip.

When the meat was half gone, suddenly he looked up. "Where's Jonathan?" On his smooth face and eyes that matched his wavy chestnut hair parted in the middle, his faint emotion of surprise and concern seemed to be reflected, like a dim light on shiny metal.

"Jonathan's been disobedient," said Lucia. "He's joined the riots."

"Dear," reproved Sarah. "How can you say such nonsense?"

"We're all worried about him. Why shouldn't I say so?"

"That kind of a damn fool he's not." Reuben cut himself a chunk from the rye loaf.

"Reuben!" Sarah was harsh. "Profanity! And your brother is *no* kind of a fool."

"Time will tell. Time will tell," Reuben intoned profoundly, his shal-

30

low eyes beaming. "What a day it's been! You know," he turned to his father, "they say there's a deal behind all this. Fernando Wood, Oakie Hall, all the bully boys of Tammany and Mozart Hall—including that coming-up young firefighter Tweed—are supposed to be in with the silk-stockings, starting with the Mayor. A sort of bear maneuver to beat down the market, and then buy it up."

"No," said Joseph. "Mayor Opdyke's an honest man."

"So are we all." Reuben grinned. "I'll never forget this day."

"A nightmare," said Sarah.

"A dream! I turned the best deal of my life—"

"You're forgetting your brother—"

"Oh, Jonathan will be all right. Maybe he's learning something that ain't in books."

"Isn't," Lucia corrected.

"Darby Sleip gave me a hand," Reuben informed his father.

"Where did Mr. Sleip get his start?" asked Joseph.

"You'd be shocked, papa, if I told you."

"Then don't tell us," said Sarah.

"Do!" cried Lucia. "I always suspected—"

"He and his wife used to be pawnbrokers."

"That's no disgrace," said the mother.

"To be exact, they were *fences*. He went to jail, for receiving stolen goods."

"Reuben!"

"When he got out—he wasn't in long, a slice of real estate they had bought up, including the southwest lot of Central Park, was in the name of Judge Mickle, the man who got him out on a writ of error—they all cleaned up. That was the fresh start."

"Sarah! You let our children—"

"Come, papa," beamed Reuben. "That sort of thing is happening every day."

"Not to everyone." Joseph's cheek was pale and his hands trembled.

"Indeed, not to everyone!" said Sarah.

"Is it a wonder," Joseph's voice was soft, "the city burns? the people rise in wrath? We have lost touch with God. All those people's hopes—"

"Thank your President," smiled Reuben. "You voted for him," and

31

he gave his plate to Frieda for more roast. "Delicious, Frieda. Thank your wonderful Abe Lincoln. He got us into this war."

"You blame President Lincoln?" Joseph's voice was shaking.

"I ought to be grateful," Reuben smiled. That morning he had cleaned up more than enough to pay his draft exemption. His mind went back to Darby Sleip: why was the quicksilvery little Dutchman with the Irish first name and the Irish wife so good to him, letting him into that deal? He saw Lucy Sleip, the shapely springtime flesh in crinolines and flounces. She liked him, and her father worshiped her. Maybe that was it. Well, why not? No one helps—or loves anyone for nothing.

The doorbell gave a tremulous long ring, stopped, rang again. Frieda put down the remnant of the pudding.

"It's Jonathan," said Sarah; half rose from her seat; made herself sit down again. "Everyone stay at table. I want nothing said."

They heard the front door open: Frieda's cry. . . .

Suddenly, Jonathan knew he was safe. —I must find Evan! Although the mob was gone, the hot waves of bodies still surged against his stomach. Had the soldiers marched over him? In the empty street lay débris of the battle: staves, workmen's tools, workmen's hats, wagon parts, and a huge organic smell of sweat and flesh that the low sun simmered. Then Jonathan saw Evan. Evan was on his back, his eyes gazing upward peacefully; near his head a pickaxe, at his feet a ripped skirt. One hand pillowed his neck.

"Are you hurt bad?" Jonathan leaned down.

The boy did not answer.

"Evan!"

"Where's Paddy?"

"Are you hurt?"

"I'm taking it easy."

There was no blood, and his eyes were clear. Yet—internal injuries? . . . the most dangerous. "Paddy ran over to the soldiers. Remember?"

"The blessed little Judas! Father'd give him a dollar. Wait till I get him!"

"Evan, can't you get up?"

"Why should I? I'm comfy."

Jonathan placed his hands under Evan's shoulders to raise him. Evan winced. "You *are* hurt!"

"Who isn't hurt?"

Jonathan looked sharply at Evan's head. Had he gone crazy? Not a scratch.

"*You*'ve a smudge three inches long on your forehead," said Evan as if he read his thoughts.

"Please get up."

"Football hurts more 'n this. Do you play football? Lots less fun. All right. I don't want you to *cry*." He clasped Jonathan's arms with both hands and hoisted himself up.

They walked, Jonathan half supporting his friend who kept on talking. "I was asleep, I guess, and I heard music. Do you ever hear music when you sleep? It's the best. I guess you're a serious chap, you don't like music."

"That's not so."

"This kind of mess is made by serious men who don't like music."

"Gee, Evan! I hope you aren't really hurt."

"Not a chance. When you're knocked down, be sure you drop into a nice soft pile of music. Breaks the fall."

The square was empty, and Jonathan was angry. No one to help him! Suddenly he let go of Evan who comfortably lay down on the cobbles. A wagon from downtown was making its way through the wreckage toward them. When the driver saw the boy ahead, he lashed his horse forward. One of the wheels struck an overturned cart, the wagon dangerously tilted, the woman beside the driver clutched the seat, and Jonathan took his stand in the direct path of the horse. The driver brandished his whip; then leaned back heavily on his reins. The horse's breath touched Jonathan's face.

"Are you crazy, boy?" His round hat was like a pudding on a plate and his cheeks were ruddy dumplings. "Get oudt of my vay." The woman sat pale and thin; behind them in the open wagon were bundles, boxes, a trunk.

"Please," said Jonathan. "My friend's hurt. Please help me take him home."

33

"Where do you live?" asked the woman. Without forethought, Jonathan gave his own address. "That's not out of our way, Rudolph," she said.

"All righdt, but hurry." The man filled his cheeks as if to blow a trumpet.

"I can't carry him alone." Jonathan pointed to Evan, lying as if prostrate on the cobbles. The woman climbed down; she was hard and very thin in her black dress that had no hoop, no spread to it at all. Jonathan knew she was kind. With little help, Evan walked between them; and when they were all squeezed in the seat:

"Why did you lie about his needin' to be carried?" asked the woman.

"I was afraid, if I went alone to get him, you'd leave us."

"You're a smart one."

At Broadway they turned north past Mr. Stewart's Marble Palace. It was safe, all right, with a whole guard of armed men around it. Jonathan feared the effect on Evan of the cart's rattling and joggling. Again as if he read his mind, Evan said, "I'm enjoying this ride. Only I wish it would never stop."

There was the Hartt house: three stories of red brick, flaking iron rail before the areaway. Jonathan had had time to find reasons, if Evan objected, for bringing him here: Mr. Cleeve was probably out, Mrs. Cleeve was sick in bed. Better let his mother decide how hurt he was. But Evan asked no question. He sat on the curb, looking at the man and woman while Jonathan said, "Thank you. Oh, thank you!"

"Dot's noddink," the man smiled. "Dot didn't take us chust on'y a minute oudt of our vay."

"Here," Evan held up a greenback.

"Nein!" said the man.

"Why not?" said Evan. "You helped us a lot. Let us help you a little."

The man, caught by the authority of the voice, not by the argument, looked up to his wife, and read a sign in her imperturbable face. He pulled a leather wallet from his shirt, unfolded it with his workman's sensitive rough hands, took the dollar and laid it away. With sudden speed, he leaped the wheel to his seat, jogged the reins, and the wagon rattled eastward.

. . . Frieda's cry had drawn them to the door: Lucia and Philip, then

34

the mother, more slowly the father because his legs were stiff, and Reuben because he was lighting his cheroot. They saw Jonathan, his jacket ripped, one of his stockings down, the other torn, his head bare and sweat-smudged but whole, and his protective arm around the strange boy whose eyes peered whimsical yet courteous from a dirty face.

"Mama! My friend! He's hurt!"

Sarah searched her son; the disgrace of his condition was annulled by his safety and, somehow, by the lad whom he supported. Thanksgiving glowed in her sharp face; then she was the cool commander.

"Reuben, help me and Frieda carry Jonathan's friend upstairs. Lucia's room. . . . Careful."

It was on the second floor, next to her parents' room: brown in the gray twilight; the cumbrous book cabinet, the chairs, unfemininely heavy. They laid Evan on the bed; Sarah, first removing his soiled shoes and jacket, opened his shirt. The bruise on his chest was slight. Deftly, repeating: "Does it hurt?" she felt her way on the white flesh from the shoulders to the abdomen. "You'll be all right," she said.

"Hadn't I better go for Doctor Wolf?" whispered Jonathan.

"He'll have enough to do, this dreadful day. What your friend needs is a good sleep." She turned to Lucia, who stood modestly at the door beyond sight of the bared body. "Lucia, you will sleep with me tonight. Bring fresh sheets. Papa can sleep in Reuben's bed; Reuben can double up with Philip. Frieda, a kettle of hot water and some weak tea."

"Who's your friend?" Reuben with his cigar took Lucia's place at the door.

"His name's Evan."

"No family name?" Reuben sneered.

Jonathan hesitated. "If you must know, he's Evan Cleeve; Grosvenor Cleeve's son."

Reuben's face registered a seismic shock, as contempt and doubt quaked into reverence. *"The* Grosvenor Cleeve?" Jonathan did not answer, but Reuben knew! the boy resembled his great father. He whistled and his eyes gleamed at his younger brother with wondering respect. Frieda had rushed to the kitchen with little Philip; Lucia fumbled for fresh linen, dazed by this glamorous invasion of her room;

35

Jonathan helped his mother undress the patient who lay with open eyes in what seemed the greatest comfort.

"No hurt, anywhere?"

"No, ma'am."

"Internal injuries?" ventured Jonathan.

"That's what I felt for," Sarah shook her head. "Get one of your new nightshirts, they're a size too big for you. Hurry."

When Frieda and Philip returned, Evan lay in fresh sheets and shirt, his handsome head at ease on the pillows. Sarah bathed his face, shoulders, arms, and hands; fed him weak tea with a spoon while Lucia stood again in the door, glorying in her brother, her beloved brother, who had turned naughtiness into a triumph.

Evan said, "This is fun. I've never had so good—" His eyes closed.

"You're to sleep here tonight," said Sarah without smiling. "You need rest. I'll write a note to your mother. You have a mother?" Evan's mouth stirred in peaceful silence. "Why! He's asleep already."

"He has a mother," Jonathan answered for him. "She doesn't know—"

"I see. Two disobedient, selfish sons! Well, she won't worry long. Jonathan, to bed at once. I'll talk with *you* in the morning. You probably need rest as much as your friend. Frieda, get dressed immediately to go out. You'll take a message to Mrs. Grosvenor Cleeve."

In the hall, Jonathan met Reuben coming down, dressed in his new suit.

"I'd break my date tonight, really I would, if there was anything I could do. But there ain't."

"No."

"I guess," laughed Reuben, "you're not so slow after all."

"Where are you going?" asked Lucia.

"Wouldn't you like to know?"

"I know."

"Then why do you ask?"

"You ought to be ashamed of yourself."

"Leave that to me."

"You might at least ask mama if there's something you can do. All you think of is yourself."

36

"Who are *you* thinking of?" Reuben's smile was cruel, as he ran lightly down the stairs.

Jonathan hated to go up to his room. —I'm not sleepy. He wanted to stay by his friend's side, to see his face while he slept, to know at last how Evan really looked: to *know* him (—I rescued him!) and to know this fabulous day. If he went to bed, the day would be over. As he approached his floor, he heard weeping; Frieda's door was open, and he saw the tiny hall room. Dove-blue curtain, pink-covered cot, on the bureau a perfume bottle shaped like a bird, a porcelain postman holding a card, and a florid framed daguerreotype of a Teuton with rhetorical moustaches, all seemed to touch the girl's body sobbing on the cot, her face in her hands.

"Frieda!"

Tear-drenched eyes glanced at him; she hid her face again and wept louder. A white slip covered her corset. The boy, drawn closer, looked into her bosom.

"Frieda!"

Through tears, she smiled up at him.

"What is it, Frieda!"

Again, she hid her face; her breasts drew him. Even the little black crucifix, with a silver Christ, that hung between them, suspended from the silver chain about her neck, could not repel him. —Catholic! "All the ignorant are Catholics," he heard his mother. But he heard his father, "All religions look for the way to God." His gentle, good father seemed to be fathering his hunger. He was confused.

"It ain't fair," she sobbed.

"What's not fair? Tell me, Frieda!" He touched her bare arm above the elbow. Instead of pushing him back, she placed a hot palm on his hand and pressed it into her flesh.

"It's not fair. All those *Lumpen!* It wasn't even safe on the streets in the day. In the night-time—" She looked full in his face, and the boy felt himself deliciously, terribly, suspended above the open menace of her body. He understood: she was afraid to go out to deliver the message.

"Don't be afraid, Frieda." He spoke also to himself. "I'll take the letter."

Her hand pressed his deeper into her arm, until his words sank in.

"But they could hurt you, too. Look what they done to your friend."

37

"No, Frieda. That was a regular battle. Between here and his house, I'll be safe."

"Oh, Master Jonathan—"

"You'll do what I say, Frieda. You take the letter from mama. Mama mustn't know. She wouldn't send you, if she knew you were scared; she'd go herself. You give the letter to me." The girl was silent. "I'll get ready and come to the kitchen. I order you, Frieda." And then, there was between them only the knowledge of his hand under her hand, in the flesh of her arm. Frieda stood up; he could not see her face, it was confused and fused in the mist of her closeness. She put her arms around him, he felt the overflowing rondures of her body.

"Oh, Master Jonathan, you're so good—so good." Her lips touched his brow, then she pushed him gently from her.

His mother's letter clutched in his hand in the side pocket of his good suit, Jonathan for the second time that day turned toward Stuyvesant Square. Clouds massed in the east, smoke brooding in the west, weighed on his head and made the evening hard to breathe. But if it was hard to bear, it was because of a new burden: his sin! He had looked with lust on Frieda Memel! who had embraced him, forgetful of her half-clothed body, because she was frightened and grateful, because she was innocent and trusting. —Punish! For six weeks, starting tomorrow—no, day after tomorrow, I'll get up a half hour earlier and devote it to study.

Emma Corthuis Cleeve sat up, propped high by pillows, and opened the envelope under the blue globe lamp beside her bed.

> Dear Madam,
>   Your son is safe and not seriously hurt, I am quite certain. But when my son Jonathan brought him to my house after they were caught in those dreadful riots, he was so worn out that I put him to bed and he fell right asleep. I do not feel he should be disturbed tonight but in the morning he can surely go home. His clothes are very soiled. Will you please send him a fresh suit, shirt and stockings by the person who delivers this?
>   With expressions of respect, I am,
>   Your Obedient Servant,
>   *Sarah Stern Hartt*

38

"Who brought this, Banto?"

"De young Massa—"

"It must be a servant."

"No, Miss' Cleeve. Him no servant. Him Massa Evan's fren' I done seen dis afternoon wid Massa Evan in de stables."

Emma was puzzled? —'The *person?*' "Let him come up, Banto." She smoothed the silk magenta puff on the bed, drew tighter at her throat the lavender negligee over her nightgown, as the door opened.

Jonathan, with the Negro boy to lead him, had risen from the splendor of the entrance foyer to the stair that lifted him to a broad carpeted hall with chairs and tables in it and doors on either side; now he felt the oblique impact of the muffled room with a lady, all silk and beauty, holding out her hand from her throne-bed.

"You're Evan's friend? You're Master Hartt? How can I thank you? Do sit down. Draw your chair closer. You must excuse me. I'm Evan's mother, an old woman receiving you in this informal way because I couldn't wait to hear what happened."

"It was a kind of battle, ma'am. But your son's all right. My mother knows!"

"So you boys go to battle?"

"Not exactly, Mrs. Cleeve. The battle came to us."

"So the Rebels are here!"

"Not the Confederates, ma'am. It's the people, poor people—"

"He *is* hurt!"

"He was knocked down. I brought him home in a Dutchman's wagon. He is all right. You can trust my mother."

"I trust you, also. I'm glad you're Evan's friend. You're good friends?"

"Oh, yes, ma'am."

"He's so headstrong. I'm sure he led you into it. And *you* saved him. Where was he hurt?"

"Just bruised, when the soldiers came and the people ran."

"Soldiers! Did they shoot?"

"Yes, ma'am."

"God in Heaven." She closed her eyes, and opened them. "What can we mothers do? Our sons in the streets, where there are battles!

39

How your mother must feel. She must be very brave, sending you out again—"

"She didn't send me." Jonathan's face, from pale, flushed red. "She told our Frieda to go. . . ." Mrs. Cleeve studied him, as he mumbled, twisting his cap. "Frieda was afraid. So—"

"So once again you're on the streets without your mother's knowing."

"It's all quiet now."

"I shall send Banto home with you."

"Oh, no, ma'am. Please, no."

"To carry the bundle—Evan's clothes?"

"Please, no."

"You're a brave boy. How shall I ever thank your mother? I'll write her a little note. But I can never tell her—"

"It was nothing, Mrs. Cleeve."

"Nothing?" She leaned back on her pillows, her heavy eyes with their long black lashes almost closed. Jonathan saw tears welling. "You needn't wait, if you wish to go alone. I have your address on your mother's letter. I'll send the clothes with Banto."

"Mrs. Cleeve!"

She waited, puzzled by the fervor in the boy's dark face that made it luminous and tender. "Banto—he is that colored man?" She nodded. "Please, Mrs. Cleeve, let me take Evan's clothes. They won't be heavy. Don't send Banto."

"And why not?"

"They're hurting the colored people. The rioters are! It's much safer for me."

She gazed at him sternly. "I hope you will always be friends with my boy. I hope you will bring him back tomorrow. Will you have lunch with us?"

"Oh, thank you!"

"I'll not send any colored man, Master Hartt, I promise. I'll send the coachman with the clothes. He's Irish, and he's six foot; no one would dare touch him. Now, I must write to your mother."

Jonathan got up. The queenly lady—Evan's mother!—was holding out both her hands to him. "Be his friend," she whispered. "He needs it so!"

40

Careful not to make a noise, Jonathan closed the door; the great curving stair wafted him downward to the foyer. With unseemly brashness, someone was turning a key in the front door; Mr. Cleeve stepped in, tossed his hat and stick on the table, saw the boy.

"How do you do, sir? how *do* you do? Glad to see you're still here. I hope you have dined properly in my absence, with my son? Just going? Step in, step in, a moment. Have you seen my books?" He waved Jonathan ahead of him into the library. (—Bart? A young Hebrew. Bartstein?) "One look at you, sir, I know you love books. There is the art of men. Music for women. Paintings for . . ." his face darkened, "deceivers. Books for men. This is not my law library, these are for relaxation. Up there are the Greeks. Aeschylus, Sophocles, Aristophanes, Euripides, Plato. And down to the latest giant: Dickens. Have you read *Pickwick Papers?* But *Oliver Twist.* What power! Life is real, life is earnest."

"Oh, yes, sir!"

"Sit down, sir. (—What the devil is that name?) A glass of madeira before you leave? Washington's wine. And mine, sir. I won't coax you to stay long. A storm is brewing." He smiled. "The storm you two young men, with perfectly understandable curiosity, were exploring before I met you this afternoon (—Bart? . . . Peabody— *Hart!* . . .), that social storm is about over. I'm referring to a meteorological one about to break, my dear Mr. Hart—an honored name that your father has made worthy in our great city. Meteorological storms, we can afford, eh, sir? They ripen the grain and fruit, water the livestock." He put down the cut-glass decanter with the silver monogrammed collar. "Your health, Mr. Hart," he handed the boy a stem glass, shaped like an inverted pyramid, in which the wine glowed like a gem: the lawyer's stately head, the square, high-ceilinged room, its walls eloquent with books, all an elaboration of the wine. "The other kind of storm: regrettable, but I fear inevitable from time to time in a nation's salad days. Too much blood. Must be let. Ah—" He sipped with his dry madeira the satisfying plans they had perfected in the house on Jones Street, after the Governor and Mayor had gone leaving their approval; plans to turn the riots into national advantage. "What an America is going to be yours, young man! The

41

world's greatest, freest, richest land. What a privilege to be young today. What a challenge!"

Jonathan, drinking but not tasting his wine, stirred uneasily in his chair. Must he not tell Mr. Cleeve about his son? How could he stop him long enough to tell him? And did he want to stop the man whom the Republican press called "Counsel for the Commonwealth"? Should he shrink the great man's attention from these national vistas (with *him* in the foreground) to a personal confession in which he shared the guilt of disobedience?

". . . You must know what the confidence of the younger generation means to us old 'uns, whose battle days are almost over. Mutual confidence! Tell me your plans, sir? Will you read the law?"

"Yes, sir; after I graduate from the Free Academy." He saw the Gothic stone pile within its fences and trees, so near where he stood now. If his professors could only see *him* drinking madeira with Grosvenor Cleeve! their surprise would catapult them through the narrow perpendicular windows, or up through the four turrets.

"I knew it! I think you can trust me to know a lawyer, when I see one. I wish I were as sure of my own son's avocation. After Harvard, of course, he'll go to the Columbia Law School." Jonathan saw another building: four stories of gray stone within the rising lawns between the Fourth and the Fifth Avenues near Fiftieth Street, and himself coming out from the lectures, *with Evan beside him!* "I drink to your success, young man. Success, in America, can be won only by advancing the country. Mill would call it enlightened self-interest. Or is it Bentham?"

"Any of the political economists, sir, would agree. Adam Smith, Ricardo." That was a pause long enough to tell Mr. Cleeve his son was not upstairs! When he knew the truth, could he face him? But who could say this fabulous time would ever come again? How could he spoil it?

"You have read 'em all, I see. You know how to work, I see that too, Hart." The dropping of the *Mr.* was another triumph. "The great asset of our country, do you know what it is? Iron and coal? No. The new West and its gold? No. The natural gas and petroleum oil they've discovered in Pennsylvania? No, and no! If our wealth

42

were ten times more immense, it wouldn't be our great asset. The capacity to work: that's our Big Bonanza. And you share it." He grew pensive. "You're my son's friend! Probably you know him better than I. It's hard for a father to know his son. I don't know why, but it is. And yes, it's hard for a son to know his father. If you could help make a worker of Evan—" Grosvenor Cleeve rose and put out his hand. Suddenly, his attention was elsewhere; his manner was remote. "Glad to have seen you, sir."

Jonathan was alone in the foyer; and on the library floor lay his cap, where he had placed it when he took the wine. The door was shut; he could not go back; could he ever go back! All unreal . . . but Evan was really sleeping in Lucia's bed. He must . . . he could not go back!

He stood at the open door with its brass bars and lock. Slowly, as if it was an end, he shut himself out. The night was black, rolling, as he went into it, to thunder. The rain . . . roaring . . . smote him.

Frieda Memel heard the rain, then the basement bell; she shut the kitchen door to the yard where the water was beating in, and raced through the dark hall. Martin Schmitt stood at the areaway gate, already drenched. "It's you!" She led him back to the kitchen.

"Who did you think it was?"

"Master Jonathan."

Schmitt was a tall, thin man of thirty, with mouse-colored hair and small eyes that turned stiffly as if they were on pivots. His sensitivity without vigor gave the effect of indolence and gray age. He took off his wet coat, hung it on the back of his chair; and Frieda again opened the yard door, breathing the free vibrance of the drenched night. If Master Jonathan came home wet, she must somehow dry his suit and press it before the Mistress knew. The moment in her room when she had stirred the boy suffused her thinking, made her happy.

"You better shut that door; it's raining in," said Martin.

"It'd be too hot. I can wipe up the floor later."

They listened to the rain's strokes on the city, to the distant flowerings of the thunder. But only Frieda smelled the storm's freedom. Martin was smoking his pipe.

43

"Martin," she smiled at him, "why don't you say when we get married?"

"You sure you like it on a farm?"

"Didn't my mother and father live on a farm, before they came to America? Have you found it?"

"Last week, I saved four dollars sixty cents. I'm making good money with all the cabinet work I can do. There's no hurry. It's good to have some savings."

"But where will we go?"

"There's fine land over in Jersey; and there's fine land right here, north of the city. Washington Heights, Manhattanville, Morrisania."

"That'd be fine."

"The soil's not so good like in Jersey."

"But wouldn't it be easier to bring things to market? No Hudson River to cross."

"That don't make no difference. From Jersey, you run your wagon right on the ferry."

"And maybe the land costs less than north of New York?"

"Land's cheap anywhere. That makes no difference. Why, you could squat right down near the East River south of Harlem—and pay nothing at all."

"Then why don't we, Martin?"

"First, I save a little more money."

She came up to him, and touched his hair. "Will I make you happy, Martin? You don't seem very anxious to have me."

He puffed his pipe. "I'll have you all my life. You're my whole life, Frieda. That's why there's no hurry."

—Hurry. The girl was thinking of Jonathan in the storm.

. . . Amity, Green, Wooster, Mercer Streets, where the prostitutes usually plied ("cruisers" they were called), were empty. The rain bounded from the pavements, dug channels and sorties for itself in the muddy gutters. The two theaters to give performances this night were crowded: Laura Keene's *The Wives of Paris,* Niblo's Garden where Mr. Wheatley still played his huge success, *The Duke's Motto.* Mr. Barnum had cautiously shut his American Museum and the rain ravaged the billboards of "General Tom Thumb and His Beautiful Little Wife, late Miss Lavinia Warren; Commander Nutt and Tiny

44

Minnie Warren, Sanford's Ethiopian Opera and a Score of Other Splendid, Sumptuous, Educational Attractions." Not far away, in Paisley Place, an alley of shanties, in an attic room that had hoarded the heat all day, and the rain now dripping through the cracks, a gentleman wrote at a bare table a letter for *Harper's Weekly*. The storm inspired him; he was inclined to believe it was the wrath of the Lord seconding the people who this day had begun to rise against their oppressors. The trouble with the country, he wrote, was the Jews; they were the ones making money, making shoddy, making deals in gold—keeping the War going. The prophet wore a soiled sock round his throat which was sore; the sweat of his body was cold; he was always too hot or too cold, but he comforted himself with knowledge that whom God loveth He chastiseth. He finished his letter, and signed, *The Lounger;* in a rightly constituted world, he would of course have been a man of letters . . . that is, a gentleman of leisure. The straight way to such a world was mapped in the magazine at his feet; it was called *The Imperialist,* datelined New York, and it lay open at the editorial page, where the gentleman's left toe, as it peered through its torn shoe, might have read: "Democracy has proved itself a failure. Nobody wants it. The people despise it. The plutocrats exploit it. What America needs is an Emperor like glorious Napoleon III of France." He recalled hopefully the Fourth of July meeting in the new Academy of Music on Fourteenth Street, packed to aisle and platform. How the orators—Governor Seymour of New York, clean-shaven little man except for a ringlet of beard under his soft chin, and ringlets like a wreath on his bald head (he had pulled his punches, he was a rich man after all); Clement Laird Vallandigham, the Ohio eagle; Congressman James Brookes who edited the *New York Express,* and George Ticknor Curtis—had excoriated the demagogue Lincoln and his crooked generals and politicians de termined to keep the War going as long as there was blood in the poor, boodle in contracts. Their message rang clear as a bell. How Lincoln must have trembled, when he read the speeches in five New York dailies, seven New York weeklies!

. . . In Jonathan's room, at Jonathan's desk, where Lucia sat, it was almost as close, but the rain did not come in. Lucia was proud of her own desk: with its glass-doored cabinet for books above and

45

drawers below, its massiveness was a sign she was a serious person. Jonathan's friend was in her room, and this was thrilling. Tomorrow, perhaps, she'd have a chance, before he left, to show him her prize possession, the New American Cyclopedia (editors, Charles A. Dana and George Ripley), the last of whose sixteen volumes had just come: all bought and paid for with her own money, earned by teaching workingwomen's classes in Reading, Writing, and History. She did not mind sitting at Jonathan's desk. She did not mind becoming his secret ally, when he told her, "I must go out. Frieda's afraid. Don't tell mother." She'd do anything for Jonathan. She only hoped he realized all women were not fraidycats like Frieda. She was a little worried about him in the storm. She wanted him always under her eye; after all, she was his *older* sister. A girl of seventeen is a woman; a boy of fifteen is a boy. She had brought up from her room a pad of yellow foolscap paper. In ornate capitals, she wrote, "The Portia Club" and beneath, *Rules and Regulations*. Philip, shifting noisily in his bed in the far corner, slumbered on. That showed you the injustice of those arbitrary divisions: Philip would be a man; who dared say *he* would have more brains than *she?* yet he was the one supposed to study science, to vote. . . . She turned in her chair. Philip had thrown off his sheet and lay sprawled, his fat blond legs bare, his mouth open. He looked like a country bumpkin, a rather sweet one. Lucia stole over to him, drew the sheet modestly again to his chest, and went back to her paper. They were going to re-form the Club at the next meeting; each of the nine charter members was to bring her ideas for the new constitution. They were all older, except Sadie Smith, daughter of the famous surgeon, Dr. Chester Smith; and there wasn't much to fear from *her* when it came to *ideas*. As for herself, she was going to follow her adored Miss Millicent McNutt, New York's greatest woman; she was going to write her ideas right into the Rules and Regulations. If mama only knew what some of them were, she wouldn't have been so friendly when Miss McNutt spoke at the laying of the cornerstone of the Hebrew Orphan Asylum. Women at work or play shall have the right to wear trousers! (Not those baggy horrors of Miss Amelia Bloomer; not skirts over trousers like Dr. Mary Walker when she worked among the soldiers.) "Don't compromise," said Miss Millicent McNutt. "All it does is get you in debt with

46

yourself." Women in professions or business shall have the right to keep their maiden names. Women shall vote, and receive equal pay for equal service. Men who associate with fallen women shall be known as "fallen men." Upright women shall associate with no men who drink alcohol or smoke tobacco. No, mama could rise to no such radical heights. But Jonathan might. He had already resolved never to smoke, like papa and Reuben with their awful cigars, and never to drink anything stronger than beer. He'd even said he saw no objection to women voting at the municipal elections. Why, that was close to one of Miss Millicent's dearest ideas. Women's place, she said, was the home; and our cities are our homes. Women should keep them clean! Women mayors, alderwomen, women streetcleaning commissioners, women police chiefs (with men under them to do the rough work). Lucia wrote: *Preamble and Resolved.* She breathed hard, not feeling the heat, not hearing the storm.

. . . The top floor of the White House near the Five Points was being rapidly flooded. This blind, fetid warren was so named, according to one school because no white object could survive in it, according to another because it was a home of the proletariat—the true "President" of the nation. A little leakage did the top rooms good, especially in summer when they were unbearably hot. But now the straw pallet beds were floating, the fires were out, small children at their usual play were in danger of drowning. The whole top floor moved down a flight; wet babes doubled with dry ones, wet mothers squatted on stools with dry ones, dry men shared bottles of ale and whiskey with the flooded. Soon, the water would seep down through floor and stair with plaster and soot, often with dead rats and hordes of drowned vermin; it would distribute itself equably through the whole tenement on its way to the two-tiered cellars where the very poor lived in perpetual darkness and the drain of sewage. Then the top floor could go home again. But usually, before this, the inter-mediate tenants staged a party. This night was certainly the occasion for a party. Most of the tenants were recent immigrants, unskilled rustics who had not yet learned a trade, or craftsmen unsettled by the sharp transition from Irish or German village. The new American air had changed their habits violently, as new soil will variate plant or insect to which it has been blown. More than half the White House

47

"presidents" had returned, before the storm, with bruised heads and hands—and booty. It varied. In the humble cases, it was a couple of bottles of rum from a raided saloon; harness or rope, dishes, a hat or a pair of shoes from an upset peddler's cart. But some men brought splendors to their women: furs, silver candlesticks and brushes, satin slippers, gold-framed miniatures, majolica vases, chignons, ruffles, hoops, tins of French sardines, flasks of perfume, lace handkerchiefs, flowered hats, made their first appearance in the White House. In every room that could afford a candle, girls and mothers had knelt before the glories of the city, theirs at last! Women sprinkled Parisian scents on sweaty armpits, pushed patent leather pumps over heels horned with callus, placed cashmere shawls on unwashed hair. But many of the citizens could afford no candles; they spent their nights in the dark or in the open. Before the storm, they had turned the yard into a wild bazaar. On one side was a small slaughterhouse (death to stray dogs and cats), near it a butcher shop and a row of latrines, each contributing an individual smell to the stench of the hot day. And even the blind ragpickers from the cellars, the whores whose charge was a quarter, the pickpockets and beggars, joined the festive swarm. The moralist who told them, glorying in their booty, that they were unfortunates would have been met with jeers of anger: unhappiness was the one unnatural crime in this green slum of drunkenness, knifings, child-death, and incest.

The rain drove the women prancing indoors, the new bracelets on their arms, the new mantillas on their sweaty shoulders, the children guzzling bonbons from gay boxes, the men knocking gold-foil necks from bottles of champagne. The storm turning the day to night molded the ebullient motions into dance. The slaughterhouse man, rushing to rescue his beeves hung on the side of the outhouse from the churned mud, seemed to dance; the bread man, rolling his wheelbarrow of stale loaves indoors where he would sort and price them according to staleness, was of the dance. Song started with a girl in a new hat, a man with a new bottle, a woman with a new ring on her old hand; song ran like fire, weaving all the mouths, all the breasts together. Old songs and new—*Doo-Dah, Dinah and Her Villikins, Susannah Don't You Cry, Bells Will Go Ringing for Sarah, Red, White and Blue*—drowned the roar of the rain, painted the black of the

48

thunder. They organized their music. On the rickety stair to the third floor, an old Scot played the bagpipe, a blond-bearded German scratched his fiddle, a consumptive Yankee spat into his flute (stopping every minute to send his racking cough into the melodious ensemble). The whole house danced. The halls were too narrow; every door was thrown open; the dancers flowed through the rooms. In one, a very old woman lay dying; the weaving dancers carefully avoided her mattress; in one, three children, entirely naked, greeted each couple with shouts of delight; in one, a drunken woman sprawled, legs wide, on her cot, inviting the men, cursing the girls. In the few empty rooms, windowless and dark, some couples lingered, while others danced in and out: the laughter and groans of love, the shouts of happy and half-frightened children, the wails of the lost and trampled, the merry music, mingling with the enstormed sky that drove down rain and thunder.

. . . —My good blue suit! what will mother say? Something made it not matter; something Jonathan Hartt carried from the Cleeve house and Evan's father and Evan's mother, something related to Evan's sleeping in his house, and something in the storm: in its pure violence which he did not resist, letting the waters drench him. He was in a well, a black well, and he could see the stars! That was the wonder: the well raged yet was serene, and his mind and heart were clairvoyant. His mother would forgive his petty disobedience, for in all great things he was going to obey her! He was going to be the lawyer, the statesman she wanted! —I'll buy a dozen new suits. No; not money . . . service to my country. But in America, did they not go together? The great men—Washington, Jefferson, Marshall, Webster—were not poor men. Mr. Lincoln had earned good fees from the railroads. Jonathan felt the rivulets of rain run down his back and chest; if you didn't think of your suit—if you thought of the new dozen suits, it was pleasant! —What's a little water? it won't melt me. He had seen violence. —What's a little violence? the city and the nation stand. Jonathan knew he loved his city. Under rain, and riots, and war, there it lived! It had given him his mother, it had given him Evan, it had given him his destiny. Warm summer water from the clouds, and blood, are good conductors. Jonathan did not figure this out; but the unity he felt within his world was fed by the storms he walked

49

through. He walked, loving the houses shut and aglow; he walked, loving the distant docks and river that a horn and the salt smell brought to him. The city was everything he loved and would fight for! and the city was everything, for it touched the seas—the Atlantic that brought Europe, the sea that was America. Jonathan's heart expanded; feeling his feet slide in drenched shoes, he laughed; —I hope they don't fall apart. What if they did? "Barefoot boy." He heard the voices of his America, and loved them. His mother's voice, and Jefferson's. His mind, lucid in the storming well, jumped to the little pamphlet she had given him for his fifteenth birthday: *Education for a Lawyer,* written when he was a young lawyer by Thomas Jefferson himself. Some of the books Jefferson recommended were superannuated; but his precepts for improving each shining hour would live always! From seven in the morning till midnight! He thought of his sin with Frieda. Jefferson, of course, had never looked on a woman with lust. Well, for penance, he was going to get up at half past six! Jefferson had written the little book for a young boy. Grosvenor Cleeve, whose grandfather might have known the great Virginian, had talked to him in the same way. It was as if Jefferson talked to him! Jefferson, his nephew Peter Carr for whom he wrote the letter, Grosvenor Cleeve and Evan, himself . . . one family! Today, he had protected Evan; and the great Grosvenor Cleeve had given him his confidence, and the greatest of them all, Thomas Jefferson, was talking! "Read the Bible, as if it were Tacitus or Livy, with open noble mind." Jefferson, and his mother, and Evan. Person glided into person, words of a strict syllogism, and the Bible brought his father. His gentle, clumsy father, a little lost in the city, in the great emphasis of his mother and Jefferson: Jonathan knew he loved him. Jefferson writing to his nephew: "For example, in the Book of Joshua, we are told, the sun stood still several hours. Were we to read that fact in Livy, we should class it with showers of blood, with statues that speak. But, it is said, the writer of that Book was inspired. You are astronomer enough to know how contrary it is to the laws of nature that a body revolving on its axis, as the earth does, should be stopped, should not, by that sudden stoppage, have prostrated animals, trees, buildings. . . ." So clear the words of Jefferson; so gentle his father who believed the Book. He must love them both. Oh! he must love them both. He would never lust after Frieda again. Instead, he would help her. That carpenter, Schmitt, with whom she kept company; he would help them get married, he would save every penny of his twenty-five cents a week allowance—and give it all to Frieda. The rain was softer. He had reached the north edge of Stuyvesant Square. Through the rain and the trees, between the black clouds and the city lying like an herbivorous beast, he saw on the south horizon a strip of pale blue sky; he felt the breeze on his face as if the blue beyond the storm breathed on him and the city.

. . . Evan Cleeve half awaked as Mrs. Hartt, having shut the window, closed the door behind her. She had heard his breath, gentle in sleep as a healthy child's; she had stood a moment near his bed in the dark, wondering at this secret life of her son: this strange boy in Lucia's bed. Must Jonathan grow away from her knowledge? Not from her will! She must accept his growing, as her will's growing. She went down the front basement stairs, heard Frieda's voice and a man's (Frieda was back quickly from her errand)—and returned to her husband who again lay on the bed.

"The storm should cool the city," she refreshed the cold compress on his aching brow, "and cool off those ruffians."

"Sarah," he protested mildly, "there *is* something else besides 'ruffians' in what's happened."

"Yes? What else, dear?"

"There's mighty poor people in this city."

Sarah silently massaged her husband's forehead.

"Take those longshoremen who want a dollar and a half a day instead of the dollar they've been getting. You know how prices have gone up. The new greenbacks don't buy much, Sarah, do they? And then, they put those poor darkies to work in their places. *They* don't know what they're doing; only yesterday they were slaves. But neither do the poor whites know—aren't we all still slaves?"

Sarah was thinking of her son and his new friend; she was used to these mumblings of her poor good man. It was going to be hard to scold Jonathan in the morning as, of course, he must be scolded. After the young gentleman had left. . . . She heard her husband:

51

"People in this country ain't found what they hoped."

"You have to *work* for that," she said sternly, but her hand on her man's brow was gentle.

. . . It was the music, more than Mrs. Hartt, that half awakened Evan. He had been following its volumed splendor, thinking: —As usual, it will wake me, and then it will be gone. There was always in his music this presaged frustration, this certain failure to hold it. It was not quite yet·lost. It was a weave of several themes, one lilting high among the violins, another holding horizontal, bastion-strong, with the trumpets and horns against the treble above and below, the cellos and bass viols rolling away down a deep abyss that their sonorities illumined. While he heard it, Evan knew that he was happy; he did not exist and therefore he was happy; the music only was real, and himself not the hearer (until he awaked and it was gone); rather, he was partaken of by the music. To cease to be oneself: this was happiness, and only the dreamed music brought it. Already, as always, within the happiness, the thought: —If I could only hold it, when I wake! and the thought already the waking and the loss. The storm, one balanced instant, helped his symphony: rumble of kettledrums, scintillance of triangle and cymbal. Then it plunged, tearing the fabric; and Evan opened his eyes. —Where am I?

The immense instant of not knowing and of needing to know who and where he was (the music losing itself in huge cascades . . . into ripples . . . into the grain of silence) filled with his whole afternoon: the Hartt boy, the battle, the Hartt home. He lay peaceful in the dark, as if the memory of bliss were all one needed for bliss and for answer to Where? Who am I? But he heard a window shut, he heard rain beating on metal, the strange house enarmed him. The house of that boy Hartt: nice chap, what was his Christian name? They seemed to get along together. Vaguely, he recalled the tight little woman with the dry face: no mother like his! and the ugly girl, unpleasantly tense, the sister. "Lucia's room," he remembered. —I wonder what it's like. No recollection; it was pitch black with almost no light from the window. Hot. He felt cooped up, and getting hotter. —We get along. The boy's face was like certain chords in that new sensation from Germany, Richard Wagner: thick, a bit muddy and dark, yet with filigrees of light racing contrapuntally through them. Hartt must be

German; not a Yankee. Spanish, perhaps? Anyway, —we get along; he felt at home in this room he had no physical sense of. It almost held on to the music. He was cooped up and hot, but his head free as if he were far above his body. A faint dizziness wafted him to sleep.

. . . Jonathan in the now gentle rain saw the pale blue strip of sky transform the city. It was the subtle vibrance of lighter air, kindling the dark mass of houses; and the vibrance was within the houses, making them faintly a-dance. A girl danced. He knew he did not see her, he knew it was a break in the storm; yet the girl danced. She was pretty like Frieda. She was miserably dressed like the women behind the barricade; and she danced stiffly as Frieda's beau, Martin Schmitt, might dance. Jefferson's clarity! how could the earth against all astronomy stop at Joshua's horn? The girl danced. His mother was going to scold; his work waited. Evan was in Lucia's room! The girl danced . . . the city was dancing. . . .

II

MIRAGES

JONATHAN HARTT STOOD IN THE ROTUNDA OF THE County Court House, where Evan Cleeve was to meet him. The milling lawyers, clerks, litigants, witnesses, had carried the December weather with them up the great stone steps on Chambers Street; slush and cold steamed in the heat of their talk on the fouled floor. —Seven years old, thought Jonathan, and the gray walls already peeling; the arrogant structure was a symbol of the man, William Marcy Tweed, who had stolen the taxpayers' millions while he built it. Waiting in the misty clamor, Jonathan recited 'the figures to himself: thirteen millions for a three-million-dollar job! for safes, carpets, furniture, seven million dollars; for a few thousands' worth of lumber, four-hundred-and-sixty thousand dollars; for city printing and advertising, three-million-one-hundred-and-sixty-eight thousand dollars! At least, the Court House was there; millions had been appropriated for schools, hospitals, docks, which existed not even on blueprints! Well, Tweed was in Ludlow Street jail, his ring was scattered; but Jonathan knew the war with Tammany was not yet quite over. Here, all around him, was the muck in which grew the Tweeds, the Halls, the Connollys: these pushing lawyers, lobbyists, bullet-head judges in billowing black robes, followed by wood-faced attendants; these plaintiffs, defendants, appellants, and respondents, their hot eyes all out for the main chance. —But we've won the first battle. To break Tweed and Hall was Gettysburg. The good men, Henry Ward Beecher, cartoonist Nast, the *New York Times,* William Tilden, Grosvenor Cleeve, William Havemeyer . . . —*We* are winning!

Evan Cleeve came in by one of the basement doors from the Park, and for a moment the City Hall was background to his fur-lined coat and ruddy beaver. He kicked the snow off his fleece-lined galoshes, freed his long head that had sweated under the hat. From the County Clerk's office, as if by shared intuition, stepped a putty-faced young man in a black coat too tight for him.

"Respects, Mr. Cleeve."

"Hello," Evan was gruff; took from the other a long envelope bulging with greenbacks, and slipped it carelessly into his greatcoat pocket.

"The gov'nor'd like to know—"

"Well? I'm in a hurry."

"*Re* that Kingsbridge, Morrisania, and West Farms annexation—will it be sustained? The option on all those lots expires next week. The tax sales—"

Evan smiled and touched his pocket. "Is the head of the firm's opinion on that included in this?"

"Oh, no, sir! A similar honorarium—"

"I've consulted him, without his knowing it." Evan paused, like an artist leaning on his effects. "It's certain. Off the record."

"Off the record, of course, sir! Thank you, sir! Good day, sir."

Evan marched up the wet steps to the rotunda and Jonathan's face brightened. It was a face apt for both shadow and light; the gray eyes were heavy and luminous; the mouth in the short ruddy-black unkempt beard was sensual and sensitive.

"I've just learned," he held Evan's hand, "the argument's tomorrow. Before Justice McHugh."

Evan laughed. "That means you'll have to spell every letter of the law. Don't forget, Justice McHugh's still 'larnin'!"

"If he's willing to learn—"

"You know what his old man, the sewage contractor, said when he got his son on the Supreme Court? 'If bein' a Judge don't larn Mike the law, then I don't know what will.'" He laughed, and Jonathan's face darkened.

"Evan. Will you appear with me? You know how important the case is."

"You know more law than I do, old fellow."

"I doubt it. And you know more human nature."

They brushed their way through the throng down the great stairs.

"The snow's turning to slush," said Evan.

"Good exercise, nonetheless."

"You can't let yourself like anything, can you," Evan teased him, "unless it's good for you."

"I suspect that's all we should like; certainly not what's bad for

58

us. Or are we stupider than the animals who never do anything that's not functional?"

"Of course, we're stupider. That's the prerogative of man's free will."

They turned their backs on the commercial palaces of Broadway and struck southeast through the Park to Nassau Street, whose mixed new and old buildings, once residential, stood dim in the slanting sleet. Icicles garlanded the telegraph poles, horses with muted slog drew carts and cabs through the afternoon. The two young men, at one with a world turned somnolent by the snow, loved this walking. Walking had reknit their friendship at the law school, after the separated years of Jonathan in City College (once the Free Academy) and of Evan at Harvard. They had walked from the legal portico surrounded by the bare lots of Madison and Fifth Avenues ... walked home together, Evan to his mansion in Gramercy Park, Jonathan to the narrow old red brick house off Stuyvesant Square. Winter afternoons, they had tramped through the mud, spring days through the bloom of a city still close to its earth. They were silent or they argued; they seldom agreed; but they got on together.

"Tell me the main points of your brief," said Evan. "But I'll have to read it, too."

The case was *Golding Brothers versus Mendis Toys, Ltd.* After the War Between the States, Valentine Mendis, who had lost his fortune in Confederate bonds, came to New York from Charleston, South Carolina, borrowed money from the bankers and began a new importing business in toys with his three sons, Raoul, Alfred, and Sylvester. The business grew; the father died; the sons learned that their loan contract with the Goldings perpetually gave all their profits above a bare minimum to the bankers. The Mendis boys brought suit, and were thrown out of court. A year ago, Jonathan had met Raoul and his sister at a charity bazaar; Raoul brought the young lawyer home and introduced him to his mother and Sylvester (Alfred was in Europe). To Jonathan's surprise, Raoul came to his office: a single room with a bare table and pine shelves for lawbooks, in an old building behind Exchange Place, and asked Jonathan to be their lawyer. Jonathan studied the case, and advised, "Let *them* sue. Don't pay them a penny more!" It was a complex problem, Jonathan's first of importance; but the beauty of the law involved, the justice he heartily desired for the Mendis widow and her children, even the good start victory would bring to his practice, did not quite explain Jonathan's passionate interest. Evan knew this, and said nothing; he had noted his friend's warm praise for the "gracious" Mrs. Mendis, for "stalwart upright" Raoul, for "lovable" Sylvester—and never a word about the youngest in the family, Greta. He knew his Jonathan. How could he speak of the girl he was thinking of all day, and dreaming of all night?

They reached Wall Street. Frozen snow almost blanketed the sedate pillared brownstone houses: the Manhattan Company, the Merchants' National, the Bank of New York, the Bank of America. The great bend of Broad Street southward was a whirl of wires, snow, huddling and hurrying bodies. Here, at Kiernan's Corner, in the new home of the Western Union Telegraph Company, whose name with DIRECT WIRES beneath spread over both six-story façades, Grosvenor Cleeve had his offices.

"Wuxtry! Wuxtry!" A boy in a ragged jacket with torn soaked stockings ran up, and Evan bought a paper: the sensationally successful *Evening Telegram*. He chuckled and handed the sheet to Jonathan.

"ESCAPE OF TWEED FROM JAIL!" Jonathan read aloud. "I can't believe it." He looked for the story. "It's just a stop-press headline. Not a word. Just some more of James Gordon Bennett's dirty journalism."

"Here's hoping," Evan laughed.

"What do you mean?"

"I hope it's true, and he makes it."

"Evan!"

"Tweed's no worse than a hundred others, beginning with our fool President Grant and most of his crooked Cabinet."

"So, because justice isn't brought to all, you'll have it for none?"

"Don't be so rational. There was something magnificent about Tweed: his solid gold Tiger watch-charm, his 'What are you going to do about it?' flung in the face of the public."

"They'll catch him, even if it's true. They must!"

"Didn't Tweed have the decency to refuse that statue the citizens of New York wanted to put up for him? Catch Tilden or Evarts or Grant doing that."

"Evan! With whom are you comparing those good men!"

They stood in the shelter of the Telegraph Building entrance. The network of wires wove in the wind and sleet an almost opaque roof to the dark street. "A good day for an escape."

Jonathan said, "I don't believe it."

"If it wasn't robbery, I'd bet and take your money. Well, old man, about your brief—"

"I'll run over and get it."

"Bring it home tonight. I'll drop in early. I won't keep you from your engagement."

Jonathan was blushing. "Why not come along?"

"Where? You haven't told me where."

"You know, you scalawag."

"Say it."

"Why should I tell you, if you know?"

"Confession's good for the soul."

"There's nothing to confess. I'm sure you'd be welcome. Perhaps there'll be music."

"Music? By whom?"

"You know, curse you!"

"Say it!"

"You know Miss Greta sings."

"How the devil should I know Miss Greta sings?"

"Well, she does. Like a bird."

"That's too bad. Nightingales and larks have meager repertoires."

"Go to the devil. But you will come along?"

"I'll be at your house for that brief."

He climbed the moldy stairs and opened a door on which was painted: *Cleeve, Fenston and Fenston.* Behind the wooden rail sat a thin man in black, almost bald, with red-lidded eyes, his hands like talons within a pile of papers.

"Hello, *rara avis,*" Evan greeted him and pushed through the swinging gate.

"You've been calling me that for three weeks, sir. I know what it means in Latin. I don't see the connection."

Evan went to his desk in the far corner beyond the barrel-stove, threw off his dripping coat, his drenched hat. "The bald eagle"—he leaned down to unbuckle his galoshes—"preys on fish, mice, chip-munks, fowl, and lambkins. You're a bald eagle; and all I've ever seen you eat is paper. That makes you a *rara avis*."

The clerk was flattered. "The governor's back, and was asking for you, sir."

Evan looked toward the door with beveled glass where his father's name was printed in small letters. "Hell," he shrugged. "Well, *sui amor fati*."

"Love of fate. What's the connection there, sir?"

"Not love of fate, Cicero, love of one's own fate. That's the desid-eratum. People are fond of saying they love life. What do they mean? Good times, good food and drink, outings on sunny days, successful love affairs. Since when is that life? Love of life means love of dirty weather, love of love jilted, love of poverty and heartache, not forgetting the toothache. That's life! Love life and you love that."

"Is it all so bad, sir? It has been, I suppose, since the panic. But surely we'll get over it, sir."

Evan laughed. "So you think if Jay Cooke and Company hadn't failed just by chance on Black Friday two years and two months ago, dragging down with him the railroads and banks, there'd be no toothache, no heartache; no dirty weather and no dirty people?"

"All in reason, sir."

"Do you look out of the window, Blackstone?"

"I'm mostly too occupied, Mr. Cleeve."

"Have you ever looked out?"

"Of course."

"What do you see?"

"Broad Street and Wall Street."

"Solon, you're an incurable asset to a thriving republic a hundred years young next July, and already assembling mountains of rhetoric and gewgaws for the celebration. Broad Street, Wall Street . . . fiddle-sticks! Look out that window, here's what you'd really see: mud and slush, men and women in wet, hideous clothes hiding pot-bellies, sunken chests, and fallen arches. Faces raked with worry and greed. And hearts full of figures: not the mystic numbers of Pythagoras, but bills, debts, schemes for piddling profit. You'd see buildings whose bricks and stones add up to dullness. You'd see a circle of Dante's

62

Inferno. Oh, yes, you'd see wires, the wonderful telegraph wires. If the Morse code were visible, what would you find? Buying and selling. Wheat futures dealt in by men who've never worked a wheatfield. Railroads and industries in the hands of men that have never known an honest day's sweat." The clerk listened entranced, as if to music. Evan thought: —What's the use? He actually enjoys hearing his world insulted! It's clowning in a circus ring, for him. "If you looked *inside,* Demosthenes; if you looked at yourself—?" Evan saw the clerk's hand scratch the ruff of hair over an ear, the dandruff fall to the shiny coat collar, while the face wavered between the spell of Evan's words and a faint fear. Evan got up, gave him an affectionate slap on the back, laid a couple of cigars on the papers, and went in to see his father.

Grosvenor Cleeve, now President of the Association of the Bar, was to his son as an old glove to a new one. His close-cropped blond hair had turned gray, his generous features were clamped close together: the nose toward the mouth, the chin toward the nose, the eyes caverned beneath the brow. "Sit down. I want to talk with you, Evan."

Evan lighted a cigar without offering one to his father.

"I had a successful trip to Washington."

Evan watched his smoke ring break in the drafty air of the room.

"I saw the President," Mr. Cleeve went on. "About the Union Pacific, of course. I found him most reasonable—"

"You mean, he won't oppose further Federal gifts of the people's land, timber, funds to the poor untaxed railways?"

"Put it that derogatory way, if you like to ape the Anarchists."

"Don't flatter me."

Mr. Cleeve chuckled, indulgently. "He's a strange man. An enemy to General Grant is still a soldier on the other side of the battle lines. If you're on his side, you must be his friend. And friends can do no wrong."

"Richardson, McDonald, Belknap, for instance, though they're crooks. While Bristow and Jewell, because they pack guns against the friend-crooks, get booted out."

"I guess that's about it. But don't forget, Evan, in the larger sense, Grant is always right. I'm not defending McDonald's whiskey scandal, nor Belknap's bribery and that Indian Territory concession. But who's

63

building the country? The railroads. Grant's for them, as he was for the Union. There was plenty of blundering in that fight, too."

"All right. God bless U. S. Grant. What else?"

"Congress will require an estimate of costs for the new line from Omaha to California. We need a man in Chicago. How would you like to go?"

"Why Chicago? Why not engineers who know the mountains and prairies?"

"I thought you'd understand. It's not *exact* costs we're after. It's the banks who can figure best how much credit the country can take; it's a subtle equation of potentials and actual confidence. You may have to make a trip to St. Paul and Omaha, but the men in Chicago have their fingers on the pulse. Congressman Oakes Ames of Massachusetts—"

"—You mean, of *Crédit Mobilier*."

"Well, he's out there already. A sound man on free suffrage for the Southern Negro and free enterprise for Business. You'll win the friendship of those fellows and their confidence; you're good at that. If we tried to figure our Federal grants here, we'd grossly underestimate."

"And the more the Government gives, the more stock you sell."

"That's a problem Fiske and Gould have already figured out. You know we don't issue stock on assets and capital—"

"As the law humbly suggests—"

"We're an expanding country, Evan. Law, by its nature, inclines to remain static. That's why the law needs dynamic lawyers. And since Grant knows it, history will forgive him his little errors of judgment. Railroads must issue stock on the basis of earnings in the future."

"The sky's the limit?"

"Something more substantial than the sky. The continent, my boy. Well, Evan, this is your big chance."

Evan got up, and looked out of the window. "Thanks, governor. I don't want it."

"You won't have to *live* in the West. Six months will do it. When you come back, you'll have enough to build a house of your own."

Evan turned round. "What's the matter with the house my mother lives in?"

"You're welcome there, of course. I merely supposed that a young man of twenty-eight, a future partner in this office, would be planning his own home; dreaming perhaps of sharing it some day with a wife."

"You'd give me a half million if I left your house tomorrow. Not that I disturb you; just to distress mother."

"We'd better get back to the point."

"I've got used to the stinks of New York. I'd miss 'em in Chicago. I'm not doing so badly here."

"Chicken feed, my boy. Think it over. It's time you cut your apron strings."

"I've cut too many strings; an *E*, an *A*, a *D*, and a *G* string. You've had your way there. That's enough."

"What are you talking about? You can still play your fiddle."

"Jigs and mazurkas and Vienna waltzes."

"Very pretty, I'm sure."

"I don't need strings for them. Didn't you know? For the dances, you need skull-and-bones. Tattoo. Bone on the skull." Evan had come back from the window and was leaning over the desk, close to his father, his fingers thrumming the wood. He looked down, and saw an open telegram.

"You may read it," said Grosvenor Cleeve.

Evan thrummed a few more measures of a waltz by Johann Strauss; he picked up the yellow paper, and turned pale.

> MRS. CLEEVE IS SERIOUSLY ILL. RECOMMEND YOU
> COME HOME AS SOON AS YOU RECEIVE THIS.
>
> DR. HARLEY

"When did this come?"

"An hour ago."

"And you sit here talking of your skullduggery railroads!"

"The afternoon is almost over. Business must be attended to. You know how much your mother's sick."

Evan went to the door. "You needn't hurry."

"Have *you* no more business? Is your desk clean?"

"Clean?" Evan shouted. "What do you mean by 'clean'?" He slammed the door behind him so hard that a crack forked upward in the glass like lightning. Grosvenor Cleeve saw it pierce between his first and last names. He cringed as if struck, his features clamped closer, and his hands twitched. Then they grew firm again and took up the papers before him.

Evan found a cab on Broadway and told the driver to race. The snow had stopped, the sky was iron-gray, a cold clear night was shaping, slippery underfoot; but the horse made good progress past the flamboyant new Post Office, the gracious City Hall with its wings and poised clock tower, the arrogant Court House where he had been with Hartt. So old Boss Tweed was out? He had heard rumored plans of collusion with the police. Why not? The difference between Tweed and Fiske, Gould, Vanderbilt, his father, was that Tweed was more stupid and more clumsy. —That's why I like him better. Stewart's downtown store was already ablaze with gas lamps . . . Ittner's restaurant, the gay Saint Nicholas Hotel: —I need just one drink. He stopped the jehu and jumped out, strode through the marble public hall of the hotel to the bar, downed a glass of whiskey, and was back in his cab. Niblo's theater, Brooks Brothers, Stewart's uptown store, Grace Church, the ornate money houses shouldering it. . . . Past the Roosevelt mansion and the rich hotels of Union Square: "Go up Irving Place," he told the coachman. A block before his house, there was a saloon, rather rowdy, that he liked. He paid the cabby an extra dollar for his speed, and went in for one more drink. At the bar, men with sweaty hands swapped stories. He had two drinks. The street was quiet, the brownstone houses stood sedate with their filigreed iron balconies garlanded in ice. Were they all hypocrites, like his own house? The world he lived in, solid in its greed and its sham, made him dizzy; the alcohol made him sober. If the respectable ones—many, like Cooke and Daniel Drew, pious churchmen—admitted they lived for money, always more money; if the ladies admitted their virtue was backboned by husbands who lived for money, would there be fewer silver candlesticks in the warm houses, and less music? That was the trouble; he, too, needed the warmth and the music. He thought of his favorite composer whom it now hurt him to play; Mozart knew, weaving his music gay as ordered, and slyly letting the blood of his humiliated heart suffuse it. He thought of his mother, the weak woman; unlike Mozart she had not triumphed over her humiliations. She had tried, she had wanted her son to be like Mozart; but he was closer to his mother.

66

Emma Corthuis Cleeve was sitting up in bed, the gas lamp's luminance on her black hair. Unlike Grosvenor Cleeve who was aged beyond his years, Emma at nearly fifty looked less than forty. Her features had not declined from their measure, her bust was still firm; but the preserved harmony of her flesh was due to a rigidity, her beauty was frozen—intact because devoid of movement and of the ravage of expression. Evan realized his father had been right: here was no crisis demanding that a busy lawyer put aside his work and rush uptown—and hated his father the more.

"What have you been up to?" He kissed her and drew a chair to her side.

"It was nothing. You know how worrisome Dr. Harley is."

"If you had to call him, it was something."

"Marie called him. She couldn't wake me this morning."

"And why couldn't your maid wake you?"

"I took a few sleeping powders too many."

"You call that nothing?"

"Here I am, Evan," she smiled wanly.

"Did you know it was too many?"

"So you're a lawyer, now, even with your mother?"

"With you, I've got to be a criminal lawyer."

"Criminal!"

"You took those too many powders on purpose. Is that a crime?"

"Suppose I wasn't here for you to scold? What difference would it make?" He took her hand and pressed it. "You're hurting me, Evan."

"You're hurting me, mother."

"That's all that's left, isn't it?"

"Won't you tell me? What happened?"

"Nothing."

"But something must have made you—"

"Nothing." She moistened her heavy lips with the tip of her tongue. "Perhaps I suddenly knew, nothing will ever happen."

"No quarrel?"

"I never quarrel with your father. You know that."

"If you really told me, don't you see?, that would be something happening. Maybe something good."

"My dearest!"

"Are you quite comfortable? How about another pillow? Are you thirsty?"

"It's too warm. Open a window."

It was not warm for Evan, but he lowered the upper sash of one of the windows and sat down again. He was a little cold; he needed a drink.

"That's better," she said. There was long silence. The woman, high on her pillows, her face unmoved, gazed before her, seeing nothing. The young man watched her, the nerves in his mouth, his eyes, his hands, faintly twitching.

"Tell me, dear," he murmured at last.

For the first time, her heavy eyes met Evan's, and at once dropped, gazing on the foot of her bed.

"As usual, I couldn't sleep." Only her lips moved. "I seemed to see each second like a grain of sand. Each grain like all the others . . . endless grains of sand, heaping on me. If you take a powder, I thought, a few thousand grains of sand will fall on you without your knowing. But then you'll wake, you'll know the grains of sand again. . . . If you take many powders—" She gazed long, motionless, before her; then slowly she turned her head and her eyes stayed with Evan's.

It was a contact, tremendous as if lightning rent the room's air, and they were clapped close together. He felt his mother's bosom rise and fall; he could say nothing.

"That's all," she whispered, her dim gaze again before her. She moistened her lips. "Something goes on for years, moment after moment after moment. Suddenly, you see—not the moment: the years. All of them, at once."

He needed to protest. How could he, knowing her words true?

"I've lost, all along the line, Evan. I didn't want you to go to college. I didn't want you to be a lawyer. I didn't want you to be unhappy."

"What right has anyone to demand happiness?"

"You've given up, too!"

"I wasn't good enough to be a musician."

"We're not good enough. Only the lawyers and businessmen are good enough."

"Mother dearest, we love each other; we have each other; we can keep close—"

"We're not close. I've lost you, too. Your hate for your father and what he stands for binds you nearer to him, than love binds you to me."

"Mother—!"

"You're not close to yourself." Now she spoke free, and her eyes were full on her son's. "Everything you love, you are away from. Everything you hate, you are close to. Your whole life is closeness to what destroys you, distance from what loves you."

"I live with you. . . ." He heard his words small and thin, and despised them.

"Can't you tell the truth?"

"Isn't it the truth?"

"I don't know what you do, I only feel it. Why do you drink so much, to cover up what? There's something dark in your life, Evan. Desperate. Desperate as dying."

"I'm a practising lawyer, since I wasn't good enough or brave enough to be a practising artist. All right. That accounts for eight hours of the day. Not so much, that. The factory workingmen are pleading now for an eight-hour day. They'll probably get it, if they stop parading and orating—and *strike*. Eight hours, they say, we'll feed the machines in your smoky, filthy mills. That leaves us sixteen hours to sleep and love our wives and drink beer. I'm like a workingman who's won his eight-hour day; only I get paid more for it. That leaves me sixteen hours—"

"Evan, stop it!"

He looked down, then again slowly up at her. "All right, mother, I'll stop lying."

For the first time, she reached for his hand and held it. "If you were only a little less clever, there'd be more hope for you, you could believe in something. Like your friend, the Jewish young man. *He* can be a lawyer, because he believes in justice, in serving his country."

"What makes you think he's not clever?"

"Beside you, he's dull. Very solemn. And how wonderfully he glows with his faith. Can't you be like him?"

"You know I can't."

"Just a little . . . a little less clever?"

"Jonathan's no fool."

"You're a fool, because you won't be fooled."

69

"I'll see what I can do about dousing this wonderful cleverness of mine."

"I wish you could be like him. I'm not joking. You see, I was wrong, I haven't quite given up hope."

"What do you hope, mother?"

"That Jewish boy, I've seen him often enough in your study. He loves you. Ever since that time he saved your life, he loves you."

"Yes."

"Love him! Entwine your life with his; at least your work."

"If I thought there was a chance of getting him into the office. There isn't. Not because he's a Jew; least of all, that. He's not our kind of lawyer. If he did get in, he'd march right out again."

"Evan, I don't want him in your firm. I want you out."

"You mean?" he studied her. "I see what you mean. Jonathan Hartt's partner."

"He loves you. The best of you loves him." Now, there was movement in her mouth and eyes; it made her look more alive, and older.

Evan got up and went to the windows, smiling. Unconsciously, he stuck a cigar in his mouth; remembered where he was and put it back in his vest pocket. He returned to his chair. "So you want me to quit one of the city's richest practices?"

"Yes, Evan."

"Mother dearest, you don't get the point. There's a difference of philosophy between us. If one's going to hang, why not for a sheep instead of a lamb?"

"I said you were too clever."

"I enjoy my cleverness, mother. It keeps me from smelling too bad. It's a bath, of course, and as soon as one goes out, one starts getting dirty and smelling bad again. It's more honest than Jonathan's godliness, I mean his delusions that the law has an organic connection with justice. That doesn't mean I don't like him." She was gazing ahead of her again. "Mother! What are you staring at?"

"The grains of sand."

In the silence, there seemed nothing to say. He too felt the heavy falling seconds: not of sand, they were stone. He needed a drink.

"Can't I get you a glass of water? You must be thirsty."

"Yes, dear."

70

He went into her bathroom, lit the gas within the blue globe on the wall. Blue curtains muffled the window; the porcelain washbowl and tub, cased in wood, were blue-veined and the faucets were brass. He opened the medicine chest: bottles, lotions, medicines; a box labeled *The Powder for Insomnia. Take One Only;* a dark bottle with rubber stopper labeled *Poison* over a scarlet skull and *Carbolic;* he found the little cognac flask woven in straw, poured a stiff drink in a cut-glass tumbler, drained it, rinsed it, and refilled it from the gallon jar of Saratoga water. Forgetting to turn off the gas-light, he returned to his mother; when he saw her he recalled the insomnia powders and regretted he had not removed them.

The brief absence had changed their relation. Emma lay lower in her pillows, tears glistening in the lashes of her half-shut eyes. Her mouth, more pallid, was still as death. And Evan felt his mother, as if she touched his throat; she was cold, now, her plea about his friend was a flame that was gone; with exacerbated sharpness he sensed her calm, feared her distance. He wanted to say, "Mother, I'll do it. I'll make him my partner!" Not pride, not reluctance to do anything however foolish, stopped him; but distance. She was too far away.

He said, "Here is your drink," and lifted her. She drank, it seemed to him, not because she was thirsty, but because she was will-less: one swallow led to another until the glass was empty. She kept holding the glass until he took it from her. She closed her eyes.

"Mother, should you sleep? Those powders—"

Not opening her eyes, she said, "He took them away—"

"Away?"

With effort she smiled. "Not very pleasant. If you must know—the stomach pump."

"You won't take any more? Never again, more than one powder?"

Her head nodded so faintly, he could not know if it was more than the stir of her heart.

"Promise me, mother. Promise you'll never again take more than one powder."

She opened her eyes. "I promise." Her eyes closed.

As her head sank lower on the pillows, the flimsy folds of her negligee parted. Evan leaned and kissed her mouth, seeing the round white breasts. —Small for a mother, weak for a mother! Conflict roared through him; he covered her bosom with the quilt, touching and loving and hating her weakness; he turned out the light.

On the stairs, he met his father coming up.

"Mother's all right," he stopped him. "She took an overdose of sleeping powders. But she's all right. She's resting."

"I'd better go and see her."

He barred the way. "She's fallen asleep; a natural sleep."

Grosvenor Cleeve hesitated. "Perhaps you're right. I'll not disturb her."

The father and the son walked down the stair together, the unison of their steps for Evan an intolerable discord. He flung on his coat and left the house.

Jonathan was at the stoop of his home when Reuben closed the front door and came down. Since his marriage to Darby Sleip's daughter, Reuben lived in his own house on Hamilton Square off the Third Avenue and Sixty-sixth Street. He owned a large parcel of land in that remote uptown and was sure, with his father-in-law, that some day it would be worth good money. Reuben in his blue coat, silk hat, looked what he was: a prominent citizen. His father never forgave him for marrying such a *goy,* the child of an unprincipled speculator; but the young man's health and happiness made it clear that his city forgave him. His mother, who had never thought highly of him, regarded him a little more as he prospered in the hard years of the panic. And Reuben continued to be a dutiful son. Regularly twice a week, he stopped off at the old house on his way home from business downtown, and chatted pleasantly with the old man (who lay on his bed for a half hour before dinner) with never a word or gesture to reveal that he was hurt by his family's disapproval. Appearances were honored. On special occasions, like his parents' birthdays, Lucy accompanied him to the house and amiably discussed servants with Sarah, women's rights with Lucia, now a full-grown spinster. He tried to be materially helpful. During the war, he had done his best to persuade his father to convert his little factory from "ladies' dress trimmings" to soldiers' uniforms. He had offered a loan and help in getting contracts. "You'll make two hundred per cent a year." Joseph, running his little hands through his thin beard, answered, "I don't want to make money out of war." In the years that followed, with the West opened by the railroads, the South conquered by the carpetbaggers, and greenbacks pouring from the banks, Joseph Hartt suddenly responded to the long-discontinued arguments of Reuben. On his own initiative, he borrowed, enlarged his workshop on Duane Street from one floor to three—all in time to be caught by the collapse of 1873. He could not dispose of his stock, he could not meet his loans. "Bankruptcy," Reuben recommended; and when the old man took the proposal as an insult, he shrugged his shoulders. "So you're better than Jay Cooke? Nonsense, papa. Bankruptcy is part of the capitalist system." When Joseph still refused, Reuben offered to finance the business with a lien. Finally, Joseph cried, "You come to see us. You're our son. But no word about money. Never!" He turned to Jonathan, whose meager savings now went to keep his father solvent. The urgent debts were paid; Jonathan persuaded the creditors that if they waited, they would receive one hundred cents on the dollar. It was hard for the apprentice lawyer, but Joseph Hartt's name remained "unsullied."

"How's things?" asked Reuben. "You're late, you must be pretty busy."

"I am busy," said Jonathan.

"I'm glad to hear it."

"How's your wife?"

Reuben's eyes warmed. "*She*'s busy. Busier than you and me. Charity bazaars, whist parties, afternoons at home. Evenings, when it's not a dinner, it's the Opera. Busy business all the time."

"You seem to thrive on it. One'd never guess to look at you these are hard times."

"Hard times are building times, my boy. Prices are low. They'll be high."

Jonathan laughed. "That's the queerest reason I've heard for going to the Opera."

"It's the only good reason. You'd be surprised what a lot of good will you buy with a couple of stalls at the Academy of Music."

"I wonder how much longer—"

"The hard times? They won't change till after the elections. When the fear of the Democrats' getting in—"

"Why shouldn't they get in? Haven't Grant and the radical Republicans made mess enough of their eight years? Look at the scandals, at the South, at that Cabinet."

"Why look at them?" Reuben smiled. "They're of no importance. Only one thing counts, Jonathan my boy: confidence. There's money again for large-scale investment, now that so many bad debts are written off. All money needs is a guarantee there'll be no dickering with the tariff, no more cheap paper to help the farmers out of debt."

"Why shouldn't they get out of debt?"

"And you went to college! Those debts are the backbone of a hundred banks. As to scandals, seems to me the Democrats are as good there as the Republicans. Your friend Tweed, I see—"

"He's no friend of mine, and you know it."

"How about the great Henry Ward Beecher? I suppose you weren't an admirer of *him*?"

"I still am. You forget the jury failed to find him guilty. Until a man's proved guilty—"

"Adultery's hard to prove—thank goodness!" Reuben snickered and his brother blushed. "The point is, who cares? What if the old preacher did sleep with Mrs. Tilton? Don't that leave him a great preacher? Stability, Jonathan: there's Republican statesmanship in a nutshell. Don't rock the boat."

"Wherever it's headed . . ."

"You know damn well where we're headed. Toward national greatness."

"To hear you talk, Reuben, one would think it was the Wall Street plungers who were winning the West."

"Who else?"

Jonathan thought of the men who cleared the forests, laid the rails, fought Indians and storm, the men who sowed the wheat. They were good men, better than Reuben. —Better than I. He stood with his brother on the street, barely hearing Reuben invite him to take Lucy to a concert at Chickering Hall ("I've got a conference on the new Elevated Railroad financing. . . . The Ninth Avenue's clear. Trains will be running soon all the way to Fifty-ninth Street. . . . The Second, Third, Sixth Avenues . . . snags. . . . I know you love music.") Music—and Greta, who might sing tonight; he stood before their old house where they had been brought up . . . the bleak night falling, the slush on the

74

sidewalk freezing—silenced by his guilt. Guilt, because he felt himself better than his brother, because he had never truly loved him, and was not sure envy did not tincture his disdain. Guilt, because he could not overcome his joy at the hour ahead when he would see Greta Mendis again; and guilt because he loved her. How dared he dream of marriage (he heard his mother's voice: "You, Jonathan, are the real head of the family now"), when there were his father's debts, and Lucia was unmarried. Lucia, approaching thirty, would remain unmarried! Neither she, corresponding secretary of the Portia Club, nor their mother, was much disturbed by this, as long as their adored Jonathan remained where he belonged: at home. But the deepest guilt of all: how could he speak even to his heart of Greta, when he was unclean! He declined Reuben's invitation, and slowly went up the steps, thinking of Frieda. . . .

Frieda Memel had married Martin Schmitt. They had moved, not to Morrisania or Harlem, but to Shanty Town, east of the Second Avenue, north of Forty-second Street: a region of crude cabins on rocky hills and grassy gulches where goats and pigs roamed by day and carts were stored at night. Sarah, in those more prosperous days, gave Frieda fifty dollars for a wedding present; Jonathan, who had rigidly avoided any possible temptation again in Frieda's room, added five dollars saved from his earnings as a teacher in the Workingmen's Night School. With his little capital, Martin Schmitt, who loved farming, fenced a half acre of loam on the slope toward the East River; built a decent one-room house on posts above the damp; and, in a year, the couple were successfully truck-gardening for the city markets. The first year at law school, Jonathan brought the amused Evan for a visit.

By then Schmitt had built a second room, where their infant, Marius, peacefully slumbered.

"How'd you happen to call him that?" asked Evan. It was a wet March twilight, and snug in the kitchen, the smoke of Martin's pipe and Evan's cigar fusing with the aroma of nuts, dough, and butter baking.

"Marius is Roman," said Martin. "The Romans was the greatest people. They conquered the whole world, and brought law and justice."

"Our Marius will grow up and bring law and justice, like you."
Frieda smiled at Jonathan.

Martin went to the nearest saloon on the Third Avenue for a can of beer.

"How are you getting on?" Jonathan asked Frieda.

"Good. My husband's a good man, he works hard." She turned from Jonathan to Evan, and quickly away as she read in his eyes the recognition in herself of what he had no right to know.

The beer made the young men jolly. Evan sang a song:

> *Oh, Marius, said the girl,*
> *Oh, Marius, said the man,*
> *Since you're already here,*
> *To make the title clear,*
> *You should marry us, if you can.*

Frieda laughed; Martin, not sure the young swell wasn't mocking, tried to smile.

"Speaking of titles," said Evan, "have you got one to this place?"

"Title?" Schmitt repeated dully; and Frieda looked anxious. She drew from the oven a tin plate of Jonathan's favorite almond-studded cookies.

"Do you *own* this land?" Evan translated his question.

Martin fumbled. "We just come here, like everybody else. The house, now, I built that! I bought everyt'ing that 's in it."

"Frieda's a beauty," remarked Evan as the youths, full of cakes and ale to lard them against the blustering wind, turned south toward town. "She's crazy about you, Jon."

"*You're* crazy. Frieda's married and has a baby."

"Must 'a' been an immaculate conception."

"What are you talking about?"

"Nothing. All I say is, I can't quite visualize that woman sweet as a field in clover being plowed by that old buzz-saw."

"Your metaphors are mixed."

"So are your perceptions."

Jonathan saw her: kneeling to draw the cookies from the oven, her breasts crowded in the soft red blouse, the full free breasts of a nursing mother, and the fire from the stove lighting her hair and mouth.

76

"I say, are you listening?" said Evan.

"Of course, I'm listening."

"You didn't hear a word I said. Well, then, repeat it."

Jonathan was stumped, and Evan crowed with laughter. "Here's my idea. They're nothing but squatters on that land. Squatters often have rights, but almost never know it. That's why they're squatters. Wouldn't it be fun to search title for that acre, and if possible get a deed for the old buzz-saw?" Now, Jonathan was all ears. "Old Fremont in father's office—he isn't really old, he was just born that way; he's a whizz at searching titles. We'll get him—"

They had the property surveyed; and Fremont, who knew it would be smart to please young Cleeve, future partner in the firm, went to work. The Schmitts had been lucky; the estate of the Wuytgens, a Knickerbocker family reduced to two ancient spinster sisters in a house too big for them on Washington Square, ended at the ridge west and south of Martin's loam which, probably, the eddying river had pushed up since the Dutch days. Late August—quick work for the law—Jonathan returned from his vacation with his mother, Lucia, and Philip at Long Branch, to find a registered envelope, postmarked Newport, from Evan. It contained the deed sent by Fremont from the office, and Evan's note:

> Here it is, you old duffer, clear as your soul. Don't take it to Schmitt, he might kiss you out of gratitude and even if it's summer you'd be sure to catch pneumonia. Find out some day when the walrus is selling his turnips at Fulton Market and give the deed to Frieda. If she kisses you out of gratitude, don't get cold feet, it wouldn't be polite. Better persuade her to lend her immaculate conception to one of the neighbors—every shanty up there has babies, and one more won't matter—goats eat everything but babies; and take Frieda to a beer garden. For your innocent information, there's Union Park at Sixtieth Street and the East River, Landmann's Hamilton Park at Sixty-eighth and Third. The coziest is the Bellevue at Eightieth on the River. They have music there, every afternoon. Wait till they play a waltz by Strauss; give her brandy, not beer. Then let the good deed do its work which, as you know, is to shine like a candle in the naughty world.

Next day, the document safe in his pocket and a bottle of red wine

77

in his hand to celebrate the occasion, Jonathan took the Third Avenue horsecar to Forty-second Street. Brown from the sand and the sun, hardened by his long swims beyond the breakers, he climbed the rocky hill and looked down on the river where the moored sailboats swung sidewise to the green slopes of Long Island. It was four o'clock, and Martin would surely be at home; yes, if he'd been selling turnips not only at Fulton Market, but at Washington Market, Center Market, Tompkins Market, all the markets of the city, he'd surely be at home!

Lusty little Marius, who resembled his mother, sat in the shade of the house, toward the river, in a tiny chair at a tiny table his father had made for him; a good part of his dinner smeared his ruddy face. Frieda knelt on the ground and fed him mashed peas, mashed potatoes, a bowl of milk. She placed a pork chop bone in his pudgy hand and got up when she saw Jonathan. "Give me your coat." She took it in the house and brought out chairs. They watched the little fellow chew at the bone.

"I'm glad he's finished with *me,*" she smiled. "That's the way he used to dig into *me.* I couldn't stand it no more." She touched her breast; he felt her body warm and his blood hot.

"Where is Martin?"

"Martin's brother, Rudolph, up the Hudson near Poughkeepsie, he's sick. The letter come yesterday, Martin should hurry up if he wants to see him alive. Martin won't be back till tomorrow."

"Then I must give you this." He drew out the deed with its red seal and red ribbons.

"What is it, Mr. Jonathan? Look at my hands."

"It's your home, Frieda. It's the paper, all regular and proved, that makes this really your home. And here's some wine for you to celebrate with Martin tomorrow."

She did not know what to do with her greasy hands; her mouth trembled and tears filled her eyes. "You're so good, Mr. Jonathan."

"You must thank Mr. Cleeve. It's all his doing."

She did not believe him. "You've always been so good!" She knelt again and finished feeding her son. Then she lifted him, his head like a too heavy flower drooping on her bosom—"Now, won't you *sleep!* He's a wonderful little sleeper"—and carried him into the house. She

78

returned with clean hands, and silently took the envelope and the bottle. In a moment, she was back, with a cup full of the red wine.

"But this is for you and Martin!"

"You won't drink our good luck? I put baby to bed; then I come and we drink together."

After the wine and the cool breath from the river, the house was hot; it was a body relaxed yet firm enclosing them. She filled his cup again.

"You must stay and help me eat the chops or they'll spoil. I got them yesterday before the letter. And there's a huckleberry pie. You used to love them. Your mama never quite thought they was proper because they make your teeth blue." She laughed, setting the table.

"Next year," he said, "Martin must build a second story. That'll keep the first floor cool."

"Do you mind the heat? It's good, the heat. Only, you mustn't fight it. Just give in."

"That's an idea." Jonathan felt the heat good.

"You never give in. I'm lots older than you. I can scold you a little, Mr. Jonathan? You never give in."

"That's an idea," he heard himself repeat, and told himself his talk was stupid, and it didn't matter. He thought of his different house: his father who was never truly at home in the house that was his mother's, his father's old shepherd's eyes longing for the hills and skies of Palestine that they would never see; his sister whose blood was turbid; his mother whose will forever prodded. He was relaxed here, as never at home, as not even at the seashore. (Philip was relaxed at home, but Philip had no brains. Here, he had no more brains than Philip.) He sat opposite Frieda at the table and consumed the succulent pork, the applesauce, the red wine.

"No use keeping any of it." She filled his cup. "Once it's opened, it'd only turn sour. And Martin don't care for wine."

"What a cook you are, Frieda! We've never had another like you."

"Then you miss me, sometimes?"

"Mother often speaks of you. She says, 'I hope Frieda's happy.'"

"*Ach*—happy?"

"You will be, now. You needn't worry any more about your home. Even if there are hard times, people must always buy food."

79

"I don't worry about that."

"What then, Frieda?"

"I didn't say I worry. You're such a funny boy. You have a beard now, but you're still a boy. Always so stiff; always so worrying. You're too thin. You work too hard."

"There's lots to do, if you want to be a lawyer. And I teach three nights—"

"I work hard, too. I'm not thin. It's because I never worry."

It was as if she commanded him: *"Look at me."*

"I'd like to make you fat, I wish we have a real farm, far away from the city. You'd come there."

"I'd love it."

"You help with the cows. I make cheese for you. I make you sleep under the apple trees."

"I'd love it!"

"Your brain would have a rest, that smart brain of yours."

"Don't praise it for what it didn't do. I tell you, it was Evan—his idea and his doing."

"Mr. Cleeve, he's smart all right; so is Mr. Reuben. But you've got the heart; you've got a heart and brain that's got the *whole world* in it!"

Jonathan threw back his head, a little dizzy, and laughed.

"The whole world! Go ahead and laugh at me. The others, they take little pieces of the world that's right under their noses, and fit 'em together so they can have good times, make lots of money. That's not like having a brain with all the people in it."

He looked at her eyes that were serious, at her body that was sweet.

"With love, your brain's full! I'm nothing but an ignorant German girl, but I know a thing or two. I know what you're always studying for, worrying for, with your brain full of the whole people."

"Go on," he laughed. "It's all nonsense, but I like it."

He ate half the pie.

"Now your mouth's all blue." She got up and kissed his mouth. In the close room, enclosing their bodies, nothing was changed. She kissed him again; her mouth smelled of milk and berries; her chemise strained with her breasts. He saw, between them, the little ebony cross with its silver Christ, so small, so unavailing.

80

"So," she crooned as to a child, but her eyes looked as to a master.

His will was against this swelling summer of her flesh and his, but it was like the crucifix, powerless and outside. When her hands, opening his clothes, touched him, the air between them was an abyss through which he must fall to lie in her, as he needed to live; life, for the miraculous first time, was no burden as he sank in the sea of ecstasy within her that bore away all burden. He lay in tenderness. . . .

Slowly at last he emerged back toward the world of his will; he put on his clothes, the lamp she lighted hurt his eyes. When she took his hand, the touch was the pain of ineffable lostness.

"Jonathan!" She called him from far off. On the river, a steamboat whistled, and it was nearer than she and himself.

"I'm afraid for you, Jonathan. You're going to blame yourself. You're going to swear never to come back to me."

He looked through the open door; the stars too were nearer than she and himself.

"Don't see me again, if that's the way you must feel. But don't blame yourself," she pleaded.

As he walked toward the cars on the Third Avenue, toward the home where his conscience waited, he carried a burden worse than his sin: his body felt laved and good! as if it were cleansed, as if it were healed. This was the terrible burden!

Before he went to bed, he knew he was going to sleep—to sleep well, as only a pure conscience should sleep! This was the terrible burden. He opened his journal at a new page. His mouth warred sternly with the glow in his relaxed eyes, as he wrote:

RESOLVED: a beginning of penance due from this moment until the
day I die—:

1. For twelve months from this inst. to curtail my sleep by one hour, not remaining in bed more than six hours maximum, the extra hour to be employed in study, incl. Saturday nights.
2. To give up candy for one year.
3. To take a cold bath every night, winter and summer, before retiring.
4. To wear no gloves even in the coldest days, next winter.
5. To refuse for twelve months from this inst. invitations to all dances

81

or any parties where my presence might pollute the innocence of maidens and good women.

6. To give what I have held back for pocket money from my earnings at Night School either to my father or to charity, retaining only the necessary carfare—and an occasional five cents for beer with my friend, Evan Cleeve, so as not to make him ask questions.

7. In a word, to strive to become at last what my Mother and Father think I am: a *M a n*.

One day, Reuben had asked him: "What about that title deed you said you and your friend were going to clear for the Schmitts? Did you manage it?"

Jonathan flushed and murmured, "Yes."

"You mean it's done?"

Jonathan looked away.

Reuben whistled. "Do as well for yourself, my boy, and you'll get somewhere!"

It was not long before Reuben casually mentioned that he had paid a visit to Frieda and her husband. Jonathan's temper flared. "Since when are you and the Schmitts friends?"

"Do you own 'em? I happened to be in the neighborhood, and just dropped in."

Then, his sin flowered! His mind, if it had not been clouded by a guilty conscience, would have told him that Reuben paid no visits to a former servant in Shanty Town to pass the time of day. Not Reuben! If he had not been guilty he would have seen Frieda, would have learned from Frieda what was brewing—in time to prevent it! Guilt kept him from inquiry, as guilt kept him from the house he had dishonored. Long later, too late, he learned what happened. Reuben ingratiated himself with the Schmitts; respectively out of gratitude and nostalgia, Martin and Frieda welcomed and trusted Jonathan's brother. Reuben encouraged Martin to expand his business; to buy a cow, a large wagon, a new team of horses—and lent him money, in the form of a mortgage on his land. Reuben secretly arranged with a commission merchant in Union Market on Second and Houston Streets to give Schmitt a large standing order and, a year later, to drop it. The panic had done the rest. Prices went to rock bottom, Martin could not meet his eight per cent interest charges, Reuben foreclosed on farm and house. And Jonathan had known none of this. How could he, since he never visited the Schmitts and guiltily avoided mentioning their name?

One casual day, Evan dropped into Shanty Town and found a new tenant in the house who told him its owner was a Mr. Reuben Hartt. What had become of the former occupant? He didn't know. . . .

. . . Now, from the head of the stoop, Jonathan, having refused his brother's invitation to take Lucy to the concert, saw Reuben turn the corner. Reuben was troubled by no guilty conscience. Jonathan could almost hear him: "The man borrowed money, didn't he? No one made him. When he couldn't pay, I did what the law prescribes. *Your* law, my boy. What would you have? The shiftless run the world?"

Slowly—his own sick conscience tiding upon him—Jonathan went up to his father's room to take him down to dinner. The old man, past his allotted three score and ten, lay on the bed, his white beard unkempt but his brow and his blue eyes clear.

"How are you, Jonathan? Time to get up?" He kicked the knitted shawl from his knees.

"How are you?"

"Tired. I don't know why I'm so tired."

"You work hard."

"I don't think so, Jonathan. I don't think I've ever worked very hard."

"Not even when you used to sleep on the counter and clean store before it opened?"

"I wasn't tired, then. I took it easy."

"Well, papa, we're not as young as we used to be."

"That's not it! We don't live right! That's what it is!"

"True enough of a lot of us. Not of you."

"Sometimes you don't get the point; as if you were stupid."

"I wish I were as bright as my family thinks me."

"Don't say I've lived right! No man lives as God wants. But that's not what I mean. Even if a man did try to live according to the Lord, it wouldn't tire him, no; but living in a time when most men don't even try, he'd be tired. D'you see?"

"We'd better hurry. Mama will frown."

"I don't get as hungry as I used to. That's bad."

"Perhaps you should cut down on your cigars."

83

"Smoke's the best food, when you get old. Don't try to interfere with my cigars."

"I won't. But smoke's no food, father."

"Sometimes everything gets to be smoke. Not so good as cigar smoke." Joseph smiled and took his son's arm. "You'll come to it yet, my dear. Smoking."

"Your friends in the Old Testament didn't smoke."

"What do you mean! You don't know smoke when you see it. That's the trouble with you modern fellows full of philosophy. You lose your senses; your eyes don't see and your noses don't smell. No smoke in the Bible? Why, when Jacob and Isaac and Abraham smelled the green grass, that was smoke from Jehovah's pipe, and sweet. When He spoke to Job out of the whirlwind, that was smoke. The old Hebrews smoked the Lord's pipe with Him. We can't do it any more. So we need tobacco."

They entered the old dining room, where Sarah and Lucia and Philip already sat at table.

Emma Cleeve was not asleep when her son, thinking she slept, stole from her room; this was neither sleep nor waking. She let him go because, absent, he was no less with her; present, no more with her. He was lost, wherever he was, whatever he did; and whatever he did, wherever he was, still with her. She did not understand why she had suddenly pleaded with him—it had never occurred to her before—to make that Jewish friend his partner. As if it could help! He had laughed; even if he had accepted, he would manage before long to laugh at it. Evan could not change, she could not change, Grosvenor—nothing could change. In this new consciousness, she lay: it was neither sleep nor waking, because there was no room in it for change. Her sleep and her waking had always been troubled, therefore full of motion or of the need for motion. Sleep without drugs was the worst; it was seeking, straining, and never arriving: a knot of tangents that bound her restlessly and loosely until she broke into the restlessness of waking. Now it was peace; for nothing—nothing in her, nothing in Evan, changed, and nothing needed to change. It was new! Her euphoric nerves recorded the dull thud below, the impact of air when the front door opened: it was her husband. Would he come up to see her?

84

He must know, the doctor must have told him her feeble attempt—bungled like all else—on her life. Of course, he would come up; but when he stood there with his hateful tailored courtesies—"How are you, my dear? What can I do for you, my dear?"—it would be the same, and he would not be there. She heard a murmur of voices: Grosvenor and Evan? and when her husband did not come, still it was the same, her husband was there, as much and as little, as if he stood in the room. Then, the second thud of air: that was Evan leaving the house.

Emma lay quiet in her pillows, nursing her revelation. It was as wonderful, this peace, as the long ago when she had lain in this same bed nursing Evan. He lies warm in her arms: fragile, small, immense. —Careful how you move. Do not move! you might wake him. If you slept and moved, you might crush him. Yet he is stronger than you, more vast in time and space, within your arms and breasts that hold and feed him. She breathed as low and quiet as she could. The little helpless body was greater than her body; the frail slumbering breath was her breath. Peace . . . wonder. Oh, let this never change! And let never change this revelation, new as birth, of changelessness: whatever Grosvenor does is the same, whatever Evan does, beating himself this way or that way against life, is the same. —Whatever I do! There lay the danger. She must go on doing nothing. Hold!, hold the changelessness, hold the infant in her breast.

She lay a long time; but she lay in the deep of time, not in its length at all: in the deep that never changes, has no measure, from instant unto hour.

When she got out of bed . . . —Quiet! Do not wake him! . . . she knew this was the way to hold the changelessness forever. She walked, her steps sure, through the dark room (Evan had turned off the light). —Careful, do not wake him! She opened the bathroom door (Evan had turned on the light). —Take care! The medicine chest was open (Evan had opened it for her). A moment, she held the bottle with the red skull label in her hands. The infant slumbered in her breast, changelessness perfectly slept. She took out the rubber cork, the rank smell smote her. And for an instant, she swayed away from the deep chasm of changelessness, losing her balance, threatened by the abyss of length where love moved and tore her entrails, where love painfully longed. The crass acid odor raking her membranes gave her the strength she needed, settled her back into depth. She knew how to anchor herself there forever, how to banish the abyss of moving and of longing into the endless lengths forever ending and beginning. She put the bottle to her mouth; she sensed her throat red, her throat flaming, her throat spreading, a flower, in orgasmic explosion; and then whiteness fell like windless snow and covered her forever.

Evan aimlessly turned toward Irving Place, the discord of his words with his father annulling for the time his memory of his hour with his mother. On Cyrus Field's house, as he glanced at it, the latticed balconies hung with icicles, the vestibule of Peter Cooper's home shone in its own lamp-glow. From his favorite saloon as he swung the doors came a drunken Irish voice:

"God bless the bloody ol' Sixth Ward."

At the bar Evan ordered a whiskey, and an old man sprawling alone at the nearby table talked defiance to the stove: "I'm one, and ye're a hunderd. But ye're rats and I'm the terrier. Come on!" He shuffled his feet through the sawdust, brandished his fists at emptiness. The stove went on glowing; no one laughed at the old man.

Around a table farther off four men from the slaughterhouses east at the river, their drams of whiskey ludicrously small before their mallet-fists and beef-bodies, listened respectfully to the very drunk gentleman in their midst, whose gray stock set with a pearl pin, frock coat of excellent vintage, and raveled silk hat, were framed by their bloody leather aprons. His overcoat, garnished with black Persian lamb, was half on the table, half on the filthy floor.

"I'm telling you," the gentleman said, "New York's—Augean stables. Ten years we've had—shtreet-cleaning 'partment, the stench is thicker'n ever. No Board of Health can clean our gov'ments, city, state, and nation. Just this afternoon, sirs, I had 'ccasion—visit that sink of human 'miliation known eu-phe-mist-ic-'ly as the Cattle Market. Cattle Market, indeed! If steer came from barns foul as these human homes you'd refuse 'em, you'd refuse 'em. But when honored chitizens like Mr. Bryant want the pesthole condemned, what does our leg-is-lature do? Listens to—tinkle of coin in—hands of—owners. Down goes reform. Nothing mus' interfere with divine rights of rent and profit." He downed his dram. "Le'sh have—drink I'm thirsty." Evan watched him

86

hoist himself laboriously from his chair and navigate to the bar. "Five double whiskeys." His hand shook as he pulled a roll of bills from his pocket and in the confusion of paying and carrying the drinks back two at a time to the table, several greenbacks fell on the floor. One of the butchers got up, carefully gathered the money, and stuffed it into the gentleman's coat. They were taking care of the rich swell, they had a paternal feeling for him, he'd leave that saloon, Evan was sure, with his bankroll intact.

Perhaps Jonathan was right, and men in the raw were lovable. He recalled his mother's wish; by God!, he'd surprise her and do it. *Cleeve and Hartt,* Counsellors-at-law. Why not? *Item:* it would please his mother. *Item:* it would displease his father. The little entertaining jobs of selling secret information would be a bit awkward if he was no longer in the office. He'd manage; he had other connections. The proposal would overwhelm Jonathan: that was the one uncomfortable point. Jonathan was a fine fellow but every now and then there was a canine whiff in him as if Hartt somehow, for all his Jeffersonianism, felt himself inferior or an outsider. He'd get over it. After all, how should he know that being the son of Knickerbockers put no marrow in one's bones? He, by the way, was the son of Abraham and Moses: surely something to be proud of. But the Hebrew prophets meant nothing to Jonathan, whose prophets were Jefferson, Darwin, and this new Herbert Spencer.

Warmed by the drink, Evan waved farewell to the four slaughter-house butchers and their genteel ward, and walked south. Too early to go to his friend's house; he turned east, then south, following the brick and wood disorder of Avenue A into Tompkins Square whose mean bare trees and wood church froze in the leaden sky. *Cleeve and Hartt:* it might even be fun, although his mother'd see soon enough that it solved nothing. Quite a counterpoint: himself partner of the upright Jonathan to whom practice of the law meant "public service." He'd go on, of course, like his father, and Tilden, yes, and Peter Cooper!, cutting the juicy melons of American expansion. Four hundred thousand head a year the immigrants poured through Castle Garden: the true wealth of the nation. They needed buttons and houses, railroads and newspapers, mountains of food. They produced what they needed, of course; but they were hypnotized, the fools, by private property and leadership, whose false premise was that the earth was not theirs. Why did all men not know they *were* the earth? Look at those fellows in the saloon picking up the rich man's money, putting it back in the rich man's pocket. Not a hundred years could teach them the money was *theirs!* —Counterpoint is the wrong word for Jonathan and me together. Counterpoint means harmonious themes, or there's no music. What he did, what they all were doing—and Jonathan's ideals—had no common key. To become his partner would be a damned dirty trick. —Jonathan's too decent.

The Hartts were still at table, silent over their coffee, when Evan rang the bell. The dinner had been unpleasant, as Jonathan knew it must be when he announced that he was going out.

"Again!" said Lucia. "Another Mendis party, I suppose."

"I know they're your clients, Jonathan," said Sarah. "But is it necessary to give them so much of your time after working hours?"

"How often do I go there?"

"In the past seven weeks, my boy, you've visited the Mendis home four evenings." Sarah was precise, like her hair drawn tightly back, like her face sharp as a steel engraving: thin nose, frosty eyes. "You used to spend more of your evenings at study, my dear. Have you learned *all* the law?"

Jonathan tried to be light. "Perhaps some things are to be learned that aren't in books."

"Not in law books, anyway," Philip defended him; and Sarah in quiet anger turned against her "baby"; usually a hard look was enough to make him retreat into his lyric clumsiness. Since high school, Philip had worked with his father; he was an excellent salesman and the merchants liked him. "If only he had some *executive* ability," his mother disposed of his humble success. She was troubled by Philip; Lucia had told her of strange books in the boys' room that surely were not Jonathan's: inflammatory pamphlets by dreadful Germans, Marx, Most, Engels. Could it be that Philip was being victimized? And here he was daring to talk back!

"You needn't look at me that way." He had a trick of twisting his head sidewise like a spaniel. "There's lots that ain't in law books."

"Ain't!" sighed Lucia, raising her eyes in grief.

"I suspect, my dear son, there *is* a lot you could learn by paying more attention to your father's business and forgetting all about books."

"Now, now," old Joseph shook his head, "Philip does the best he can."

"Perhaps," retorted Sarah, "his best isn't good enough. Perhaps his best would be a little better if he didn't befuddle his mind with *Socialist* slander. The idea! Bringing that European hatred to our land of opportunity."

Lucia was not interested in Philip; she veered the attack back to Jonathan. "Anarchists and Communists aren't the only people bringing us trouble from Europe."

"I say nothing against Europe's culture," Sarah smiled at Jonathan.

"Europe's *vultures,*" cried Lucia. "They come here, despising us, using us, just to make money." Anger brought red blotches to her sallow skin. Her father's large features, gentle in him, were harsh in Lucia; her mother's strength, prim and graceful in her small face, was forbidding in the daughter.

"Whom are you referring to?" Jonathan suddenly blazed.

"You wouldn't be so angry if you didn't know." She faced him square and her eyes filled. "You wouldn't know, if my description didn't fit."

"I know. Not because your description fits the Mendis family; but because I know *you.*" He saw the pain in her face, and he was sorry for her. "Mrs. Mendis and her daughter do love Europe's grace of living. Isn't that natural, since they spent so many years there? Wouldn't you care to visit Paris, Vienna?"

"Of course, Lucia would," Sarah hastened to intervene. "And some day, Jonathan, you shall take your sister. We must plan for it. When times get better."

Joseph said, "They're good enough for some people, now. They'll never be good for some. . . ."

Sarah ignored him. "Perhaps you can take Lucia on at least part of Mark Twain's tour in *Innocents Abroad.*"

"Mama!" Lucia was mollified. "He's so vulgar!"

"But funny," said Jonathan.

"And that's important, too," Sarah added. "We mustn't get too serious. You work so hard, dear Jonathan. Yes, it shall be arranged—Lucia and you. And you'll send us letters from Windsor Palace."

"Good times may be a long way off," said Jonathan, who sensed the true meaning of this mythic journey: if unto the dim future, he took his vacations with Lucia, he must be free, and both of them unmarried.

"Perhaps not so long; they *must* get better," concluded Mrs. Hartt. "Meanwhile, it's a sin for us to complain! We have our beloved home. We have each other."

Lucia's eyes were again beaming. She and Jonathan and Philip had their father's eyes; Philip's were now veiled in a stubborn brooding; the old man's shone with gentle irony; Jonathan's again were angry. With Lucia's pain and dangerous temper averted, he could once more resent the insult to the Mendis family and the easy way Lucia and his mother disposed of him, even his future vacations! He was a lawyer not without promise; already he was active in the Reform ranks that were struggling to consolidate against Tammany, against Sweeney and the new boss "Honest" John Kelley who "assessed" every man who wanted a city job, and had just named a saloonkeeper, a strong-arm bully, a probable murderer, Richard Croker, for the fat office of Coroner. But what was the use? His family owned him! Joseph's financial troubles troubled them not at all, with their Jonathan to manage; Lucia's spinsterhood troubled them not at all, with Jonathan to fill her solitude. More than once, his mother had sighed complacently that she could die in peace, knowing that Jonathan would be there always to take care of Lucia, Lucia of Jonathan. He sipped his bitter coffee, thinking of the more aromatic brew that Mrs. Mendis served. And suddenly, as if she had read his thoughts, forgetting her effort to make peace, Mrs. Hartt blurted out:

"I'm not so certain about this superior European courtesy! Mrs. Mendis, who has lived so many years in Europe—well! if she had what I call proper breeding, she would invite Lucia to accompany you to her parties. She would call on me. Her sons would call on us."

"Why don't you invite her?"

"You know we can't entertain. Do we have the money for soirées?"

"They haven't any more than we, mama. Their kind of hospitality doesn't cost money."

"They serve collations, don't they? Perhaps you think cakes and salads are given away by the stores. Look at these chairs. They're falling to pieces."

Lucia chimed in: "They probably have money, when it suits them. And when it suits them to ask favors, of course, they have nothing."

"Don't!" said Jonathan.

She was aroused. "You're an innocent fool. You'll ruin your career."

"Lucia," Sarah reproved.

"Falling into the hands of adventurers from Europe!" Now Lucia's tantrum was released, it must run its course. "You men are all alike. If women are spineless, and fall into a faint at the slightest provocation, they can get what they want. Dickens heroines! Little Nell and Dora!" Her face was livid in contempt for those pale beauties. "Dressed-up lies! We have brains too. But if we show them, men don't like it. You prefer dolls. You'll never know what you missed."

"My dear," Sarah waited for the squall to subside.

"I hate all men. Conceited lords of the universe. And what a mess they've made of it."

"That's true enough," Jonathan smiled, his resentment again vanished.

"The front-door bell," warned Sarah. "Lucia, my dear—"

"If it's Mr. Cleeve," Jonathan said to the servant, "let him come in."

Grosvenor Cleeve sat alone at the long board set for two, before the silver candlesticks, and ate in silence. After the turtle soup, the butler in white gloves brought him broiled sea bass garnished with parsley and bacon, and poured Pouilly into the green fluted goblet; then venison steak (the gift of a Connecticut client whose factory Cleeve had trebled in value by persuading the railroad to run a spur through the town) with two glasses of dry Pommard; then a *baba au rhum*. He enjoyed his dinner no less because he was alone; enjoyed it, he feared, a bit too much: he had twinges of gout. Yet surely he deserved these little compensations. He had done more than his share in guiding the country's industrial expansion and keeping it solvent (what a fight it had been to bar the depreciated greenbacks—all right for wages—from becoming legal tender instead of gold for the national debt!); but no one could say he had been blessed with personal felicity. His wife he had written off, long ago. But his son and heir! And the devil of it was that Evan had a first-rate legal mind; all he lacked was good will. It was Emma's fault, Emma's "revenge." Well, he had his little com-

91

pensatory pleasures: this tawny port, for instance—how it merged with the Colombian coffee! And Henrietta Dexwith, whom he visited once a week. Even here, there was trouble. The little Bijou Opera House ballerina had gone to the great Moody and Sankey revival meetings in the Claremont Avenue skating rink in Brooklyn; and damned if she wasn't getting religion! She needed an annuity, she said, to snatch her from sin and the stage. He lighted a long Havana. No annuity for little Henrietta. "If you want to be a Christian, my sweet," he'd tell her, "you should earn your own bread. I'll give you a present for a starter." A thousand? Five hundred would do. He was getting a bit old, anyway, for that—that's all it was: that very moderate pleasure. Amused, he figured out how many boxes of Havanas, how many cases of this port, he could buy for five hundred dollars. He'd finish his smoke, then have a look at Emma. Pure formality. If she needed anything, she had a bell at her bed. Then he'd go over the brief in the appeal of the Pennsylvania Natural Gas case. A pleasure, too, the fine points of the law; a nobler one than little Henrietta. And it brought him many more five hundreds than Henrietta cost him.

At his wife's door the gray light through the window curtains showed him the empty bed. —She's in the bathroom. Better knock. Might be ill. . . . He crossed the room . . . knocked . . . louder; he called, "Emma!" He tried the door, and it opened. The rank smell of carbolic: before his eyes went down, he knew. Then he made himself see. His wife lay, her body crumpled and contorted as a green leaf by flame. Her glazed black eyes were toward him; her dead mouth was open, shouting at him.

Evan removed his coat that radiated the street's cold, took the chair and the cup of coffee. He was never quite at ease with the Hartts whose pervasive subtle ways seemed forever hinting that he was better than they and that they were better than he. Not the unobtrusive old man, however, whose mild eyes met him with neither self-abasement nor self-assertion.

"You're going with Jonathan tonight?" said Mrs. Hartt, cordial as she could be to one whose chief reality was that he was Jonathan's friend.

"It's my duty. This young man, I've learned, has a secret life. He's a regular knight-errant out of Tennyson, or is it Longfellow? He needs watching."

Lucia thought: —If only *he*'d fall in love with that girl, and save Jonathan! Not likely. Evan was tall, blond, handsome, a rich gentile. But the glow in her brother's eyes, the glow in her brother's mind— who could match them?

"Young man," said Joseph, "aren't you a mischievous young man?"

"I am," said Evan.

"Get Jonathan into a little mischief."

"Heaven forbid! Tonight, I'm his guardian angel."

"He needs a little mischief." Joseph wagged his head. "You know the Bible?"

"Not well, I'm afraid, sir. I'm too busy laying plots and snares for the new Prophets, like your son, to rail against."

"No, it's not in Proverbs." The old man drew his fingers through his beard. "It must be a Midrash. It says, 'No child is born except through pleasure and joy.'"

"Joseph!" Sarah reproved him, and Lucia blushed.

"The teaching," Joseph went on, "is that pleasure and joy are good."

"Splendid doctrine! Is that Judaism?"

"That's why my son's not a good Jew. He hasn't learned yet. He's too solemn. Lead him into mischief."

Evan roared his laughter. "By Jove, Jonathan! Why didn't you tell me? It seems I'm a better Jew than you are."

The young men walked downtown; Jonathan handed Evan the brief in the Mendis case. Evan carelessly slipped it into his coat; Jonathan, a little nervous, began to discuss it.

"Not a word!" said Evan. "Not till we leave your friends' house. We're going to be rare sons, tonight: we're going to heed the voice of the father. You'll be jolly, if I have to choke you."

"That'll do it."

"What?"

"Choking—will make me jolly."

"Can't you quit being logical for an hour?"

"Let's try. We're bound for Lafayette Place. It's downtown. Suppose we get there by going uptown?"

"You're getting cold feet about going at all—because I'm along."

93

"Perhaps because it's cold."

"Too logical, again."

"What was your deduction that I'm getting scared?"

"Direct observation," said Evan.

"Wrong. Deduction from observation. Hold on! Don't put your foot forward. That's logic, too. You can't walk without logic."

"I'll dance."

"Logic no less. I don't want to walk, I want to move: *ergo,* I'll dance."

"Wouldn't strict logic be: *ergo,* I'll crawl or run? Dance is the extra-logical, the non-logical factor."

"Perhaps," Jonathan smiled. "But your differentiating words *extra* and *non* prove the logical base. We're logic bound."

Evan chanted:

> *"Logic to right of us,*
> *Logic to left of us,*
> *Logic in front of us,*
> *Volleyed and thundered."*

"Don't crow over it," he went on. "Look what happened:

> *"Stormed at with shot and shell,*
> *Boldly we ride and well,*
> *Into the jaws of death,*
> *Into the mouth of hell."*

Jonathan laughed. "You forget the last stanza:

> *"When can their glory fade?*
> *O the wild charge they made!*
> *All the world wondered."*

"Yes," said Evan, "but when Tennyson made his pretty jingle, most of them were *dead.*"

The slush on the streets was frozen hard, the night crackled; gaslights in little shops were dim; through frosted glass the street lamps carved wreaths in the rough dark. Past Cooper Institute, they came to the colonnaded mansions of Lafayette Place.

"Here we are," Jonathan's voice suddenly hushed.

Evan saw the Middle Dutch Church, a marble Grecian temple with twelve granite monoliths on the portico and a mean wood spire; and beyond, the white and brown residences, muffled and aglow as far as Great Jones Street.

"So she lives in a church?"

"What makes you say that?" Jonathan was not ready to have Evan's animal spirits overflow into the demesne of Greta.

"You said, 'Here we are,' as if we were souls at Heaven's gate."

"Come on!"

In these marble-pillared mansions, only a few years ago, had resided friends of Evan's parents: members of the Astor family, Van Wirt, who often entertained his cousin Washington Irving; Governor Morgan, David Gardiner—all now dead or removed to the Fifth Avenue and Murray Hill. "Come," repeated Jonathan as if he himself needed urging. Evan looked up at a second story from whose stone porch with wrought-iron rail the fluted columns stood clear in the high glowing windows; the rest of the house was dark. Jonathan pulled the bell; they heard a faraway jangle; the silver-knobbed mahogany door opened.

Jonathan stood somewhat lost in the high-ceilinged over-furnished room. He saw Mrs. Mendis enthroned on the black horsehair sofa and her bare shapely arm upraised as Evan in true European style bowed to kiss her hand; he saw Raoul, the black hair bristling on his square head, his rigid dignity making him look taller and older than he was; and Sylvester, short and already plump at twenty-nine. He did not see whom he wanted to see, and Mathilda Mendis, aware, smiled at him playfully. Raoul relighted his mellow meerschaum pipe; Sylvester offered a Corona to Evan who took it.

"I can recommend this cigar," said Sylvester.

Jonathan stared at the plum plush portières on the door, as if they might be hiding someone.

"I know," said Mrs. Mendis, "from looking at you gentlemen that it's stopped snowing, it's getting colder, and you walked. Your dreadful New York winters!"

"You don't like them?" asked Evan.

"I do! But it's a one-sided affection. They don't like me."

"You're from the South, Mrs. Mendis?"

"Charleston. I was born near Charleston, in a little place called Summerville."

"I've been there. It was spring, when we got there—"

"From winter here, I suppose?" Raoul puffed his pipe.

"I remember the azaleas and dogwood blooming beneath the darkest blue pines."

"Spring almost smothered our house: the azaleas, the jasmine, the wistaria, the japonica, the roses." Mrs. Mendis wore the uniform of widowhood: black lace, black taffeta skirt billowing below her bodice like a hoop. Yet she was cool and young, except her dark eyes.

Jonathan felt his ill humor growing. "Is that all you remember?" he asked Evan, and instantly regretted it.

"You were there too, Mr. Hartt?" cried Mrs. Mendis. "You never told us."

"We went down together," Evan answered. "I was sick, the doctor prescribed a sea voyage; it was vacation time at law school, and Jonathan came along."

"I remember the flowers," said Jonathan. "I remember also the poor shanties in the swamps, where the Negroes lived."

"Prancing with song," laughed Mrs. Mendis. "The darkies don't need flowers."

"You were born there, too?" Evan asked Raoul.

"It depended on the season where our children were born," Mrs. Mendis answered for her son. "Summerville was safe only in the months when there's no fever in the country. Raoul, Carlo, and Alfred were born in Charleston in the house on Legaré Street. Carlo is my oldest; he was killed early in the War. Alfred's in Germany—Dresden. Sylvester and Greta were born in Summerville."

"Where *is* Miss Greta?" burst from Jonathan, and they all laughed. Mrs. Mendis went on quickly, her wise eyes twinkling to Evan:

"My husband was born in Charleston, too. But his great-grandfather, Jacob Mendis, who settled there came to Charles Towne—that's what it was then—from Nieuw Amsterdam."

"He might have known my mother's people!"

"What was their name, Mr. Cleeve?"

"Corthuis."

"It might well be."

Jonathan knew Evan was consciously playing a game against him. Evan asked, "Why did he go, I wonder?"

96

"Charleston was a much better place for trade," said Raoul.

"It was a place of music and good wines," added Sylvester.

"The Mendis sons," continued the lady, "were always importers of fine things from Europe. Carriages, wines, laces. But there was a better reason. He liked Charles Towne's constitution. Who wrote it, Raoul?"

"It was drafted by Sir John Colleton and Lord Ashley. But his secretary deserves most of the credit: John Locke."

"Locke! I never knew that!" cried Evan.

"It granted 'freedom and citizenship to all who are Deists—' "

"Purposely omitting creed and church."

"That was better than New York."

Jonathan had lost his chance to get into the talk with the name Locke; he knew more than Evan—any of them—about Locke. But at the moment, he was shifting his chair to plain view of the door, and he was gripping himself: Greta must be home! If Greta were ill or absent, courtesy would require of Mrs. Mendis to say so. Mrs. Mendis was a gracious lady, she had not said so; *ergo*— He was more at ease, and logic had done it, even though Evan might not approve. He heard:

"Greta was nine. That was the third year of the War." What had he missed? He had begun to hear at the name 'Greta'. . . . "My husband was abroad. Mr. Judah Benjamin had sent him on a secret mission. They were great friends. Neither believed in slavery; they were quite sure it could have passed peacefully."

Raoul said, "As it is passing in Brazil."

"Neither owned slaves. But they did believe the South, when it was free, would become a wonderful country. An American Athens. Countries can be too big, my husband thought. Don't you agree, Mr. Cleeve?"

"With some, the smaller the better," Evan laughed.

"With some, the larger the better," Jonathan retorted; and blushed; and again held his silence.

"Miss Greta," Evan teased, "you said was nine—?"

Jonathan suddenly was frightened. Why this elegiac tone about Miss Greta? Was he mad? Was she dead? Had he heard the news of the disaster and lost his mind?

". . .We were to meet Mr. Mendis in London; Raoul was already
97

there. The Yankees had just shelled Charleston. Below Calhoun Street our carriage wheels made a fearful noise in the night, as they crushed shattered glass and the horses stumbled on bricks and beams. At the Battery, we crept into a rowboat: Sylvester and Alfred were big boys, but Greta was such a baby! The Yankees were blockading the harbor and I told little Greta if she cried a big cannonball would send us all to the bottom. The men rowed with muffled oars for hours—it was so cold and wet we seemed to be under water. Past the forts, we rowed to the *Marion Bradley*. That was a blockade-runner of which my husband owned a share."

"Miss Greta didn't cry?" Evan glanced at Jonathan.

"She sneezed! I nearly smothered the child in my shawl."

"And the good ship *Marion Bradley* sailed you safe to London?"

"Stories don't end that quickly," Mrs. Mendis laughed. "They have to run two years."

"Two years—!"

"It wasn't quite that long. The skiff, that's all she was, dropped us at Norfolk. We rode in a farmer's wagon to Maryland, under crates of chickens that made so much noise the children could sneeze all they wanted. They were too tired even to cry. I don't remember how many boats and trains we took before we came to Jersey City. At the hotel, I read the list of recent arrivals in the guestbook. I suppose I was lonely and a little afraid, and foolishly hoping to find a friendly name in that horrible dirty town. Our steamer sailed in the morning, Raoul met us at Liverpool, and papa was not in England." The emotion had made Mrs. Mendis fall into the familial appellation of her husband; her eyes glanced toward Jonathan. "Not hearing from us for so long, papa had worried and come to America. He was staying at the hotel in Jersey City when we arrived there; but he had been warned not to register his real name. Next day, when he came back from New York to the hotel, he learned we had sailed."

—Why this story to Evan? What does she want *me* to learn from it? Jonathan's imagining how the wife and mother suffered—and the husband and father—after their dangerous journeys when they found they had missed each other, weighted only his own anguish. Could mischance be so cruel and definitive? Could it come between him and Greta? Restless, Jonathan got up; turned for the first time from the

98

door, and in that moment Greta entered. She walked the length of the room; with his back toward her, he heard Mrs. Mendis introduce Evan.

"Where have you been!" He spun around, and flushed because he had no right to ask. Greta laughed, and gave him her hand. She knew him: already he would be planning some self-punishment for his rudeness and indiscretion. Jonathan's eyes, angry and humble, made her strangely and deliciously alive; thrillingly sure of herself, as if she were riding safe through the air; made her see herself with his eyes: the young woman fragrant in her cream-colored close-lashed dress, her hair heavy and redolent above her fragile face, her full bosom blushing.

"I'll tell you where Greta's been," laughed the mother, "although she'll scold me. She's been in the kitchen. I know you two lawyers are bookworms and not interested in food. But my two young men get mighty hungry every night. Well, sirs, our servant is green as Ireland, and she thinks cakes and meat should be tough like peat. Greta is the real cook in this household. Of course, you, Mr. Cleeve and Mr. Hartt, can look on, if you've no appetites. But it will hurt our feelings."

Greta said, "Then there's Doctor Foray."

"Of course! He's sure to drop in."

Raoul explained: "He has the attic room that goes with our flat."

Evan remarked, "Isn't it a strange residence for a physician?"

"He's a strange physician. I don't think he has many patients."

"If he did have," Raoul was a bit gruff, "I don't think he'd drop in with such regularity when the smell of food goes up from the kitchen."

"That makes him," said Mrs. Mendis, "not only our lodger, but our star boarder."

"A fallen star?" asked Evan.

"The word's much too precipitate." Mrs. Mendis smiled and her eyes softened. "Doctor Foray slowly comes down the stairs, the way the steam of the viands goes up."

They all laughed, except Raoul and Jonathan. He understood the situation. They had rented the room, because they needed the money. Doubtless, what he ate cost more than the room brought them . . . if the rent was paid at all.

"He's an interesting gentleman," Mrs. Mendis explained to Evan. "He's from a very good Richmond family, and he was an army sur-

geon all through the War. Instead of returning to his practice, he came
to the North. He's terribly alone, as if he bore some brooding wound.
I think the dreadful things he saw—"

"He's a good man," said Greta. "I know it, when he listens to music."

"Jonathan told me about your music," Evan said.

Mrs. Mendis went on, "Perhaps those who die are not the war's
worst victims."

Evan suddenly was serious; Jonathan knew he was thinking of his
mother.

"Well," Raoul puffed his pipe. "Now, peace will begin."

"What makes you think so?" asked Evan.

"Disraeli's Premier of England. He's a conservative man, and he'll
keep the British Empire quiet. France is making money: look how she
paid Prussia! So will Germany be quiet, now her territorial ambitions
have been satisfied. Italy will grow peaceful, too, with the Pope in his
place. When good times reach America again, the whole world that
counts—"

"—will be peacefully making money?" Evan interrupted.

"I think you're right," Jonathan said to Raoul.

"It's reasonable," said Evan.

"Exactly," Raoul nodded.

"Have you ever heard of man?" smiled Evan. "I guess not. He's
not reasonable, you see."

Jonathan noted: everything Evan said, jocular, extravagant, pleased
Greta. As if, under his words, there were a music for her. He did not
like this evening. —It's showing up my worthlessness. I'd better like
it! How splendid Evan looked, how could a girl like Greta fail to be
impressed, even without the common bond of music? Jonathan felt
his own sins. —Evan, too, is a sinner. I'm doing what I can for the
family; more than is just. It was logical, it did not satisfy. Here, too,
Evan who laughed at logic, had the better of it. Evan was enjoying
himself, talking mostly with Mrs. Mendis, and mostly aware of Greta.
He too, like Greta, knew Europe; and knew music. What a couple
they would make! —Let be what has to be! He thought of Lucia,
and himself, like Lucia unattractive. Evan's blond head and Greta's
sumptuous chestnut tresses; Evan's tall body and Greta's flowering
form. Jonathan felt himself small, dark; and when Greta's eyes were

on him warmly: —Don't be fatuous. Of course, she likes you as a friend of the family, one who is helpful in a crisis. What has a girl's heart to do with economic problems? Perhaps she feels sorry for you. Suddenly, Jonathan felt better. —I can do it! Let's have it all clear in the open. I can do it! He said:

"Miss Greta, you will sing? I've especially promised Evan you would sing for him."

"Sing for Mr. Cleeve? Not for you?"

"For me, too." Jonathan blushed and knew he was blushing. "I gave only the strongest reason."

"Oh," Greta's face clouded; and when her little features were crossed with discomfort, Jonathan observed, she was less pretty; as if light were her chief loveliness. She got up. There was a timid knock on the door.

"Come in, Doctor Foray," Mrs. Mendis called.

A man, extraordinarily tall, cadaverously lean, black-bearded, came in stiffly erect; his exquisite hands in the frayed cuffs trembled; his eyes were blue like a break of clear on a dark day. He bowed, taking no one's hand, and sat down close to Mrs. Mendis, who said, "Greta was just going to give us a little music." He nodded; Evan observed that his head kept faintly nodding, as his hands kept trembling. He was so tall in his chair, he appeared to dominate the others; Jonathan felt his own shortness.

"Are you, sir," the doctor asked suddenly, "the son of Grosvenor Cleeve?"

"I am."

"You look much like him. I have seen his picture, in *Harper's Weekly,* I believe. I remember, because in the same issue there was a portrait of Edwin Forrest who had just died. That must be two or three years ago. I noted the resemblance, not so much in feature as in temperament, between the great Thespian and the great lawyer."

"I'm certain," said Mrs. Mendis, "Mr. Cleeve is too much a man of the world to take offense at that."

"The law's a stage," Evan smiled. "A stage without music, without dance."

"That's good, sir. Very good," said Doctor Foray.

"Very bad, I call it."

"Very true, sir."

"Then I'm glad I'm in business," said Sylvester, lighting a fresh cigar, not offering one to the new guest.

"But you businessmen," said Evan, "are letting the lawyers steal the show."

"What does he mean by that?" Mathilda Mendis turned to Jonathan. "Something deep, I'm sure!"

Jonathan glanced at Greta. "I suppose he means, although business runs the country, it lets lawyers hold the chief offices, make the rules."

"Not the rules," said Evan. "Business makes them. But there's jealousy and dissent among the businessmen. The lawyers are called in. They patch up compromises."

"I'm afraid you're a cynic, Mr. Cleeve," Mrs. Mendis shook her head.

"Business ain't that bad." Sylvester peered at his cigar and let the smoke drift through his nose. "Be good friends with a fellow, laugh at his jokes, sympathize with his troubles, make him laugh, and you can sell him!"

Jonathan said, "You're both forgetting the people. The people are behind both business and the law."

"How far behind, old man?" Evan laughed.

"Greta," said her mother, "these gentlemen are either too cynical or too serious tonight. You were going to sing?"

Greta went to the square piano and began to raise the revolving seat. Evan stood beside her. "What will you sing?"

"Schubert?"

He explored the albums on the rack. "What's this? Let's have this."

"You like *Fidelio?*"

Evan hummed an aria.

"You know it?" She moved to sit down.

"I'll accompany you."

"But I always accompany myself, Mr. Cleeve. I'd be nervous."

"How can a young lady sing, sitting down? Jonathan says you sing like a bird. Does a bird sing sitting down?" He twirled the seat again, took his place at the piano; turned the pages. "*Abscheulicher!* Can you do that?" He struck the chord.

Jonathan, farthest from the piano, felt his cynical mood: Evan was sure that Greta's voice was small; he had selected Beethoven's opera to show her up.

She stood hesitant; yes, she was like a bird. Slim, but the corsage of ivory-colored rosebuds at her bosom, the flounce of lace, the peplum ruffled into the tiniest bustle, made her seem plump and feathered. Her eyes were not large, her red lips were small, the heavy gathered ropes of her hair dwarfed her face. And Evan was treating her a bit too cavalierly. She breathed deep:

Abscheulicher, wo eils: du?

Doctor Foray's forever-nodding head sank in meditation; Mrs. Mendis glowed, full of the life she loved; Raoul, serious, none too bright (Jonathan thought of his father; were the *smart* businessmen all like Sleip and Reuben?), let his pipe go out. And Evan's face, visible over the piano, became relaxed yet harmoniously tensioned as the music cleansed it of all conflict. Where did her passion come from? how did Greta know of the fiends and the love now pouring from her throat?

Evan followed the intricate score carefully; Greta sang free and secure in his accompaniment; and when the aria was over, they looked at each other, full of the experience that had joined them. She removed the *Fidelio* album and opened Schubert's *Winterreise*. Evan merely nodded. They were too close to need words; the room was forgotten. She sang:

> *Ich träumte von bunten Blumen*
> *So wie sie wohl blühen im Mai*
> *Ich träumte von grünen Wiesen*
> *Von lustigen Vogelgeschrei.*

Her voice was sure as a young tree, her voice was tender as its leaves, and ruthless as its roots. Jonathan's eyes went from her fragile face, sweetly strained by its burden, to the calm, deep-breathing bosom. Here was the source, here was why he loved her. The hearty *A major* was overladen, and fell with sensuous, delightful sorrow to *A minor*.

> *Die Augen schliess ich wieder*
> *Noch schlagt das Herz so warm,*
> *Wann grünt ihr Blätter am Fenster?*
> *Wann halt' ich mein Liebchen im Arm?*

Mrs. Mendis as the music began had taken a piece of embroidery, drummed to a ring, from a capacious bag of maroon velvet; in the hush after this song, she went on working and smiling at the half-realized flowered pattern. No one moved, except Sylvester who always fidgeted a bit when the music was not what he called jolly. Greta folded her fan into her elbow and walked toward the rear door. Evan, still at the piano, turned the pages of the Schubert.

He said, "One more song?"

"Oh, but everyone must be hungry!"

"How do the Germans put it?"

She faced him and laughed—"*Alle guten Dinge sind drei*"—and came back to the piano.

The song was called *Muth:*

> *Klagen ist für Thoren . . .*

She sang now with her eyes on Jonathan. And when she stopped and ran to the door, and only her side, then her back, was visible, not her throat and bosom, she seemed to Jonathan slighter: her singing had had volume, and she had left it behind her.

Sylvester got up and followed Greta. "I'm assistant, consultant cook."

Then the back doors slid open; Mrs. Mendis laid her embroidery aside and summoned her guests to the dining room. The table had been laid for a collation, with coffee cups clustered about the silver urn, the dishes uncovered, and the chairs to the walls. Sylvester stood carving a strange bird, dark within cold jelled gravy.

Evan peered at it, puzzled when the knife cut straight through, as if the bird were boneless. "What *is* it?"

"Taste it, sir." Sylvester carefully laid a slice, not disturbing its mosaic, on a plate which Greta garnished with celery, shelled walnuts, and a spoonful of creamed cucumber salad.

Mrs. Mendis, triumphant and amused, watched Evan. With his fork, he took a portion of the meat, placed it in his mouth, tilted his head as if listening, while he slowly chewed, to its succulence subtle as mangoes.

"I still ask: What *is* it!"

Greta cried with delight, "You're a musician. Tell us."

"It's perfection." Evan took another forkful. "No, it's a dozen perfections."

"Not quite a dozen," said Raoul, eating his slice. "To be exact—"

"Six," said Sylvester.

"Has it no name?" Evan noticed that Doctor Foray, slighting the delicacy, was devouring rye bread, cheese, and cold salmon. —The man's hungry!

"A simple name," said Mrs. Mendis. "It's a Charleston dish. And if you like it, Mr. Cleeve, the South has won another friend. Like Mr. Hartt."

"Which of the six elements do you recognize?" asked Jonathan

"Blasphemer! I'm not analyzing. I'm adoring."

"*That's* blasphemy." Jonathan laughed again. Greta's song had given him strength in his resolve. He loved her, for he knew her womanhood welling in her breast. If she was meant for his more brilliant friend, perhaps the better man—richer in gifts, infinitely richer in gold—so be it! he would bless them, serve them both forever. But if some miracle beyond logic, outside the universe of Spencer, Darwin, Mill, gave her love to him, not his sister, not his mother, not his father's debts—

"We shall tell you, Mr. Cleeve," said Mrs. Mendis. "First, you must learn the traditional way to eat it." She poured him a glass of claret from the decanter. "A little wine held in the mouth." He obeyed. "A little crumbled walnut. Now, the fowl."

Evan rolled his eyes upward. "If this is the South, remember me in thy orisons."

Raoul said, "It's called simply Preserve of Fowle."

"You begin," Sylvester could not hold back, "with a dove."

"A dove!"

"You bone it"—Mrs. Mendis silenced her son with a look—"and slip in a long slice of bacon. You bone a partridge, and place the dove inside the partridge. You bone a guinea hen, and place the partridge inside the guinea hen. And *that* goes in the duck: a mallard, but a canvasback will do. The duck fits in the capon or goose. And then, over all, the turkey."

—Mad, dear people! Jonathan thought. They'll live on bread for a week to pay for it.

"Being such an artist," cried Sylvester, "I'm sure Mr. Cleeve wants more details. Each bird's got to be seasoned and basted separate. White and dark meats alternate. Then the whole's roasted in all the gravies."

"First, song; then, symphony," Evan smiled at Greta. . . .

The two friends, warmed by the many foods, stood in the cold street; the moon, invisible behind the houses, freezing the city to its substance, claimed the universe.

"Let's walk," said Evan and started without waiting. Instead of east toward home, they went west on Eighth Street past Aberle's Theater, a pyramid with a monstrous square tower (it had been a church) and north on Broadway.

Jonathan's thoughts and fears, seething together, confused him into silence. The music, because it was beautiful, brooded pain in Evan. This girl, he thought, probably a small soul in her small pretty body, had yet been the vehicle of greatness; as his mother, ineffectual and feeble, was yet mighty upon him. He resented the beauty, the lovableness of woman: weakness that mastered and created! —I'll do what she wants! He knew his impulse was resentment, the stubborn wish to prove his mother wrong, a defiant pressing on a hurt with a hurt of his own.

The two friends walked. Union Square, trees glistering with frost, was color of moon; Madison Square balanced its mansions, many still aglow, and the great façade of the Fifth Avenue Hotel, between the sky and the hard snow. A night hack crunched past them and vanished uptown in the dark spell of the commercial buildings.

"I'll read your brief tonight."

"When will you sleep?"

"To hell with sleep."

Jonathan needed to thank his friend; needed to know what Evan thought of the Mendis family, of Greta. He did not trust the confusion of his impulse—fear, anxiety, envy, hope—to ask a question. They strode in silence.

At last Evan said, "It'd be good to put that gracious lady back where she belongs—in a house of her own."

"What is it in Mrs. Mendis?" Jonathan ventured. "Europe or the South?"

"Maybe it's just herself."

"The years abroad didn't harm."

"They certainly helped the girl's singing. We don't have that kind of regimen here."

"She *is* an artist?"

Evan strode on. Then: *"You* had better not think of her as an artist."

"What do you mean?"

"You know damn well what I mean. Believe in yourself, old man."

"Thanks, Evan."

"What makes you so goddamn humble? Oh, I guess I understand. It's in the story books: the noblest swain feels himself the most unworthy. But so's the happy ending in the story books. You'll make your way, old blunderbuss, if that's what you're worrying about. You'll be able to buy her the dove, the partridge, the turkey, for every day of the year."

Again Jonathan was silenced. How could he tell his friend, close though they were, about his father's debts, about Lucia's problem, about his own sinful part in the miserable fate of the Schmitts?

"We can't miss making money," Evan went on. "In the last few years, a million and a quarter immigrants have come through Castle Garden. *They* are our money. To hell with panics. All we got to do is scoop it in."

"That may be true for you."

"I'm talking about *us.*"

"You speak as if Evan Cleeve and Jonathan Hartt were in the same boat."

"Let's be," said Evan.

"Well, we are, since we're friends. But—"

"I'm talking business." Evan stopped on the street.

A boat whistled in the harbor, its voice through metal air; and Jonathan felt, sharp as sight, the ocean, the docks, the continent converging upon where they stood, pinnacle of a pyramid. . . . "Let's form a partnership," Evan was saying lightly.

—Pinnacle of the world! "You mean—?"

"I mean, dammit, what I say. I'm asking you: Let's be partners at law. If you don't want it, say so. I'll not blame you; in fact, I'll understand. We'll be just as good friends."

"Evan!" said Jonathan. Evan strode forward again. "Can't you stop a minute, Evan? Are we bound for the Adirondacks?"

Evan stopped; his face, as Jonathan turned to meet his eyes, was vague and shadowed.

"Evan, when did you first think of this?"

"Can't you ever be simple? What the hell's the difference when I first thought of it? Long enough to mean it."

"You want an answer now?"

"Think it over as much as you want."

"I've got my answer, Evan. I don't need to think it over."

Evan put out his hand.

"We'd better get home," said Jonathan. "I've got to be fresh for court."

"There's a hansom," Evan hailed it. "I'll take you home."

"You go. I want to walk."

"You just said—"

"Who's being logical now?" smiled Jonathan.

"All right. Will you come for me at the office at nine-thirty? I'll get there early; I may want to look up some precedents. Nine-thirty tomorrow?"

"Today." Jonathan held his friend's hand a long moment.

Evan climbed in the cab, the doors folded down on him. The moonlight in his face, framed by the hansom's black interior, made it gaunt, pain-haunted. . . .

Still submerged in the wonder of what had happened, Jonathan raced through his breakfast, ran for the stage, not stopping to buy his usual *Times* at the corner, and got off at the Park because he was much too early. He made himself walk at a slow pace down Broadway, and at nine-twenty-four he entered the office of Cleeve, Fenston and Fenston. Behind the rail, the bald man in black pierced·him with red eyes.

"We don't expect him today. Haven't you *heard?*"

Jonathan's heart sickened. "Heard what?"

The clerk pulled a paper from a pile of documents and thrust it into Jonathan's face.

Jonathan handed back the paper without a word, and groped his way down the moldy stairs to the street where he bought *The World*, *The Times*, *The Herald*. In *The World* the story struck him, next to the headline that Tweed had escaped and was probably on his way to Cuba. Jonathan stood against the swift, harsh crowds of Wall Street; he could not yet meet what his friend's tragedy must mean. He made himself read first how Tweed, accompanied by two jailers on his customary constitutional, had gone to his ornate home on the Fifth Avenue and Forty-third Street, left his guards in the parlor while he went upstairs to his wife who was supposed to be sick, shaved off his beard, donned a blond wig, and by a back door driven away in the waiting cab to the Weehawken ferry. Jonathan looked at the artist's crude image of Mrs. Cleeve. Then he raced down the column, feeling himself poisoned by the bad air of the allusions to "the famous society belle" and to her husband's nefarious career as a hard-money man and legal brains for the Bankers' Ring, running and ruining the country, and enough to drive any lady to destruction. —What must I do? This blow on this crucial day! Jonathan hated himself for thinking of himself. —*Help Evan!* Before his mind cleared, his legs seemed to know his course. They carried him, still blind with indecision, to Justice Mc-Hugh's chambers.

The Judge sat at a roll-top desk, pigeonholed with papers, and with bland brown eyes in his mild face smiled at Jonathan. He raised his small hand: "Your friend's taking it hard?"

"He hasn't come to his office."

"Who's the opposing counsel?"

"Joseph Choate."

The Judge's eyes gleamed with a malice that Jonathan did not find unpleasant. "Mr. Choate, the young partner of Mr. Evarts? Mike!" he called.

The clerk, a little Irishman, quick, bright, red as a chipmunk, popped in from the outer office.

"We're continuin'—" The Judge had forgotten the name of the case, and turned to Jonathan:

"Golding Brothers versus Mendis Toys, Limited."

"—for a week. Will that do, d'ye think?"

The clerk said, "Mr. Justice, Mr. Choate's already in the courtroom."

"Do him good," chuckled Justice McHugh.

"I can't tell you, your Honor, how much I appreciate—"

" 'Tis a sad t'ing," the Judge's voice keened, "when a lovely woman tells them that loves her she can't abide this world with 'em." His eyes sharpened on Jonathan. "Better find young Cleeve, if he's yer friend. Find him, and hold him."

Jonathan felt guilty. He had always sneered at this Judge hoisted by Tammany corruption onto the Bench to "learn the law." Well, he seemed to be a man.

"Evan Cleeve adored his mother, your Honor."

"More than his father, I'll bet." McHugh rolled his eyes, as if he agreed with *The World's* interpretation.

Jonathan found Raoul Mendis in the rotunda.

"While he was with us! While he was accompanying Greta! While he was enjoying the Preservè of Fowle!" Raoul could not solve this mystery of multiple events. He seemed to be suggesting that the great lady's suicide would have been natural, if her son had been with her.

Waiting for the horsecar in front of the Astor House, Jonathan saw the guests, fresh from luxurious breakfasts, step into the sun, hail cabs, walk away. His surprise that life went on was as witless as Raoul's which he had inwardly patronized a few minutes before. —Nobody counts and everybody counts himself number one: that's the world's mechanics and its tragedy. The city went its course, heartbreak and gaiety commingled. How could he count? How make himself count? As the horses with liquid hoof-blow trotted the long car up Center Street, east on busy Grand Street with its stores, up the Bowery— tenements and saloons already filling, he saw the individual drama, comic or tragic, sealed in each passenger's face (—I have mine, too), and the unmoved city: the car cold and close with foul straw to warm the feet, the snow thawing in splotches on the houses, in rivulets to the gutters; and all the countless motions of matter and men the sun absorbed to a repose beyond any man, any motion.

A group of reporters lounged on the lawn before the Cleeve home. The butler, hostile and unafraid, peered through the chained door, recognized Jonathan, and let him in. "Them newspapers, sir! They been here steady since midnight. Try all sorts of dodges. One borrowed the baker's apron and tried to barge in with the bread."

"Do you think Mr. Evan would care to see me?"

"Lord, sir, he's not here." The man, who was English, looked up the stair and then to the anteroom across the hall from the library. His face was tired; he was glad of a chance to talk with someone he could trust. "Come in, sir." He shut the door of the paneled room behind them. "I wisht he *was* here, sir. I wish you'd find him."

Jonathan had never before pierced the butler's formidable armor, although he knew it consisted mostly of his own mingled awe and contempt for this parasite of the rich, this separate species. Now the butler, too, was human.

"I'll tell you all I know, sir. After the doctors and the authorities had gone, Mr. Cleeve ordered us servants to bed. But I waited up, right here, leavin' the door a bit ajar, just in case I was needed. Mr. Evan come in, late. Mr. Cleeve takes him in the library. Not more'n a minute, Mr. Evan comes out again, his face like a ghost. The governor follows and says, 'You'd better not go to her room.' Mr. Evan turns round on the stair. 'I said that to you, when she was still alive. If you'd gone up, you might have saved her. We're both murderers. You've seen what you've done. Why shouldn't I?' 'Suit yourself,' says Mr. Cleeve and shuts himself into the library again. Still wearin' his coat, Mr. Evan goes up. I don't know why, but I stayed on. A long time. I was about sure Mr. Evan'd retired to his own room, when down he comes again, still wearin' his heavy coat and what he'd seen—I can't put it no other way, right there on his face. He puts on his hat that he'd left on the table, and out he goes."

"Where could he have gone!"

"It wasn't much after two, sir. There's plenty places he might have gone."

"Tell me. I'll find him."

"You're his friend, sir. Didn't you ever—go with him?"

"At that hour?"

The butler sadly shook his head. "I see, sir. You was his friend, but not his night companion."

"What are you driving at?"

"No offense, sir. This is no time for it. But if you knew more of 'is 'abits, you'd 'ave more chance to find 'im!" In his confusion, the man dropped his aitches.

"I know Mr. Evan was fond of night life: concert saloons, taverns. He couldn't have stayed—"

"He often stayed, sir."

"But not last night!"

"He 'ad real friends, like, sir—bosom friends, you might call 'em. He used to say to me, 'Dulham, when you get low, seek out the low.' "

The strangeness was growing more familiar. Last night, he had dreamed strangeness, forms unseen, emotions visible: joy of Evan's proposal, pain because it could not be, because Evan was not Evan; joy in Greta, pain because she could never be his wife, because Greta was not Greta. The dream-night strangeness was going on; he must go on. He saw Dulham, the body a little too soft, the face pale-sweet as if the man lived preserved in a bottle; he disliked discussing Evan with a butler! He listened carefully, as to a lesson, while Dulham named the places where the young master might have spent the night. How did Dulham know? Feeling his doubt, the butler hinted Mr. Evan sometimes took him along; and this hurt Jonathan; and the dubiety of why it hurt him hurt him more. . . . At last, still within strangeness, Jonathan found himself on a Twenty-third Street cross-town stage, putting the names and addresses in order, so as to avoid unnecessary retracing of steps:—the *Cremorne, Sailors' Hall, Tom Gould's, McGlory's, The Pig and Whistle,* while the old topheavy stage swayed and rumbled. Most of all, he was troubled that even now his chief emotion was egocentric. Dimly: —Is that why it's all strange and unreal? If for *one instant* I could think and feel for Evan without myself in the picture, would the strangeness leave me?

At the Seventh Avenue, Jonathan walked uptown. He came to a row of two-story houses, red-brick, or blue and greenish-yellow plaster, with dormer windows in the roof, areaways sunken beneath iron rails, and Georgian marble cornices. It was hard to believe these could be places of ill fame! But the shades were down at eleven of the morning, and several had placards above the basement gate. Here was the first on his list: *The Frenchman.* Jonathan went up three steps to the white vestibule, after a long pause rang the bell, and looked at the tall, shuttered windows. He rang again. A Negress in a green wrapper opened the door against the chain. Jonathan put a quarter into her hand. "I'm looking for a friend; a tall light-haired young man. . . ." "Ain't nobuddy stayed hyah las' night. Light-haired *nor* dark." She made a face at the coin. "Wha' yo'all *mean* 'sturbin' de neighborhood in de middle ob de night?" and slammed him out.

Jonathan turned the corner into the Sixth Avenue. He was amazed at this solid realm of dives and dance halls, right up into the Thirties and along the side streets. Dreary they were in this late morning that was night for them. At last, after many failures, he came to a saloon which according to Dulham was a particular favorite of Evan's. Chairs stood on the tables, the floor was foul with sawdust; behind the bar a huge man in rope sleevelets that crimped the blond curly hair on his arms was methodically, delicately polishing glasses; and the place seemed to reek with aphrodisiac dregs. Jonathan asked his question, and the barman, shaking his head, looked to the rear where someone on the floor was mending a crimson-curtained Punch-and-Judy booth with one of its sides staved in.

"Mr. Evan?" said the carpenter. "I think you'll find him at Dan McGlory's."

Jonathan walked nearer. . . . "Martin Schmitt!"

"Good morning, sir." Still on his knees, Schmitt laid aside his hammer.

"How are you, Martin?"

"Fine."

"How is Frieda?"

Schmitt picked up the hammer, dropped it again. "She was fine when I seen her last. That must be five year."

"You mean—?"

"I thought maybe you was seein' her and the boy."

Jonathan shook his head. "What happened?"

"Nothin', Mr. Jonathan. After I went back to carpenterin' and the boy was bigger—you know that big concert saloon on Delancey off the Bowery, *The Four Seasons?* She got a job there as waitress. She

113

was workin' most o' the night; we didn't see much of each other." His old hands groped for his tools. "She went away."

"With Marius?"

He turned the screw on his plane. "She wouldn't leave *him!*"

"I'm sorry, Martin."

"That's all right, sir." Schmitt placed a level on a board, and began planing.

"Martin, is there nothing I can do?"

Schmitt straightened up on his knees; he had always seemed old to Jonathan, he seemed no older. "It's a long time"—he stopped, glanced forward at the barman—"I was sorry to read— Try McGlory's," he bent again to his work.

As Jonathan went out, the sunlight struck him in the face. He had ruined this man, and no man knew, no man cared. There should be a God to care! He had been cheated of his farm, had lost his wife, his son; and delicacy had stopped him from divulging Evan's name before the barman. There should be a God to care!

Jonathan had, of course, heard of Dan McGlory and his "emporium for sin": a favorite topic of crusading pastors. More than one committee had tried to put him out of business, but the police knew better; and the notion that he owed his immunity to the large sums he passed down from aldermen to patrolmen missed the point. Dan had been baptized Elam Smith by his father, a Methodist parson in an Ohio village. He was at the head of his class when he was expelled from the theological seminary for writing a theme entitled, "Give the Devil his Due," in which he quoted chapter and verse to prove that Christians who "rendered unto Caesar the things which are Caesar's" must not stint Satan. Despite the antinomianism of this thesis, his good marks might have saved him, had it not been for several faculty members who owed him considerable sums lost at cards—each unbeknown to the others. Smith came to New York, and after cloudy years a poker winning made him the proprietor of a sailors' dive on Water Street. In the scent of spices, among the bowsprits, Smith got religion. He rechristened himself Daniel, son of Glory and opened a new lion's den on Houston Street, closing the place Sundays. The sinners didn't approve; too many were off ships with only a day on shore. Dan kept open Sundays, and salved his

114

conscience by delivering sermons at 11 P.M. with his girls to sing hymns. The feature was such a hit that Dan introduced fifteen minutes of devotionals every midnight. Dan believed in glory in dead earnest. Any customer who sneered at religion was soon out on the street at the hands of the bouncer, a big black Negro who sang the spirituals. But any man who could discuss exegetics with the boss was welcome to drink himself into prayerful silence. Dan prospered, moved uptown to the new Tenderloin, and knew the Lord was in it. "My place is in the world," he said. "Since man is so utterly depraved that only faith can save him, where can he see the need of Grace better than in the home of open sin?" McGlory touched no liquor and no women; he gave credit to all who asked and was never cheated; he slept in a truckle bed in a small room near the bar, and gave to the poor not the Biblical one-tenth tithe but a half of all he took in.

McGlory's was on the next block near the corner; Jonathan walked up and down and could not find it. The meeting with Schmitt had confused him, blurred the clarity of his resolve to help Evan. Who was he to help anyone? Was this unworthiness the reason why he could not find him? At last, on the Sixth Avenue, between a druggist's with red and green globes in the window and a shop for artificial limbs: livid false legs, a plaster loin wearing a truss, he saw what looked like the entrance to a tiny chapel. The stained-glass panels showed a youth safe among lions, and two thieves, one in bliss, one writhing, on their crosses. Beneath, the Gothic letters said: THY FAITH HATH SAVED THEE. Jonathan found himself in the dark passage; feeling his way, he sensed Frieda and Martin, Greta and his mother, terrifyingly present. He opened a door into an immense empty room. Far off, on a platform with a piano and music stands, two Negroes sang as they scrubbed the floor. Others wielded mops beneath the balcony that ran round the dance hall on ugly plaster columns. The balcony's open scarlet curtains revealed little cubicles, each with a table and a divan. Behind the bar at the left, on a high stool before a stack of papers, sat a bald man with a blue-black mustache, a pencil in his hand; and far to the right, surrounded by tables with chairs on them, was Evan with a bottle and a glass.

The darkies, McGlory, and Evan, looked up; the darkies went back to their rhythmic swabbing; McGlory's glance connected the intruder with Evan and he returned to his figures; Evan peered through a mist.

"Hello, Evan." Jonathan came close.

Evan got up, set a chair from the next table beside his own, and Jonathan sat down.

"McHugh," Evan said. "Bad—"

"The hearing's been continued for a week."

"A week. That'll give us time." His hand fumbled to his pocket, drew out the brief, and placed it next to the glass of whiskey. "Dan!" he called. "We got a week to decide a matter of life and death. Can we stay here a week?"

"The table's yours for a week." Dan did not raise his voice nor his head.

"Evan, I didn't—"

"Have you had your lunch?"

"Jim," said McGlory quietly. "Take the gentlemen's orders."

"Have *you* had breakfast?" asked Jonathan.

Evan poured whiskey into his tumbler. "Can't you see I'm drinking mine?"

A svelte brown man in a red sweater and a jockey cap stood over them. "What'll it be, bosses?"

"Don't ask 'em," Dan still did not look up. "Kidneys and scrambled eggs."

"Yassah!" Jim went away.

"You gotta eat, my Jonathan." Evan spoke as to a child. "Don't you know you can't spend a week on a matter of life and death without eating?"

"I didn't come here about the case, Evan. Nor to eat. But if you'll have something—"

"You came here to feed me?"

"I came—"

"To feed me. You're an honest man. Don't start lying. You came here to feed me."

"That's not how I'd put it, Evan. I came . . . I thought . . ."

"Dan," called Evan again. "Meet my good friend, Mr. Hartt. Jonathan, meet Mr. McGlory."

116

Dan made a neat pile of his papers, and came toward them. He was tall, lean; his linen and his black suit were immaculate.

"You should have met," said Evan, "long ago. Old and New Testament should meet."

"I'm mighty glad to meet you, Mr. Hartt. Any good friend of Cleeve's."

"Sit down, Dan. Eat those kidneys and eggs you ordered for me."

"I think he needs them," suggested Jonathan.

"I told him: he's come to feed me."

"I'll eat 'em." Dan sat down and turned to Jonathan. "Whiskey's not a bad breakfast once in a while."

"There's the difference between the two," Evan shook his head. "Old Testament orders: 'No matter what you want, bread for you—stale bread.' New says sweetly: 'Drink what you like. If your spirit's right, 'twill turn to milk and honey.'"

"That's a mighty sensible interpretation," said McGlory.

"It's a miracle, and I've seen it. I've just seen it." His eyes were distant and peaceful, and Jonathan, who had never seen them so, was frightened.

"Do you know what I saw?" He poured more whiskey and with effort focused his eyes on Jonathan. "Dan knows; don't have to tell Dan. By God, he's been telling us for years: the whole damn city. You're the man, Jonathan, 's got to be told. Do you know what turns to milk and honey? *Carbolic acid.*"

—Come to feed him? Jonathan suffered. —What have I to feed?

"Of course," Evan went on, "it takes a bit of courage. Most of us don't have it. While it's in the bottle, it stays what it is. When it burns the throat, it stays what it is. You never see it change!"

Jonathan felt McGlory's eyes, black, intent, as he leaned, listening, back in his chair.

"I saw it change, old fellow. Milk and honey at last."

Jim came in, a tray on his high palm. He set three plates before them, toast, cups, a pitcher of cream; he poured the coffee.

Evan drank whiskey, McGlory ate, only Jonathan could touch nothing. —Perhaps he's all right. But Jonathan trusted his fear. As they sat in silence, he forced himself to taste the coffee; the brew was delicious.

117

McGlory got up. "I better get back to my accounts. You're welcome here, brother," he said to Jonathan as if he meant it.

"Mr. McGlory," said Jonathan. "I want to—don't you think—Evan needs some sleep?" McGlory looked down at him, patient, with no answer and no need to answer. Jonathan alone was ill at ease; constrained to speak. "Don't you think he ought to go home?"

Evan burst out laughing. "Old Testament! Old Testament! Commandments. Didn't I tell you, Dan?"

"You two boys fight it out."

"Fight my friend? Why, we were going to be partners."

"A mighty smart team, I'd say."

"That was long ago. When I was practising law."

"Well, you're still friends."

"Unto death. But you can't have a dead partner. You wouldn't want that, old fellow?"

"Let's talk this out," said Jonathan.

McGlory sat down again. "That suits me."

"Daniel," Evan laughed, "if there was silence in heaven and good talk in hell, you'd choose hell."

"It wouldn't be hell. Hell's silent."

"I hadn't thought of that. Music's good talk. All right." Evan turned to Jonathan. "We're listening."

"I still think I ought to take you home and to bed."

"Listen! No more word about home."

"I'm sorry. I understand. How about coming to my house? Like that time, long ago, Evan, when you were hurt?"

"You think I'm hurt now, Jonathan?"

"Of course, Evan."

"Hurt is the word?"

"Yes, Evan."

"And you want to put me to bed again, like that time we were kids? A good sleep and I'll wake up all right?"

"Not so quick this time—"

"But sooner or later?"

"I hope so, Evan."

Evan looked at McGlory and smiled. "Tell him the truth. He thinks a man can be healed."

118

"Not in this world, brother."

"Where, then?" said Jonathan.

McGlory looked up, then his black eyes drove at Jonathan. "Not in this world."

"I know what he means." Jonathan appealed to Evan. "That's not for us. We don't believe in the hereafter."

"You're both wrong," said Evan. "But you're worse, Old Testament. Dan's got faith in the hereafter. Well, maybe. Who knows? You can't prove he's foolish. You believe in the present life. That's an idiocy that can be demonstrated."

"Evan!"

"You think you're the hard-headed logical one; you think Dan's the ninny. Well, it's the other way round. He may not be betting on a sure thing. But you're betting on a horse that's not in the race."

"*There's* at least a beginning of wisdom," smiled Dan.

"Evan! In yourself, is there nothing to live for?"

"Dan?" Cleeve turned the empty bottle upside down. "Your whiskey is weaker than your sermons."

"Jim!" called McGlory. "A bottle of the eighteen-year bourbon."

"I know how you feel," said Jonathan. "No, Evan, I can't know. You'll feel this way a long time. Some day it will change. Till then, I'll stay with you."

"Suppose I tire of your company?"

"Sorry. I stay."

"Old Testament, Old Testament, I wonder why I like you? You're dull. Mother admitted that. You're a bore." .

"I know it."

"You can stay, if you like."

"Thanks, Evan."

"This is a whiskey!" Evan tasted the fresh bottle. "Eighteen years a-slumbering in the barrel. Think what a man would smell like after eighteen years in a barrel. Eh, logician? *Ergo:* corn mash is superior to man."

"A tree or a mountain stay sweet much longer."

"You're right. Man's at the bottom of the list. What a creature. A fly can fall a hundred times its height and not be hurt. If a man drops from a second-story window, he's pulp. Why, without years of hard labor, a man can't even play the fiddle!"

Jonathan smiled. "We can't all be trees and flies—or even whiskey in barrels. We've got to accept what we are."

"Who said so?"

Jonathan glanced at McGlory, smiling and at ease in his tilted chair: *he* had an Authority who said so. Jonathan saw the Negroes at their rhythmic work; they'd quote the same Name as McGlory. He almost wished Evan would get religion. No! They were rational, modern men; reason was their authority. Why couldn't he say it? He would say it!

"It's good to be a man."

"Who said so?" Evan's head sagged a little.

"It's good to be a man, Evan, and have to prove it to yourself, out of your own reason and responsibility."

"You're a fine feeder."

"Evan, you've found it good to be a man. You will again."

"Who said so?" Evan's head was near the table.

"Why are you suffering now? Because you loved your mother. That's good, Evan: to love. You wouldn't have it otherwise, though it hurts. That's being a man."

Evan raised his head, put down his tumbler without touching it. His hand was steady, his eyes were firm on his friend. "I'm not sure. If I'd really loved her, I'd have saved her."

"Don't take that on yourself. A man's imperfect. You said it. Then his love's imperfect, too. That doesn't wipe love out. Any more than man's imperfection wipes man out."

"I take it back, Jonathan, you're a rotten logician. Man *is* wiped out, because he is imperfect. Love kills, because it isn't love."

Jonathan pleaded: "To demand perfection of ourselves is as arrogant as to demand it of others."

Evan's head was again sinking. Softly, as to himself, he said: "Wouldn't love have known? Would it have let her die?" He was seeing his father on the stair: "She's asleep, a natural sleep." He heard his own voice, saw his body barring the man who wanted to go up, who might have saved her.

Jonathan saw again in Evan's eyes the dangerous distance as Evan

120

poured more whiskey, found in himself anger at McGlory, whose presence seemed to erase his words for Evan. They had to go through McGlory; when they reached Evan they were worthless. He'd stick it out, he'd have the last word! Meantime, he'd be silent, now he knew Evan wanted him to talk—as he wanted the whiskey. Evan's mother! What could Evan find to hold on to in himself, to wrench him from the precedent of his mother?

The empty hall had a rancid odor that was not the air, not the sawdust the darkies scattered and mopped up. Jonathan knew what took place in the balcony cubicles when a man and woman drew the curtains. Was this the lingering smell? And McGlory deodorizing this foul world with otherworldly prayers! A man came in, mounted the platform, took off his coat and began to play the piano. This music compared to Evan's! (Would Evan hear it?) McGlory signaled to Jim; Jim went up to the pianist who instantly stopped, sitting still on his stool, his back toward them. Perhaps there was kindness in McGlory, after all? Evan's head sank to the table, his eyes wide open.

McGlory said to Jonathan, "There's always a cab waiting on the Avenue." He placed an arm under Evan's arm; firmly, tenderly they lifted him.

With McGlory's and Jonathan's guiding arms, as if he could not see, Evan walked between them to the door, and into the cab. All the way home, his eyes were open and he saw nothing. Unchanged, he let Dulham and Jonathan lead him to his room, undress him. —Until his eyes close or his mind clears, I don't leave him. Jonathan was alone with his friend.

. . . He was alone with the room; always before when he was there, Evan had filled it. Evan, now open-eyed in bed, was strangely absent. In the law-school days, Jonathan came here frequently to study with his friend; Evan would take his violin when they were tired, and play with passion parts of Mozart, with precision folksongs of Hungary and Spain, holding their wildness captive. Later the violin spoke less often; the music stand stayed in the corner between the bookshelves and the writing table with its brass student's lamp, but the music cabinet was moved to the corridor, and in its place stood a mahogany chest with glasses and bottles of madeira, whiskey, armagnac. Nothing else in the room had physically changed, but with Evan's face a mask on the bed

beneath the tapestried headpiece Jonathan was aware of the long gradual changes. Something like despair had grown within this house. The
mother's frightful end was fruit of a long gestation, and was not the
end. Jonathan knew he was fighting death. He must save Evan!

He sat in Evan's comfortable chair, forward, his elbows near his
knees, and tried to marshal his resources. McGlory's religion would not
do; its victories were all beyond the grave. And Evan, although he did
not relish Spinoza's geometrical metaphysic, agreed that the good man
thinks not on death but on life. There, Jonathan's father's religion was
in accord with Spinoza; but like the philosopher's intricate logic its
archaic ceremonies could not touch this crisis. Jonathan could neither
pray for Evan, nor argue him into salvation. Nothing . . . nothing
would do but to stay with him blindly . . . lovingly. Yes, he loved Evan,
and that poor thing was all he had for him. The learning, idealism,
ambition . . . summed to impotence; and Jonathan knew they had
never been the life of their friendship. From the beginning when he
had led him into the rioting city, there had been violence in Evan: the
mob, his iconoclasm cynical and loving, the passion of his music, the
adroit daring with which he already practised the law, his fondness for
the underworld dramatized by McGlory, his hatred of his father, his
loyalty to his mother, and her horrible end: all violence, now turning
inward, threatening to destroy him. —*Why are we friends?* Jonathan
thought of his own moderate ways. . . .

Evan would have been the first to crow over this victory of illogic:
"You see," Jonathan could almost hear him, "when it comes to some-
thing real, you don't act by reason." Evan then was right? Evan knew
more about life than he did? He sat crouched in the chair, gazing at
Evan's face which was sardonically alive with eyes open and unseeing.
—Watch. Wait. Only so, can you help Evan.

Dulham came up at last with a tray: a chop, a bottle of ale, a slice of
apple tart and coffee. "Do you think, sir, we'd better send for the
doctor?"

Jonathan shook his head, although he knew this was, again, illogic
. . . rationally it was indefensible not to lean on medical science.

"No. Not yet."

He let the food grow cold.

A pallid sun, sinking, cast its rays into the room, brokenly. Warm and still, the room became a vibrant chiaroscuro; a death was in it, but also it was womb-like. Then Evan's eyes closed, his breath grew softer; and Jonathan breathed in unison to uphold his friend's breathing. In the deepening gloom a shard of sun stood higher, touching the row of paper-covered books on the top shelf. These were Evan's favorite French authors. Evan was fond of living in their "golden day of France" as he put it: the same Evan who wanted now to die. Jonathan thought: —Drinking is a little death for him, a death in homeopathic doses.

Evan's arm stirred; he raised it from the coverlet to his brow. He brushed his hair back, and his eyes opened.

"Hello," he said. "You still here?"

"Hello, Evan."

"I'm getting old. Can't hold my liquor."

"Who could hold a quart of whiskey on an empty stomach?"

"Two quarts! Don't undervalue me. Not empty stomach, empty mind! If your mind's full and in focus, you can drink all night."

"I repeat: empty stomach."

Evan sat up. "Jonathan, you're priceless! You think you're an idealist. You're the world's perfect materialist."

Jonathan smiled; Evan seemed normal, robust. "I'll bet you've eaten nothing since the 'Preserve of Fowle.'"

Evan got out of bed. He put on the brocade dressing gown Dulham had laid on a chair, pushed his bare feet into leather slippers, and stood steady. He seemed to be recollecting. The fingers of his left hand lightly tattooed his forehead.

"I'm all right. Just a little headache."

Jonathan waited, looking up from his chair.

"You can go now."

Jonathan did not move.

Evan's old ironic smile. "Are you camped here for good? Don't you have any business to attend to?"

Jonathan's mouth twitched. At last he said, "I'm afraid to leave you, Evan."

Evan sat on the side of the bed. "You think I'm going to kill myself?"

"Until I'm sure—"

"How in hell can you keep a man from killing himself, if he really wants to?"

Jonathan did not answer. Evan looked with disgust at the tray of cold food. "I'm thirsty."

Jonathan went to the bathroom and came back with a glass of water. Evan drank it.

"I'll take your word, now, Evan."

"That wouldn't be very shrewd. If a man was going to die, was practically dead already, and was sure death was the end, why should he hesitate to give his word if it made the going easier?"

"I'll take your word."

Evan's eyes wandered over the darkening room, as if he had never seen it. The sun was gone from the yellow-covered books; a last dim glow on the top of the shelf touched his violin case. His mouth quivering, Evan reached for the case and drew from the white silk scarf that covered it his glowing Amati. As if it were a weapon, he raised his arm.

"What are you going to do?"

"I'm going to smash it. Any objections? If you wish, I'll wait till I'm alone."

"I've no objection. Only—"

Evan waited.

"Why don't you play it one last time?"

"You want to hear it?"

"Yes, I want to hear you."

Evan took his bow and at once, mechanically, he began to play the Mozart seventh sonata in F major. The strings were out of tune. Jonathan saw in the shadow his eyes lighten with focus; he stopped, tightened the bow, and tuned the violin. He started again, mechanically; the music won him; he played with strict passionate precision to the final note of the *Allegro*. He tossed the violin on the bed and came close to Jonathan. Now it was so dark Jonathan could barely see him.

"Are we going to be partners?" said Evan.

"Yes."

"You're a fool. I mean it. You'll regret it. I mean it." He paused. "I'll probably drag you down in the mud."

Jonathan was silent.

"I'm no good . . . I mean it. . . . What have you got to say?"

"I'm not arguing with you."

"Are we going to be partners?" said Evan.

"Yes," said Jonathan.

Jonathan stood up; he did not dare to wipe the tears from his eyes; but Evan could not see—he hoped he could not see them.

The two young men stood in the dark room together.

"You've given your word, haven't you, Evan?"

"If everything else I've said goes with it."

Jonathan put out his hand and Evan took it.

2

THE CENTENNIAL EXPOSITION IN PHILADELPHIA HAD opened with a shout heard faintly round the world. From faraway Bayreuth, Richard Wagner sent a March; John Greenleaf Whittier, the Quaker bard, from a realm more remote, composed a Hymn:

> *Oh, make Thou us, through centuries long,*
> *In peace secure, in justice strong,*
> *Around our gift of freedom draw*
> *The safeguards of Thy righteous law;*
> *And, cast in some diviner mould,*
> *Let the new cycle shame the old!*

With an orchestra of preponderant brasses, Theodore Thomas played, in alphabetical file, the airs of Argentina, Austria, Belgium, Brazil, Denmark, France, Germany, Great Britain, Italy, Netherlands, Norway, Russia, Spain, Switzerland, Turkey, and "Hail Columbia." Before two hundred thousand uncrowned heads and one crowned, Dom Pedro, Emperor of Brazil, President Grant started the nation on its second century: "While proud of what we have done, we regret that we have not done more. But our achievements have been great enough to make it easy for our people to recognize superior merit wherever found." He pulled a lever, the great Corliss engines moved, and all America knew the humility of his words was good sales talk for Europe, but hogwash: the United States was the richest, strongest, brightest land on earth. The rain clearing, under a balmy fifth-month sky among the throng stood a gray man, his body prematurely aged by his excessive labors nursing soldiers in the hospitals of the Civil War, and his eyes fresh as a child's. He had hobbled on foot a good part of the way from his home in Camden across the Delaware. He too had made a song for the Exposition:

> *After all, not to create only, or found only,*
> *But to bring, perhaps from afar, what is already founded,*
> *To give it our own identity, average, limitless, free. . . .*

Long, long, long, has the grass been growing,
Long and long has the rain been falling,
Long has the globe been rolling round.

Come, Muse, migrate from Greece and Ionia;
Cross out, please, those immensely overpaid accounts. . . .

Away with themes of war! away with War itself!
Hence from my shuddering sight, to never more return, that show
of blackened, mutilated corpses! . . .

Away with old romance!
Away with novels, plots, and plays of foreign courts!
Away with love-verses, sugar'd in rhyme—the intrigues, amours
of idlers,
Fitted for only banquets of the night, where dancers to late music
slide. . . .

To you, ye Reverent, sane Sisters,
To this resplendent day, the present scene,
These eyes and ears that like some broad parterre bloom up
around, before me,
I raise a voice for far superber themes for poets and for Art,
To exalt the present and the real. . . .

All thine, O sacred Union!
Ship, farm, shop, barns, factories, mines,
City and State—North, South, item and aggregate,
We dedicate, dread Mother, all to thee. . . .

But no one heard Walt Whitman.

During May and June, Jonathan Hartt was far too busy to go to
Philadelphia. It was true: commerce still lagged and would, until the
Presidential elections in November, but the depression was passed,
America was rising again, and the practice of Cleeve and Hartt thrived.
Even Sundays, Jonathan spent an hour or two in the library of the
Bar Association; and since his proud election to the new Civic Com-
mittee whose task was to clean the town of corruption, he had little

time even to visit Greta. But this July Fourth, he was going to the big show, with Lucia, of course, and Philip; at the last moment Reuben and Lucy had invited themselves along. It was to be a great day, almost as great as the opening of the Exposition; Bayard Taylor would read an original poem, William E. Evarts and Grosvenor Cleeve deliver the orations.

Fresh and resilient dawn sang through the open windows; Jonathan jumped out of bed and shook Philip by the shoulders (it was the only way to wake the big "baby"—he was twenty-four—who seemed to sleep at the bottom of a magic well, that perhaps opened on the Elysian Fields). Sarah was already in the kitchen, preparing the early breakfast.

"Your father had a poor night; he didn't really sleep until almost daylight."

"That means *you* had a poor night, mother."

Mrs. Hartt stirred the oatmeal porridge. "You needn't worry about me."

"If father's sick, perhaps we'd better not go."

"Did you wake Lucia? Of course, you're going. Lucia is looking forward to the day; and you can't disappoint Reuben and Lucy."

"Oh, Reuben and Lucy! They can get to Philadelphia without us."

"Don't think of it, Jonathan." Time had wholly healed the mother's coolness to Reuben's marriage; and she was glad of any occasion that brought all her brood together. Reuben had more than justified himself: not only was he successful, but Lucy, although a little common, was a good wife, a good mother to her two baby daughters. (Jonathan did not know it had been Sarah's hint a few days before that had made Reuben invite himself and Lucy to go along.)

"But father's not really sick?"

"Here, Jonathan, you can cut the bread." The maid had gone to spend the holiday with her sister at Coney Island Beach. "I don't think so," Sarah answered.

"You say he's asleep now?"

"Yes."

. . . Evan Cleeve lay on his back, asleep. He had quit his father's house at the same time that he left his father's office; Grosvenor Cleeve

128

remaining alone with his servants, his wines, and his mixed memories. Evan could have gone to a luxurious hotel, or moved into one of the newfangled French flats near Union Square and Murray Hill; his choice was the plebeian Earle's House, headquarters for Western cattlemen and Southern politicians; and from the Gramercy Park mansion he took only his clothes, a few books and his Amati. Through the windows of his bedroom the breeze, converging on Center and Canal Streets, stirred the soiled curtains; a cart and a stage rumbled, the surrounding commercial buildings slumbered in sordid holiday trance. Evan had thrown off his sheet and lay, arms out, as upon a cross. He was walking with Jonathan, the weeds grew monstrous; he was hemmed in by green blades sharp as knives and high without end, no sky above them. Jonathan beside him, who had somehow brought him here, walked on normal lawn. Evan could not communicate with his friend, could not make him know the towering green blades that prisoned him and cut him. While Jonathan kept comfortably walking, talking of his work on the Civic Committee, "I must get out of this," he muttered, and Jonathan did not hear. "I'll get even with you yet." Evan opened his eyes . . . lay relaxed, seeing the bleak hotel-room furnishings and the breeze on the curtains. A fly circled over his face, between his face and the low ceiling; he forgot his dream. Deftly he caught the buzzing creature in his fist; about to crush it, he changed his mind, went to the window; saw the long gray façade of his hotel: five stories, then four; let the fly go and went back to bed. —Fourth of July; nothing to do. His hands clasped back of his head, he lay contentedly on his pillow, and recalled the night before. He had had a gay time at the house of Coroner Croker, an up-and-coming man! They had gone to Union Square to see the parade and fireworks; the huge crowds had broken the police lines, and several patriots in their fervor to celebrate the nation's hundredth birthday had been burned by rockets. Croker said, "A crowd's a fool. Let's go home." Far into the night, Julius Kleinberger who aimed to be Sheriff, August Dinger who had a program for city-wide adult education through public lectures, Patrick Eustis, the red-bearded alderman who engineered franchise sales, and he, had drunk mint juleps and argued about everything while Croker listened, enjoyed, and said nothing. Croker, only five years older than Evan, the son of a blacksmith from Cork, seemed to know what it all meant: business, politics, the fireworks, even Dinger's plan (with himself at the center) for universal uplift: a paying show if you don't get hurt. Croker himself had put up so good a show of imperturbability two years before when they were trying him for murder, that the jury, despite the evidence, let him go. Without recalling his dream, Evan's thought switched to his partner. Jonathan today was visiting the Exposition; he'd hear the old man roar his rounded rhetoric. —What shall I do with this all-sacred Fourth? Evan jumped out of bed again, took his fiddle, and played a *courante* from a Bach suite. Perspiring, he bathed, shaved, rang for his breakfast. —I know! He had a friend on South Street who rented rowboats. He'd take a bottle of red wine, a French loaf, a sausage, and spend the day skirting Manhattan Island. When it got too warm, he'd come home, bathe again and drive Sylvia or Ophelia (it didn't matter) behind his new trotter to the road house near Dobbs Ferry.

. . . Jonathan, Lucia, and Philip boarded an almost empty horsecar (folks stayed home on holiday mornings; besides, Jonathan had noted the steady ebb of crosstown traffic as the railroads boomed: fewer bowsprits hemmed the city, more and more seven- and nine-story buildings bristled skyward). Through the dirty windows of the car, while the horses dawdled as if they resented having to work on the nation's hundredth birthday, the sun came already hot over the dumbbell tenements of the East Side, most of whose rooms never saw the sun. Philip held his bright-banded straw hat in already sweaty fingers; Lucia looked uncomfortable in her polonaise of gray-blue with bright white plaitings and ribbons. Soon she would celebrate her thirtieth birthday, and she had made a scene when her mother casually remarked that it would be her twenty-fifth: "I'll have none of that! I'm going to be thirty, and I'm not going to be married! Why should a woman hide her age, any more than a man? The greatest women never married." Reuben was never on time. At the ferry entrance Jonathan, Philip, Lucia waited warmly while the foot passengers and farmers' wagons going home empty from the city markets filed to the broad, flat boat that reeked of manure and tar in the hot morning. At the last whistle, a hackney coach bounded up; Reuben jauntily stepped out and helped his wife to the filthy cobbles. Lucy's vivid body looked toothsomely cool in a pale lemon organdie dress trimmed with blue ruching under a Scotch straw bonnet and a striped blue parasol; her white fingerless gloves reached from palm to elbow, where the pink arm was naked up to the puffed sleeve at the shoulder.

She kissed her sister-in-law. "What a gorgeous day!"

"It's going to be hot," said Lucia.

"Good!" Reuben mopped his brow with a silk handkerchief. "That'll give us an excuse for drinking plenty of iced punch. How are you, Judge?" He clapped Jonathan on the back.

Lucia and Lucy went forward to the ladies' saloon; the three brothers stood on the rear platform in a little oasis free of horse dirt and fouled straw; behind them the tall stack of the boat belched smoke into the morning; before them the flank of the city spread as it receded, the new iron-girded office buildings and hotels challenging the church steeples. A two-masted, two-jibbed sloop glided among steamers topheavy with their funnels and tiered decks; tugboats tough as bulldogs churned the water; a pied blanket of pipes, whistles, bells, lay on the scudding whitecaps; into the horizontal day of tide and windy sky, the city thrust perpendicular and wilful.

"Quite a sight," Reuben philosophized, putting a match to his small cigar. "There's your city of the future. Skyscrapers! They'll be solid in a generation."

"Where will the people walk?" asked Jonathan.

"Tunnels, bridges. . . ."

"How about sun?"

"Coal to heat 'em, natural gas to light 'em. Who'll need sun?"

"Jiminy crickets!" cried Philip, "Ain't there *room* enough in the country?" and tugged at his stiff collar.

They passed a dory; two men at ease in undershirts smoked their pipes and fished while Philip gazed at them with envy. A hoarse horn sounded, an ocean liner swam athwart the stern of the ferry. They were near the Jersey shore; beyond the big ship, each deck and porthole visible, the city hid in the sun's haze. To Jonathan the great liner was Europe: Tower of London, Temple Law Courts, Versailles, clear as a printed page; while his New York, murmurous in the morning, was the unknown. Reuben figured: —If I stick to the pay-dirt of Manhattan real estate, I can buy Lucy and the little girls the best cabins on that boat! New York to him was plain as rising prices.

131

Philip, as the steamer glided past, heaving huge waves that tossed the dory into danger, worried about the fishermen who dropped their lines and held on to the gunwales; the dory righted itself. . . .

The Jersey terminal was a cave that led to the hot, panting iron locomotive, to the cars tense to spring into speed. Then the engine screamed through the liquid green Hackensack marshes, the glaring meadow-wide morning. Jonathan reminded himself that he had reason to be happy (and knew his need to argue the point refuted it). *Golding versus Mendis* brilliantly won, his father's debts in hand, his acknowledged good work on the important Civic Committee (its youngest member), his possible nomination at the next Democratic caucus for Congress . . . were in tune with the train's speed; and the summer morning embraced his love for Greta, his knowledge that Greta loved him. The cars, scudding from Trenton, sloughed off, into the past, dirty street-corners, decayed warehouses: these excreta of progress would be cleansed, sure as the sun rises. The course of train and day toward the Exposition . . . toward the new era of the nation that was his, fused with the course of his own life.

Philadelphia seconded the omen. The dignified pressed-brick houses with white shutters, marble steps, fan-shaped portals, the stately Mint and Custom House, Independence Hall rising in porch and double-pillared pediment to clock tower and cupola, its galleried wings joined to gracious red brick mansions, more than New York brought home to him the nation's Jeffersonian beginnings. The new Girard Avenue bridge, one thousand feet long, one hundred feet wide, fifty feet above the waters of the Schuylkill, tilted the crowd to the turf and trees of Fairmount Park; Landsdowne Glen, George's Hill, the foliaged high banks, all spoke of the nation's lush rising into power. There, at last, it was! The sun beat on the twenty-one-acre glass-and-iron Main East Building! Clumsy, the one-hundred-twenty-foot towers at each corner; an oven the half-mile immense interior with the sun burning the huge tin roof. But of the throngs milling in a Bengal fervor of fecundity among the many inventions, no one complained (except Philip who kept asking, "When do we see the animals?"). —I am part of this greatness! exuded with the sweat of the ten thousand bodies. Jonathan, holding Lucia's hand in order not to lose her, following Reuben, felt the wonder of being an American . . . tried to live the wonder . . . and found beneath the phantasmagoria of machines, charts, models, promising America's promise, his need of Greta who for him must be its home. Without her, the American promise would flare off from him parabola-wise into space like a comet.

Only a week before, he had been with Greta a whole hour alone. Mrs. Mendis was indisposed in bed; Raoul and Sylvester were out. "Please sit down," she had said. "I'll ask mama if you can stay." She came back promptly, placed her work basket beside her on the sofa, and began to darn a sock. The silence did not trouble her; her hands and her smile were sure of their place in her world; and Jonathan sensed that he must join her in it, then his own suffering from his silence would cease. It was a world beyond his thoughts, beyond his feelings, beyond time. Even his sight of her sweet body made him suffer. But here, within reach, was a closeness that was timeless. For an instant he held it; then his problems at home, his plans, his hunger for the woman he saw, came back: again, he suffered in the silence.

She laid her mending away, and looked at him. "You're so tired, Jonathan. You work too hard." She was taking pity, leaving her perfect ease of silence to partake with him of the more troubled world of time and words.

"There's always more and more to do," he said.

"But you can't do your best at *anything,* if you're too tired."

He could not say, Be still; in your silence I must learn to find rest. Within this infinite present beyond time and sense where for an instant he had been with her forever, there was another infinite, smaller, more intense: the need to hold and die within her body that must perennially renew the need. The one infinite was too alien to his mind and sense to be borne, the second was too consuming of his flesh—devouring all and still demanding all. He tried to escape them both.

"You're scarcely idle, yourself."

"Oh, yes, I have lots to do."

"Your household, your music."

"I read, too!"

"How do you find time?"

"I don't know. Everything just swims along."

133

"No, Greta, the good things don't just swim along."

"No?"

"We have to work hard for the best which is the rarest."

"Oh, Jonathan, the best is easiest—and most common! Sunlight. Fresh air. Except, of course, in this dirty city." She smiled impishly. "But I love the city. I love to long for the fresh air and sunlight, in the city."

"But we're not trees or rays of the sun, Greta. We must improve ourselves."

"I know it. I work hard at my music. Only it's not *real* work."

"Don't you practise exercises?"

"When mama's around."

"You're slandering yourself."

"A song teaches me much more. Especially when it's fun. Then each note tells me what it means."

"I didn't know you were so conscious an artist."

She opened her eyes wide, not understanding. He was fighting off their closeness with his preachings. Why did he have to influence, make her over . . . when their closeness had been as easy as the sun? He loved her for what she was; he had to justify his love by making her what she was not! Dimly he sensed his mother in this—his need to please his mother who would destroy their closeness; and his need to please his will which would not care what died if only it had its way. But most terrible of all, she was feeling his will, she was striving to conform! It proved she loved him!, and because she loved him, would she allow his love to maim what he loved?

"You tell me, Jonathan," she said demurely, while he suffered, "what I do that's wrong, what you don't like in me?"

"Greta! what I don't like?—what could I not like?"

"I want to improve myself, too. I know—"

"What, dear Greta?"

"Singing is not everything."

She was beginning to tire; her small features were peaked. At that instant, Jonathan saw the abyss: the life of his love and his love's doom were one! She could not save them, because she loved him, accepting even his will against herself! He could not save them, because even the heartbeat of his love was impure with time—with hungers—with his will against her! More was needed of his love than love, and more of her love than love, to let love save them. The ultimate closeness was in her!; for an instant he had reached it and at once fallen away. How could he stay in her until he was close? How could he be close until she had already saved him?

Leaving Greta, he had thought with nostalgia of his father, who let them all live in their own way. And pity for Greta overwhelmed him, not because he loved her; but because she loved him. . . .

Lucia, Jonathan, tall Reuben, Lucy, still miraculously neat and cool, disgruntled Philip, moved from exhibit to exhibit, from building to building. When they approached the Memorial Hall where France, Italy, Spain had sent treasures of art, and Lucia was already exclaiming her delight, Philip slipped away. They were half through the pageant of Raphael, Tintoretto, Velázquez, when Lucy cried, "Philip has run away!"

"I'm worried," insisted Lucia as upon her woman's rights.

"He's not a child," said Jonathan.

Reuben laughed, "He's probably communing with the cows."

"It's all right," Jonathan appeased his sister. "Didn't I take the precaution of giving each of you a return ticket?"

"Mama will be angry," said Lucia, "if we come home without him."

"Heavens!" Lucy was amused, "you'd think Philip was ten!"

"We don't know our baby Philip," observed Reuben. "The cow he's communing with is probably a two-footed heifer."

"Reuben!" protested Lucia.

The argument had brought them to the exit. An open-air restaurant beckoned with gay-colored parasols on the tables, as if confident of its strategic place for relaxation after the sublimities of the Renaissance. Lucia and Jonathan looked hot and mussed. "I invite you to something cool," said Reuben, nearly as unwilted as his wife.

"Jonathan," insisted Lucia, "couldn't you walk around and *find* him? We'll wait for you here."

"That's all right with me," said Reuben. "So long as the cold drinks hold out."

"Please, Jonathan!"

"This is a rather big place—"

"Please!" Lucia stood her ground.

"We'll restrain ourselves and save you a couple of beers," Reuben laughed.

"I'll have one first," Jonathan tried to compromise. They had reached a large round table.

"Then *I* shall go!" Lucia's face was firm as a martyr's. "The longer we wait, the harder it will be to find him."

"Oh, very well," Jonathan ignored the waiter and rushed out. His afternoon was ruined. He hoped he would not find Philip; then why was he looking for him? —I'm not free, I'm not free. He felt humiliated. But he went about his task with conscience: he searched the Farm Exhibits, then the Labor Pavilion where models of prospective workers' tenements from Germany and Sweden drew his interest. Outside a Norwegian farm, the lawn sloping to a bower of trees above the water, he noted heavy clouds over the sun from the west.

"Did you look *everywhere?*" Lucia asked when he returned.

"I think you'd better trust me, Lucia."

"Here's to Philip's happy afternoon," Reuben raised his glass.

"If it's happy for him"—Jonathan dourly drank his ginger beer, not tasting it—"he's the only one."

"Come now, we're all happy! Ain't we, Lucy?" Reuben drained his glass.

"It's been perfectly wonderful."

"And how about you, sister?" Reuben went on. "You ought to be happy, too. Why, you've even found something to fight about."

Lucia scowled and Lucy was radiant; she enjoyed these Hartt quarrels as she enjoyed the antics of the acrobats at Proctor's.

A heavy raindrop sounded on the taut, striped canopy above them.

"It's going to storm," said Jonathan.

"That'll make everything perfect," Lucia was sardonic. "Now, they won't be able to give the orations."

"Jonathan will give us a private one on the way back," teased Reuben. "After all, he's practically in the Grosvenor Cleeve family, seeing Evan Cleeve is his partner. How about it, Judge?"

"Everything's going wrong." Lucia was grim. "I feel it."

—You want it, Jonathan felt like saying.

The storm fell on them. The garish dyes of the table parasols ran in the rain; the posts on which they were suspended snapped in the wind; the waiters in white coats scampered for shelter as the canvas wall of the pavilion, picturing a Swiss châlet, ruminant cows, cowherds with alpenstocks on a background of snowcapped mountains, ripped and collapsed, revealing a row of garbage cans that alone stood stolid in the rout. They bolted to the exit, the whole Exposition suddenly revealed as a papier-maché world in which the possibility of wind and rain had not been reckoned. The Hartts swept with the drenched crowds to the main building, could not get in; Lucy laughed as her cool dress wilted in the flood; Lucia, feverishly holding Jonathan's hand, cowered from the drench as from an insult. They looked at the gimcrack buildings, now caricatures of splendor, and waded through rivulets of rain and débris, over the park sonorous with storm, toward the station. The waiting cars with windows shut at once became cauldrons for their steaming bodies. Those who found seats were the enemies of those who stood in the aisles; those who wanted the windows open, although the rain was waterfalls, became a party against those who preferred to be dry. Men lighted pipes and cheroots, and Lucia roused a faction of indignant ladies against smokers. Each group spoke its wish with the authority of exclusive virtue. These, thought Jonathan, are the same men and women who a few hours before joked at the jostling, found crushed hats and toes a pretext for gaiety. The rain had washed away their thin gloss of brotherly love; self-love was naked. He thought of Philip, who, he suspected, had left the Exposition grounds, followed the river below the park to a fragrant spot of trees, perhaps contrived a hook and line for fishing. The rain he was sure did not trouble Philip, possibly it brought worms for bait to the surface of the ground and made the fish bite. What Philip had done was a rebuke for all the Exposition stood for, and the raw mood of the crowds in the train gave Jonathan the fantastic notion that they felt it. Jonathan never could despise the recalcitrance of Philip. Philip, too—his individualism—was part of the nation's riches. But the behavior of the crowds when a little water doused them showed what the unformed American greatness needed. Discipline! Not only Philip—and Greta. All America lacked discipline. Tweed's ring was broken, but the city and country were full of men in high places waiting their chance at the same game. The War Between the States was won, chattel slavery was abolished, but

137

new schisms, new slaveries, threatened. Look at the railroad war over preferential rates for grain: Chicago fighting by every foul means to beat New York and Boston. Look at the labor troubles. The brand-new air brake of George Westinghouse they had seen today was very good, it would make train travel safe; it was no substitute for the brake of discipline. The new models of fireproof steel buildings before which Reuben had stood, reckoning costs and rents, were very good; they would make tall houses—twenty, thirty stories!—safe for human habitation; they were no substitute for discipline's inward structure. Jonathan forgot the beery German's breath, the voluminous lady's wet cape entangling him; he did not hear Lucia's mutterings, Reuben's gallant jests to keep up her spirits. He had the key! Evan, too, lacked discipline; dear Evan, who had everything else! Brains, money, charm, connections. Why did he drink when he wanted to relax; why did he love the company at the Earle's House bar? Wasn't he like the nation? Without order, without foresight? —I'm his partner. That means something, too. *My* contribution! I've sat in Grosvenor Cleeve's library, drinking his madeira. I'm part of this new world, part of the promise! Jonathan's mind exulted, gathering proofs that he was right. Not only Evan; not only business with its orgies of greed and its panics engulfing national heroes like President Grant: a saintly leader like Beecher lacked discipline. How else could scandal touch him? Yes, even Ralph Waldo Emerson . . . those edifying essays on Nature and the Over-soul—a gaseous overflow of good intentions that never came to grips with the pigsties of politics and commerce. The train settled into a swift lacing motion over the ties as the storm waned; the ill temper of the passengers dried into muddy meditation; through the now-open windows the wet earth breathed the crass energy of growth. —*I* belong, I *belong*. Discipline is my function. And Greta . . . he knew he must win her, not only as his wife but as his helpmeet, make her so perfect even Lucia will have to love her. She must learn discipline, too!

As Lucia and Jonathan opened the door of their house, they knew something was wrong. He saw the strange hat on the hattree and ran up the stairs; the doctor appeared, put a finger to his lips and went down, followed by Jonathan, to where Lucia, breathing heavily, waited.

"Your father's had a stroke. He's been asking for you." Even now, Jonathan noticed resentment in Lucia; the doctor, looking at him, had left uncertain whether their father had asked for them both.

A small oil flame burned in a glass on the table by the bed, the street glowed palely through the farther window, Sarah Hartt sat beside her husband. Jonathan read her thought clear as if she had spoken: —Where are the others, Philip and Reuben? The death of the man with whom she had lived her life was also a family function: no one should be absent.

Lucia lifted the old man's hand to her lips; the arm moving hurt him, and his eyes overbrimmed with tenderness. His brow was unfurrowed, his beard on the turned-back sheet was soft as swirls of smoke; his hands were his years, dry and gnarled, unschooled and gentle. Jonathan did not know if the eyes saw him. He leaned and whispered:

"Father, Reuben went straight home from the train, we'll send for him. Philip decided to see the Exposition his own way; he will be home soon."

The old man made no sign. Sarah got up.

"Father must have a strong beef tea. Come to the kitchen with me, Lucia. Jonathan can stay with father." She walked to the door and Jonathan followed.

"Does he hear us?"

"I'm not sure. He asked for you, Jonathan."

"He doesn't seem aware—"

"I think he is. He brought this on himself. I wanted him to stay in bed after his poor night. He insisted on getting up at noon. To hear the *Sängerbund* celebration at the Academy of Music."

"Did he go?"

"He fell as we were ready to leave. If he had listened to me—"

"Yes, mother." This, too—the mother's inevitable lesson—was part of any family function; Jonathan did not resent it, but he wanted it short.

The door closed, he was alone with his father.

The dim night-flame beside the bed, the breathless glow from the street, the humid bedclothes, the immense vainglory-bubble of the Exposition, burst by the storm and by Philip's silent dissent, swathed in death the old man's body. His head was unmoving yet relaxed.

139

The sole life was the eyes. Their gaze was upon everything and nothing. Jonathan touched his father's hand; it opened and closed on Jonathan's; the eyes did not stir yet were not staring. Jonathan knelt, his hand within his father's hand, his eyes within his father's eyes. He knew this ineffable ease was closeness to his father, but they were not more close, this was essence only of the closeness that had always been and that would always be. Could he bear it? The dying old man could bear it! Jonathan fought his need of diluting and dissolving words. He thought of his momentary closeness to Greta which he had not endured, and which had made him think of his father. Joseph's lips were dry and heavy like old rubber. Dead. . . . —Do not look to his mouth. The hand holding his was absolutely still, and cooler than the air. —Look to his eyes! How could his father bear it? The weak, fumbling father, failure in business, follower in the home! His eyes' unbearable tenderness was strong to bear this unbearable closeness. Perhaps it would kill the old man, but he was ready to die. Could it release the son, and bear him into living? Suddenly, Jonathan was afraid; the words in his throat were like the infant's cry from the womb: "Father, father!"

Joseph heard and the vast tenderness of his eyes sharpened and shrank to pity; the dead lips struggled: "It is good."

But the son wondered what his words and need of words had killed, although his father blessed him.

A cataclysm wrenched the rigid chest of the old man; breath was a cornered beast hideously fighting to get out. The eyes' tenderness modulated with pain into a new sweetness not to be borne: an essence of living that could not live in its home. A glaze came to Joseph's discarded eyes, the body suddenly was smaller. . . .

SPRING IN THE CITY! GRETA MENDIS RETURNING FROM market felt it less in the streets, less in the sky, than in herself. She hummed Mendelssohn's *Auf Flügeln des Gesanges,* slipped to another *Lied:* a bird she was, with songs for plumage. Her blue bodice with closely-woven vertical bright stripes darkened her hair (she was between blond and brunette); her puffed sleeves stood out from the shoulders like gusts of a blue breeze; her bustle, very small, gave her body the appearance of plumpness (she was neither thin nor heavy); her skirt of brilliant yellow plaitings hid the white kid tops of her diminutive shoes. She lingered as much as a young lady dared on the gruff street, three boys passed her and leapt on the back of a dripping ice-cart. Spring was in such a hurry, hurrying toward summer (she did not like the heat); hurrying toward autumn (she did not like the cold). Why not live always in the spring?

Greta was happy; but Greta was twenty-two, and her happiness also hurried, like the spring, to an end. You can't sing all the time, although song is spring and spring is now! There was nothing to do. Jonathan did not make her happy.

> *Du, du liegst mir im Herzen,*
> *Du, du liegst mir im Sinn.*

Stern, solemn, rigid, complicated, passionate, tender, helpless Jonathan! Wherever he was, came problems! All summer, all winter, he was!

> *Du, du machst mir viel Schmerzen,*
> *Weisst nicht wie lieb ich dir bin.*

Yet, though there had been a hundred other men suing for her hand: richer, gayer, simpler, happier men—she knew that only he must be her husband.

She had better hurry home and get the hamper ready; today was the picnic with Jonathan and Evan Cleeve. Her mother had consented:

"Jonathan will be his own chaperon," she laughed. "Besides, you're practically engaged."

"Mama!"

"I know he hasn't proposed. It's about time. When he does, it will be news—as if he said, 'My name's Jonathan Hartt.'"

"He'd have proposed long ago, if I'd let him." Greta's pride was hurt.

"I know. You know. Raoul and Sylvester know. Even Jonathan knows—"

"You talk as if he were an idiot! *'Even* Jonathan—'"

"Well, when a brilliant young man, so brave in his dealings with the world, lets an arrogant old mother and an impossible old maid of a sister run his life as if they owned him—"

"You wouldn't want him to be heartless, mama. His sense of duty—"

"That's where he's mixed up. Jonathan's duty as a man—"

"Please, mama—"

"You're right. Why should I be in a hurry if you're not? Should I be in a hurry to lose my only daughter?"

"You'll never lose me, goose!"

"I'm an old woman. I'd like to see my baby settled—"

"You an old woman!"

"A widow of fifty-two, who has had a happy life with the best of husbands, and three sons with prosperity before them, and a dutiful daughter, can afford to be an old woman."

Greta put her sewing aside, jumped up, and kissed her mother. "I wish some young people I could name had *your* young heart."

"I know—"

When Joseph Hartt died last summer, Mathilda Mendis, who never bothered about protocol or pride when her heart spoke, had taken Greta to visit Jonathan's mother and sister. They sat in the bare, almost dingy drawing room, in the July heat, and felt chilled. Mrs. Mendis tried to fight her discomfort with candor.

"I've felt for so long, Mrs. Hartt, that we should know each other. Your son has meant so much to us." Silence. "I know how he must feel about the death of his poor father."

"My son's a good son."

"You can't know Jonathan without being sure of that."

Mrs. Hartt grew even cooler: she resented hearing her son called by his first name; she resented being forced to say that her son was a good son.

"We're an old-fashioned family, Mrs. Mendis."

"Surely there are no fashions in families!"

"I fear there are, Mrs. Mendis. Haven't I heard my son say that one of your boys lives in Europe?"

"Of course. Alfred's in Dresden."

"That's what I mean."

"I'm afraid I don't understand?"

"I can't imagine any member of our family breaking it up."

"But you don't understand!" Mathilda's voice was full of surprised good nature. "Alfred runs the business abroad. He's married to a charming German lady and has two sons."

"Precisely."

"Precisely what, Mrs. Hartt?"

"I said we were an old-fashioned family. I'm not criticizing. Far be it from me. I know, in these modern times, business, even personal attachment, comes first. I don't say they shouldn't. Only in our family, duty comes first. You see?" She smiled sadly. "I'm afraid we could never understand one another."

"Perhaps understanding's not the right word, Mrs. Hartt. But I did want you to know—how grateful we are for your son. If there is ever anything I can do—"

Mathilda Mendis, walking fast despite the heat to discharge some of her rage, had been silent all the way home. Greta knew it was because she did not want to speak her mind before her daughter; and Greta suffered.

That night, when Raoul and Sylvester were home, suddenly it burst:

"Raoul," Mathilda asked, apropos of nothing, "is Mrs. Hartt a Duchess?"

"She's a good lady." Raoul relit his pipe.

"I truly think the Jews are the proudest people on earth. No one is good enough for them."

"Didn't papa have Jewish blood?" Greta asked eagerly.

Mrs. Mendis laughed. "So he used to say. Mendis, in Spain, was Mendez, and he used to joke, saying the only people in Spain who had no Jewish blood were the pigs. Really, it made no difference—"

"What difference *can* it make," cried Greta, "if one is good?"

"She sits in that dingy parlor as if she were on a throne."

"I'll bet the food's pretty tasteless," Sylvester laughed.

"God help him!" Greta knew her mother meant Jonathan. "God help you, my child!"

Greta's little mouth curled in struggle as she bent over her embroidery. Suddenly, she ran from the room.

. . . And now it was spring in the city! At Greta's left Evan Cleeve held the reins taut to the black horse who champed his handsome head and flicked foam toward them; at her right, Jonathan squeezed into his corner lest he touch her—as he longed to touch her. The day smelled of tar, of leather and lilacs, of salt water and Evan's cigar; the wheels skimmed the cobbles and Belgian blocks, the brownstone and brick houses were softer than the air. At the Scholar's Gate of the Park (Fifth Avenue and Fifty-ninth Street), the fresh-foliaged trees suffused them in cool music. Up the hill to the blockhouse that had seen battle in the Revolution, over the Harlem Kill, Evan held the eager horse to a walk. Past the Warrior's Gate at Seventh Avenue and One-hundred-and-tenth Street, he relaxed his reins: hooves tattooing, wheels spinning silent on the new asphalt, they flew past shanties, truck gardens, pigsties, irrelevant clusters of city houses. The wind made Greta's veil a pennant, billowed Jonathan's heavy hair (he had taken off his cap) and teased his beard. Greta felt him near as her breasts.

Evan, that morning, had had a pleasant conference with his friends, Sheriff Kleinberger, Justice McHugh, and Dick Croker. They had met for breakfast at Varney's on Broadway and Canal Street, a saloon said to be as magnificent as any in Nevada's Virginia City. An immense circular mirror, framed in gold, crowned the mahogany bar and was flanked by two Bouguereau masterpieces: nude nymphs sporting with satyrs in a dingle, and mermaids whom amorous dolphins chased through crested waves. On the bar was painted a hundred-dollar bill and any bartender who cracked a smile when a customer tried unobtrusively to lift it, was out of a job. In the paneled redwood recess, under a bronze chandelier spangled with silver stars, the four men worked out a scheme for buying up real estate along the still unpublicized extension of the Third Avenue Elevated and the Harlem River Railroad. Evan by now was an expert in franchise law, Croker and Kleinberger controlled the Aldermen, Justice McHugh had influence in Albany and with his neighbors in the Annexed District where he owned a farm. Not the least pleasure in the deal for Evan was that Jonathan's brother Reuben, with old Darby Sleip, of course, was in it.

A mechanical orchestra of levers, wheels, pistons, and pipes, all solid silver, blared Irish ditties: *The Land of the Shamrock, Why Paddy's Always Poor,* and Varney's favorite, *Don't Sell My Papa Any More Rum,* to which Evan had composed an antistrophe, *Make It Bourbon.* Silex Varney helped the statesmen's deliberations with the best mint julep in town; and Dick Croker passed around cigars of the special Havana vintage which poor old Tweed had discovered and which the Queen of Spain was supposed to smoke in bed with her serial lovers. Evan lived at the same hotel in a suite of rooms that he had comfortably furnished for himself. Evan liked the Earle's House, because, he explained to Jonathan, no Sapolio was used to scrub its floors; in its lobby he never ran into his father or Jay Gould or Collis P. Huntington or J. P. Morgan or John D. Rockefeller or any of the new "Sapolio scrubbed thieves." The bellboys adored him, the drummers from Cleveland and Elysium amused him; the Bowery was near; the Buckingham (New York's finest, where Dom Pedro and the Empress had stayed in 1876), the Hoffman House, the Fifth Avenue, the Grand Central (New York's largest: an eight-story mansard-roof giant with three-flagged turrets, a marble front, and rooms for a thousand guests, on Broadway between Bleeker and Amity) were all at a safe distance.

With conflict in his own life, Jonathan unconsciously loved contrast. Evan's somewhat crude taste in friends pleased him; Jonathan was sure it was a kind of emotional escape and harmless. For that matter, it was probably true that more honest men lounged in the lobby at Earle's than in the gilded uptown places such as the Hoffman House, Bang's Bar, the White Elephant across the street from Daly's Theater. It was good that Evan Cleeve, the aristocrat, got along well with common men. Jonathan, who served them on the Civic Committee and in his Good Government Club, wished he had the gift. Since Evan's hand never touched boodle, why should he not shake hands with Tammany sachems? Jonathan had learned there was no black and white in public life. The case of his boyhood idol, Beecher, had taught him, although the lesson was bitter. Even Tilden, he knew, had played shady

145

tricks at tax-dodging; Abram Hewitt, the iron-master, was no saint, as the strikes of his oppressed workingmen showed; but Jonathan agreed that in a democracy where the ballot is free, strikes were not the way to justice. Strikes were "for Europe," he believed, apt for the feudal old world, although, unfortunately, the Paris Commune had given class violence a romantic glamour everywhere. Contrast and conflict: Jonathan had not read his Hegel for nothing; he knew the logic of progress, peace from violence, order from disorder. The world of scientific power burgeoned like the spring in this Harlem village they rode through. Bicycles were spreading. The Elevateds were thrusting far north beyond the city along four great avenues: Ninth, Sixth, Third, and Second (the latest). Roebling, nearly a year ago, had laid the cables for the Big Bridge that would bind Brooklyn to New York—in time, they would be virtually one city. Only a few days past, Bell had lectured on the Telephone at Chickering Hall; exhibited his long-distance Voice Machine to two hundred amazed guests at the Hotel St. Denis. Bell had predicted conversations from New York to Chicago —even to San Francisco! Already there were six telephones in the city; a decade would bring thousands. And there was talk of an incandescent electric lamp to replace gas, itself a wonder less than a generation old! The world progressed. And contrast was of its essence: look at the foul slums, look at the corruption of public life, look at his own life! He loved the pure girl at his side, yet he had sinned with another man's wife; by a subtle concatenation of cowardice and remorse he had brought disaster to them!

The Seventh Avenue ended; at Macomb's Dam Bridge they looked into the Annexed District—to be called the Bronx. Evan's thought of the deal at Varney's was blotted out by the sight of a sidewheeler gliding through the drawbridge while they waited. Two men fishing in a flatbottom boat made Jonathan think of Philip. The farther bank of the Harlem River, rising in flowers and shrubs to the elms of Macomb's Farm, a square white mansion with iron balconies, made Greta think of the houses in the South which she could not remember. They watched a little sailboat tack close to shore; the triangular drawbridge with a turret at its apex creaked back into place and they cluttered across. In more than one way, the city was far behind them. Evan made an occasional joke, Greta and Jonathan were silent; this drive through

146

the spring, this easy closeness within spring, was too good for words. They rolled along Jerome Avenue, the ledges of Washington Heights above them.

"Aren't you boys hungry yet?" asked Greta. "Remember, we have a hamper."

"Why do you think Aladdin has trotted so fast?" said Evan.

"Oh, I didn't forget him. There's sugar for him and cake."

"Do you want to civilize my horse into a parlor pet?"

"The sugar won't hurt him."

"Horses, too, can be corrupted. Although it's a lot easier with human beings. Animals have no original sin; you have to work harder to spoil 'em."

"I've been looking forward to feeding him with my own hand. He won't bite?"

"Not a chance. If you curl your fingers over the sugar, he'll wait patiently till you uncurl them."

"And you say he isn't civilized!"

"Are civilized creatures gentle? Prussia's the most civilized nation on earth and it's gobbled up Austria and France."

"Animals fight, too," said Jonathan.

"No arguments, please," Greta laughed. "Not today!"

A path barely wide enough eased the cart into a grove of maple and blooming dogwood, and then a field with bees cruising the clover. Evan halted the hot Aladdin at the shade's edge and jumped out. He removed bridle and bit, loosened the traces and, letting the cart sink on its shafts, tethered the tense horse to a tree and spread oats for him on a blanket. Meantime, Greta, not far away, found a carpet of grass for her checkered tablecloth; opened the hamper and arranged a large bottle of wine, a smaller one of lemonade, two broiled chickens in quarters, a pot of mayonnaise, sandwiches of sardines, pâté de foie gras, plum jelly, strawberries which she dished into small tin plates with mounds of sugar, and portions of chocolate layer cake wrapped in paper. Beside each plate, she folded a red-and-white checkered napkin and opened a collapsible tin cup. The sparrows in the trees discussed the intrusion; the clouds south over the meadow drifted from the sun as if it were too warm for them.

"The gentlemen are served. Sit down."

"Why the lemonade?" asked Evan.

"For Jonathan."

"Let's see if Aladdin likes it." Evan took a varnished brass-rimmed pail from the cart and poured the bottle; the horse thrust his mouth in, the red nostrils snorting, and with one noisy draught half drained it.

"But you mustn't water a hot horse!" cried Jonathan.

"There's no law against cooling his nose with a little lemonade. That'll do, son; no more. You see? He likes it." While Aladdin champed in protest, Evan emptied the remaining liquid on the ground. He came back to the others. "Now you'll have to drink wine." He sat down and took the cup from Greta.

"I don't mind," Jonathan smiled.

"He doesn't *mind!* Most excellent médoc in most excellent May, and all he can say to the good Lord is that he doesn't mind."

"That's all I can *say,* perhaps," Jonathan's eyes basked in Greta's.

"You've got to say what you mean."

"Leave him alone, Mr. Evan, and have some chicken."

"Never, Miss Greta! Not referring to this admirable bird. Thanks, I'll have the second leg. Imagine the catastrophe of living with false teeth, and not being able to enjoy chicken bones. Wouldn't it be better to be blind?"

"Oh, no!" Greta shrank.

"Do you hear that, Jonathan? Miss Greta disapproves of blindness. My 'never' was to your command that I leave him alone. It's our duty this afternoon to reform this reformer."

Greta shook her head and her eyes twinkled.

Evan went on: "I know. You think reformers incorrigible. We mustn't give up hope. This plum mixed on the palate with the browned crust of chicken is a pretty harmony. It's true, I suppose, the reformers try to change others because they find it easier than changing themselves. So *we* must help them."

Greta laughed and blushed; Jonathan, a sandwich in one hand, a drumstick in the other, finished his wine.

"You don't get off so easy, old fellow. You need deeper help than that." Evan refilled Jonathan's cup.

"Don't give it all to me; there won't be enough to go round."

"No?" Evan got up, righted the halter rope which Aladdin had tan-

148

gled in his foreleg, and returned from the cart with a half-enclosed pail in whose icy water was tilted a bottle of champagne.

"Extra sec, and still cold." The cork popped loudly and he poured the iridescent bubbles into three stem glasses.

"Oh!" Greta was a little frightened.

Evan stood over them. "I said you needed help, old fellow. I didn't mean a glass of Pommery would do it. Let's drink to Miss Greta's happiness"—Jonathan brought the opalescent wine to his lips—"and to yours. Go ahead. Both of you." They drank in silence. "You know, you old fool," Evan smacked his lips and sat down again, "it's all one: Miss Greta's happiness and yours. Can't be divided. Have you seen that piece of plumber's piping they've recently unveiled in Central Park, calling it Daniel Webster? It's on the West Drive, near the lake at Seventy-second Street. Sure you've seen it. Makes the old owl look even more leaden than he was in life: quite an achievement. Well, there's a good phrase under it—"

"What?" asked Greta.

"She's asked me what. I have to tell her, don't I? Raise your glasses again."

"To you, this time," said Jonathan.

"To me, in good time. I've still got the floor, even though I'm squatting. Raise your glasses. Here's what it says: 'Liberty and *Union*. One and Indivisible. Now and Forever.' "

Jonathan was angry.

"He's going to attack me. Will you let him, Miss Greta? No arguments, you said, today."

"But look here, Evan—"

"All right: look here, you dunderhead. You've got your problems. Who hasn't? Are you going to get the courage to begin to live when your problems are all solved? That'd be like saying: I'll start to live when I die."

Greta was blushing.

"I repeat my toast—a famous line from the literature of American oratory, hence certainly acceptable to Jonathan Hartt: 'Liberty and *Union*. One and Indivisible. Now and Forever.' Drink to it."

Greta drank.

"You see," Evan shouted. "Greta's accepted!"

"Accepted?" Jonathan jumped up. "The toast?"

Evan smiled and kept silent. Jonathan looked at Greta; her lips trembled, but her eyes met his squarely.

"Greta," Jonathan whispered. "You mean it?"

"Yes," said Greta.

Evan was laughing. Greta, between laughter and tears, tidied the crumpled picnic cloth, set the bottles in safer places; suddenly she stared beyond the two men. Her face filled with horror; they turned and saw four figures, blurred by the sun behind them, approaching from the field. A grim black-bearded man came up, carrying a bundle on a club which he shook till the filthy clothes fell from it to the ground; at his side a younger tramp with a face chalk-white began to giggle, the slime dribbling from his teeth; the two others lagged in the rear.

"Sorry if we scared the lidy," said the black beard, and motioned the others up. "All we asks is a inwitation for a drink and a bite."

Greta saw Jonathan turn pale.

"If that's all you want—" he began.

The black beard sneered, the idiot beside him snorted, the two laggards shuffled closer. Greta's heart stopped as Evan, who had sat a little to the side, suddenly was gone, leaving Jonathan alone between her and the ruffians. All four lurched forward, the drooling idiot closest, his opaque eyes upon her. Jonathan leaped to his feet, grasping a bottle.

"No," he shouted. "No, you don't!" and pushed the idiot back into the arms of the black-bearded leader.

"No, is it?" With an agile thrust, the big man's stick struck Jonathan's bottle and it fell in splinters. Greta ran to his side, and gave him a second bottle.

"We wuz hopin' fer a perlite inwitation from the gentleman," said the leader, slowly swinging his club. "But one of youse seems to have had another inwitation, and youse fergettin' yer manners. Maybe the lidy—" He stepped toward her, closely flanked by the others. Jonathan, guarding his second weapon, prepared to strike; a report rang out, and Greta saw the red welt like a flame on the faces of the two forward men, then Evan, swinging his long whip for a second blow. The tramps, more frightened by the voice of the whip than by its bite, did not wait. Down the path they tumbled till the dust hid them, and Greta found herself in Jonathan's arms.

"You've ruined your coat. Dear! Oh, dear!" She laughed and cried.

"So I have," Jonathan soberly examined his jacket splashed by the wine from the broken bottle. His body and his voice were trembling; this made him ashamed and he was too proud to admit his right to be proud.

Evan was gay. "What will your mother say when she sees it! 'My son's a drunkard! Spills red wine on his best blue coat!' Her tears will wash out the spots, old fellow."

Greta had drawn off the jacket and was sprinkling salt on the stains; Jonathan, with nothing to do, stood tense between Greta and Evan who went on talking:

"The red wine's spent; the champagne is intact. A symbol!" He poured the rest of it into the three glasses. "Do you grasp it, Greta? Now the day is perfect. Red wine represents the common things of life. It must be spilled to get rid of the ruffians—"

"Your whip did that," Jonathan said.

"By God, man, if you spoil my symbol I'll let you taste my whip. Besides, it's not true. You with your bottles held them off, and grouped them, till I could finish them with the whip. Ruffians are common troubles; common wine to chase 'em. What remains? The luxury, the Pommery. . . . Drink." He handed them the glasses. "That's the ultimate in human life, and all that counts. Not the necessary which we share with the brutes or lose to deal with them. The superfluous, the champagne—"

They sat again and drank the last drops of the wine. And now Jonathan was afraid. Suppose Evan's whip had missed? Suppose Evan had had no whip? Suppose the men had grabbed or broken the second bottle, overpowered Evan and himself, kidnaped Greta? No such unrealities made him afraid. He was afraid of the real. He knew it! This drop of wine marked the beginning of their union. They were together, the woman he loved and he, now and forever. No wonder he trembled.

Greta was gaily waving his jacket like a flag. "See! it's quite presentable. Perhaps your mother won't even notice." She laughed and Evan laughed with her. He, who was the blessed one, could not laugh, and must tremble. . . .

3

JONATHAN HARTT SAT ALONE IN HIS OFFICE AND looked at the safe. The wall of lawbooks, bound in yellow leather, faced above a black shiny sofa steel-graved images of Jefferson and Chief Justice Marshall; a long pine table was littered with papers, bundles of envelopes, a china water pitcher, three tumblers, a magnifying lens with a brass handle, law digests, and a worn briefcase. Near Jonathan's hands on the desk stood two framed photographs. Greta was in her bridal gown, holding her bride's bouquet; the tight silk bodice and hips with long seams and a basque front, the apron over the skirt cut in turrets and trimmed with orange blossoms, the surplice of crêpe lisse, the square neck, the lace sleeves, the orange and gardenia headdress, made Greta's face look flat and lifeless. In the other photograph, a boy of four—velvet jacket, bare legs, and patent-leather slippers that pinched the little feet—stood on an upholstered chair, a hand on its carved arm. Jonathan's eyes went from the safe to the photographs and softened; returned to the safe and hardened with hurt. Ten years had changed him. His unruly curling beard of a young poet and prophet was now the trim Vandyke of a successful lawyer, the hair toughened by much barbering, the ruddy glow of it dimmed. The eyes that had been in tune with the beard were poignant strangers in this careful face, and the hands on the clean green blotter showed the same dissonance: groping hands without rest and the reward of finding.

At last, the eyes stayed on the safe, and the hands came together. Jonathan got up, opened the safe door, and, returning to his desk with a large yellow envelope letterheaded *The Civic Committee,* drew out three sheets signed *Evan Cleeve* and studied them as if desperately seeking in their known contents some new word against their irrefutable meaning. His eyes went to the opaque glass door of his office, then to the portraits of Jefferson and Marshall. A terror in them melted to sadness. He consulted his large gold watch, snapped it shut. So late? He must be the last in the offices of Cleeve and Hartt, and this was what he wanted. Slowly, as if in pain, he got up, hunted the briefcase from the littered table, placed the documents in the envelope and the envelope in the briefcase. Clasping it tight, he went to the window. Across the court rose the brick windowed wall of other offices like his. He raised the sash, looked down the seven stories to an iron grating through which the rubbish of years had fallen. If he tore and dropped the papers in his hand they would be rubbish with the rest; time would dissolve them. And they would make him rubbish as surely as if he lay down there beneath the iron grating. He shut the window, took his overcoat, buttoned it close, pressed his slouch hat on his head as if he were already in the cold of the street; gripped his briefcase again and left his office.

Down William from Pine, he turned west on Wall Street, walking stiffly (those who disliked him said that Jonathan Hartt strutted). —What am I going to do? Whatever it was, he was walking toward it, and must walk erect. At the corner of Broad Street, a big man muffled to his chin in a black coat stepped from J. P. Morgan and Company; Jonathan recognized the tapir-textured face under the silk hat, the hard porcine eyes, the proboscis. Next to him was a lithe little man with a badger-brush beard; in different clothes and a poor street his terrier-quick body would have made Jonathan think of a pickpocket or a racing tout; he was, Jonathan knew, the uncrowned king of Pittsburgh steel. Andrew Carnegie and Mr. Morgan paused an instant to look at Jonathan Hartt as if his eyes disturbed them; then they walked ahead toward Trinity Church that thrust the nostalgia of its steeple into the January gloom. At Broadway, crowds pouring down Rector Street toward the two Els became unreal as the graveyard under the lead sky that the gone sun's glow lesioned like a cancer. The winter night, the city which it gripped, were the real, the two masters of gold and iron were the real; Jonathan's heart flinched: what was he, what were these crowds, against them? Elemental forces did not rule, they *were* this world! For four years Grover Cleveland had been President; Jonathan had worked hard for his election: a strong man, at last, in the White House. The forces that were the real had moved on. Railway workers struck in Chicago, a bomb was thrown, policemen were killed, and Cleveland, precisely as his Republican predecessors would have done, sent Federal troops to restore "law and order." Jonathan had stumped for Abram Hewitt, from the old Fifth Ward to the new

153

Bronx across the Harlem River; and Hewitt was Mayor of New York, a sounder man than his opponents, the theoretical Henry George, the theatrical Theodore Roosevelt. But who went on running the city? Ask Richard Croker—and Evan. . . . He had forgotten Evan. How even for a moment could he forget? How could he remember? What he knew about his partner and friend, and what the letters in his briefcase told him, were impossible together, and true! No wonder he could not think the unthinkable; the contradiction was a spike in his brain, threatening to split it. Evan was deep in him. What could he touch, deep and dear, without touching Evan? He had always known his friend's taste for the town's gamy elements (he remembered McGlory). But that Evan Cleeve could be involved in dirty money was impossible as that this crowd of clerks, lifting him up the already squalid steps of the Ninth Avenue El past the ticket-chopper's urn into the sooty car—the boxed-in engine puffing, whistling—should turn into a galaxy of angels. Yet it was proven! They raced through grimy blocks, swung over housetops, shops, and slogging traffic. He must unite the contradiction of what he knew of Evan and what he knew he had done . . . or go mad. He must tell Greta. He quailed: to speak of the impossible, still smoldering and slumbering in his mind, would make it altogether real! It was obvious Evan could not have taken money for money. Jonathan thought he understood corruption (his Committee had facts to prove that upwards of seven millions passed each year through the steady hands of Croker). As Jonathan figured it, need made men afraid, and when the need went the pattern of fear remained, turned unconsciously into greed and lust for power. That could explain a Croker, not a Cleeve. Some driving force more organic, more universal, must be there: something closer to what he had sensed a half hour ago linking Morgan and Carnegie with the city and with the sun! To make sense of Evan, must he tear down his whole rational psychology of ethics? They clattered over the switch at Fifty-third Street, climbed the grade past the Church of the Paulist Fathers high in the foreground of vacant lots and shanties falling steep to the river. Again, the impulse to drop his briefcase; to fall with it. And again, the knowledge without words that this death-wish was illusion: the lower he sank the letters and himself the closer the force that would not let him sink.

At Seventy-second Street Jonathan left the car (the few passengers remaining were Italians bound for Little Italy in Harlem). On Columbus Avenue stood the new brick tenements of six stories, railroad flats they were called, against the lots and rocks of the side streets. Jonathan had seen these modern homes: the dark stair, the bedrooms dark as closets, the parlor at the end of the dark hall, breathing the soot and sparks of the El engines. The city was growing without order, except "every man for himself." The country! "Business for itself" hunted the wealth created by the millions pouring in from Europe. The railroads with the trusts rigged dishonest rebates to crowd out the little men. Labor was contriving its own version of "every man for himself." The farmers' way was cheap money. But the farmers were helpless against the middlemen and the small bankers; the small bankers were helpless against Wall Street; and labor had no chance with every hand against it. Here in the metropolis, fish-peddlers and house contractors paid tribute to the politicians whose power was based on their "protection" of the saloons and brothels. "Every man for himself," the "equilibrium of interests" the political economists spoke of, added up to chaos. Poor people got scared, needed coal and good food for the baby; the fear stratified into a pattern of greed long after the threat of cold and hunger was gone. —You're back where you started. . . . Some fear in Evan? *How about me?* Fear explains me at this moment! What's troubling Jonathan Hartt right now is "every man for himself."

As he went up the stoop of his new home: —Better start with yourself. Since Evan did what he has done, what's wrong with *you* that it should shatter and split you? What fear, what hunger, hiding Evan from you? Jonathan took the big brass key from his pocket. He felt he understood for the first time the poor devil on the corner who voted the way the Tammany captain told him. Hadn't he saved his son from jail when he got drunk and smashed the drugstore window? . . . The farmer in the West who followed the Populist heresy of Free Silver: how else but with cheap money save his home from foreclosure? A rush of feeling brought him upon Greta. He must explain everything to Greta: the corruption of "every man for himself"! Greta understood Evan better than he: were they not both musicians? She would help him; she would save them. No use looking deeper: those thoughts about elemental forces beneath morality would lead to metaphysics and religion: they were politer versions of dropping the letters out of the

155

window or himself into the Hudson. Without farewell, the dim sense he had caught on Wall Street that to be real his ethics needed revision, faded away. He needed Greta! He opened the front door. At long last, at this crisis, he would bring Greta close. They had been too busy, he with his professional work at day and Committee work at night, she with her household and her music. He loved his wife, she loved him. Still the longing to be close! His need to discipline her animal spirits, to bring her more into his plans: what was it but the need to give her himself and to win her? In each individual item, his will won; and the sum—which should be closeness—always added to failure. He had wanted her to make a home for him, here it was. He had wanted her to be the mother of his children: their first-born, little Sarah, died at two months, but little Jeff thrived; and no son could have more loving care. He had wanted her at all costs to make peace with his mother and Lucia; warm-hearted Greta, used to adoration, had borne snubs and even insults, and now his mother and Lucia and Philip lived with them in the new house! He had wanted her to help "make Evan happy." She had done all she could: persuaded him to move uptown, found him a spacious apartment in the near-by new Dakota, made a real home for him, selecting the curtains, furniture, dishes, finding the sedulous Augusta who, at least when he was there, fed him decent homecooked food. No man could have a more loyal, more competent wife; even his mother admitted it. "Greta," she said, "makes a dollar go farther than any housewife I know." When he came home late at night from the Good Government Club or the Civic Committee, Greta did not complain. When he took on the added responsibility (and honor) of membership in the Grievance Committee of the Bar, Greta did not complain. When he invited important guests to dinner, Greta was in the kitchen with the cook before she appeared upstairs, the shining hostess. And when, after her long labors and the brilliant dinner, she was asked to sing (with Evan usually at the piano), her song hushed the chatter on Tariff, Servants, and Sound Money. And yet—and yet! The heart of his heart did not know her; was alone and needed her. Again he remembered Evan whom also, loving him, working with him, he could never have known. . . .

Before taking off his coat, he called, "Greta!"

In her blue housegown, bound by a gold girdle under the full bosom, she came down the stairs.

Above them, the gas illumined the red, green, yellow diamond panes of the lantern-chandelier; beyond them, the hall was dim. She took his coat, hung it on the rack and followed him as he walked slowly upstairs holding his briefcase.

"How was your day, Greta?"

"Just fine." He felt her hesitation.

"And everyone?"

"Jeff fell in the Park, Jon, and scratched his face badly. He came home all bleeding. I really think Fräulein is careless. I think he was knocked down."

"You need some evidence. Did you ask them?"

"But Jon—"

Standing with his wife in their bedroom, he saw the danger: every moment of every day and night, there would be a need, a problem, a pleasure! They would go on to meet them, one by one; and at the end of years, still . . . still . . . this distance. Greta was saying:

"I think Fräulein lies. I think she let Jeff get out of her sight, probably while she flirted with a sparrow-cop. I think he was in a fight with those toughs."

"What toughs?"

"You know. Those dreadful people from Columbus and Amsterdam Avenues. The boys go in gangs and they steal from the well-dressed children."

"Why not ask Jeff how he got hurt?"

"I did! But he's such a little man."

"He's nearly seven!"

"He'd think it was tattling to tell."

"I'll ask him." Jonathan took off his shoes and coat, Greta brought his soft leather slippers with elastic sides and his plaid house jacket with elaborate braided buttons.

"I'm worried about those toughs. You don't know, Jon—"

"I'll find out. Man to man, Jeff will tell me." Jonathan smiled, then he frowned. The little immediate problem always just ahead. And the great crisis? But nothing could be done until after dinner. "How is mama?"

"She's in her room. She's all right."

"And Lucia?"

"Lucia and Philip are at Reuben's for dinner."

He got up for his customary ritual: first to his mother's room to report his health and day, then he climbed to the fourth floor.

The phases of his son's brief life, jostling one another, had already crowded his room. Toys outgrown and discarded, tin soldiers with broken guns, fire engines that had lost their drivers, shared a corner with muslin picture books and blocks of vari-colored stones that could rise into Gothic castles. Shelves held Mother Goose, several volumes of fairy tales, tracks and cars of a mechanical train which it was forbidden to leave on the floor, stuffed bears and lions, and an illustrated *Bible for Children* which Jonathan read to his son in deference to the memory of his father. A sleek white horse, its mane real horsehair, its saddle real leather, its stirrups real metal, pranced at the foot of the bed where little Jefferson lay, a strip of court plaster under his blond hair, another across his nose, and, with gray eyes sensitive-bold, intelligent-anxious, looked at his father.

"Hello, papa," he faltered. Each night, he had to give a report of his behavior: "Good today" or "Bad today."

"Sorry to find you in bed."

"I hadn't ought to be in bed. It's only my face."

"Mama knows best."

"Even Fräulein says—"

"Mama knows best." Jonathan sat on the bed and looked at his son sternly, feeling the warm sure close room fended from night and the world. His heart was full with love for his boy. And love, as toward his wife, engendered strictness. "I suppose you were good today, since you didn't say you were bad. I suppose you just forgot?"

"Papa, this wasn't my fault."

"That's good."

Jeff loved his father near, when he was sick. He wasn't really sick, but he supposed he should be, when mama had put him to bed. Mama was too anxious, when you were sick; she made you tired. Grandma Hartt made you feel you were sick because you'd been naughty. He wished he was sick, now. His father took his hand, and the boy was happy. He had wandered away from Fräulein to fly his kite. Suddenly, all around him were a lot of boys in ragged pants and coats, some without coats. They were after his kite, and he was scared. If he pulled it down, they'd grab it; if he let it go— The string slipped through his fingers and off it sailed! That made the gang mad, and he had to fight his way through the ring of them. He didn't fight much, he just pushed; but he cried, and the crying was what made him ashamed 'o tell Fräulein. He said he had fallen on a rock; he knew it was bad to lie. They rescued the kite. If he hadn't cried, he could have told his father.

Jonathan did not press him. —This is already not my room; this is my son's: his thoughts, all that comes to him, already not mine.

"Well? Did he tell you?" Greta and he went down to dinner.

"I didn't ask him."

She smiled and was glad. "I'm *sure,* Jon, it's those awful toughs. Of course, he wouldn't tell, the little man. They're dangerous!"

To reach the dining room, they had to pass through the library. Two gas jets of the wide chandelier burned low over his mahogany desk in the center of the room; the walls, where his books stood, were in shadow. Year after year, since his boyhood, they had gathered, organic like his years: the Greek and Roman classics, the Encyclopedia Britannica, the British and American Statesmen Series, The Federalist; Goethe, Schiller, Lessing, Jean-Paul Richter, Heine, in the original German; Shakespeare, Milton, Pope; the Essays of Bacon and Lamb; the novelists (to Jonathan this meant Scott, Dickens, Thackeray, George Eliot, and Bulwer-Lytton); the American poets, Longfellow, Bryant, Lowell, Whittier, Holmes; the works of Emerson; fat brown volumes of Washington Irving; close to the one window, the historians and thinkers: Macaulay, Green, Gibbon, Buckle, John Fiske, Prescott, Herbert Spencer, Huxley, Mill, and Darwin. One of Evan's standing jokes: "Jonathan has the perfect library; not a book in it to read." "Shakespeare?" Greta laughingly protested. "That's what *he*'d say if he found himself in such company." "Dickens?" "You don't read Dickens, my dear Greta. You *eat* him, the way you do a pudding." If Evan's library at the Dakota had been merged with Jonathan's, there would have been remarkably few duplicates. Evan's novelists were the eighteenth-century Englishmen and the nineteenth-century Frenchmen, his English poets were the Elizabethan dramatists, the Metaphysicals and the Cavaliers, his thinkers were Descartes, Voltaire, Rousseau, the Encyclopedists. Jonathan extinguished the dim lights over his desk (he was saving of gas) and found he agreed with Greta; the muckers had attacked his son; he felt them tearing and defiling his books! Evan knew the District Police Captain. He'd speak to Evan. *Evan!* Again, he had forgotten! Greta ladled the good soup: he smelled the meat stock, brown and strong with okra, carrots, potato, soup of the Mendis tradition. "Every man for himself." Next to him sat his mother, shrunken and dried by the years. Annie, the maid, a pretty Irish girl with a lace cap on her black hair, handed him his portion; he took the heavy silver spoon and began to eat the good soup.

He had carefully, not without flourish, sharpened the horn-handled knife with the steel foil, and was carving the roast beef, medium well done as he liked it, slicing it paper-thin with skill and pride, when the front-door bell rang.

"Who can that be at this hour?" asked Greta, and Annie went out to answer.

Philip, his shoulders hunched in sheepish defiance, came in and took his customary place, which had not been set.

"Philip!" said his mother. "You were expected with Lucia at Reuben's! Didn't you go?"

"I went."

"What's wrong? Where is Lucia?"

"Don't worry. Reuben will bring her home." He looked at Annie. "I don't want any soup."

"The proper person to tell that is Greta," Sarah said sharply.

"All right, what's the difference? Annie's the waitress, ain't she?"

"It's very good soup," Greta beamed. "It's no trouble at all. Annie, just bring up a plate. See that it's hot."

When Annie was gone: "Now," said Sarah, "kindly tell me what happened."

Philip shook his body like a big dog. "I just can't stand it in that house."

"*You* can't stand it!" said his mother, while Greta who loved Philip tried hard not to laugh. "As handsome a house as there is in New York."

"Oh, I don't mind the bric-a-brac, although it's worrisome not to break the stuff, there's so much of it. And you don't have to look at the pictures. But you *do* have to listen to Reuben."

"Another quarrel," Sarah sighed.

"No quarrel at all." Philip looked up brightly, enjoying his memory of what had happened, and aware of Greta's smile. "I didn't say a thing."

Annie returned with the steaming soup; Sarah bit her lip, forced in the silence to listen attentively to her son's noisy eating. Jonathan suspected he was exaggerating the noise, using his hurry as a pretext; and he was quite sure Greta was a bit unseemly in her enjoyment of her mother-in-law's displeasure. Philip finished his soup when Annie finished serving the meat; she gave him his portion and again withdrew to the pantry.

"Now," said Sarah sternly.

Rebellious child, Philip implicitly accepted the authority he opposed. He took a long ruminative bite of the beef (he preferred it rarer) and obeyed: "We were all in the *sa-long* on the second floor; you know, the all-Jap-and-Chinese one with those bamboo chairs you don't dare sit on. Reuben began on the Knights of Labor, how they ought to be abolished, and Powderly and Gompers were nothing but murderers—"

"I must say," remarked Sarah, "after what happened in Chicago—"

"So I said"—Philip gulped a large hunk of potato—"I said: Business combines. The Supreme Court has ruled a trust is a person, and you can't interfere with its natural rights to pursue its happiness, which means to make money. Then, I said, a trade union is a person, too— Well, that sets Reuben going. A regular speech. I think he's planning to go into politics. That's all right with me. But he shouldn't practise on Lucia and me and the butler."

"The butler!" pealed Greta.

"In the middle, he comes in with glasses of sherry on a tray. He starts handing 'em round. Just then, Reuben says something like there was a whale of a difference between a combine of successful men studying new ways to increase production and a gang of failures conspiring to cut down hours and production. The butler shoves the tray at me with one glass left on it. I'm sorry. Something happened. I guess I got mad. I didn't mind the talk so much for us, but it seemed the butler might have feelings and if he had they were being hurt." Philip chewed and swallowed. "Anyway, my foot goes up, and so does the tray with the glass. The glass smashed, the sherry spilled on the carpet."

Sarah Hartt hid her face for shame in her hands.

"I'd have said I was sorry." Philip's lush body twisted like an embarrassed boy's. "I will, honest! when I see Reuben again. I just went out. . . ."

Greta said: "Next time you'd better stay *home*," and smiled at him, and rang the service bell for Annie.

Jonathan understood: Greta wanted Philip to feel her home as his. She was grateful to Philip who had spontaneously accepted her at once, oblivious to his sister's and mother's opposition; but more deeply, she liked him for what he was, and perhaps most of all for his shortcomings. After old Joseph's death and the final liquidation of the Ladies' Trimmings business, Philip drifted through several brief ventures. He was a good salesman, until for one unreasonable reason or another, his interest flagged. His most successful work was covering New York State for an Ohio buggy manufacturer; suddenly he resigned with the startling declaration—which made his mother doubt his sanity—that buggies were too old-fashioned. After a nebulous year, he again found a happy berth with a company of job printers in Wooster Street and soon was expert in the intricacies of layout and type. Several of the men were English and German radicals, who pitied Powderly of the Knights of Labor as a sentimentalist, and despised the little Jewish cigarmaker, Sam Gompers, as a bourgeois opportunist. Pamphlets by Johann Most, Karl Marx, Daniel de Leon, appeared again on the bureau of his bedroom. Finally, in a great scene, Sarah revolted against the disgrace and scandal of a Hartt lowering himself to be a mere workman. It had never happened, she said, and it was going to kill her. She persuaded Reuben to take Philip into the real-estate offices of Sleip and Hartt; and with odd docility Philip acquiesced. In six months, he walked out with the casual observation that Reuben was a thief. When he offered to explain, his mother shut him up. The real-estate business had led him to Henry George, whose panacea for all ills was the single tax on real estate; Socialist and Anarchist booklets began to gather dust on his bureau. At present, Philip's economy was doubtful. He remarked vaguely that he was "selling printing." But Jonathan knew Greta took nothing for his board and hall room on the fourth floor; he suspected she gave him pocket money out of her household allowance. The "family baby"—only three years his junior—certainly had no vices. And there he sat, careless of his mother's hurt pride and his brother's Chinese carpet, wolfing his second plate of roast beef and potatoes with hunks of rye bread to clean up the gravy: his skin clear, his eyes fresh as a child's, he was to Sarah a gratuitous insult to their name, to Jonathan a challenge strangely lovable and disturbing, and Greta's pet and ally.

As they rose from table: "Son, I must talk with you," Sarah said to Jonathan.

Another of those footless consultations on what to do with Philip? Somewhat too sharply, Jonathan replied, "I'm busy tonight, mama."

"You have no time for your mother? Very well, dear. Your mother can wait."

Annie was lighting the library chandelier, then the artificial gas-logs —he heard the little explosion. They were Greta's pride and her one difference with Philip who, when they were recently installed, called them "a bad imitation of a fire." "But they're so much *cleaner*, Philip, and lots cheaper."

"Greta," Jonathan said, "will you wait for me in the library?"

It was an invitation to his mother and Philip to disappear. Jonathan slowly climbed the stairs to his bedroom, burdened by the fantasy that the one who could help him was not his wife, but Philip! Perhaps he was losing his balance? In the dark, he found the briefcase and went down to his wife.

Greta had made herself comfortable near the gas-logs. At her feet on the floor was an old Huyler's candy box full of buttons, hundreds of miscellaneous buttons, and in her lap was a bundle of Jeff's clothes to be mended. Jonathan placed the briefcase on the desk. The moment had come. . . .

It was hard to accept. He opened the briefcase, Greta sewing and humming.

"Have you thought, dear," she asked, "what to do about those toughs?"

"I have something more serious to discuss with you."

She looked up, surprised and unbelieving: more serious than their son? Then she smiled. "Poor Philip! He's a good boy."

"It's not about Philip." Jonathan was getting angry.

163

"Darling, I sometimes wish you smoked. Not cigars, of course." She puckered her little mouth and nose. "A pipe is so restful. Like Raoul. You never *will* relax. Is that wicked of me? I'd love to get you a big meerschaum, I'd cover it with chamois, you'd sit quiet for hours doing nothing but smoke while it got colored."

"Can't you be serious, Greta?"

"I was a great success at the Hospital Benefit Concert, Jonathan. It was this afternoon, you know, and you never asked me how it went. Professor Dietmann accompanied me! He's Sembrich's teacher. He said—I daren't tell vou what he said."

"Tell me."

"He said I sang the Hugo Wolf as well as Sembrich!"

"You *are* an artist, my dear. Don't think I'm not proud of you. But today—"

"Even when you're not there, I sing for you. I imagine you there—so far away only my voice can reach you. Guess who sang, too."

"Tell me."

"I want you to guess."

"Greta, tonight—"

"You're so good at guessing. Do guess."

"Greta, I—"

"You know you approve of guessing as a scientific game of questions. It improves your mind."

"This evening, I can't think of improving my mind. Greta, today—"

She broke in: "Mrs. Loring! You know how vain she is of her voice. She studies with Fraterni . . . spends loads of money. She sang a Schumann cycle. She didn't get half my applause. Probably she didn't notice. But after, we were drinking tea and Professor Dietmann came up. He began to praise my singing, and she was right beside me. He said nothing to her. It was *so* pointed."

"Greta"—his words were heavy and tired—"you know my work on the Civic Committee. We've been trying to trace Tammany graft to its sources. I have some dreadful documents . . ."

Her hand held thread and needle in the air.

". . . incriminating Evan."

She laid the sewing in her lap, swallowed, and hushedly said, "What do you mean?"

164

"You know the word 'incriminating'?"

She shook her head.

"It comes from the word 'crime.'"

The small face shrank from the blow it could not absorb.

"Evan?"

Her eyes were a tame animal's before a cruelty it was not used to; they sought his, wandered about the shadowed room, went to his nervous hand on the briefcase.

"You have them there?" Already they were brighter.

"You mean, the incriminating evidence?"

Her voice leaped: "No one else has seen them?"

His breath stopped; she took his silence for assent.

"Oh, how fortunate, dearest! You scold me for never being able to keep a secret. You'll see! Oh, Jonathan, I'm so glad you could confide in me. Often, I've wept because you didn't tell me *everything;* I've always known when you didn't. It won't make any difference between me and Evan. He'll never guess I know. Not a soul—"

"Greta, what are you saying?"

"Don't you understand?"

"You mean—you think—? Yes, the letters are here. You mean, Greta? . . . What do you want me to do with those letters?"

She breathed fast, but a stubborn firmness held her mouth.

"Greta, what do you mean I should do with those letters? I want you to answer me." His voice rose so high, she looked to the door, fearful he might be overheard.

"He's your friend, isn't he?" she whispered. "Your best friend. He's your partner."

He held his voice low. "I want you to tell me." And her face broke, her eyes filled with tears; she was of another world—an animal you cannot reach.

"Greta," he tried to call her back.

"Why did you tell me, then? What *can* you do?"

Anything was more bearable than her distance. "You think I should destroy them?"

She would not be trapped, she kept her distance. "Jonathan," she wailed.

"Dearest," he said, "I want you to understand. I want you to help me." He knew he should get up and take her in his arms; that would win her closeness. He did not dare; he needed and now he feared her closeness: he, not she, would be won by it. He began to argue: "This is no private matter. The Civic Committee is a public organization; you know that, and I am its trusted servant—a servant of the people. What Evan has done is not a private matter, although secret, dreadfully secret. What have I been doing for years? What is my whole career? Did you think I was practising law solely to make money? Oh, Greta, I have tried to serve the city. Every lawyer is an officer of the courts and of justice."

She murmured, "You know how proud I am of my husband." But through her tears, she glanced at him and her eyes were shrewd; she was not on his side.

"Now the servant of justice, a member of the Civic Committee and of the Grievance Committee of the Bar, finds that his friend, his partner, has had his hands on unlawful money; plotted with the enemies of the people."

"Poor Evan!" she sighed, as a mother who knows a child to be clumsy might sigh when she sees it stumble.

"Greta, isn't this a time when we must stop thinking of ourselves, and of Evan?"

She looked around the room, still safe and warm. Twice a year, she took down every book from those shadowed shelves and dusted it. It was her home, and clean! Why could a man not see that nothing else mattered?

"But Jonathan, what would happen?" She clasped her sewing, trying to be calm.

—*Help* me! he needed to cry.

"We must think it over," she pursed her lips, trying to thread her needle—and succeeded. "You must do *nothing*, till we can think it over."

"What does that mean, Greta? The evidence is absolutely clear. Do you imagine, if there were the slightest doubt—?"

"You must consult with—trusted people."

"Who, for instance?"

"Reuben! Mr. Grosvenor Cleeve! He is so powerful." She basked in this comfortable power. "Not Evan!" She knew her Evan. And it came to him that, of all her gamut of emotions which he had clearly followed, surprise at what Evan had done—surprise that had almost split his sanity—was not included.

"How can I hide it from Evan?"

She got up, letting her work fall to the floor, and as she bent to gather it: "You know how wild he is!" Again, the mother talking of a child. "You look all worn out, dear. I noticed when you came in, but I didn't want to speak; you always get so angry when I suggest you are working too hard. I thought it was only that."

The gas-logs flickered on her face, tear-stained, not pretty with her eyes red. Her body . . . the full bosom, the lithe waist . . . poignantly drew him. He suffered.

"Come upstairs," she said softly. "We can talk better, upstairs."

The door opened, Mrs. Hartt came in and shut it instantly. Greta flew toward her.

"Mama Hartt!" she cried. "Help me with Jonathan! Evan is in trouble. Jonathan wants to send him to prison!"

He saw his mother look back anxiously to the door, as Greta had done, fearing, above all, not the news but that the news be known. Hallucination-sharp, the city pressed on him: the grinding streets, the upthrust of houses, the swarms of flesh and mind grovelling, pleading, snarling, "Every man for himself!" He was alone. He thought of his father who believed in God. He was alone.

Greta was blurting out all she had vowed to keep secret. At last the two women were close, they loved each other; from this day his mother would be the ruthless ally of his wife. "Nobody else knows . . . all in that briefcase," he heard.

Sarah Hartt quietly sat down. "Why are you both standing? Do take your chairs." When they obeyed: "You mustn't be angry, son, with Greta. Isn't it natural she should turn to your mother?"

—The mother, he argued with his aloneness, of your career. . . .

". . . We must do nothing rash. How fortunate you spoke to your dear wife and she opened her heart to me."

"What do you suggest?" His voice was dry.

"I don't know, dear. But you must put things in their place. You have your duty to your Committee. Your mother doesn't need to be told that. And your mother knows her son doesn't need to be told. You also have your duty to your family, your career—"

"Toward Evan!" cried Greta.

"You're more than just partners."

Greta said, "I'm sure he meant nothing really bad!"

"You must look at this from all sides. And that takes time," said Sarah. "I should think, the first one to see might be Evan's father."

Jonathan forced himself to be calm. Some day—his dearest aspiration—he hoped to sit on the bench of a high court. A judge must be calm. "Perhaps you don't quite understand," he said. "There's nothing left to discuss; the evidence is in. A dozen men for months have been piecing it together. One link was missing, between parties criminally engaged in a conspiracy to defraud the city in the allocation of certain contracts and franchises. Well, the link has been found; Evan's letters irrefutably prove it. Whom is there to see? What is there to do? Except submit the evidence or compound the felony and suppress it!"

"Mama Hartt." Greta went over and took the old lady's hand. "We really mustn't talk with Jonathan any more tonight." His words to her were symptoms of a sickness. "I'm going to put my husband to bed."

They had not noticed the bell, now they heard the door, and Reuben's voice and Lucia's in the hall: "Tell mama I've gone to my room."

In the moment before Reuben appeared, Jonathan was conscious of the wheezing irregular *tock . . ticktock* of the grandfather's clock in the adjacent dining room. He had forgotten to wind it tonight. He saw his father, who never forgot, in the old house draw down the rustling chains that pulley-wise lifted the brass weights; he felt the old man's hand over his, the pressure of his eyes in his last hour. He waited for the old clock to stop, it was time for it to stop, it was tired. . . . Reuben was with them.

"What's the matter?" Reuben rubbed his hands and smiled with willed buoyancy. "A funeral or something?" He supposed the gloom on their faces to be due to Philip's outrage at his house, and he had come resolved to make light of it, to give this dazzling further proof that he was a good son, a loyal brother. Reuben had not "run down." Year by year he had risen in the world and from his mother's contempt to esteem; and Jonathan had to grant that her esteem meant more to him than his money. In a daze, he heard her telling him the bad news, as if it were his right, and his presence a godsend; watched Reuben take it as all in a day's work. From his vici-kid boots topped with suède gaiters to his slick colorless graying hair, Reuben was one with his Madison Avenue house; his elegance was like its booty of Oriental art bought on the trip he had taken with his wife. Fortune he had already; politics was the next rung of the ladder. Not that Reuben hoped to run for office. He was worming his way into the good graces of the Republican Party by private services and campaign contributions.

"Why don't you ladies run along? I'll have a word with Jonathan."

"He's so tired." Greta was fearful.

"I'll send him up to you in a jiffy."

His mother's dry lips on his cheek brought a blur of hate to Jonathan and at once a shattering shock of recognition and of refusal that he could hate his mother. Greta, more shrewd, came a little closer to where he still sat at his desk, and, not touching him, whispered, "I'll wait for you, dearest." The two brothers were alone in the room from which the shadowed books had vanished.

At once, Reuben's tune and tempo changed. Pacing energetically up and down, his hands clasped behind him, he said, "What the devil, man—what the devil do you *mean,* letting the womenfolks in on this?"

Jonathan passed a hand over his face. "I guess you're right, Reuben."

"I thought you had more sense. I can't make you out. You *have* more sense. You're a damn good lawyer. You must need a vacation."

"I suppose this isn't exactly news to you—?"

"It *is* news that Cleeve could be idiot enough to put his John Hancock to incriminating letters. I thought *he* had more sense. Although I've never trusted him."

"How about the facts of the case?"

"Look here, Jonathan," Reuben kept pacing. "Are you a practising lawyer in New York or are you a schoolboy?"

"You knew about it?"

Reuben faced him. "Maybe I was in it. If not—I don't know the details—it's simply that I can't be everywhere. Wish I could. Human enterprise has its limits." He came close to his brother and beat a fist into a palm, "Great jumping Jehosaphat, man!, instead of playing the melodrama, you should be studying what to do—how to turn this to good. It can be done. You can't burn the letters; that would be to muff

Dennis who knows, and who can be reached, and who must get into our hands—not you into his. Lucky Kleinberger's Cleeve's real friend. It may cost money. Don't worry about that; I know you have your mortgage on this house. The first thing to do, as I see it, is to go ahead —whatever we *do* do—without a word to Cleeve. When it's all sewed up, you give him back his damn letters and tell him what's what, and to be a good boy next time. But really, Jonathan, what made you blab to the ladies?"

"Haven't you forgotten the Civic Committee?"

"Damn useful. The public needs to have its confidence bucked up from time to time. I'm not saying a thing against reasonable exposures, even convictions, even reform legislation. I'm in favor of 'em when they don't hurt business. And it's the luck of all the angels, as old Sleip would say, that you're on the Committee." He struck his hand again, and again began to pace up and down before his brother. "When I think what Joe Pulitzer and Dana would do, if they got hold of this."

"Stop pacing like a caged lion."

"The Committee's brought you *kudos;* now it can begin to *pay.*" Reuben drew up the chair in which Greta had sat and relaxed into it.

"You're right, old man."

"But what *did* you mean, bothering the ladies? Lose your head?"

"My heart, maybe."

Reuben got up from the too-easy chair; took a straightback one and, his long legs forward, sat so close to Jonathan he could touch him. Jonathan saw the sharp creases in his gray-striped trousers, the trim cut of his white piqué vest with its heavy gold chain, the precise folds of his ascot tie, smooth on the starched shirt.

"You know, Jon, the one thing that worries me is Evan Cleeve. You'll have to talk turkey to him. Sometimes he acts like he was a musician or a playboy in college. He hates his father so, he's likely to pull down the whole town just to give the old man a bump on the head. He's useful, don't I know it? Don't *you?*" Reuben smirked and tapped his brother's knee. "I'll bet eighty per cent of the fees in your office come through Cleeve's clients. But to get down to brass tacks: the first thing is not a word *yet* to Cleeve. Get Dennis to your office and stall; say you need time for procedure. That may make him show his hand; he's on the make, is Dennis. Anyway, it won't hurt."

"Hurt what?"

"The problem is, not to bury this; that'd be easy as rolling off a log, if—as I presume—nobody knows except Dennis. The problem is, to come out *stronger*."

"What do you mean by 'stronger'?"

"With *all* the interested parties. Cleeve's crowd, of course: you can show them easy enough what they owe you in the future. But I'm thinking of Grosvenor Cleeve. He should know. The old boy has two prides: the family name (that'll make him want his son saved) and his reputation as a reformer. It's mixed up. . . . I've got it! Tell Grosvenor Cleeve, and tell him you're the one who on your own responsibility has suppressed the papers. D'you see? That'll save his face as a reformer, and make him your debtor without hurting his pride."

"And the Committee?" Jonathan stroked his beard.

"You'll have to find someone you can expose . . . make a big noise."

"Maybe Walker of the *Cosmopolitan* could be persuaded to print an article on Jonathan Hartt, the great reformer."

"Why not? Look how Reform is paving the way for young Theodore Roosevelt."

"Precisely."

"Just what you cook up, I can't advise you. But don't scare prospective clients. Be careful."

"Like Theodore Roosevelt. I understand. I've watched him when he was Commissioner of Police. He was very careful; he exposed little enemies and even little friends—nobody big."

"That's it," beamed Reuben.

"Brother mine, you just naturally assume, don't you, that I'm one of you?"

"I hope so. Of course, we're in different parties. For that matter, Roosevelt's a Republican, but his game ain't mine, and, off the record, I don't like it, and we're going to give him rope to hang himself. He's too rash."

"I guess you're right. I've been one of you."

"You're a lawyer, aren't you? You want to make real money, don't you? Which means, you need clients who *pay*." Casual and relaxed, Reuben's eyes fell on the briefcase on the desk. "Don't tell me those letters—"

"Yes."

"For God's sake, man, keep those papers in your safe! Suppose they fell into the wrong hands. I'm not so sure your safe at the office *is* best. Maybe you were wise; there's many a political and journalistic burglary these days. Give them to me, Jon; I'll take care of them. I have a new Mosler at the house."

"Thanks, no."

"Have you a clerk you can trust? Have him deposit them in his own name at some bank."

"How about showing them around first? Consulting someone else, before I buy off Dennis?"

"Who?"

"This has been a sort of family confab." Jonathan stroked his beard. "Greta, and mama, now you. Why not consult Philip?"

Reuben's face cracked in a broad smile; then his eyes hardened. "I've been scared more than once, Jon, you had something in you of Philip."

"Not much."

"Are you trying to insult me?"

Jonathan sadly shook his head. "It would be hard."

Reuben got up. "I hope you realize, if this went wrong, what it would mean to your practice, your family."

"Don't worry, Reuben. I'll not trouble Philip."

Reuben recovered his smile. "I promised Greta I'd send you up to her. Have a good sleep. I'll tell you what. I'll come by for you at eight-thirty. We'll drive downtown in my coupé. We'll have clearer heads in the morning."

Slowly, as if his knees hurt, Jonathan got up from his desk. "Don't come."

"Why not?"

"I doubt if I'll be here."

The older man, smooth and cool, studied his dark, bearded brother whom he had known all his life—and never known. Only Jonathan knew this; only Jonathan knew how he had suffered from his guilt in Reuben's fleecing . . . long years ago . . . of Frieda's husband.

"Thanks, just the same," Jonathan made himself say.

Reuben was not much worried: Jonathan would be safe; Jonathan

172

would not tear down his own house. Maybe he thought he would, but he wouldn't. Jonathan knew why Reuben was not much worried. . . .

"Can I get you something?"

"A glass of water."

She stood beside him while he drank; she was not there, and her absence made her standing at their bed in her nightgown indecent. She turned off the gas; darkness revealed and weighted the sound of her feet approaching, the creak of the mattress, the shift of the covers, the warmth of her body close to his. Monstrous since she was absent. "Dearest," she whispered, "I want you to try to sleep. Whatever you decide, Jonathan, you know I will accept. With all my heart and soul. I'm your wife. Now sleep."

Good words of the good wife. But where was she? A rush of compassion overcame him. His judgment exiled her, and by what right did he judge? She was defending their place in the world. Women were moved by a personal logic; at least the premise was love for something sweeter than power and self-esteem. —Then take her in your arms and make her real again! He lay on his back, awake and rigid in the dark. She was so close, the back of her hand touched his; she was so far, it would be violence to touch her. The breach brought dizziness, the dizziness brought breach; the room slowly swung about his rigid eyes and the frozen world beyond the windows (the pale street) swayed from the warmth of his home. Come close to his wife? He was not close to himself! He had worked hard and well, many years; the energy that united him to his deeds and thoughts was monstrously missing. Call it hope. Hope had driven him, and now it was unreal like the God of his father. So much more rational and precise his hope had seemed, than that prehistoric voice of Sinai and the Prophets, less rejected than ignored because it was not needed! It had served his father, given him answers; his father, beside a wilful wife, had never been alone, as he beside this loving one. How naked he lay! Not his career, not Greta, not the covers, not the bones of his body, not the hard skull infinitely far from his thoughts, touched him! A projectile, he had been propelled from mystery; the hope he had named his motion was less bodied than his father's Jehovah! The real was the mystery, infinitely far, that had propelled him. Infinitely cold!

173

He had the excruciating sense of his flesh, of his bones, of his fragile open eyes, of the brittle bone-box of his brain, and of thoughts vaguely tentacling the ether . . . all cold and alone in space that was absolute meaninglessness and absolute cold, and absolute dark loneness. He could not bear it. —*Give in! Don't try to decide.* Now at least, not forcing himself to decide, he could live again, and with the reprieve came Greta. As if her body heard in sleep, she turned toward him, her hand touched his breast, her whole body came to his embrace. The moment, wrought of pure body, was pure spirit. The spirit, wrought of flesh and time, was fleshless and timeless. Again thought came, as the union waned; thought and time again corroded them. Greta fell away to her sleep, and nothing of what they had been ineffably together survived. In their union, which was pure flesh and without body and without time, there was no need and no need to decide; even the decision not to decide had fallen away. But with Greta asleep and her face turned, what had the moment given? Oh!, to be able to bring it whole into the world of thought and action. Thoughts swarmed conflicting . . . balanced him . . . numbed him at last to sleep. . . .

When Jonathan awoke, a gray day was heavy in the room. He jumped out of bed and Greta opened her eyes: again the wife of the evening, of the home, of the alliance with his mother. Wounded with feeling that was two-edged judgment . . . because he must not judge her . . . he dressed, the moment of their union the memory of a memory. Greta too got up; and as she reached the door to go to the bathroom, he said:

"I won't be here for breakfast."

"You're going to Evan's?"

"Yes."

This was not unusual. When he wanted quiet talk before they reached the busy office, Jonathan dropped in, unannounced, to share Evan's breakfast.

"Very well, dear." She compressed her slight features into a smile whose loyal resolution made her ugly. "Aren't you going to kiss me good morning?" ·

He put his arms around her. Although she was distant again and unreal, memory of memory made her sweet to him. He would not believe his hunger, he refused it the substance of hope. What might it not demand that he give up? He thought of his son, upstairs.

"Kiss little Jeff for me."

"Did you sleep well? Are you all right?"

"Yes. How are you, Greta?"

"I'll be all right." She smiled bravely.

The brownstone houses, the vacant lots with a few cabins clinging to the rocks . . . now the Park, gray wall and bare trees, made an iron morning; the winter on his hand clasping the briefcase (Jonathan never wore gloves, not in the coldest weather) was iron against him. Evan's sitting room, where he waited while old Augusta announced him, was a confusion of warmths: the books in morocco and levant with paintings and etchings above them, the grand piano, a Sevillan flowered *mantón* draped on it, and the bronze figurine, the thick magenta curtains. . . . Evan came in, whistling a theme from *Don Giovanni*.

Jonathan unstrapped his briefcase and brought out the letters.

"I wanted to bring you these. They're for you."

Evan slipped them into the pocket of his houserobe, looking at his friend. "Couldn't they wait till the office? They must be damn important."

"Yes, Evan, they're important."

"You chose a good breakfast. Augusta tells me there are kidneys. 'Gott sei Dank, I got *enough*.'" Good-humoredly, he mimicked the old housekeeper's accent.

"Aren't you going to look at the letters?"

"I'm not going to let *you* spoil those kidneys. You don't seem to realize what Augusta would do to me." He opened the portieres into the dining room, where a second place was set. The Tiffany glass chandelier low upon the table made shadow of the oak-paneled walls, the walnut sideboard; the Sandwich glass decanters of sherry and whiskey, the ornate silver bowl of fruit, were dimly visible; only the table, the heads of the two men, the high white ceiling, were illumined.

They ate, Jonathan silent and strained, Evan at ease. He had put on flesh under the rule of Augusta, his hair was a little more thin and less bright but his mouth was still boyishly volatile and gay, his eyes had the same freshness.

175

"Evan," said Jonathan at last, "I must ask you to see what I've given you."

Evan smiled indulgently. "Great Scott, man, don't you think I can guess?" He took a swallow of coffee. "You come here like an undertaker into the house of the dead. You eat Augusta's broils as if they were straw. I know what's in my pocket."

"You've been my friend and partner, Evan. I should have known. I should have saved you from yourself. I assume my share of the responsibility."

"You have my sympathy, old man. I know what it means to you. I don't blame you for thinking of yourself."

"If I were thinking of myself, would I be here? Would I give you the letters?"

Evan's eyes narrowed. "Why not? You're a hard taskmaster for yourself. You love your conscience; you love your loyalties also."

"You're insulting me."

"I don't mean to. What's the good of a showdown—which you evidently want—if we don't talk square?"

"*Talk* square! That's all right with me. What about *acting* square?"

Evan smiled, a little nervous. "It's hard, isn't it? Now you know."

"Why was it hard for you?" Jonathan's voice rose. "You have everything. You—"

"Don't lecture me, not with nonsense anyway. I'll take the lecture. But talk sense. On the evidence, I did not have everything."

"Good God! Do you mean to say you needed money?"

"Good God, indeed. Who said I needed money? I've more than I know what to do with. I don't believe in charity, except the sort you take out of your pocket and give to the bum on the street. The girls I occasionally sleep with are grateful when I give 'em a hundred-dollar bond—if they'll take that. Augusta complains she has too much household money and gets angry when I refuse to look over her accounts." Evan stopped short, there were tears in Jonathan's eyes. "Old fellow," he went on softly, "didn't you come here for the truth?"

"I'm here to save you. I can't go on with it, Evan. I've given you the letters."

"They're safe in my pocket. Jonathan, dear Jonathan, don't you know anything about me?"

176

"Because I didn't know? So you place the blame on me? Maybe you're right."

"Must there always be blame?"

"And 'right' as distinguished from 'wrong'? That's wrong, too?"

"You're not yourself, this morning," Evan laughed. "Hamlet said conscience makes cowards—must it make one dull?"

"Be patient. Teach me."

"I'm sorry. I don't want to hurt your feelings. I want you to understand."

"I knew, of course I knew, you were friends with many of that crowd: the men we're fighting. I knew you liked them. I rather liked your liking them. I don't know why. I've always liked everything about you, Evan. Even your faults and weaknesses. I suppose when a man loves—" He stopped. —Greta's faults and weaknesses, *do I love them?*

Suddenly tense and clear, as he could be in court with an adverse witness, Evan leaned forward, both his hands on the table: "You see? What I said is true: you're thinking of yourself, you're seeing only yourself."

"How can I see you straight till *I* get straight?"

Evan relaxed in his chair. "Go ahead."

"I never dreamed, while you played poker with those crooks and went to their beer parties and clambakes, you shared their corruption."

"Dear old man, don't we all?"

"It's the truth."

"The banks and commercial houses we represent as counsel, are their hands what your ancestral Prophets would call clean?"

"It's true. I'm guilty also."

"But there's a difference. You feel there's a difference."

"I wish I were surer of the difference. Then I'd know what to do."

"If I can, Jon, I'm going to help you."

"I've got to think of myself, Evan. Because *I'm* involved. There's something deeper here than the difference between those who stay within the law—"

"—and those who write incriminating letters?"

Jonathan cried, "Why did you do it?"

"I wonder . . ." Evan poured fresh coffee from the silver urn.

177

"Let's find out! Evan, let's both find out! Where both of us stand! I swear to you, what's tearing me to pieces is that I don't know. How can I know what to do?"

"You've loved a weak man, Jonathan. That's a clue to your own weakness, if you insist on bringing yourself in. I'm weak. I've always been." His voice went low. "That's why my mother killed herself. She knew I was weak. Because she knew *she* was weak."

"I didn't come here feeling righteous. I've never known the man, not personally, I would call strong. Perhaps those I think strong, if I knew them—"

"Why did I write those letters?" Evan's voice, flexible as music, modulated to an adagio of contemplation. "Deals like the Morrisania one, I've been in them, on and off, for years. Why not? It seemed snobbery to carouse with the bunch and refuse to do business with them when they asked me. There was nothing to stop me. But I always stayed on the safe side. Like some of your friends, and most of our clients. . . . Like my father. There's the key, perhaps!"

Jonathan watched him.

"Maybe"—he went on—"you didn't understand what I meant when I said I was weak. If I'd been strong I'd not have told my father to go to hell; I'd have simply gone my own way, which was what my mother always wanted. I'd not have studied law, certainly not practised it. I'd have played my fiddle—for a living if I had to; or done nothing, if I'd dared. I was weak. I insulted my father, and followed him in the law. I practised law, and got my weak man's revenge by breaking it. Even before I left his office. Then I left . . . asked you to be my partner . . . and kept on following my father. I obeyed my mother, and wasn't strong enough to resist the temptation of proving she was wrong. That's why I wrote those letters."

"I don't see—"

"I'll have to stop following him now." Evan's smile was gay. "I've smashed my career. I didn't have the guts to do it clean. Like the weak one I am, I had to concoct the circumstance that would do it for me."

"You mean, you wanted to be disgraced?"

"I couldn't get clear, the clear way. It was a foul trick on you."

"Don't worry about me."

"We'll come to that."

178

"Evan, nothing irrevocable has been done. If you know your motives, you can remove them like a surgeon. As to the immediate situation, only Dennis—"

"I guessed that. Dennis can be fixed. But don't you see, I don't *want* it? A surgeon's not in love with the tumor he cuts out. *I* want to be out. I need to kill my life, and I can do it only as I have—messily. That's my way, that's what I really am and what I really love."

"You think you'd be free?"

"Not for long," Evan smiled. "But I haven't your passion for permanence; it's not in my race. Sure. In a few years, if I went away—became a fiddler, for example, or just loafed, I'd find myself in a new condition of servitude, and murder it—"

"You know. . . . And yet—"

"There's the theme of my life! 'To know . . . and yet'—"

"Evan, I won't let you go on. You're going to step out of your vicious circle. I've got you where I want you."

"How do you figure that? If I love it?"

"You may love to victimize yourself. You don't want to do it to me."

"You've always been my victim, Jon."

"You don't want it. You've explained mighty well why you don't mind ruining yourself. Will you let me sit here at your table and hear you say you don't care if you ruin me?"

Evan looked at his friend calmly. "Yes," he said. "I love myself, too, and I'm not sparing myself on that account. Why should I spare you?"

"I don't believe you."

"Besides, your smash-up isn't necessary. If it were—but it's not. You can get out of this."

"Wash my hands of you—after twenty years?"

"Twenty-five, isn't it—a quarter of a century next summer? Remember the Draft Riots? You'd better wash your hands of me, old fellow. I've said you've always been my victim. Why, even here, even this morning, I've fed you a lot of sophistical half-truths to the effect that you're as bad as I, and you've believed them! You're a better man than I am. I don't say you're a saint or a hero; such vacuums don't exist in nature. Compared to me, Jon, you're strong and you're decent. This smash of mine, if you keep your head, needn't damage you too much. It may even prove the one time you're not my victim."

"I can't make head or tail—"

"I'm going to give you back the letters, Jonathan. And through the regular Committee channels you're going to release them."

"What if I refuse? I can get to Dennis—"

Evan laughed. "You get to Dennis? Dennis will get to *you*. You'll have to persuade Dennis to do his duty."

"And if I don't—"

Evan kept on smiling. "If you don't, it won't save me. For God's sake, believe me. I'm doing what I need to do in my own dirty way. Thwart me and I'll find another . . . dirtier. It won't save me if you suppress those letters; and it *will* ruin you. How can you go on bullying your clients, Jon, if you've lost your sense of being decent? How can you feel decent, if you suppress the letters? And how can you practise law if you can't go on bullying your clients?"

"I don't feel like joking, Evan."

"You think only solemnity is serious. You don't know even your own nature." Evan got up and brought the decanter of Scotch whiskey from the sideboard to the table. He poured a half tumbler and downed it. "Do you know why you good men—you are a good man, Jon—fail and always will fail? Because in your heart, you think everyone is like you. You can't bring yourself to believe the evil of men, because it's not like you. So your arrows and lessons fall wide of the mark. That goes for even the best: for instance, your co-religionist, Jesus (he's yours, not mine). He spoke to men as if they were all potentially good: therefore, eager to be saved, eager to hear the Good News. They crucified him for his good intentions. Then evil men took him over, organized him; *they* were listened to."

"Let's leave men like Jesus out of this. I'm a practising lawyer in a corrupt community."

"You're a good man. Which means, you not only don't know men—and me; you don't know even yourself. Good men never do."

Jonathan was silenced, and mortified that it was so. He had not been able to prevision this talk, but certainly he had not dreamed he would be the student, the subdued. He needed to save Evan, and for this, he needed to know! —What do I know? "Your passion for permanence," Evan had said; keenly right as usual? What frightened him at this moment: was it change? change in his home, change in his office, change in his role of respectable reformer, change in Evan's life! What would become of Evan? Why did this frighten him more than it did Evan? His heart sank as if he faced death.

"What do you propose to do?" He spoke low, hearing his clouded accent and Evan's lucid:

"I'll clear out."

"Where?" (Why should it be Evan who spoke clear?)

"What does it matter? I'll have to go somewhere, won't I, once the letters are public? I don't exactly relish Sing Sing." Evan's look was affectionate. "I'm counting on you; you won't go back on your old friend? I've got to repeat, Jon, although I know how repetition exasperates you: I've not had the guts to clear out of my own free will, so I've blown myself out. But I've not thought only of myself. The mess will bring you trouble, of course. You'll lose clients: some, like Dodson of the Empire State Bank and probably the Clipper Navigation crowd, because they'll be scared of a man with your zeal for righteousness; others, because they were my men. My father will do what he can to hurt you. But you're a damn fine lawyer, and New York's beginning to know it. You'll get on."

"I'm listening, Evan; I'm not agreeing."

"Greta—you'll have trouble with her, at first. She won't understand your action, as she does me—instinctively. Good women haven't the same limitations as good men; good women are closer to us bad 'uns. But she's a loyal wife—"

They saw Augusta at the door; the small gray woman with a hard face and large soft eyes looked reproof at Evan.

"You never mind the time, when Mr. Hartt comes for breakfast. It's half-past nine." She marched up to the table and lifted the decanter of whiskey. "For breakfast! For shame!"

Evan laughed and got up; it seemed to Jonathan that he was happy. How could it be? Was it his freedom from the fear of change? —All life is change? to fear change is to fear life? to welcome it for itself is to love life for itself? Who here is the weaker man?

Evan was at the door. "Let's walk to the El at Sixth and Fifty-eighth Street. We're so late we might as well be later." He drew off his silk robe, felt the bundle of letters in his pocket as if he had forgotten them, and took them out. "Here. I hope I can trust you with them."

The boy at the reception desk: "Mr. Dennis to see you, Mr. Hartt. He's waiting in your office." Jonathan felt Evan's smile as he passed to his own room, remembered Evan's words: "Get to Dennis? He'll get to *you*."

The executive secretary of the Civic Committee, its one salaried officer, was a lean man of about thirty in formal morning suit and spotless linen; his narrow head reminded Jonathan vaguely of McGlory. Jonathan found it hard to listen . . . polite circumlocutions . . . at last: "—more harm than good. Mr. Cleeve, of course, and Dill to whom the letters are addressed are not what we're after."

"So you judge—?"

"In all conscience, Mr. Hartt! We mustn't drive ahead like a bull in a china shop. That'd be all right if our aim was to break a few cups. It's the whole shop—"

"Excellent metaphor, Dennis. You should have been a poet."

—Poet? The man don't seem to mean it as an insult; after all he's smiling. Dennis went over his scheme; and Jonathan surmised he had already hinted it; he recognized that for Dennis subtlety in greed was greatest virtue. For some reason, Dennis figured, Mr. Hartt was a bit dense this morning. He was forced at last to be explicit:

". . . If we win their confidence by burying the letters, I'm assured— I can tell you this in private—it's absolutely straight: Tammany will throw the Democratic nomination for State Senator to me. You know, my district's normally Republican. The voters can be divided into three parts—"

"Like Gaul?"

Again a bit bewildered, Dennis was again reassured by Jonathan's smile: ". . . the straight Republicans who'll never vote Democratic; the straight Tammany voters; and the independents of both parties. They decide the election; and they're sure to vote for the man endorsed by the Civic Committee."

Now, Jonathan had it. Dennis was ready to do away with the evidence; Tammany would pay by slating him on the regular Democratic ticket (it was a by-election to replace Senator Darling, deceased) and he would win with the independent vote, if the Civic Committee endorsed him; Jonathan's price for the service of saving his partner was to swing the Committee for Dennis. And it was all for the best, because they weren't after a few teacups, but the whole shop. While Jonathan, oddly dense this morning, was figuring it out, the elegant executive secretary stretched his spidery legs forward, and wriggled his toes delightedly in his patent-leather boots. It was a good world.

"Thanks," said Jonathan.

"Not at all! Not at all! That's why I ran right over. I knew you'd understand."

"I want you to."

Dennis got up. "I've taken enough of your time. You needn't say another word, Mr. Hartt."

"I'd better, before you leave my office."

Dennis narrowed his eyes.

"You've made one thing clear." Jonathan placed his palms on his desk. "You're fit for no endorsement by the Committee. You'll never get it."

Dennis looked at the little man who seemed to be strutting while he sat. For a moment, the black eyes of Dennis showed panic; they eased, and he again sat down.

"I don't think you know what you're saying. Those letters—"

"I know just as far as I've said."

"If you tried to destroy those letters, Mr. Hartt. . . . I earnestly advise against it."

"I've said nothing about destroying them. What I've said referred to your endorsement by the Committee. I'm sure it was clear."

Again panic in the little black eyes; again a smile of confidence wiped it out. "Maybe not. Maybe I've not understood. . . ."

"Your plan shows you to be an unprincipled scoundrel. Is that understood? Do you really think, if you cheated your way into the Senate at Albany, you'd be the kind of man good government can look to? When would you start to be clean?"

"I guess you don't see where *you* stand."

"I'll find out." Jonathan stood up. "There's your hat." He pointed to the table. Dennis got to his feet slowly; close to Jonathan, he made him look small and, his casual face against the other's passionate frown, outlandish. At the door, he turned and gazed at Jonathan again. He could not believe his ears. Was this all perhaps a game to save "face"?

"I'm going to forget what I've heard from you today." He smiled.

"Tomorrow, you'll have thought better of it." He slid out of the door.

They were all sure of him—except Evan! Not his wife, not his mother, differed essentially from Dennis in what they thought he would do! He believed he had read Dennis's thoughts: "The pompous little Jew . . . has to have his noble moment. But when Cleeve gets to him, and he sees the mess staring him in the face, he'll drop the letters like they were fire. And when I get my nomination and my friends ask the Committee's endorsement, he'll be in the bag . . . he won't dare lift a finger. He's just got to have his moment, the damn little Jew. I've got him!" The one person who believed he was honest was dishonest Evan!

. . . To gain a little time, to think a little more, Jonathan that evening on his way home from work left the train at the Fiftieth Street station. Ninth Avenue under the El was a cave of winds, cold and hot: the north wind cold with the snow it promised, the breath of men and women hot with the rebuke of sordid poverty against him. Saloons stank into the street; through swinging doors, a woman was hurled backward to the gutter and as she lay, Jonathan saw an infant pillowed on her breasts. Irrelevantly, he thought of Frieda. Gas lights bleared the small provision stores whose shoppers issuing into night were part of the night, part of the tenement walls. A train casting cindery sparks shattered overhead, and Jonathan felt the lesion of his world: the fine words, the noble laws, and this avenue rotten ere half ripe. Now the lesion was in him! A boat whistled. —What am I going to do? He was substanced of conflict, suddenly strange to himself; the island rock beneath the city, between the wheat fields westward under the snow and eastward the sea, was more real than himself.

It was strange that his key fitted the door of his home, strange that his wife came to him and embraced him, strange to see his boy (the court plaster removed) run down the stairs and greet him: "Good today!" His slippers fitted and warmed his feet; his housejacket with the braided buttons fitted his body . . . strange.

Everyone at the dinner table was in strange good humor. Lucia unconsciously rejoiced in the rift she sensed between her beloved brother and his wife; Philip's bucolic ease was always buoyed up by excitement. His mother somewhat too ostentatiously rubbed him the right way with little remarks about her day's shopping with Greta who was so wise at economical buying, and about Jefferson, the little man who had so patiently helped his old granny with her knitting yarn.

Sarah said, "Jonathan, my dear, you're going to have a visitor tonight. Such a distinguished visitor! Mr. Grosvenor Cleeve."

This must be his mother's doing; such initiative and such invasion of his business were alien to Greta. But he lacked the energy to ask or to scold. Stronger returned the mood of last night: "Don't decide; don't try to decide." Was this the reason of his strangeness to himself: that in this crisis he was functioning beneath the limen of decision? Annie had had her orders: all the jets in the library burned and the gas-logs blazed their brightest. His desk was freshly tidied and—as usual—his papers out of order.

"We'll leave you alone, dear," said Sarah.

He felt pity for his mother: to do what she had done, to be so quietly self-righteous—pity engendered a cold cruelty.

"Greta, stay," he said.

The old woman took her exclusion gallantly. "That's a good idea. Your wife should receive Mr. Cleeve. You can excuse yourself, Greta, after a few moments."

They were alone at last: Jonathan and his wife, waiting and without words. In the background of his thoughts Ninth Avenue, and this home Greta had made for him, confusedly mingled; and in the foreground, as if he were making a speech, stood Grosvenor Cleeve. A few weeks ago, he had spoken at the Windsor Hotel banquet honoring him on his seventieth birthday. Jonathan had missed it, being in Washington to argue an appeal before the Supreme Court; but the papers had carried the eloquent words: *I had intended, if such an occasion as this offered, to employ it to announce my retirement after fifty years of practice of the law: fifty years, may I venture to say, of devotion to the law. I do not find it in me now to give that word of resignation. Our nation is too threatened. New forces of strife, yes!, of secession from the wisdom of our fathers, loom on the horizon, particularly the Western horizon.* (applause) *We are threatened by cheap money, which would make our name a byword for shame among the respectable nations. We are threatened by such anarchy as a peacetime income tax, which would choke to death the initiative that alone has saved us from the ruins of civil war. . . .* He had closed: *So long as our Union is*

185

thus threatened, whatever strength my declining years vouchsafe to me I dedicate . . . Now was he coming here to plead for his son—perhaps subtly, circumlocutorily?, the great lawyer who had known Webster and Clay!

Annie announced him; Jonathan, who had not seen him in a decade, was shocked as Grosvenor Cleeve came in. Precarious above the perfectly groomed Prince Albert coat, the bright bosom shirt with a pearl stud where the satin lapels met, the weary sagging head!, between the down-bearing nose and up-turning chin, the thin drooped mouth; the watery eyes, the caterpillar eyebrows, the gray hair brushed from the creased forehead and long at the ears: it was the mask of an actor playing the nobleman, his art staled by too many years of routine repetition. And in structural resemblance and qualitative contrast, it was a bitter caricature of Evan.

Greta, naively flustered but too resilient and naturally poised to fail as hostess, offered her guest a glass of port.

"I wager, Mrs. Hartt, your husband has forgotten the time I offered him a glass of madeira. A quarter century it must be!"

"He couldn't forget," cried Greta. "But how could you remember?"

"I was very proud of that glass," said Jonathan.

"You were proud then; I am proud now. . . . Proud of what a good prophet I was."

"You've been a good prophet more than once, Mr. Cleeve. But I don't follow—"

"If I recall correctly, I prophesied about *you,* sir. You were nothing but a lad. I looked you over, and said you would go far. You have gone far."

"You are very kind."

"I'm not a kind man. I have not found life kind." He swayed his ponderous head toward Greta. "I've been satisfied with justice. Soon or late, if you look for it, if you help it, you find it. This afternoon, I was having a long talk with our Mayor. Mr. Hewitt—"

Greta got up. "If you gentlemen are going to talk politics, perhaps you will excuse me?"

"I'd regret it, Mrs. Hartt. What I was going to observe was merely a point of human nature. Surely, that concerns the ladies? And doesn't politics belong to human nature? If you good women realized that,

186

you'd condescend—not to take active part in politics, Heaven forbid!, but to give us men your counsel. Behind every good man, isn't there a better woman?"

Greta, glowing, sat down again. "Oh, I *am* interested, Mr. Cleeve! The one fault I find with my dear husband is that sometimes he doesn't tell me more—not to burden me."

"As if it were not woman's glory to be burdened!"

"Oh, it's true," she sang.

"I was minded of my talk with Mr. Hewitt. He should be known as our 'angry Mayor.' He's always so out of temper and so full of charm. And usually"—Mr. Cleeve's head, turning from one to the other, came to Jonathan—"usually he's right. . . . Just before me, he had seen Commissioner of Police Murray. He told me what he'd said to him. 'Bill' —that's Commissioner Murray, Mrs. Hartt—'Bill, I want your help in cleaning up this city. I know you've stolen three-hundred-thousand dollars. Now you can afford to be honest.' "

Greta smiled her puzzlement; Jonathan frowned. Grosvenor Cleeve poised his audience and continued:

"So there you are. Mr. Hewitt intends to clean up the Department of Health, the Department of Streets—"

"Oh, how they need it!" Greta interrupted. "They're filthy."

"—the Comptroller's Office, filthy, too, Mrs. Hartt; and even the Police! All with the aid of a man who, having had his fling and learned the ways of the unworthy, can afford to be honest."

"Perhaps," said Jonathan, "an act of desperation?"

"Anger." Mr. Cleeve lifted a tremulous hand. "Anger can clear the air like a thunderstorm; leave it cool. Do you recall, Mr. Hartt, when Mr. Hewitt drafted the Tariff Reform platform?"

"It elected him to Congress."

"And your President Cleveland betrayed it. Do you recall? Abram Hewitt was so angry he wanted to resign from Congress."

"So the papers said."

"It's true. And suddenly, Richard Croker named him for Mayor. What's less well known is that election frauds were needed to put our clean angry man in office."

Jonathan no longer frowned; he had expected Grosvenor Cleeve to be subtle. Was he being profound? At least he was entertaining; Greta, who surely could not understand what he was driving at, since *he* did not, sat enthralled.

"You mentioned, dear Madam, the discreditable condition of our streets."

"It's dangerous! All the time tearing them up! I'm so afraid of malaria for my boy."

"The cycle of progress, perhaps?" Jonathan tried to be light. "We excavate for water pipes, and fill in. Along comes gas. We excavate for gas pipes and fill in. Along comes electricity. We excavate for electric wires—"

"That ought to be *all*," sighed Greta.

"I doubt it, my dear Mrs. Hartt. So long as there's New York, we'll be tearing up our streets—and our governments—and our tempers. One thing we must never tear up!" The old man paused, looked at his hands and clenched them. "Our faith—our faith—"

Jonathan suspected tears in Greta's eyes, because she suspected tears in the old man's, who must be thinking of his son. Grosvenor Cleeve tossed his mane and smiled:

"I was saying . . . I must get back to our Mayor. I want to give your wife this little anecdote to show her how profoundly politics is human nature. Where was I—? Ah! Mayor Hewitt. In regard to the condition of our streets, he's in a losing battle. For instance, the car tracks: he wants them sunk below the level of the pavement, so our carriages and carts aren't shattered every time they cross. The Companies don't want to spend the money; Tammany's Aldermen back them, the Mayor loses. He wants to stop the filthy custom of scattering sand on the tracks, that soon becomes mud. 'The horses will slip,' say the Companies. 'Get more horses per load,' replies the Mayor. And loses again. Cleveland, Richmond, a score of cities have electric trolley cars. They're swifter, cheaper, safer than horse and cable cars. 'Too much money invested in present rolling stock,' say the Companies and the Aldermen (who ought to know) back them up. Our Mayor loses again. And now comes the biggest need of all: Home Rule for our city—to free it at last of our intolerable condition of servitude to envious hayseeds from Essex, Oswego, and Oneida counties. Well, Mayor Hewitt is going to Albany on that paramount issue with Croker and Tammany behind him! He'll win the big fight, because he was willing to lose the little ones."

"Wonderful!" acclaimed Greta.

"And, of course, when he's won the big cause, the little ones will follow."

"How wise of him!" Greta sang.

"And who implied, dear lady, that ladies have no ear for politics?"

Jonathan was not concerned in arguing the fallacy of Grosvenor Cleeve's lesson. His mood grew more contemplative: let him hear what was to be heard . . . in time he would hear his own decision.

"I'm afraid, just the same"—he said to fill a pause—"we'll not get Mr. Hewitt a renomination."

"We'll go forward—under his successors." The old man's eyes on Jonathan were sincere, Jonathan was sure of it . . . sure also that Evan's view of his father was essentially correct. The contradiction was solved in the man's capacity to believe whatever his will proposed: the rightness of that *will* was what he never challenged; hence the rightness of whatever contradictions tuned with it. Jonathan felt himself exceptionally lucid—about everything except his crucial problem. (—Do not trouble, decision will be there!) He thought: —Is this the basis of success in politics? Never to question the main premise either of one's will or of the common laws? That would make statesmanship manipulative, rather than creative. . . . Greta was saying:

"I know nothing about it but I'm so sure you're right! How can an American ever lose hope in the future?"

"I have never lost it."

"That is why—" Greta blushed.

"Say it, dear Mrs. Hartt."

"That is why you are so young, Mr. Cleeve."

"My hope is always young." He tasted his second glass of port. Jonathan amusedly observed this was quite a case of love at first sight between his wife and the gerontian. As if Greta were aware of it, she rose, faintly flushed.

"I really must go now."

Grosvenor Cleeve rose, too, and kissed her hand.

"Hartt," he said, the moment they were alone, "you don't need to tell me what this is about. Evan's gone too far?"

"There are letters—"

"Please!" the old man raised his hand. "I don't want to know. I mustn't! You have said, 'There are letters.' That is a factual generic statement tantamount to saying, 'There are leaves,' or, 'There are bottles of port.'"

"I understand."

"Hartt," Cleeve again sat down, "your charming wife has turned a very painful visit into a pleasant one."

"That will gratify her."

"I've really nothing to say. It's not easy for a man like me to find himself, suddenly, for the first time in a long life—ah—in a position which a less intelligent man than you might—ah—misinterpret as that of a suitor."

Jonathan was silent.

"I'll not disguise the fact that when my son left my office, where he was in line for a partnership, I thought he was mad. I've often thought Evan was mad: a way—sometimes the only one—to excuse him. Partnership with you, I'll not mince my words, seemed to me then a very one-sided proposition."

"I quite understand."

"It's turned out the other way round. As I would have told you long ago, if I'd had the opportunity. You steadied my son, kept him on even keel; at least, so it appeared."

Jonathan did not trust his voice.

"This, of course, has taken you completely by surprise."

"Yes, Mr. Cleeve."

"You more than me. I am sure of it! You more than me. I had more occasion to experience his original nature. Which you cannot change." The old man paused; Jonathan observed in his bland, almost elegiac eyes the swift shrewdness. "If anyone could change him, it is you. Last of all his father." Again, Mr. Cleeve rose, holding his glass in a tremulous hand. "Strange, how impotent a father is toward his son. If this—ah—business were in my hands, what could I do but proceed by the iron rule of justice? In a way—have you thought of it, Hartt?—justice is the makeshift of ignorance. Men must be just, because they know so little. If they knew more, they could dare to practise a more godlike mercy. If they knew all, as the Frenchman said, they would pardon all."

190

A little wine spilled over on his wrist. With acute effort, Grosvenor Cleeve steadied his hand, and was about to place the glass on the desk when he noticed that it might stain the bright mahogany. He found the tray; then he clasped both his hands behind him.

"You've seen a side of me," he said, "few know about. That's as it should be. You're not a stranger. You're Evan's dearest friend." He paused, and Jonathan saw that his eyes dimmed. "I'm not as strong as I appear. When a man's old, his oldest ties are strongest."

Jonathan, too, got up. "You're telling me, Mr. Cleeve, you love your son."

"He is the son of his mother." The hand that had trembled came forward again, steady. "I ask nothing. I know nothing; therefore, I can ask nothing. Good night, Jonathan."

Jonathan found it hard to meet the hand waiting for his. Why? Was it not true that nothing had been asked?

The old man's hand dropped again. "I venture one word. I—and my colleagues who, thank God, have more years and more force ahead of them: we are not men without eye, and without memory."

Jonathan opened the door.

"You have a handsome house." Mr. Cleeve stepped into the hall. "I've never had the privilege before of being in one of these new West Side houses. Very handsome." At last, having put on his coat and hat, he gave his hand and Jonathan took it.

"It's going to snow," said Mr. Cleeve and went out.

Jonathan hated his house. He bolted the door and stood alone in the hall and hated his house as if it had been soiled. "No," he muttered, "nothing was said, nothing was asked."

Slowly, heavily, he went up the carpeted stairs to the bedroom where his wife waited. . . .

The sun was there, and Greta's face looking down at him. "I thought you'd never wake up. It's late. It snowed, but it's a beautiful day."

He lay trying to find his night. He had dreamed a horde of dreams, and as swift as his mind reached for them they vanished. "You haven't forgotten, darling," she said, "we have tickets for the play tonight." He recalled how hard it had been three weeks ago to get them; *Shenandoah,* the great hit: the Civil War and Charleston before the bombardment of Fort Sumter; Greta's childhood and his own. Of course, he had to take her, why should he not take her? He groped for the difficulty. Why did he feel gratitude toward Greta? She had asked no question. Grosvenor Cleeve: he remembered! He had come up to her from his talk with Grosvenor Cleeve aching with fear lest she explore his thoughts, his decision; and she had let him go to bed in silence. His wife, with whom he longed to share his thoughts—and he was grateful, not that she had helped him, that she had let him alone! He remembered the consciousness of stain: Grosvenor Cleeve's hand, what had it meant that he took it? Had it been worse to withdraw his own suddenly than not to give it at all? Did Grosvenor Cleeve notice? And what was the matter with his house? He had lain, eyes open in the dark, seeing nothing clear within him, sure he could not sleep. He had slept suddenly and deep; the storm of conflict did not touch him. It was a mystery: he should have been sleepless, he had slept; he should have been tortured by indecision, he was rested as if he had decided. . . .

Jonathan walked across the Park through the shallow snow that still lay pure on the paths; in tree and bush it glistened, garlands of ice. The stain on his house? He recalled his wish, several years ago, to move out to a farm on Washington Heights that would have cost less than his brownstone house. They would have had horses, cows, chickens, an experienced couple to take care of them. (Today the farm would have quintupled in value.) Greta refused, although he explained to her that the Harlem River Railway solved his problem of getting to the office. She needed, she said, to be near her friends, her music masters; she could not bear, he knew, such solitude with him. His resentment had quickly faded; why now did it return with the irrational thought of his soiled house? Greta had received Grosvenor Cleeve in it? Greta, when she refused to move with him to a farm beyond the city, had shut herself out from their home? . . . opened it to invaders? The sun made the snow blue. Simple peoples worshiped the sun as god; God is love, said Emerson's disciples. His heart ached for Greta because his love had not more closely won her. —Somewhere I have failed. The decision about Evan? Deeper than this! When this is passed, I will look deeper into failure? Or I could speak with her, I would have no problem that is mine; all problems would be ours. Without awareness, he was responding, now in the cold morning, to the warm bed when Greta had waked and leaned over him, remote in his dreams. She loved the dark fire in her sleeping man; she mourned that he must always burn alone; near enough for her to love him, too far to bind them close except in the passion that passed as if it had not been. "Why," she had murmured as he slept, "can I not make you happy?" In the snow drifted from the north against the rise of ground at the Fifty-ninth Street gate, Jonathan stumbled. How suddenly the body fell to earth! Like gravity drawing him, gravity everpresent and invisible . . . was his decision in him?

In the middle of the morning, Evan came into his office with the brief for the appeal in *Lawson versus City Bank*. He explained, precise and original as always, how he had used the common law on torts as a rebuttal of the precedents that had made the State Supreme Court find against the appellants. Then he sat down, at ease on the horsehair sofa, and lighted a cigar.

"Well," he said, "what's the news?"

"Your father came to see me last night."

Evan whistled and gave a little grimace of disgust.

"It was my mother who asked him. He quite won Greta's heart."

"He looks handsome at a distance. Like a picture on a billboard."

"I suppose if you were drowning you'd joke with your last gasp."

"Why not?" Evan's smile was gentle.

"Have you noticed, Evan, when you and I argue, I'm usually on the side of reason, yet you usually have the best of it?"

"There's a reason."

"You have the better mind."

"Not at all. I have the better case."

"I've done nothing, Evan. I'm still in the dark."

"You're nearing the end of the tunnel."

Jonathan's eyes moved about the walls . . . lawbooks and portraits of revered lawmakers . . . where he had practised law and loved it, knowing always the presence of the loved man in the next room. —Tunnel? Tunnels are dark. If one loved the dark, could one not somehow keep it . . . call it light? Evan was saying:

"I don't want to hurry you. But you mustn't delay too long. You've got Dennis worried, and a worried rat can be nasty. If he really fears

193

you're going to leap, he may jump first. Besides, I ought to be gone in time. . . ."

Jonathan got up. "Evan! Evan! Where are you going?"

"Don't worry about me. I'm going away."

"You won't tell me where you're going?"

Evan lifted himself from the old sofa, and the two men stood close. For the first time, Jonathan felt the struggle in his friend.

"Haven't you any sense?" said Evan. "You mustn't know where I've gone. Do you want to have to lie, when they ask you?"

Jonathan could not help it, the sobs were in his throat; he placed his two hands on his friend's arms, and the sobs rose.

"I'm going to miss you," said Evan, and drew his arms away.

III

THE WATERS FLOW THROUGH
THE LAND

ELYSIUM'S SYMPHONY HALL WAS IN A PART OF TOWN
that had run down. Vine Street and Independence Place still had
spacious square brick mansions built by Germans and Yankees from
the Western Reserve before the War of the Rebellion; now they were
Negro tenements, and the magnolias received in their green altars the
incense of nearby slaughterhouses. The Ohio River, once the town's
main traffic artery (even the hills studded with clapboard villas had
felt its lush ponderous rhythms), now flowed aloof between train
yards. Cindery children romped on the chipped stone of once haughty
stoops; a saloon displayed an immense stemmed bumper of painted
beer with the caption *Biggest Five Cent Drink in Town*. Over the
lugubrious waterfront stalls for the doomed cattle reigned the dark
iron smoking vibrance of locomotives, and far away were the visible
copses of bare birch on the Kentucky hills. The tall man, muffled in
a fur-collared coat, leaning against the corrugated winter wind, passed
a bakery oozing lard, a bookshop called *Schuberth* in Gothic letters,
that mixed in its windows German classics with novels by Laura
Jean Libbey, Anthony Hope, and Marion Harland's Cook Book;
passed a derelict row of whilom mansions now carious and frowsy
behind their rust-sponged piazzas; and stopped at a white brick
pseudo-temple with Corinthian pillars. He shifted his violin case to
place the cold hand in his pocket, and raised the broad brim of his
slouch hat to let the raw air cool his forehead.

The dusty wing backstage reminded him of theaters he had seen
in London and Vienna. Ever since his arrival in Elysium, the Heming-
way House like old commercial hostelries in Liverpool and Hamburg,
Froshart's, where he ate knackwurst and drank beer, like the Bavarian
bierkeller, the streets of heavy Germans, cosmopolitan Jews, made him
feel the Old World near, as if he had gone East from New York; and
Europe, not New York, had heeded Horace Greeley's "Go West,
Young Man." He reminded himself jocularly he was a young man
only by the coincidence of his going West and the fact that for the

first time in his life he was down to his last ten dollars and looking for a job: customary concomitants of youth. Did the stolid Germans, he wondered, have in mind the necrophilous meaning of Elysium when they named their city? Happy resting ground for the dead: perhaps this fitted him? Well, if he was dead, he could bear it.

The ruddy little German, only half again as big as his French horn, came back smiling. "Herr Riese now will see you."

Of course, the man with the violin knew of Anton Riese. The Philharmonic had tried to lure him to New York; the great man had explained to an interviewer: "How can I go? I have everything a conductor needs! good players, *natürlich,* and a whole city that listens to good music." Could one claim that for New York, or London or Paris? The week in Elysium had expounded the great musician's meaning: Elysium was a town that "felt" like music. The "bottoms" of warehouses and workers' slums, the piers where huge Percherons dropped manure and stamped their flowery hooves in mud that reflected themes of the sky, the hills terraced by canons and fugues of cottages, brick streets, cottages again; the wood, coal, soot, stench of cattle and toil, pungent as mellow cheese within the rivery rind, were notes of an organic medium in which the music of Anton Riese could live. Of it were the players he now passed, mostly Teuton squareheads with festooning mustaches, who were packing their instruments after the rehearsal or going over a hard passage; and the climax was the little man he approached on the podium, in shirtsleeves and suspenders, his small skull, half forehead, shining with sweat.

Anton Riese peered down at him through thick glasses that reverberated his eyes blue-clear as triangle notes.

"Do you have an opening for a second violin?"

"*Second* violin?"

"I doubt if I'm good enough for first."

"Play something." Herr Riese's high voice made the dark auditorium a cave behind a single candle.

The man slowly removed his heavy coat, unpacked his violin, and played the solo of the last movement of Lalo's *Symphonie Espagnole.* Riese let him go on to the end, only once raising his hand to bank a *diminuendo.*

"You don't like *rubato?*"

"Not for this modern music."

"For what you like it?"

"Not much for any good music."

"Chopin is not good music?"

"I suppose so. If he wrote for the fiddle, I don't know it."

"But you don't like Chopin." Riese did not ask; he stated. Then he reached down his chubby palms with their contradictory gnarled knuckles. "That's a fine fiddle you got." He fondled the Amati lovingly and peered at the man, then at the rich coat he had thrown carelessly on the rough floor. "What's your name?"

"Corthuis."

"A Dutch name."

"Yes, sir."

"Why do you say *second* violin? . . . Can you read?"

"Not too well."

"Can you keep time?"

"That's my weakest point."

"You try *not* to keep time in my orchestra! Next Monday at eleven. On time, hear? On time every minute! See Mr. Dokin."

—I got my job. Too damn easy. Evan wrapped his violin in its white silk kerchief, and laid it in the case. The world was flowing easy as the river, he along; and yet, if the world was to have meaning, it must be against the flow, against ease. Had he done what he had done . . . what had brought him here to this hour . . . to move against the flow and the ease? and . . . flowing, easing on . . . had he merely fooled himself? It was not easy to stand against ease, to stand against flow. Did he really want to? Had he merely indulged a whim, his whole life a whim, against ease? and by indulging it flowed on with ease? But he was stifling; life was stifling as it flowed; stifling because it merely flowed. An instant's impulse gripped him to smash his violin. He saw Herr Riese peering at him; he snapped the case shut.

Backstage again, a tall gangling youth was cleaning his flute.

"Can you tell me," Evan asked, "where I can find Mr. Dokin?"

"He's with the chief, ain't he?"

"The chief sent me to find him."

"Here comes Mr. Dokin."

199

The particulars of salary and rehearsal were soon settled, within earshot of the young man cleaning his flute.

"I heard you say you got no address."

"I've checked out of the hotel."

"Want a place to sleep and eat?"

"I suppose so."

"Why not come along with me? I'm Tam Liebling. My ma's Mrs. Liebling." He said it, as if the name must be familiar, like Beethoven or the new President, Benjamin Harrison. "We'll walk, if you ain't in a hurry. You a stranger in this town?"

"Never been here before. I feel at home."

"Ma'll make you feel at home."

The town was ripe. Horses plowed through the cobbled streets and the crowds, like slow barges on an easy river. Electric trolleys sent liquid bells slow through thick air; the brick and brownstone houses were soft banks of an easy river.

"Should we have a glass of beer before we go 'home'?" suggested Evan.

"Here's Ludwig's."

Along the immense mahogany bar receding into shadow, the barman slid the frothy mugs of beer. Tam slid a dime back.

"This was my treat," said Evan.

"This is my town," said Tam.

The men talking, drinking, were a comfortable thick agglutination far back from the bar to the shadows.

"Where you come from?" asked young Liebling.

"New York."

"They ain't got no electric trolleys in New York."

"That's so."

"They ain't got no Anton Riese."

"That's so."

Evan treated to a second beer, sliding the dime along the wet wood.

Tam blew the foam. "Just the samey, Elysium ain't what she used to be."

"Plenty of it still here, seems to me."

Tam put down his mug, serious. "When I was a kid, we slaughtered more head o' cattle than Chicago."

200

"What happened?"

"The railroads," said Tam. "Eighteen railroads come here. Elysium had ought to be a river town. There used to be so many packets from St. Louis and New Orleans you could hop-skip-and-jump the decks clear over to Kentucky."

"Who'd want to?"

"Don't you run down Kentucky. Where do you think our distillers get their corn?"

Evan glanced around at the comfortably gesticulating and imbibing crowd. "I don't see much whiskey being drunk?"

"We make it, sell it; then we buy beer."

"And make music?"

"There's not half so much music to a railroad engine whistle like there is to a steamboat horn. Don't spoil your appetite." Evan was building himself a sandwich from the free-lunch platters on the bar: a slice of ham, a spread of mustard, a slab of cheese on rye bread. "Ma'll be hurt, if you don't eat hearty."

"She's scarcely expecting me, you know; unless she's a seeress," Evan laughed.

Tam's quiet solemnity was unshaken. "No, she's just ma. But you'll never guess when you walk in she wasn't expecting you."

Warmed by the cool beer, they climbed Summit Street. The area-ways had brass rails, trees brushed tall second-story windows muffled in curtains and crowded the iron lattice balconies. Below them the town hummed; the river was a sinuous *legato* on which the sun flashed grace notes. Tam opened a gate, led down a brick path, in whose interstices dry grass was tufted, to a wide wood porch. He opened the door (it was unlocked) and Evan stepped into an air of comfortable cooking.

On the marble-top table lay letters; a tree of deer antlers held bowler and slouch hats; high under the roof they heard a woman singing scales.

"Ma," yelled Tam. When there was no answer, "Come on up. If she was downstairs, she'd a' heard me."

He took the carpeted steps two at a time. Halfway up, in a niche, a painted plaster ragamuffin, cherubic and slightly chipped, offered a newspaper from the stack under his arm.

"That's a genuine Powers," said Tam. "Ain't he *natural?* Mr. Duvenick gave it, when he left us. He died six months later." Tam seemed to point the moral of such folly as leaving. "Ma!" he called again.

A liquid voice through the door said, "Come on in."

Tam opened, and Evan saw in a room ablaze, after the dark hall, with the sun of two bay windows a woman standing over a chair cutting the gold hair of a youth bundled in towels. Her green wrapper revealed her plump arms and bust; beside her on a table was a tumbler half filled with whiskey.

"I brought a new boarder," said Tam.

Mrs. Liebling slithered the scissors and snipped. "That's fine." She dropped the morsel of hair on the carpet, and took a swallow of her drink.

"How do you do, ma'am," Evan bowed.

"Just fine. Hope you're the same. This is my Jacob, he's my bairn. Dinna turn your heed, you fool, I'll nip your ear off; the man's no' goin' to rin away. You can ha' the wee room at the top, six dollars a week. *Keep* quiet, Jacob."

"I'm sure—" Evan began.

"What did ye say your name was?" The lady with the German name and the Scotch burr went on before Evan could answer: "It's no' the best room; fact, it's the wor-r-st. Next month when dear Mrs. Goldberg's leavin' to be married, ye can ha' her room that's got the sun i' the winter and a breeze i' the summer. It'll no' cost ye. any more. She's marryin' Herbert Dole, imagine! That sweet Jewish lady marryin' a tight cockney; she'll live, please the Lord, to regret it. She's old enough to ken her ain mind. When ye move in, you'll no' have to pay more though ye should eat more, I hope!, livin' in the sun."

Said Tam, "Mr. Corthuis is a new first violin."

"The hoose is so noisy no one'll hear ye practice. If ye can hear yersel', that's the question!" Her laugh chimed with the clip of her scissors; she seemed to fondle each little snippet of hair before she dropped it on the carpet. "There now, ye're through." She knocked on the blond head as one knocks at a door. "Get up, ye big gangling lubbert and may no woman ever shear ye but yer mither. Rin doon, ye'll still ha' time to baste the meat."

202

Shedding towels from his shoulders (the towels shedding curled tufts of golden hair soft as thistledown on to the red carpet), Jacob got up; Jacob kept on getting up until six foot six of him, resilient and callow, rose above his mother. Tam now came on her other side and kissed her. The sun unified the dust, the chairs littered with clothes, the bric-a-brac and papers on the tables, and the unmade bed, into a subdued dance about the woman, sweet and springlike in her loose hair, loose wrapper, loose slippers, flanked by her two sons.

"Ye'll just ha' time to wash up before supper. No' that I want to hurry ye. What did you call yersel'?"

"Corthuis, Evan—" He could not understand her smile. Suddenly, as if remembering a joke, she recalled the proprieties and bowed. "Pleased, I'm sure, to meet you, Mr. Evan." He returned the bow in the best Gramercy Park manner which he had carefully avoided in Gramercy Park.

He stood alone in his room, and liked it. The room itself was part of the charade he seemed to be living, a fantastic specially concocted scene. Above the bed, not two feet from the pillow, the ceiling bellied and the walls, at an obtuse angle, narrowed to two legs; at the end of one a high stained-glass skylight window, at the end of the other a huge oak chest. The floor was of blue tiles, the walls were whitewashed, the ceiling was walnut like a vault. Opposite the bed in the belly of the room was a washstand with a cracked bowl and in the half-open cupboard a slop pail and a chamber pot not emptied since the last tenant had used it. The towels on the washstand rack were clean, the linen of the iron bed was spotless; the tiles gleamed and little heaps of gathered dirt stood where the cleaner had forgotten to remove them. On the oak chest was a row of books: a Bible, several paper volumes of Beadle's *Dime Novels* and Nick Carter, *Little Lord Fauntleroy,* and Emerson's *Poems.* Crowded above on the wall were the room's two pictures, both luridly colored: a moving van drawn by prancing horses, its façade showing George Washington Crossing the Delaware (the ice floes sharp as alps) and a framed fashion plate of six stiff caparisoned ladies whose big bustles and small heads made them dragon-armored insects. Propping the books was an alarm clock and as it ticked its charade time, the room on its two legs creakingly revolved like a windmill in a slow wind. Evan smelled the stale urine, the cold air, and felt himself revolving with the room; even the new job on the Symphony was part of it, and the charade was pleasant; the charade would go on until he found the name it spelled; and to find it, must be desperately avoided. He placed his violin case on the chest, washed his face and hands, and went down to dinner.

At the head of the long table which filled the basement room sat Mrs. Liebling, now in corsets beneath the same green wrapper. As Evan stood at the door, she introduced him name after name to her boarders. Over their heads on the mirrored mantelpiece he saw a row of Dresden figures. He heard: Mrs. Goldberg, Herr Marks, Madame Dolores, Miss Madden, the Count . . . and saw the china shepherdess, the roaring lion, the fiddler, the pierrot; saw them doubled by their reflection in the glass. When Herr Marks, unlike the others who were content to nod and smile, jumped up and took Evan's hand in a hot moist clasp, Evan felt a disturbing violence in this extrusion from the norm of the charade. Jacob appeared in the kitchen door, ducked his head to pass, and set the huge tureen before his mother. Evan took his seat, the savor of the soup fusing them all together.

Mrs. Liebling's husband had come from Austria, a young man expert in the making of pipe organs; her meals were the Scotch woman's reverence to the dear departed. (He had died when the boys were in kilts, leaving her not a penny to run the Summit Street house he had bought on speculation.) The scones, barley broths, kippers, meat and kidney pies of her girlhood deepened to a flavor more Vienna than the Highlands, and harmonized with the goulash, the blinde Haase, the Gänse Grüben, the sweet-sour beans, the Rotkraut, the Kartoffel Puffer, the Linzer Torte, and coffee with whipped cream; and even the food became for Evan a scene of this charade of ease spelling the word he was afraid to look for. When he left New York, he had given Augusta five thousand dollars, all his ready cash except the roll in his pocket; and told her not to dare cook her good meals for anybody else. "I'm corrupting you on purpose," he told the weeping woman. "I'm hoping you'll not put the money in the bank—not right away at any rate. Enjoy yourself. Have a fling. Learn to be lazy and drink Schnapps. When the money's gone, maybe you'll have contracted bad habits and won't be able to take care of your next boss as you have me. That'll be a comfort." She understood not a word of his jesting (she was used

204

to that); now the joke was on him! For Mrs. Liebling's cooking was strikingly like Augusta's. Of course, he missed her care. Augusta had mended his socks, sent his clothes to laundry and tailor, supervised his diet, scolded him for his late hours, put out his rubbers when it rained, his woolens in winter. Mrs. Liebling, so far as he could see, took care of no one, including herself. The house was dirty and disordered; guests were perpetually asking if letters had not been swept off the marble-top table in the hall—but never leaving despite their suspicions. Since the lofty Jacob was the waiter, and sober Tam the house steward and treasurer (Evan was not permitted to pay a cent until he had been there a month. "Ma won't like it if you pay till you're permanent." "What if I clear out after a week?" "Nobody does," said Tam.)—how did Mrs. Liebling fill her days? She inspired the cook in the kitchen; she sensed by instinct every boarder's secret —and if she didn't like it, the room was "reserved" for someone else after a week and the unwanted boarder went; she wandered up and down stairs with her glass of Scotch and water; she lay long hours in bed with sentimental novels of *The Fireside Companion*. She did nothing, she *was* everything in the warm, tumultuous house whose human ingredients were varied as one of her famous stews (beef or lamb, potatoes, carrots, peppers, okra, parsley, tomatoes, scallions, chives, and innumerable herbs from her backyard garden), to which she gave fanciful names: "We're carvin' a fine roast pheasant tonight."—"Would you like to ha' some more, Count, o' the grilled antelope?"

Soon Evan found her spirit, incarnate in her sweet lax flesh (corsetless except at dinner), beyond the house through the whole town. Tam's presence in the orchestra, their constant goings and comings together to rehearsals, reinforced but did not inspire Evan's frequent thought of the Scotswoman while he played a scherzo of Haydn or a slow theme of Gluck. The town itself kept her before him. When he wandered alone, drinking in the saloons of the "bottoms," watching the dance in a music hall near the great potteries in the South Bend, he thought of Mrs. Liebling: —Tomorrow's Friday, there'll be kippers for breakfast. And when he saw her with her sons, easing along through every day, he thought of the Ohio River. The ease went on, amazing if he had known how to stop and behold it. But it immersed him wholly. How long? For the time being. And nothing before had immersed him; he had been the analyst of himself and his world—New York, college, summer trips to Europe, his mother, his father, Jonathan —because of his separation from them. All that . . . including himself . . . was an "other world" he had beatifically lost. Dimly, his mind hinted *it* was the real, and this immersion the charade. But the capacity to know this, and to say this, was of that "other world," an echo alien to this total music which made no echo, which gave no memory, which he did not follow since he was wholly in it.

At the month's end, when Mrs. Liebling said to him: "I'm grieved, son [he was as old as she], to ha' promised you Mrs. Goldberg's room; she's no' leavin', she's no' goin' to marry the doleful Dole after-r all, thank the Lord! The bonnie Jewess, what'd she ha' done wi' an accountant in bed?" (Mrs. Goldberg was forty-five, dry, homely, with a mustache; only the Scotswoman's clairvoyant heart could see her as bonnie). Evan answered, "You couldn't pry me from my room!"

"Why d'ye like it so?"

He could not say, it's part of my new body, change would hurt like a dislocated hip; he made an effort and said, "I sail out of that stained-glass window over the whole town."

"You're a male witch?"

"The room's bewitched. You had something to do with it."

"Go on wi' ye! When my man lived, we used that room for storin' things."

"Nothing else?"

Mrs. Liebling's smile spread over her past, her eyes twinkled at him shrewdly. "I used to go up there wi' him when we had a bundle to throw out. He'd play a game o' courtin' me like we wasn't married; steal a kiss, like it wasn't proper doonstairs."

"I told you."

"Well, it's a dirty uncomfortable cot for a man that's a gentleman, even if he do play the fiddle. An' it will be awfully war-r-m, come summer. Ah, ye dinna ken what a boilin' pot this river toon is, till summer comes."

Sudden, after a late March blizzard, summer came. . . .

Every Saturday, Mrs. Liebling made her Jacob take the evening off, and before long it was his habit to call for his brother and Evan at Symphony Hall and lead them on a lyrical carouse. Tam, who was shorter, less blond, perpetually sane; who had gone to school, had a steady job and earned and handled money, accepted his somewhat inferior rank in the heart of his mother. If he had shown ambition, if like so many of the orchestra men he had supplemented his meager earnings by teaching or playing at private concerts in the homes of the rich, she would have admired him less. But even if he had turned banker, she would still have loved him, since he was part of herself. She loved Tam, she loved her house, she loved herself, all as *part* of herself; only Jacob, who was pure enough to play his pipe through life like Pan, did she love as *all* herself. She had never sent him to school; he had learned what reading and figuring he had, like walking and talking. She denied him nothing; but when he was slow in knowing his own hungers, she prompted him. Two years ago, when he was sixteen, she had pushed him gently into the bed of an amorous lady boarder who could safely give him an experience he seemed to need. But she was not sorry when the lady left, as if she wistfully regretted she could not, herself, serve her darling in this as in all things. Jacob remained unspoiled as fresh-drawn milk. He was an excellent if capricious waiter. He made her morning tea in bed a sacrament by bringing it to her. She deplored as a limitation that her periodic sips of Scotch left her sober, and took delight in Jacob's bouts.

"I love to see a sweet lad roarin'," she crooned to Evan when they loaded the boy upstairs and into bed. They undressed him; Jacob's flesh, pink and benign as a babe's, lay in the sheets; he raised his long head, shaped like a colt's, and neighed.

"Is it no' the fine music!" she purred.

. . . That first "popular" Saturday afternoon concert of the warm weather series (much Johann Strauss, Délibes, Mendelssohn, Offenbach, Meyerbeer), Jacob was waiting for them. The two youths and the older man stepped from the windy stage into the last remnants of the blizzard oozing in soiled rivulets away under the premature warm dusk. The brothers locked arms with Evan and, their feet in the muck, their eyes clear, they walked singing *The Drunkard's Child,* then *Drill, Ye Tarriers, Drill,* till they reached Froshart's.

With the second goblet of Glühwein, Jacob began: "Madame Dolores came down to lunch today like she was goin' to a funeral."

"If you mean she was gloomy," said Evan, "it must have been her own. Anyone else's would cheer her up."

"She wanted Mrs. Goldberg's room; ma's letting the new lady have it."

"Mrs. Goldberg's really gone?"

"Not to get married. She's cashier of a new candy store out Dauphin way. Too far to her place of business."

Evan laughed. "So she was in love with figures after all, even if she jilted the accountant?"

An acquaintance came up; they bought him a drink and got rid of him. Sooner or later, Jacob always came back to the boarders, and no outsider could hear his intimate information.

"Madame Dolores had two devils sitting on her shoulders."

"That's because she's Spanish," said Evan. "Spain goes from one civil war to the next because of the two devils on every Spaniard's shoulders."

"But it's the men, ain't it, who make the civil wars?" Tam asked seriously. "Madame Dolores calls her shop *French Hairdressing.*"

Jacob brushed aside these irrelevancies. "The little devils on Madame Dolores' shoulders don't talk either Spanish *or* French."

"How do you know?" Evan challenged.

"I heard 'em." Jacob slithered his long tongue inside his empty glass.

"Another round." Evan smiled at the barman.

"What were they saying?" Tam's face was solemn.

"They was having a dreadful fight. The little 'un on her left shoulder kept jumpin' up and down and yelling, 'You dirty little devil, I got as much right to this here body as you!' He was scrawny; t'other on t'other shoulder was fat as a pig, rounder'n high. He smiled and licked his lips like he was gettin' ready for a feast. You know how Madame Dolores eats." The others laughed; Evan made a noise that was supposed to imitate a steamshovel excavating earth. "Every time she took a gulp of the soup—we had lentil soup with those leftover sausages, they had to be eaten today, it's turned so warm—the fat 'un acted like he was eatin' too. The thin 'un on the left got nothing. 'You gotta stop,' he yelled. 'You gotta give me a chance!' The Count comes in, late like always. You know how Madame Dolores feels about the Count." Again, the listeners laughed. "She gives him the soft eye and the skinny devil perks up. Just then ma says, 'Won't you have a little more sausage, Madame Dolores? They won't keep.' Madame Dolores passes her plate, forgetting the Count, the fat devil rubs his belly, the thin 'un gets madder and thinner."

"She's never made the Count look at her," Tam observed.

"She's tried," said Evan. "Remember that dinner after she'd visited the shop where the Count cuts marble tombstones? How she kept slyly hinting that her figure was like the lovely lady angels?"

"She's too busy eating," Jacob concluded with finality. "She gets all mixed up; she thinks of men like they was food."

"Who's the new boarder? What's she like?" asked Evan.

"Ma tells me she teaches school," said Tam.

"Her devils," said Jacob, "ain't friends with Madame Dolores' devils. So Madame Dolores' devils are mad."

"Not she, but her devils?" asked Evan.

Jacob peered through his glass as if it were a crystal ball. "It's never us who get mad, it's always the devils. *We*'re all together, we are!"

They walked down Linden Street toward the "bottoms"; the twilight textured of the punctuating puffs of invisible locomotives, of the lowing of doomed cattle in the pens, was a warm fume over the still cold earth. At Pete's saloon, as usual, the Negro longshoremen drank and sang. Three big fellows leaned over the bar, over their small drams of rum, their clothes exhaling a sweet chaos of tar, sweat, wood, and horse manure, their lowly faces bowed, and their voices in *Deep River* wove the world together. They hummed as if they were praying. Evan took his fiddle from the case and played a delicate *obbligato*. They kept on humming; suddenly they raised their faces toward the white men and the song burst, lighting the room's rafters. Then there was silence. Evan motioned to the barman, a dwarfish German, to refill the glasses. One of the Negroes spoke:

"That fiddle got silvah wings."

"Wings"—hummed the others—"*All God's Chillun Got Wings. . . .*"

Between the wharves, in a turn of the river, lived a pocket of old-time houses: red-roofed clapboard dwellings with oleander and magnolia in bloom, and a white church steeple joining the cold earth to the warm dusk. Heavy horses drew heavy wagons through the heavy mud, whips quivered the moist warm flanks of the twilight; they could hear the river, heavy-laden, lurch around the bend.

"We're going to have floods," said Tam.

They stopped; through the solstice of the wine they had drunk, an exquisite pause of time making the grain of each moment visible, they felt the river bearing down on them: with them, the thicket of piers behind and ahead, the little group of houses from the past, and the whole town rising in gas-lit hills, seemed to lie beneath the river.

"We always got floods," said Jacob. "We ain't a river town; we ain't a railroad town, we're a flood town."

They walked against the river.

Jacob said, "We're a flood house, too. Our boarders, they're like what the river brings when it goes over the levees."

"I've never seen a flood," said Evan.

"Sometimes," said Tam, "a whole house comes floating down. Trees, cattle, chicken coops, cradles. . . ."

"Dead chickens, dead babies?" asked Evan.

"You never know what's dead," said Jacob. "It's like our boarders."

The Rainbow was a celebrated roadhouse that had been a station of the Underground during the War Between the States; in its cellars, still stocked with generous wines, runaway slaves from Kentucky spent the night on their way North. The tables had checkered red cloths; the bottles over the bar were festooned with flags and interspersed with mounted heads of deer and fish. A complicated mechanical orchestra walked, like a brigade on stilts, through the *Rakovsky March*. They ate prawns seethed in wine sauce with a bottle of Liebfraumilch, duckling stuffed with celery and apples, cucumbers in cream, with a bottle of Pommard. Evan was proud that his stomach weathered the many wines as well as his young friends'. He laughed at his pride. —It's true. I'm over forty! I could be Jacob's father.

"Why do you laugh?" asked Tam.

"That's a personal question," said Jacob.

"And why not a personal question?" Evan smiled.

"The mattress floating down the flood asked the floating cottages, 'Why's your roof upside down?' 'That's a personal question,' the house said, 'but if you gotta know, I've lost my cellar.' "

They ate tiny wild strawberries in yellow cream.

"The Governor of Ohio come here last spring," said Jacob. "They give him some of these strawberries and he tries to put sugar on 'em.

They took him out and lynched him. Then they're a little ashamed. 'After all, he was only the Governor, he didn't know no better.' They was a little scared, too. 'After all, he *was* the Governor.' So they cut him into little pieces and the head they hid in a cornfield, the heart in an apple orchard, the hands and legs in a melon patch."

"That was too good for him," Evan laughed.

"It was too bad," said Jacob. "The corn in that field, all its kernels was india rubber; the apples of that orchard was lead; and the melons —they tasted like piss."

"Jacob'll never vote Republican," said Tam.

"I'll never vote! Why don't they let the cows vote? Anybody that can make this lovely cream—"

"Do you think they'd want to? Even if we passed a constitutional amendment?"

Jacob, always solemn, shook his head. "They don't like us, the cows; they don't like our smell. They say we eat the wrong food."

"Milk and roast beef?"

"Only dogs like our smell. They got a taste for us, like we have for liquor. It's unsettled 'em."

A gentleman came to their table from the bar. Under his florid face and florid vest, his legs in tight gray trousers carried him like stems of a topheavy flower.

"I couldn't help overhearing you gentlemen." He bowed courteously and spilled some of his mint julep on Jacob's shoulder. "I'm delighted you're not Republicans. What this state needs, suhs, is a Democratic administration."

"No hope," said Tam.

"Why not, suh? May I ask, why not, suh? Didn't the country elect a Democrat in 1884? Won't we put Grover Cleveland back in the White House where he belongs in 1892? Never lose hope! We Democrats must never lose hope."

"The cows won't vote," Jacob wagged his head. "I've argued and argued with 'em. They say they'd rather be milked than vote."

"How about the bulls?" asked Evan.

"Seriously, gentlemen—"

Jacob shot up like a geyser from his seat, shouting, "Who's not serious? Ain't we been serious?"

The gentleman recoiled in terror.

"Sit down." Jacob's voice was mild and dulcet. "Have a drink." He removed the fiddle and flute from the ôdd chair.

"There's our hope." The stranger winked at Evan. "The younger generation. *They* won't be blinded by sectionalism. They'll be Democrats."

Jacob said: "I was talking t'other day with an old brindle Guernsey; calved five times; done her patriotic duty, she has. 'Now take the clover,' says she. 'It's sweet and it's strong; why don't it *abolish* all that sourgrass?'"

"I'm an Ohio man," said their guest, "even though I was born three miles from Henry Clay's home in Lexington County. I've lived in Elysium twenty years. Up on Tamaril Heights is my home; Dalton's the name, suhs. Colonel Jeremiah Dalton, wholesale hardware." He took out his wallet and extracted a card.

"We ain't got cards," said Jacob. "This man here," pointing to Evan, "lost his name in the flood. Tam and me ain't been named yet."

Colonel Dalton laughed, peered closer at Evan, and down to the violin case. "Now I know where I've seen you! Front row of the orchestra. You're all musicians?"

"Only me," said Jacob. "Tam uses his flute for a toothpick. Evan, who lost everything coming down the flood, uses his fiddle for a raft."

The Colonel roared with laughter. "I tell you, it's splendid to find musicians interested in the public welfare. I heard you about that varlet, the Governor; how he ought to be lynched. Splendid! Say, my youngest: Daphne's her name, she's musical, too. She takes violin lessons from an old maid; I wouldn't name her, 'twouldn't be polite, but she's got no more music in her than she has juice. How about giving her some lessons? I'll pay your price."

"You're very kind," said Evan.

"You got my card. There's a telephone in my office, suh! Or just call on me: the Dalton Building, you must know it. Monday. Of course," he winked at Evan, "if one of those young bloods was the fiddler, maybe I'd not dare have him round the house."

"Evan's the youngest man in Elysium," shouted Jacob. "My brother and me, we're bringing him up. He's never had a drink in his life, and this is his first square meal. Only got his teeth last week."

When they were alone, after the Colonel had insisted on opening a bottle of brandy, "Tear up that card," said Jacob.

"Why?"

"The man lives uphill; that's not the right direction."

"Think how much farther you can slide, if you start uphill."

"That's where you did start. You had nothin' to do with it, so it's all right. Now you're supposed to slide—"

"Dear Jacob," Tam smiled, "you're wonderfully drunk. We can go home."

Evan said, "We'll take ma a bottle of this cognac."

. . . The night had become cool; Jacob looked up at the lucid stars and said, "The sky's wearin' a girdle of white roses." They led him to a cab, folded him through the door: "If I could get my nose out of this wine, I could smell the white roses. They mean a wedding."

Tam kept a hand firm on his brother's as on the string of a kite to keep it from flying away. And while Jacob sailed, embroidering visions, Evan found himself in a dark corner; the Colonel from Kentucky (he touched the card in his pocket) had exiled him from these boys half his age, from this city more immersed in the muddy river as the cab creaked up the steep street. Suddenly he felt homesick; the pang of his mother bled with new blood and it traced Jonathan, Greta, his old world: he alone was traceless.

They found Mrs. Liebling in the kitchen drinking "java" with Herr Marks, the Count, Madame Dolores, and a small young woman in gray. The Count looked the Sicilian nobleman he claimed, without pride, to be. Tall, iron-limbed, with black sideburns, a prognathic jaw and inset hard black eyes, he was arguing like a hot pump with Herr Marks.

"We don't need more laws, you're right. We need *one* law, the will of *one* man, to tell every idiot every minute what to do. It'd better be a king. Upstart dictators have to be cruel, because they rely on the young. Kings are considerate, because they rely on the old." The Count was indolent, dissolute, and clever; he worked a few hours each week carving angels for the tombstones of the rich; most of his pocket money he procured from lavish lovers, and he kept his body lean and hard by constant sexual bouts.

"No man," shouted the sweaty German, "is good enough to make a

213

single law. Laws make everyone bad. If your king was the best man in the world, just making laws would make him bad . . . bad as a Congressman." Herr Marks, a disciple of Max Stirner and Bakunin, worked ten methodical hours a day drilling Latin verbs and German grammar into the skulls of dull boys.

"You think men are good," sneered the Count, "you think they can be left alone? I say they're cattle and love to be slaves. God made them slaves."

Mrs. Liebling enjoyed the fracas; she kissed her sons and told them to keep quiet; she passed cups of fresh coffee, and began feeding Jacob with a spoon. Madame Dolores swayed in the argument of the two men, her eyes closed, her body rhythmic with the words of the Count.

"There is no God," shouted the Anarchist.

"All right, there is no God," said the Count. "That only proves I'm right. Why was God invented? Because men wanted to be slaves. Why did they make up the divine rule of kings? Because they're only happy when they're on their bellies, groveling, worshiping."

"That's when they were children. Now they're grown up. They don't need any more toys like gods or kings." Herr Marks flourished his saucer and the cup jounced to the floor, pouring the hot liquid on his quivering knees. He did not notice.

"Who's grown up?" sneered the Count quietly.

Mrs. Liebling rescued the cup and was nearly trampled by the German jumping to his feet, shaking his fist in the Italian's face, shouting:

"Not men like you. Barbarians! Degenerate aristocrats! Loafers!"

"Pooh." The Italian did not flinch. "We had a great empire when you German savages were jumping around in skins."

"We smashed your empire."

"We civilized Europe—all except you Germans."

"You enslaved Europe, you with your Holy Rome. We freed it with our German science. You say *Pooh,* I say *Pfui!*"

"Count," cried Madame Dolores, "he's going to bite you."

"What about Galileo? Was he a German scientist?"

"Your Popes made him eat dirt!"

"Is it no' the bonnie sight!" Mrs. Liebling smiled at the little gray woman beside her. "Such brotherly love!"

The German's red face was very close to the Count's; his hairy red fists milled up and down, ready to strike. The room was tense. Then the Count, holding his ground, burst out laughing. Everyone laughed, except the German who seemed to collapse and retired to his chair in the corner.

"It's a victory for you Quakers, who believe in brotherly love!" sang Mrs. Liebling. "Why, my dear, I've forgotten to introduce ye. These are my boys, Tam and Jacob. Jacob, are you too drunk to get up? For shame! You can roll in the gutter or into bed, for all I care; but if you fail to bow to a sweet lady, I'll—biff ye!" She looked at Evan, and paused. "Mr. Evan Corthuis. It's he, dear, didna want the room you got. It was his by rights. You can thank him for it."

Evan looked at the little person, and saw himself: tall, tending toward corpulence, no longer young. "Rachel Lorne," he heard. Was she a woman? She was a girl. Her gray clothes too old for her, her compassionate face, dark like his mother's, had made him think her a woman.

He bowed carefully, and repeated, "Miss Lorne?"

LITTLE JEFFERSON HARTT (HE WAS NOT TALL FOR HIS nine years) rang the basement bell and waited. One mittened hand held a waterproof schoolbag, the other arm clasped close to his body a portfolio of music. School was over at one, but on Wednesdays after his lunch there was drawing class at school and piano lesson at Mr. Bendolph's. Already in the basement hall he heard the din of the ladies; this was his mother's "day at home" and a score of feminine voices all talking at once carried down the narrow stairs a world as remote from his own as a tree full of birds. A world fabulously happy: they didn't have to study, they didn't have to struggle to "be good," they weren't "little men" burdened with the awful destiny of growing up and being like papa. And they had all the good things served to them on silver platters. Jefferson knew what they were consuming at this very moment: chocolate with whipped cream, almond cookies thin as paper, wonderful little hearts, triangles, and stars of snowy bread spread with tomato, sardellen, salmon, chicken, olives, and anchovies. Cook, after letting him in, went up the back stair to help Annie, the waitress. For his supper, there were generally leftovers from these "days at home;" but that was a long time off. Jeff dropped his bag and music on the kitchen floor, just as if he had never been taught and taught and taught to be neat, and stole to the big closet at the foot of the pantry stairs behind the kitchen. He heard the two servants talking overhead, but they would not hear him, he figured; they were too near the noisy ladies. The closet smelled like heaven: shelf after shelf of jams and jellies (put in jars each autumn from cauldrons on the stove). He found a tablet of chocolate, broke off a big piece, and let it melt in his mouth while he rummaged for cookies. Then he had an idea; he ran back to the kitchen for his schoolbag and filled the interstices between the big thin Geography, the little fat Reader, and the pencil box, with raisins, chocolate, cookies, and a big banana. An orange and apple he stuffed in his coat pockets. Cook was coming down the winding steps; breathless with fear, he ran back to the kitchen and stole up the front basement

216

stair. At its head was the library door: if only it was shut! It was open. No danger they would hear him in their own noise, but they might see him. Hunching his shoulders ·to make himself invisible, the boy emerged into the hall he must pass. Even if he were seen at the farther end, from the parlor, he could run up the next flight; but here, for an instant, he stood helpless. His mother, pouring coffee from a silver urn, looked past a lady in a flowery hat, and saw him.

"Jeff!" she called.

The chatter ceased, a dozen pairs of eyes turned on him; he hated his beautiful mother.

"Jeff, come in, darling."

·The stolen goodies in his bag must be visible, too; for the eyes of the ladies gloated. He took a step inside the threshold.

"This is my little Jefferson."

They took him as they took their hot chocolate and cake. "What a fine little boy. . . . How he has *grown!* . . . My dear, he's the image of you. . . . Don't you remember me, little man? I have a big boy at home just your age. . . ." In the armchair by the window, aunt Lucia looked on and said nothing; she knew he was suffering, she was sorry but she was glad, too.

"How was your music lesson?" asked his mother. And before he could reply: "Jefferson takes piano with Mr. Bendolph. Yes, he is talented, although he loves his drawing lessons more."

The ladies smacked their lips as if he tasted good.

"Soon my little man will be able to play for my friends."

"Oh, Greta, *do* sing for us."

"Yes, dear, *do* sing something."

He stood there, already swallowed and forgotten. . . .

On the second floor, another danger: grandma's room was open! and there she sat, the little dry old lady, all in black, under the gas, peering up from her knitting through steel spectacles.

"Good afternoon, my boy." Now, he must go in and kiss her. He loved to kiss his mother who tasted like flowers; he did not like to kiss papa because his beard and mustache prickled; aunt Lucia, who seldom kissed him, did not taste at all; but grandma tasted hard and clean like a dry brush.

"Did you have a good day, my boy?"

217

"Yes, grandma."

"Did you learn well?"

"I guess so, grandma."

"You must work hard, Jefferson. Your papa always worked hard." He did not speak. "It's all very well, your music lessons . . . you must not neglect your *real* studies."

He understood: music, to her, meant his mother. She was looking fondly at his bag; in it, she thought, were books. That meant papa.

"What did you read today?" The dangerous lady pointed at the bag. "Let me see." The boy turned pale.

"Come," she held out her hands.

"W-we had g'ography . . . America. . . ."

"*All* America? Show me."

"I don't want to."

The smile, now, was gone. "You don't *want* to? Is that the way you're taught at school to speak to your elders?"

"We're not taught that. We're taught g'ography, and reading, and fractions."

"I suppose so; it's not the school's fault, I'm sure." His turning too fast to escape made the keen old lady suspicious. "Well, I'm waiting."

Jefferson clasped his bag as if her hands were on it.

"*Well,*" said Sarah. Pinioned, he saw his grandmother place her ball of yarn, her needles, and the gray strip she had knitted on the floor, saw her raise her spectacles to her forehead, and get up. Her hands were on his bag.

"No!" He struggled. But he did not struggle well; part of him wanted her to take the bag, as she did; wanted to watch her open it, drop her spectacles again to her eyes, pull out the chocolate, the crumbled cookies, the crushed banana. In her old shriveled palm, she held the raisins mixed with dust and crumbs. She placed the stolen goods on the table and quietly sat down.

"Where did you get these?" Silence. . . . "From the kitchen?" Silence. "I hope you know, you're a thief. Not a common thief. They steal, I suppose, because they're ignorant and have no good example to follow in their father. You're a disgrace to your father." Still silence. "What have you in your pockets?" Docile, he took out the orange and the apple and laid them with the rest. "You're a bad evil boy."

218

His continued silence she took for agreement. "Now go to your room. Take your books and do your homework. Then, for punishment, you will go to bed without supper."

"I won't!" he shouted and Sarah glanced nervously at the open door. "Mama promised me chocolate with whipped cream."

"You think you deserve chocolate with whipped cream? You deserve a glass of water, a bath, and a whipping."

"You aren't my mama!" His tears rising from a wail to a scream, the boy rushed into the hall and upstairs. In his room, he shut the doors and barricaded them with chairs. He sat on his bed, gazing in anguish at his desk. How could he do his homework with his books in grandma's room? He could never fetch them; if she brought them, he could never let her in. He was a thief, he was lost. . . . His eyes went to the open shelves between the windows, where his wonderful new menagerie stood: the giraffe, the springing tiger, the lion. How could he do his homework? He got up, held the elephant lovingly in his hand, and flung it down. The trunk broke. One by one, he hurled his beloved animals to the floor and stamped on them. The world turned black, the crushed creatures were himself. Part of the ecstasy of madness, the chair he had placed against the door fell back, and his mother's arms were around him.

"She called me a thief!"

"You're not a thief! My darling!"

He wept on her bosom, knowing that his tears stained her party dress; and because she did not mind, an immense joy merged with his grief. He kept on quietly weeping.

At last: "I've spoiled your dress."

"It's nothing, dearest."

"I *am* bad, mama."

"No, sweet, you did nothing. *Nothing.*"

"I've spoiled your dress."

It was a gown of rose silk with creamy chiffon from the height of the bosom to the ruching collar; and on the breast were his tears. Never had his mother looked lovelier to him.

"May I go now, darling? I'll be right back, soon as the ladies leave, and I'll bring you something *very good* to eat."

The boy's sensitive mouth was breaking again: his homework, his slaughtered animals. . . .

"I don't want you to study today, dear. You can stay home tomorrow. I think you've been studying too hard. You shall have another menagerie! Why, darling, you're all wet. Undress, before you catch cold." She swiftly opened his bed.

With the door shut behind her, like a child's, Greta's face broke into tears. This was too much! On her day at home! on Mrs. Darwin's first call for which she had waited so long! If only the library and parlor doors had been closed! "Mrs. Hartt is going to sing. . . . Have you *heard* her?" The hush, as she opened the piano. Then the boy's shriek! She had lost her head: all mother, not artist at all. Greta went into her own bedroom; thank God!, the door into mama Hartt's room was shut. "You're spoiling that child, indulging his tantrums!" would come later. —Now, collect yourself. You must go back to your ladies smiling. "It was nothing. My boy fell and bumped his head. Nothing." She saw her face in the glass. Oh, if only that were all she had to smile away! —Evan, how could you do it to your dearest friend?, knowing Jonathan, knowing how Jonathan must act! It had been hard enough before with mama Hartt and Lucia. If she had won that silent battle, she would have won her mother-in-law forever. Now, everything was her fault: because Jonathan had lost so many clients, her doing; because while Reuben was getting richer, Jonathan was poorer, her doing; because Jonathan lived under a cloud, her doing. —*Keep your hands off my boy!* If she thought of that, she'd cry again. What was her crime before God? If she prayed, she'd cry again. God did not want her to cry with her ladies waiting downstairs; God wished her to be happy. Her mother, with troubles ten thousand times worse, how radiant she had always kept her home! She missed her mother, gone to spend the year with Alfred's family in Dresden. That great English philosopher, at the banquet Jonathan took her to, had said, "You Americans have not learned to be happy." What was his name? Herbert Spencer. —Don't think of mama; it will make you cry again. She loved her husband, she loved her home—if only it were hers! She kept it in perfect order with just two cheap servants; she kept up her singing, she kept up bravely entertaining. It wasn't easy. Lucia did nothing; housework

220

was beneath the champion of women's rights. Mama Hartt found plenty to criticize. She didn't care. —*But leave my boy alone!* She would slave for her husband, she would live in a slum for his sake. She would never understand why he had acted as he did. What good had come of it? Ah, the harm! Yet had she blamed him? Had one word from her lips blamed him? He must do what he must do. But why, when he forgot himself (—Yes, he loves me!), when he let her give him happiness in her arms, why did he wake next morning as if they had sinned? Why can't this house be happy? The answer was beyond that door. In the clairvoyance of her momentary hate (Greta could not hate long) she saw the self-righteous woman in her chair: the woman who did not believe in happiness for others, because she had missed it for herself. Now her boy, too! —*I won't have it!* Anger, the brief moment it could survive in Greta's breast, dried Greta's tears. She saw in the mirror the stain on her dress and, beyond, the bed which threatened more tears. She took the Paisley shawl from her drawer, the gift of Lucy and Reuben after their wonderful voyage to the Orient. It was almost the color of the soiled chiffon; it would hide her boy's tears. How she would love a journey on one of those palatial steamers! Now, they could never afford it. She clasped the shawl at her throat with her cornelian cameo: the carved profile of a lady. —I'll sing *Du Bist die Ruh'*: for my encore, *Ich Liebe Dich*. Humming, she forgot the woman next door, and her boy. With a last look at the set of her shawl, she tripped smiling downstairs to her guests.

At the close of a dull day, Jonathan was clearing his desk when the office boy announced Mr. Samson Isadore.

"Let him come in. And you may go."

Isadore, an old friend from law-school days, never an intimate, was a clever lawyer with a gift for ironing out the conflicts of acquisitive men. Those who disliked him called him "oily"; his admirers spoke of his organizing genius. He specialized in railroad law; among his clients were the Mid-West and Pacific System with its supporting bankers, and he made a minimum of a hundred thousand a year. Ten days before, without preamble, he had come to Jonathan's new small office on Broad Street (a vestibule for the clerk and boy and a single room with the same furniture, the same pictures, the same lawbooks dimly looking out on Exchange Place), and offered him a partnership in Romney, Dulac, Isadore and Fenner.

"Jonathan," he had begun, characteristically mingling forthrightness and ingratiation, "you're a fine lawyer, you'd make a great judge if knowledge of law and character were what made judges in this country. But you're a poor handler of men"—he smiled—"and that means you'll never be a judge—not until some Governor or President appoints you out of sheer altruism, which *may* happen if—if you stop making enemies, to put it bluntly. What you need is a berth where you can practise *law* and leave your fellow mortals alone. We have what you need, and we can use what you have. You'll be our office man. Financial details, I'm sure, old fellow, can be worked out to your satisfaction."

"It's good of you to want what I have. These past couple of years, I've wondered if anyone did."

"Don't put on the humble act. You know your own worth. You insisted on a fight and fighters must expect to be hit."

Needing to get his balance and perspective to judge this sudden turn of fortune, Jonathan had veered the talk to general matters. They discussed the growing problem of the railroads, the effect on them of the new Sherman Anti-Trust Law. The interlocking combinations pilloried by the Pulitzer and Populist press: Standard Oil, the Morgan bank, the Steel Trust, the Lumber Trust, the Sugar Trust, the Whiskey Trust, the railroad systems, did they not rise of necessity from the expanding, centralizing trends of machine production and interstate free trade? Jonathan agreed. How else could the country grow? Where else lay America's potential advantage—to be pressed *now* before the new century or lost forever—over the frontier-broken economy of Europe? Jonathan nodded.

Isadore said: "But you can't fight the American faith in individual free enterprise. Not frontally. We've got to *use* it. That means three kinds of jobs. The politicians must persuade the people to identify their interest with Big Business prosperity, their freedom, with freedom for Big Business. The job of men like me is to get the big fellows together, make 'em see that's the only way each can win what he wants. The job of men like you is to keep expansion within the law, interpret the Constitution along economic lines. When the long-haired dreamers like

Governor Altgeld of Illinois or that young ass 'Lochinvar' Bryan from Nebraska threaten us with impossible laws, *smash* 'em in the courts. Most of our judges need to be shown the light. You're young still, Jonathan. Who knows when you just naturally will shift from bar to bench?"

It seemed providence, it seemed retribution, a chance so golden that Jonathan dared not trust it. He saw his mother kind again to his wife. How Greta needed kindness, praise, applause! Her brothers had spoiled her. Often he had felt in her a longing for that warm home on Lafayette Place. She was an artist; artists, everybody knew, were children. Was that what had been wrong with Evan? —Why do I love artists? Sitting with Samson Isadore, keeping the talk general so he could think, Jonathan had an intuition: —Did I love in Evan what ruined Evan? did I love in Greta what I'm forever "correcting"? They could redecorate the house, as Greta longed to do: get rid of the gloomy mid-Victorian furniture, the dark walls. They could install electric lights . . . How many clients he had lost! and others (like pressing on a tooth that hurt), he had thrown out of his office. The little men were afraid of his courage, his honesty and his brains. Not Isadore, who represented the only banking and railroad group that dared stand up to Morgan! If he was cool and hesitant, the offer might be withdrawn. Isadore was so obviously looking *him* over, and so was Jonathan—looking himself over! scarce aware of Isadore. He couldn't help it.

"But there's something real behind their distrust, isn't there? Even the Populists. The banks, for all their clamor for the gold standard, aren't they the real cause of the trouble? They're the ones who've depressed the farmers' earnings by withholding credit except on terms that mean big mortgages—and foreclosures. They're the ones who manipulate the watering of stock."

Isadore's voice was suave and velvety; he'd have made a good doctor for rich old ladies, a popular preacher for a rich congregation:

"What you call 'water' turns to blood and bone all right when business can go ahead. It's nothing but preparing for the future. Lack of confidence in business, labor troubles: *that's* what turns new stock issues into 'water.' Take the railroads. Vanderbilt, Huntington, Crocker, Hill, Villard are builders of the future. All they ask is for the public to underwrite them."

"I see your point, Sam, but isn't it true—take the farmers for instance: isn't their trouble that they have to sell in an uncontrolled world market? Wheat prices are made in Russia, Argentina, but the prices *they* must pay for their goods and their loans are made here."

"And why do those prices go wrong? Because they're interfered with by a lot of politicians under the Interstate Commerce Act; by labor union demagogues: first it was Powderly, now it's Gompers."

"There's poverty among workers," Jonathan smiled gently. "Even here in our Empire City."

"Why wouldn't there be, with Tammany mulcting forty cents boodle out of every dollar? I don't have to tell *you* that. And we don't have to tell each other that a bunch of laborers who haven't the brains in this free country to become bosses aren't likely to have the brains to fix proper prices and hours of work."

Within the wavering yellow glow of Mr. Edison's incandescent lamps, Jonathan saw the man who had been his law-school comrade. Isadore, short like himself, had lush full features, black bushy hair, black velvety eyes and a thick curved black mustache hiding his mouth and inviting conspiracy and confidence. Even his voice was velvety and dark. Isadore had barely passed his examinations for admittance to the bar, not because he was dull but because he was too busy with plans and contacts to spend more than the necessary minimum of time on his studies. (Jonathan and Evan had both ranked in the first ten.) These past two years, their careers had been antitheses. While Jonathan was forced to place a second mortgage on his house, Isadore acquired a hundred-acre estate in Hastings-on-Hudson. While Jonathan was dropped from the Civic Committee, the Grievance Committee of the Bar, and was refused the anti-Tammany Fusion nomination for Congress that had been virtually promised him (all this the work of Grosvenor Cleeve and his friends), Isadore was named vice-president of the City Bar Association and counsel for the important Non-Partisan Commission of Public Works appointed by the Governor to keep Dick Croker within city bounds. While Jonathan suffered, as from personal pain and loss, in Tammany's overwhelming defeat of the "forces of decency" in the last mayoralty election (vice, boodle, graft, working with the police, and the Comptroller's Office Croker's private clearing house), Isadore had complacently declined a Federal Judgeship offered him by President Harrison because "he could not afford it" (how Jonathan would have jumped at it!). And now, this shining mirror of his failures sat in his office, asked him to be a partner! (There was, Jonathan reflected, in the electric lamp both vibrance of duality and glow of unity.) Jonathan did not know if he was superior or inferior to Samson Isadore; but Isadore evidently assumed they were equal! What did it mean?

Isadore unbuttoned his coat that muffled him to the chin like a priest, as if even his body were a secret; drew forth his gold watch:

"It's been good, talking with you again, Jonathan. As I've always said, there's no great difference between a *good* Democrat and a Republican." He got up, smiling.

"You must let me think this over."

"The partnership? Of course! I didn't come here today for your answer. There's absolutely no hurry. Why don't you have lunch with Romney and me, some day next week? We won't talk business at all."

"I'll let you know."

When he had a problem to solve, a black mood to fight, any motive whatsoever for not hurrying home, Jonathan took, not the Ninth Avenue express, but the slow Sixth Avenue El to Fifty-eighth Street, and walked west across the Park. Here was a problem he must face alone; no word of·it to Greta or his mother, unless of course he accepted the golden offer. Why did he hesitate? —I'm a practising lawyer . . . If he wished to support his wife and son, his mother and sister as they deserved (Philip was no longer a charge: with his usual wordless sensitivity, he had felt the situation and gone to Raoul, and now he was a salesman . . . a successful one . . . for Mendis Toys, and paying Greta for his board), he must have clients who paid. —Yes, Sam Isadore understands me. I'm not a mixer. I'm a man of law. Of course, much of what Isadore said was sophistry. The railroads were thieves. They had robbed the people of public lands, hundreds of thousands of acres, buying the immense wealth of their right-of-way from Congress as cheap as the street railways bought their franchises from New York's boodle Aldermen. They watered their stock for power; they were far more concerned with cutting their rivals' throats than with serving the nation. In the rate war of the roads to Boston and Chicago, the ones with the banks behind them lowered the cost of transportation until the field was theirs; then up went the monopoly rates. But they did "open the country." (In the most expensive, inefficient, unethical way!) You could also argue that Tammany "helped" the poor family that appealed to the ward-heeler for coal or a loan or a word to the judge when a son got jailed in a drunken brawl. At what price? The city putrid with corruption, vice protected on every street by every patrolman, and the crooked leaders spending millions on the races and gambling tables at Saratoga. At what price were the railroads and steel mills "developing the country"? Every industrial town was a slum; workers on the Wabash and in Chicago were shot down for asking an eight-hour day or protesting a slash in wages (with prices rocketing). And the waste of public wealth was not the worst of it: by far the worst was that the country was growing in a way that identified greed with strength, corruption with expansion, theft with success! It was in the papers, in the schools, in the American air: this dangerous confusion! His little clients were no better than the big fellows: merely less lucky or less shrewd. The chap who ran the stationery store on Amsterdam Avenue, the labor leader, had the same cloudy values as the Fifth Avenue merchant. Or was failure a virtue? success an intrinsic evil? —Look out, Jonathan! To love poverty for its own sake makes a good monk, not a good lawyer. The Park was lonely . . . naked trees and the dim lamplights of winter night; and Jonathan felt lonely. If only he could speak his innermost thoughts to Greta! He saw himself with his beloved wife in a cheap flat over the Columbus Avenue El—but together! the thoughts and fears of each open to the other. How good it would have been! Half aloud, he spoke the words of Goethe:

> Es wär' so schön gewesen,
> Es hat nicht sollen sein . . .

Eighth Avenue was booming: apartments flanked the one that stood alone when Evan lived there (—What is Evan thinking? is he at least aware that, thanks to his father, no legal action was taken against him and the scandal soon quashed even from the yellow press? I want to tell him. It's worse, this not knowing where he is, than if he were dead); a great hotel, handsome five-story dwellings, were

226

crowding out the squatters' shanties and their goats. He thought of Frieda. Why was that guilty embrace, long, long ago, a comfort even now? as if his giving in to his weakness had brought him strength. On a vacant lot between two new houses, a billboard announced the revival of *Shenandoah*. Jonathan's heart recalled. . . .

The evening two years ago of his decision about Evan, Greta and he had gone to *Shenandoah*. At dinner, he said nothing. Silent, they rode downtown on the El to Fourteenth Street; walked east to the Star Theater. They sat through the first act:

. . . Greta's childhood Charleston, the gracious room and verandah, lights from the city and the distant harbor, soldiers and lovely ladies waiting for the shot on Fort Sumter that would begin "the irrepressible conflict," all strangely mingled with *his* waiting beside Greta: his own "war" with the war on the stage. The shot came; Southern and Northern characters stiffened for the struggle that divided while love bound them. . . . Curtain.

"I've sent my report to the Committee," he fired his own shot—quietly, not looking at his wife, while the applause died, men stood up, put on their tall hats, and the ladies began to chatter.

Greta said nothing. He heard her breathe, he dared not look at her. And the silk-hatted men returned, the darkening house quenched the murmur of the ladies, the curtain rose again. Cannon offstage grew louder, soldiers' words were passionate: he heard the sobs of Greta. He wanted to touch her hand in the dark, she might sob louder, and he did not dare. For a moment's intermission between scenes the curtain went down, but the theater remained dark and he was thankful. Now the battle before them! Dusty bloody soldiers blue and gray, drawn swords, smoking guns, men wounded, men dead. When the curtain fell and the lights kindled, Greta sat beside him infinitely distant. He was afraid to speak lest the sobs in her bosom rise again to her mouth. He should have said nothing; having waited so long (the dinner, the long ride downtown) why not have waited a little longer? But even if they were now alone, what was there to say? Because there was nothing to explain, had he spoken in the crowded theater? Its pasteboard war seemed no more frivolous and unreal than what he had done to his wife, to his friend, to himself. —Oh, Greta, Greta! understand and *love* what I needed to do! The curtain rises on

227

the last act, the War is over, and here they all are . . . all the principals, alive and in clean clothes. None of them maimed, none of them dead; only the minor actors were paid to bind their false fatal wounds, paint their false bandages red, die their false deaths. Here is a sunny room in Washington: skies blue, the storm has passed and freshened the green lawn. One by one, the enemies of the early acts come in, graceful, clean and smiling: two by two, the Southern and Northern lovers embrace to live "happily ever after." Jonathan took his wife's arm, and led her to the street. It had snowed and sleet was falling, the street was full of slush, they could find no cab. They had had to ride back on the El; wet and bedraggled, they had stood in the hall of their home and faced each other, the cruel exposure of their bedroom before them. . . .

Now, walking home through another winter's night, Jonathan thought: —I despised the play's "happy ending" that wiped out the blood and horror and death of the Civil War. The "happy ending," I was sure, lied. Was I wrong? *Isadore was really in my office!* New York quickly forgets! The city of hope! Wealth and even power are in my hands again—the happy ending!

After that night at the play two years ago, Greta never spoke of what he had done; only by allusion did he learn that she never understood; and she "accepted," being the dutiful wife, as doubtless she would "accept" if he were sick or bankrupt or disbarred . . . or successful! It would make no difference between them, because she had never spoken, because she had never understood, above all because she "accepted." For a week, now, after Isadore's offer, Jonathan went about his business . . . home to office, office to home . . . suspended in an abyss. Greta did not notice. Jonathan was amazed to find that he was not really thinking out the problem of his decision (he did not call Isadore for their lunch engagement). He knew all the answers; they all were for acceptance; and they were all irrelevant, incompetent, immaterial. On the night of the seventh day, Jonathan sat alone at his library table. Greta had gone to the Opera with Reuben's wife (she had given up her own season tickets); his mother and Lucia were at Reuben's; Philip as usual was out and Jeff was sound asleep. Jonathan drew a piece of writing paper toward him, his eyes distant. Like a medium whose hand clumsily follows the pressure of a "spirit," he wrote to

228

Samson Isadore, declining the partnership. He read his note, it sounded stilted and abrupt; without revision he sealed it.

All the next day and the next, he carried it with him. A little before closing time, he sent his office boy to deliver it by hand.

That was yesterday. Here again was Samson Isadore, smiling toward him, his hand outstretched . . .

Isadore sat down in the same chair, quite at home; unbuttoned his hermetic coat, drew forth a leather cigar case, selected his *perfecto,* ran it along his nose. "You don't smoke? You don't know what you miss." With the gold cutter at the end of his gold chain, he groomed the cigar; from a small gold box he took a wax vesta and got the savory tobacco evenly alight. All this time, he kept his lush eyes on the bearded man at his desk whose 'hair, unlike Isadore's, was already thin at the crown.

"Jonathan," he said, "you know me too well to misunderstand this visit. We can get along without you."

"The boot's on the other foot," Jonathan smiled.

"This is a friend's visit. I really would like to know how the devil you could decide as you have."

"If you suspect I've better prospects somewhere else, or just as good, you're mistaken."

"Is that the truth? Well, frankly, I'm damned if I see."

"That's about how *I* feel."

"You want to grow, don't you?"

"There's the rub. What does it mean to 'grow'?"

"Don't split hairs. . . . Perhaps I left some misunderstanding—"

"I took your offer exactly as you made it. You're not confidence men. And I could do the work."

"None better."

"I'm grateful for your saying that."

"You won't grow on gratitude."

"Sam, I can't bind myself, that's all. I've got to be free to go ahead any way I need to."

"There's only one way to go ahead in this country, and that's to fall in with the forces that are going ahead."

"There are many forces; not all of them are right. They conflict."

"I'm not urging you to reconsider. You've given your answer, it's on Romney's desk and I assure you he's not tearing his hair. My partners didn't send me."

"Call it freedom, Sam. I've got a miscellaneous practice that leaves me free."

"For what?"

Jonathan considered. "I couldn't tell you. Don't we have to *become* free to learn for what?"

"Don't talk like a philosopher or a Socialist."

"I'm no Socialist, Sam. I believe in our system of private enterprise and in the Constitution. Maybe your railroads are the Socialists and don't know it."

"We're developing the country; we're growing with it. Call us anything you like, *that's* the future."

"I don't see it so clearly."

"When do you think you will, Jonathan?"

Jonathan's smile was wistful. "Probably too late to do anything about it."

Isadore nodded. Pessimism and resignation were, to him, a sort of disease, fortunately not contagious. Jonathan Hartt was simply not well; but he'd get over it: he *was* one of the best lawyers in the city.

"These last days, while I was debating my decision with myself—"

"Only with yourself?" Jonathan caught Isadore's shock of surprise. "Why didn't you talk it over with your brother?"

"*We* know what Reuben would say."

"Reuben Hartt's a big man, Jonathan. If the Republicans win in '92, he's in line for something fat."

Jonathan felt his temper rising. No matter what he did, what he said, what he refused, could he not pierce this man's placid assumption that they and their values were alike? —Why does it anger me? *because it's true?* A sudden sadness softened him into the need of self-bestowal.

"Sam," he looked him straight in the eyes, "you say you came here to understand why I refused your offer, probably the best chance I'll ever get in my whole life; and you keep talking about my brother. Don't you see that if I gave a damn for his advice, I'd have said Yes to you without needing to consult him?"

"I see, old fellow. I think I do, anyway. You love your 'freedom' best. Your work in our office would be specialized, of course."

"These days, while I was mulling the matter, going over the pros and cons—the pros had it by a landslide;" Jonathan smiled, "all there was against them was a memory that kept recurring. Where were you, Sam, in the summer of '63?"

"That's a long way back . . . '63? Why, I suppose I was in New York. My folks didn't have money to take us to the country."

"And now you live in a country estate of your own, big as four square city blocks."

"That's what America means, Jonathan."

"Where were you living?"

"In '63? Why—Saint Mark's Place."

"Not far from me, east of Stuyvesant Square!"

"We probably bumped into each other more than once. Did you ever play on Tompkins Square?"

"That July, Sam, do you recall it?"

"Not particularly."

"The Draft Riots?"

"We were kids!"

"I was out in the trouble, and so was Evan Cleeve. That's where we met. Evan got hurt, and I took him to my house. . . . The memory that keeps coming back from all I saw, nothing but a boy: buildings in flames, men shot and hanging from lampposts—the memory, *all* the memory, is of a kind of hope. There was a hope rising in the city. It was mine, and I loved it."

Isadore was waiting for the point of the queer tale.

"Well?" he said at last.

"I guess that's all," Jonathan kept on smiling. . . .

He came home late; the talk had depressed him. It would have been wiser, since he *had* to refuse (why did he have to?), to leave Isadore with his suspicion that Jonathan had better prospects elsewhere. Now, in Isadore's flat mind, Jonathan was a fool . . . or obliquely trying to insult him . . . or, worst of all, inscrutable. He'd resent that; he might even become an enemy. . . . Jeff did not come down to make his daily report. One look at Greta, following him up the stairs to their bedroom, told him there had been trouble again at home.

231

"I had to put Jeff to bed. Mama Hartt made a terrible scene; and on my day at home! The ladies heard it! The boy put some things from the kitchen in his school bag."

"Why did he have to do that?"

Greta flared. "I don't know. And what's the difference? He could have eaten them downstairs; he could have asked for them; well, he wanted them that way. Does that make him a thief?"

Jonathan smiled. "Technically, perhaps."

"Well, that's what your mother called him. And a child doesn't know what 'technically' means. Neither do I."

"Greta!"

"I can't bear it, Jonathan." The tears came. "I do the best I can. I can't bear it."

Sarah came into the room and kissed her son. "I did what I thought was my duty. If your son's mother doesn't approve, that's her right. *She* is the mother. Only, I cannot change. I'm too old to start pampering a child when he does something vicious."

"He's not vicious!" cried Greta.

"I didn't say he was vicious. Stealing food *is* vicious. If it becomes a habit, the child who grows such habits—"

"Weren't you ever a child?"

"What I was going to say, my dear," old Mrs. Hartt ignored her, "—if I must change my lifelong convictions not to offend your wife who is the rightful mistress in this house, I had better leave."

"Mama!"

"You know how long Reuben has been wanting me. Perhaps it will be better. I'm only a strain here on your wife. And a drain on you."

"Please, mama."

"Reuben can afford to have me better than you. What good am I in this house?"

"I won't hear of it."

"Yes, you will!" Greta stood by the bed, supporting herself by both arms on the footboard, as if she were too weak to stand. "She says it to insult me. You'll hear it, and you'll hear it."

Abrupt as she had entered, Sarah left the room. And more deeply hurting than the pain of the scene, Jonathan knew that he feared being alone with his wife.

232

"I'll go up to the boy." Jonathan groped through a mist for the red volume plainly before him on the table. It was *Shakespeare for Young Readers,* and he had brought it down the day before to read ahead and to judge if the text was adequate for his son.

"Don't speak of what happened," said Greta; and Jonathan was aware that she was aware of her son's trouble—not at all of his.

Little Jeff in bed had heard his mother's song rise glowing through the house. The house so full of stern faces, stern orders, grandma's, aunt Lucia's, papa's: "Be good! Work hard!" even mama's: "Don't spill your milk! Don't put your feet on the sofa!" . . . but when mama sang, the house was transfigured: he was safe in his room, the gaslight warmly breathing; his room was safe in the world, the terrible outside world, he was now safe and muffled in the rumble of the El, the rattle of a wagon. He fell asleep in his mother's song; he waked in her bringing him his supper on a tray.

When his father opened the door, Jeff was glad. Papa was strict, but not now. When you were sick, papa was strong and quiet, he made you feel safe like mama singing.

Tenderly Jonathan took his boy's hand, leaned down and kissed him (his beard smelling of the world) and sat beside him.

"Feeling bad?"

"I'm all right, papa." He wasn't really sick and he knew it. He wished he was, but he wasn't.

"That's good."

The boy lay silent, gazing at his father. Maybe he was . . . just a little . . . feeling sick.

"Did mama give you enough for supper?"

"I had left-overs!"

"Lucky boy."

"Won't you have any left-overs?"

"You have to be a privileged character for that." —Better not read to him tonight. He might feel he must say yes, if I ask him. Jonathan placed the red book on the floor (they were half through the abridged *Merchant of Venice*).

Jonathan held his son's hand within the quiet rhythmic pressure holding his own hand. Jefferson closed his eyes. If papa was best when he was sick, why not be sick always? Then you couldn't play games, you couldn't swim and have ice cream and candy. Better be well. Then everyone was strict. Bother! Jonathan's mind rankled back to what he had said to 'Samson Isadore. Why had he suddenly spoken to Isadore of *hope?* He·looked at his son. Nothing in his well-planned life had come out as he hoped; not his career of public service, not his friendship and partnership with Evan, not his marriage. Something somewhere along the years had gone wrong. He remembered the last silent word of his father: what had it been but hope? His father had never known him; his father had had faith, his mother had had will; the two, faith and will, were not enough, were no substitute for knowledge. —I must know my son. Jonathan knew his hope, articulate and breathing, in this body of his boy soothed toward sleep. He held his hand; from that fragile contact his son's life went like a parabola beyond him. To grasp at it crudely would be to crush . . . or lose it. His own father prayed; he did not believe in prayer; something like prayer would be good. This truth he touched with his hand, holding in gentleness his son's hand, touching his son's life on its mysterious orbit beyond him—yet his own! as their hands were together: was prayer, for them who could believe in it, like this? a humble hand upon an unknown Hand? Too poetic. Hell is paved with metaphors. —Know your son! What do I know of him? . . . only my own hope?

2

THE HILLS' DANCE WITH THE OHIO RIVER DREW
them south, then west, then north by east, finally south again where
the waters spread wide and slower. It was the day of Mrs. Liebling's
picnic, the same day each May and always sunny. Evan asked: "Suppose it rains?" "It never does," she answered. "It can rain on the
Fourth of July, but it canna rain on my picnic." "That sounds like a
blasphemous boast." "God gets bored with solemn prayer. The Lord
likes you to get fresh wi' Him." "How do you know?" "Look at those
hills. Naethin' solemn aboot them."

They had just arrived at the old farmhouse five miles from town,
high up, nearer sky than river. Evan's eyes followed the fields flaunting
their wild flowers; saw the copse of dogwood a-bloom as if there were
no such threat as frost, the little companies of aspen and birch chattering in the breeze and, far below, the sumptuous girdling willows.

"Maybe you're right. The land's fresh—"

"—and no' afraid."

Across the water, a hill leaped with a cloud on its head.

Tam superintended the unloading of the hampers from the surreys,
with Mrs. Goldberg, Madame Dolores and Rachel Lorne to help, while
Evan and Mrs. Liebling talked, and the Count and Herr Marks laid
themselves out on the grass to start their daily battle.

"Why don't we eat outside?" Evan asked Jacob who, like the leading
actor in a play, awaited his cue as cook (the cook had a day off).

"You can if you wish. But good food needs a stove and *concentration*. If you like, *you* can take a chop in your hand and go swimming."

Jacob disappeared with Tam into the house. The Count took off
his coat, collar, and shoes, and lay with the grass as if he loved it;
Herr Marks, his jacket buttoned, the band of his straw hat already
showing sweat, hunted four-leaf clovers.

Evan watched a crane far below trace an arabesque of white on the
blue-brown waters. "You're a pagan," he said.

"The Lord loves me," answered Mrs. Liebling.

"I take it back. You're a Calvinist sure of Grace."

"You wi' your big words! Why do ye ha' to plaster 'em all over the landscape?"

"Defect of a faulty education."

"It's safer no' to ha' any, surely!" As she smiled on Evan, he lost the sense of boundary between her blond flesh and the air, the susurrant grass, the apple tree blossoming behind her. "But *you*'re comin' through."

"What does that mean, sibyl?"

"I dinna ken wha' sibyl means; but don't you r-realize how well all's gone wi' ye since Tam brought ye to the hoose?"

"I do! What I don't know is what it means."

"Dinna ask!"

"You're right."

"Just take—and ho'd onto 't."

"Asking questions is an old habit."

"One way only to ho'd on to a loved thing: love it!"

"You're wiser than the sibyls. Answering questions was their stock-in-trade."

"You ken too much and too little, Mr. Evan. You throw what you ken at what you ha', like stones to kill."

"Perhaps what I have is not what I am."

"Questions answered never told a sad man what he is."

They both saw Rachel Lorne come toward them from the house with two different-shaped glasses and sandwiches on a tray.

"Like honey to a bee," Mrs. Liebling continued, "is sadness in a man's eyes to a woman."

"I don't know what you mean."

"Thanks be to ye, Rachel dear." She took her tumbler of whiskey and water.

"Why didn't you bring a glass for yourself?" Evan tasted his dry chablis.

"Thee knows I don't drink alcohol, Mr. Corthuis."

"You serve it."

"I don't object to others' drinking it in moderation," she smiled her motherly smile.

"Broadminded Quakeress!"

"Lucky for you," laughed Mrs. Liebling, "or we'd ha' you drinking lemonade."

"It wouldn't hurt him."

"Ah, but it would!" laughed Evan. "Anything weaker than wine makes me weak. You're strong, Rachel; you don't need strong drink."

"Thee could be strong!" said the young woman.

"I'm going to ha' a wee sleep in the grass," Mrs. Liebling moved off. "I got up air-r-ly; terrible air-r-ly."

Tam went to the horses tethered in the shade of the trees, and gave them their nosebags of oats. Madame Dolores and Mrs. Goldberg talking with Herr Marks and the Count made, below Evan and Rachel Lorne on the hill's brim with sky above them, a music apart: soft, sinuous, hard, explosive.

Evan said: "You follow me around like a Fury."

"Yes."

"I wish you'd leave me alone."

"The Furies were only the Greek idea of conscience."

"Is that what you teach your children?"

"Yes."

"Magnificent! The Quaker schoolmarm from Ohio converting the Athenians."

"Saint Paul tried it. All Christians must humbly imitate—"

"The Furies had no connection with your sickly Christian conscience. They stood for natural force, far deeper, beyond morals—"

"Thee are more learned than I."

"If your Paul had got to Athens five centuries earlier, and had converted them, there'd have been no Greek tragedy, no Greek philosophy, no mathematics. You wouldn't have cared?"

"If they were Christians, of course not!"

"I'll buy you a ticket to Greece."

"They're Christians, now."

"Ah, but not Quakers! Not *pure* Christians."

"There is plenty for me to do here."

"Seriously," he turned toward her, "if I buy you a ticket will you go to Athens?"

"It's much more expensive than thee knows. Thy salary on the orchestra, even with the private lessons—"

237

"I can afford it. Anything to be rid of you."

"Thee may have other expenses in the future."

Evan drained his glass. "You drive me to strong drink. I need some whiskey."

"Will thee stay here till I bring it?"

The black hair molding her large head and curling upward heavily at the shoulders, the white skin in the gray frock, the seethed red mouth, the height of her breasts, were a vortex that drew him. He needed to embrace and to crush her. He thought angrily of Mrs. Simeon Law to whom he gave lessons and with whom he went to bed: why did she not satisfy—and defend him? of Colonel Dalton's sixteen-year-old daughter who tempted him; she was only a child, it would never do, it would be safer than this.

"Will you bring me a tumblerful?"

"Half a glass. On condition—"

"That I wait here?"

"Yes."

"You're a shrewd bargainer."

The others twenty yards away: why did he not join them? He knew they would leave him alone; it was best, they had learned, to leave the advances to him. Rachel Lorne came back with his drink.

"You're generous," he said. "The glass is more than half full."

"Thee needn't drink it all."

"For God's sake, must you say 'thee'? Can't you talk like other Americans?"

"It's the way my mother and father spoke."

"It drives me to drink."

"That's not true, Mr. Corthuis."

"Well, that's the reason at the moment. Before you, I admit, there were other reasons."

She looked up at him with her quiet gaze that was neither submissive nor assertive. He thought of his mother: had she driven him to drink? He poured the whiskey on the ground; then he was angry.

"Listen, little Miss Lorne, you're a born schoolmarm. You're at home with children because you can exert your will on them. Perhaps it's a good will, I'm not sure: good anyway according to your conventional ideas; but it's *will*. You're the sort of mild unconscious tyrant who

238

can be happy only lording it over inferiors. Children are your best meat; their inferiority is veiled by nice words like helping them to grow. What I can't stand is your turning me into a child. I'm sick of it. Even your 'thee' is a badge of saintly condescension."

Her gaze in his eyes was steadfast; only her mouth revealed the faintest tremor. He saw that her mouth was beautiful.

"I don't know where you come from," he plunged on. "Probably from some community of boors who couldn't hold their liquor. Probably you don't know there are countries where wine is as common as bread and no one is ever drunk."

"Yes!" She was eager and grateful, as if he were giving her a history lesson. "France, Italy, Spain—don't they drink wine as part of their meals? Sometimes the Bible—"

"Well?"

"That's not thee, Mr. Corthuis."

The victory again was hers; he had not even hurt her.

She took the glass from him. "Shall I bring thee more?"

"Good God! aren't you glad I didn't drink it?"

"Not that way, of course."

She was gone again; again Evan waited, knowing he could join the others. She came back with a glass more than half full.

She said: "I've been thinking about 'thee'—I mean the *word* 'thee,'" she blushed. "Perhaps thee are right. It is a badge of pride. Be ye separate, Saint Paul said; but our Lord warned against show even in our prayers ... I shall learn to say 'you.'" There were tears in her eyes.

Evan took the glass and drained it. Then he looked at her mouth. He led her by the hand down the other slope, out of sight of the group on the lawn. He clasped her shoulders harshly, and pressed his mouth, moist with the liquor, on her mouth. Then he thrust her at arm's length and looked at her: nothing in her had changed, not spirit, not body. He wiped his lips dry and took her in his arms. Still she did not resist, still she did not respond....

"Dinner!" tolled Jacob's voice. He had not kissed her again and there had been no words; they walked up the slope together, and down toward the company. Evan found that he felt well ... and hungry.

The others were already at the long pine table, assaulting the baked

239

jelled ham armored in cloves, the roast beef crusted brown and red inside, the bowls of asparagus and peas, the earthen jugs, beaded with moisture, of milk and beer. Before Mrs. Liebling was her inveterate tumbler of whiskey and water; beside her sat Mrs. Goldberg, the dark little lady, hot and vibrant as a bird, in whose peaked features Mrs. Liebling saw beauty. Next to Madame Dolores in flowered taffeta that made her look like the bad fairy masquerading as a girl, sat the indifferent Count; Herr Marks had his bulbous nose in a mug of beer; Tam carved; Jacob hovered in with deep-dish rhubarb pies. Through the open windows, the cool southeast breeze brought dusk.

"I cried all the way through," said Mrs. Goldberg. "Even when I was laughing at that Dick Swiveller, I cried."

"Dickens is wonderful," Herr Marks announced.

The Count said: "Children are all savages. There never was a child so impossibly good as Little Nell."

"And the villains?" asked Evan. "Quilp, and brother and sister Brass: are they impossibly bad?"

"That's not the same," the Count snickered.

"He painted a true picture of England," said Herr Marks, "—after the industrial revolution."

"You've got him all wrong," said Evan. "As a reporter and historian, Dickens was a liar."

"You just can't stop," Mrs. Goldberg shook her head. "Every chapter just *throws* you into the next."

Evan went on answering Herr Marks: "Dickens is good, because his poetry came right out of an old Merrie England living on farms, that danced around barbaric maypoles and drank strong ale for breakfast. His mind knew the sordid towns; stunted children in factories, respectable misers smelting gold from the sweat and blood of slaves; but what he really *saw* was the dance and song of Merrie England. Don't let Dickens fool you. His characters are as fantastic as those in *The Tempest*. Caliban becomes Quilp with an office on the Thames, Ariel becomes a potboy with a noble widowed mother, Miranda is Little Nell. The realities of industrial England—the dirt, the poverty, the injustice? mere stage effects like the tempest."

"Then," said Herr Marks, "you don't take his social conscience seriously?"

Evan laughed, feeling Rachel Lorne's eyes on him. "Just as seriously as the rich bourgeois who felt noble when they'd said a prayer on Sunday, and put a pound in the poor box."

"That's not serious! That's frivolous," protested Herr Marks.

"Dickens was frivolous, Dickens was false," said Evan; "only it's all forgiven, because Dickens was a poet."

The Count raised his glass. "It's the miracle of the ages: how England always has poets."

"Self-defence," laughed Evan. "They generate poets, the way the blood of a sick man generates phagocytes against germs."

"Will you talk," Mrs. Liebling scolded, "so a body can understand?"

"Anti-bodies against dullness, that's what the Dickens characters are: as fantastic as the elves and fairies in *Midsummer Night's Dream*. Only he dressed 'em up in modern English clothes, gave 'em umbrellas like Mrs. Gamp's, had 'em drive a hackney coach like Mr. Weller—so Herr Marks wouldn't protest."

"I've never had the time to read Dickens," said Mrs. Liebling. "His books are too long. If I canna read a story all the way through after I go to bed, I forget what it's all aboot. But Mr. Evan, you're talkin' nonsense, I know! Is real life no' the real fairy story?"

Jacob put on his coat and took the chair between Evan and Rachel, who poured him milk from the jug. The room suddenly was silent. . . . They heard Jacob swallowing his milk, they heard through the south windows a quick gathering of birds in the trees and a riverboat hollowly calling round the bend. Through Jacob who barred his view of her, Evan was aware of Rachel as if Jacob's body magnified some subtle sense. Mrs. Liebling at her end of the table loomed over Herr Marks at the other, tilting the board like a boat. They sailed through time and twilight; the side where Evan, Jacob, Rachel and Mrs. Goldberg sat, outbalancing the other. Within the instantaneous exposure of the silence, each man and woman was an apparition; flesh was transparent, a revealing hunger not animal, not spirit. Madame Dolores felt herself darkness dressed up in a bright frock, the Count felt the ancient plowed soil of his Sicily more present than his years of attitudes and fornications, Herr Marks stared at the joys he never had, the sole security, and at his logic of revolution, its brittle surrogate, Tam knew himself a flute hollowly filled with other people's breathing,

241

Jacob was his food and milk merging with his body to make a harmony causeless and reasonless and in love with itself, Rachel was root in earth seeking sun, and Mrs. Liebling was sun immense and never waning. "An angel's flying through the room," she laughed; again they talked, their nakedness was covered.

Except with Evan, who felt his emptiness and that it could not last. Emptiness was want of pain, emptiness longed toward pain that would fulfill and destroy it. Across Mrs. Goldberg, Evan reached his hand toward Mrs. Liebling who clasped it and smiled toward Rachel. Evan felt doom. He needed to see the sun before it set, as if it would never again rise. Stark-shadowed against low sun, he saw his mother and father and Jonathan; then he saw himself get up from the table. "I'm going for a bit of a walk," he said. "To see the sun set." On the lawn he waited a moment and Rachel joined him.

They followed the brow of the hill westward to where they saw the river turning south again. Here the sun was still high; and they watched in silence the green earth foam into purple forest, subside to mist that fused it with cloud on the horizon. They stopped and Evan had the sense of tilting vastly downward. Near him, in a small wild cherry tree, a horde of caterpillars swarmed, ready to devour the tender blooms. And near him Rachel stood, part of the far, part of the near. . . .

"What do you want?" he said.

Rachel kept silent.

"You followed me. I didn't ask you."

After a long pause: "Does thee—do *you* want I should go back?"

"No."

Between each response, there was silence and it seemed the silence that spoke; their words were an echo of their silences, talking long, far away.

"Let me stay," she said.

"What do you want?"

"Let me stay."

The pause grew even longer, an echo from always farther.

"Do you know what you say?"

At last: "Let me love thee, Evan."

They did not see each other; they looked toward the sun falling and seething, the earth rising to sun in mist.

"I don't want you to love me."

She was silent.

"If you love, you expect love. I have no love for anyone."

"I ask," came her slow words, "only what I said: Let me love thee, Evan."

"Whom do you love? Do you even know that?"

"I need to love thee."

"You don't even know my name." He turned half toward her, and she was smiling. "You don't know my past, a damned hurtful past. You don't know me."

"Yes," came her echo at last.

"You're a fool," he said.

"No," she answered quickly.

"What do you want?" he said again.

Her body near him was a blessing; he did not believe in it, but there it was. The loathsome caterpillars swarmed, ready to swarm the leaves and blossoms. He believed in the caterpillars, he knew her body was a blessing.

They stood while the sun more swiftly fell in its own fume. Cloud suddenly obscured it, an immense shadow raced across the land like a shudder and Evan's struggle turned to fright. His hand touched Rachel's hand and clasped it. She withdrew her hand, and he was cold; she put her arms, warm as sleep, around him.

JEFFERSON WALKED SLOWLY. HE LIKED THE PARK, this October afternoon, and he did not like where he was going. He liked the wind, somehow white and watery, the leaves that were scuttling copper wheels across the grass, he liked the rocks that were breakers of the wind, and the trees that cast off their garments to dance with the wind. He had shot up to be a tall lad for his slender fourteen years, already as tall as his father; his tweed cap did not hide his blond hair, its peak shading his eyes brought out their blue from the gray. He dawdled, opening his jacket. A little of Grandma Hartt was a lot, these weekly duty calls were a pain in the neck, there was nothing to say: a rigmarole of questions always the same. The Park was fun. A squirrel trilling up a tree reminded him of peanuts: winter was coming, and the wonderful little beasts, he knew, buried the food in a hundred secret places that they never forgot. (It waved its tail as it now climbed downward like a flag.) At the lake, he bought a bag of peanuts for a nickel; he ate one, a little ashamed—they were the squirrels' winter food! He crossed the pretty bridge into the rocks and cavern-region of the Brambles. He stopped, held a peanut in his palm, showing it to the beast who came forward, all vibrance, darted back, forward again, its tail a feathery flag. He felt the little feet grip his stocking, clamber to his sleeve, whisk the nut and flash away. A man was at his side, he was a big fat man with a full-moon face all bright with smiling. Then Jefferson recognized the button on the man's lapel: a large silver disc of the face of William Jennings Bryan! He was a man who was going to vote for Bryan! If Bryan was elected, Jefferson knew, they would all be disgraced, money wouldn't buy peanuts, factories would close, grass would grow on Fifth Avenue and Broadway. Yet the man was a nice man, smiling because Jeff knew how to make the squirrels climb into his hand. He must be a wicked man to be for Bryan. Jeff went forward scowling. How could it be? a bad man with a nice face who was kind and liked squirrels? He turned back to see. The Bryan monster was walking quickly toward the path

244

on the hill where a young woman ran down the stone steps toward
him. She had her arms out, and so did he: they embraced. Jeff saw his
derby hat tilt her hat upward; he fixed her hat, she fixed his hat, and
they were laughing. But Bryan was a—what was it?—a demagogue!
Bryan was a thief who wanted to steal from everyone who wore a
clean shirt and give it to loafers in dirty shirts. If Bryan became President— The man had his arm about the woman's waist, and they were
walking away. He had a nice broad back, and his hat was a little on
the side of his head like a funny man in a vaudeville show at Proctor's.
His hair curved on his reddish neck like a saucer.

Uncle Reuben's where grandma lived was almost straight across the
Park from home. As you came to it, you could see Park Avenue; if
you passed it, you saw the green plot with an opening for the tunnel.
Jeff was late but he went past uncle Reuben's house. Each block up
and down Park Avenue had a green plot and an opening. Far downtown, a jet of smoke rose; he waited; now the smoke was a block
nearer! Goody! the train was coming uptown. He watched the smoke
leap upward, block by block. Now it was where he stood, now it was
rolling away . . . uptown . . . farther away: the wonderful train. It
would come out of the ground at One-hundred-twenty-fifth Street; it
would cross the river; it would speed across the country, all across the
land that was going to be disgraced if Bryan—if that nice man with a
full-moon face and a saucer haircut, who loved his pretty wife and
who laughed—

Uncle Reuben's butler opened the door. Even the door was different
from at home where it was wood with red satin over the glass panel,
here it was all glass and iron with frilly creamy silk to cover it. Inside
was a Chinese rug and Japanese shields of bronze dragons on the
wall and big blue vases on the stairs. You had to be careful not to
touch anything: everything at uncle Reuben's was worth millions and
millions of dollars. The steps were hard shiny wood. On the first floor
the electric lights in ornate globes; and on the second floor grandma's
room. That was another world, with the same gloomy furniture she
had had at home·before she went to live with uncle Reuben. You had
to kiss grandma's cheek, although it smelled of soap and wool. She
was a very old lady in a rocking chair, with a gray shawl on her sharp
shoulders; and she always asked the same rigmarole questions. Today,

mama had told him papa would be there to take him home. That was something. . . .

As often as he could, at least once a week, Jonathan went to see his mother straight from his office, taking the Third Avenue El. As he climbed the stairs today, Reuben called him from the sitting room.

"Hello, Jon."

"Hello, Reuben."

"Have a seat. Mama can wait; your boy's with her."

Jonathan felt the room, his brother's glory: spoil of his two visits to the Orient which had made him in Washington and New York an authority on China. The tables, the bric-a-brac, the vases, the rugs, the chairs, were Chinese or Japanese; silk portraits of Chinese worthies hung on the silk walls. The room shrilled like an aviary with a different voice in each of a hundred cages; but the owner (who knew the period and value of each curio—always more than it had cost him) drew the cacophony together. Reuben, at fifty-three, was a handsome man. His hair lay smooth, parted in the middle, above a bland face. His body was slim in its white vest and corded velvet housecoat and striped trousers. On the right hand an ostentatious seal ring touched off the clever quiet of his fingers; the left hand poised a cigar.

"Can I offer you a glass of sherry?"

"Gladly."

"You look tired, Jon."

"It's not the crowds on the El, it's the bad air."

"I know."

"Our traction systems are a disgrace."

"What isn't?" Reuben smiled.

"You'd think Hugh Grant, not our own William Strong, was Mayor."

Reuben kept on smiling. "You forget: Croker's always the boss."

"I know," said Jonathan. "I've learned that lesson long ago."

"You have, and *I* know it. I can't tell you, old man, how gratified I am that you've bolted the Democrats and are for McKinley."

"That's not quite the way to put it. I'm not *for* McKinley; I'm *against* Bryan. A vote for McKinley is simply the sure way to beat Bryan."

"Put it any way you like."

"It looks bad, though."

Reuben smiled more broadly. "I saw Mark Hanna last week. We have nearly four million dollars in national headquarters here, and in Chicago. Four million dollars," he rolled them on his tongue, "can do a lot of persuading."

"How about the tens of thousands of miles Bryan is talking through the country?"

"I'm confident."

"Of the good sense of the people?"

"Of their instincts. They see what money wants; they trust the money. They know where money is, the brains are."

"It's an astounding business, this thirty-six year old madman appealing to all the dissatisfactions in the country."

"The country's sound, Jonathan. Don't judge it by New York."

"The farmers aren't sound or they wouldn't listen to a hawker of patent medicines. They're broke."

"We have to expect a crisis of this kind, every ten years or so. One time it's financial; then it's political. Hanna is confident. And Mark Hanna's a *man*."

"Mark Hanna's a coal mine, an iron mine, a railroad, a shipyard, a bank, a newspaper—and an opera house thrown in for good measure."

"Then Hanna's the U.S.A. That's even better."

"And McKinley, what is he? You saw him in Ohio?"

"I had a talk with him; I had ten minutes with McKinley, alone . . . Jonathan, I'm going to let you in on a secret. Absolutely in confidence. Your brother's slated for Minister to China!"

"That's a great honor, Reuben," Jonathan said at last.

"Yes, Jonathan, it is."

"You've earned it."

"Well, I wouldn't say that. But I've paid for it."

"You've never been afraid to pay."

"You have, Jonathan. That's been your trouble. You wanted—what we all want. When it came to paying the price, you always expected it as a gift. From the gods. You've never learned to pay."

"I guess you're right."

"Lucy mustn't know! Can't tell such things to a woman. But she'll be happy in the Orient. She loved China."

"Have you told mama?"

"I couldn't resist. But that's different. Mama can keep a secret."

"She must be glad."

"She's proud."

"Well, if McKinley wins—my congratulations."

"Thank you, Jon."

The brothers looked at each other, the years of their divergent wills immense between them. Jonathan thought: —*This* is the price I'm paying. To save the country from an illiterate demagogue, I must support privilege, patronage, money. Reuben thought: —Life is good.

As Jonathan got up, Reuben, still seated: "Not a word to a soul, remember! You know the sanctity of political commitments."

"Yes, commitments to campaign contributions are sacred. Not promises to the people."

Reuben got up. "We'll take care of the people."

"By the way, there are a lot of people in China."

"I suppose so," Reuben went on smiling, and stroked the delicate blue vase on the table.

. . . Jonathan stood with his son on the dark street, the lamplights fluctuating in the wind; under the glow of Reuben's door he took his watch from his pocket, snapped it open. "Should we walk home? There's time. Mama won't worry, she knows I'm with you."

Jonathan walked slowly against the wind blowing cold, strewing the iron sky with shreds of cloud and stars. He did not want to go home. He was glad to leave his brother's house, he did not want to go home. Before his mother, while they talked of this and that, he had felt guilt. When she said: "The campaign is going better? There's no danger, is there, son?" he had felt her exultance; her cool excited eyes probing him like steel to learn if he knew Reuben's secret. He had agreed reluctantly to let her live with Reuben; Greta and Lucia were both more at ease without her; but it hurt, another defeat, to let his mother leave; *he* had always been the favorite, the family provider. —Am I envious of Reuben? of Reuben's house? He had contempt for them both. Reuben, for whom his father had no blessing; Reuben, whose first deal in New York real estate had meant a fraud on their old servant: now United States Minister to China! It was grotesque as his house of misplaced curios. . . . While he went on with his humdrum law: all about somebody's profit, somebody's loss, somebody's hope of profit, somebody's fear of loss. The honorable profession of the law. "You are all servants of justice," he heard the valedictory words at law school. In certain slave societies, the masters often could not read: their slaves did the figuring and the writing. That was the lawyer's true status in America! And Reuben the chosen one for public service! Six years ago, he had refused Samson Isadore's offer. No, it was not envy clamping his heart: it was the iron, the irony of knowledge.

"You're hurting my arm, papa."

"I'm sorry, my boy."

They were in the Park. The irony went deeper. He had married for love; something, long ago, had gone wrong with him and Greta. Reuben too had married for love. But Jonathan knew love would not have counted, if Lucy Sleip had not had a rich promoter for a father; not brought with her sweet body a certain capital. . . . Yet Reuben and Lucy were the happy ones! the harmonious home was theirs! —Are you quite sure it's not envy?

"Can't we walk a little faster, papa?"

"I'm sorry, my boy. Are you cold? That's a light jacket."

"It was warm."

"You never can tell in October. A wind from the west and north, where the land's already cold, can bring frost; a wind from the east, from the warm sea, brings days like summer."

"Yes, papa."

"You set the pace."

"Papa, what sort of people are for Bryan?"

"Many kinds."

"Are they all bad?"

"Oh, no."

Jeff walked silent a long moment. "But you said Bryan was bad."

"Not as a man, Jeff. He'd be bad as President. Many people are for him, not because they're bad, because they're mistaken."

Jeff thought of the jolly full-moon man. . . . —How do you know *you're* right?

"Are you interested in politics? I was, when I was no older than you." The days of Civil War, the Draft Riots: —*I was Jeff's age!*

249

"Papa, where do the squirrels sleep?"

"What? Oh, I imagine they have a favorite branch in a tree."

"But the baby squirrels would fall off. You never see the baby squirrels."

"I never thought of that."

"Haven't they nests?"

"Now you speak of it, I think they do. Only the mothers for their babies, while they're very young."

"Then they go away and forget. And when the female is going to have babies again, she builds another nest."

"You see? You know more about squirrels than your father."

"I like the Park when it's night."

"You must never come alone; not at night. You'd better not tell mother. You know mama. She'd worry."

"I won't tell."

It was good that the boy already showed an interest in public affairs: a straw in the wind.

"Tell me what you know about the campaign. Why is Free Silver dangerous?"

"I suppose, if it was free, everyone would just spend it."

Jonathan smiled; in the dark path, the trees straining and sighing with the wind, it was safe to smile, the boy could not see. Nor could he see his son's face! He gripped Jeff's arm again, shaping a simple explanation of Free Silver.

"Gee!" Jeff freed his arm, "it'd be fun to camp out here all night. We could build a fire."

Jonathan did not hear; he was hurt that his son had forgotten politics again, and that he had drawn his arm away. It troubled him, unreasonably, that he could not see Jeff's face. How make the boy know his love and his need? The gas lamps blinked and faltered in the night's blind commotion. Love must not be blind. Love was born blind, like so many young. Until it opened its eyes, it was not love. He would learn to see his son and know him. —Be brave. Practice your humdrum law. Be the provider. Jeff will grow. Jeff will do better than I. . . .

250

3

RACHEL LORNE SAID: "WHEN MY CLASSES ARE OVER IN June we can be married."

"Yes," said Evan.

"I've sent in my resignation. Mr. McAllister was so nice. He is sorry to see me go."

"Why not stay on? We'd have July and August for our honeymoon."

"A wife has no time to be a teacher."

"You'll miss it."

"Yes," she said quietly.

"You may be sorry."

She smiled at the irrelevance. Teaching had been her life; now her life was to be marriage.

"In fact, you're sure to be sorry."

"I've found such a dear little cottage, Evan. It may not stay unrented long. Could thee come with me to see it?" She still relapsed, when she was moved, into the Quaker idiom.

"So you've been house hunting? If it's right, why need I see it?"

She nodded: "I'll make the down payment."

Evan reached in his pocket.

"I have money in the savings bank," she said.

He gave her the roll of bills, all he had; she counted it: one-hundred-and-five dollars.

"That's too much."

"Take it." She took it.

The next Saturday after breakfast, she said: "I think we should tell Mrs. Liebling. She'll be so happy. And that will give her plenty of time to rent your room and mine."

"Go ahead."

"Please come with me, Evan."

"When?"

"Now."

She took his hand, twice as big as hers, and led him up the stairs.

The sun in Mrs. Liebling's room exalted its permanent disorder; the clothes dropped on chairs, the miscellaneous objects in corners and on tables, the very dust on the carpet and woodwork, danced in the sun. Mrs. Liebling sat up in bed, waiting for her tea; her wrapper loosely guarded her lush bosom, her hair waved like a windy summer field.

"*Good* morning, bairns," she sang. "Sit ye doon. Throw those things on the floor, Rachel."

Still standing, Rachel said: "Evan and I are to be married."

Mrs. Liebling's head went up and down in meditative assent. "The Lord ha' mer-r-cy on your souls."

Evan laughed. "Do you know who speaks those words? The judge in England puts a black cloth over his head and says them, when he sentences a man to death."

"Is it my fault, when your silly judges take the name o' the Lord in vain?" She reached for Rachel's hand.

"Why don't you advise Rachel to save herself?"

"These men are such clowns!" She smiled tenderly at Rachel.

Evan knew she was right; he was playing with the fantasy of separation, as a child plays when it says: "I'm going to cut myself in two." Mrs. Liebling was asking questions, Rachel was answering with a fullness of detail she never gave to Evan. He was in the hands of the women.

"I have to see the hoose! I'll get up this minute and ga' wi' ye to see it."

"But it's so early . . . you never get up before—"

"This ver-ry minute! Mr. Evan, go on away so I can get oot o' my bed."

He retreated to the door. "Do you know, Rachel doesn't even know my name?"

"Hoot!" Mrs. Liebling's eyes met Rachel's, and they laughed together. "She's no' wedding a name. Maybe she kens your real name better than you."

"Yes," said Rachel soberly.

"Perhaps I should take her name?"

"We leave the namin' o' things to you men. That gi'es you something to fight aboot from age to age. Now, like a good boy, tell Jacob no' to

252

bring me breakfast. Tell him I'm no' sick, and I'm no' daft either; but am getting up and will drink my cup o' tea in the kitchen."

... They were married on the first of July in the Friend's Meeting House. Rachel in her customary gray carried a nosegay of white rose-buds, the gift of Jacob who, alone of the Liebling household, did not come ("You have to be a churchmouse to be happy in a church," he said; "I'm a kitchen mouse."). The wedding breakfast was at Elysium's best restaurant. They drank Rheinwein and champagne (all except Rachel) and were jolly, and Rachel said no word, though her smile slumbered as if she were at home forever. Evan told tales of the harp houses in New York's Chatham Square; Mr. McAllister (Rachel's principal) sang solemnly *Sweet Adeline, She's Only a Bird in a Gilded Cage, Down Lover's Lane We'll Wander;* Mrs. Goldberg voraciously ate and dropped tears of vicarious joy into her dish; Mrs. Liebling, caressing Rachel's hand, made jokes about the food and the exorbitant prices and the obsequious waiters. When the last bottle was spent, a coupé with the new married couple creaked up Locust Hill, the city and the river in lowering cadenced glimpses at each turn of the road, toward their new home which Evan had not seen.

It was one of a row of identical houses on an unpaved street; pipes still exposed in the dusty sun, the slim fronts newly sodded, with a few saplings like crippled children in iron bands amid the discards of car-penters and masons. Evan saw, between the slate roof and the brown wall, a peering dormer window that made him think of a prisoner's face. He paid the coachman—the shrill sun, the shrill grass in his eyes, and thought of death whose shadow was a suffusion within sun too fine to dim it. Of the same order of being was his closeness to this girl he could not see, as he could not see his blood. She opened the front door. Now he saw the varnished lobby and stair, the cheap garish furniture: sofa, tables, lamps, miscellaneous and irrelevant to him as if they stood in a store window. The wine in his stomach turned, a faint nausea brought sweat to his forehead.

"I hope, dear," he heard, "you'll find the chair by the lamp com-fortable. But your den will be upstairs. I didn't know how to furnish it, till you told me. There's room for a piano."

He saw her in one of Elysium's department stores; the sallow sales-

253

man, smelling of musty woolens and cottage cheese under a Prince Albert coat, guides her among the beds and bureaus with discreet, prurient advice. All this, it occurred to him, she must have paid for with her savings.

"Won't you come up?"

The bedroom's difference from downstairs surprised him: the maple bed with white candlewick cover, the maple chests of drawers, the prim little rocker near the white mesh curtains, bespoke a delicate awareness, an assertion of herself utterly lacking in the clumsy hardware of the living rooms below. Was this a symbol?

"See from the window."

Beyond the terrace of weeds, the dishevelled roofs of lower streets, flashed the river.

"Isn't the view wonderful? And Evan, we can have a rock garden; I'll plant perennials in the fall."

Evan went back to the center of the room, to the foot of the bed. A fly buzzed under the white ceiling; the ceiling was low, he could thrust his hand through and let the fly escape. Rachel shut the window.

"We must have screens. Don't thee wish to see my kitchen?"

"Can you cook?"

"I have no references, but indeed I can! And bake!"

"Don't bake too much for me. I'm an old man, you know; old men must watch their weight. Do you want a *fat* old man for your husband?"

At last her eyes veiled with tears; his every gesture since he came into the house had aimed to bring them. If the tears thickened into cataracts and sealed her eyes, he must fall into darkness. But only because they looked at him; before, he had done well enough. If her eyes could look away again. . . .?

The fly in long lunges kept knocking at the ceiling. Evan thrust his hand up, the fly was a stain on the white ceiling. The faint nausea in Evan rose to his throat.

"I've already soiled your room."

She smiled: "There's nothing here that can't be washed."

"Nothing?"

Her smile became wan, as if his "Nothing?" drained it.

"Washed in the blood of the Lamb," he hummed to himself. Once

254

he had teased her, calling her a Salvation Army lassie, needing only a bonnet and a drum. He felt the furniture below as if it heaved in a hoofed pachyderm dance. —*Get away!*

"Come here," he said.

She came at once close. Close her hair and enclosed by it her brow, her prehensile, passionate mouth and her eyes that saw for him, her throat. There was a way to be free: not to kiss her eyes and mouth but to press her throat till it burst in his hands.

He let his hands rise sidewise from her waist past the swelling of her breasts. His fingers touched the breath and heart-throb in her throat; his fingers clenched; then, he kissed her.

After a timeless hour, he raised himself on one arm from the bed, and tried to see. Rachel lay asleep, her moist hair near her mouth, her closed eyes' seeing blent through her throat to her breasts and all her body, so that her breathing became seeing. He saw the blood on the sheet beside her, but pain had not marred her perfect taking. How was it possible? how could this girl, ignorant and innocent, have taken him so firmly and so deeply? how could he, corrupt and too knowing, have won this sacrament, this marriage? He looked up from the blood on the bed to the stain of the dead fly on the ceiling; and he was afraid. Their separate bodies had come together, kindling within storm a peace ineffable; but only the storm lived, and now their bodies were again apart, the storm neared. He lay beside her, breast to naked breast; saw the garden of her loins whose organ had wonderfully clasped him, pinnacling them together through ecstasy of struggle to ineffable peace; but now only the apartness, only the storm. He got up; drew the sheet over her body whose suffused seeing filled the room; dressed silently and quickly.

Closing the door softly, he went to the unfurnished chamber that was to be his "den." In the bare whitewashed walls, a twilight paled from the east window; the floor smelled of varnish. Let his "den" stay empty, only storm could fill it! He went downstairs. How often, in the kind of store he never entered, in the kind of home he despised, he had seen furniture like this! The strange constriction of his heart he knew was pity: pity for Rachel? pity for him? —Hold on! The ecstasied union he had known upstairs in a strange room, in a strange body:

what bearing did it have with pity? He went to the kitchen. A new range of white enamel, bright papered shelves with colored cannisters, a brand new icebox . . . he opened it, the cool of the ice touching his heat and making him aware of it: he saw eggs, a block of butter, a head of lettuce and carrots, lamb chops in festive paper frills, bottles of Bavarian beer. Pity again; he needed to hurt someone, he sensed that he himself must be the weapon. He went back and opened the front door. He could walk out, could walk away, down the row of ludicrous cottages to the foot of the hill; he could never come back: lose himself as he had lost Evan Cleeve. That would hurt Rachel—with himself as the weapon. Their embrace had wounded time and momently found peace. Would peace be in this violence?

With the door still open, he took a few steps down the walk. Across the way, a man in his shirt fastened the hose to the spigot under the porch and began to sprinkle his lawn.

"Good afternoon," he said.

He was a plump, middle-aged, middle-sized man; the eyes in his round face were stupid and quick like a bird's.

"You're the new neighbors, ain't you?" Above the stream of water: "Glad to see you've come. Henry Smith's my name."

Evan said nothing.

"You'll like it here." The column of water, brittle as tinder, broke on the porch, splintered on the bed of hectic geraniums. "We got the best air in Elysium. Ten years from now, these here houses'll be worth ten times what we paid for 'em." He did not seem to object to Evan's silence. He turned off the cock. "If there's anything Mrs. Smith and me can do to help you get settled . . ." He studied his young grass. "All this block needs is some rain. Hope 't won't be a dry summer. They say the bend in the river draws the rain."

Evan saw the immense Ohio serpenting, pushing through hills for one purpose: to break the clouds to rain on this particular lawn.

Having shifted his hose, Mr. Smith was watering again. "I didn't catch your name."

Evan said: "It's a hard name to catch."

"Must be the noise of the hose. I'll turn off the water."

"That's right," said Evan. "You got it right. Don't stop your watering."

"Waterman?" said Mr. Smith. "Did ya say Waterman?"

Evan walked back into the house; the click of the front door latch woke Rachel. She did not stir in her silence and the knowledge of her body whose miraculous joy caused her to close her eyes again. She touched her breast; her husband was here within her. She waited, while the thought of little things: the supper, the first supper, how to prepare the chops, the salad dressing, should she serve beer unless he asked for it? pleasantly rippled her calm. Suddenly, knowledge left her body, she was frightened and cold; her eyes, looking up, pried at the future. Her body was a wound of craving for what had wounded it. Her eyes rigid on the ceiling where there was a stain to clean, and her mind revolving the little supper problems, spun her as upon a slow wheel, and made her dizzy. Like a mother tenderly wiping the spilled food from a child's face, she passed her hand over her mouth and eyes. God came back; God had given her this knowledge of her body. —I am his wife, her mouth whispered. God took the place of future.

Evan in the foyer stood balanced, between the hideous furniture and his hat on the table. He can still take his hat, go down the walk, Mr. Smith with his hose will scarcely stop him. Hurt Rachel? They are joined, and it will mean to rend himself. For an instant, he gave up; he felt union again. And with its new strength, lucidity to fight its source. He knew, while Rachel lay alive in her bed, he could not leave her; nor could he destroy her. His hands, ever again, if angry and clenched on her throat as they had been, would stay to make love. He saw in himself an obscene depth of darkness; a horror for the light, a need for the light. The conflict of being worse . . . and better . . . than he had dreamed to be, tired him. He sat on the clumsy sofa, facing the stairs. . . .

At last, Rachel came down, a bright blue apron over her housefrock. She kissed him on the forehead and went toward the kitchen.

"It won't be long, dear, for supper."

"Rachel."

She turned, her hand on the kitchen door.

He said: "Let's go out for supper."

Less than a moment she paused and her mouth opened. Without a word, she went upstairs again. She came down in a new costume, gay for her: a voile of gray with embroidered flowerets blue and yellow, and a wide-brimmed straw hat on her black hair.

He took her to Rudolph's, the noisiest German restaurant in the city. Rachel felt herself and Evan at the bottom of a bursting well. Dark Gothic walls rose above them to a balcony cluttered with people beneath the beetling rafters; and in between, a quintet made boisterous music, waiters in hip aprons bore trays of beer and heavy meats, knives and forks clattered, service doors swung on the miasma of the kitchen, the crowded bodies were plethoric with gutteral in-take of food and out-take of words. Rachel sat silent with her husband who saw her unmoved and patient, not even asking why he had brought her here. He loved her; she was suffering; he knew the ugliness in his need to hurt her. And when they returned through the naked summer night under the eyes of the stars to their gewgaw street and house on the hill, to their serene cool room, Evan watched again his lowness, his lust to wound, transfigure into the white purity of union: changeless and without identity, fragile, perfect, and doomed.

For three days, he insisted that they eat in alien German restaurants, where Rachel barely touched the ponderous food. (The Symphony was on vacation; his private pupils were away.) He stole into the kitchen, saw that the meat was gone. Again pity, a sweet paining, shame, that would all rise into their peace together. Then, he went down the hill to the butcher and came back with chops (like those she had thrown away); Rachel cooked their first home supper.

It was all easy, incredibly; but he could not know if it was life or death. He lost his bearings, he was in a calm in a sea whose tides he could not reckon, a sea without sun, lit by its own phosphorescence. The summer was dry; he bought a hose and watered the shrill young grass like Mr. Smith. He bought a piano, and helped the movers fragrant with sweat hoist it through the foyer beside the flamboyant sofa. The furniture's ungainly gesturings he no longer noticed; his den remained bare. The river, with monotonous insistence, flowed through the land; the sun made its daily round, the stars paled and brightened as the moon waxed and waned. Within this ease, this same huge rhythm of the world, Rachel became pregnant. They dwelt without high or significant words, and without friction, together. They walked, they read a poem, they ate, they sat, he with his glass of beer, she with her knitting, through hours that always led to the hour timeless as death. Rehearsals of the Symphony began, his pupils returned from northern lakes and eastern beaches. Evan on his way home from work stopped at saloons. The drinks were mere enhancers of the ease, the ease he could not name, not knowing if it was life or dying.

The growing quantities of knitted clothes at which she constantly worked were abstruse signs of an event unreal and beyond him. And when she held him deep and the storm rose in whose pinnacle was peace, he was sure no life burgeoning where he lay could ever replace him. Yet the signs multiplied. His den . . . one by one, a crib, a painted bureau, a bassinette, a washable rug, lavender curtains . . . became a nursery. He wondered if Rachel ascribed his refusal to furnish his den to a delicate prescience of its new use. He wondered if this had been his motive. How could she know, when he did not know? Their intimacy lived below the limen of questions.

The summer held through the year's fall. Imperceptible was the slow burning of leaves and the sere of the fields, while the nights lengthened and the moon swung from crescent to crescent. He looked at his wife's belly, still slim although more firm, still articulate to take him and transform him into the mysterious peace now less sharply different from his hours apart and from his hours of drinking. He brought her the ample money he earned; she made him keep a share, and it went to the saloons. She knew; she was his accomplice; and nothing was said. She encompassed his ease and its growth, as she encompassed his child, as she encompassed his flesh.

In late November, like an over-ripe fruit, summer suddenly rotted into winter. The rain was cold and incessant, the town shivered in its bowel of earth, there was no sun and no moon. Great mists rose from the river, under their drench the hills hardened. But winter could not touch him, as it could not touch the life in Rachel's body; he too was sealed in a warm, secret birth. He had lost his sense of separateness from Rachel; he did not separately know her, he had no separate thoughts about their future. He was the violent seed whose fruit was peace, and he was peace. Yet he did not believe in peace, although he loved it and used it, and knew it was there. In his hours alone, he drank more steadily, never becoming drunk; the warm mists of his mind, when he drank, affirmed his organic moving. Toward what birth, he did not know; but knew that birth was not this ease; was violence and the fruit of violence. The unborn child also was preparing for a violent act, and did not need to know it.

Rachel loved her house. She had no aesthetic measure; the house was simply hers, was comfortable, she could keep it clean; only its too much sun before the winter rains had vaguely troubled her. God's world for her was dark, its light was secret and not of this world; therefore, without knowing why, she approved of the dismal furniture downstairs, of the kitchen's and pantry's dark woodwork; therefore, she had attached brown awnings to the bedroom windows to dim the white walls and the "colonial" maple. All she loved was dark, and all she knew: her childhood, her blond man, the life in her womb. Darkest of all, the flame and pain, the fierce annihilation, of their clasped souls and bodies.

Rachel had always worked since the small child lost her mother and helped her father on the farm he did not even own. He was more preacher than farmer; the Word of the Lord in his scattered community of Friends took him on long journeys through the countryside and brought him sparse food. When Rachel was fourteen, he sold his chickens and his cow to send her to the city to a better school; at sixteen, she was already teaching. Rachel worked hard, living on almost nothing, and hoarded her savings until they amounted to the downpayment on her father's farm. She put her money in her bag, returned to the bare house, and learned that her father was dead. She saw his hours and his years since she had left him; the straw mattress from which he rose to the dawn; she lifted the frying pan and kettle in the hearth where his hands prepared his food, his old hands warming themselves, shaking the ashes from the grate. She heard the footfall to the barn, the clank of the mule's harness. And while she had half starved for him in secret, he had closed his Bible, he had died in secret. God's ways were dark. She did not think actively of her father, she never spoke of him to Evan (he knew as little of her past as she of his); but the decayed and silent house in which she had stood, the vain money in her hand, was a dimension of dark depth to her moving about her own home as she made the bed, dusted, set the new loaf to bake, sat near Evan's piano knitting a tiny sweater.

When the life in her flesh stirred, she loved to set aside her sewing, to be idle for hours, not thinking and not feeling. Her husband would be away all day, he would return perhaps swollen with liquor; but the house was ready for him, the roast was ready, and she . . . spirit and flesh . . . was ready to receive him. He was part of her, he could be left to his own processes like her swelling womb and breasts. The organic immanence of her father who was dead, of her child who was not yet born . . . and of God . . . were one with her man: the least seen, the least judged, the acme of all living.

Not always this victory: Rachel encountered days when every object rasped. She awoke, her heart burning, her body a burden, Evan's nearness an intrusion. He was never rude, he asked to help her, but he did not resist her hurrying him away. Now each household task was an offense, and the food she must take for her child's sake choked her. Original Sin lay heavy on her world; she wondered why God did not send a second Flood. Then she remembered Christ, and she knew she had sinned, thinking of a Flood. Man might destroy himself with his self-love turned hate; Christ would not allow it! She wept at her ingratitude; so deep was her sin she found herself almost wishing Christ did not love her: then she could die. Christ's love an intolerable burden? Sinner! Sinner! Thought of Evan . . . teaching, rehearsing, in the afternoon soberly drinking his way to soddenness and to her . . . how could she bear it without love? Her womb weakened. In this lucidity, like certain winter days when each bare tree stood clear in the dun sky, she saw Evan going down; and what of the child of this father? Her own father's opposite way became a rebuke and a warning; her passionate submission to love became sin and betrayal. She was lost and she was frightened. Her child, her love, her father . . . the contrary of self . . . parted her from self and left her torn. Then she dared not call on God. Does a woman sin, loving and joying with her husband? What would Christ say? Rachel had no theology, but she knew Original Sin to be enmeshed in every joy, in every virtue: right bore the sin of pride, love bore the sin of lust, happiness made one a coward fearing to lose it. What poison would there be in the milk of her breasts for her child? She sat, weeping. She feared her body that had known delight. And when Evan came, she was so weak that brazenly she welcomed the oblivion in his arms.

As her time neared, the strength of her child overwhelmed her weakness; she became the unborn, the helpless one. Over her misgivings and all that Evan was, the child conquered, the child commanded. She knew the dark ecstasy of being a slave.

Well-being returned to her in humbler terms. Now she went about her housework, bearing her laborious body, dutiful, no longer proud. She received her husband, submissive even to her own passion, no longer glorying, therefore no longer anguished. The elements of her life; Evan's descent into wayward distance, her womb's growing, the sacrament of her father's last years (in her foreshortening mind, now, he had actually died that she might live), were again unified, but darkly. Her forebodings for Evan and the child retreated to the future. And the taste of fresh bread, the touch of the little woolen shirt awaiting the tender body, the new vibrant spring on the river, the sound of Evan's voice after the day's silence, were the immediate joyous moment.

Such a moment was the birth, all its twenty-four hours of rising rending travail. She could see the light in her womb; it was breaking through the walls of her flesh that were all pain, but it was light. One by one, the walls broke, she saw their anguish, but she was with the light. Then her hands were on the light, and her breasts were fed by it; her hands guarded it fragile and immense, her breasts fed it, infinitely hungry and strong. They called the child Rebecca.

Evan's descent was swifter, as if Rachel's absorption in her child released him. He came late to the Symphony rehearsals, a sin to Herr Riese more heinous than playing out of tune.

"What's the matter with you?" he asked, his eyes misleadingly kind in his square head. "Three times now, you come in when we already work. Got trouble at home?"

"We've got a baby, if that's trouble!"

"Is the baby sick? . . . . Is the Missus sick?"

"Not that I know of."

"A well baby's no trouble. What's the matter with you?"

Evan's remote sardonic smile: "Maybe it's another baby that's causing the trouble."

"What you talking about?"

"A baby inside *me.*"

"You're crazy, my dear fellow."

"I'll try to come on time. If I don't, throw me out."

262

"I can always do that. I don't want to, unless I got to." Riese's smile was ice. "You're a good fiddler."

"Thanks. Am I really good?"

"You're good. You're not sure on time; I always got to keep my eye on you, and a conductor should never got to notice any one string. But you play well. I can hear you."

"That sounds as if I must be playing a little off key."

Riese pursed his strong small mouth and looked into the distance. "Maybe you do, a little. Just enough to give *width*. After all, there are a hundred tones between halftones. That's what gives the music size and color."

"It's a charitable idea."

"When rehearsal's at ten-thirty *punkt*, ten-thirty is no idea!" Herr Riese dropped his knuckle from the stationary wrist to the table with a tap like a baton's.

After several weeks (it was autumn and Rebecca nearly a year and a half old) Evan was late again. Riese did not appear to notice, when he somewhat noisily took his seat in the midst of the first movement of the difficult new Brahms. The next day, the rehearsal over, Riese suddenly stopped while passing him, backstage.

"You," he said abruptly, "are you rich? . . . No? . . . Not any more, eh? Milk and coal, winter coats, doctor bills sometimes, for the wife and baby . . . they cost money. Remember!" He was gone.

Evan was late again, and a third time. That Saturday, his pay envelope contained a note initialed by the conductor: "Your services will no longer be required."

Evan stepped into the November dusk, into the blustery wind smelling of snow. He thought of the men he would no longer play with. At first, he had been amused by them: the violins, violas, cellos and basses, the oboes, trombones and horns, the kettledrums and flutes—what a dull pedestrian lot converging on the strict ladders of time to make Beethoven and Schubert, whose words were not so much remote as infinitely alien from their drilled fingers, their minds stuffed with vanities and petty rivalries. These men making music were like the town; of its innumerable chaotic appetites making a music too. He had despised their audience, that nervous, erethic rhinocerous mass beyond the platform, digesting its hay, rumbling its flush bowels to the *obbligato* of Mozart's graceful agony! He had found even Herr Riese incongruous; except for the man's forehead, he too was routine and shrewdness. Now, collectively, he liked them. They all made music together, some of it sublime, only because they all "made" milk and coal and winter overcoats together. The contradiction was the warp of life, and of music. —It's been too easy for you; he put his face to the blustery wind smelling of snow. Now, are you satisfied? Winter and no job. Now it's not going to be easy. . . . He wasn't sure he minded; and he was sorry. Alone on the street corner, the wet night raw in his face, the home-hurrying men and women a confused gyre like the bacilli seen by a microscope in a drop of water, he knew he did not care; everything was still easy, except to care, which was hard. His way of life was a way toward death, because he did not care, because he needed to care. But even for this, he was not responsible; had he made the universe or himself? He tested his feeling about Rachel; he did not care if she was troubled by the loss of his job. He said to himself: "I have a daughter . . . a daughter," and what he felt was the burn—it hurt—in the throat of his mother dying on the floor of her bathroom. —I'm not unhappy. Rachel would call it "Original Sin" that even now he could say, I'm not unhappy. Only he who cares lives? Rachel would say, he cares because God is in him. Smiling, Evan jumped on the cable car that climbed up to the Lieblings.

Jacob was in the kitchen, basting a joint. Mrs. Liebling came in.

"Hello, you! Stay to supper."

"I will, if I can have Jacob tonight."

"What's the celebration?"

"I've lost my job on the orchestra."

Mrs. Liebling nodded. "You're a kind thorough family man. Does Rachel ken?"

"Not yet. Why am I kind and thorough?"

"You're gettin' your wife and daughter all ready."

"For what?"

"Aye! for what?"

Leaving his fiddle at the house, Evan with Jacob went down to the "bottoms" where the colored folk caroused on Saturday nights. The snow was holding off; behind corrugated cloud the moon cast a harsh

264

spell at the wooden shanties on stilts above mud, warmly, secretly hugging their dim oil lamps. It was a world humiliated by the world, yet serene in self-acceptance. —If I lived here . . .? *when* I live here . . .? thought Evan. A lean cur barked at them, Evan heard explosive resilient freshness in its voice, a strange contrast to the mangy yellow hide that the street light spotted. The dance-barn they entered reeked of sweat, cheap perfume, and corn liquor; the couples in short, thumping, ponderous circles made it reel. Evan bought a bottle and placed it on their table.

"It's a wonderful thing," he said, "to be alive and able to ask questions."

"There are no answers," remarked Jacob.

"Not in life. All life, every bit of the living universe, is just questions."

"Only men."

"I don't know. Take space. When it gets to the end of itself, where there's nothing, not even space, doesn't it ask a question? Isn't space, every inch, asking a question?"

"Singing a song," said Jacob.

"All right: singing a question: *How can I be? how can I be?*"

"How could I not be?"

"That too," laughed Evan.

"It's a good song."

"We're part of it; that's why it must sound good to us."

The colored couples danced with clumsy grace, some the grace of bears, some the grace of bumble-bees from flower to flower. Evan hummed, Jacob's eyes gleamed the music of their feet.

"I've got an idea," said Evan. "A good one. Scientific. Want to hear?"

"Oh, I can stand it."

"You old diamond! You can stand anything."

"I can't cut glass."

"You don't have to. You see through it."

"I can tell you what I like about you, Evan."

"Go ahead. But I'll get back to my great scientific idea."

"Most folks talk nonsense. Your *life* is. That's better."

"My life is nonsense?"

"Wonderful rot! That's why ma likes you. That's why dear poor Rachel Lorne married you."

"You talk as if she were dead."

"I talk as if she was alive."

"She's used to my irregular hours. I think she likes 'em, hers are so regular. Babies do that to a house, and it's a crime. They're even plunked on the potty according to schedule."

"I agree; it ain't fair."

"Babies love to defecate. It's their love-making; it's their world-making. What right's a mother got to make 'em take their pleasure when *she* wants, *where* she wants?"

"You don't have to wash the diapers."

"That's irrelevant, old diamond."

"It's true," meditated Jacob. "A baby's turd is sweet as mud. We put worse things in our mouths."

Evan poured from the bottle. "This, for instance."

"Maybe," Jacob sipped and mused, the dance brightly mirrored in his eyes; "maybe men make governments because their mamas wouldn't let 'em crap in their panties."

"Sort of revenge?"

"Sort of habit."

Evan laughed. "That's an historical discovery. I'm jealous. Here's my scientific one. Motion—"

"Motion?"

"You know what motion is?"

"Don't bother me," said Jacob.

"None of us do. It's an insoluble mystery. So we name it."

"Animals don't." Jacob took a long drink. "Does that mean they know what it is?"

"They die, too, don't they?" Evan pounded on the table. "Their motion also tends toward death. That means they too ask questions, and don't know."

"Well, they don't mind. I don't mind. Why do you mind?"

Evan filled his glass with corn, and forgot to touch it. "Listen!"

Jacob listened, and all he heard was the heavy music, laden with shuffling feet and shifting bodies.

Evan drained his tumbler, smacked his lips. "The best we can name

266

motion is to call it an elementary *trait* of matter. The substance of matter, the men of physics say, is force, energy, gravitation, electricity, inertia—all motion, either potential like a seed or blossomed like a flower."

"Sure," said Jacob.

"You follow me?"

"What do you care? Go ahead. *Move* ahead." Jacob smiled peacefully.

"Here it comes. Listen hard! To ask a question: what is it but a sort of motion?" Jacob looked at him fondly. "A motion or a tending toward an answer."

"You're heavy tonight," Jacob smiled.

"Yes! A stone's heaviness is its capacity to fall; its potential motion."

At the next table, a big black man leaned to a frail brown girl and whispered words that came to Evan and Jacob as a murmur of music. Jacob looked at Evan and listened to the music.

"Space," said Evan, "is the question in physical form: *What beyond?* That question is motion. It can have no answer, for then it would stop, which is impossible. That's why space seems limitless."

Jacob turned toward the black man and the frail brown girl. "Go ahead."

Evan continued: "It's a mistake to think that the impossibility of an answer to the question, *What beyond?* applies only to the *end* of space. For precisely there is no *end* of space. The question that has no answer . . . no end . . . is in every inch of space; the unanswerable mystery of space *is* space. The substance . . . the motion . . . the question that has no answer . . . are one."

Jacob said nothing and held out his glass; Evan filled it.

"We're part of space; our minds are. The motion aspect of our minds is to ask questions."

"—no one can answer."

"Our blood is part of space. The motion of our blood is to hunger, to long, to make new blood—"

"Or spill it."

"Make new life with old ones. All men's questions are the motions of life. If there were answers, they'd be the motionlessness of death."

"Why do we think there are answers?"

"We get tired; we want to stop, which means to die. It's our insanity. It can't be, God damn it."

Jacob kept his eyes on the dark couple. "Can't we die?"

"Isn't the whole world trying? And what does it do? Increase and multiply."

"I don't know no history," said Jacob, his eyes still on the next table. "Then," he mused aloud, "scientific questions are sane? but scientific answers are crazy? . . . Let's ask 'em over for a drink."

Evan followed Jacob's eyes. "Sure," he said and got up, and bowed to the black man and the brown girl. They understood him; the big man serious, the frail girl smiling; and sat down at Evan's and Jacob's table. The black man spoke, the voice mellow as a violoncello; they all spoke: suddenly Evan was aware that he understood no spoken word, all he heard was a music. It was a tender music, without melody; each voice spoke its own theme, and yet there was fusion. The big black man who did not smile was completely at ease; the brown girl (like a flower close to earth and yet transcending) smiled and was less at ease. The black man's hands covered the girl's hand on the table; it was as if the girl vanished within him. For an instant, Evan fought the strangeness. —I've had too much to drink. Then he submitted, and it was easy: the music without words of their voices invaginated him as the man's hand the woman's.

. . . The night had calmed when he walked home up Locust Hill. Separate from his body, he watched his limbs, muscles, nerves and senses navigate him surely along the rising grade and then along the level row of houses. His legs were steady; all of him was steady; life was easy.

Rachel came out of the nursery (that was to have been his den) with an empty bottle of milk.

"Rebecca awoke and cried. She was hungry. How are you, Evan?"

He understood her words, he was angry. —All I said to Jacob tonight was nonsense. The opposite is true. No: the opposite is also true.

"I've lost my job with the Symphony," he said.

"Oh!"

"You don't seem surprised."

"Should I be, Evan? I'm sorry."

"Are you?"

268

"I think I'm sorry."

"I have plenty of private pupils."

"Yes." She was still. But he heard, like the harmonic of a note that is played: "Plenty remains to lose . . ."

They went into their bedroom; Rachel removed her wrapper, turned out the gas and lay in bed beside him. The dark, and she, were good . . . were easy. —I talked nonsense to Jacob.

"Rachel," he said, "are you asleep?"

"What is it?"

"You know, I think I'm a happy man."

She made no answer.

"Or is it, that I'm a very unhappy man?"

She lay with the dark, immersing him.

"Odd that I shouldn't know. Rachel, are you happy or unhappy?"

"I don't know, either."

He lifted himself a little from the pillow. He saw the glow of her black hair in the less luminous dark; the fire of her mouth. —She is lovable. But what he felt was beyond happiness and unhappiness: was a world beyond them, as the words in the dancehall a music beyond words.

From the next room came Rebecca's crying.

"I hope the child's not ill! Perhaps I was wrong to give her the milk." Rachel got up, threw on her robe: "You'd better go to sleep," and shut the door behind her.

Within ten days of her arrival, Rebecca was a recognizable human unit. She had her father's head and—rare in a newcomer—a nose in miniature the aquiline of the Cleeves; but the close cap of her hair was dark and the eyes that blinked, stared, slowly focused to sight, were her mother's. Rachel held her at her breast, in the moment before the infant, sated, slept; and received the revelation of a being strange to earth but intact, and helpless on earth not because it was weak but because it was a stranger. Its body, the mother saw, was a pitiful prison, an instrument unwieldy and inadequate; and Rachel's love for her child was born in the ecstasy of compassion. That her Rebecca could not lift her head, could not perform the simplest human skills, was to the mother mystery akin to the mystery of Christ inferior to men, despised and tortured on the Cross. Life luminous in powerless flesh, beauty that fouled itself and fumbled, truth that could only wail and whimper: because she was a Christian, Rachel knew, although she could not understand nor consciously state, this paradox of spirit.

As the infant became a baby, its life merged with its body; as its reflexes, gurglings, recognitions established body contact with the mother who fed, who bathed, who comforted, Rachel's love, also more physical, lost its secret insight (never articulate enough to be words or deliberate thought). The baby awoke hungry at dawn, diapers had to be changed, diapers washed, the house must be kept, food must be bought, prepared, clothes made, mended, laundered: and with Evan drinking more of what he earned, all these manifold duties crowding the day and the night must be performed without help and with care for every penny. Rachel had embraced in a swift revelation the infant's transcendency of spirit; now they were bound together in things to be done. Rachel saw the intricate, endless labors of her child learning to live. Rebecca, when she was awake, was as busy as her mother! To focus in the light, to know and to touch objects, to connect hand with eye, to turn her pitiful body, to convey food into her mouth, to digest it, to reckon sounds and distance, finally to cope with the outrageous indignity of discomfort and pain! no wonder the little soul needed to sleep so many hours! The baby's work and progress every week made the efforts of older children whom Rachel had known at school idleness by contrast; and as to adults: they in comparison were static, when they were not *un*learning.

While the work of mother and child wove months (too crowded with action to leave room for measure), and the months wove years, Rachel's relation with Evan moved in a diverging system: a star's, close to hers and her child's whose different velocity gave it a different time. More and more, the sense of spirit, strange to the traffic of earth, which Rebecca had awakened in the mother and the mother now lost in her crowded busyness with Rebecca, fixed on Evan. He was her husband, he was her beloved; she was his loyal, at times passionate wife; but the place of his soul in his own life as in hers was the helpless one of an infant's spirit in its unwieldy body. Rebecca grew geared to body and home, learning to live; and Evan grew ungeared.

One by one, Evan lost his private pupils: more precisely, he let them go. His bearing as teacher was exemplary; he was never late for a lesson, never sensibly under the influence of liquor. But with one child he was bored; with another, burdened by the responsibility. "I'm nothing but an amateur, you need a better teacher," he said when there was talent; "I'm not a drillmaster," he said, when there was none. He could not win distrust, although he tried; but he lacerated the vanities and illusions without which few, even the gifted, will give time to an art. He saw too clearly the ties within himself of his music and his self-indulgence. If he had not played the fiddle, would he not still be living the completer, hence more honest degradation of a lawyer? Music in him, he told himself, was no pure language; it was fused with his every weakness. As a musician, he was certainly no honest man. Other musicians, he knew, even the best, were as bad. Leaning in their youth on their reed of talent to escape humbler work, they soon turned it into a trade as crass as the shopkeeper's. And their cabined lives, their dealings only with self-indulged little monsters like themselves, kept them from the clean open air that blows through even the meanest shop. By the same token, he despised most music; and, not hiding his contempt, humiliated the bad taste of his pupils. When one loved a sentimental piece and had worked long to learn it, Evan might say: "This is the equivalent of 'the moon is silver and the sky is blue'." When another practised a difficult concerto, Evan might observe that the hard-won passage was "empty rhetoric." He mortally offended a young married woman who adored him by saying: "Wagner is full of florid masturbation."

At last, Rachel was heavily in debt to the butcher and the grocer. They had to move from the sunny house on the hill, from the bland demesne of Mr. Smith, to a much humbler cottage in a dark street of the old town, within the river's malarial miasma. Rachel breathed no rebuke, took the descent of fortune as a word of God more legible than the sun, and considered a return to teaching. Rebecca was old enough now for kindergarten and could be left alone for hours. If she was ill, in this poor depth of Elysium, there were helpful neighbors to be relied on. Her old principal, Mr. McAllister, more devoted than ever, urged her to return. But Rachel was reluctant. Her life with her child was too close knit for absence and for duties elsewhere; she would be torn, she

271

would bleed. Evan, always without specific word from Rachel, sensed her struggle. One evening, he came home:

"I've got a new job I'm going to like."

"What is it, dear?"

"Incidentally, it'll pay the bills."

Rachel looked at her husband. He had grown paunchy, his muscles softening into flesh; he stooped a little; his eyes' poignance had deepened with pain and humor forever waking within strangeness, forever looking out upon strangeness. His eyes held Rachel. In one of her moments of cloud, she had wondered, were her husband blind, if she would love him, and known that even if his eyes were lost . . . even if *she* were blind . . . she would see them and love him.

Evan's new job was in the 'orchestra' at Rudolph's. The leader and pianist was Max Schmehl, burly and plethoric, who adored sentimental German and lascivious French music, as he did dark beer and slim girls. Simeon Smith, the contrabass, was a Yankee from Vermont, thin as his big fiddle was fat, with a long skull all but visible beneath its parchmenty skin. The cellist was Luchansky, a long-haired Ukrainian Jew with black fingernails and a snivelling tapir nose (he had once toured the nation as a virtuoso). Théophile Lesueur who played the clarinet was a Gascon with rat eyes who, before the concert began, loved to sit at the piano and play harpsichord and clavichord polyphony by little-known masters earlier than the Bachs and Buxtehude. He touched the keys without pedal in a cool cleanness that contrasted with his dirty and loud linen. Wielding the drums, the triangle and cymbals, was Chris Doppel, a big brutish blond German, bullet-headed, pop-eyed, whose secret delight was to torture stray kittens and puppies and whose sense of time was perfect. Each of these men, Evan reflected, was the decay of a great tradition—himself included: the traditions had built Europe, pioneered America; now, here they were serving music soft as rancid butter, false as the platitudes of a patent-medicine hawker, to the stomachs, the itching palms, the lubricious genitals of the diners. The irony wounded the poignance of Evan's eyes, sharpened their recovery in humor. He felt himself, when he played, solid and secure in corruption.

Now that he worked half the night, slept half the day, and was away on Saturdays and Sundays from noon to midnight, Evan saw less of

Rachel and almost nothing of Rebecca. Could he see his child at all?

Very soon, the infant's black hair (like Rachel's) had turned to the color of wet hemp (an approach to Evan's). The child was tall for her age, her body promised to follow her father's. But her fair skin had an undertone of shadow that reminded him of Rachel and his mother. Could he see her at all? Rebecca was elusive, her eyes suffused a quality of mist. She was a quiet child. She did not care for dolls, she was not playful, she seldom cried or misbehaved. For hours, she sat at the kitchen table content to watch her mother work. She loved to squat on the floor with one of her father's books, and color the black-and-white illustrations with crayons, muttering little phrases meant only for herself. A book of colored animals, which Evan gave her, she rejected. He gave her another with plain drawings which she soon gaily colored. Evan was by no means certain that he loved her; she gave no sign of loving him; she took his presence cloudily, like her opalescent eyes. The child's will seemed unaware of his existence. Yet she was charming. Evan liked her equivocal and unobtrusive presence near his wife, as if she enhanced the shadow that was his ease, his habitation.

Evan was never late to work at Rudolph's. . . . Before mounting to the alcove where the sextet plays, he stands at the bar and quickly downs a couple of drams of whiskey (gratis). This is his passport to the comfortable irony ahead, of playing *lagniappe* for guzzlers. The main floor tables are already well filled; the steams of roasts and stews are tinctured with the acid scent of beer; and talk envelops all, the restaurant's main organic substance. Even if he could hear its individual strands of gossip, prejudice, coarse humor, sexual persuasion, it would mean nothing; the talk is the noise, the animal noise, of human life itself. Evan winds up the narrow stair, places his hat and coat on a hook; Max Schmehl is arranging the scores, Simeon Smith leans on the wall and picks his terebrate teeth, Lesueur, whose body holds its own within the rising fumes from tables and kitchen (he wears a loud checked suit, a striped shirt and a diamond pin beneath the wing tie), sits at the piano and softly runs through a piece by Boccherini. Doppel, always the last, bursts in, conveying as usual to Luchansky (in whom Evan amusedly reads it) the fear that if a screw got loose in his big wooden body he would go berserk, break chairs and heads, instead of beating the drums and clashing the cymbals.

The first selection is a waltz from Vienna. Evan wonders, as his bow and fingers deal out the symmetrical design, why he likes it: it is complacently sure of itself, squat, without height or depth, and its appeal is, not to experience or passion, but to their memories comfortably diminished. The waltz is a defensive lie, pleasant because successful . . . the fantasy of Doppel running amok among tables and bodies stays with Evan as he plays: if the restaurant were in fact a shambles, would not this indulgent music be a soothing plaster? The falsehood of the music, the falsehood of the decency of the really brutish diners, multiply to a truth as negatives in mathematics multiply to positive.

Long past midnight, Evan walks through the deserted town toward his house in Glass Street, bearing his mood along. The 'decency' of the diners, the Viennese waltz, civilized lies, scabbarded a truth savage as Doppel's secret vices! and now, these somnolent houses: he does not believe in their stillness! they too scabbard ferocity and explosion! He thinks of his mother's violent end fashioned by the elegancies of his father (he hums the Viennese tune); he thinks of his convivial nights with the Tammany boys building what violence for Jonathan and for himself, here, a fiddler of waltzes from Vienna. He thinks of Rachel's quiet spell upon him; the violence within it, and Rebecca. . . . He opens the door of his house, carefully climbs the rickety stair to his bedroom and Rachel's. Quiet! He does not believe in the stillness, but let it go on while it can! Hum a waltz from Vienna under your breath while you quietly undress, to let the unbelieved-in stillness go on. . . .

The next day was Evan's day off. When he awoke, it was gloomy afternoon, slush on the streets. He went to the kitchen, the one warm room, with a new German book he had discovered, settled himself in the rocker and lighted a cigar, while Rachel prepared his breakfast. The house had a basement in lieu of a cellar, a porch at the head of a stair whose steps were rotted, a living room hot in summer, cold in winter, that led to the more livable kitchen whose windows looked on a yard; on the top floor the two close bedchambers had a sloping garret roof and each a dormer window. Evan ate his breakfast and returned to the rocker with his book; Rachel placed her ironing board near the stove, Rebecca on the floor colored the animals in her new picture book.

"Still at it?" Evan looked up.

274

"Wecca in the lion," the child stated to herself, and pointed to her garish red beast with yellow mane.

"And still calls herself Wecca."

"That's because we always said Rebecca; it's a hard name for a baby."

"Isn't she seven?"

Rachel tested her hot iron. "She called herself Wecca before she was two."

"Wecca in the wolf." The child pointed to the next picture she had colored. She gave no heed to the grown-ups.

"I remember," said Evan, "a long time ago; she couldn't have been more than three or four, when she said the same thing."

Rachel ironed, and Rebecca turned the page.

"I'm no expert like you on children," Evan again laid down his book. "But isn't it unusual? wouldn't most kids put it the other way?"

Rachel looked up, questioning.

"I mean: wouldn't most kids say, *I* am a lion; not, I am *in* the lion? Increase their identity, not lose it?"

Rachel smiled. He went on:

"Maybe the child's going to be a saint, sinking herself in humble creatures." He looked at his book. "Not a saint . . . I could make a bad pun. Wecca in a child's speech is wrecker. By Jove, she agrees with Nietzsche!"

"Who is he?"

"A new German. Or was. I think he's mad now, or dead. He didn't believe in humanity. He was something of a punster too. He spelled pray with an *e*: P-r-e-y! Man must become Superman, he said, and the way to it, so far as I can gather," he brandished the book, "is to turn beast. My dear, our daughter is a philosopher."

"I'll be satisfied if she's a Christian."

"According to this Nietzsche, Christian morals are the curse, the slaves' spell on the world, which the Superman will conquer. Be hard, selfish, brutal."

"And that beast's way leads to God?"

"The Superman, my dear, kills all the gods."

"Please, Evan."

"She never hears me, don't worry."

"I'm not sure."

275

A giraffe had turned livid green with scarlet spots; the leaves it nibbled from the high tree were blue. "Wecca in the giraffe," said the child.

"By Jove, the kid's a prophet."

"She may hear more than you think."

"Rebecca," said Evan, "Rebecca!" The child slowly looked up. "Did you hear what I was saying to your mother?"

Rebecca looked at him calmly and long. "I don't like you."

"Darling!" cried Rachel.

"Why don't you like me?" Evan's smile was warm.

The little girl kept on gazing at the man; except for the twist of her thin mouth she was without expression. At last, "I don't like you," she repeated, and turned the page to a tiger.

"That's all right," Evan said. "I don't blame you, dear. But won't you tell me why?"

"Evan!" Rachel put the iron on the stove.

"Why shouldn't she tell me?"

"I won't have it! of course Rebecca loves her father. You've hurt her feelings."

The child drew stripes of yellow on the tiger. Without looking up, she said: "You don't like mama and me."

Rachel's eyes filled with tears. "Darling, of course papa loves us. But he's so busy; he has to be away so much to earn money."

Evan smiled. "The German was right; Christians are cowards and liars. But your world's ending. Leave it to Rebecca. 'Out of the mouths of babes and sucklings—'."

There was a knock on the porch door.

When Rachel came back, her face was very pale. "It's a gentleman to see you."

Neighbors frequently dropped in on Rachel, sometimes an old friend from school. But Evan never had a visitor.

"Well, let him come in."

"Don't you think, Evan, you'd better see him in the other room?"

"And freeze? It's warm here."

Rachel took her child's hand. "Come, Rebecca."

"What is this?" Evan was irritated. "Why should *you* go? Stay where you are, both of you, and let the man come in." Rachel was trembling, and he smiled at her. "Have I secrets from you?"

The morning coat and striped creased trousers of the young man meant New York. He came in bowing, his derby hat in his hand. Rachel sprinkled water on a shirt and began to iron; the child stared at the new face and, not interested, went back to her pictures. Evan did not get up.

"I have a letter for you, Mr. Evan . . . Corthuis."

Noting the hesitation in the name, and what it meant, Evan took the envelope.

"My name, sir, is Dusenbery. Cloyd Dusenbery. I am—"

"Do I have to hear who you are?"

The envelope, with the name and picture of Elysium's newest hotel, had a small wavering script which Evan knew.

The young man stood waiting. At last: "I believe an answer's requested."

Evan tapped the letter on his knee.

"Won't you please read it, sir?" the young man said. "I was instructed to bring an answer."

Evan kept tapping. Rachel at the stove moved a pot and her shoes creaked. The man's eyes wandered about the room. Evan's eyes caught them, white with fear. He could hear the man's breathing; he could hear his own. Rebecca turned a page. Evan got up so suddenly his chair almost toppled. The young man backed and Rachel screamed. Evan gripped his collar, turned him about, and pushed him to the open door.

"Don't!" screeched Mr. Dusenbery, scrambling half-suspended through the next room and on to the porch. Rachel and the child heard him clatter down the steps, heard the front door close, the kitchen door: Evan returned to his rocker.

"That's the worst of violence," he said. "When you're not used to it, you do it badly."

"Did you want to kill him?"

"Not him."

Rebecca turned back the pages, and looked admiringly at her work. "Wecca in the wolf."

277

Rachel, ironing again, said softly: "You must read the letter from your father."

Evan smiled. He knew she had read it in his face at the moment he read it on the envelope.

"The old man must be in town," he said. "Did you know that?"

"When you did."

He opened the envelope ... read ... tossed the letter on the ironing board. She read:

> My dear Son,
>   I am in town for a day on business. Can you dine with me at the hotel? If you care to bring your wife, I shall be happy to meet her. If more convenient for you, come after dinner. I want to see you.
>
> Sincerely yours,
> *Grosvenor Cleeve*

He got up, took the letter from her hands, tore it and dropped the pieces in the stove. Then he went back to his book.

Rachel at last fed the child her supper and took her upstairs to bed. She returned, prepared food for her husband and herself, and they sat down together. When they had eaten, she said:

"Evan, you have to go."

"I'd like to know why."

"He's your father, and he wants to see you."

"I don't want to see him!"

"It will be hard for you."

"Why should it be hard? I have nothing to say; nothing to hear."

"It should be hard. But you must do it."

"You're sending me?"

They heard Rebecca, upstairs, crying; this was unusual. Rachel went to her. When she returned, she poured fresh boiling water on the tea and brought it to the table.

"Put on your good suit, Evan."

"Aren't you afraid to send me?"

"Yes," she murmured.

"You saw what I did to that poor wight, his secretary."

She was silent.

278

"I might do worse to the old whited sepulchre."

"I'm afraid, Evan. But you must go."

Evan got up, leaned over her, and kissed her. In the hard years, she had not aged, she had not changed save that her breasts were softer.

"I never even told you I had a father;" his voice fell: ". . . or a mother. Do I talk in my sleep?"

"No, dearest."

—Sleep. He did not talk, he *lived* in sleep. In sleep he had come here, in sleep married this woman, made her a mother. What he feared was not to wake, but partial waking. That was the disease of the world: its partial waking.

"I wish I knew you well enough," he smiled, "to ask you a few questions. We're not on speaking terms, are we?" His hand caressed her hand that held her cup, and some of the tea spilled: she put the cup on the table.

Evan had never seen the brand new Damon House; he avoided such palpable reminders of his past. The lobby was a blaze of brass, crystal, soft upholstery, flamboyant curtains, sleek men, embroidered women, over the marble floor punctuated by tall cuspidors. At the desk, a huge slab of genuine Carrara, bobbed the bland faces and ascot ties of the clerks. On the way to it, Evan saw Dusenbery in a crimson chair beside a vast vase turned lamp with tasseled shade. As he went up to him, the young man gripped the arm of his chair and lifted sulky eyes.

"Don't be scared. I just want to apologize."

"I'm not scared. If you start anything here—"

"I'm twice your age. You should have thrown *me* out."

"Do you think, if it hadn't been *your* house—?"

"I never thought of that. You shouldn't be so conventional. It stops clear thinking and good works."

"I think you're crazy."

"No, you don't. You're just bewildered. I hope you weren't hurt?"

"I'm all right."

"More bewilderment. I guess you're hopeless, my boy. Is the governor upstairs?"

Dusenbery nodded. "I didn't tell him, by the way, what you did. I just said you'd been rude."

279

Evan smiled: "I'll keep our little secret. By the way, how is he?"

"Vigorous."

"Good appetite? Still drinks his bottle of claret?"

"I think you're crazy."

"That's the second time you've said that. To a man you really thought was crazy, you'd not dare say it once."

The sulky eyes shifted.

"Bet I missed a good dinner;" Evan strode on.

The muffled elevator wafted him upward like a gentle falling. The carpeted broad hall, gray-paneled, gave him the sense of a soft decline. Evan thought of a rosewood casket, silk-padded, the kind in which members of his clan were buried. —Too bad I like this luxury, I must be preparing to die. He saw the room before he saw his father: gray and silver, the walls of brocade, the heavily shaded lamps, the thick carpet, and he felt a quaver of ease before he realized his father's face, the exaggerated nose, the paler lips, the watery sharper eyes, as if the years through which he saw were a cruel telescope.

"Sit down," said Grosvenor Cleeve. "Sorry you couldn't come and dine with me. A cigar?"

He sat down opposite his son. Evan lighted the cigar, the pleasantly good cigar after the years. And with the dry body of his father (in a dressing gown of purple silk)—the head too heavy, all the sap of the man gone to it, he felt the room coffin him.

"Perhaps you're curious to know how I found you?"

"It couldn't have been hard, if you hired good detectives."

The old man nodded. "It took quite some time. Five months, approximately. You see, the trail was cold. Then one of the operatives found the name Corthuis in the old Symphony lists. The rest was easy."

"You hadn't looked before?"

"No."

"What made you start, after all that time?"

"I'm going to tell you. Tell me first, Evan: how are you?"

"Pretty well," said Evan, "for so busy a man. The Missus says I work too hard. She says she'd be satisfied with half what I bring home —say a mere fifty thousand a year, if only I'd stick around a little more: show my face once in a while at her soirées and musicales."

"Evan, I'm old. Next year, if I live, I'll be eighty. I realize you're here because I asked you; you didn't seek me out and I know appeals to sentiment—"

"Stop it! I presume you're the same man you were, only a good deal shrunken. How can you talk of sentiment to me?"

"I assumed, at least, you wouldn't come here, if you did come, in ·a mood to joke."

"And why not?"

"I happen to know something about your fifty thousand a year—or is it a hundred thousand? I know where you live. I know about your wife. From the reports, she's a very fine woman and deserves more than you give her."

"Is it for her sake?"

"I didn't say that."

"But you assume a poor man can't be in the mood to joke?"

"I didn't say that, Evan. Your poverty, as a matter of fact, is a sort of bitter joke."

"I'm glad you see it. Admit the jest all round; that should make it easier for you to say what you have to say."

"You've forgotten me. I've never had to have things easy. I've gone my own way, too."

"You've been a man of strength, it's true, because you've always traded on the weaknesses of the country."

"You'll not discourage me, Evan. I tire quickly, I'm not good for much longer, and when I go, I'll go quickly." The old man placed a steady hand on his heart. "Until then, I'm *here*. Because I have something to say to you. I'm here for my own sake, primarily; not yours, not your wife's and child's. There's such a thing as the concurrence of interests. Will you stop—at least, will you stop talking to your father like a rebellious boy?"

"*Touché.*"

"I'll begin at the end: the proposition to be proved. For the sakes of all concerned, you should come home."

Evan let the smoke curl from his mouth, the smoke of the pleasantly good cigar.

"To dispose of a first item: you needn't worry about what you'll find in New York. You needn't have left. Nothing legal was ever brought against you."

"Your doing, of course."

"Where you live, how you live—you can work out such particulars in any way you like. The least conspicuous, the most gratifying for your wife, it appears to me, and what I wish, is to turn the house over to you. It's big enough for us all. It's a large house to be alone in."

"So mother found it."

"I'm glad you mentioned your mother. You never had much respect for me, Evan. Do you know, that would have been impossible—to the extent, I mean, of your hatred for me, if you'd not had much of me in you?"

"When did you learn that?"

"I've not been a soft man. You're harder. Don't be too hard."

"So we're alike? I'm a variation of the theme?"

"You have a wife, you have a child, too. Has it occurred to you: in your artistic, romantic way, you might be doing to them what I did to mine?"

"It's an interesting thought."

"Your father's no fool, Evan."

"A most interesting thought."

"You think you've changed. You've changed your name—to your mother's. You've become a fiddler, as your mother wanted."

"Not too good a one."

"As I suspected, when I had you study law. You live in a cottage (I've a photo of it) whereas you were born in a mansion. But I'm the one who's changed most."

"If it takes nearly eighty years, I've not had enough chance."

"If it did, as it has me, that would only mean again, you were not so different from your father."

"Your mind still runs."

"Listen to me, Evan."

For the first time since he had come into the room, Evan's eyes left his father; from the soft-napped carpet and the curtain-muted windows, they wandered to the sideboard.

"Would you care for a drink?" the old man asked, and without waiting for an answer got up; with steady hands he poured whiskey,

282

siphoned seltzer, into two tall glasses and carried one to Evan: the other he placed on the floor beside his chair in which, with painful knees, he sank again.

Evan took a long draught of the bourbon, the best, the pleasantly best he had tasted for years. He wiped his mouth: "You've been clear and concise. You're a good lawyer, still. Here, I take it, is your brief: Essentially, we're alike. Two positive charges of electricity, we've shot off from one another—or I, the weaker one, from you. There's the tragedy: being alike, we belong together, but we're antipathetic? Now, you've changed. You've had your fill of greed and flummery. In my way, I've been equally vile. (I'll grant that, at least.) So I'm to change, too? But then," he drank, wiped his mouth again, smiled broadly, "don't you see? we'll still both be alike: two negative instead of positive charges, we'll still shoot off."

Grosvenor Cleeve moistened his dry lips with his tongue (he had not touched his drink): "You're a good lawyer, too, Evan. We both know how specious an argument can be, that's based on analogy by metaphor."

"You mean—?" Evan appeared to be following, like a pupil.

"You might change, as I've changed, in such a way that we *won't* fly off from each other."

"I see."

"Help yourself to the whiskey."

Evan got up and half filled his tumbler, not touching the siphon. He walked toward the windows, he examined a painting of sheep a-browse on a field. He turned back to his father: "You assume the premise of change. Perhaps I don't want to. Granted everything you've said, granted your change is real enough, perhaps I don't want to change."

"I never thought of that." The old man's gaze rose from his fur-lined slippers. "I thought you'd suffered enough."

Evan's eyes quickened. "Oh, did you?"

The old man's gaze shifted from the strange smile he did not understand.

"You're still a hypocrite," said Evan. Grosvenor Cleeve's eyes went back and held to his son's. "What you mean is you thought *you* had suffered enough."

"Does that refute my conclusion about you? A man knows the suffering of others through his own."

He wet his lips again; he was visibly growing weaker, his great head heavier on his body. "It's always been a mistake of the moralists to plead with people about other people's pains. Make men aware of their own."

Evan nodded, but the flicker in his eyes grew hard.

"Of course, I've come to your unhappiness through my own." His voice died: "—to your mother's, through my own. Of course, if I could bear it—"

"It's a pity you're going to die; you could write a great book, father. Reform the world, by making each man know how *he*—not the piddling other fellow—suffers."

"You don't need to die," the old man smiled. "You write the book."

Evan laughed, and Grosvenor Cleeve anxiously clasped his chair: "Again, you're assuming your premise: that I *want* to go on from you, from *your* change."

"Don't you know yet, Evan, how unhappy you are?"

Evan drained his glass and smiled at his father: "No."

The handsome old man suddenly looked ugly, as if he had been struck in the face.

"I'm grateful to you, father; you've given me an insight. Let me follow *that* through. I don't want to change, because I don't yet know my own suffering. The revelation comes to one at the brink of the grave. It's too late for one to use it. You want to pass it on. But perhaps it can't be passed on, like a fortune or a disease. Perhaps that's the tragedy of man; or is it the farce? that the truth heals: but no man finds the truth till he's past healing."

Grosvenor Cleeve was very tired, the tensions of life faded from his face, leaving it a hideous gray chaos. He reached for the glass at his feet, his hands shook, he could not grasp it. Evan got up, held the drink to the wrinkled mouth, and Grosvenor Cleeve swallowed like an infant. The tremor of his hands rose to his head.

Evan went again to the sideboard. With an elbow on it, he looked at his father, and seemed to take aim with his words:

"We can know how we suffer only in the light of hope. That hope is born in the tenderness of a mother's breast and we lose it soon

284

enough. If the hope comes back before we die, it lights only what is lost. Where's that maggot of yours: what's his name? Dusenbery. Should I call him?"

"I'll be all right," gasped the old man.

Evan brought the bottle to his chair and sat down. He drank, watched his father, and drank again.

The shaking of the old head slowed; the hands quieted in his lap; the mucilaginous lids of Grosvenor Cleeve's eyes closed on their gaze.

Evan looked at him long. He saw the hands faintly pulsant, the hard protuberant blue veins, against the purple silk of the dressing gown; he saw the ruined body, the wrecked head, within the silk and silver of the room. Suddenly, he saw the room wrinkled with age; the curtains, the upholstery, the carpet, the walls, wrinkled and obscenely pulsant. The room was decayed like the old sleeping body. He picked up the half-empty bottle of rare bourbon and went through the door into the bedroom. His father's rich leather bag lay open. He found what he wanted: a large silver flask with the Cleeve arms and much rococo tracery. He poured the brandy into the washbowl, rinsed the flask and returned to the old man stifling in his chair, his mouth open, his eyes shut, his triumphant chin that had prowed through so many battles, now slavering against the haggard corded neck. He poured the bourbon into the flask and slipped the flask into his pocket. The room, its silk walls and ceiling, was obscene with wrinkles. He took his hat and shut the door behind him.

When Evan awoke at dawn beside Rachel, he recognized a well-being more terrible than pain. All the elements of his life seemed about to join together; the collisions, the corrosions, the assaults, seemed about to cease; but all he had known—pleasures and sufferings, all he had been used to, would be gone; the union would be like death. He remembered the night; he had walked, when he left his father, strange and inaccessible streets; he had met strange and inaccessible emotions. Life was at pause, the past and the future equally fused and destroyed in this present which held a secret ecstasy. Close to his house, it had come to him: —*My father is dead*. Did I deliberately torture, tire . . . kill my father? He lay now in bed in this frightening birth of well-being. Rachel got up, he heard her go to the porch for the milk, and to the kitchen. He heard Rebecca, her mother answering. All the familiar household sounds came unified; he was detached and heard them clearly—close, as never before; he heard them as if he were dead. There had been a flash of lightning; now the pause before the rent airs came together. Then there would be union: shattering thunder.

He lay long in bed, dozing, waking. At last, silently, he dressed and without going to the kitchen for his breakfast, he stole out of the house. The streets too were in waiting. Traffic and walkers moved as usual, yet in silent waiting. He bought a late edition of the morning paper, and without surprise read the black type of a stop-press bulletin:

GROSVENOR CLEEVE DIES IN CITY

Evan walked the streets, till it was time to go to Rudolph's for the noon concert. He desired neither food nor drink; they belonged to time and this pause between lightning and thunder . . . this pause before union of all within his life . . . was timeless. But thoughts spatially, visibly, occupied him. He saw Rachel and her womanhood, a warm mist within winter clarity; he saw his child and understood her: will was the fierce small flame of Rebecca, flame-colored, flame-fierce will. And he saw Jonathan; Jonathan Hartt, he saw, was still alive and still loved him, and wanted to be with him. He must see his old friend; this too was part of the impending union.

When he got home, reporters crowded the cold living room. He smiled at them and sat down. As they fired their questions at him, calling him Mr. Cleeve, he realized with a pang (his nearest approach to pain since he had seen his father) that this pause of timelessness was not an instant; it had depth, it lasted, and while he lived it, he must go through a routine of act and sense that simulated his old habits. Thus, he had walked the streets, knowing how to place one foot before another; thus found Rudolph's; thus played his violin in tune and in time. Thus, now, not having eaten all day, he was hungry.

"Just a moment, boys," he said to the reporters, and opened the kitchen door. "Dear," he called to Rachel, "could you bring me a sandwich?" He turned back to the men. "I'm hungry. I'll not say a thing, not even nothing," he smiled, "till I've had a bite. Meanwhile, you tell me: what do *you* know?"

They told him. Cloyd Dusenbery had sprung the sensation: he,

286

violinist in an Elysium bierkeller, was the son of the great lawyer; was himself a one-time prominent New York lawyer. The old man had come to town to plead with him to return. He had spent the evening alone with Grosvenor Cleeve, found dead in his chair by his secretary-attendant.

"Thanks, boys. That's all correct. You've got the whole story."

Rachel brought a tray with a sandwich and a glass of milk: she left them at once.

"What've you got to add?"

"Nothing."

"Why did you leave New York?"

"Nothing."

"Didn't you see the old man was sick?"

"Nothing."

"Why didn't you call a doctor?"

"Nothing."

"When exactly did you leave? . . . The police will be here any minute. What'll you say to them?"

Evan got up. "Nothing. Now good-by."

"You can't do this, Mr. Cleeve. Grosvenor Cleeve was too big a man."

"Thanks for the advice, boys."

"Won't you sit still just a minute more, till I finish this sketch?"

"Certainly, if you hurry a bit."

They left with no word from Evan, and yet not angry, so relaxed, pleasant, even gracious, had been his manner.

At five, two plain-clothes officers bulged through the door. They had orders to be polite, and it made them clumsy.

"But my dear men, if I go with you now, what becomes of my job? The guests at Rudolph's must have their dinner music."

"Can't someone take your place?"

"Lots of men could. But how find one, at this short notice?"

Evan promised to be at the District Attorney's the next morning. That night, many eyes oozed through the smoke of Rudolph's orchestra alcove. Chris Doppel was obsequious with respect, Sim Smith was chillier than ever, Lesueur smirked, Luchansky was afraid to look at Evan.

The papers next morning spread an ugly story. The son, Evan Corthuis Cleeve, had left New York under a cloud of scandal. There was bad blood between the great man and the wayward son; his mother, whose name he had taken, long years ago had killed herself. Was Evan his father's heir? What had happened in the room at the Damon House? (a diagram showed the position of the body). The glass at the old man's feet was being analyzed by police chemists. Had the son handled it? . . . Dusenbery, it was plain, had had plenty to say, he was taking his revenge. Rachel at breakfast said nothing unusual to her husband; forbearing, as if Evan were bereaved and sick, she did not seem aware that newspaper reporters and the police had invaded their home. She was very clear to him, her warm womanhood, but at an immeasurable distance.

In his private office, Evan found District Attorney Dowdie, an ambitious little man who seemed to feel around him such vastnesses in his authority that he was afraid of losing his way or being knocked about like a loose package. Margining him were two assistants and a stenographer; standing beside his desk loomed the Police Chief, a German whose truculence was fashioned on what he believed to be the manner of New York's "finest." Dowdie, with a gesture denoting dignity, waved Evan to a seat where he had the light in his eyes.

"We've just heard from New York," Dowdie began. "The will has been opened. You're your father's chief legatee."

Evan said nothing; the sun glare would not disturb him, he figured, if he kept his eyes relaxed.

"Suppose you tell us just what happened between Grosvenor Cleeve and you in that hotel room?"

Evan clipped a cigar and put a match to it. "Is this a criminal inquiry?"

"I didn't say that."

"Then I'll tell you nothing. I can't see that it's any of your business."

"You may find it is."

"I'll wait and see."

"Do you want a lawyer?"

"I'll be my own lawyer."

"Why won't you cooperate with us?"

"What in? What's this all about?"

288

"We've had a report on that glass of whiskey."

"Indeed?"

"Did you poison your father?"

"Was my father poisoned?"

"You tell us."

"Listen, Mr. District Attorney, I'll tell you nothing until I've been informed how this matter concerns you."

"You were on bad terms with your father."

"That's none of your business."

"You profit enormously by his death."

"Perhaps I do. If you mean I profit financially, you're a fool."

"Why call us names?"

"Sorry," Evan smiled into the glare. "I've been out of touch with men like you so long, I've lost the light touch."

"Would you mind telling us, now you're known and have all that money, what you intend to do?"

"I'll tell you nothing."

The Chief, trying to be an Irish bulldog, lunged forward: "Did you kill Grosvenor Cleeve?"

Evan blew smoke into the air: "Stop barking."

"Do you deny you killed your father?" asked the District Attorney.

Evan paused: "No. I deny—and admit—nothing."

"That glass your father drank from: did you give it to him?"

Evan's mood changed; he was no longer defensive: "I don't believe I did. He was the host. He handed out the drinks."

"Did you touch your father's glass?"

"Come to think of it, I did! Why, of course! The old man had a kind of seizure . . . like palsy. His hand shook and I helped him." He smiled. "The way you feed a baby."

"So." The District Attorney was outdistanced.

"What'd you put in dat glass!" bawled the Chief.

"Did I put anything in it? Did anyone put anything in it? You tell me. Come clean, Chief. Was there anything in that glass besides most excellent bourbon and seltzer?"

"Did you know your father was dead?" asked Dowdie, afraid of laughter.

Evan smoked and pondered. The question appeared to interest him;

289

not the questioner, not the questioner's purpose. "I seem to have known . . . if you could call it knowing. Just before I got home. Interesting! The thought popped into my mind. What was the cause of death?"

"You're not here to ask us!" the Chief shouted.

"Sorry," said Evan. "Don't tell me, if that's how you feel."

The District Attorney tapped a self-conscious finger on the edge of his desk. "Perhaps," he said in what he hoped was an ominous undertone, "you had better get a lawyer, Mr. Cleeve."

Evan thought of Jonathan . . . Jonathan who loved him and whom he suddenly longed to see. In this moment of fusion of all the parts of his world,—this pause between the lightning and the thunder that had now lasted two nights and a day—Jonathan had a place. But not here! The District Attorney took Evan's silence for hesitation. The bluff had worked? the man *was* in trouble? He began to congratulate himself (—You'll go far), when Evan answered:

"Don't be unkind, Mr. District Attorney. I'm a damn good lawyer, myself."

"I can take you to Police Headquarters," growled the Chief. "We'll know how to make you talk."

"You'd better watch your step; you might fall and put out your brain," said Evan.

The District Attorney began another tack: "Why did you change your name?"

"Unless you think you have evidence that I did so to defraud, it's none of your business."

"Does your wife—"

"None of your business," repeated Evan.

The Chief was boiling over. "We'll show you damn New Yorkers we know how to take care of our town."

"Come, Chief, have I soiled it? Are you as fragile and fragrant as that?"

"We'll let you go for the present," said Dowdie. "Don't try to leave—"

Evan got up, laughing. "Why don't you two get together? The Chief thinks I'm a blot on the city; you beg me to stay . . ."

"You heard me," the little man glowered.

Evan leaned over his desk. "Won't you tell *me? was* there anything in my father's glass, that didn't belong there?"

Nobody answered.

"I suppose not," Evan turned toward the door, musing; forgetful of his audience, he murmured: "That makes it serious. That makes it a problem—"

The Chief tried a last lunge. "Who's it a problem for?" he shouted.

Evan quietly ran his eyes over the big paunch, the small head. "Not for you, I'm afraid, Chief," he smiled gently. "Why, if I were a Catholic and you were a priest, and I faced *you* in confession, not even God could get my message." He turned back to Dowdie. "It's an idea, Mr. District Attorney. Why not recruit your police officers among men trained along the lines of theological seminaries? It might get results."

"You wait!" muttered the Chief who had understood no word of what he knew was an insult.

"It's hard to wait," said Evan. "That's why my temper's a bit short. Forgive me."

In the corridor, the reporters closed on him.

"Sorry, boys," he pushed his way through. "The District Attorney and the Chief of Police wouldn't tell me a thing."

THANK GOODNESS!, THE REDECORATING WAS FIN-
ished just in time to solemnize Jonathan's fiftieth birthday. For the
parlor, Greta chose green tapestry panels with wall brackets of fluted
imitation candles, each holding a tiny pink bulb like a flame. Near
the windows, curtained in green, lined with gray satin, stood her new
Steinway grand. Jonathan's books in the library were still housed in
the old ponderous dark shelves (Greta would have liked to throw
them out, they just collected dust!, in favor of bright glass-enclosed
Globe-Wernicke cases); but at least the walls over the books were a
rich crimson like damask. (His new Chippendale desk was banished
for the evening celebration to the basement.) The dining room was
brown: walls in imitation leather with imitation brass knobs, walnut
chairs with leather seats, and on the walnut sideboard a silver fruit
dish and tall silver candlesticks (never used) like Corinthian columns.
Greta, Lucia, ancient Mrs. Hartt, Reuben and his wife Lucy, were all
agreed that Jonathan must have a splendid birthday. Were not the
clouds of the Evan Cleeve misfortune gone forever? (They had trembled at the recent flare-up when Grosvenor Cleeve was found dead in
an Elysium hotel, and his son discovered playing the violin in a beer-
hall and living in a slum under his mother's name with some woman
and a child. The yellow press had hinted foul play; then the black
sheep vanished, refusing to touch his father's money; the newspapers,
unable to digest such hyperbolic nonsense, dropped the story—and from
beginning to end, not one, thank goodness!, had mentioned Evan
Cleeve's old partner.) Jonathan was prospering again, Greta had been
able to give the swell Fifth Avenue decorator, Mr. De Launay, *carte
blanche*—well, almost. The hall room on the top floor that Philip
occupied when he wasn't traveling for Mendis Toys, was unchanged,
at Philip's insistence; Greta's and Jonathan's room on the second floor
had the same bed (Greta would have liked twin beds but did not press
her wish). But Lucia's and Jeff's rooms on the third floor were done
over, there was a second bathroom with a built-in tub; and the back

room on their floor, where Grandma Hartt had lived till she moved to Reuben's, was now a charming sitting room with a bed-couch of rosewood and Japanese prints on the walls.

The folding doors into the dining room were closed while the servants and the waiter from Sherry's prepared the supper collation; the paneled glass doors with brass hinges from the parlor to the library and hall were folded open. The new inlaid parlor floor shone; the new electric lights of library and parlor sang like canaries on the guests, a good three score, who wallowed in their own effluvia of voices, the men's rumbling, the women's rustling and piercing.

Sarah Hartt sat in state near the library window and smiled benignly as the guests, one by one, greeted her, congratulated her, hoped she was well, and lied about her looks which were older than her eighty years. Her face, between the black satin dress and the black lace cap, was yellow parchment; her eyes and nose and mouth, dried and precise, were peaceful as a mummy's. In the parlor, Greta's mother, Mathilda Mendis, whose years seemed at least twenty less than Mrs. Hartt's (she was seventy-three), held a circle of delighted listeners with her gossip about Europe. She was back after two years abroad with her son Alfred and his family in Dresden, and with her son Sylvester, who had opened the London branch of Mendis Toys and married an English lady addicted to horseback and lawn tennis. So much more *happens,* Mrs. Mendis implied, in Europe! There, people *live;* here they are merely *busy.* She tapped her Spanish fan on the knee of Belinda, Reuben's serious elder daughter (twenty-five and still unmarried!) and Belinda agreed, although her way of putting it would have been: "There, people *think;* here, they merely run around." Mrs. Mendis smiled into the receptive faces of her audience. She had seen Queen Victoria, very near, at a Charity Bazaar. The old lady, she said, was a pious fraud; what she really would have liked was a glass of ale in a fairly respectable pub. Nobody believed this iconoclastic version of the Queen; but it was thrilling and somehow assertive of American democracy to hear a woman who had *seen* her dare to be irreverent about it. Sarah Hartt would have disapproved of Mrs. Mendis's chatter; Lucia, who sat alone under the picture of Washington in the library, would have found it bad taste to be disrespectful of a sovereign who had done so much to increase respect for woman. Her sparse gray hair tight on her head, Lucia more and more resembled her beloved brother, Jonathan. Few spoke to her; she sat in dignified repose, the storms of her frustrate years happily past. If Reuben had heard the remarks of Mrs. Mendis, he would not have confined himself to silent disapproval; he would have felt it his duty to defend the Queen. Reuben was home on his first visit since President McKinley sent him to Pekin as Minister. He stood near the blazing gas-logs in the library, with by far the the largest group—all men—around him, their eyes and ears drinking the wisdom of his words. Not one but was grateful for his presence; not one but was saying to himself or implicitly feeling: This man knows the President; this man has met the Emperor of China; here he is, I can touch him! he knows *me!* Reuben was Minister to their greater glory. They were asking him questions about the crisis in Cuba, about the mystery of the recent sinking of the *Maine* in Havana Harbor, about the disgraceful, incredible letter of Spain's Minister to Washington, insulting the President. Yes, said the Honorable Reuben, the letter is authentic, even though it was Hearst who published it in his unsavory *Journal.* The country's wish for righteous war, he said, was mounting like a fever. Great names . . . John Hay, Whitelaw Reid, Henry Cabot Lodge, that magnificent statesman War Secretary Alger . . . rose from Reuben's casual mouth like flares from a Roman candle. He knew them all, yet here he stands, warming his distinguished long legs at Jonathan's gas-logs. Reuben oozed confidence *(entre nous);* he knew everything, of course: yet his listeners received no certainty on what they wanted to know: Would there be war with Spain? no help in what really worried them: Would war be good for business or bad?

Jeff, down from Harvard for the great day, sat on the carpeted stair in the front hall with his beautiful dark cousin, Hortense, younger daughter of Reuben. The same step would have brought their bodies too close together, but Hortense on the step above felt her elevation not quite enough to symbolize the difference between them: Jeff, a mere freshman and seventeen, she a senior at Smith and twenty-one. Yet she liked Jeff, he was distinguished and terribly clever; and besides, who else was there to talk to, in this gathering of old men and women?

"What's it like at Harvard?"

"It's kind of bewildering at first."

"Do you have to work hard?"

"You can do what you like. No one pays much attention."

"That must be wonderful."

"I guess it is," Jeff agreed doubtfully.

"All those wonderful boys from the oldest families! Do they have old colonial chairs in their rooms?"

"Lord, no! you grab what you can from the second-hand dealers or the chap who had your room before you."

"I thought at *Harvard*— But there must be fascinating talks. Literature and—"

"Football."

"Why, Jeff! Harvard's the *brains* of New England, and isn't New England the capital of culture?"

"I guess so. There's all kinds there. You don't get to know most of 'em."

"What kind are you?" She smiled winningly down at her cousin.

"It's true, we don't know much about each other."

"If I tell you what kind I *think* you are, will you tell me if I'm right?"

"I'll tell you what I think; but maybe *you*'d be right." He hoped his hair was smooth (he'd put enough water on it to hold it down), and his white tie in order. He was uncomfortably aware of his stiff shirt and of the tails he was sitting on.

"Well," began Hortense, "I dunno."

"Yes, you do."

"I guess lessons—kind of bore you."

"Not all! I love History, and the History of Art."

"Are you going to be an artist?"

"I'm going to build houses—new cities."

"That's even better."

"Architects are artists."

"What will uncle Jonathan and aunt Greta say?"

"Mama'll love anything I love. Pa sort of hints I should be a lawyer, go into politics, reform the world. But I can manage him."

"Didn't he used to want to reform the world? Papa says so."

"I guess he's outgrown it."

"I like uncle Jonathan. I don't see why we see so little of uncle Jonathan and aunt Greta."

"You *live* in a grander world. China—"

"Pooh! I haven't even *been* to China; maybe I'll go when I graduate —but not for long, you can bet! Before ma and pa went to China, I'll tell you a secret: most of the people who came to the house were stuffy. Your ma and pa aren't stuffy."

"Thanks awfully."

"Aunt Greta has a beautiful voice. That's a lot better than spouting political speeches. And your pa—I guess I like sad people."

"You're not sad."

"Oh, aren't I? That's all you know! Because a girl has a beautiful home—"

"—and a beautiful face."

"Shut up, silly boy! Because she's *popular,* you think she has *everything?* I didn't suppose you were so materialistic."

"I'm not! Really, Hortense, I'm not."

"I know you're not; not really. I couldn't talk with you like I do, if you were. It's so natural to talk with you, as if we saw *lots* of each other; as if I were talking to myself."

"Gee, Hortense, I'm glad. Do you think it's good that I'm going to build houses?"

"I think it's wonderful. I hope they're like those wonderful old houses you see in Boston or even in little villages like Litchfield. Full of the most wonderful Windsor chairs and hooked rugs and lowboys and old, old canopied beds."

"I'll build you a house, some day!"

"That'll be wonderful. But oh! I'll never need a house, I'm never going to be married."

"Gosh, Hortense, how can you talk such rot!"

"All the men nowadays, all they think of is money or politics which is even worse. Or football and baseball." Hortense shook her head and her dark velvety eyes met her cousin's, and retreated.

"I know that's most of 'em, and they're not your kind. But there's always one exception, Hortense—even like you're one exception. He'll come along."

"You *shall* build us a house!" Hortense said gleefully. "We'd better go back to the others. Oh, what a bore!" She leaned forward to rise; her hair touched the boy's cheek, her breast skimmed his shoulder; a pleasure poignant as pain stabbed him and she felt her spell on him. To hold it, she held her closeness, her body forward between and sitting and rising; and in that moment, they both saw Jeff's father step from the noisy incandescent parlor into the hall below them. Unaware of them, he strangely surveyed the new hat-tree, the bronze Chinese shield beside it (a house gift from Reuben and Lucy). They felt his suffering, that shielded them from his vision and was strangely akin to the poignance of pleasure in their bodies. This secret harmony was too strong to let them feel confused or unpoised, when at last he saw them.

"Hello, my dears." He took without surprise their apartness from the others and the closeness of their bodies, as if also within the spell of the harmony between them. "May I join you?"

Now they sat on the same step, and he below them, sidewise, his profile toward them. The evening was ripe (soon Greta would sing, then the supper), and Jonathan had moved through it, his discordance from it ripening along. All day at the office, he had been depressed. A profitable day: he had completed a contract for the sale of a ribbon factory, solved the problem of a lien on a remunerative patent (the inventor long since dubbed off with a pittance). His work, serving the fat of the land, seemed to him without dignity, but this was nothing new. He had imagined Greta at home in her efficient preparations for the party; and now he saw her, the happy hostess; but the disillusion of their twenty years of marriage was not new, why should all this trouble him today? He told himself these friends and dear ones were offering their congratulations not to the successful lawyer, not to the happy husband; but because they loved him. Why did their affection, which he wanted, draw his disaffection? He should by now be used to not knowing where Evan was. But all day Evan had pressed on him, making an irony of the feast, as if he were here—, as if he were dead. When Grosvenor Cleeve died, he had read every word of the affair, procuring the fuller accounts in the Elysium papers. For a day they were dangerous and ugly: a man who refused his inheritance from his father, they "wisely" said, must have his reasons. That was the last word of the gutter press, which dropped the story. Jonathan had given in to his impulse to write to Evan a simple word of friendship, which he asked the executors to forward. Cranston, in the Cleeve office, confided that Evan had quit his bierkeller job, probably driven out by the publicity, and that they did not know where he was. Then, on the impulse again, Jonathan wrote to Evan's wife. "I'm your husband's old friend. I cannot feel that has changed. It must not change. If there is anything a friend can do—" This also was forwarded, and never answered.

The proper host, he drifted through the crowded rooms, chatting with everyone. He felt sorry for Lucia who disdained to talk servants with the ladies ("a greenhorn fresh from Ellis Island" . . . "a *treasure, my dear, yes, Irish, but how she can work!"*) and could not talk business with the men. He was amused by the spectacle of Reuben, monarch of all he surveyed: he seemed to judge him with Evan's eyes. He joked pleasantly with Lucy, who alone took no pride in her husband's greatness (Reuben to her was Reuben and her husband): he liked Lucy Hartt, shrewdly at peace with nature, man, and her God.

"If I dared," she laughed, "I'd play *Brown October Ale* to celebrate your birthday."

"Why don't you dare?"

"On Greta's new grand?"

"That's from *Robin Hood?*"

"Yes."

"You go ahead and play. But make it chopsticks."

He saw his brother Philip also wandering from group to group. Philip was alone and congratulated by nobody for nothing, yet Philip had the ease he lacked, and liked everyone, and deserved—because he did not need—congratulations. At forty-seven, Philip was a soft easy man with a growing inward solidity that showed in his quiet eyes. His jowls hung like a comfortable hound's. Of all those present, he was the one most master of himself. (Several times during the evening, he had stolen into the dining room and the servants, who adored him, gave him a slice of salmon, a dish of salad.) . . . All this now in Jonathan, sitting on the stair below his son and Reuben's handsome daughter.

"It's a lovely birthday party, uncle Jonathan." Her dark, somewhat heavy features reminded him of his father's. He liked her.

"That's why you run away from it?"

"This isn't exactly running away. After all, Jeff's here—and so are you."

"You talk like a diplomat; you frighten me, my dear. The sins of the father—"

"I *am* having a good time. So there!"

"Aren't you, dad?"

Father and son looked guardedly at each other. In the man, with his trim Vandyke beard, his hair thinning and graying, the dreamer had retreated to his eyes—and to the youth on the step above him. Jonathan was dark and tense; Jefferson, already considerably taller, had a supple blond grace; his large eyes gave him an upward lyric lilt that the years might wear down to nervousness.

"But the best's yet to be," laughed the boy, when his father did not answer.

"Aunt Greta's singing!" said Hortense.

"How about the grub?"

Chords of the piano fell on the rumbling rooms, not quite smothering the chatter. The piano was still; now came the opening measures of a song by Schubert, but not till Greta's voice rose was there silence. This *Lied,* Jonathan remembered, she had sung in Lafayette Place, the first night he brought Evan. It was as if Evan were there again, at the piano. . . . Greta's voice took the song and molded it with her own flesh. This was Schubert; but also this was the woman. She sang a Brahms, a Hugo Wolf; the passion was never born, the tears never shed. Why had he not lived with this Greta? Her singing was her body as she had been on their wedding night: the firm free breasts, the swelling throat, the thighs concealing. . . . Her singing was her life, never attained by him. Greta, he knew, had accommodated herself to living with his absence. She was not only faithful, she was happy with his absence. The sorrow, the passion, the tears, which should have been his food, that his own sorrow and tears might be born wholly, were in her music, forever forming it, never discharged. He looked at her listening son. There lived the unborn, which he called his love and his hope.

The voice stopped, the applause lapped over it, irrelevant. In the library, he knew, sat the dry old woman who never applauded; he could feel his mother's rigid silence. He heard Greta: "You must all be hungry," and the crowd in chatter, laughter, shards of words, tumbled from song toward the food.

Hortense sighed: "It was too too beautiful."

Jeff said: "But you *are* hungry?"

299

Hortense laughed and got up. They were gone, and the music quite gone.

To be again the dutiful host, Jonathan made his way from the almost deserted parlor through the crowded library and more crowded dining room. The men stood with plates in their hands; most of the ladies sat, expansively smiling, daintily eating. He heard fragments of the talk: "The Greater City's *first* Mayor, a Tammany henchman like Van Wyck! . . . Disgrace." "Altman's *is* reliable. But I assure you, the sales at most department stores—" "The new District Attorney at least was honest enough to say, To Hell with Reform." "Why, I heard only last week—" "That disgusting Mrs. Humphrey Ward." "Well, the *country's* sound . . . The G.O.P. . . . McKinley and Lincoln." "A bear market would be dangerous." "Senator Thurston of Nebraska said, 'War with Spain will stimulate every industry and domestic commerce'." "*Trilby* was immoral, of course; but so brilliant!" The music quite gone . . . Philip also did not seem to be eating. "What's wrong, Philip? No appetite?" "I guess I've spoiled it." He squirmed like a happy dog. "Annie gave me an advance." Greta on her bright way from guest to guest: "Jonathan dear, is everything all right? Why don't you have something? Get yourself some lobster salad." She was gone. After the twenty years, on his fiftieth birthday, she did not remember that her husband ate no lobster. Belinda was arguing with Lucia. Small, blond, intense, a new kind of "modern woman," Belinda despised her aunt Lucia and despised her father. Jonathan was afraid of Belinda. Raoul, good plodding fellow, who looked so tired ever since he married his young wife, talked with Reuben. The "Ambassador" was probably saying: "So long as business is sound; so long as the gold standard—" —If Bryan had been elected; if grass had grown on the streets . . . Grass. All flesh is grass. That was Isaiah. His father. The gentle bearded face. Jonathan longed for his father; for the old house . . . Evan slept in it, thirty-five years ago, the day of the Draft Riots. Evan called him "Old Testament;" his father, not he, deserved the name: his father, the gentle failure. The Old Testament was hard. Survival of the fiercest. Darwin proved it. But where is the saber-tooth tiger? Greta was coming toward him with a plate. "Here, darling, your favorite *chicken* salad." She did remember! The little canapés were hearts, triangles, stars and crescents; anchovy, salmon, Westphalia ham, tomatoes, made them gay. Greta was gone again. Someone in the library was striking with a knife against a glass. Persistently. Asking for silence. It was Reuben.

"Friends," came Reuben's voice, "I wish to propose a toast. To our Birthday Child."

Everyone applauded. Annie, the waitress, was at his side, her dark Irish face flushed with trouble. "Mr. Hartt," she whispered.

"What is it, Annie?"

Reuben was speaking . . .

"—at the door, sir, the basement door," said Annie.

"A tradesman at this hour?"

"—years of incorruptible service to our city—"

"He says, sir, just to say: it's Mr. Evan."

Jonathan was standing in a vertical silence; far overhead, as from the surface of the sea to a diver at the bottom, Reuben's words quavered:

"—of loyal love and devotion to his family—"

Jonathan went down the basement stairs.

He was standing in the dim hall, a weak light on his face. Jonathan took his hand which was hot.

"Evan!" he said.

"You're having a party? I could hear the racket from the stoop. That's why I rang the downstairs bell. I'm not dressed for a party."

"You're not well. Come upstairs."

"I'm not dressed for a party. What's it for? Anything special?"

"What's the difference? My fiftieth birthday. I don't mean: join the party. They're all busy eating. We'll go up to your room, where I can have a look at you."

"My room?"

"Start arguing tomorrow. It's late, and if you're not sick, you certainly are tired."

Jonathan smelled the moist soiled clothes; he was sure Evan had not undressed in a long time.

"I'm a bad birthday present, Jon."

"You're the best. Shut up and come along."

At the first step, Evan stumbled; Jonathan placed his arm around his friend, sensing the strange humiliation in his body. He half lifted him upward.

301

Toward the head of the stair, the noise of the guests struck them like shattered glass.

"Wait," said Jonathan, and closed the door into the library. He was running a gauntlet, like little Jeff. (He had sat on Jeff's bed, one night, while little Jeff told him the story.) He felt himself small, stealing along the hall beside large Evan. Evan's clothes smelled of rain and sweat; Evan smelled of sorrow. They came to the steps where he had sat with his son and his niece. No one in sight in the parlor.

"I was expecting you," he said, helping him up.

"Old Testament prophet. Old charlatan!" Evan smiled.

In the second-floor sitting room, Jonathan shut the door and turned on the light. "Lie on the couch. Are you hurt?"

"That's a devious question." Evan sat on the couch.

"Are you hungry?"

In Evan's face, haggard and unshaven, the eyes glowed with fever. Slowly, his body sagged; his head sank sideways. Jonathan took his hot wet hand and looked into his eyes. The eyes shut; he breathed quietly; he was asleep.

Jonathan drew off the muddy shoes, the matted socks, and, with difficulty, the coat and vest. He found a knitted wool comforter in a drawer, and covered his friend. Then he opened the window an inch from the top, quietly shut the door, and went down to his guests.

4

EVAN'S EYES OPENED UPON HIS DREAMING; A SPHERI-cal music, heaving him within it, spun upon itself and welled parabola-wise outward. Dissolved in the sound were visual coagulations that he knew were memories. Schmehl, the leader, lifted his shoulders flush with his ears (he seemed to have no neck) and threw his soft palms up: "It's the boss's orders. I'm sure sorry to have you go, Mr. Cleeve. You see how it is. Crowds at dinner-time is fine, but you can have too much of a good thing. Most of 'em don't come to eat, they come to look. I'm awful sorry. It's the boss's orders." Rachel darned Rebecca's woolen stockings, and said nothing: only her usual words, household words, mother words, but he could hear her silence, the one dissonance in the music. Her sufferance, like an animal's, had no dimension be-yond the immediate present, and he was already beyond. Her word might have stopped him before they were no longer in the same space, the same time. He was going backward through time. —This isn't dream. You're dreaming, but this is true. The split parts of his world, widening, were coming together; nothing mattered, but that at last they must all come together. Part of them that said "I" still moved against the enveloping motion; precarious as if he stood on an icefloe against a hot storming current, he that was "I" suffered but must melt, must vanish. He came into Jonathan's private office, they discussed a brief. The name of the case was fantastic (he forgot it as the dwindling floe passed on), but Jonathan was palpable: his heavy eyelids, his dark lips with too much blood in them. They discussed the law in the case; Evan was glib with nonsensical words, quoting statutes, precedents that never were on earth. But the music was true. He sat in the saloon on Irving Place and went over the new franchise with Dick Croker's handy-man. Dangerously easy—fun because of the danger, not the ease, was the fat roll of bills he slipped into his pocket. The streets of Elysium flowed past; days and nights were welded to the houses, were dragged by them forward uphill toward Mrs. Liebling's; but he knew in his dream, this was delusion: *he* was the one moving, falling backward

303

and down. "You can't go back like this without tearing your life!" he spoke with his mother's voice. Yet she beckoned him back, she was a station toward the unity against which the part of him that said "I" stood out. And there was his father, quietly, with dignity, lying down to die beside his mother's flaming throat on the bathroom floor. "Evan, come and join us. Haven't you suffered enough?" The District Attorney found no evidence which proved he killed his father . . . and his mother. He must find Jonathan, to kill him. "I haven't suffered enough."

Evan lay, his eyes shut again, not sleeping now. He knew he lay in a room of Jonathan's house. How had he got there? —You're out of tune, you're ahead of the music. No: he was in the counterpoint that moved upon two planes, his present memory of the weeks since his father's death and the weeks' factual procession. He refused to touch the inheritance. Jonathan's letter came: "I've not yet reached the space to answer it;" the past he was going back to, where he would answer Jonathan, was spatial. Rachel showed him her letter; he put it in his pocket: "I'll answer it." Rachel was paying the bills, now, from her own savings; perhaps borrowing; she had good friends. He reached Jonathan of his boyhood; he scarcely glanced at this new stage of his regression: with the others, it would pass. But Jonathan's face held him: it was like his mother's. The present—his lying half awake in Jonathan's house with his dreamings—merged into the past; separate they impinged upon each other; and now an impingement of bodies also separate yet united. This was the unbearable transition! he must escape to perfect separation or to perfect union! And even this pain was both separate (living in his memory of the weeks and in their factual procession), and united. What he felt now he had felt the last time he tried to talk with Rachel.

"Of course he died of natural causes. But I helped him. When I saw I was hurting him, I hurt him more; when I saw he was tiring, I wore him down. Rachel, I killed him."

Rachel failed him. All she said was: "Yes. When we are hurt, we go on hurting. We are all responsible for every unhappy death."

He wanted to cry out: "Help me to suffer! Then I'll stop falling back." He was silent, and she went on:

304

"That is why Jesus died. If only you could know, dear, and find comfort!"

He did not want comfort! The icefloe must melt and be lost.

She said: "The Jews didn't kill Christ nineteen hundred years ago. I kill Christ now! We all kill Him, each day and hour. And He forgives us."

He did not need to be forgiven. He needed to suffer until the widening fractions of his world fused into one. Now he knew: Rachel with her praying and her need to comfort barred his flowing back. Even to tell Rachel: "I must go back to New York" would halt him. He said, simply:

"Give me some money."

"How much do you want?"

"Not much. Say fifty dollars."

"I'll get it for you. Can you wait till tomorrow?"

He saw her, concise and remote: she did not ask even herself, What is the money for? She did not worry about food or her child or their future; she was as sure of her inheritance under God as he was sure she too would never touch a penny of his father's. She was a monster, this Christian! he felt no pity for her. A moment he knew, were he strong, he could embrace her and her child in the unity he needed. He was not so strong. Only the wreckages could he gather in; not her outrageous purity. Therefore she must be excluded. The moment of revelation went, leaving no regret, leaving only a cold fury against her.

Next evening, when he came in from his usual wanderings through the Elysium streets, now a palimpsest with the remembered streets of New York seething with commerce and civil war, Rachel went at once to the broken teapot on the shelf and gave him the money he had asked for. The kitchen was warm, the rest of the house cold. Rebecca sat at table before a bowl of oatmeal and a glass of milk.

"Thanks," he said.

"Supper'll be ready soon."

"Did you have a hard time getting this?"

"No, dear. Mr. McAllister let me have it. I've been so fortunate! There'll be an opening in his school in February. I'll pay him back from my salary."

"I won't ask you for more."

305

"If you need it, Evan—"

"I won't need it."

"That's good. Have you found something? I should think, by now, you could go back to Rudolph's."

He knew she did not mean it; she was "making conversation" as if they were already strangers.

"Do you want me to go back?"

"I didn't say that. But you were happy there?"

"Do you mean, happy?"

"I don't know."

"Do you think I should be happy, Rachel?"

She was busy, her back turned, at the stove. Now she brought two plates of beef liver and potatoes to the table. That was all her answer.

"You forget," they sat with the child between them, "there's more money than we can possibly use, waiting for us in New York."

She smiled and began to eat.

"What if Rebecca needed it?" he asked.

"Rebecca won't need it."

Evan cut the tough meat and chewed it long. They were strangers, "making conversation."

"Mama," said the child, "I don't want to finish my milk."

"It's good for you, dear."

"I don't want to."

"Aren't you hungry any more?"

"I want some pudding."

She took the half glass of milk and poured it into the bottle on the ledge of the window. She brought the bread pudding to the child.

There was no dessert for them. She said: "You have one bottle of beer left. Do you want it?" When he made no sign, she brought it and emptied it into a huge stem goblet he had carried away, long ago, from a saloon that boasted "the biggest five-cent beer in town." Even with the foam, the glass was little more than half full. Suddenly he knew it was tonight; and Rachel knew! this was their last supper. He tried to force his mind to focus on their years together. He had loved this woman; this Christian monster in his arms had given him delight, ecstasy, peace, utterly beyond what he had known of women who lived for love of men. He had loved this woman; and it was nothing! Re-

306

motely he remembered, as if he were looking at some alien life poorly focused in telescope or microscope. Perfection was dead; more dead than all his failures! For her, the perfection lived. Then, there was a grace for happiness, as there was a destiny for hell? Grace! another word, like hell; which suddenly had meaning. Evan looked at the mean kitchen, the child at the bare table; they were part of him, yet could not touch him. —This is hell? His suffering touched Rachel, she was filled and whole with it. —This is grace? He tried to flay himself with the cheerful cottage on Locust Hill where they had loved, and that he had destroyed, as wantonly as if his hands had torn it down. It could not touch him! Since it could not fill him, he must be emptied of it. He finished his beer. The last supper.

"It's bed time. Come, Rebecca," said Rachel.

Evan got up and put on his coat and hat. Then he went back to the table, and lifted the child high, face to face. He kissed her; her eyes were cool and glanced from him like ice.

"Goodnight," he said.

The child twisted her body to be let down.

He placed her on the floor. He went up to his wife, held her face in his two hands; instead of kissing her mouth, he looked into her eyes. He saw the questions in them: —Where are you going? Oh, what are you going to do? For a moment, pity . . . an exquisite elation . . . won him. Pity for her? for the child? for himself? He did not know, but it was a precious gift. He could not afford it. Pity was the kingdom of heaven; but to possess it, he knew, meant to rule it! meant all the responsibility of rulership. He was a beggar and weak, what could he do with a kingdom?: he wanted a crust of bread. Consciously, he knew this. Failure and death is easier than the kingdom of heaven. Rachel freed herself from him, came back, while the child stood staring, and gave him his violin. Then she knew! she was nourished and whole, knowing his plight and suffering for him? Then the graced ones in their heaven needed hell; knew there was hell and used it! She seemed to him infinitely cruel. She seemed to him, in her greater cruelty, helpless as he. Pity did not fade. It was the moment to go. . . .

He lay awake, more aware. Had he come to New York to see Jonathan? Then he'd managed pretty well, since he lay in Jonathan's house. He heard the rattle of an elevated train approach, subside. It was painful to breathe deep, and he needed to breathe deep: he was thirsty. Too bad he'd not brought along some of the rain of his walk . . . his clothes? he passed a hand over his side and found he was warm and dry in a nightshirt. Dear old Jonathan, half a foot shorter and thin: it could scarcely be his. Had they borrowed it from their cook, big as a tun? Perhaps from Philip. The rustic, rhythmic Philip: he dimly remembered him at the door, handing Jonathan something, while in the hall a woman whispered. He recalled the basement, the noisy rooms they had passed (Jonathan's fiftieth birthday!). Then, the superb parabola music, congealing, shrinking now, in the rattle of another train. If that was the progress from dream to waking, did he want it? He heard the door softly open. He drew a hand from under the covers to show Jonathan he was awake; and Jonathan came in, bundled in a red bathrobe.

Jonathan placed a hand on Evan's brow. "How are you feeling?" Before he could say that he wanted a drink, Jonathan held a glass before him, and Evan, raising himself heavily, drank the painful imperative coolness. Jonathan drew a chair close and sat down.

"You have a fever. You'll have to stay in bed till the doctor sees you."

"I'll get up. This is no place for me, particularly if I'm sick."

"Don't talk like a fool."

"All right. Don't get excited. I'll stay anyway till you get back from work. I guess I wanted to talk to you, or I wouldn't be here."

"There'll be plenty of time for that."

Evan looked at his friend. Highly respectable lawyers with trim beards shouldn't show their skinny legs and pallid feet. He saw in Jonathan's face the memory of what scene, perhaps with Greta? He would never know, and why should he want to?

"Till the doctor gets here you mustn't expect much breakfast. A glass of hot milk won't hurt you."

"Could you put some brandy in it?"

"The doctor'll be here soon."

"Stop talking like an idiot. Do you think I came to New York to see a doctor?"

"Guess you're not very sick; you sound like your old self." There was a pause between them, full of the years, mirrored in their different smiles. "I'll see about the milk." Jonathan left him.

308

As he went past the parlor and library where last night's party lay, a painted corpse, down to the kitchen (the servants having worked late were still in bed), the last scenes of the evening were with him. Reuben had finished his toast, glasses were raised to Jonathan, all eyes sought him, and he was not there! When he appeared at last, he joked it off: "I thought Reuben could slander me better behind my back," but Greta was harassed, Reuben was cold; he had to tell them. Reuben nodded sagely: "Strange, very strange. Look out, my boy!" Greta, fighting tears of anger (in her new ease, Evan too was distant) exclaimed: "Just tonight! Why did he have to come just tonight? Thank goodness, he didn't spoil the party." Philip had helped him undress the prostrate Evan; Greta refused to come into the room; Lucia remarked: "He hasn't hurt you enough." When he turned out the light and lay in bed beside Greta, her last word: "It *was* a success, dear. Everybody thought it was just modesty, your slipping away when Reuben made that wonderful speech."

The doctor came at nine. A severe bronchial infection, he reported: "No danger of its reaching his lungs, if he stays in bed and keeps warm for a week."

"A week!" Greta wrung her hands.

"Do you think we should have a nurse?" asked Jonathan.

"N-no. That's scarcely indicated, I should say."

Jonathan took the tray from Annie and brought the milk toast and weak tea.

"You still here?" Evan looked up from a doze. "I thought you had a law practice."

"Mind your own business."

"It must be late. Aren't you going downtown?"

"Maybe I need a morning off."

"You're a damn liar."

"If it's my holiday, why not? Think how truthful I've got to be at the office."

When, early that afternoon, Jonathan returned from work, Evan said, as if continuing a dialogue: "You'd want it."

"What would I want? How are you feeling?"

"You'd keep me here, a burden to your good wife. You'd cure me by the doctor's standards. You'd have me put my affairs 'in order' as you call it; bring my wife and the child; settle down, like you, and live happily ever after."

Jonathan felt his lips tremble.

"Good American! Trying to find out what it's all about: that's America's sin against the Holy Ghost. You've stopped trying, haven't you, Jon? I needn't ask you what you've been doing all these years."

Jonathan opened his mouth.

"Don't!" Evan interrupted. "For God's sake, none of your platitudes. Don't you realize, when a man stinks with rottenness, like me, his flesh is sensitive? platitudes can't be borne by soft sinners, only by hardened good men. Jonathan, a man can't do much about how he lives. Whatever he does, it's part inheritance, part circumstance, all nonsense. Happy or unhappy, successful or a failure, only at the end does he have his chance of freedom: to make sense of the sound and fury. Life's like a German or Latin sentence: the verb's at the end."

"You're a long way from that, even if it were true."

"Jon, you used to try to understand. When I laughed at you, called you 'Old Testament'?"

"What do you want me to say: that I hope you'll die?"

"Don't coddle me. Kill the bedside manner. I have a fever. What of it? Do you get the truth by watching people buy eggs at the grocer's? If you could take their real temperature, would you find it normal?"

"Anyway, they've got to be well enough to go to the grocer's."

"The only truth open to a man is his last gesture. At the grocer's, it wouldn't work: folks would say, He's dropped his eggs—how clumsy! Only the hero can make his gesture of truth in the midst of life. And then he dies. I'm no hero."

From his chair close to the bed, Jonathan leaned forward. "Evan, what is it you want?"

"Help me."

"Of course I'll help you, Evan. But can't I help you get well?"

"You're not trying to understand. All you hear is your own habits of mind."

"It seems to me: values may differ from one man to the next, but it's never his death that counts; it's his life."

"We know nothing of lives: nothing but sound and fury, till the verb at the end."

"Evan, it's too easy."

"Why should it be hard? What is man that he should presume he can do difficult things?"

"You speak of heroes. They die, but they don't seek death. They fight death. They love life. Their death is a part of their love of living."

Evan closed his eyes and smiled. "Don't worry, old man. You don't hear me, all that's real to you is your routine. But you'll probably have your way. I'll get well, if you can call it that. I'm not one of my own heroes. It's not enough to die, you're right there; a man's got to die at the true moment. I'll miss it, and rot gradually."

Day after day, when Jonathan returned, Evan began as if he were continuing; as if Jonathan were always present. And he found that Evan's words were always an approach, an assault, from another direction toward the same besieged center. Jonathan felt himself on the defensive—and gradually losing ground.

Evan said: "Do you remember the first day we met? The sweat and blood in the streets fascinated but disgusted me. You were the one who understood. You've forgotten."

"No."

"You heard hope, you saw hope, in the mobs. Hope of what? It was a kind of love affair, a clumsy rape; they wanted to be united with their city. You *have* forgotten."

Another time:

"Maybe it's the Jew in you. Your race had to struggle so hard to live, it's carried the cult of life into idolatry. Why did they deny Jesus, who told them what they'd known for centuries? If they'd accepted, they'd have been crucified, like Jesus. They preferred life to truth— refusing to die, they stopped living."

Jonathan at work in his office, or suddenly awake at dawn in his bed, found himself asking: —Evan's wayward life, faithful to a search, however impotent: is it nobler than mine? And who was he to call it impotent and wayward? This at least he knew: despite his sometimes violent name-calling, Evan was not arrogant; Evan was humble and suffering—and was begging!

Rachel took the letter from the postman and went back from the porch through the cold room to the warm kitchen. It was Saturday, the child and the sun were there together on the floor. Rachel needed both, but the ten days Evan was gone had strangely made Rebecca remote—as impossible to talk to as the sun. Not once had the child asked "Where is papa?" Perhaps if she had, Rachel might have begun to speak; perhaps the child had not asked because in her inscrutable way she knew her mother could say nothing. Evan is gone, Evan is gone, her mind and her heart told each other; and neither believed. . . . His going had left her empty.

Did Rebecca feel the difference in the touch of her mother's hand, brushing her hair, dressing and undressing her? She looked at the hand now, holding the letter (not from Evan; from New York, from the "law offices of Jonathan Hartt"). Her hand, brushing her child's hair, making her food, wove an invisible garment on Rebecca. If the hand is dead; if, severed from her heart absent with Evan, it is dead, what will it weave on her child? Rachel turned her face from the letter in her hand. If a moment came she could not bear, and if the moment was forever?—Christ, be close to me! She saw the cracked plaster of the ceiling stained by soot and the leak upstairs. She looked down at Rebecca in the sun and the sun in her child.

"Who was it, mama?"

"The postman."

The child's precocious eyes went to the envelope, to her mother's eyes; and returned to her picture book. She said nothing.

Rachel went back to the cold room, and opened the letter.

> Dear Rachel,
> I feel I must call you that. [—He doesn't know what to call me: Mrs. Cleeve? Mrs. Corthuis? Miss Lorne? I am nameless.] You are the wife of my dearest friend, and therefore I am your friend. Evan came four days ago and has been with us since. He is sick. The doctor says it is not dangerous; a bronchitis. But he remains in bed with a slight fever—about 100°, and doesn't yet improve. If you feel you should come to him, or if there is any way it would help, you will be welcome here to both my wife and me. Your daughter, too, if you cared to bring her. I enclose a check to meet the expenses of the trip, if you do come. You can consider it a payment from your husband.

Or, if you don't wish it that way, a loan from Evan's friend, which you can repay at your convenience.

Sincerely yours,
Jonathan Hartt

She folded the check in the letter, folded the letter and placed it in her bosom. It was very cold in the front room; her flesh shuddered. How terrible is cold! The world without Evan cold forever? —Jesus, give me warmth! She resisted the need to rush back to the kitchen warmed by the stove, the sun, the child. —That is not warmth for my soul. God is here, since He is everywhere. God's nearness to me is not enough; I must come near to God. And for that, do I need what is in the other room? She stood shivering, and her tears welled. Tears of defeat: Rachel went back to the kitchen (—Oh, the good warmth!); knelt on the floor and took Rebecca in her arms. "I don't care," she murmured against God.

Jonathan moved in the orbit of his home and work, an eye upon him, and the eye was Evan's. He saw himself, he did not like what he saw. He saw a little man somewhat below average height, not much, except in the measure of the eye of his tall friend in bed on the second floor of his house. He saw a man who walked stiffly, his shoulders too far back, a man pushing conscientiously along, a man ashamed. Evan's eyes were barred from no secret. When Jonathan studied a mortgage or the investment problem of a client's fruit ranch in California, Evan's eye was on him; intimate, it knew; distant, it devalued merely by its own perspective. With the same eye, Jonathan lived with his wife. Greta lived in the world of the present; Greta had no history. He was a man forever bearing the past with him, forever straining toward a future. And therefore, he needed her and loved her; and therefore his will, rooted in past and future, had tried to engulf her. He had not succeeded; he had merely exiled her; while his heart, despite his head and will, craved the nurture of her living in the present. None of this Evan told him; with Evan's eye in his house, he saw it.

The doctor made himself comfortable in the library (he deserved it, his gestures said, after the long day's work); lighted his cigar and looked at the anxious faces of Jonathan and Greta. "There's no cause for worry. The infection's stubborn, the man's run down. He must be

313

a heavy drinker,—the worst kind, who never gets drunk. But his lungs are all right. We're keeping it localized. It's just a question of building him up: rest, warmth, good food. I wish you could make him eat." He scribbled on his gold-cased prescription pad with its gold pencil, puckering his mouth so that his fan-shaped beard went forward. "This is a tonic. It's really nothing but good port wine—he'll like that—with a few ingredients added. Give him a glass, three times a day. And how are you, Jonathan? You don't look too well, yourself."

"He's terribly worried," said Greta. "He rushes home from the office and sits for hours in that room. They even have arguments."

"That won't help."

"He seems to need it," Jonathan nervously tapped his knee. "He seems to have to talk things out, things on his mind. If I simply listen, he isn't satisfied. He knows my ideas; he wants me to speak out so he can speak out."

The doctor nodded. "He's a strong man. Give him his head. It's only a question of time."

Greta said: "Do you think a nurse—"

"He wouldn't stand for it," Jonathan said sharply. "A nurse would only drive him out of the house."

"There's really nothing for a nurse to do," the doctor smiled soothingly at Greta. "So long as he remains quiet and warm. A sudden change of temperature: that's the one danger."

The first week passed unchanged into the second. Jeff, immediately after the party, had taken the night train back to college. But Philip, before he went south the next day on a sales trip, had a pleasant talk with the sick man.

"So you sell toys now? It's a useful job."

"What do you mean, 'useful'?"

"I suppose they're only for the kids. That's a mistake. Couldn't you persuade the grown-ups to change over?"

"Over from what?"

"From the grown-ups' toys. They're dangerous. But I don't see why I should worry."

"Grown-ups' toys?"

"Oh, railroads and steel mills, newspapers and warships. *You* know." Philip smiled. "If the people can get hold of *them—*"

314

"The people won't, my dear fellow. *They*'ll get more and more hold of the people. The toys'll get bigger and bigger. More and more people will be used to make them, to run them. And the men in control will get more and more like the iron toys they make. A machine can't create. A machine can only destroy or lie. Even the press—and books, now they're turned out in the millions by machines, will get to be more and more like the machines that print them."

"You don't have much faith, do you, in the people?"

"Not in their brains, old fellow. They'd have to grow mighty fast— their brains, I mean, to get on top of the factories and armaments. To grow, they'd have to be fed the right food. And what do they feed on? The product of machines—which of course makes them more and more not masters of, but food *for* the machines."

"You're cheerful, Mr. Cleeve."

"That's because I'm looking at you, Philip. And my name's Evan. You're a sight for sore eyes. And what place does this modern world have for you? It lets you sell hobby-horses and dolls. They ought to put you in Congress."

"No, thank you!"

"You see? Not only does the world reject the man of good heart; *you* reject the world. Poor world!"

Philip stared at Evan like an affectionate dog that understands not the words but their warmth.

Lucia, loyal to her own resentments, never came into the room. But Greta liked him again, now that she saw him again. Evan, out of her sight, was out of her heart, an abstract disturbance to her present. But now he was here, her warmth needed to warm him. She brought him food and sat with him; she tried to reach their common ground of music, telling him of her new maestro; she longed to make him speak of his wife and child although she was too diffident to name them. He listened politely and did not respond; he was at ease in silence; his music, like his wife and child, seemed dead to him. For hours, she told Jonathan, he lay alone on his bed-couch, needing nothing.

One day she said to Jonathan: "It's a pity Evan didn't bring his violin. He's not so sick he couldn't bundle himself up warm in a bathrobe and play. It might help him."

315

The next evening on his return from the office, Jonathan asked: "Where is your violin?"

Evan's beard had grown, unkempt and curling, not unlike the darker beard of Jonathan's youth. Within it, his face was gaunt, his eyes smoldered. He looked both younger and older than he was; as if the beginning and the end of life were crowding out this present.

Now, he did not move his head on the pillow.

"Isn't it here?"

"The violin? Certainly not!" Jonathan was frightened.

"That's strange. I took it with me."

"Are you sure? Then it's lost, by Jove! Can you remember when you last had it? We'll trace it. We'll publish a reward."

Evan did not hear; again he was with the parabola-wise music bearing him outward. He saw himself in the night of the Elysium streets, walking, walking; and here at last was the face of Rachel, still turned away like the far face of the moon; yet now he saw it, broken with her anguish! He must walk swifter away. The unity he needed, the unity toward which he moved, could not contain her. At dawn, the sun came up on the mean street of an eastern suburb, stirring its clotted meditation. He kept on walking east. Clouds massed over the sun and it began to rain. He went on walking through rain, away from the pang of the hidden face of Rachel. Then it was dusk; he remembered the lights in the shop windows of a town beneath rain; the horses, the men and women, slogging doleful through rain. The whole world was subaqueous slime. He knew he was wrong: there was a way to unity that reached the sun, embracing Rachel. Like Rachel's hidden face and the far face of the moon, the sun was beyond this rain. He knew he had failed. That all his living had suffered from want of union; that his sickness was his craving to be whole and his refusing all fragments, he knew and knew it was good; to reach unity by exclusion he knew was failure. He loved failure. . . . He saw himself in a saloon, shocking his flesh to fire with glass after glass of whiskey. He saw the man, black and gleaming like coal, smelling of wet hides, and his huge voice melting in the music. He must have left the violin with the man. He remembered telling him: the music must go with Rachel and the sun —and with the black man, all together. At least he was sure, as he rode in the day coach toward New York (he heard the throb and rattle of the country, solid dark, glide past the steadfast windows; he saw the men near the lamp silently playing cards and sharing a bottle; he saw the woman with peaked face press her babe's mouth to her mighty breast), the violin was gone.

"No." At last he heard Jonathan and answered.

"But my dear fellow, it's an Amati! It's worth—"

"No! Don't you dare trace it."

Jonathan thought it wise to drop the subject; he went down to dinner.

Evan lay quiet. The last music was gone; even the knowledge of the other way that led to union. He had dangled long enough. Since he loved the way he was going, let him be shrewd, fiercely loving, and get there.

Jonathan returned, the smell of coffee in his beard, and sat at the side of the bed.

"Why don't you smoke?" he asked. "Didn't the doctor say a cigar or two a day wouldn't hurt?"

"I've lost my taste for tobacco."

"Well, I suppose it's wiser."

"I like fresh air in the room. There's not enough of it."

"Doctor's orders."

"Don't you see even yet, the good doctor doesn't know what it's all about?"

Jonathan was silent.

"Be a good fellow. Open the window a little more."

"It's a fine evening."

"You see? Let me have a taste of it."

"You're right. If it's sunny tomorrow and you really want to, you could get up and take a little walk. I don't think it'd hurt you."

"It's the truth."

"Of course, I wouldn't let you," Jonathan smiled.

"What a false son of the Prophets! You no sooner get hold of a truth than you deny it."

"We'll have to start with homeopathic doses."

"Right! Start at once by giving me a taste of outdoors."

"What do you mean?"

"Open the window wider."

Jonathan drew the counterpane to Evan's chin. "Will you stay covered?" Close, he saw the face, purified and worn within the strange young turbulent beard; and the eyes that saw him. Evan closed his eyes, Jonathan sensed the airless moist gray of his body—somehow sepulchral. Jonathan went to the farther window and opened it from the top a full foot. The clear night rushed in. He sat near his friend, his back to the window, and felt no draught. Evan did not move, he seemed to have gone to sleep. Quietly, Jonathan got up and went to the library.

He sank at once into study of the papers he had brought home from the office. Greta and Lucia were at a concert, he was alone. The deep brooding walls, his books, the glow of the gas-logs, his house solid and close as an extension of his body, matrixed his working, made it secure like a sleep. The problem was the threat of a bank to call its loan from his client who planned to convert his business to the manufacture of automobiles, the bank claiming the risk was bad and constituted a misrepresentation of the property on which the loan had been made. Not for nothing had Jonathan formed the habit thirty years ago of playing his mind on intellectual problems; now it was delight to indulge his habit. As he marshaled his argument, the thought stirred that to prepare the case for the bank would have been equally enjoyable. But did not his client, who believed in the future of horseless vehicles, stand for progress? He denied himself this salve. He was a good lawyer, as he might have been a good chess player: he was better paid for his games, that was all the difference. Bitterness slowly seeped into satisfaction, until at last—as if the intellectual play had been a dream, it woke him. He looked around the silent room, heard the flicker of the flames, and thought at once of Evan. He had opened the window unusually wide; he found he was afraid, not for Evan's health (the evening was calm and mild) but because he had obeyed a mood in Evan deeper than his mere wish to have the window open; the impulse was hidden from his view, he had not understood it, he had not questioned . . . he had obeyed it because it was attuned with a hidden impulse of his own! His disquiet analyzed no further; it became motion; he went up the stairs quickly.

Evan was breathing softly. From the open window, a gray hand of the night touched his face. Stern and pallid, it seemed asleep, and to sleep on, as Evan opened his eyes.

"Hello, Jonathan."

"I didn't mean to wake you."

"Why not? I've plenty of time for sleep."

"How are you?"

"Mending. Definitely mending."

Jonathan walked to the window.

"Don't shut it!" he heard.

"I'll leave it open, as usual, a couple of inches. This is still winter, you know. Before morning, it might be blowing twenty degrees colder."

"The air's doing me good. Don't touch it."

Jonathan stood by the window and looked out. The back yards of his block and the next were shapes of shadow confused by the varying lights from both rows of houses (when one light went out, or another went on, the whole configuration changed), and by the fences that crisscrossed, reflecting, barring. From this common city sight suddenly eerie and chaotic, he looked inward on a mind more shadowed. —If I close the window, Evan might easily get up and widen it again. Why would I prefer this, although it means more exposure than if Evan stays in bed? Why is Evan tonight less docile than he has been? Why all this to-do about nothing? Vaguely aware that he was moved by some impulse beneath his reason that cast a confusing shadow upon it, Jonathan left the window untouched. He groped for a spare woolen rug on the closet shelf, and laid it on Evan.

"Be sure to stay covered." He left him; went straight to bed, and fell asleep so quickly, so soundly he did not hear Greta who came in almost as soon as he had darkened their room.

... Evan partially awoke, within an urgency that had matured while he slept; it moved him out of bed and to the window. Gusts of black wind, fragmented against the opposite row of houses, fell upon him. He stood in the torn air and felt the steadfast city; now that it was beyond him he dwelt with it and loved it. The wind was cold on his hot chest. He stood with bare feet and let it, harsh as iron, flail him. It was hard not to retreat to the warm bed. He stood it out, dwelling beyond his eyes with the city. Until his chest was no longer hot, the wind no longer cold; until the city beyond his seeing—its innumerable murmurs and designs—was in him close as the cells of his brain. Within the city he felt the void of space; lightless and without warmth or cold, it too

319

was good. Only his body now was the outsider. He came back casually to his body. It was numb with resentment, and he laughed at it. Thoughts in the foreground of his mind threatened to blur his ecstasy. Of Jonathan . . . "Good Jonathan," he murmured. Then, to his surprise, he thought of Jesus. —Even Jesus couldn't manage it alone. Even he needed collaborators: Judas, the Jews. It didn't worry him a bit that for their helping him to die, Judas and the Jews were cursed. He went back quickly to bed, in order to stop thinking.

Jonathan awoke somewhat later than usual from dreamings about Evan that suffused and confused his whole night. Evan was dead and Evan's mother blamed him: "You opened the window. . . ." The wind blew, he tried to shut the window, it would not budge. . . . Evan tried to get in through the shut window, and Greta cried, "Open the window," and he would not allow it . . . because a storm was blowing. He got up and went to Evan's room, and shut the window. (This was so vivid, he was not sure it was dream, except that the storm was hot with lightning and scalding rain, and it was linked with a scene in which the doctor told him the shut window had stifled Evan to death.) His head heavy, Jonathan forced himself out of bed (Greta was already downstairs); put on his bathrobe, saw that the weather had turned extremely cold and clear, and went into Evan's room. He heard Evan's stertorous breath and saw the window as he had left it. In the air hard and cold as ice, Evan lay half uncovered, between fever and coma.

The doctor came speeding; soon a nurse. Jonathan rang for a messenger and despatched a telegram to Rachel:

> Evan has sudden relapse. Dangerously sick with pneumonia. No reply to my letter. If not received wire for money for fare and come at once.

By the second post came Rachel's letter, written two days before:

Dear Sir:
  Thank you for your letter whose goodness and sincerity I cherish with all my heart. I have considered what you say for a long time and tried to search my heart and prayed for Divine guidance. It would not be right for me and my daughter to come to New York now. My husband went away because he needed to be alone and to be near his old life again. If he wants

320

us he will send for us or return to us. If I came without his word he would only be angry. I must not force him, Mr. Hartt. I pray God for strength not to be tempted to force him.

With all gratitude I beg you not to be offended if I do not take the money. I respect my husband's feelings about his father's money. I could never touch it. And we do not need it, Sir. There was a sudden opening at the school where I taught and where I was going to go back next term. So I am working now, and my child and I will not lack.

Very truly yours,
Rachel Lorne Corthuis

To Jonathan's telegram, no reply.

Doctors and nurses invaded the house, made it theirs, and could not reach the man unconscious on his bed. Greta wrung her hands and wept, within a sorrow she could not fathom. Lucia brooded in her room, hearing the attendants lug ponderous oxygen tanks up the stairs. Jonathan moved, his voice shrunken, his pain dissolved, among shadows.

That night, before dawn, Evan Cleeve was dead.

PART TWO: AFTERNOON

IV

BREAD UPON THE WATERS

I

JONATHAN HARTT SAT IDLE AT HIS DESK, IN HIS
right hand a pencil and beyond it the brief his clerk had placed there
an hour before. His clerk came in. Ben Dantry's skull was like a jack-
o'-lantern and his dry, long bones in his seersucker suit seemed to rattle. Jonathan had advised him, two years ago, to set up practice for
himself, promising to send him work and even clients; but Dantry
liked to work for Jonathan Hartt, he liked even his not infrequent
bursts of temper.

"Don't scold me, Ben," Jonathan touched the brief with his pencil.
"I've not looked at it."

"Tomorrow's Saturday; it can wait."

"I'll do it now. Why don't you go home?"

Dantry stood hesitant.

"By Jove, there *is* something else! That matter of the house—"

"Yes, sir. But it's really settled. Mother's found one that'll do, since it
has to. On Ninety-fifth Street, between Amsterdam and Columbus. It's
smaller than yours; only three stories. Not half so suitable, of course.
But it'll hold us and our four regular tenants. I'm almost sorry ma saw
your house. If she hadn't, this one—"

"What's the price on this one?"

"Just what we can pay: six thousand cash, fourteen thousand on six
per cent mortgage."

"Bean and Parman saw mine. They say they can get forty thousand."

"I don't doubt it, Mr. Hartt. I'll tell mother—"

"It means a lot to you, Ben, to please your mother."

"I guess it does."

"If you'd gone into practice for yourself, your mother wouldn't need to be taking in boarders."

"You don't know the old lady; it's her life. She wants not less but more of them. There are two friends begging to be taken in, for years. Your house would have made it possible."

"The house is yours."

Dantry stared. "You mean—?"

"You heard what I said. What do you think I mean?"

"But at what figure—?"

"Where's your mind, you dunderhead? Did I say, it's yours if you pay *my* figure? which I know you can't;—or did I say, it's yours. How you make me waste breath!"

"Mr. Hartt—I'm—Mr. Hartt—"

"Draw up the papers. You said six thousand cash, the rest—fourteen thousand—at six per cent mortgage?"

"Mr. Hartt, I oughtn't to let you do this."

Jonathan raised a hand to his trim beard. "Don't be an ass, Ben. Besides, present day prices won't keep, you're not getting such a bargain. Everyone is moving into apartments; they're going up by the hundreds. If you hold on to your house long enough it will be worth just about what you paid for it."

Dantry was accustomed to these abstruse ironic jests. "I can't tell you how grateful mother will be."

"Go home and tell her. Tell the typewriter to go, if you're finished with her. It's hot! I'll run through the brief and shut up the office."

Jonathan drew the papers a little closer. He was getting farsighted, but he resisted wearing glasses, as he refused even in the coldest weather to wear gloves. The heat through the open window brought the spiced scents of Pearl Street and the docks where the West Indies boats unloaded; brought the symphony of whistles from the dogged little tugs and of the horns of liners whose voyages . . . Liverpool, Hamburg, Buenos Aires . . . were bright cool ribbons through the afternoon. It was hard to concentrate in this caldron of a day that the red sun simmered. Jonathan looked at the two framed photographs on his desk. He had replaced the one of Greta in her wedding gown by a still earlier one of the girl he had seen first in Lafayette Place, the girl of the sensuous mouth, the eyes vivid as birds, who, in order not to change, had withdrawn subtly into her hidden world. Beside it was his son's photograph taken a few months ago for his graduation at Harvard. Greta and her son were the same age; both were youth, and a new century begins. Jonathan let his mind wander with guilt (the brief) that sharpened his enjoyment as the effort to awake sharpens delight in sleeping. There had been learned arguments to prove the new century would not start until 1901, four months ahead. The people knew better and had already had their celebration. He looked at his son's face (a few weeks and he sails for the École des Beaux Arts in Paris); Greta's youth was timeless, it had retreated from time and from her husband, but Jeff proved the people were right; the new century was rising! and he, whatever his opinions, was rising along. This time he was going to vote for Bryan; Bryan, this time, on his anti-expansion, anti-imperialist platform would be badly beaten, and he, Jonathan Hartt, was going to profit by the forces that beat him. His practice, these two years since Evan's death, had nearly doubled his earnings. As soon as Jeff sailed, they were moving into a new apartment, straight from the cottage in Amityville on the Great South Bay, and at the same time Lucia and Philip, after all the years in the old house, would go to their new flat at Eighty-third Street and Central Park West. The new country, the new century, was rising. Suddenly, Jonathan looked at his hands; the joints wrinkled and enlarged since his first attack of rheumatism, the hands of a man past fifty, seemed to drag him back from the rising new world. He thought of Evan: his obscure collaboration in Evan's death. "Out, damned spot!" Merely the hands of a man not getting any younger: he smiled at his morbid conscience. He must hurry or he'd miss his train. He saw himself rushing uptown to the East Thirty-fourth Street ferry, the fetid old boat wheezing across the river, Jeff and Jeff's mother as usual at the station. Before he knew it, Jonathan had pulled the little lever on the wall behind him for calling Western Union messengers. He took a yellow blank from his desk, and wrote:

> Do not expect me tonight. Delayed at office.
> Will stay at house and take noon train tomorrow.

If the boy hurried, the telegram would arrive before Greta and their son climbed in the buckboard and its high spiderweb wheels began spinning to the depot. The messenger boy did not come . . . was not coming! Jonathan's watch told him it was too late for the messenger service; he would have to take the telegram to the nearest office. Now Greta will worry. The train subsides at the Amityville station; smoke and passengers disperse, the engine crouches and growls a bit as it pulls out; Jeff in white flannels and a bright blazer puts his hand on his mother's waist: "Don't worry, mom. Pop must have been delayed;" and back they go behind the high wheels smacking little pebbles off the road. But if he hurries now to send it, a boy in blue on a bicycle rolls up to the cottage on the bay and delivers the yellow envelope; Greta's half hour of worry is over. —Why are *you* worrying? It's not so serious. He looked at his old hands, got up, and put them in the pockets of his coat. No pushing and sweating with the crowds on the car, on the ferry, on the cindery train: not tonight. A good dinner at Whyte's, and early to bed, alone in the old house soon to be Ben Dantry's—at twenty thousand loss: well, fifteen thousand. Why not? He could afford it. He leaned down, shut the safe, twirled the combination to make sure it was locked. Tonight he needed and was having a brief vacation—with the new century? Part of it . . . so long as he kept his hands (Out, damned spot) in his pockets.

Jonathan walked to the telegraph office; Nassau Street's curve, its not yet modernized houses, many with the flamboyant granite base of the pre-steel stone age, were in tune with the years of his youth. He sent his message and found that he was hungry. The famous chophouse was open to catch the trade of the newspapermen and a group filled a long table, their coats off, their shirts drenched, their beer mugs keeping the sweat and the talk flowing. From his place between the wall and a pillar, Jonathan sensed their cynicism, soft beneath the surface: product of fear and adaptation to a competitive life. How luminous Jeff would shine among them! Yet these journalists were in a work closer to what he had dreamed for his son than the work Jeff was choosing: they expressed social needs, they shaped public opinion! In the almost empty restaurant, he caught fragments of their talk; the subject was politics, the mood was hilarity or derision. His mutton chop was savory, the famous chutney pleasantly stung his palate. The ale's bitterness was good, he ordered a second stein, telling himself

328

he could afford a tubful. Strange: he had made his money, and each year a balance went into bonds, yet he had never got used to having money. "Bryan!" shouted one of the reporters into the loud argument. "Bryan . . ." he repeated, and when he had their attention, in the general hush his voice sank to a whisper. He was telling some off-the-record story. Then sudden laughter. Last year, Jonathan had met the Great Commoner: the expanse of starched shirt glossy and none too clean beneath the low-cut vest, the black ribbon tie, hair slicked up from the bulging forehead and curling at the ears, the dimpled protrusive jaw that made the brow recede—and the eyes too close together, had reminded him of a Temperance dominie compensating his under-thinking and no-liquor with plus-talk and over-eating. Yet he must vote for him; vote against his opponents, rather, who were buttering *his* bread. The conflict did not come quite clear, it was part of his slight dizziness (he was not used to so much ale) as he walked west on Park Row to the El. At the street's end, a bloated sun bled on the deck of a ship; the city was a ship on a sea of the Atlantic and the American mainland; he felt it rise and dip, the topheavy narrow island, between the waves of the ocean and the waves of the West. The El swung him softly, deliciously above houses already in shadow, the sun was visible only below in the gutters. The train tilted into Fifty-third Street with black heads blooming at dark windows; then, as it straightened farther to the west, again the sun and the river. Everywhere summer fermented the refuse of the streets. Not so long ago, under Mayor Strong, they had been clean; Jonathan recalled Street Commissioner Waring's proud parade of his "White Wings." He had done a better job, scrubbing the Belgian blocks and the new macadam, than Police Commissioner Roosevelt. It hadn't lasted; New York had celebrated its coming of age as Greater New York by bringing the rascals back. But the streets should be filthy, it was more honest! How, a while ago, had Rudyard Kipling put it? "New York is governed by its worst elements with occasional insurrections of decent citizens." Perhaps Governor Roosevelt, who knew how to straddle, was right? Then Senator Tom Platt probably was wrong, thinking he had shelved him forever by naming him for Vice-President on the McKinley ticket. Roosevelt's moral scruples were even weaker than the Great Commoner's brain! The Tammany wardheelers raked graft from the saloons and brothels. Roosevelt as Police Commissioner had noisily enforced the Sunday closing law, arrested a few saloon keepers, a corrupt cop or two—on the front pages of the papers; and played along with the big bosses. But what of it, if the new century was in him? He had shown where he stood when the Good Government Committee asked him to run for Governor on their ticket: the hero of San Juan Hill refused. Jonathan recalled the Lotos Club dinner when, in place of the silk-stocking swell he had known as Police Commissioner, he sensed the fiery tough body (tougher than Bryan), the energy rhythmic like a fine machine's . . . the new century?

"Hello, Mr. Hartt! Bully to see you again."

"It's good to see you, Colonel. But not where you are."

"Not where I am? That'll never do!"

"With your ideas, Colonel," Jonathan said, while the guests clustered around, "you belong with us Reform Democrats."

Roosevelt gave a roar of laughter and placed a hand on Jonathan's flattered arm. "You, sir, are suffering from what I call the Jeffersonian 'optical illusion.' You think bigness is the same as badness. That was his fallacy: small farms, small business, small men, small country. Even Jefferson didn't live down to it: who made the Louisiana Purchase? No sirree! Is a four-foot negrito in Africa a better man than a six-foot American? Is one of your two-by-four pithecoid Carribean republics a better place than continental U.S.A.? Which is the better ship, Columbus's tiddledewink caravel or the new *Deutschland* which the Kaiser says will make Plymouth-New York in five days?" Roosevelt bared his teeth in a smile that was a brandish, flashed his magnified eyes behind glasses, and slid on to the next group. His speech that night seemed aimed at Jonathan: "To the strong man in business, I say: be strong, *but be good*. To our strong nation, I say: *be stronger*. No: *be strongest!*" Perhaps it was as simple as that? —Perhaps the new century will iron out conflicts and complexities like mine, as the giant *Deutschland* plows through the waves?

Jonathan stood under the El at the corner of his block, now serried rows of houses. Through a saloon's swinging panels, he saw drinkers' boots draped on the bar-rail. The alcohol and the gas in the hot night turned his stomach, bringing a faint nausea: a drop of brandy might

330

help; he went forward as a woman, her face unveiled and painted under a huge black hat, swung the doors out. Her breasts seemed to touch him and to shape all his anxieties into a hunger. What the woman had for sale he wanted; wanted to die in this flesh that asked a simple price with no responsibility, no future. The woman was gone (she had seen at once the little man was not her meat) but Jonathan's need was to escape this new fierce need that she embodied. With his hand pushing the panel, he saw above the bar two colored pictures festooned in American flags: John L. Sullivan, a barrel body topped by a head like a bung, and a rodent visage with diamond eyes that he recognized as Gentleman Jim Corbett. Jonathan turned away and walked down the block to his house.

Greta, the good housewife, had swathed her home against summer; Jonathan stepped from the city's fever into a death still and cool. Newspaper covered the pictures and the bronze shield in the hall; through the glass doors the piano, the chairs, the bric-a-brac cabinet, stood in their gray shrouds. Their bedroom lay stagnant as a tomb; he went through the sliding doors into the room where his mother had lived, Evan died, and opened the window which had helped him to die—opened it only from the top as on that fatal night; at once returned to the front room and sat near the bed in which he and Greta had slept together since their marriage. It was covered by only a sheet; and the lamp from the street shed a vague vibrance upon it, while from the window in the other room the air stirred like a ghost. Jonathan took off his coat and shoes, collar and cuffs; it was cool here, as if the heart of the night's heat were chill. Yet he opened one of the bay windows, feeling the hot street sounds come in. He had been part of it for over fifty years, yet he heard the city as for the first time, a woman's voice in steel anger, a man's crass laugh, the El train more softly rising, falling, the bark of a dog, a piano: *Take me out to the ball game,* a blurred scuffle. . . . Then Greta was lying on the bed. He looked at the sheet which was smooth, but he wanted her so sharply that she was there . . . forever beyond him. And there, not for the first time, was the death—his collaboration in the death of Evan.

When he heard the scrape of a key in the front door, he was startled only as in a dream one knows one is dreaming. The front hall door opened. He turned his head, not his body, and saw reflected in the hall beyond his room the light downstairs. "This is the parlor," he heard, and the glass doors edged on their hinges.

He got up; walked down the hall toward the head of the stairs, and caught the faint odor of heliotrope. A woman's voice said: "Who's hat is that?" "Don't be afraid," said Jonathan. Her eyes followed her voice. She was a young woman, hatless, her black hair heavy, the rondures of her creamy shirtwaist slashed by the hall light. Ben Dantry stepped back from the parlor. "Mr. Hartt! We didn't know—"

"Of course not. I didn't either. I suddenly decided to stay in town. It's quite all right, Ben."

"I thought I'd show—. Louella, this is Mr. Hartt. My cousin, sir, Mrs. Lake. We thought we'd stroll over. Mrs. Lake wanted to see—"

"Go right ahead."

"Oh, no, sir! We'll come some other time."

"Nonsense. Show your cousin the parlor and the library. I'll be right down."

He went back to his chair, and while Greta watched him so that he seemed to see himself, he put on his shoes; his collar was wilted, he decided against collar and cuffs. The vibrance on the empty bed where Greta lay without form held him against going. "I won't wear either coat or collar," he explained to Greta. "That'll make it all right." He was perfectly aware that he was speaking nonsense; one should not appear half-undressed before a lady.

They both rose when he joined them in the library. "You should have opened the window," he went toward it. "Too bad I can't offer you something cool to drink." He lifted the heavy sash; the damp heat of the yard breathed in his face. He turned and looked fixedly at Dantry.

"Sit down, both of you," he said. "Well, when we meet again in this room, it's you who will be saying, sit down."

"I shouldn't have left so early, Mr. Hartt. If I'd stayed, you might have caught your train."

"I didn't want to."

He made himself see the young woman. "Are you used to our New York summers?"

"My cousin's from Charleston."

"Charleston! My wife comes from Charleston."

"Indeed?" came the furred voice.

"Oh, she left a long time ago. Before you were born."

"Mrs. Lake is going to live here. Until she finds a place of her own, she's staying with us."

"A charming city, Charleston."

"Yes," she murmured.

The books on the walls, shrouded in sheets and shadow, fought the hot electric pressure of the lamp on the desk; but the woman's eyes, round and vague, suffused the room and relaxed it.

Dantry got up. "We'll not disturb you any longer. Please excuse us."

When they were gone, Jonathan bolted the front door, and returned to the library to shut the window and put out the light. The dark at once filled with the heliotrope that pressed and suffused him like the round vague eyes of the woman. The scent was herself still there in the dark and Jonathan had the insane notion that the woman might have remained.

He went upstairs; Greta no longer lay on the bed. . . .

Greta managed everything for the new apartment; Greta who could do a good deal more than sing, whose household ran like clockwork, and whose cuisine was famous among their friends. Jonathan was not allowed to trouble even about his books. "You have *your* work," she told him. And one September afternoon (Jeff already on his way to Paris, Lucia and Philip in their new flat with much of the furniture from the old place), Jonathan changed his route on leaving the office: instead of the Third Avenue El to the Thirty-fourth Street ferry and the Long Island train, he took the Ninth Avenue El to Eighty-first Street and walked west to Riverside Drive. (Soon he could use the almost completed subway so much closer to the river.)

She heard his key in the door (the thin key symbolic of the new, as the ponderous key was of the old) and ran to lead him to his new library. His old library transfigured! the same pictures, the same desk, the same mahogany bookcases on three walls: but the two windows westward broke the magic. The old library had been dark with its purblind eye to the yard; its true somber light was the books. Here, through the windows, the sun ruled and the river, breaking through amber curtains, compounded the light of the cream-colored woodwork, of the white ceiling, of the bright new rug: the books were mastered. While Greta stood in the door to her adjacent music room to hear his verdict, Jonathan stooped to a shelf; picked out a brown old Herbert Spencer much fingered in his student days. It did not belong in this room; he put it back. In the correct corner, he found his Lamb; noted as never before Elia's shabby binding and poor print. . . .

"Are you satisfied?" Greta could not wait.

He replaced the Lamb, slowly walked over and kissed his wife.

"Try the chair"; she turned away her cheek. "If it's not comfortable, I can exchange it."

He sank in the new armchair beneath a new bronze lamp.

"That's much better, isn't it?"

"It'll put me to sleep."

Greta gave her musical laugh. "And why shouldn't you sleep? You've earned it."

—Old man, nodding over his old books? That was what she saw? Perhaps he would die in this chair; they'd find him with Macaulay or Herodotus or Hobbes open on his knees. "I hope *you'll* keep me awake," he smiled up. "Your piano's right next door."

"The door is thick."

"My dear! when have I ever wanted not to hear you sing?"

"Some day, I won't sing any more."

He saw tears in her eyes, and as always did not like them; his reception of her miraculous transposition of his books had hurt her.

"Don't say that! You will always sing." He tried to rise from the deep chair, his knees made it hard.

"I'll leave you." She recovered. "When you get used to it, perhaps you'll like it more."

"But dear, I like it now! Aren't you going to show me the other rooms?"

Their old bed was gone; blue enameled twin beds stood separated by a painted table with a gay parchment lamp. There was a new chaise longue in blue satin, and a chifferobe which Greta proudly opened, revealing the clever drawers and compartments, large and small, shallow and deep, for his shirts, collars, handkerchiefs, underwear, and socks.

"Isn't it *nice?* You can find anything."

334

"What a lot of work you've done, my dear."

"I've got rid of a couple of your old suits, I hope you don't mind, they were *rags*. And those dreadful worn-out slippers."

"They'd scarcely do, on this bright floor."

"Sit down," she said. Jonathan obeyed, and Greta on her knees unlaced his shoes, drew them off, tried on the new soft leather slippers. He saw the gray in her hair; within the fold of her housegown, the creased flesh of her once resilient bosom.

"Are they all right? Walk around."

"Yes, Greta."

"Now go back to your library, I have to see Anna in the kitchen. You may find some books placed wrong. But I don't think so."

"How did you ever manage?"

"I managed."

Their lives rose with the rising city. Bryan was beaten again, badly as Jonathan had predicted: four more years of the Full Dinner Pail with McKinley and Roosevelt. Towns boomed; Detroit poured motorcars on to rutted dirt roads; the silent electric cab, the stertorous "steamer," the malodorous gasoline buggy, began to knot the traffic. Coal rose from mines in mountains, became steel and speed. American troops still fought in the Philippines (the ever-outraged liberals wondered how a war begun against the oppression of Cubans by Spain could close by our oppressing the Filipinos), until one day General Funston lured Aguinaldo to a parley under the white flag, broke the truce and captured him: the American people adored this new hero for his treachery and were proud of the "White Man's Burden." In China, John Hay, the great statesman (so much more the gentleman than his first chief, Abraham Lincoln), saved the peace against the megalomaniac Kaiser who told his army *Gott ist mit uns*—but without injuring Germany's healthy power: after all, it might be needed to balance Russia and France. But all that was on the other side of the world, the side going down: we without violence were the new century, the new world going up. The Gold Standard was saved forever, gold bonds, being eternal, were at a premium. Oh! there was some trouble: a hundred thousand coal miners, mostly Polacks and Bohunks, struck for the right to organize and become a "trust" (they called it a "union") in imitation of their masters; murder was endemic in the city slums;

335

but all this, it was agreed, was "the fault of the foreign born," the "not yet assimilated generation." Everywhere in New York, the buildings, the institutions of the old century remained: rancid airless tenements, foul gutters, stuffy business structures with small arched windows, shedlike terminals, shaky piers, sun-stifling Els, cantankerous cablecars, jerrybuilt real estate gamblers' blocks uptown; and the same rivers fetid with sewage, the same minds and hearts festered with passion. But the new city was rising. Subways cut their electric rails under the avenues; new slender buildings draped on steel soared and looked down on the old town. Cable and horse cars turned into comparatively capacious trolleys. The arc and electric light stared out the gas. Park Row had a skyscraper twenty-nine stories high, whose roof commanded the Palisades, the Jersey hills, and south beyond the Narrows, Sandy Hook and the Ocean. Invisible miles of wire wove the telephone from house to house and from the island city clear across the continent. The new century was rising.

Jonathan's reputation grew as a counsellor skilled in the most intricate services and disagreeable to his clients. Prospective ones were warned to leave their vanity behind. "Mr. Hartt—if he takes you at all —will treat you like dirt and bring you gold," a manufacturer of buttons said to a manufacturer of paints. Jonathan eliminated trial law from his practice; he could no longer tolerate the crawl and limp of most judges' minds, and he despised juries whose collaboration, he felt, should be reserved for criminal cases where they were more at home. Many kinds of work he would not touch: for instance, divorce; and he threw out a lucrative practice among theater men, finding them "gamblers in disguise." He wanted no connection with great corporations; the independent "going concerns" had, he knew, no more morals than the trusts, but "I can get along with a man who runs his own business; I don't like boards of directors." What he meant was that he could handle individuals as he wanted; from the huge impersonal combines he could not derive the emotional satisfaction of being arrogant, ill-humored. This was not the way to get rich; but he found he was not interested in wealth; the zest of legal problems, his independence among a multiplicity of clients, carried him forward.

Dantry came one day, shifted his bony body in his loose-hung suit, and said nothing.

336

"What's the matter with you?" Jonathan smiled up from his desk. "Have you found the house I sold you is made of cardboard?"

"Oh, no! Nothing like that, sir." Dantry was always solemn. "Mr. Hartt, I want to ask you a favor."

"Well, what is it?"

"It's about my cousin, Mrs. Lake. Do you remember her?"

He had forgotten that night, as one forgets a dream; a word, a chance sight, unlocks it and it looms. Jonathan remembered and was silent.

Mrs. Lake, Dantry explained, was in trouble—like so many widows, Jonathan reflected. The estate of her husband, a Charlestonian more than twice her age, had gone entirely to his children by a former marriage (its chief assets were the ancestral house and a plump New York insurance policy) and Mrs. Lake had lost the first round of her legal battle to win a share. As a favor to Ben Dantry, would Mr. Hartt look into it?

She came, an afternoon when the wind hard with threat of snow besieged his office. She came with the scent of heliotrope that was all he remembered; he saw her round face as if he had never seen and was not seeing it now; like an animal he recognized her by her scent. She sat down, her gloved hands demure in her lap, her eyes vaguely fusing with the room's pulsing warmth, her quiet in contrast both to it and to the blustering day outside the window.

He said sharply: "I promised my clerk I would hear about your case. I'd do a good deal for Ben Dantry. That doesn't mean in the least that I take it over, or that I'll even find anything to be done which your Charleston lawyer hasn't done already. And of course, in any eventuality, I shall do nothing without first consulting him. Is this clear?"

"Yes, sir."

"Now, all the facts . . ."

She pressed her small upper teeth, a child's teeth, against her lower lip, a child's thin quivering lip; drew off her gloves as if she were getting down to work (her hands were small) and, after a long pause, gave him the details of her suit with a precision that surprised him. He did not interrupt her.

When she had stopped, slightly tilting her small head as a bird does when it shifts its vision, he said: "Leave me the name and address of your attorney."

She drew it, already written, from her bag and placed it on his desk. Then, hesitant, she showed him a small bundle of documents banded by an elastic.

"Here," she said softly, "are all the papers, and a copy of the will. I won't trouble you with them, sir. But—"

"Leave them."

She got up and came close to the desk. "Thank you, sir. There's something further I ought to say. Even if you do nothing more than having listened to me now, I owe you money. If I lose, I'll pay you, but a little slower. For it'll have to be out of my own earnings."

"You work, Mrs. Lake?"

"No, sir, but I can work."

"Sit down again. What could you do?"

Standing, she answered: "Anything: I can sew, embroider—"

He smiled at his image of this handsome woman at a sweat-shop's sewing machine.

"I could run a tea-room, sir; or a specialty lady's store. I could take care of *myself,* and I could pay you, even if I lose—." Her hesitation seemed to float and draw him.

"What is it, then, that's troubling you—?"

She drew back as if he had touched her; then she seemed to yield. "You see everything!" she murmured.

"Sit down, and tell me."

"It's my half-brother, Jack. He's eighteen and he's ready for college. But he won't go, unless I can send him. He's interested in automobiles; he says he can earn lots right away as a mechanic."

"Why not, if that's what he wants?"

"I'm sure you'll understand. Jack's not a bad boy, but he's not steady yet. He's just a kid. If he makes his own money now, he'll get into bad company. If I have the money to send him to college, he'll be loyal; he'll grow steady." She rose again, with the same startled air as if he had touched her.

"Thank you, Mr. Hartt," she seemed muffled in her furred voice. "I can't say how to thank you."

Jonathan took himself for a conventional man: a good lawyer who,.

338

if by miracle he had his wish and became a judge, would be a good one . . . no more, although good ones were rare these days with the bench fed by venal politicians (even an independent Democratic Governor in Albany or a new Cleveland in the White House would use his appointments to pay political debts); a good husband who, if by strange mischance he should be tempted from the faithful path, would know how to deal with the monster. Jonathan did not believe in miracles nor in strange mischance nor in monsters. If someone had asked him what he thought of strangeness, he would have said it was what we called the objects of our ignorance; if pressed, that strangeness, being everywhere, was nowhere. His mind and his convictions kept him unaware of strangeness in his moods or in the world; as to miracles, he was too busy to regret them; as to monsters, his life— except for his rheumatism—was too pleasant to fear them. His mind dismissed, having no place for them, his own subtle intimations of conflict and of question. Thus, the fact that of the three plays he had seen recently with Greta: Richard Mansfield in *Jekyll and Hyde,* Mary Mannering in *Janice Meredith,* Weber and Fields in *Barbara Fidgety,* it was the "idiotic nonsense" of the last he most enjoyed—as if it had been the most *real,* moved him to no self-search; thus, the fact that he found the operas of Richard Wagner oppressive and unclean moved him to no question about the public taste or his own; thus, the fact that he found himself juxtaposing such items of the news as Queen Victoria's death, Carrie Nation's splintering of the woodwork of saloons with an axe, the oceans of oil gushing into the Texas skies and the vogue of ping-pong among the new century's youth, meant to his conscious mind only that it was wandering. The contradictions in his feelings, barely noted, barely disturbed him. Each enthusiastic letter from Jeff in Paris, the gist of it always Europe's superiority over America, left him for an hour vaguely resentful (addressed to them both, the letters usually spoke more directly to Greta). The new alliance between Greta and Lucia (the kind of alliance in which both parties keep their arms), although he welcomed the end of hostilities that had caused so much heartache, depressed him, as if the two women had come together only by losing each an edge, a dimension that was part of her, and dear to him. Philip, when he was not traveling, came to dinner with Lucia regularly every Friday night; but he asked Philip no more questions about politics, about the books he was reading.

Serene in serious problems, Jonathan was irritable, often irrational about little things—and his lucid mind did not bring the paradox to his attention. He had practically tossed away fifteen thousand dollars in selling his house to Dantry; his charities and his allowances to his wife and son were generous, but he went from room to room at home turning off unused electric lights. He prided himself on his part in the new century, but he resisted the installation of a telephone in his apartment. If the matter came up, even with guests at table, he launched into violent attacks on the telephone's intolerable intrusion of one's privacy at home or in the office. "But you have one, dear, at your office," Greta sweetly countered argument with sovereign fact. It was, finally, through Reuben that Greta won that battle. Reuben had hurried home from China, when his wife became seriously ill. The doctor diagnosed cancer, and Greta insisted on her need for daily reports. As a concession, the clumsy instrument with its bulging box was installed in the pantry, between the dining room and the kitchen. Almost the first voice to come over it was Reuben's, announcing his wife's death.

Old Sarah Hartt now seldom left her room in Reuben's house. When the Minister and Lucy went to China, when Belinda went to London to continue her studies in economics, and Hortense married, the old lady was often alone in an establishment of servants and Oriental curios. She had despised her son Reuben as a "mere business-man;" now she lived among his spoils, but neither she nor Jonathan discussed the irony. At least twice each week, he visited his mother to report the family news; and her dry fleshless body in starched black made a recurrent wound within him. Unconsciously, he needed to re-member the tender flesh and blood that must have borne and suckled him. He came away with the emotion that his mother had always been this shrunken relic: the woman tender, upright, true, who had chosen him and destined him to his career, was the delusion. It was an irra-tional horror that he quickly forgot—until he saw her again.

And contradiction invaded his trivial business with Mrs. Lake. Her Charleston lawyer approved his strategy to get the case into New York by suing the New York life insurance company. One day Jonathan had walked to the Tweed Court House of many memories and made good his claim to a hearing. But Jonathan did not notice how, when Louella Lake sat demurely in his office, he broke his custom of giving his clients no details of his plans. He gave her lengthy details; she answered brief precise words when he asked a question; her vague round eyes were never sharply focused on him. Each time she came and drew up her veil, he had again forgotten her face; each time she left, her scent of heliotrope immersed him, momentarily moving him away from his own life. But the spell soon passed, leaving no conscious mark. If Jonathan had been asked by a good friend what he thought of Mrs. Lake, he would have considered and said he did not trust her, certainly did not like her. She was a woman without a face, probably for cause . . . She did not need a face. . . .

One morning the telephone bell rang when Jonathan was still at table drinking his breakfast coffee. Not yet used to her new toy, Greta jumped up, and came back, her face solemn.

"It's Reuben," she said. "He wants to speak to you."

Reuben was still in New York, having delayed his return to Pekin; first, in order to get Belinda's reply to his long letter urging her to come back with him to China (her expensive cable said: "Sorry cannot interrupt studies and Zionist Congress coming which must attend"); and now because of his mother: Sarah had had a stroke that left her blind, and was rapidly failing.

Jonathan wiped his mustache and set aside his napkin. You had to hurry with this arrogant contraption; if a man called on you without notice he could cool his heels, but any voice at the end of the electric wire was always in command. Jonathan slowly adjusted the vulcanite receiver to his ear, and said: "Yes?"

"Hello, Jon. You'd better rush right over."

"What's happened?"

"Another stroke. The doctor's here now, he advises come quickly."

Jonathan went back to the table, resenting the form of the conveyance of this word (the buzzing voice strangled to wire-size), in order still not to face the word. He heard the grandfather's clock, he saw his wife, her lavender housegown adorned with lace, between the old clock that his father used to wind and the silver coffee urn. He drank the last swallow of his cold coffee.

341

"Mother has had a second stroke. The doctor warned us the last time this would probably be all. Do you wish to come?"

Greta glanced at her hands, and his eyes following hers saw the broad gold wedding ring, the diamond solitaire engagement ring above it. She got up and went back to the telephone. "Is this Danegan's Livery Stables?" he heard her. They had added a few auto-cabs to their carriages. She ordered one to be sent over.

"You mustn't wait for me," she said. "You see, dear, how useful the phone is?"

The squat electric hansom (driver on top, large rubber-tired wheels) rolled him through rows of prosperous houses, gray and brown and red, with boastful stoops and bosomed bay windows; resisting the wind and the first lance of the cold spring sun, they stood in the weight and complacence of their shadows. At Central Park West and Eighty-first Street, he veered into the gray of the transverse road. Over the stone walls, trees strained in their scant leafage, clouds scudded like scared animals in a blue field. They dipped through a tunnel, its rough-hewn rock echoing the drip of water; and suddenly with Jonathan there was a crowd, gathered in the city's womb, of men and women emerging with him. He knew them, the unseen: they were the rioters of his boyhood, the soiled prisoners of hope who burned houses, hanged Negroes, on a distant day when he brought Evan home to his mother. They were coming with him now to see his mother die.

A maid opened the door. Jonathan walked up the stair, feeling the cold chaos of Reuben's booty: the vases, the sculptures, the paintings, remote as China. In the library, Reuben, Lucia, and Philip were waiting, Philip at the mantel, his bucolic head flanked by a Manchu bronze of playful dragons and a blue amphora from Korea. Reuben clasped Jonathan's hand in both his (Reuben was a great handclasper); and in the poignance of distaste Jonathan sensed the suffering man. Reuben's marriage had been singularly happy, and his wife was gone; Reuben had won his mother who had despised him, and now she was going; Reuben lacked a son to carry on his success, and his two daughters were making of their lives a deliberate rejection of their father. Belinda, the intellectual, called herself a Socialist, and that was bad enough: but now she had become involved with those violent malcontents, Herzl and Max Nordau, and become a Zionist! a way to flout not only her father but her dead Catholic mother. She had even, in a brochure she had written on *The Economics of Palestine,* changed her name to Hadassah Hartt! And beautiful Hortense was married to an extremely clever lawyer, Irving Brock, born in Kishenev, brought as a babe to this country in the steerage by a father whose name was Brodsky! Even Reuben's political day was over, having been nothing but the reflected light of such men as Harrison, Hanna, Platt, McKinley—now all gone. Roosevelt moved at a swifter, more contrapuntal pace than Reuben had ever learned. In fact, Reuben had secretly decided not to go back to Pekin, but to retire on the pretext of his bereavement and ill-health, before the White House perhaps brutally recalled him. A twinge of sympathy for his brother went out from Jonathan—and died. Against his own obscurity to himself, Jonathan more and more saw the world about him clearly; and he sensed that Reuben's suffering was blunted even now by complacence. Reuben had an answer for every sling and arrow of outrageous fortune: he had lost his wife but he had been a good husband, he was losing his mother but he had been more than a good son, his daughters had drifted away but he had done what he could for them, his political hour had tolled, but was it his fault that the bullet of a crazy anarchist named Czolgocz had shot the quicksilver Roosevelt into power? And fused in his complacence like copper in bronze there was always that prime proof of excellence: his money! A tawny Persian cat, luxurious as a muff, wafted through the open door, followed by a nurse, all stiff white, who signaled them to come. Led by Reuben, they filed up the carpeted stairs. And Jonathan knew that all his life had been a dialogue with his mother who was dying.

Sarah Hartt lay propped up in the same bed, surrounded by the same furniture and pictures she had brought from the home near Stuyvesant Square to Jonathan's and then to Reuben's. Her eyes, open and unseeing, made her head a skull on which the white hair, the yellow skin and lips, were a grotesque addition. Her hands jerked on the sheet like the talons of a bird that has lost its head. Reuben and Philip stood at one side of the bed, Jonathan and Lucia at the other.

"We are all here, mama," said Reuben.

"Reuben, be still," she said sharply. "Have respect for your father."

Jonathan saw the pain in his brother's face, and felt in Lucia be-

side him a surge of triumph: the old order, in which her beloved
Jonathan had ruled, was re-established!

A word struggled to come out from the old woman, a deeper one:
the dry breast rasped, the throat corded, the lips broke. When it came,
it was: "Joseph."

"Joseph," she repeated, "you must forgive Reuben. He needs money
so much more than you do."

Reuben's pain froze on his face, he could no longer absorb it.

"Philip," said the old woman, more easily, "kiss me. You never
needed your mother."

Philip leaned down, relaxed, and placed his quiet mouth on his
mother's cheek, lingering as if to warm it.

Her hand groped: "Where are you, Lucia?" Lucia's face, as she bent
down, softened with tears; was the face of the girl again who could yet
flower. The frustration of the years was annulled; Jonathan saw the
suddenly freed face, and loved his sister.

"Children," the old woman spoke again, "your mother is dead."

Had she forgotten her favorite?

"Joseph," she said, "why don't *you* kiss me? Can't you forgive me,
Joseph?"

They stood, all four, the orbit of their mother.

"You were always a good husband, and so wise!" she pleaded; and
they had never heard their mother plead. "I was less wise; I had to
try harder. Forgive me, Joseph. Kiss me."

Lucia was the first to understand. Feverishly, joyously, she pulled
Jonathan's arm down; and her clasp exclaimed: —She means you!

He was not forgotten. In the perspective without time or space
where Sarah Hartt looked on her life, her son Jonathan was her husband Joseph. He stooped to kiss his mother. But she had said: "Forgive me." It was true: long, long, he had resented her will and her
betrayal, resented the tenderness that she had never given. Now here
was his own will and want of tenderness, betraying! Could he achieve
her miracle of union? could he be his father's tenderness? His face
came close to hers, his eyes near her blindness, his life upon her death.
She was ugly to him, she was no longer a womb. Forgive me, she
had pleaded. "Forgive me," he whispered desperately in his tears, "if
I cannot forgive you." Then his mouth touched her brow, his mother

vanished. If he was son and husband in her moment when life and death fused and became neither, she was now all that she had never been, and that he needed because of her, and that could be only because she was. Beauty was a womb about her ugly death, and gave it birth. Letting his tears flow as never in his boyhood, he kissed his mother. Her hands were on his head, and he felt them die. He raised his own hands, clasping his mother's, and laid them down on the breast of the dead woman.

Greta joined them in the library, waiting for lunch. Reuben had tried to save himself by saying: "Poor mama was out of her mind;" their silence disavowed him. Their mother's death had forced this holiday, this closeness of their distances from one another. The room was a sardonic witness: between the windows a mandarin presided on silk; above the sofa where Lucia sat, the portrait of Reuben's wife with her two small daughters managed after the Gainsborough manner to be both wooden and shrill; Chinese vases sang irrelevantly over bookshelves. To distract himself, Jonathan looked at the sets, mostly in green crushed levant and red morocco: the Earl of Beaconsfield in eleven volumes, Bulwer-Lytton, Charles Reade, Dickens, Thackeray, George Eliot, Wilkie Collins, Shakespeare, Gibbon, Buckle, Longfellow, Lowell. They looked as if they had never been touched, but Jonathan had read them, and now they were remote as the bric-a-brac above them. Yet these books were his age! but he felt strangely young, his mother's retching breath had released him. Also, he felt insecure, all his foundations hollow, his strange freedom breathing him outward into the unknown. Greta sat with them, her demure tailor-made suit by contrast accenting her vivid verdure: and his freedom leaped toward her . . . fell back; Greta was inaccessible.

She said: "I telephoned your office, dear. Mr. Dantry suggested for you not to come down today; to take a little rest. He said there is nothing urgent. Of course, I told him I couldn't speak for you. Do you wish I should telephone and tell him you're not coming?"

Jonathan was about to say yes: and recalled that Mrs. Lake was due at the office to sign a paper. The paper could wait, or Dantry could have her sign; he knew for the first time that he needed to see her.

The need and the knowledge were obscure, somehow involved with the body upstairs whose blood was already clotted in its veins; and with Greta, as Greta, involved with his brothers and sister, with this room, moved him toward Mrs. Lake. He did not answer his wife's question. But after the dainty luncheon prepared by Reuben's Chinese chef, served at the teak table with individual doilies in lieu of tablecloth, Jonathan took his leave. He kissed Greta, and her coolness (obscurely his staying away from work all day would have been a triumph for her) at this moment when her body stirred him, made her painfully remote—part of a yesterday when his mother was still living.

He walked east to the Third Avenue El. Spring was winning over the harsh wind, the houses seemed softened, the city was relaxed and subdued by the spring sun; well-dressed children with nurses, their uniforms a pressure on their soft contours, walked in a slumber. The train between the tenements was a wooden cradle a-swing, the guard, opening and shutting the door, calling the stations in incomprehensible Irish, clanking the iron gate, beneath his dirty shirt was earth. Jonathan got off at Hanover Square; through the station stair in the street gutter he saw a crowd wreathed about the bleeding body of a man. A querulous voice at his side said: "Probably one of those damn automobiles. Outrageous!" and he looked up at the sideburns and savage eyes of an old gentleman in a high hat.

His pad told him Mrs. Lake was due at four. She arrived a few minutes late. He made her wait a half hour.

"Sit down," he said when she came in; "you were late. You know I'm a busy man. If you can't be on time, Mrs. Lake, I may not be able to see you in the future."

She sat without even raising her veil. And he talked on; in order not to stop, he went into technical details such as he never discussed with clients; in order to hurt her, he spoke with contempt, as if he were the umpire in a contest between ignoble players. She listened without words, without movement.

At last there was nothing further, except the one thing she had come for.

"Here, sign this." He shoved the document toward her on the desk, not explaining its nature.

346

Mrs. Lake got up and leaned toward him. To see where she must write her name, she at last lifted her veil, and he saw that she was crying.

In June, Jeff came back from Paris (he had been away twenty months, and would be gone again in September). For weeks Greta had lived in a state of desperate happiness: how could the time in which she would have her boy be adequately filled? and would it ever come? On the day, Jonathan telephoned to the *Nord Deutscher Lloyd* and learned the *Fuerst Bismarck* was in quarantine earlier than schedule and would dock at noon.

Greta's excitement sang over the wire. "Oh! So soon! Oh! I must rush out and get some flowers for his room. Oh! is there time, Jon, to get flowers?"

"You have plenty of time, my dear. Now listen carefully." He gave her exact instructions: when to leave the apartment, what train to take, what ferry. "I'll meet you at the dock, where they collect the permits. . . . *Naturally* I have the permits."

He settled down for a half-morning's work, beneath his calm not less stirred than Greta. Nearly two years is a long time. What will his son be? and why did he know that the eye which saw his son would not see clearly? The eye that sees truly is seen, and sees itself. —What have I to hide? There was no reason in this smoldering trouble; hence no reason could combat it. And if he *had* something to hide? —Is my son my judge? Our hope is our judge. Because our hope is trust. He sat at his desk, thinking of this deeper meaning of the word trust, and of his son who was his hope and therefore his judge; making a swift inventory of his life, and angry at himself, and angry at Jeff, for whom he made it. Evan? (Not a day without Evan in silent dialogue, together with his mother.) His practice of law which no longer made pretense at public service? How could he be used? he was willing, he had fought, to be used! Greta? . . . He thought of Mrs. Lake and said aloud: "Nonsense." He had never seen the woman outside his office: he forgot the first time. (—What if I never saw her again?) There was something indolent, false, at least hidden, in this airless young woman. (Faint, he caught the heliotrope, heard the furred

347

voice.) —She's a client; what of it? (—Some day, the case will be finished. Then I'll not see her again.)

Jonathan set aside his work, took his gray slouch hat (he never wore a derby) from the old rack in the corner. In the outer office, Ben Dantry jumped up; he was perspiring and Jonathan wondered where in that dry-bone body the juices came from.

"I'm sure you'll find your son in great shape."

"Paris is supposed to be good for Americans."

"We have a big picture of the Eiffel Tower in the hall. Mrs. James —she's one of ma's star boarders—brought it back with her from the Exposition, and ma had it framed. That tower sure is a dandy. Higher'n anything on Broadway."

"Give us time. We'll beat it."

"Everything 'round it, according to the picture, sure is flat."

"Why do you have it in the hall? Aren't you afraid someone will hang his hat on it?"

Dantry began to reply, saw the joke, and beamed.

"By the way, Ben, what are we going to charge the Climax Cement Works for the supplementary proceedings?"

"You're right, sir. We'd better put in our claim now. I'll figure it out."

"Don't be modest."

"We saved 'em. I'll remember."

"Remember also they're not worth saving."

"Oh!" Again, Dantry saw the joke, and the effort beaded his square brow with perspiration.

The crosstown horsecar that jangled Jonathan toward the river reassured him. If life was problems stealing away conscience: father and son, husband and wife, lawyer and woman client, man and friend, public service and politics, *Sapolio* gave you Spotless Town with no need of a Civic Committee to clean out the thieves. *Jim Dumps* was a sour old soul, life's problems had worn his body thin; but *Force,* the new cereal breakfast food, could be purchased anywhere for a dime: *Now he is Sunny Jim.* The weazened clerk who sat opposite with a mouth hard as a bird's bill, the weary woman all of whose energies seemed to have gone into her flower-garden hat, needed only to look up and take their choice for all their troubles to be over:

Three United States Senators Praise Peruna. And *Lydia Pinkham's Vegetable Compound* solemnly declared: "Mrs. Pinkham is able to do more for the ailing women of America than the family physician. Any woman, therefore, is responsible for her own suffering who will not take the trouble to write to Mrs. Pinkham for advice."

Jonathan stood on the forward ferry deck, near the chains, and let the river embrace him. Next to him two horses, harnessed to a dray, stamped in their manure; the sweet sweat of their flanks, the smell of the Irish driver, tinctured the June air opalescent on the waters, mist on the Jersey shore. In the south distance under the sun the gently riding steamers fumed into mirage; on his face the salt and the tar and the tang were an aphrodisiac kiss. Life was good; here between his city, the Jersey mainland and the sea, life poured down, life lifted up. It smelled good and tasted good. A little carefully at first, Jonathan caressed the muzzle of the huge gentle Percheron, brought his face close to the velvet-soft flesh; the drayman's wink seemed to say: "I understand you."

He had come early because he knew his Greta: and there she was, a little moist and breathless as if the steamer were already on its way back to Bremen. In her straw bonnet trimmed with daisies and ribbons trailing, her white veil lifted to her brow, her creamy peek-a-boo blouse with flounced short sleeves and white. elbow gloves beneath them, her marine green skirt revealing pretty ankles, and over all the canary silk parasol wtih bamboo handle, she was not June, as she tripped toward her husband; but certainly not autumn. Jonathan smiled, thinking of a buxom widow past the time of mourning.

"Where is he? Has the steamer come?" she said before she reached him.

"My dear, I've just inquired. The steamer won't dock for two hours!"

"Oh! But you said—" Somehow, it was his fault.

"I said what the office said. You never can tell exactly how long quarantine and the immigration officers will take. There's probably been a slight delay."

"Oh! oh!" she repeated.

"We have plenty of time, my dear, for a good lunch. I know of an excellent bierkeller in Hoboken. I've never been there, but I'm told it's good."

She stared at him.

"I hope you're hungry?"

"No," she said.

"Well, you must be thirsty, it's so hot. We'll find a cab. We have more than enough time."

"Isn't *this* where the ship docks?"

"Of course."

"Then why should we leave? Can't we wait here?"

"You're not listening, Greta. The ship docks in *two hours*. Madame, I invite you to honor me with your company for lunch."

Greta's eyes often troubled Jonathan; now, they hardened like an animal's scenting danger. She looked about the waiting room (two battalions of windows, shut and dirty, kept the June day out) and sat down in one of the long rows of benches. "We'd better wait here. I'm not hungry."

"But I am, darling. The official said—"

"They were wrong once, weren't they, saying Jeff would be here at noon? I couldn't eat a thing. They might be wrong again."

Jonathan knew it was useless to explain the difference between an early office guess and definite dock news. Greta had stacked her gay parasol on the bench beside her, peeled off a glove, and was daintily mopping her face with a lace kerchief.

"I saw a soda fountain outside. Will you bring me a lemonade?"

Jonathan was piqued; he had planned to make Greta, whose acquaintance with alcohol was almost nil, a little tipsy before she met her son (a wine-cup disguised as lemonade would do it). As he walked out of the empty waiting room, his wry smile admitted that if this was his plot in taking Greta to lunch she had been right to refuse. At the counter, he bought two sandwiches, a cold bottle of Moxie, *The Ladies' Home Journal* for Greta, and for himself *Everybody's* and *McClure's*.

"Didn't they have any lemonade?" But she cheerfully poured the drink into the glass, placed the sandwiches open in their paper on the bench, and spread her lace handkerchief. "M-m, it's not bad," she smiled. "Sit down, Jonathan. It tastes like sarsaparilla." The brown foam on her upper lip made the faint hairs visible.

"I brought you this, to kill time."

Without looking at it, she tossed the magazine on the next bench. And he remembered that Greta never read the magazines, never read the papers, cared little for novels, not even Dickens; the news and nurture of her world were elsewhere. Feeling excluded and rebuked, he sat down, ate his sandwich, opened *McClure's* at Ida Tarbell's "History of Standard Oil." He glanced at the clock. 12:17 . . . a long vigil.

"What time did they say?"

"Not before two."

A German, ponderous as a grenadier, with square-cut *pince-nez* that a broad black ribbon attached to his lapel, marched up, a little girl trotting beside him, and they sat at the opposite end of the room. Others filtered in. The hot air smelled of gray paint. He read the shame of Rockefeller's ruthless chicanery, more "shame of the cities" that the public was enjoying with a zest that went with pleasure rather than with shame. It was obvious that people loved or at least envied the villains. Why could he not be happy, having Greta and his son? He put down the magazine, and looked at his hands: Evan, his mother: —Am I so much better? Greta jumped up (he had forgotten her) and ran to the windows.

"Jonathan!" she called across the room. "Look!"

The crowd that had grown while he "wool-gathered," moved to the river side: squat and puffing as if short of breath, the *Fuerst Bismarck* lay athwart the pier while little tugs yelped and poked at her flanks, edging her in. Greta placed a hand on her husband's arm; she was trembling.

"You see? I was right! And the food at that restaurant would have been awful!"

He looked at the clock: it was *1:20.*

The covered pier, into which they jostled, was a cavern of bales, barrels, crated machinery, vibrant with sweating laborers and horses, and on its open side with the sun's myriad detonations upon water. After a void of waiting, they saw the gangplank's conduit thrown up from themselves, who were the land, to the ship; and at last the passengers trickling down, transfusions from the sea-creature's distance. Jonathan again looked at his watch: *2:07.*

He heard Greta gasp and saw his son at the deck's congested entrance to the gangway: jaunty straw hat with red-speckled band, silken thin mustache, this strangeness, this *Europe,* was his son? In the flash before the head vanished, Jeff looked bewilderingly like Greta. And Greta, to Jonathan, had always been Europe in a way (although her people came to America long before his): her education, her *Lieder,* most of all her gay acceptance of life for life's own sake. He had always inarticulately felt that in his marrying Greta, America had conquered Europe. Suddenly Jeff emerged on the pier close to them: three inches taller than his father, a camera strapped from his sloping unpadded shoulders, his brown tweed coat tapering at the waist into the tight trousers of a lighter brown, almost beige. —I paid for this smartness, Jonathan found himself feeling, and felt shame. Jeff freed himself from his mother's long embrace, kissed his father, turned at once back to his mother whose eyes twinkled with tears that did not spoil them. "Younger than ever, by gad! and prettier!"

They stood waiting for the customs inspector, and Jeff opened his French leather trunk with brass knobs.

"That won't last long in this country," said Jonathan, "when our baggage-smashers get their hands on it."

"Plenty more where this came from," Jeff smiled. And again Jonathan felt shame at his irritation that the boy took *his* money for granted.

The open trunk displayed smart cases for collars and handkerchiefs, socks of silk and English wool, monogrammed shirts. "I might as well show you your presents, while we're waiting." Jeff lifted the trunk tray, and Greta saw tiny gloves, suède and calf, gem-like flasks of perfume, an exquisite bead handbag. She held it against her body.

"Anyway, the bag fits," Jeff laughed. "I hope the gloves do—and this," he pulled out a filmy sweater of green merino.

"It's a dream," said his mother. "Everything will fit."

"I had fun, picking it out. I took a guess on your gloves, I was sure I remembered your little hand," he clasped it tenderly. "For the sweater, I picked out a salesgirl—a young one, very pretty—about your size and had her try it on. Told her it was for my mother in New York, and maybe you think she believed me. Oh, no! But she loved what she was sure was a lie. Women have no moral sense, do they, dad? You were harder. If you shaved—there are some wonderful new safety razors,

English, of course; or smoked—Algerian briar is the best in the world. I saw some bully Russian pantoufles, fluffy wool inside, but pop, I couldn't for the life of me remember if you had big feet or small." While he talked, he unstrapped his steamer-blanket. "Here's what I got you; you still read French, I hope?"

Conscious of the cavernous dark pier windy with moving, talking men and women, Jonathan saw the boxed set of seven little volumes in red leather. He picked one out, opened it; the exquisite type on the gilt-edged page seemed engraved rather than printed.

"You don't have 'em *all*, I hope?" said Jeff.

Jonathan read the titles: *Pensées* by Pascal, Montesquieu's *Esprit des Lois, Caractères* by La Bruyère, *Réflexions et Maximes* of La Rochefoucauld, Bossuet's *Sermons,* and two volumes of Montaigne. "No, I have Montaigne in English, I'm sure one should know him in the original. Montesquieu I read, of course, when I was studying law. I've forgotten him, I'm afraid. Thanks, Jeff."

"Just imagine! The personal anxiety of Pascal, revealing the absolute loneliness of every soul—the incapacity of reason or science to heal or even touch it in even the highest civilization; the social and international wisdom of Montesquieu; the psychological analysis of La Bruyère; Montaigne's gracious irony and insight; La Rochefoucauld's delicate, desperate cynicism; Bossuet, pure and devout as the best music of Bach—all in one little box of books! Only the French could do it."

"How about the Old Testament?"

"The Bible?" Jeff looked surprised, and his mother, as to defend him, took his hand.

"Leave out the New Testament. What of the Law and the Prophets, the Psalms and the Proverbs, the wonderful little stories of Joseph, Ruth, Esther, Jonah?"

"I must *read* the Bible!" Jeff laughed; and Jonathan was silenced by his own outburst. As if *he* were religious or even a good reader of the Bible!

The inspector came; Jonathan kept irrationally thinking: —He could buy gloves for his mother; he didn't know if my feet were large or small . . .

353

Jeff stood alone in his father's library, the Hudson before him and in his heart the Paris he soon would see again. To reach his rooms in the Rue de l'Hôtel Colbert he passed between a tiny laundry, misting sweat and *lessive* even in winter, and Henri's fish stall where Martine, his daughter, worked while she hummed an air from Charpentier's *Louise*. Martine was flat-chested and homely; and Jeff knew where the flowers came from that he occasionally found in a tumbler of water on his drafting table. Martine brought him flowers as she burned candles to her Saint. She was more familiar with the Saint, could ask him favors; whence the pride, the dignity, that somehow saved her inarticulate devotion. The passage between the fish stall and the *blanchisserie* led to a *cour* of moldering walls, each tier of windows aloud in the polyphony of Paris. In one corner of the *cour* an ancient wooden pump, in another Henri's malodorous cart, everywhere mud and shadow. Three dark stairs, then his door and at the far end of his room the tall uncurtained windows that gave him the Cité, the *parvis* Notre-Dame, the Châtelet to the west, eastward the tenements of l'Ile Saint-Louis, and ahead (he could almost see them) the seething streets of Les Halles, of the Boulevard de Sébastapol, of the Porte Saint Denis, of the Boulevards Extérieurs—to the north sky of Paris. On clear afternoons (they were rare) the sun leaped the town from Issy and Boulogne, flaming the gargoyles and slate roofs within the bastions and buttresses of the Cathedral. Sun or no sun, the quais glowed, the old Pont Neuf rang its romanesque refrain. At dawn when he was home from a night's passionate talk with friends, the day slanted in from distant Ménilmontant and La Villette, bringing over the still quiet city to the open windows the murmur of workers who had finished their *croissant* and *café au lait,* or the morning's first *vin blanc.* . . . Jeff was just back from a walk up Fifth Avenue to the Park between rows of buildings that he found to be masqueraders. French châteaux by the dozen; a façade of the Antwerp Cathedral; Roman columns (on banks and jewelry shops); the Campanile of Venice, a copy of the Carnavalet Museum, Italian palazzi! One shop masqueraded as a corner of the Place de la Concorde—with a few extra stories thrown in for good measure. And when he got to the River at Seventy-second Street, there was the Château of Chenonceaux! What frauds, what imposters! And the avenues in between were even worse. The dismal down-at-the-heel brick of Sixth Avenue under the El, the crass chaos of Eighth and Columbus! New world? But he would show them! He'd clean out the false feathers of the masqueraders, the squalor from Amsterdam Avenue to Chatham Square. —I'm not worrying, he murmured half aloud. —There's just time. And found he was carrying on a dialogue with Corinna Kennedy whom he had met in April and who listened (her part of the dialogue) so understandingly, so warmly!

Almost at a run, he went through the dining room, snatching a pear from the silver bowl on the sideboard; it was half devoured before he reached the pantry and the ponderous telephone. (In Paris, the telephones were more graceful and more practical, too, with their single hand apparatus: one end for the mouth, the other for the ear.) While he waited for the number, he heard Cook in the kitchen, and smelled what he imagined to be roast duckling stuffed with sweet-sour apples. Yes: any sidestreet bistro in Paris gave you a good *gigot* and a clean beaujolais; but you couldn't complain about the food in his mother's house!

"Hello? Is this the residence of Mr. Aloysius Kennedy? Is Miss Corinna there?"

"Hold on, sir."

A sign, her being home!, his sudden impulse was to be rewarded. He wondered while he waited why he liked Corinna so much more than any woman he had known in Paris? Including those you could sleep with. —I guess it's because she is not only wonderful, but *home*. We're both in this together. There were plenty of Americans who stayed on in Paris, and Jeff had sized them up: they were so secure, they didn't need to belong and to contribute to a world-in-the-making; or they were too empty to know they didn't count in Europe.

"Hello," his voice softened almost like a prayer. "How are you?"

"All right. How are you?"

"You know who this is?" It was intimate and delicious not to have to name each other.

"Of course."

"We have a date for Thursday. Remember?"

"Of course I remember."

"This is Tuesday."

"I know even that."

"Day after tomorrow's a long way off."

"Is it?"

"Corinna! I was thinking—could I see you tonight?"

"Oh, Jeff; I'm busy tonight."

"I've got something important to . . . discuss with you."

She was silent.

"Can't you *manage?*" Again silence. "It *is* important."

After a pause: "Papa has guests to dinner. I must be hostess, you know."

"After dinner—?"

"They're just business friends. They'll play cards or go to a meeting."

"Then I can come?"

"If it is *so* important."

"I'll be there at eight-thirty. All right? But Corinna, listen!"

"I'm listening."

"Tonight doesn't cancel Thursday."

"Oh!"

"Promise!"

"We'll talk about that."

"All right, but I *mean* it."

"Jeff, I have to go. The butcher was late, and he's just come."

"What are you having tonight?"

"Steak."

"We're having duck, I think. Can you smell it?"

"Of course! Smells awful good."

"Good-by, Corinna."

"Good-by, Jeff."

He wanted to say, "Thank you." That would be servile. He looked at the forgotten, half-devoured pear in his hand—badly mangled; put it in his mouth, seeds and all, and returned to the dining room, cleaning his hand on his handkerchief. His mother had just come in.

"Jeff dear!" she raised her face to be kissed, "don't you know fruit spoils linen? Anna would have given you a plate and a fingerbowl."

"Sorry, mama." He kissed her. "When's dinner?"

"As always. At quarter to seven."

"It'll be on time? I've got to go out."

"I thought we'd take a walk along the river. With papa."

"How about a walk with *you,* now?"

"My dear, I'm nearly dead. I've been shopping—in this heat! I found you three lovely ties."

"Let's see 'em."

"Silly. I didn't *bring* them. They'll come tomorrow."

"Thanks a lot. I'll wear all three of 'em at once. Too bad I can't use 'em tonight."

"And where, if I may ask, is my young man off to tonight?"

"I'm calling on Miss Corinna Kennedy."

"That's nice. You met her, didn't you, in Paris? Tell me about her."

"Some day I hope you'll meet her. Her mother's dead. She runs the house for her father; a big house, I gather, down on Stuyvesant Square."

"What does she look like?"

They had strolled to Greta's room, and Greta, before her mirror, was taking off her hat and powdering her face.

"Well," Jeff sprawled on the chaise longue, "she's big and fat, with a long nose. In fact, she looks just like you."

Greta laughed. *"Really,* Jeff."

Suddenly Jeff was pensive. "It's funny," he looked tenderly at his mother, "I don't know. Do I know what *you* look like?"

His mother leaned down and kissed him. "I hope not!" she laughed. He jumped up. "No walk? Sure?"

"All right, dear. Give me half an hour to rest. It'll be cooler then."

"I'll read—and wake you up in half an hour."

"I'm not going to *sleep,* silly! Come in just half an hour."

"Don't you let that cook sleep and delay dinner."

He flung himself on his couch and opened his book. His room was as his mother furnished it, just before he left for the Beaux Arts, mostly with the treasures of his callow days before Paris made him a man. On a little stand draped by a dove-blue altar cloth squatted his bronze Buddha, above the divan with vari-colored cushions Manet's *Olympe* lay on her bed. The bookshelves had old textbooks and miscellaneous volumes of Swinburne, Francis Thompson, George Moore, Meredith, Anatole France, Daudet, and Gissing. The room was no longer his, he had outgrown it: in fact, it was as much a masquerade as Fifth Avenue. The new beauty was function. —Just wait, New York! Another

357

year of Paris, learning the skills of Europe, and I'll be ready for you as you are ready for me! . . . He opened his book. It was Volume One of the latest novel by Henry James, who had saved himself by living in London and Paris where he was accepted by the giants: Turgenev, the Goncourts, Flaubert. But an architect must come home: *homes*—and business homes—were his material. Already he knew what *The Wings of the Dove* was about (you couldn't call it a story, it was a tapestry of music, fugues of mood, canons of tragic circumstance). Milly Theale was the heiress of all the ages (—that's what we are, we Americans) and in full view of it all, was doomed to die. The poignance and the pity! —But Milly is a woman and sick; I am a man and well! I shall fulfil where she fails. The room was warm in the waning afternoon, aromas stirred him from the kitchen, Jeff let the book fall and his eyes closed. —I'm happy, I'm grateful. His mother had given him health and talent. His father had given him more than the chance to study and make himself the builder he was to be: the old man *did* have a mind, although of course his epoch never taught him how to use it. Perhaps a decent lawyer never *could* be contented: what a shoddy business, the law! America was like a house where the drains don't work (politics is plumbing) and all the bungling burghers do is talk about the drains—argue about the drains—and elect bunglers to patch up the drains. Some day they'll learn to hire experts and leave the job to *them* —like in France, where no intelligent man or woman would be *caught* in politics. Then Americans will think of more important matters. *His clients* will come to him: "I need so and so. I have so much money to spend." "All right," he'll answer. "Now get out of my way, and let me go to work." The practice of law wasn't like that: he recalled his father's saying that in America lawyers were servants of business, not experts in law. Poor pop! could he even understand these first hundred pages about the broken wings of a dove? —Those books I brought him? Perhaps it wasn't very tactful. Pop belongs to a generation that thought Dickens was a *writer!* I'll make you proud of me yet. Why is he so hard to get at? is he jealous of my luggage, of my education? He gave them to me. People aren't logical. You can be jealous *and* proud; proud *and* disapproving. Jove! you're getting stuffy: what have you done to make the old man proud of you? Give me time. . . . Drowsing, Jeff thought of Corinna Kennedy whom he was going to be with in a couple of hours. As if he were there, he saw the comptoir on the Quai des Grands Augustins where he sometimes ate his breakfast *croissant* and *brioche* with *café-crême* (*sans sucre, s'il vous-plaît*—sugar spoils coffee); he sat on the terrace under the awning; the *sapins* and an occasional puffy auto sloshed through the rain, the people under umbrellas (*sous cloches,* like mushrooms) huddled across the filigree Pont des Arts; and Corinna was beside him. "You see, Corinna? These men and women aren't better than us Americans. But look at the Louvre, the Institut, the rue Mazarine, the Pont Neuf, the Cité; what are they but the grace and wisdom of generations made steadfast as stone, to hold all the volatile motions and emotions of the people? That's what culture is, Corinna: the *best* made permanent to house and hold the everyday. Now, if there was a war—which of course there won't be, and all these buildings were smashed, the French would become creatures of their passions like anyone else—like us: a basket of crabs. The French followed their *best:* men of the Church, aristocrats of the mind, wherever they were born. We can't do it, the same way. But we must learn, too, to be led by our *best*—not the best shouters and flatterers and liars. Then we'll build permanent structures for *us* to live in. That's why my work is important!" And Corinna listens with such understanding! He takes her hand, and she does not withdraw it. She grows large; large until her mysterious deep breast merged with the silhouette of Paris in the rain; surrounded and lulled him. . . .

Jonathan opened the door, and saw his son sleeping. Greta had told him to wake their boy for the short walk before dinner; but Jonathan found it hard to wake anyone: sleep had a beauty too close to his heart's hunger. He stood in the door and watched his son at peace in a far world. Even when Jeff was awake, even when they talked (and he was always yearning, always planning to talk more closely with his son), his son was in a far world, like a sleep, where the father could not touch him. He saw the face, its vibrancy relaxed, sensitive, not yet strong. All youth was a sleeping; youth built a world of its own from the substance of sleep, then youth awoke into a world alien to the world youth's sleep had builded. He also had been young, and he was waking; his heart went out in compassion to his son, still in youth's sleep. Carefully, he shut the door and went back to Greta. . . .

Just in time for dinner, Jeff jumped from his couch, burst into his parents' room, good spirits exploding; hugged his mother and asked her forgiveness, threw his arm around his father.

"Why shouldn't you sleep?" said Jonathan. "You're on vacation, aren't you?"

"You work hard enough in Paris!" said Greta.

"Not all the time, I hope?"

"I should say not!"

Jonathan tried to see his son, when he was not working in Paris. Perhaps he lay in bed, not with a prostitute—with one of those free, gallant, generous women for whom Paris was famed. *Petite amie,* they called them. He could not come near enough to see. Suddenly he thought of Frieda and of Mrs. Lake: shame blurred him.

They sat down to table. The dinner tonight began with a novelty: half grapefruit flavored in brandy, a red maraschino cherry at its center. Then came soft-shell crabs broiled in butter and lemon. The *pièce de résistance* was not duck (as Jeff had guessed) but guinea hen in browned sweet-sour sauce, with asparagus and a bottle of Rheinwein. Cold Nesselrode pudding set the stage for the coffee.

"*This,*" Jonathan savored his cup, "I'll bet you can't equal in Paris."

"Your father would leave home, if I didn't give him his good coffee."

"No, dear. But without this coffee, it wouldn't be home."

"You didn't know your father was such a materialist, did you? Why, I have to buy the berries green, roast them in a flat pan before we grind them."

"Poor mama! I suppose there's no time left for your music."

"Oh! that's of the least importance."

"Greta! Jeff will believe you."

"No, he won't. He knows when his old mother is joking."

"Joking aside," said Jonathan, "why shouldn't food and drink be important? Don't they go into us and help make us what we are?"

"The Germans say: *Man ist was man isst,*" Greta beamed proudly.

"Don't you believe it," said Jeff. "Man's more than what he eats. He's what he hears, what he sees, what he lives in."

"What he loves?" murmured Greta.

Jeff glanced at the grandfather's clock; thrust his unfolded napkin aside, kissed his mother, and was gone.

360

With no more words, Jonathan finished his coffee and got up to go to his library.

Greta asked: "Jon, do you know anyone named Kennedy?"

"Kennedy? There are hundreds of Kennedys. It's a common Irish name."

"No, but this must be *some* one."

"There's a rich contractor named Kennedy. Aloysius Kennedy. Very close to the Tammany gang."

"Where does he live?"

"How should I know where he lives?"

In his library, where Greta never disturbed him, it was too early, this June evening, to turn on the lights; but in the corner where he had ranged the little books Jeff had brought him, it was too dark to read the titles. At hazard, Jonathan drew one out and went to his chair. He read: *Pensées*: Blaise Pascal. . . .

At last, Jeff looked up at the row of red brick houses. The dim lights of street lamp and vestibule made no headway in the dusk; it was hard to read the numbers. He pulled an old-fashioned patient brass bell, his impatience heard it reverberate remotely. A young man with a red face and a brown sack suit that needed pressing, a soiled napkin on his arm, opened and said "Come right in, sir."

The dark hall smelled of heavy food and cigars; in the parlor, except for the light from the street and the back room, the furniture looked both unused and worn.

"They're still at table, sir," the man said. "You're to go right in." The brightness of the rear room revealed Corinna coming toward him.

"Hello," she clasped not his hand but his arm to lead him; he felt her strong and pervasive. From the round table over which the chandelier hung low, a short man got up. His wrinkled red face, beaked nose and twinkling eyes, his hair between straw and gray and parted in the middle, did not, it seemed to Jeff, resemble his daughter.

"Mighty glad to know you," he held out his hand. "You'll join us in a cup of coffee?"

The light, focused on the table, revealed crumbs and stains; the walls with their looming furniture were shadowed. And part of the

361

shadow were the two large men who sat back from the table, glasses before them.

"Judge, this is Mr. Jefferson Hartt, who met Corinna in Paris. Supreme Court Justice Dobbitt. Dan, Mr. Hartt. Dan Scanlon. Can I tempt you, Hartt, with a spot of very good Irish?"

They were all seated and Jeff, next to Corinna, took a sip of the aromatic whiskey.

"What were you doing in Paris?" Judge Dobbitt's voice was gruff as the whole man was gross: his pachyderm gray skin, his powerful long head with rough-hewn features.

"I'm studying architecture at the Beaux Arts." Jeff tried to adjust Corinna in her home.

"It's a grand thing," Kennedy smiled at the Judge, "when our young men go to the old countries to bring back the best."

"When it's the best," growled Dobbitt.

"We can put it all to good use, even the worst." Scanlon's face of an overblown cherub beamed. "That's what democracy means."

"Scanlon," said Kennedy, "is our philosopher. The philosopher of the Anawanda Club we call him."

"I guess I'm pretty ignorant," Jeff glanced appealingly at Corinna. "What is the Anawanda Club?"

Dobbitt grunted, Scanlon brightly laughed, Corinna's father said: "We've got to be there tonight. If you weren't busy, we'd be glad to have you join us."

"I've really not lived in New York much, these last years. Not since I left high school."

"The Anawanda Club," Scanlon said, "is the gathering place of the princes of the city." He made a fat small circle of his mouth and blew a perfect smoke ring.

"That means," said Dobbitt, "carpenters, masons, longshoremen, clerks, slaughterhouse workers—"

"In other words," Scanlon interrupted, "the Dominions and Principalities, Archangels and Angels."

Jeff blinked helplessly at Corinna who sat at her ease among these men, smiling and secure. They could not be laughing at him; she, who was on his side, would not allow it.

Kennedy said: "We get used to Dan's lingo; he's a sort of poet, too. Which doesn't mean he don't run his ward business-like."

"You're a doctor, sir?" asked Jeff. "A hospital ward?"

Judge Dobbitt slumped his body in his chair, and his face flushed.

"To shift the metaphor," said Scanlon, "you might call the Anawanda Club a nursery. It nursed Judge Dobbitt here, for instance, and Mayor Van Wyck, not forgetting Tim Sullivan and Bill Devery and Dick Croker. Charley Murphy and Al Adams got warm in its blankets. We got our swells too, like George McClellan, son of the General, and shipbuilder Nixon."

"That's Tammany!" Jeff put down his glass abruptly.

Corinna's father laughed. "You see, Judge? Just because a fellow goes to school in Europe don't mean he can't catch on."

Corinna said "Mr. Scanlon is our district leader."

"And in this district, young man," Dobbitt warmed, "that *means* bein' a philosopher."

"Wait a minute," said Jeff. "Isn't this what's called the 'gashouse district?' "

"That's right," said the Judge. "And where do you live?"

"Riverside Drive."

"Where would you say you'd find the best brains in the city? I suppose you'd guess your silk-stocking districts where the boys go to Harvard and Yale? You'd guess wrong. The highest ratings in the civil service examinations are here. That proves Avenue A has more brains than Fifth Avenue."

"Quit boasting, Judge," said Kennedy. "Even if young Hartt comes from a Republican bailiwick—"

"Oh, but my father's a Democrat. Perhaps you know him, sir? Jonathan Hartt."

There was a heavy silence. Corinna's father broke it:

"Isn't Reuben Hartt your uncle?"

"But he's a Republican." Jeff was getting more confused.

The Judge: "He's a good man."

Kennedy: "Many's the time I've done business with Reuben Hartt."

Scanlon: "Foxy Reuben's been no stranger to the Anawanda Club. Remember his partner, dead now, Darby Sleip?"

The somewhat soiled manservant placed a pot of fresh coffee on the table.

"It's getting late," Corinna's father looked at his gold watch and got up. "Come again, young man. Glad to have known you." He went to his daughter who put her cheek to be kissed. "Go to bed on time, mind? Don't wait for me."

The Judge rose to his full six-foot-three and clasped Jeff's hand. Jeff felt in his crude features intelligence and melancholy, the travail of a man who has broken his way up, alone, from the gutter; he was not sure he disliked Judge Dobbitt. Scanlon clapped him on the shoulder. The heavy, disparate parts of this household came together, and the catalytic agent was Corinna, daughter of this fond father, hostess of respectful guests. Jeff thought of home on Riverside Drive: the better taste that brought no ease, the good books and the good music that never touched each other, the indubitably purer ethics of his father that brought him no peace. Here ease in acceptance of contradictions; there, in the strain for unity, always only strain. . . . Jeff felt weak, insecure.

"We'll go up to the sitting room," Corinna said. "It's cozier," and again her hand on his arm drew him. Upstairs in the dim light of blue and red frosted globes, the majolica urns, the obese upholstered settles, the inlaid tables with gyring legs, the red carpet, each to his taste a "horror," were innocuous beside the serene reality of Corinna. Her smooth dark hair, her large and shapely head, without the vibrance of too great sensitivity or of conflict, gave her a plastic beauty, yet her flesh was warm, and her maternal repose was youthful. Corinna felt his trouble and his need; this was enough to incite her.

"You don't have to tell me that special news until you want to, Jeff," she said. "Although of course I want to hear. I mean: I'm glad *anyway* you came tonight."

Jeff went with his mother to the mountains, to a bright hotel on a shaded Adirondack lake, and Jonathan (in August he would join them for a brief vacation) remained alone under the care of Cook. It was one of Greta's many gifts (Jonathan's mother had never had it) to keep her servants faithful and efficient, and Anna was devoted to Jonathan, feeling for him in the way of peasant women a mingled

pity and respect. She knew without asking what he wanted for breakfast and ought to have for dinner; when he was tired or bilious, she
knew and fed him accordingly. So unobtrusive was she that Jonathan,
perfectly cared for, had the perfect sense of being in an empty apartment. He was glad to feel alone; it was a relief, although he did not
tell himself from what; it was even a luxury, although he did not
know what weakness it indulged. He finished his coffee, carefully
slipped his napkin into the gold-plated silver ring, shaped like an oak
leaf, that Lucia had given him so long ago all the gold was gone, and
went to his library. The evening was cool, with the breeze from the
river: a good time at last to tackle that Pascal. Deep in his chair, he
opened the gem-like volume which pierced him with two distances: his
son and his neglected French. To his surprise, he could understand.
He read at hazard:

> *Je blâme également, et ceux qui prennent parti de louer
> l'homme, et ceux qui le prennent de le blâmer, et ceux qui le
> prennent de se divertir; et je ne puis approuver que ceux qui
> cherchent en gémissant . . .*

—A bit stiff. Translate:

> I blame equally—those who take the part of praising man,
> those who take the part of blaming him, and those whose aim
> is to entertain themselves; I can approve none but those who
> seek—in sighing.

> *Il est bon d'être lassé et fatigué par l'inutile recherché du vrai
> bien, afin de tendre le bras au libérateur.*

> It is good to be wearied and worn by the useless search of the
> real good, in order to hold out one's arms to the redeemer.

—Pascal was a devout Christian; by "libérateur" he meant Christ.
How could so deep a mathematician, one of the masters of modern
science, really believe that myth? And Newton, mapping a topography
of Hell? and Kepler, plotting the end of the world in the Book of
Daniel? Were there men of genius, before there were men of *sense?*
Good sense is modern? But why, if Pascal knew his "liberator," his
approval only for those who seek in sighing? Another contradiction?

365

As he turned the pages, Jonathan thought of the Jews who had never found, who had only hoped and suffered for their redeemer. What had been the "liberator" of his gentle father? The Mosaic Law? to the modern as impossible as Christ. (His mother's will-for-success, his own Jeffersonian and Darwinian "progress"—were they firmer?) Most of the gentiles he knew were certainly not Christians—not in Pascal's sense of reaching out their arms to Christ. They leaned on other supports, as he did. They sighed less, because they had the strength of the majority. They who had Christ did not appear to need him, so much as those who did not have him, and who had lost the Law of his father. What made the Jews not need him? Did the gentiles not need him, precisely because they had him? Jonathan smiled at his sophistry. —Pascal's tergiversations are catching. The Jews . . . he saw the word *Juifs* . . . read:

> *C'est une chose étonnante et digne d'une étrange attention, de voir ce peuple juif subsister tant d'années, et de le voir toujours misérable: étant nécessaire pour la preuve de Jésus-Christ et qu'il subsiste pour le prouver, et qu'il soit misérable, puisqu'ils l'ont crucifié; et quoiqu'il soit contraire d'être misérable et de subsister, il subsiste néanmoins toujours, malgré leur misère.*

—I don't quite get it: go on . . .

> *C'est visiblement un peuple fait exprès pour servir de témoin au Messie. Il porte les livres, et les aime, et ne les entend point. Et tout cela est prédit: que les jugements de Dieu leur soient confiés, mais comme un livre scellé.*

—Is it important? Why trouble to translate? Because Jeff gave you the book?

> It is astounding and worthy of strange attention, to see this Jewish people subsist so many years, and to see it always miserable: it being necessary for the proof of Jesus Christ, and that it must subsist to prove him and that it must be miserable, since they crucified him; and although it is a contradiction to be miserable and to subsist, it subsists nevertheless always, despite its misery.

Jonathan smiled. —I suppose in Pascal's day, the Jews he knew were miserable. Not now! Not by a long shot! (True: there were still the poor devils under the barbarous heel of Russia, but that would change soon: they were pouring into America, and even Russia some day must catch the infection of progress from Germany and the West.) In Pascal's day, all the nations believed in Christ and all the Jews were miserable. When all the nations finally cease to believe in Christ, will all the Jews' misery be over? . . . Go on:

> It is visibly a people made expressly for a witness to the Messiah. It bears the Books, it loves them, and does not understand them. And all this is foretold: that the judgments of God be confided to them, but as a book that is sealed.

Troubled, Jonathan turned the pages. *Les juifs . . . les juifs . . .* the great Christian was certainly concerned (—more than I have ever been!) with the Jews. He read:

> To prove that the true Jews and true Christians have only the same religion.—The religion of the Jews seems to consist essentially in the fatherhood of Abraham, in circumcision, in the sacrifices, ceremonies, the Ark, the temple in Jerusalem, finally in the Law and the Mosaic treaties.
> I say: that
> It consisted in none of these, but only in the love of God, and that God reproved all else.
> God did not accept the posterity of Abraham.
> The Jews, if they offend him, will be punished like the gentiles. . . .
> The gentiles will be accepted of God like the Jews, if they love Him. (Isaiah lvi.3.). . . .
> The real Jews find their merit, not in Abraham, but in God only. . . .
> Even Moses told them . . . (Deuteronomy x.17.): "God regardeth not persons nor taketh rewards, sacrifices . . ."
> The Sabbath is but a sign. . . .
> Circumcision is but a sign. . . .
> Circumcision of the heart is required (Deut. x.16; Jeremiah lv.4).

Jonathan closed his eyes, the little volume in his hands as if he were still reading. —I am not miserable, I am a Jew. It's hot and I sit after my good dinner high above the Hudson. Tonight, on the East Side, thousands of men, women, and children will carry their rags from windowless rooms, fetid kitchens, to the tenement roofs, gasping for air and for sleep: I'll go to the best bed money can buy and in my cool sheets think of my wife and son in their luxurious hotel in the cool mountains. I have my grip on this wonderful new world rising. Miserable? Why take Pascal so damn seriously? He dates. His redeemer, his sighs, his unattainable search: how he dates! Miserable? a Jew? Evan was miserable and not a Jew.... Now he had thought of Evan, Evan remained; and the obvious:—I am not miserable, became uncertain. —Am I a Jew? The utterly denied became the fact: —I am miserable. His eyes opened on the handsome room, he moved his head slowly as if it hurt and saw his head swaying . . . his father's head swaying in prayer. Jonathan dropped his book, and his hand went to his eyes. The loved head of his father! —When his eyes see me, I am a Jew and miserable . . . and for all the happiness of the world, I would not lose my father's eyes! In my father's eyes, Evan is a Jew, all men are Jews! Despite the new century, misery subsists; despite the redeemers and the freedom from redeemers. Jonathan sat with his father's eyes open, not seeing his room, seeing himself: and every part of him was now ambiguous like the certainty, *I am not miserable*, which had become the truth, I *am* miserable. He had had a nervous day at the office. Mrs. Lake was there and remarked on his looking tired. Their business was settled, no reason for her return; but he had found a pretext for her to come again. —To seek in sighing. His relation with his wife, with his son, with his dead ever-present friend, with his practice, with Mrs. Lake: all cloudy, and the cloud hid foulness. Greta had stunned him with a casual remark on Jeff's interest in the daughter of a Tammany contractor, whose hands were soiled with the same filth he had fought and that had ruined Evan. How had he fought it? with his ambition and pride? how clean were they? —To seek in sighing. Even now, what rankled most in his resentment? Pride? possessiveness of his son? Jonathan leaned down for the little volume fallen on the floor, a twinge of rheumatic pain made him sigh. He walked to the corner shelf to replace the book, seeing himself with the eyes of his father. He knew: this was what he wanted most and needed most, though the sight was not good.

Jonathan slept well and woke, feeling himself. But the doubt of the undoubted, the presence of the never-there, was a lesion within him. A darkness began to bleed into his usual life. Hidden within him, it was also hidden in the city whose heat was less summer than fever: millions of men and women like himself were lesioned by doubt of the undoubted, by presence of the never-there. At times, he knew that he had always known this bleeding darkness; never believed in the brightness of his apartment, his career, the new city; and that everybody knew what he did: the brightness was a lie ever more desperately needed as the dark lesion bled. Good Anna thought the master was working too hard; she gave him light dinners with a somewhat tiresome insistence on salads. The coffee tasted less good and when he asked her, she admitted that she was serving him Kaffee Haag, a brew without caffeine.

"But, Anna, I sleep very well!"

She turned to the kitchen door, the stubborn old peasant, and said: "You will get used all right to the new coffee."

Mrs. Lake came to the office, and as always he could not see her unremembered features; but now he knew if he tried he could see, and that he did not want to try.

"Mr. Hartt, may I say something?"

"Of course."

"You don't look well."

"I guess I'm a little tired. This heat wave has lasted a long time."

"Why, Mr. Hartt, it broke yesterday! It's positively cool. You *are* sick."

"I've never been sick in my life."

"Mr. Hartt, may I stay just a few minutes longer?"

He smiled wanly. "It's against the rules, during office hours."

"I know it. You're so strong. That's why you can stand all those rules. But you don't know how they wear even you down. May I break the rules, just a little while?"

"They're my rules, not yours." He kept on bravely smiling.

"You've been so good to me." She looked down at her hands and when her eyes lifted, her face again was strange. "It's not fair. You're

369

not being generous, Mr. Hartt. I mean—" her small round teeth bit into her lip as it trembled: "when you've been so good, I mean it's hard to take it all as just professional. Never, never to be allowed to think of it as coming a little from a friend."

"Lawyer and client don't have to be enemies."

"I know. But you've been so good; I mean—you see, if it had been a friend who had done it, I could never repay, of course; but I could try to give *something*."

Jonathan was silent.

"That would be generous of you, Mr. Hartt. That's what I mean. That would be kind."

Still Jonathan was silent, but relaxed: —Let her say, let her do what she wants.

"You're so tired. Your family, I know, are away. Strong men can never watch out for themselves."

His relaxation was almost ecstasy. If he said: Next week I shall join them in the mountains, it would vanish.

"You've never even seen my little home, which I owe to you! It would be so kind, if you'd come up—you'd have to walk four flights! —just long enough to drink a glass of something cool with me, or a cup of coffee. That's what I mean by being generous. I'd *seem* to be doing something for a friend."

"I love good coffee. Anna, our cook, what do you think she's been doing? Giving me some concoction in place of coffee, for my nerves—"

"As if that's what you need!"

"Do you make good coffee?"

"Oh, yes!"

"You tempt me with your coffee."

Laughing, her voice for the first time seemed free: "If that's temptation, Mr. Hartt, won't you please let me tempt you?" Again the furred murmur: "It would be *kind*. . . ."

Jonathan walked up the first flight; gray stairs between rough brown plastered walls that hurt the quick of his nails. Walking up with effort, he was falling into the darkness long . . . too long . . . within him. He felt shame and he needed to be close to shame, to understand it. The dark toward which he fell, climbing step by step, had a glow.

370

The light of his years—all his knowledge—had been phasma, ignis fatuus; adoring, he had been blinded by it; he needed to heal his eyes in this darkness. He climbed (his knees hurt him) because he needed to fall. Shame in the darkness was a kind of sleep. He climbed because he needed to sleep. 2A, 2B on brown varnished doors. . . . He obeyed the stair upward. Reason told him his forebodings were absurd. He was going to drink a cup of coffee with a woman client whom he had helped and who wished to thank him. Perhaps he could never see her face because he could not face an illicit longing in himself; perhaps he distrusted her because he distrusted himself. What of it? Will and reason were his, to keep such darkness in place. Even if he were right not to trust the woman upstairs (but how not believe in that moment's free laughter?), was he not a man of reason? The whole world was coming together with reason. He thought of the plans for the Panama Canal, soon to draw East and West, North and South, together within reason. President Roosevelt had granted amnesty to the insurgent Filipinos; even Japan opened her gates to reason and progress. The whole world— Man still could not avoid natural cataclysms like the eruption of Mont Pelée, forty thousand human beings buried under lava, but man was mastering his own volcanoes! Suddenly, he saw his cloudy part in Evan's death. What had moved him to open the window wider? beneath reason (that told him the night air was mild) had it not been a sign of acquiescence in Evan's will to die? and had not reason covered up . . . protected . . . the dark shared impulse? Evan must have got up from bed and stood in the cold blast. And before he left the room, while he worked in the library, all through the dreaming night, he must have known! or rather, he would have known, *but for his reason. 3A, 3B* on the brown doors. I can go back if I want. He climbed on. Violence? what was there in this of violence, and why did he fear it? Evan had been a violent man because the one unity he could reach was death. Evan had spread death: his mother, his corruption, his father, probably his marriage, at last himself—and he, Jonathan, had been involved in it. But why did he feel violence, climbing these stairs? *4A, 4B:* he paused on the landing. The woman he wanted was Greta. He had lived with a willed image, not with Greta. And Greta was still there. —Turn back! Take the train to the mountains! He sees himself at dawn leaving the sleeper, boarding the little spur-line train. He sits by the open window behind the wood-burning engine; he plunges into the forest of pine, into the morning coming down (the woman's laughter), and the forest rouses with the sun. The train lopes past a mountain lake; the cool water, the vibrant woods, laughing with sun, draw him away. He was climbing the last flight of stairs, already he saw 5A. Greta is waiting at the station: he will see her as she is, he will delight in what she is! He knocked at the brown door. . . .

2

REBECCA LORNE WORKED IN A SMALL ROOM ON THE
top floor of The Fair, Elysium's leading department store. From the
inside partition which did not reach the ceiling, came the din and
clatter of the main business office; from the open window—it was
June—the street sent its thresh and clang and thud of traffic. Suddenly, the silent typewriters, the shuffle of feet, made Rebecca know
it was closing time. She went on working at her tilted table on which
was tacked the sketch of a woman's head wearing a large mushroom
hat and a chenille veil. Her pencil lavished dots on the veil, over the
chin, the whalebone collar, the shoulders. She heard the door open
and shut; she knew who it was breathing close to her hair.

"You're blotting out the face with all those dots; and it's a pretty
face."

"I want to." She kept on working. "This is an advertisement of a
hat and a veil, isn't it? If the woman who sees it in the paper sees
the face too clearly and it's not like her own, she may decide the
hat won't be becoming. If the face is vague, she'll put her own in
its place."

"You're right. You're smart, Rebecca."

Her pale lips puckered wryly, she went on spacing the dots.

"Nearly finished?"

She felt the man's breath, smelled the pomade on his black hair.

"You shouldn't work after hours. I don't pay you any extra. You
can finish tomorrow."

"Thanks."

"Don't thank me. I want to *talk* to you."

"Go away," she said.

He was a glossy young man in a herringbone suit and white piqué
vest. He shifted his hands from his pockets to behind his back; then
forward again. She went on dotting the veil designed to protect lady
automobilists from dusty roads.

"Why do you talk to me like that?"

373

"Because I want to."

"Can I walk a ways with you?"

"I'm not walking, Mr. Pearl. I've got shopping to do and must hurry home."

"You always have an excuse, don't you? Lunch—supper: it's always the same."

She brushed against him, getting up, as if he were not there; drew her work smock over her head, its coarse cloth impeded by her heavy breasts, and went to the wall where a hat hung on a hook. With her back toward the man, she placed the hat on her hair, color of wet hay in the sun. When she turned again, he caught a green glint in her eyes.

"All right, I'll talk to you here." She waited, strangely motionless for a young girl. "I don't like to talk to you here. After all, here is business, I'm your boss here."

"What on earth are you driving at?"

"As if you didn't know!"

"I'll know what you tell me."

"Whatever I tell you, it mustn't spoil your job. I want to be fair. Promise?"

Her smile was a faint twist of her thin mouth. "I thought I understood English, but—"

"I'm crazy about you, Rebecca."

She half turned toward the door.

"It's not what you think, Rebecca. If you'd give me a chance, maybe I'd want to marry you."

She faced him again: "You're crazy. You don't even know me. You've never even tried to kiss me."

The young man's conventional features seemed to decompose; he went up to her, she did not move, and he kissed her mouth.

"Now will you let me go?" She pushed him away.

"Rebecca!"

"I don't like you, Mr. Pearl. I let you kiss me to see if I was wrong. I didn't feel a thing." She smiled at the wound she had inflicted. Then she shut the window, drew down the shades, dusted her hands, and left him.

At the corner, a man stepped out from the loading platform between two lorries. She did not slack her pace and he walked beside her, a big solid workman, smelling pleasantly of tobacco and raw wood and sweat.

"Hello," he said.

"Hello yourself."

"You're in a hurry."

"Ma's sick again. I got shopping to do."

"You're a good gal, Rebecca."

"Thank you, sir."

"Rebecca, listen."

They crossed the street in a lull of the traffic.

"Are you listening?"

"Sure."

"I got a wife and a couple o' kids. They're all right. But I swear, if I could have you and the price was tossin' 'em out, I swear I'd do it."

"Why should you have to pay a price like that?"

"Rebecca! Do you mean—?" They went on walking, till his hand engulfed hers and wrenched her toward him. She stood facing him.

"You mean—? Good God, girl, you mean—"

"I like you, Bill. If I was ready, I'd give you what you want, and there'd be no price at all. Why should you leave your wife and kids, just if we liked each other? But I guess I'm not ready."

"Girl!"

"I don't guess. I'm *not* ready." She smiled and looked past him to the next corner. "There comes my car." He watched her tall young body running.

The room where Rachel lay in bed smelled of sickness. Rebecca dropped her parcels on the table, flung open the window, then leaned and kissed her mother. Bill belonged in this June, not Bertie Pearl, son of the owner of The Fair, not this woman. Rebecca thought her mother beautiful; now that fever parched her skin and mouth, even her hair and eyes, she was more beautiful, but the girl could not abide her. Rebecca's world was June. But June had many mansions, and Bill's share was a hovel. One had to wait, hard though it was. The

375

girl channeled her unrest in quick tasks: set a broth on the stove, tidied the kitchen and her mother's room, fed the cat; then placed a tray on the chair beside her mother's bed and ate with her.

There had never been many words between them. On Mr. McAllister's advice, when Rachel returned to teaching she had resumed her maiden name; and when Rebecca entered a new school she used the name of her mother. It was her one expression of how she felt about her father. But the refusal did not negate his continuous presence. That first year after his disappearance, when she remembered him as one hears a storm in one's sleep, the child had come back from school and asked her mother: "Why did you call me Rebecca?" "Your father and I thought it a lovely name." "A girl at school said it's a Jew name. Am I a Jew?" "No, dear, we are Christians. But Rebecca is in the Bible; she was a good woman; and we Christians believe in the Bible." "Did papa believe in the Bible?" Rachel turned away: "If only he had! if only he had not mocked it!" And that night in bed in the dark, the child lay awake and figured it out. —Papa mocked the Bible; I have a Bible name; papa mocked me. Her mother's silence and acceptance, in which devotion glowed, her refusal to marry Mr. McAllister who had always loved her, her little chance proud words: "Your father was a genius," then a sigh; "You're very smart, my darling. Well, no wonder." . . . thinking of her husband, fused pride with humiliation in the growing girl; merged the glamour of secret value with the mocking of defeat. The ambivalent silent dialogue with her father wove into her years. And now, unconsciously, her mother's illness fitted the same pattern. Her mother had been brave, she had kept beautiful, and suddenly she lay defeated! Sickness was insult. Her mother had not won after all; her mocking father had won!

Rebecca washed the dishes, freshened her mother's bed, and went to her hot room. First she made her own bed (there was no time in the morning); then, in the dusk, she sat by the open window. The prospect of backyard fences and chimneys was not fair, she did not see it; she did not hear the voices of crowded poverty. She heard June in herself. She thought of the two men who wanted to make love to her, and of a pamphlet she had read: "The New Hedonism" it was called (whatever that meant) and the writer, someone named Grant

Allen, was a sissy. What he said about free womanhood was true, but why so excited, why so solemn about it? When you talk of woman's right to love, why flutter the flags? Rebecca hated anything that trembled: Bertie Pearl's breath, her mother's sick voice. —No one's going to make me tremble! She was a new woman of the new century. And even the writers who wrote about it, you could see, had been brought up by the old: they were so damned sentimental. Her mother had tried to be new, earning her own living, but in such old-fashioned pious ways! submission, loyalty to a dead man. (—Catch *me* ever loving a man one minute if he stops loving me!) No wonder she was failing.

The summer was hateful. It cheated the spring; sordid with the sweat of cheated men and women, it cheated them all of spring, and her mother was dying. Hurry, Rebecca, don't let them cheat you of spring! Mr. McAllister came every evening and sat with the woman he had loved and never touched . . . never really helped, thought Rebecca, or she'd have married him and they'd have gone to live in a decent house. (He was a gray weak man beside the bed where Rachel grew more beautiful as she burned away.) What the old man and the woman said to each other was lies: their talk of school, for instance, when all school really did was prepare the children to be cheated. (—Not me!) The doctor came more often, and he lied too with his pills and encouraging words, when he knew the one way to save her mother was the impossible way of sending her to a sanatorium in the mountains.

—I am going to be alone! I am going to be free.

Will cannot grieve; will can be sullen and resentful, and at the same time dutiful and careful. Rebecca carefully nursed her mother.

One day, Rachel smiled: "Darling, I feel sorry for you," and held her daughter's hand. "Not what you think; you'll be all right without me. It's not that. It's because of all you do for me, and yet not truly loving."

"I love you. Whom else?"

"No one, not even yourself." Her eyes, brimmed with tears, were still dry in their fever. "I've been luckier than you and your poor father. He also couldn't love himself. Men are losing God, running after many inventions, and only in God's love for us can we love—

even ourselves." Rhythmically, with the diastole and systole of her heart, she pressed her child's hand and her eyes, now tearless, were strong seeing her daughter. . . . "If only you could see Jesus, not as the Son of God, but as the truest man. He gave up everything to life because he loved life. He let himself be used even by men who hated him, because he loved them. He had deep love for himself or he could not have died for love of others."

Her words meant nothing to Rebecca: it seemed to her she loved herself more than her mother loved herself. Look at her mother's life! an abject memory of a few years with a man whom she still thought better than she (his whole coming to Elysium and his marriage was a mysterious aberration!) and then a poor cottage on a mean street. Rebecca loved herself better than that. She'd go on loving herself. Her mother was wrong.

Toward the end, Rachel said: "Life is beautiful, because God makes it fresh each morning; breathes into each of us each day His own breath." Rebecca heard her mother's breath come harder. "With His breath, how can we die?" Rachel said; and Rebecca saw her mother die.

After the funeral, Rebecca went to the private office of Bertie Pearl. Styles from Eastern colleges and London's *Yellow Book* were vaguely syncretized with business: a morris chair next to a commercial swivel chair, a Princeton banner and an original Aubrey Beardsley over the steel files. The walls were of imitation leather and the rug was purple.

Bertie jumped up from his creaking seat, his hands waved (he never knew what to do with his hands), and as he came forward Rebecca saw an unpleasant hopefulness in his glaucous eyes. —Maybe, they seemed to say, now her mother's dead, she'll be less proud.

"My dear, my dear, I was so shocked to hear of your loss. You know you must let us help you. Nothing personal; The Fair wants to be of service to every one of its big family. There must be large bills; excuse me if I seem abrupt. Was there—ah—life insurance?"

"I don't know, Mr. Pearl. My mother had an old friend who took care of everything."

"I see." Crestfallen.

"But you *can* help me, Mr. Pearl."

Her request changed him; slowly he went back to his throne behind

378

his desk; soberly he said: "Sit down, Rebecca. What can I do for you?"

She kept standing. "I want to go to New York."

"Oh!"

"If I've done good work here," she paused and he said nothing, "maybe you could give me a letter of recommendation?"

"Business is picking up very slowly. Not every concern has weathered last year's panic like we did."

"I know."

"Rebecca, I've been meaning to give you a raise."

"I want to go to New York."

"You'll be lonely there, my dear! New York's cold and hard—"

"I'm not afraid."

"After all, this is your home. Your friends are here. You'll need them now, more than ever."

"I have no friends."

"I want to be your friend."

"I know," she spoke vaguely.

Bertie picked the ivory Chinese-dragon paperweight from his desk and twirled it. His two roles: employer and suitor, confused him; he was playing both badly and he knew it. The reason was this eighteen-year-old girl, who should be overcome with the orphan's helpless grief and was not playing *her* role at all.

"Think it over," he hoped his smile was both fatherly and full of cryptic promise. "There's no hurry. Starting at once, you get thirty dollars a week. If a little later on you still wish to go, I have friends, of course, in the big city. Murray of *A La Mode*'s a pal o' mine. He might use you, later on, if I told him to."

"Would it be all right, Mr. Pearl, if I went the beginning of October?"

"Next week?" Bertie slammed the Chinese dragon on the mahogany and jumped up. "How can you be so sure of yourself? Isn't Elysium good enough?"

She stared at him.

"I won't give you a letter." He waved his hands. "I'll give you a letter: I'll write—what I'll write is, you've got a heart made of stone and will drop any job soon as you've worked into it and learned what it has to give."

Coolly: "I wouldn't have to use that kind of letter."

Bertie sat down. "That's all you'll get from me."

"You gave me a job, without a letter."

Bertie picked up the ivory, not broken, thank goodness. "Today, if you want it, Miss Lorne, I dictate you a letter to Murray of *A La Mode*. A grand letter. He's a grand person."

"Oh, thank you."

"You rub me the wrong way, Rebecca. I want to show you my feeling in your loss of your mother; you won't let me."

"I'm sorry, sir."

"*You* sorry?" How smart the girl always managed to look—and how careless! From her buttoned suède-top shoes, her pleated skirt a daring seven inches above the floor, his eyes rose to her full bosom and the prim stiff collar. In her face, as in her body, the same disharmony: Bertie did not know, could not analyze, the duality—frailty and challenge, vulnerability and hardness—that confused and drew him. She saw him softened; at once her need to hurt mastered her will to be shrewd.

"I *was* sorry," she said. "If you have so many doubts about the letter, I can do without it."

"You'll have your letter. It's only fair. That's our name, you know: Fair," he snickered. "Just to make you feel good, I'll tell you something: you could get a job in the big city even without a letter. It might take you a little longer."

"My work *is* good, Mr. Pearl?"

"Good?" He pointed a connoisseur's hand at the Aubrey Beardsley: a naked woman with small pyramid breasts and a red carnation mouth. "That depends on what you mean by good. The women *like* your work. And they're the bosses. *B-u-y-e-r-s* in American spells bosses."

"I'm glad."

Suddenly the man's face collapsed. "Will you have lunch with me, Rebecca?"

—The fool! "I'll be glad to have lunch with you, Mr. Pearl."

Rebecca found a seat in the day coach, arranged her coat, bag, lunch-

380

box at her side, and waited for the train to wing her through the bright new world to New York. She had made only local trips by rail; she expected more speed from this express which now ambled through the Ohio Valley orchards, the meadows harvested and golden, the villages under featherbed trees, and across roads tilting produce-laden wagons past her vision. Rebecca's face against the window-pane was a mask of youth, and all she beheld became her own hard fire. The scene changed: brick mills, chimneys, and mine shafts violated the fields. In places, the trees were delivered of their life, the summer was dead, not burning on the earth. Hills, destitute and wrinkled, huddled in the horizon; as if to escape the foreground of shanties which gathered momentum, became a swarming main street, and again shrank to empty rows of hovels, a dirty child and a dirty dog in the gutter. With vague hostility, Rebecca sensed the coach a close-knit creature with many eyes: the drummers bound for Ironton and Huntington; the Swedish farmer woman with apple-red, apple-hard cheeks and soft twin babies on each arm; the pale youth late for the opening classes at the University of Virginia; the mechanic whose rubbery mouth expanded when he looked at Rebecca; the elderly conductor, gently punching tickets, raveling them all together, all except Rebecca who shared with this coach-creature only its motion. In a day, it would dissolve and die; she alone in all the world was going to New York! With the valleys and the hills on her impervious face, the coach carried her and did not touch her.

After the bleak coal fields of West Virginia, the Blue Ridge suddenly flung its banners, the rocks crashing up, the streams torrenting down, the trees in stately yet precipitous dance, and Rebecca unaware breathed deeper. Stone jaws swallowed the sun; sky became fragmented pools of quiet left by the tiding height; then sky was gone as the train tunneled. They swam at last into night; the outside dark compressed Rebecca more completely in the coach which stretched its many limbs, fearful of the long dark hours, then curled them against the cold and shut its eyes. Rebecca slept and woke; sleep was a thin dimension, not enfolding the train's motion, the opening and shutting of doors, the platform voices, the jolts of brake and lamp, the alien vibrance of a new passenger until the car absorbed him. But the night deepened; the motion forward became night's dominant grain, persisting even when the train stood. The train would go into day—and she into her future.

The accidents of human bodies, weaving their noises and silences in the coach, became nothing, her past nothing: secure, without excitement or fear, her expectation of tomorrow was a part of her like her breasts, also pointing forward, also unawakened to excitement and fear.

Rebecca slept and opened her eyes on morning: the pleasant melody of Virginia came with the warm sun into her window. The trees were scarcely touched by autumn, the corn had yellow tassels, a village in the embrace of a church, its steeple high, outsang the passengers sodden with dregs of the dark hours. This was tomorrow! this the day she would be in New York! Rebecca was hungry and wanted to sing. She ate her last sandwich. Her body felt fresh as if bathed; a vague sweetness seeped from the car's motion through her body. Even the names of the towns spoke music: Culpepper, Warrenton, Fairfax. . . . Again she was separate from the coach-creature; it was dying and knew it, its end was Washington, and Washington was near. The Potomac was her ideal of a river: broad, steadfast, unresponding to the clatter of the wheels on the trestle. The Capitol in its distance also was impervious, the proper mood for government, she supposed: Rebecca's one political thought of all her years. In the Capitol's haughty stones she read dominion, and approved of her country.

At the start of her journey Rebecca had spread her things on the seat beside her. She soon learned that if she avoided the eye of someone pausing above her, looking for a place to sit, he moved on to a seat less innocently defended. Now, in the longer, shining red plush coach to which she changed at Washington, she deliberately filled the place beside her with all her belongings and kept her eyes straight on the window, where the iron hand-trucks laden with luggage and mailbags wove through the passengers on the platform. The car was filling; several times she felt a face hover close and, not winning her eye, move on. It was fun. Suddenly, she changed her mind: —Why *not* have someone sit with you? It might be a New Yorker! She looked up into the eyes of a young man whose smart gray Fedora revealed their blue. He was already moving on; she clutched her hat. "Don't bother," he said. "There'll be a seat in the next car." "This isn't taken," she moved to get up, to place her things on the rack. "Let me," the man neatly stacked her bag, her coat, her empty lunchbox, then his coat and safely on top of all, her hat. He had slender, very white hands. Whispering "Thanks," he sat beside her, pulled a book from a leather brief-case. Rebecca saw that it was called *The Fruit of the Tree* by Edith Wharton and that the slip of thin paper which marked his page had the pencil sketch of a building. Was the man an artist, like herself? He looked up, feeling her attention.

"The train's crowded," he said. "There wasn't a seat to be had in the parlor cars." He flushed at his indelicate remark. "Not that I always ride in parlor cars. But I do when a client pays the fare—" He slowly turned and sought Rebecca's eyes. No: she was not offended.

"Anyway," he smiled, looking again at his book, "my riding back day coach will save you money."

"Me?"

"You're an American citizen, aren't you?" He kept his eyes on the book. "It's your money pays for my trip."

"You're in the government, sir?"

"Lord, no! But I've been to Washington. . . . I won a contest, you see, for a government building—not a very big one."

She pondered this. "Why, isn't that wonderful!"

"Not bad." He raised and dropped his eyes like an embarrassed boy.

"It's wonderful," she repeated with more assurance.

He twisted his mouth sulkily. "I thought so too. After my session with those bureaucrats, I'm not so sure." She said nothing, and he went on: "To tell you the truth, I don't see why they gave *my* project the award, if they want everything changed."

"Oh!"

"You know what I suspect?" He half turned toward her and again to his book. "I suspect what they liked in my stuff was its weaknesses. So they want more of 'em!" His thin, sensitive face seemed to depre-cate its own laughter.

"What are you going to do?" She was solemn.

He shrugged his shoulders and turned a page, although obviously he had read nothing.

"Will you refuse to let them change—?"

He turned quickly toward her. "Don't you think I should, if they spoil the design?"

"What are bureaucrats?" she temporized.

"Then you don't live in Washington?" he smiled at his joke.

"Oh, no!"

"They're the little bosses—who really run things."

"Now I know! They buy buildings. Buyers are bosses."

"That's the gist of it," he laughed. "So, as an interested and good citizen, you think I should obey them?"

She was suddenly aware of the train racing (so much speedier than the first), of the sun gone, and the sky aglow like a ripe melon. "Is it important?"

"Important for what?"

"For your success?"

"It's *it*." His boy mouth sulked and smiled together.

At last she said: "Yes."

He understood and nodded, then for the first time he faced her. "See here! How do you know what I should do?"

"I don't."

"Just the same, I'm going to obey you."

"Oh, but you mustn't! I was just talking. How can I know *any-thing*?"

"Well, I have already obeyed you. It comes to that. You see, those chaps in Washington simply took it for granted I'd be so overwhelmed with their favors I'd do anything they wanted. They just bowled me over."

"You won the prize; they must appreciate your work."

"It's not so simple as that."

"Why isn't it?" Rebecca was ready to fight for simplicity.

"You want to know?" He stopped himself from what was coming. Why should it trouble him to say it? Because it did, he had better say it. Why not be open with this girl it was so easy to talk to? "Well, you see," he stumbled and then plunged, "I've got—there's a man who's a big contractor. He has influence, see? . . . political influence. Jobs come in. I suppose you don't know much about politics?"

"Only what Mr. McAllister used to tell mama: that they were ruin-ing the schools."

"You don't know much, maybe, but it's always the essence."

"I don't know anything," she laughed, "not even what you mean by essence."

"It's not even as simple as straight influence. The man I'm talking

384

of's a Democrat; the men in Washington are all Republicans. So you see—, it can't be *that* that made me win the contest."

"I should say not!"

"Just the same, Teddy Roosevelt, who's a Republican of course, likes to have friends among the New York Democrats. If the Democratic majority in New York City isn't *too* big, the State goes Republican. That means it pays the Republicans in Washington to get on with their so-called enemies in New York. Now my father-in-law—"

"Your father-in-law?"

"He's the contractor." The young man was blushing.

Confused by his facts, she was clear about his mood. "You can't have everything at once. You mustn't mind being helped, not at first. Isn't that so?"

"I've been at it five years! When does 'at first' stop? Gosh, the ideas I brought back with me from Paris."

"Is that where you come from?"

"That's where I studied architecture. After Harvard."

—My father went to Harvard!

"And what I haven't told you,"—after a long pause: "what I should, to be perfectly honest, since I *have* told you so much: my other clients, in New York, aren't a bit better than the bureaucrats." She said nothing; she was amazingly easy and comforting to talk to. —Well, why not? . . . "The ideas I brought back! I was going to change the face of New York. Build it over in its own spirit and color. Take color, for instance. Every great city has its own. Athens is aquamarine, Paris is brick-red, New York is blue." His smile as he turned to her became a laugh. "You think I'm talking nonsense."

"Oh, yes!" She fervently agreed. "I mean: oh, no!"

"You know your New York, I see."

She was silent.

"New York has a different sky, a different bloodbeat from any city in the world. Why clutter it up with masqueraders, museum pieces?" Again she did not answer, and it did not matter; again, secure in her wanting him to, he talked on: "Well, New York hasn't seen it. I'm just adding to the masquerade."

"You just wait!" she smiled for the first time.

He consulted his gold watch, thin as a wafer. "One thing we needn't

385

wait for: dinner. You've been awfully kind listening to all my troubles. Haven't they given you an appetite for something good?"

Rebecca thought of her empty box. "No, thanks, I'm not hungry."

"I am! Won't you keep me company?"

She glanced at his briefcase. "Go ahead. You eat yours."

He smiled: "It's not in here. Our dinner's in the diner. If we go now, we'll get a table."

"Let's!" She jumped up.

He enjoyed watching her in (he was sure) her first experience of a dining car. She glanced once, swiftly, at the ornate woodwork, the unctuous steward leading them to a table, the bright napery and silver; she found, quickly, what she wanted on the menu; she ate, not needing to talk, not trying to hide her hunger. Words were sparse between them as they walked back through the swaying, tossing cars to their seat, their ease was even closer. The train now flew toward the dark; the autumn dusk, the industrial towns—fitful bonfires against the dark —invaded them. Philadelphia's muffled streets were behind, too far. . . . They raced across the Jersey flats: huge gyres of steel, masses of black masonry, pyramided from the swamps to the slate sky. The train groaned, and dimmed into the terminal shed; the train died and rejected them.

They stood close together on the ferry and watched the metropolis come nearer. The water buoying them was black and more solid than the dim lights of the city; the river, sighing and soughing against the boat . . . against their own bodies . . . was a hunger that drew them from the lights, urged them seaward, darkward. They had said almost nothing to one another when they returned from the dining car; she had tried to look out of the window, he had tried to read his book; but now the time of silence would be transformed from ease to pain. The ferry warped into its pier; the crowd and the trucks sluiced through the cave-like passage into the street. He set her bag on the dirty cobbles.

"Look," he said. "New York isn't your home."

"No."

"You've never been to New York?"

"No."

"Where are you going?"

386

"To the Martha Washington Hotel."

"You have no family here?"

"I have a letter."

"You mean, you have no friends—you know no one in New York?"

The street light touched in her face its conflict of child tenderness and lacerant will. She said: "I came here to get a job. I'll get one."

"I don't even know your name."

"What does it matter?"

He was wounded and silenced: it was true, *he* had been the one to talk, to be happy freely talking of himself. But he could not help pleading: "Mayn't I tell you my name and address? Just in case I can ever—"

"Please don't," she smiled.

"I can drop you at your hotel. It's on my way uptown."

"No."

He had raised his arm to the line of waiting cabs. One drew up and he opened the door. Perhaps she was right. —I'm a married man. She got in.

"I hope you'll find a good job." He placed her bag at her feet. —What if I am married?

"I will," she said solemnly; and her face was in the lamp-glow riven between frailty and strength.

—You can still jump in and ride with her!

The cabbie, pressed by those behind him, jogged his reins. He shut the door of the cab.

3

FROM THE ENTRANCE OF HIS APARTMENT, JEFF HARTT saw his father waiting for the elevator, his hands with their swollen knuckles clasped behind his back. He nodded to the doorman in pale blue and silver buttons, hurried through the foyer whose mirrors and vases spoke the vapid eloquence of conspicuous waste, and touched his father's shoulders. Jonathan, in the moment before he knew who it was, turned and revealed to his son a glimpse of eyes alone in their life, and the view entered his son sharp as an incision. Before he felt it, Jeff said:

"Hello! What a spring day! Are you in a hurry to leave it?"

"Leave it?"

"Go upstairs, I mean. You know: curtains and womenfolk. Let's steal a swift stroll in the Park before dinner."

Jonathan pondered: "I must have my visit with little Joan and Joseph."

"How about letting your grandchildren wait for once? How about a visit with your son?"

Jonathan consulted his watch, snapped it shut, returned it to his pocket. "Very well."

Two blocks west, one south, brought them into the Park: over their silence, not disturbing it, the usual words about work and the state of the country, now the seven nervous years of Teddy Roosevelt had subsided into the hopeful ease of President Taft.

The Park was quiet, the nursemaids and children had gone home to bath and supper. A redbreast robin like a shred of sun sped on the shrill grass; a squirrel trilled down a tree and looked at them. All through his life, at intervals, Jeff had walked in the Park with his father; he knew it better than he knew his father.

Now he could name the nakedness he had uncovered in his father's eyes in the foyer: it was like the amazement in the eyes of a child or of a dog being tortured. A seed of knowledge: with the April warmth, the languor following his stiff day at the office, suddenly it flowered.

Since his engagement to Corinna, Jeff had been aware he did not understand his father. His mother had told him the old man was unhappy about his alliance with the daughter of a Tammany contractor, but Jonathan gave no sign. Later he appeared to like Corinna, but of this also he said nothing. Jeff had the sense of an abdication from both disapproval and approval. Why should this be? Then, one day, uncle Reuben had called him to his office and given him the incredible story.

"I'm telling you this, Jeff, because I think you should know; because it proves your father is a very sick man and therefore you ought to know. You must never let on to him that I've spoken to you, and you must always keep it from your mother." The woman, a client and quite a "stunner," according to report, had wormed her way into his father's graces. She had a flat near Amsterdam Avenue, not far from the Riverside Drive apartment, and there he evidently went to see her. No one knew how long the affair had lasted—if it was an affair—when the woman told him she was pregnant, that the child was his, and she needed ten thousand dollars. His father flatly refused to give her a penny (on what grounds no one knew), and when the woman threatened exposure, he still refused. Then the woman got too smart, gambled —and lost. Since she could not budge Jonathan, she wrote to the Honorable Reuben who, she hoped, might have more regard for the good name of Hartt. Without a word to his brother, Reuben hired detectives. They learned that Mrs. Louella Lake, a genuine widow from South Carolina, was living with a young gambling man whom she passed off as her half-brother. He was wanted by the Charleston police, but on no charge serious enough to warrant the expense of extradition. Gently persuaded by the threat to make the Charleston police a free gift of her lover, Mrs. Lake vanished; and only then did Reuben tell Jonathan what he had done for him. The ungracious way the saved man took his salvation (which had cost Reuben a tidy sum) was, he told his nephew, a final proof that Jonathan Hartt was a sick man. . . . That was all. But what really was this "all"? Jeff realized the bare facts told nothing. Why had his father's anger been directed chiefly against his brother? If there was a child (uncle Reuben strongly doubted it) and the child was his, would his father refuse support to the mother? If it was blackmail, why did he withhold his thanks from the man who had helped him? Was it guilt in his father that kept him from expressing both approval and disapproval of Corinna? But in this case, why his judgment against his brother who had saved him? It seemed almost, in his refusal to pay the woman and in his anger when she was shoved out of the way, that his father *wanted* the scandal! Most mysterious of all, if Mrs. Lake was a mere mercenary, how could his father, the upright, loyal, astute man, have become involved with such a woman?

But was it more of a mystery than to become involved, *as he was,* with a girl seen once on a train eighteen months ago, a girl nameless and almost without features, who had merely listened while impulse made him speak as in a dream? *La princesse lointaine!* Perhaps the woman his father went to see in the Amsterdam Avenue flat was as remote from the woman who tried to blackmail him as *his* phantom from the girl who really sat beside him on the train. At first, Jeff had despised himself for letting her go without learning her name, without giving his in case she needed him: she was testing how strong his wish was to know her, and he had failed the test, she must despise him. Then he realized he had not wanted her name; he could have insisted, could have jumped in the cab beside her, taken her to her hotel, or gone there the next day: could have looked at the guest register . . . waited for her in the lobby. That realization should have closed the story. It had not closed. The more distant the princess, the longer was her shadow. Jeff was always looking for her on the streets and always seeing her in different faces which, as they came close, dissolved. So vague was his memory he was not even sure he would know her if he really saw her. Yet she was real enough to have invaded even his intimacy with Corinna.

Father and son walked to the Park meadow where a group of boys played ball. Jeff heard the crack of the bat, a shout, a thud, as the ball struck his father's forehead.

"Cheese it!" The boys scampered.

Jonathan said: "Tell them not to run away, they'll lose their ball."

"Are you hurt?" Jeff gripped him with both hands.

"Evidently not," the rigid old man released himself. "If anything were broken, I'd not be standing telling you what to do."

390

Under cover of a fringe of shrubs at the meadow's edge, the boys peered at the enemy.

"Tell them to get their ball."

"Come on, boys," Jeff called. "Don't be scared."

A lad wiry as a terrier moved in. The ball had rolled under a bench not far away. The youngster darted, grabbed his treasure, and raced toward the others.

"It might have been bad. You're sure—?"

"I was lucky. My head was turned and it glanced off. Matter of fact, I was admiring the Fifty-ninth Street skyline. It's going up."

"I bet your head aches."

"Nonsense. My head never aches."

"You mean you never let on."

Jonathan's free hand half rose to his head, and went down. "How do you know what I mean?"

"Well, if I don't, why don't you tell me? Or am I a stranger?" The arm Jeff held as he led him toward the bench told him his father was a bit unsteady.

"Don't talk like your mother! Do you remember how she'll come home, and say: 'I was *nearly* run over' and act as if she had been?"

"I suppose you weren't nearly badly hurt?"

"Nearly . . . nearly: isn't truth nearly a lie and a lie nearly truth?"

"All right, dad. You needn't act as if it was a crime, my worrying." He saw the flush on his father's brow.

"We'd better hurry," Jonathan said; "my two pets will be in bed—and the ladies will worry."

"That's *their* exclusive privilege: to worry?"

"Yes," said Jeff's father.

"I'm an old woman, then; I'm worried about you."

"I tell you, it's nothing." Jonathan was angry.

"I wasn't thinking only about the baseball." Firmly Jeff pressed his father down on the bench.

After a silence, Jonathan said: "What is it, son?"

"Dad! Oh, dad!"

"Is it yourself?"

Jeff felt eagerness in his father: how gladly he would hide himself

again in any trouble of his son! Jeff felt resentment. The sun was going down beyond Columbus Circle; the moment of possible commun-
ion between them was also vanishing. He longed to tell him of many
things; stronger still, he longed to help his father, make him speak in
order to help heal him. There was no idiom between them.

They got up and walked slowly toward Jeff's house.

"Don't tell your mother, Jeff, about this little—violence to my head.
You know her: she'd call ten specialists."

—Little violence, thought Jeff. How great must the violence be, to
bring us together?

At the dinner table, Jonathan gulped a whole glass of sauterne; his
wife noted this unusual intemperance but knew enough to say nothing. He sat at Corinna's right, then Lucia, Philip, Jeff, Greta, and on
Corinna's left, her father. The talk rippled peacefully, chiefly propelled by Aloysius Kennedy's gracious-crude banter. He mentioned the
new hobble skirt:

"We've tricked you ladies at last, the fashion masters have! Got you
in this straitjacket, so to speak, so's you can't walk out on us."

"You're joking, of course, Mr. Kennedy," said Lucia, "but you're perfectly correct. Women are harnessed—by their vanity."

"No good woman," said Greta, "would wear one of those dreadful
skirts."

"Then we're still lost," laughed Kennedy, "for 'tis the good ladies
from whom we need protection."

Jonathan saw them all, himself included, magnified, tremulous, as
through water; the table itself buoyed up in the medium that de-
formed but convinced. Corinna's broad-beamed handsome body, he
saw, kept its maternal amplitudes, not because she had borne children,
not because she liked good food (Greta had revolutionized the Kennedy cuisine), but because she was at ease in her Zion. Corinna loved
her home, her father, her husband, her children, she delighted in her
mother-in-law; if she had troubles, she had also her Church, pleasantly
unobtrusive, to help solve them. Corinna was not sure she loved God
quite as a Christian should, but she was entirely sure God loved her
and had blessed the Kennedys for merit. Across from her, usually silent at his own table, Jeff sat, enclosed in Corinna, muffled in the bright

napery, weighted by his duties at home and in the office; Jonathan felt for him tenderness and pity, and he knew that Jeff had felt tenderness and pity for him as they sat together in the Park. His resentment that his son had not continued his own struggle and that he had married into the enemy camp had long since vanished. But in its place there was a vacuum of feeling; his tenderness, his pity, his sense of guilt, were all insulated by a void. It neutralized, no less, his feeling about Corinna's father. He liked Kennedy, who got along so well in the world as he found it; Jonathan disapproved of his world, but the conflict generated merely a flavor of pathos and distance. Philip, hugely enjoying his food, also took life as it came. In Jonathan's refractory vision, Philip and Aloysius Kennedy were close together, and so were Greta and Corinna. He and his son and poor frustrated Lucia were the outsiders! but they were not free of the world to which they did not wholly belong, they had no world of their own, except anxiety and void: they were nowhere! and insulated not only from each other but from themselves.

"You don't say! You don't say!" came Kennedy's high voice.

"But I do!" beamed Greta.

"The President should hear about this."

"Greta's a good singer and a wonderful cook," Lucia smiled, "but she's no astronomer."

"But a comet *is* coming, Miss Hartt! Halley's Comet *is* coming! In May. And Mrs. Hartt says she dreamed it."

"I did."

"You read about it somewhere, Greta. You've forgotten," said Lucia.

"I didn't read about it. I never read the papers."

"We need you in Washington, Mrs. Hartt. Taft can use you. *He* never knows what's coming. Jeff, didn't they used to have—wha' do you call 'em?—soothsayers at court?"

"Yes. In the Dark Ages."

"You don't appreciate your mother. Dark Ages? that's what I'd call a time like ours that has no prophets."

Philip put down his spoon: "They're scared in the Middle West." He was just back from a trip. "They say the comet will burn up the crops."

"What does our soothsayer say? What was your comet like?"

393

"It was like fireworks," said Greta. "Rockets and Roman candles, up in the sky."

"Did it do much damage?" asked Kennedy. "Did you feel it getting hot?"

"Cold!" said Greta. "Jonathan and Jeff were there, both shivering like little boys. I wanted to warm them. Then I woke up, and it *was* cold. It was so warm when we went to bed, I'd thrown off my blankets."

"And there," said Jonathan, "is the explanation of your dream. You were cold."

Kennedy stubbornly shook his head. "The comet *is* coming." They all laughed with him.

Jeff said: "You all joke about dreams. But there's a doctor from Vienna, a hard-headed man of science, who takes them very seriously."

"Really?" Corinna vaguely sensed a corroboration of her faith.

"His name is Freud."

"If he's from Vienna," said Lucia, "he probably writes dream-waltzes."

"One of his disciples is here; in fact, he's talking tonight—at the club where I gave my talk on the new architecture of Sullivan and Wright."

"Let's all go," cried Corinna. "We'll ask him about mama's dream."

"Nonsense." Greta blushed.

"Is that the Radical Club, down in Greenwich Village?" Lucia showed her disdain. "It's full of Socialists and Anarchists—no place for ladies."

"You're right, aunt Lucia. It mightn't be safe for you."

"How our ideas of progress have degenerated!" the old lady mourned.

"I'd go, I think it'd be safe for me, just to hear Mrs. Hartt properly interpreted, only—" Kennedy stopped. "By Jove, Corinna, I nearly forgot. H. H. Sears is coming to pick me up, we've got to go to an important meeting."

"Harrington Howland Sears?" asked Jonathan.

"The same."

"Perhaps he'll drink a cup of coffee with us," said Corinna.

"Don't you remember, dear? H. H. touches no stimulants, not even tea."

"Instead," said Lucia, "he publishes yellow journals that are worse poison than whiskey."

Aloysius Kennedy smiled, as if it didn't matter.

Lucia went on: "I wouldn't have a Sears paper in my house—"

"The comics are good," Philip interrupted. "Sometimes the front-page editorials in big type make sense."

"Wait till you meet him," said Corinna. "He's sweet."

"How is it possible?" asked Greta. "Aren't his papers full of nothing but murders and scandals?"

"Well, he is," Corinna insisted.

Greta smiled at Kennedy: "I'm sure he's a gentleman, if he's your friend."

Jonathan's head ached vaguely. "What do you think, son, of the Sears journalism?"

"I don't see it much." Jeff smiled. "But I don't feel as strongly about it as aunt Lucia."

"Isn't it poison for the masses?" asked his aunt.

"I don't think so. Not in moderation. It's dull." He smiled toward Philip. "I'm not referring to the comics, I don't know them. It smells bad, of course. But I can't get the enjoyment either that a dog does, when he noses his way along."

"Jeff!" Corinna and Greta cried out together.

"The analogy's good. Sears dishes out killings, divorces, all the stuff in human life that corresponds more or less to what a dog loves to smell."

Corinna, who loved dogs, particularly her Pekinese named China, was angry: "Dogs don't smell at murders!"

"My!" Lucia was more logical. "I must say—! It's fortunate dinner is over."

Afraid to pursue the squeamish subject, they all laughed, except Jonathan who looked at his son, inviting him to play on.

"All I mean:" Jeff flushed and smiled at his father, "yellow journalism is our folk art. The one folk art we have."

"Folk art," cried Lucia, "is beautiful and pure."

"That depends on the folk. No, not even that . . . it depends on the part of the folk, its good heart or its sick habits, that the art expresses. It's complicated—"

—The boy's got a mind! thought Jonathan.

"Anyway," Corinna laughed, but she meant it: "I won't have my dogs insulted. And you'll see, all of you: Mr. Sears is *sweet*."

The talk shifted, constantly shifted; it was never really conversation, never more than a medley of ejaculations. But Jeff could converse; and never truly, thought his father, had they conversed together. Suddenly he realized that in a few moments (they had reached the after-dinner coffee) H. H. Sears would be among them! the arch purveyor of sewage to the masses, the most corrupt and sinister demagogue in American life whose ambitions and multi-millions had one goal: the White House. The thought almost froze the fluid, wavering medium that softened Jonathan's lucidities. His friendly encounters with Kennedy had never meant this kind of confrontation. He saw his wife, his son, himself, shaking hands with Sears; then he thought of Reuben, Frieda, his own guilt—of Mrs. Lake. . . . Harrington Howland Sears came in.

They all saw the bland girl brow and the brute jaw, the very tall, strictly-groomed body with womanish rhythms, the soft hands and the ice-hard eyes. . . . Kennedy clasped the hand of the manipulator of public taste into power; Corinna the hand of her father's friend; Lucia bowed to man, the mystery, her moral inferior yet master; Philip acknowledged the good fellow if you got on his right side; and Jeff, indifferent, felt the two half-men, both incomplete and monstrous, in the one body. Jonathan alone avoided Sears' hand, and saw in the cold blue eyes that Sears had noted the exception.

"How d' do? how d' do?" his piping soprano monstrously issuing from the prognathous jaw repeated with each salute; he took the chair placed beside Corinna.

"I don't know what to offer you," she said. "I know you don't take coffee or tea. Can I offer you a cup of *Postum* or a glass of milk?"

With a gesture swift as a monkey's, Sears reached to the silver basket on the table and took a candy. "This will do very nicely," he bit the bonbon in two with pearl-like teeth. "What exquisite chocolates!" He took another.

"Much better for the health, I'm sure, than cigars." Lucia was already mollified: the man was gentle as a woman.

"But they don't taste so good!" Kennedy lighted his Corona Corona.

Sears focused his eyes on Jonathan. "It's a long time since I've seen you, Mr. Hartt. Not since the Civic Committee days."

"I'm surprised you remember." Jonathan noted the man's hair, brown like a boy's cap, although he was sixty.

"Of course I remember! You and I were always on the same side for reform. Only our methods were different."

"That's true."

"Yours was to lead the public, before you had 'em. You can't do that." He waved his maidenly hand. "How can you lead 'em till you've got 'em?"

"Good logic," Kennedy laughed. "After all, you can't drive a horse till you've harnessed him."

The hand darted for another candy. "We reformers," he bit and examined the half remaining in his hand, "are likely to make one big mistake. We've modeled our politics on the old-timers, like Jefferson and Jackson. Well, in their day, in spite of the big words, the public had no power; men like Jefferson and Jackson *were* the bosses and they could go ahead, carrying the people with them. Most reformers haven't waked up yet to the big new fact: what those old fellows wanted has come true: the people now *have* the power. How move 'em along the right way? How get 'em? And what gets 'em?"

"Candy?" Jeff smiled.

Sears giggled. "And you've got to love it yourself."

"You're a great confectioner, Mr. Sears," said Jeff.

"Delmonico to the people," Kennedy laughed. "I'm afraid, dear, we must go." He kissed his daughter and shook hands with all the others. Sears looked round the table, bowed, and followed Kennedy out. The "moral cesspool," Jonathan understood, had been sensitive enough to shake hands with no one so as to avoid stressing his own refusal.

"Jeff, why don't we have an engagement too?" They were all moving to the parlor. "Uncle Philip can take care of the ladies. That meeting—"

"You mean the Radical Club?"

"Would you like to hear the dream fellow?"

"Would you, dad?"

When they were in the street Jeff took his father's arm. "Don't you want me to take you home?"

"What are you talking about?"

"I thought—that baseball—I thought you just wanted an excuse to go home."

"I've forgotten all about that baseball." But the fluctuant medium was still around him.

"The Club's a damn inconvenient place. Rickety camp chairs and people almost hanging on to the chandeliers. Arguments sometimes turn into scrimmages."

"Sounds a bit like a dream. If you didn't want the discomfort, why didn't you say so?"

"All right, dad."

Jeff wondered why he had been reluctant, why he had almost hoped his father wanted to go home. . . . Perhaps the doctor from Vienna would explain that there were dreams more solid than fact, dreams like the girl on the train that invaded and conquered. . . .

"I feel," said Doctor Anton Freienleben, "as a man in 1500 must have felt, telling Europeans that America is discovered. In this case the America is the *unconscious:* it is not three thousand miles away but in each one of us; it is not of remote importance to our daily lives but the *controlling force* in what we think and feel; in our family relations, our pleasures and sorrows, our hates and loves, our politics and arts: the cause of all our troubles.

"So you see, the America comparison won't do. It would be better to say we have all been like puppets in a Punch and Judy show, seeing ourselves go through certain motions, hearing the words we were supposed to speak, not understanding at all well but at least quite sure the words and actions were ours. Now, suddenly, we see the strings that move us, the voices that speak in our names. Only in this case the strings, the hands that pull them, and the voices, are inside us. We are puppets only so long as we do not know that we are puppets. When we do know, for the first time in the history of man, we can be our own masters."

Long head of the fanatic, round small mouth surrounded by black beard from which the words came with a foreign accent spicing their strangeness, Dr. Freienleben was Svengali to the crowd's silence. Jonathan and Jeff sat in the center of the room dense with young men and

398

women, and each a center, a vortex. In every one of us, said the doctor, lives the vast dark hunger that has no name; no predetermined goal, not even individual life, for it can seek its own death. Pure desire it is, savage, speechless, outside good and evil, taking all shapes, generating all energies and goals, with none of its own. Because our basic life-method is sex, it acts through sex, but blindly, with no regard, until it is harnessed, for the propagation of the species. It is the infant's love for its body, for its excrement, for its mother; it is jealousy of the father, hatred of rival brothers and sisters; it is love of pain—even self-pain, and of blood, long before the word beauty can be pronounced. To society, almost all its early forms are perverse and forbidden; thus desire turns inward, hides from society and even more from the growing conscious mind that society molds. It weaves our dark dreams, our crimes, long before our laws and ideals call them crimes. It moves both madman and saint, for you cannot have one without the other, the difference being in the social acceptability of forms, not in its own substance. But the hunger *will out;* and when it is impeded and denied, it is worse than murder; it lies, twists, poisons, filling the world with men and women who lie, twist, poison. This is the state of our civilization under its security façade. The *unconscious,* working in the dark, has become a cunning animal. Some of its means of expression have their social uses: the arts, for instance, which, although they are escapes into the world of dream, teach us much about reality; or social reform and revolution which, if kept within bounds, harness desire to rational ends; even the religions that preach justice and charity, although the central idea of God is, of course, the infant's dream of being the favored child of an all-powerful Parent. Doctor Freienleben became casual: *Hamlet* and *Oedipos* hold us because we all love the mother and wish to be rid of the father. We forget our umbrella in the house of the rich friend, because we want to go back. We laugh when someone slips on a banana peel, because we're afraid of slipping ourselves, must rebuke clumsiness for our own sakes, and dare not openly reveal our fear. The doctor modulated back to the general. The insane are the sole victors over society's ban on the *unconscious:* in them, the *unconscious* "takes over" and lives its own life wholly. The neurotics are they who have made no stable balance between what the *unconscious* desires and society permits. Religious and political extremes, excessive lust for money, for love-affairs, for social position, are neurotic forms of anxiety, are irrational devotions. The businessman who lives only for profit, the mechanical crank, the prohibitionist, the aesthete, are as hysterical as the fat lady who lives for her dog, as the Anarchist who lives to throw bombs, as the Don Juan who can love no one, not even himself. . . . We are all neurotics; Doctor Freienleben paused. "Maybe there are some questions?" and sat down.

Little gusts of laughter punctuated the silence. A girl, well-hidden, said: "What must we *do?*" The doctor's reply to the effect that if we brought the *unconscious* out into the open we could tame and "manage" it, was scarcely noted: the individual vortices of the crowd swirled, each on itself, each quickened, each seeking its own outlet. The few questions were half-hearted, the crowd was in suspense. Jonathan looked at his son who was dreamily smiling while his eyes wandered over the rows of hermetic faces, in each of which a question stood and did not dare. Suddenly Jeff's eyes stopped moving, grew charged, and his father heard him breathe. Then from the opposite direction to where Jeff's eyes were fixed, a large fellow in a gray shirt stepped a little forward from the crowded wall.

"Look here," he said.

The room's temperature changed, as if the hundred vortices had come together.

"Look here," the big man repeated (only Jeff did not look). "That's great stuff you've been giving us. But your conclusions are all wrong."

His face struck Jonathan as vaguely familiar. But the general strangeness of all things, floating and refracted in the fluctuant medium of his mind, was now familiar. What the doctor had said, although he had heard none of it before, was also familiar. . . .

"What's this about our finding what we really want . . . deep in the *unconscious* . . . only to *tame* it?" the man said. The doctor, standing again, wet his round red lips. "—only to trim it to social standards? Whose standards? The bourgeoisie's? That's just what's got to go. And the *unconscious* can do it! Its desires and dreams, uncensored, *are* the new world."

Dr. Freienleben faintly waved a hand. "I'm a psychologist, not a social philosopher."

"I should say you ain't!" The man spoke in swift lunges punctuated

400

by brief pauses, as if he were both running and limping. "Why, what you recommend is the most dangerous damn counter-revolutionary stuff I've heard. . . . The old world stinks . . . All it can do, like you say, is deny. Deny our needs and our dreams. So they fester, like you say, in the dark . . . So bring 'em out . . . Swell! . . . Bring 'em out. What for? To manicure 'em? to *manage* 'em, like you say? . . . Phooey! . . . down to old-world standards?"

The crowd swayed firmly; a few brave hands applauded; faces beamed less hermetic. Jonathan saw his son still gazing in the same direction, away from the speaker.

"Ever heard of the general strike? . . . It's the great myth, the great dream of the proletarians. And who are they? . . . They're society's *unconscious*. They're dark desire. Repressed, like you say. Savage . . . One day they bust out. A cyclone. That's the general strike. . . . The capitalist class lies on the ground, dead chickens. . . . The proletarians are the new world. And you'd have 'em 'tame it down'—phooey!" The crowd roared.

The doctor smiled. "It's not so simple, my friend."

"Simple as dynamite; only a hell of a lot stronger."

"And after your general strike, my friend—?"

"There you go making the old mistake. Decide beforehand what comes after, means to shackle the new world, to kill it with old-world standards."

Doctor Freienleben raised a hand that was faintly trembling. "You talk, sir, as if the members of your proletariat were not ordinary men and women; as if their needs and values and censors, too, were not just like the bourgeoisie's—and their neuroses also. You talk as if proletarians had no parents."

"We haven't!" the man shouted. "And we haven't a damn need or value except to bust open the capitalist system and *live*. Why, even Darwin refutes you. How can a *new species* have parents? and without new species, what becomes of evolution? The capitalist world will be dead in twenty-four hours, once the strike begins. I ain't no Marxian Socialist; I don't know what's coming after the strike; all I know is, it won't be anything we *think*. Like the *unconscious,* the proletarians don't think."

"Who is this chap?" whispered Jonathan. Jeff turned toward his father and then looked at the man for the first time. He was now well launched on a speech of his own. Jeff said nothing, and his eyes swung back again to where they had been gazing. The doctor took his seat; the club chairman, a white-haired woman with the face of an angel, got up in his place. The orator champed like a stallion, his words prancing:

"... let the *unconscious* out and let it sing! let it flame! most important of all, let it destroy! ... Then you're on the side of the proletarians, of the new world. ..." He had made a space around him. His very tall, loose-knit body in corduroy trousers and a worker's jacket seemed younger than his face, and to Jonathan the face was poignantly familiar.

He stopped as suddenly as he'd begun and plunged into the crowd that applauded, got up, rattled chairs, congested in small groups, while the gentle lady chairman tried to thank the doctor in words nobody heard, and said: "The meeting's adjourned." Jonathan turned to Jeff, and Jeff was gone. Then Jonathan saw him, moving as if to follow the big fellow who shouldered his way, shaking off those who wished to praise or argue. It was the direction in which Jeff had gazed. The man stopped and talked to a girl. Jonathan picked his way closer. Jeff patiently waited: did he want to speak to the man? Then Jonathan saw the girl's face, with a disdainful smile on it, turn from the man toward Jeff and grow aware of Jeff. Two surprises shocked Jonathan, stronger than the evening's medium of strangeness: the girl was staring at Jeff as Jeff had stared, and the girl's face also was familiar.

She did not move as Jeff came forward and they began to talk. The crowd sifted away; then the big man whom Jonathan had momentarily forgotten was there again in a soiled raincoat, still bareheaded, his black moist hair athwart his brow. Jeff half turned, feeling his father's eyes on him, and Jonathan saw in his son's eyes an exultation.

He drew him closer. "This is my father," he said.

Jonathan said: "Why don't we go somewhere and have a cup of coffee?"

"That's all right with me," the big fellow was sure he was included, "so long as there's something besides the java. I missed my dinner."

They entered Washington Square, four abreast (there had been no introductions: perhaps, Jonathan ironically thought, a by-law of the

Radical Club forbade them). Jeff's hand was on the girl's arm, as if he were afraid to lose her. On the north side they passed the dignified lighted mansions and the Arch with its two Washingtons, soldier and statesman, pale in the blue night. In University Place, they came to the quaint railings of the Café Lafayette. "How about this?" suggested Jonathan.

"The java of those Frenchmen is too bitter," said the big fellow.

"They have sugar," Jonathan smiled.

"I don't take sugar in my coffee."

"There's a Childs on Union Square," said the girl.

No other word between them. The waitress took their orders. In slashing strokes, the iron shadows of the restaurant cut the electric glare, dwarfing the scattered patrons at the white-topped tables. The big fellow said:

"Make mine a beefsteak, well done."

"That'll take twenty minutes, sir."

"What's twenty minutes?"

The silence troubled none of them, Jonathan observed, for different reasons. The big fellow next to him had said his say, now he was hungry and waiting to eat. Jeff and the girl across the table were also hungry (and waiting) for a moment that must come before words. And why was he here? why had he arranged this little party? For him, was it a moment after words . . : after many words, many years? While the big fellow wolfed bread and butter, Jonathan looked at his profile: the creased eyelid as if chiseled, the tremulous nostril, the lips color of heat and privation. Between the open flannel shirt and the corded neck, Jonathan saw a thin chain, although what it suspended was hidden. The girl reminded him . . . reminded him: that tension of the eyes, that high-bridged nose. And the man. After the many words, the many years, what sat with him at this table? They were talking now, but no one really listened to the casual words. The waitress brought the steak; as the man attacked it, leaning down, his shirt opened and Jonathan saw . . . without surprise . . . the little silver crucifix.

"We're old friends," he said with a quiet irony. "But I'm an old-fashioned man. I'd like to know your names. Mine is Jonathan Hartt."

"Mine is Schmitt."

"First name Marius?" Jonathan asked.

"That's right," Schmitt nodded and without surprise swallowed a slice of potato.

Although Jeff was staring at him, with the same quiet Jonathan turned to the girl. "And your name, Miss?"

"Rebecca Lorne," she said, with an amused glance at Jeff.

"Rebecca Lorne," Jeff repeated, as if he were drinking it in; and Jonathan was sure he had not known it.

Suddenly Jonathan found that he was happy: unbearably, because inexplicably. —As if this had meaning! He needed to talk.

"What was the name of the great dream-doctor?"

'Freud," said Jeff.

"Ought to be Fraud," said Schmitt.

"In that case," said Jonathan, "you'll have to change a lot of names and words. Most of our waking hours."

"Can be," Schmitt gulped his coffee.

Jonathan left silver on the table, paid the bill at the door, and they all stood in Union Square. A cold wind from uptown had blown away the precocious mist of spring, but the open place before the mercantile houses and the field of the sky, where sparse clouds scudded, were still blue. Marius looked sharp at Rebecca and her new friend, and came to a decision.

"I'm for downtown." Without more, he left them, swinging east on Fourteenth Street with his gait of knees thrown forward, feet up, that made him seem both unsure and reckless where his next step would take him.

Jonathan pressed Rebecca's hand. "I'm for uptown in the subway. Unlike my son, I live on Riverside Drive. Goodnight, Jeff." He shook hands with his son.

At the subway entrance he turned: his son and Evan's daughter were walking west. With him going north and Frieda's son going east, they formed a cross. To his evening of strangeness came the strangest fact of all: that he, Jonathan Hartt, of rational mind, found this important!

As soon as his father had left them, Jeff said: "Where do you live, Rebecca?"

"Near here."

Pain seethed his eyes and mouth. "Won't you tell me?"

He saw her shake her head, and her lips drawn.

"I won't leave you this time till you tell me."

She began to walk and he walked with her.

"I suppose Schmitt knows where you live?"

"Yes."

"He comes to see you?"

"Why not?"

"And you won't tell me?"

They were near Fifth Avenue. The city was empty: vast stone and the percussion of home-going feet.

"I've not stopped thinking of you, Rebecca. Not for a moment." He looked straight ahead as he spoke, but his body was vigilant of hers, as if it might escape.

After a pause: "That's a large order, 'not for a moment.'"

"I know it."

They went on westward toward Sixth Avenue. "You're still living with your wife, aren't you?"

"Yes."

"You *live* with her, don't you? 'Not for a moment.'"

He gasped at her penetration. "But it's true."

At Sixth Avenue, she turned downtown; the El barring the wind and clouds, a train shattering their silence, leaving a silence.

"I suppose," he said at last, "you mean I've no right to see you."

"Why?"

"Because I'm married."

She laughed angrily. "You're nothing but a kid, are you?"

"Don't say it, Rebecca."

"I saw you with your papa. I've heard of him." A silence, while they walked. "You've never grown up, have you? That's what's the matter. No wonder you're not happy with your wife."

He thought it over. "That's not so. I am happy with her."

"Well, that's good."

"Happiness doesn't always count."

Before the round, then square, then pyramid brick turret of Jefferson Market (it reminded him of the building blocks of his boyhood), carts rumbled from Christopher Street and the river. A ship's horn blew.

405

"I'm almost home. You'd better go. You probably live 'way uptown."

"That's right. I'm not going."

They crossed Greenwich Avenue; the city became mellow, low red houses with dormer windows in the sloping roofs clustered to irregular-angled blocks, to squares with dwarf trees.

"What do you do, Rebecca?"

"I've got a good job."

"Did you find it right away?"

"Right away when . . . ?"

"After I met you?"

"Pretty soon."

"What was it?"

"I work on *A la Mode*."

"Greenwich Village is a little like Chelsea, in London. I'd like to live here."

"Then why don't you?"

"That's a fair question. Hard to answer."

"If I had lots of money, perhaps I'd move out too."

The short blocks ran askew; Jeff, no longer sure of his direction (all his awareness on the girl), began to wonder if they were walking in a circle.

"This is my street." She stopped. "Will you go now?"

"Not till I know the number."

She turned her face up toward him, "You'd better go."

"Not till I know—"

"Perhaps I don't want you to go. So you'd better go. . . ."

He took her arm as she walked again. "Perhaps you're right, Rebecca. I don't feel like a friend. But I'll try."

"You *are* a fool. Do you want a friend in a girl? does a girl want a friend in a man?"

"I suppose Schmitt is a friend?"

"He wants to make love to me, and you know it. Because I can't let him, he's a headache."

"I think I see."

"No, you don't see. . . . I'm sick of having friends." She stopped before a three-story square house, mild and quaint in the lamplight. Seeking the number, he put out his hand: "Don't talk on the stairs," she

406

said and went down three steps to the door which she unlocked. Without looking back, she led him past the musty-smelling dingy hall up two flights whose mahogany bannisters were gracious. He stepped after her into the dark room and heard her lock the door behind them.

When she had lit the gas, she took off her hat and sat on the couch covered with gray monkscloth.

"Thank you," he was near the door, and both his hands held on to his hat. "Thank you for letting me know where you live. Now I'll go."

"Aren't you going to kiss me?"

When he came toward her, she rose; when her mouth touched his, she seemed to vanish. Her body was in his arms, her lips lay passive beneath his, but his embrace—without pleasure, without assuagement— was of a void that dangerously drew him.

"Do we love each other?" He held her, not with passion; with fear, as if she might escape.

"How should I know?"

"What do you mean?"

She was both angry and tender. "You make me say everything. I'm ashamed to tell you: but I'm a virgin."

"Why should you be ashamed, Rebecca?"

She pushed herself away: "Because it means nothing! Because for a long time, I've decided not to be, and have tried not to be."

"You tried . . . ?"

She sat again on the couch, and he beside her.

"The right man," he said, "simply hasn't come along."

"The right man! How should I know? Do men stay virgin, till the 'right woman' comes along?"

Again the void drew him: the hard will armored by fragility. He embraced her; embracing not pleasure but pain, not passion he could have fought or love he could heed, but openness, emptiness. . . . Her body was thin, white emptiness. Her breasts surged, the full breasts of a mother and their small nipples, with no trace of the corolla, were of a child. In her face he saw her will watching, waiting. But the white emptiness won; he had to plunge in it and it engulfed and drained him. He lay selfless at her side near her pale eyes. He heard her say: "Is that all?" She got up, threw on a robe, and sat on the couch beside him.

407

"We must love each other," he said. "Don't question! Not yet."

There was nothing he could confess to Corinna. He was not afraid to hurt Corinna who was strong and would want to help him. But whatever he could say was a lie; the one truth was the void and if he spoke it, would it not have form? the void which was true could not be spoken.

He prevailed on Rebecca to have lunch with him. He found himself speaking to her, as on the train, in a dream's freedom. It was a Saturday and she was not returning to her office. He accompanied her home. "You care too much. That's all I felt the other night. It's no use." Rebuffing him, she drew him, and again he died in her arms.

He knew her choice had been cool as a syllogism: "I want a man because I want to be a woman; why not you, since other men haven't answered?" But he kept saying to himself, this was the surface only: she rationalized the giving herself because she was a rationalist, but she gave herself because she was a woman. And other men had *not* answered. Now a fear—fluid steel saturating, bursting his flesh—that in her disillusion she would give herself to Marius Schmitt. Along with the fear, the conviction of her tenderness if only he could reach it!

With sparse meetings between them, spring became summer. Corinna and the children and his mother were in a camp on an Adirondack lake. Jeff saw more of his father (both alone in their respective apartments) than he did of Rebecca.

One evening of hot July, Jeff came into her room and Marius Schmitt was standing by the mantel.

"Rebecca told me you were coming and to clear out. But I thought you wouldn't mind blowing me to a dinner."

"That's all right."

"I'll leave after the nuts. Soup to nuts is what I need, I'm hungry and broke. I got a date with a girl."

"Come along, but try to bring your manners."

"I don't need 'em. I have manner."

"If you had, you'd not need to mention it."

Marius laughed, spat on the bricks of the fireplace and rolled a cigarette. "That's a cinch to say for a guy like you, who's always had money to do his talking for him. I don't say you couldn't talk for your-

408

self, once you got started. But what do you know about that moment—
it can last a lifetime, you can starve to death in it or just get run over
without being noticed—before you can open your mouth and say your
say? That's when money talks for you. You had it in school and college, and when you were looking for your first job. I never had it.
Don't forget, old man, my mother was a waitress and my father was
no corporation lawyer."

"If you didn't boast about it, I could congratulate you on what
you've done for yourself."

"It's been fun. Not the first jobs, maybe. I feel sorry for a guy that's
never had the chance to find out what's in him."

"Meaning me?"

"No one finds out, till he's got to."

"That's true. But you seem to think having a dime and needing a
dollar is the only challenge."

"Isn't it though!"

"No, it isn't. Ever heard of Goethe? of Washington and Jefferson?
or Tolstoi who's just died in Russia? They're a few among hundreds:
men who never needed a dollar, but they kept pretty busy finding out
and showing what was in them."

"You can have the whole lot for olives in your cocktail."

"How about Marx—and Nietzsche? Seems to me these bourgeois
gentlemen have whispered a word or two in your ear."

"Sure: I eat pigs and chickens. I don't have to respect them for that."

Rebecca came in from the bathroom in a cool blue dress that gave
her, for Jeff, an irreducible distance.

"Not that they weren't good boys for their day; stars of slave culture.
Greek, Hindu, Feudal, Capitalist—slave cultures. We're going to
change all that: man's going to be animal again; a glorious beast, like
Nietzsche said. We're going to chuck the human dimension whose
name is God. God's dead. Without God, man is no longer man, he's
magnificently animal. Before the Greeks spoiled him, he was an unconscious animal. Now, he'll be a conscious scientific animal."

"And what's the new beast going to do?"

"Animals have three interests; don't worry. Food at all times; sex
when they're in rut; fight when the first two need a fight. The rest is
human and out."

"Well," Jeff smiled, "you said you needed food. Let's go and feed."
With Rebecca between them they walked through the soft street.

"Food, sex, and fight," Jeff chuckled. "It sounds a bore to me."

"Sure. Because you're no good at any of 'em. But you won't be here any more," Marius half chanted. "Change the word sex for the one starting with *f*: there's our slogan for you—*the three F's*."

"If it weren't taking you too seriously, Schmitt, I'd let you feed yourself. You wouldn't want to be a *fed* animal, would you?"

"Nature feeds animals; the difference is only in the force, cunning, or perseverance that it takes to get fed. You, old man, are an easy part of nature. But I don't mean to be personal. Sorry. I'm only talking of your class."

"Well, we've fed on yours, according to your theory. And we're outnumbered. We must be pretty good animals."

"You're cunning. Human cunning was the one bourgeois virtue. We're going to get rid of it. We're the kind of animals that rely on their claws and their teeth. Art, religion, ethics, philosophy—all names for your cunning tricks: we just won't need 'em."

"Seems to me, Marius, you're something of a philosopher yourself. Quite a caricature—your ideas are, of Bergson, Marx, and Nietzsche."

"You're upside down, old man! *Their* theories are the bourgeois caricature of forces they've felt in the proletariat. Marx particularly had something, when he was young and hadn't got himself organized. What you don't see is that *we* are the real thing. *We* are what Bergson spins into his pale "élan vital"; *we* are what Nietzsche blindly touched, like that old Cyclops who got strong every time he was thrown to Mother Earth. If you're outside like philosophers, then it's something to get a trace of life in your reflections. That's the best you can say for the best of what you call culture. But catch a tiger stopping from his tiger-business to reflect on *tigerishness*. Man's an animal. He's been a damn sick animal. He's getting ready to be healthy again—rarin' to go."

Rebecca said: "Why don't you stop talking, Marius, and begin to roar?"

"I am roaring!" Marius laughed.

Beyond the basement of an old brownstone house, they came to a yard, under the brick walls, filled with tables in red-checkered cloths. The waiter brought antipasto: Marius became silent, devouring the salami, anchovies, sprigs of garlic, fragrant white bread with butter, and drinking the "red ink."

Jeff smiled at Rebecca: "He's proving his point, that a man talks only when he can't eat. What do you think of it all?"

"I like to hear him roar."

"Why?" They talked as if Marius, now gulping the minestrone, were deaf.

"I don't know. He's fun."

"Nonsense *is* fun."

"I don't think it's all nonsense."

"He doesn't believe it himself. Look at the cross he's always wearing."

Marius put down his fork stacked with spaghetti. "My mother gave it to me when she was dying and made me promise to wear it. That don't mean I believe in the bloody stuff."

"You remember your mother; what animal does that? You keep promises. That's not worthy of the big beast."

"He's still an imperfect beast," Rebecca laughed. "Give him time."

"Waiter! Another bottle of the red. You're right. It's about time I chuck the damn thing. It just got to be a bad habit." He touched the crucifix within his open shirt. "I'll tell you what, Rebecca: the minute you come across, I chuck it."

"Cut it!" said Jeff.

"Oh, be yourself. You don't own Rebecca."

"You're getting drunk."

"I'll be drunk in fifteen minutes. That gives me time to tell you a few facts of life I've been waiting about fifteen weeks to tell you."

"Listen, Schmitt. Stick to your loony philosophy; don't try to bring it down to earth."

"I suppose that's how you make love to Rebecca. It's all over her face: you're a rotten lover."

"Don't go too far, Schmitt."

"That's your code, not mine. 'Don't go too far' . . . 'Don't bring your ideas down to earth.' Don't bring love-making down to earth! which means to the body, the belly . . ."

"Shut up!"

"Let him talk, Jeff. What's the difference? We don't want a fight."

"Let's have the fight—and the food—and the third *F*—"

Jeff brought his fist down on the table; the dishes danced, the bottle spilled on Marius.

"I'll shut up for the present. I still want my fruit and cheese and nuts."

"Yours!"

"Sure. The waiter'll bring 'em, unless you smash the dishes. Or get up and walk out. Why don't you? If you do, I'll just say I can't pay. Try and see what happens. Maybe Rebecca'll walk out with you."

"It's not a bad idea. Waiter—"

"Don't, Jeff." Rebecca spoke quietly.

"I'll pay. Schmitt can stay and feed."

"Jeff, you're making a lot of fuss over nothing."

"See?" There was no sneer in Schmitt's suddenly child-innocent smile. "If you walk out now, you walk alone. I told you. So the fruit and nuts are mine, although I invite you to stay and share 'em. And after we're through—" He gave his crucifix a little tug.

"And after we're through, what? Don't get the idea I'm scared of you, Schmitt, simply because I don't relish scenes in public places. Neither does Rebecca."

Marius nodded, as if convinced; held a piece of *bel paese* in his mouth and washed it down with wine. "All right. We'll have no scene, unless you make it. I repeat: after we're through here, what?" Again he touched the cross. "Here's what. Rebecca, you give me my chance. You know damn well Hartt's had his."

Jeff sickened with the sense that he was helpless. Now he knew what it meant: to be cold and to have one's insides turn to water. If he got up and left, he was not sure Rebecca would follow him: he had no hold on her. If he stopped Schmitt by striking him—ah! he knew he would not, the moment one asked oneself the chance was over. He had struck once on the table, without asking himself permission, he must patiently wait till passion of its own accord rode him again. With freezing blood, he saw that Rebecca had not repulsed the man. She was cutting her pear in halves, calmly eating. Marius went on:

"I know what's holding you back; you feel sorry for Hartt. Hell, ain't it better to do it clean and above board? Then he'll know where he's at. Besides, what right has he to object? Do you stop him from going to bed with his own wife?"

412

"Rebecca, do you want me to put up with this ugly stuff?"

She sipped her coffee. "I don't see why it's ugly."

"Decide for yourself!" Jeff flared.

"Good man!" Marius laughed. "We'll make a beast of you yet."

"I shouldn't wonder."

"It's up to us now, Rebecca dear. That mean's it's up to me."

"You don't say so!" she bridled.

"I damn well do. A woman can't know what she wants till she has it. That's up to the man."

Jeff decided to be light: "You seem to forget with your obscene nonsense that you have a date with a girl."

"To hell with it; she'll wait. You see, I've had my chance with her," he turned to Rebecca, "and I made it. So she'll wait."

"No self-doubts about our Marius," Rebecca smiled.

Flourishing his arms, Marius jumped up. Jeff threw a five-dollar bill on the plate and reached for his hat. He was angrier at the girl than at the man, and this confused him. They filed out, while the nearby diners stared their cold pleased curiosity; and this, it seemed to Jeff, was the secret of why the world suffered: because it looked with these eyes on suffering.

Before her house, Jeff said: "Now get out, Marius. The farce is over."

"I'll come up with you."

"Rebecca, this is your home. Tell him to go."

"Come up, both of you."

Jeff felt obscenity engulf him. "For God's sake, Rebecca. You're letting this fellow ruin—"

He had never seen her lips so thin: "What can he ruin? It must be pretty weak—"

"You don't see what you're doing. And I can't explain before him. You'll have to take what I say on faith. Rebecca, for once, you'll have to let me give the orders. . . ."

He turned from her smile as if it burned him. And when his eyes saw again, he was near the end of the block. He looked back: Marius and Rebecca were gone.

—What am I going to do? He knew already: nothing. He knew too much, and he was married, he had no right to her. He had the right of love; but if it had not won her? had not awakened her to acknowledge his right? Never had they become healed, had they become one, together. —Let her go! She was gone. While he paced the pavement, she was in the arms of the madman. —Oh, let it not be! His mind leaped to imagined scenes: "I tried, dear, to give myself to him; I couldn't. I needed this brutal way to prove to myself I love you." She would never say it. "Forgive me if I hurt you; I can never forgive myself." And he embraces her . . . It would never be. —I'll ring and go up. I'll throw him out. She's right to put a stop to this; whether she finds happiness with him, at least he helps to put a stop to this. I'll tell Corinna, who loves confession. I'll thank the madman yet. He has a touch of genius. Scoundrels and men of genius, Balzac said, make the best lovers. Women instinctively know. Rebecca's white body, the void, filled and fulfilled by the alien dark man-root: Jeff cried aloud in the street; a woman heard him and stopped; he did not care. —I must love her. His heart overflowed with tenderness for Corinna and the children. He must do something: the man-root in *his* flesh! A taxi cruised slowly and noisily by; Jeff hailed it, and jumped in.

"Where to?" said the driver at last. He gave the address of his father.

. . . He followed his father to the library stripped for summer of carpets and curtains. Pools of stagnant heat hid in the chairs; Jeff went to the open window and let the cool Hudson touch him. The usual questions: he knew his father would not ask, "What's wrong?"

Suddenly, without turning, he said: "I'm in a bad way."

"Yes?" His father accepted it.

"You remember that girl?"

"Of course."

"You didn't know, when I saw her that night with you, I was finding her again."

"I did know."

"This is going to shock you."

His father stood beside him at the window.

"It must have been simpler in the old days before there were 'free women.' If a woman gave herself, a woman who wasn't a whore—" Jeff thought of Mrs. Lake, but he had to go on, "she really gave herself. She was yours."

414

"Perhaps it was simpler only for the men. Perhaps we don't know what it was for the women."

Jeff knew his father also was thinking of Mrs. Lake. "God help them, if they felt what I do."

"What happened tonight, Jeff?"

"How do you know it was tonight—?"

In his father's smile, his son saw new meaning: his reserve did not mean that he wished to hide himself, it meant that he did not wish to give the wound that went with self-bestowal. This was why he wanted to receive. Whatever he said, his father would take the hurt unto his own guilt. It was absurd; with his nerves on the rack, it was good!

"You recall the big fellow?" His father nodded, and Jeff, relaxed as in the old days when he lay sick in bed, his father beside him, told his story.

They stood, gazing together at the cool flowing river.

"I don't understand him," Jonathan said. "He's no common ranter. He's an Anarchist who wears a cross."

"Not after tonight. It's a memento from his mother."

Jonathan was thinking of the cross burned in the girl's face, the memento of her father. Belated, what his son said pierced his meditation. "What did you say? If he's worn the cross all these years, why not after tonight?"

Jeff told him. Jonathan pressed his fingers to his eyes to hold there the vision of Frieda in her room of the old house . . . of Frieda in her home which (so the perspective of his conscience placed it) he had taken from her. But words came out.

"He mustn't do it, Jeff, you mustn't let him."

Amazed, Jeff turned toward his father.

"Go and see him. Tell him to keep the crucifix."

"He'd laugh at me."

"What of it?"

"If I see him again, how do you know I won't kill him?"

"Don't try to explain." Jonathan seemed not to hear. "Simply as you can, say: 'Keep the memento from your mother.' Jeff, say to him also, 'If you can love her, keep Rebecca.'"

"But if I love her—"

415

"Jeff, don't try to be happy!"

"What are you saying? I don't recognize you—"

"Recognize this man and this girl! It's the only hope—"

"You're talking in riddles. What is a cross to you?"

"I can't help you with lies, Jeff. The alternative is riddles."

"Unanswered riddles?"

"We live the answers. We don't live long enough to read them."

"You mean what you say? I'm to go to this madman—"

"Do it!" Jonathan touched his son's arm.

"And give the girl up?"

"I did not say that. Nothing must be given up. Not even the cross. So far, I can see . . . Do it!"

The lights of ships and shores were tremulous on the water.

"Sleep here tonight, son. There's always your old room."

"It's a long time since I've slept here."

"When Anna's away, she leaves good things in the icebox. Come on."

They went to the kitchen, poured cool fruit juices, sat silent at the kitchen table. When their glasses were empty:

"Goodnight, Jeff. You'd better get some sleep."

"You know, dad," Jeff lingered near his father, "when I was a kid, and you used to walk me to school and kiss me goodbye, right out on the street before all the fellows, I hated it. I was ashamed."

"I must have been a trial."

Jeff kissed his father.

In his own room, Jonathan felt overwhelmingly tired. His son had been brave to confess. When would he be brave enough, wise enough . . . to confess what? and to whom?

Jeff tidied his drafting table at the noon hour, boarded the Third Avenue El, walked past Cooper Union, climbed the dark stairs of a Bowery tenement, and knocked at Schmitt's door. It was the last day before he took the night train to join his family in the mountains. For days his chaos of rejection and respect for what his father had asked him to do (he had not mentioned it again) was without issue, and when decision came it was instinctive and sudden. "Come in!" he heard the voice, and opened the door.

Marius sat up in bed, a sheet to his waist and his upper body naked. Jonathan made himself look at the lean white vulnerable flesh, broadening to the shoulders. The crucifix was gone. To dilute his pain, he saw the miserable room, the books and littered papers on the table.

"Hello," Marius welcomed him without surprise and pointed to the one chair. "Sit down."

The room, despite the dust and the disorder, was austere; the bared body was beautiful; the pain Jeff felt was not hate, it was too close to love that caused it.

"You keep late hours," he sat down, holding his hat.

"I worked all night."

Jeff glanced at the carpenter's box under the window whose blurred glass showed the tracks of the El.

"Not at that. I'm making a study of the Wobblies. I've not had a carpenter's job for two months. The union don't like my notions, and I can't scab."

Jeff could not reconcile what he knew of Marius with a man who worked with his hands; nor his universal rudeness with the grace of a host he seemed to be expressing in this room.

"That's not a bad way for you to make a living."

"On the Wobblies?" Marius laughed. "I live on my friends, not on my comrades. There's always a dame, if not a man, to feed me and lend me a ten-spot. Maybe you will, now you're here."

Slowly Jeff took out his wallet. "I'll lend you ten dollars."

"Toss it on the table." When Jeff had done so, Marius asked: "Have you seen Rebecca?"

Jeff shook his head. "I'm seeing her tonight. She gave me your address on the phone."

"There's a girl that makes it hard for herself. So busy wanting, she don't have time to find out what she wants."

"I suppose, Marius," Jeff felt his lips tremble, "when you go to bed, you take off that keepsake of your mother?"

Schmitt's eyes hardened, then grew soft. "I threw it away like I said I would, after I went to bed with Rebecca."

It was unreal: that must be why he could bear it. And his father's request was unreal. Why then not obey it?

"You mean you took it off? Can't you find it?"

"What for?"

"Wear it again."

Marius laughed. "Not even for Jesus' sake I couldn't. And why in hell should you care?"

"You don't think much of reasons. Can't you do it without my explaining?"

"So you believe in magic! Then you ought to be glad. According to the superstitious, what I did should bring me bad luck."

"I'm not sure I want you to have bad luck."

"On my way home, I guess I was thinking about you. I suddenly remembered what you'd said when you guyed me about the cross. 'All right, old man,' I says, 'here goes.' I ripped the thing off and dropped it."

"So it was I that did it!" Jeff said, half to himself.

"It was about the time they turn the bums out of the Bowery flophouses. Maybe one of 'em picked it up and hocked it for a dollar."

Jeff looked at the dusty floor. "I'm sorry."

"What's this? the noble act? You think you love that girl? She'll tear you to pieces."

"What about you?"

"We don't mean a thing to each other. That's what was good about it."

Suddenly rage flowered; if there had been a gun in his hand, Jeff would have used it. "What about her? A life broken doesn't 'mean a thing' to you!"

" 'A life broken'—doesn't mean a thing."

"Speak for yourself."

Marius leaned forward. "Don't tell me *you* can. Whether you know it or not, you speak for a social system that doesn't break a life or two. Oh, no! It breaks 'em by the millions. Twists every child till the spirit gasps and gives up. Warps their bodies and minds into instruments for profit."

"So if it pleases you to do a little private trampling of your own, what does it matter? You wolves whose hearts bleed for humanity and are stone when it comes to a neighbor."

Marius looked at him quietly. "Really, Jeff, you don't know any-

418

thing. I'm a bullet, if that's what you mean. I'm firing myself at the enemy."

"How about being kind and tender with someone who's no enemy?"

"Hold on, Hartt, what are you driving at? do you think you've been kind and tender to Rebecca? Ask her. Your good intentions with a Harvard accent—they certainly haven't helped her. Kindness and tenderness should have results."

"If you've hurt her, Schmitt, I'll come back here and kill you."

"That's the ticket. The complete monopolist. Hands off! All rights reserved to hurt the woman."

Jeff got up and stood at the door. "No, I won't kill you."

"Don't apologize. It's the cleanest thing you've said."

"Too much of what *you* say has truth in it."

Marius met his eyes in quiet.

"I'm sorry," said Jeff, "you threw away that cross."

Marius laughed. "Think of the poor bum who hocked it."

Jeff opened the door.

". . . and thanks for the ten-spot."

When he had phoned for the address, she had seemed glad to hear him. And she was glad to see him. His days had been doubt and rage; her smile distilled them into a moment of joy. Her smile was hurt and defiance, child and age together. He sat across from her at the table and his tenderness was ready to give her up. Not a promise again of happiness could make him happy; but tenderness, whole in itself, holding no demand or challenge like love which needed to possess. Tenderness was easy; and as he sensed this, tenderness was gone, turned back into the days' doubt and anger. She was pleasantly telling him of her boss who hated her, and therein, she said, lay her security—although her work wasn't much good. The man was so afraid, she said, of being unfair because he hated her that he would not fire her. From her pale lips of an adolescent girl came these steel observations. Beauty, Jeff knew, always hurt, but not like this. Her loveliness was conflict and it drew him unbearably toward conflict. Only tenderness could save him. —A weakling's way? am I a coward parading as a saint?

"I saw Marius."

"I haven't seen him."

"Not at all? Why not?"

"He hasn't been around."

"You want him to come back?"

She pondered slowly. "I'm not sure. But if he comes I'll see him . . . I'll do anything he wants."

"You do love him?"

"I don't know what love is. I don't even want it. I don't think I love him."

"You'll be hurt, Rebecca."

"It's the leap of the heart. You have to follow it."

"Call him, then. Bring him back."

She shook her head. "It doesn't help. Look at you. The leap of the heart has no authority."

"That's why I'm here, Rebecca. The leap of the heart."

"It's a hell of a mess," the smile contorted her mouth. "My heart leaps for him, because his doesn't, perhaps. Yours for me, because mine doesn't."

"Rebecca, if you let yourself love me—"

"Don't start lying! You don't know what you'd do. All sorts of problems would come up that aren't there now. Your wife and kids—"

"So you think I'm giving you up to Marius because underneath all it's a relief?"

"Nothing so simple, I suppose. Besides, you can't give me up to Marius. He doesn't *take* people. He catches 'em and throws 'em."

"You could change him."

"He's pretty old. And who says I want to?"

"You're twenty, aren't you, Rebecca? He must be twice your age."

"You wouldn't understand; but it's really Marius—not you—who respects me. He's tough and insulting by your standards. To hell with them! To hell with the word 'respect.'"

"You're the one who used it."

"Jeff dear, I've told you all I know. Go back to your wife. You never really left her."

"That's because I never was really there."

"Go back," she smiled, "to where you never really were. Perhaps that's the good life."

"It's strange to hear you speak of 'the good life'—a Victorian phrase. Isn't it Matthew Arnold's?"

"I'm better educated than you think. My mother read me all the pious poets. Anyway, Jeff, I don't want to hurt you any more." This hurt most and she knew it. "I guess I wanted to hurt you and needed to be hurt. I've had enough of both."

"I hope it's true."

"Well, it isn't!" She was angry. "I hate men. Now I know why. If they don't stir you, you despise them. If they do, you despise yourself. I'm sick of your goodness. It's worse than mama's. Papa had culture too, but he laughed at it and killed it. I want peace. That's a lie. Anyway, if I want war, I can get enough of it without you. I'm going to throw up my job. Won't Leftings, that's my boss who hates me, be chagrined! losing the chance to fire me and to be virtuous and not fire me. I've a new job in mind with a new outfit, who may send me to Paris. My father went there when he was twenty and I suppose you did, too; but your papas paid the bills. I'll go on my own."

"Rebecca, stop whistling in the dark."

"Perhaps I like to whistle. And who isn't in the dark?"

He disliked her. It was as easy and logical as adding the figures on his check. They walked toward her room, and from the release sprang desire. "You care too much," she had said. Was that the reason for his failure with her? Then this was the mood for victory. Let him humiliate her by taking her without love! At her door:

"I want to come up," his throat was husky.

"No."

"I want to. I don't say I love you, any more. I want to come up."

"No."

So she wanted him to care too much? she did not want him to be free? she wanted him to fail? She smiled, and turned, and left him. . . .

Through the airless night on the train, into the morning of pines ablaze with the sun, he took his humiliation with him. Corinna stood on the platform and the children raced up.

His wife examined him at arm's length after she had kissed him. "How tired you look, dear. The city must be beastly."

421

They were part of the morning: Corinna, sweet, sound and large; demure Joan who was six and a little ashamed of having leaped into her father's arms like a baby or a dog; little Joe, a blond, terrier-quick lad of four, who resembled Aloysius Kennedy except for his eyes that were old Joseph Hartt's.

"How is mother?"

"Fine. She wanted to come to the station but I wouldn't let her. It's too early for her. But she'll be down for breakfast."

"I'm hungry," Joe announced.

"Of course you are. Who isn't?" asked Corinna.

Jeff reflected that he was not hungry.

"The air will get you back your appetite," she answered his thought. "We'll fatten you up."

"Do you want a fat daddy?" Jeff asked.

"You bet," said Joe.

"Daddy couldn't be fat," Joan declared. "Only mummies are fat."

"How dare you!" laughed Corinna.

"Well, you're fatter than daddy. An' granny is fatter than all my granpas."

"Than all dozen of them, eh?" said Jeff.

"I only got two, silly!" Joan rebuked him.

Their camp was one of those rough-hewn "log cabins" where every twentieth-century comfort, from tiled bathrooms to refrigerator, hides in the illusion of "getting back to nature." From the upholstered chairs, hideous but easy, they looked out on the lake and woods with the complacence of a civilization so sure of itself it could toy with the primeval. When Jeff took his boy and girl in a canoe, the canvas shell balanced them in an abyss of water, forest, sky; they enjoyed even the sun with the same sense (to Jeff) of fragile equilibrium: nearer, the sun would burn, farther, let them freeze. And the August evenings came already cold on the day's heat. . . . Jonathan joined them. In silence he observed his son. But one day, after the early supper with the children, the two men strolled to the lake; the chaos of trees, swarming insects, wood creatures dimly heard, refuted the table they had left laden with good food, the cozy fire burning in the hearth, the warm beds waiting, the mother abloom in her children, the grandmother whose reincarnation in this happy flesh made her glow like her old songs a little muted. Hard as steel, the twilight world vibrated. Jonathan said:

"I don't like your looks, Jeff. Are you well?"

"Perfectly."

With steel persistence, the lake lipped at the moss and overhanging branches. "You're not seeing Rebecca? It's over?"

"No, and yes."

"Does the wild fellow still wear his cross?"

"He kept his promise."

Jonathan watched a loon jet from the water and lacerate the twilight with a laugh. "I'm sorry."

"About what, dad?"

"About everything."

"I went to see him. I told him what you wanted."

"There's something to him, isn't there?"

"He'd thrown it away."

Jonathan said: "The night is darker than dusk, yet nearer to morning."

"I love the twilight. That's when the colors come out."

"I'm the one who should say that, son."

"That's a relic of your conventional ideas; you know you have them, dad. You're younger than I."

"You've been hurt. You'll get over it because you're young. That may sound conventional, but it's true. Time is tragic, because it devours what is timeless. I've been hurt, but too late."

"I know, dad."

"If you do, you know it can't be talked about, because it's not one thing, not one person; it's the cause of them all."

"I think I understand."

"You too must see the cause under what's hurt you. Rebecca is not cause."

He was silent a long time. "Father, I love the twilight."

"Those builders you used to praise: Sullivan, Frank Lloyd Wright—"

"Perhaps they too are younger than I."

"Jeff, I was brought up to believe . . . to *know* this American world is a dawn."

"Are you still sure?"

"There are winds blowing we had no names for. The fixed stars we navigated by are blown by them."

"Is that why you wanted Schmitt to wear his mother's cross?"

"The young can't live, Jeff, unless the old who mothered and fathered them are strong in them. That's not superstition."

"It's hope, dad. What if I don't want it?"

The word hope gave him his city, hard as the fury beneath this "peace" of nature that was struggle and chaos, trees fighting for sun, insect and beast feeding on one another. He saw again the mob of his boyhood rioting and burning. He had read hope in them; he saw the years of his city's growth, grinding him down to what he was today. Was the city of men different? was it more? was the "more" that was not in this twilight shambles of plant and insect and beast, in the word hope? He said:

"You're part of man's world! You can't deny your part. Life insists."

"Your vaunted modern world. Perhaps it's all twilight. Look at those ephemera swarming their instant. It's morning and all day for them."

"I haven't made myself clear." With deep sadness, Jonathan smiled at his son. —Until I'm clear, he thought, I must never leave him!

Without Rebecca, it was a pallid year for Jeff. Pallid in summer's bloom as a white worm in a flower; and pallid in its death, under the blue-ice crackle of the autumn nights of the reawakening city: the tall buildings coruscant, the swelling streams of motors, the brilliantly-dressed shops and restaurants and theaters. A new year began: snow that fell white and became ash, mornings of cold sun lancing the streets and prying the crowds open. Jeff did his work; the less he gave to it the more it satisfied his clients. Corinna, fulfilled, asked for little. He bought the new magazine and found a page of models sketched with flimsy grace—how little like Rebecca!—and signed with her name in that crass slanting script of hers that made him think of an animal racing to its prey. He longed to see her again, to be with her again, even in failure. And then it was spring, a whole year since he had found her again and lost her again. The same hand stared at him one morning from an envelope on his office desk. He read his other mail and put the letter in his pocket. At noon he went to the Harvard Club to lunch with a fellow member. As the man came forward, suddenly: "Perhaps she's in trouble!" he remembered the letter. "Carver," he said, "I can't have lunch with you today. Something urgent has just come up." He walked down the block to Sixth Avenue, to Forty-second Street and sat at a table in Shanley's where the noisy lunchers numbed a vibrant part of him he could not cope with. Relieved, somehow remote and watching himself, he pulled the letter from his pocket.

> Dear Jeff,
>   I wonder about you a lot, so hello! Perhaps I shouldn't say it, you may not want to be bothered. Or you might think it meant something it doesn't.
> *Rebecca*

Unable to decide, he did nothing. On the flap of the envelope, he had noted a new address; he destroyed the envelope and found he knew the address. The letter itself was unaddressed and undated. Each time, day after day, he took it from his pocket, it moved him as if fresh from her hand.

Rebecca and Marius occasionally met at the Radical Club, but he did not come back to her and she found she did not need him. She had needed him only when Jeff was there: without Jeff, not Marius. Oh! if he had come and kissed her, probably she'd let him. His brutality was knowing, as Jeff's tenderness was clumsy. Any night, if Marius came —or no night. . . .

Then, suddenly, he came. He looked at her new room (it was on Irving Place and it had white paneled walls, a high ceiling, a black hardwood floor without rugs, a white marble fireplace and a black leather cover on the couch): "What is this? A mausoleum?"

"Don't look at it if you don't like it."

"I still like you, Medusa."

"What do you mean by Medusa?"

"It was an inspiration."

She laughed. "Your name for insult?"

"Don't you know how seriously I take the ancient myths? Didn't I

425

wear a crucifix for years? I'd touch it and say: 'There is no God' and no lightning struck me. You're Medusa, but you haven't turned *me* to stone." He threw himself on the couch.

"I wish you'd go away."

He got up and kissed her. She said:

"Who was Medusa?"

He reached for the dictionary on the bottom shelf of a little bookcase in which squatted a French doll and a china dog. "Don't you really know?"

"She turned you to stone? She had snakes in her hair?"

"Listen, Medusa." He read: "'*Medusa,* a soft gelatinous hydrozoan, a jellyfish.'" He dropped the volume and took her in his arms.

. . . It had been that night, after Marius left, that Rebecca again put on her clothes and wrote to Jeff. But Jeff did not come. And when Marius returned a week later, she held him off: not a kiss.

"I want you to go and not come back."

"That'd be too bad. I came, you see, to borrow a ten-spot. If I don't come back, how can I pay you back?"

She took her purse and pulled out twenty dollars: "You can keep it. Now, get out."

She had plenty of money now . . . now that it was too late to send her mother to the sanatorium that might have saved her. That was how everything turned out: money at the wrong time, men with the wrong traits. Nothing fitted. She was nearly twenty-two, and no longer that disgraceful cipher, a virgin. Most men were futile, but she would have missed their unsavory amorousness (no third man ever touched her). Men didn't really *like* a woman, they went blindly toward you (including Jeff) as a moth to the flame. Marius liked her, that was why he could stir her, perhaps: but made her hate herself. Rebecca got ready for bed. And there were tears in her eyes.

Infinitely more than all her waking, Rebecca loved her sleep. Sleep was strange—beautiful, and the beautiful was always strange. Why had she needed to know man's love? because it was strange, therefore perhaps beautiful. Well, it was no longer strange, and it was ugly. Everything in her life was ugly: the drawings that paid her, the elegant magazine, the absurd women who bought it. She knew she had made Jeff ugly, and Marius made her ugly. Her mother died, and that was ugly..

426

Her father, deeply strange, was beautiful and she hated him. Sleep . . . Rebecca was whole in sleep. She prepared herself for bed as for a sacrament. She knew nothing about sacraments. But the eye that saw her undress, carefully fold her clothes, carefully brush her hair, lovingly don her nightgown, remove the cover from her couch, tuck the blankets a little tighter, smooth the pillow, then in darkness glide between the sheets, would have known the ritual in her behavior. She lies in her warmth, relaxed and yet with tension. She feels her body tender and immense. She gazes in peace at the dim ceiling where shapes and lights of the street are vaguely mirrored. And all that wrestles in her life subsides: her body and her head, her memories and her will, become one darkness. The eye that could see Rebecca sleeping would wonder at her face of a fresh child, bathed in well-being.

Late in June after a hot day, Rebecca, home from work, came out of her shower, put on a pale gray dress that clung to her leanness and breasts. There was a knock at the door. She thought of Marius and Jeff together: impossible! And what nonsense! as if no one else ever knocked at her door. The landlady with a message? She opened the door, her bodice still unhooked, and Jeff came in. He seemed smaller, more boyish, except his eyes that were larger. Hooking her dress without haste, she smiled. He turned to shut the door and she liked the grace of his shoulders, the dignity of his long head. She had forgotten.

"Hello, Rebecca."

"Hello, Jeff." She put out her hand.

He held it lightly, as if meditating on a distance; then drew her close and kissed her.

Carrie, who ran the restaurant in the Radical Club basement, leaned down between Marius and his girl companion, her heavy pendulous breasts brushing the girl's shoulder, and placed the pot of coffee on the table. For a moment her face, a mask of dull gray against the world, was framed between that of Marius and the girl's which was frail and bright as her spun-gold hair. From the kitchen came a raucous gramophone caricaturing Caruso's voice in *Musica Proibita*. The other tables were empty, it was past dinner time.

"In plain daylight!" Marius boomed, his dark face aflame with the intensities that were corroding it. "Stolen with the piss-ass guards all over the place and the bourgeois property-lovers down on their bellies before it."

"Hee-hee," giggled Hyacinth Lefère who sat across from him: a cat-like little man, fierce in his Anarchist convictions, violent in his periodic binges, and most of the time indolent as a Persian cat.

"No doubt of it," said Solomon Steinsohn, the solemn editor of *The Marxist,* who sat next to Lefère. "The theft of the *Mona Lisa* is a symptom of capitalist decadence."

Daniel Sollen, poet and chess player, on the right of Schmitt's girl, puffed his low-slung pipe and peered through his thick glasses behind which he seemed to hide; "They'll find it. After all, it's got to be put up for sale some time, somewhere. And all the world knows *La Gioconda.*"

"Who says so?" Marius shot back. "Who says the man stole it for money?"

"Somebody's got to see it," said Steinsohn.

"You're all wrong," said Marius. "The man who stole the *Mona Lisa* did so to destroy it."

Hyacinth Lefère sighed voluptuously; Steinsohn shook his dry head, the girl with the diaphanous hair and face gasped and turned eyes of idolatry on Marius. He went on:

"A class-conscious proletarian did it. No one else would have the nerve, the cunning. Why did he do it? Not to sell it, of course; he's no such bloody fool. Not to hang it up in his bare kitchen and adore it. He has other bacon to fry. He's cut it into ribbons!"

"Gee," purred Hyacinth Lefère and grinned like a Cheshire cat.

"It's a signal for the general strike. What was the damn thing? Aristocratic art."

"Oligarchic," corrected Steinsohn. "Da Vinci was a bourgeois employed by Dukes of Milan who were financiers."

"All right. Oligarchic. Anyway, it's the most famous work of bourgeois art in the world, and a grand thing to have it go. While the bureaucrat rats and the tourist touts looked on. Right under their noses."

"They found the glass frame," said Sollen, "in the cellar. The canvas had been neatly extracted. Maybe it'll start a new movement in art: frames without pictures."

"It's a declaration of war."

"Maybe," said Steinsohn, "the Kaiser did it. He's been rattling his saber enough."

"Then there'll be a war between Germany and France!" Hyacinth Lefère licked his pretty lips.

"International war," said Steinsohn, "is a thing of the past."

"Oh, yes?" growled a voice from the open kitchen door (the gramophone had stopped). It was Jim, Carrie's brother, whose job was to wash dishes and who sometimes indulged in self-expression by smashing them. His deadpan face, like his sister's, had the same undertone of violence. He seemed offended.

"There'll be no more great wars," Steinsohn settled it.

"Why in hell not?" Jim half-sneered, half-pleaded. "Ain't there navies and armies enough?"

"The international bankers and Big Business profit by the armies and navies." Steinsohn tried to be kind. "But war would destroy too many of their assets."

"That's not the reason," said Marius. "The armies are made up of workers. Well, they won't march, that's all. The Germans will stand at the frontier and refuse to shoot the fellow workers of France. They'll shoot their own lousy officers instead. So will the French. So will the Russians. With the officers out of the way—"

"And the bankers! And don't forget the politicians," Lefère added.

"All right. Throw 'em in," conceded Marius. "And the intellectuals too."

Steinsohn scowled. Sollen smiled quietly:

"Don't you underestimate the politicians and the statesmen? How could they make peace every few decades, if there weren't any wars?"

"Who in hell are they? They don't count," said Marius.

Sollen puffed his pipe. "A man who sees tomorrow: that's a politician. A man who sees day after tomorrow; that's a statesman. A man who sees today—and therefore the years to come: that's an unpractical poet."

Marius snorted and ignored him: "With all the bosses shot down by the workers the first day of mobilization, there'll come the general strike in all the factories. The Revolution's finished."

"Then what?" asked Jim from his kitchen door.

"Don't you worry."

"Even if it were true," said Sollen, "in a year the workers get themselves new bosses, new politicians; and the thing starts all over."

"I think you're all crazy," said Jim from his distance. "There'll be wars so long as there are countries. Men love to fight, and countries make the easiest teams. Just like boys gang up by blocks."

"The worker has no country, he has only his class," said Steinsohn.

"*You* say," sneered Jim.

"To get back to our muttons," said Sollen, "the man who stole the *Mona Lisa* will start a flock of new religions. The picture'll show up —and be called a fake. Another copy will appear, claiming to be the genuine article. Then a third 'one and only original.' Each will have its followers, and finally its armies. Some day, one of the 'one and only's' will be slashed, there'll be a war, Jim will be happy."

No one smiled; they all felt vaguely that the chess player was laughing at them, except the girl who merely stared.

Steinsohn solemnly said: "You forget the art experts—"

"*They*'re the worst fakers!" Marius was off again. "Say! the *Mona Lisa* that was in the Louvre was probably number 5: probably the one the dago painted got burned in a pawnbroker's insurance fire back in the sixteenth century. Who the hell would know—"

"And who the hell would care?" giggled Lefère.

"You don't allow," Sollen said sadly, "for the uniqueness and immortality of genius."

"Sure we do!" Marius passed a hand gently over his girl's hair. "Genius is like Mary. Sure Mary's unique. To me she's immortal all right, for she'll live longer than me. She'll die just the same. And there'll be other lovely Marys."

Carrie had come back to listen and stood over them, a cigarette drooped from her well-shaped mouth. The smoke rose into her eye, she kept blinking but did not move the cigarette. Now she said: "Smash him one for that, Mary. Don't have nothing to do with a guy that says there'll be another gal like you."

"Sit down," laughed Marius.

"Git back where you belong," Carrie tossed her head toward Jim who had edged out from the kitchen. "Make some more java." She squeezed into the bench between Hyacinth and Steinsohn. The kitchen door slammed shut. "Jeeze, I love that chawming brother o' mine.

You'd think he was doin' me a favor. I house him and feed him, and give him a dollar every Saturday night to get drunk—"

The gramophone started to play *Alexander's Ragtime Band.*

"You're an exploiter, Carrie darling," Hyacinth Lefère squeezed her hand. "You house me too and feed me and give me more than a dollar to get drunk. And I wash no dishes."

"Christ!" cried Carrie. "So I'm an exploiter because I make my brother work a little? If I killed myself doin' *all* the work, not only nine-tenths, where would you all be?"

"I don't know, Carrie darling. But that's beside the point that you're an exploiter."

"What about you? You live pretty good and don't work at all."

"Exploiters often work very hard, and don't live so good. No logic, Carrie darling. All day you jump from premise to conclusion, dumping the undistributed middles in the ashcan."

Carrie stumped out her cigarette and lighted another. "Can you beat it?" She smiled lovingly at Lefère.

At a rest of *Alexander's Ragtime Band,* a dish fell in the kitchen; then an explosion of dishes drowned the music. Everyone laughed, including Carrie—except Steinsohn.

"Jim's sore," said his sister, "because you guys said they wasn't to be any more wars."

"International, not civil," Steinsohn corrected.

"Jim always wanted to be a soldier. If they was only a war, he'd not be washing dishes. He'd be a general in a minute. You'd be surprised what that lad's read! Every campaign of Lee and Washington."

"Why didn't you send him to West Point?"

"It's too late, I guess. He's twenty-two."

"Not at all!" said Steinsohn. "If our district elects a Socialist Congressman next election, maybe it can be done. Congressmen, you know, recommend appointments."

"Oh!" Carrie dreamed blissfully.

"I always said it!" Marius pounded the table. "You Socialists are more corrupt, more respectable, more anti-revolutionary, than Tammany and the bankers. Instead of sending Jim to West Point, you ought to blow it up."

"See here," Steinsohn bristled.

431

"We'll have to blow *you* up first."

"Before the Revolution?" asked Hyacinth Lefère.

"Absolutely! The Socialists would ruin it. With their legal reforms. Things have got to get worse, quick—much worse, so the workers will strike. Reforms put off the day. Look at that imbecile Congressman from Minnesota—what's his name?"

"If you mean Lindbergh, he's no imbecile," said Steinsohn.

"Ain't he though? Look! We had a panic in 1907; it hurt the people and made Wall Street stronger. So the bankers are fixing for another. They've got together in what they call a National Monetary Commission. If their plans go through, we can expect a worse crash pretty soon. The workers will be worse off—and that much nearer the general strike. So what does this ass Lindbergh do? Like all the liberals and socialists, he protests and agitates for money *reform*."

"So what?"

"So the workers will be a little relieved. So their wrath, their *élan vital* for the Revolution, will be that much weakened. You're the worst enemies we got!" Marius raised his fist toward Steinsohn: the fist relaxed as he saw the entrance door open. "Hello! Look who's here."

Jeff Hartt saw Marius at the table and came forward.

"Comrades," said Marius, "this is Mr. Hartt, architect to the exploiters."

. . . Nothing had changed between Jeff and Rebecca except that now they knew nothing could change. Jeff told himself: it can't go on; and was ready for any stratagem, any humiliation, lest it should not go on. Marius, he learned, was again in the picture. The repetition of the last year was life mocking itself. Then, once more, Rebecca shut him out. What he did not know was that, shortly before, she had broken again with Marius. He joined his family in the same Adirondack camp. He returned to the city and rang the bell at Rebecca's house. The landlady said she was gone. On a vacation? "Moved out," said the landlady sweetly. Did she leave her new address? "Oh, yes, sir," and she gave him the name and address of her magazine. Jeff looked for Marius who also had moved; and at last, here, Jeff found him.

432

"Have a seat," Marius pointed to the chair at his end of the table. "I've been sort of expecting you."

"I've been hunting for you." Jeff sat down.

"Rebecca's gone to Paris."

"Paris!" The cry in the word exposed him to these strangers

"Her magazine was after her for a long time, but she didn't want to go. One fine day she says to herself: Why not? Paris must be quite a place. That was after I met my Mary."

"You're a damned liar."

"Sure I'm lying," Marius laughed. "Who doesn't lie about women? Don't you?"

Smiles, not unkindly, wreathed Jeff: Lefère's glitter as if he were waiting eagerly for trouble, Sollen's gentle but a bit ghoulish awareness of pain, Carrie's cynical amusement when two typical men made fools of themselves for some silly pretty woman. Only Steinsohn, the pure intellectual, had no idea what it was all about. When Jeff did not answer, Marius wove on:

"She's got a swell assignment. She goes to the races, the Opera, all the big shindigs, and sketches what the *crème de la crème* is wearing. In three months it'll bore her. By then I'll be in Paris."

"You have an assignment too?" Jeff tried to hide himself.

"I'll get an assignment all right, whenever I want. If not on a liner, on a cattle ship. Do you think the only way to get to Paris is with a first-class ticket?"

"You'll have to take me!" said Mary.

He ignored her. "Paris is the head of the Syndicalist movement. If it isn't Italy. Sorel's in Paris! I want to be there when the general strike starts. And it won't start here. When Russia gets going again," Marius turned to Steinsohn; Rebecca seemed forgotten, "—there's a case for you, Solomon! in 1905, when the Russians started their revolution, French gold gave the bosses a chance to make a few reforms and the workers were appeased. Now they won't move again till things get worse. When they do, and Russia wakes up, the U.S.A. is going to be the most backward big country in the world. Fifty years—and then, bang! But I can't wait that long. I want to see the start."

"Take me!" cried the girl. "When is it going to be?"

Marius pinched her cheek and laughed. "A couple of years, honey. How about 1914? Is that soon enough to suit you?"

Jim came in and sat at the opposite end of the table, facing Jeff.

Steinsohn said: "Your Revolution is taking place right now. It's collectivization. It's fundamental. It's gradual. And it may not even be bloody. Marx said—. One day, maybe in 1920, the people of England and Germany will wake up and find they're living in a Socialist society."

Jim spat on the floor: "Bullshit! They'll blow each other and themselves up first."

Everyone laughed. Jeff got up. He'd learned what he wanted; he had not come to hear the crackpots talk.

"Sit down!" said Marius. "Don't you want to talk about Rebecca?"

"You've finished eating. Walk a way with me."

"Not on your life! We'll talk here. In the world we're going to make, when man is a healthy animal again, we'll have our love affairs in the open. We can't do that just yet. But we can talk in the open."

The smiles now, Jeff felt, were less friendly, since he had shown his wish to go.

"Perhaps," he said standing, "I invited you to come out with me, not to talk but to smash your damn face."

"Now *you*'re lying. But if that's what you want—"

Jeff had to get out; each moment he delayed it would be harder.

"You're right," he said. "I don't want to fight you; even that would be a kind of communication."

"Wipe me out, without soiling your hands: that's what you'd like? *Presto chango!*" Marius waved a spoon in the air like a wand.

Taking his time: "That's exactly it," Jeff bowed to them all and left them.

4

JONATHAN HARTT STOOD AT THE DOOR AND CLUM-
sily removed his rubbers by prying down at one heel with the other
toe. This was easier than to lean down; the rheumatism about which
he carefully said nothing to Greta troubled him on these wretched
days. Greta was singing a *Lied* by Schumann. He kicked the rubbers
into the closet, hung up his drenched coat and hat and went to the
bedroom. Greta's voice was softer now, less brilliant (after all, she was
fifty-six) but more poignant, the artistry more complete. This was
Greta's secret: she was an artist. That overwrought tale by Wilde?
Dorian Gray remained young while his portrait hideously aged;
Greta's subterfuge was better, she remained fresh in spirit while her
sufferings, her disillusions, became the mere loveliness of music. The
word "mere" was his mother's, to whom art and artists were not
"serious." Did he accept that . . . and love in Greta what his standards
refused? Confusions under clarities. . . . He sat down by his bed.
Now he would have to lean over, he could not kick off his high laced
shoes as he had the rubbers. The singing stopped and Greta's foot-
steps were in the hall. It was like that; he never called her and she
usually came. She kneeled, took off his shoes. "Your feet are wet!" she
scolded him and drew off the damp socks. He kept thinking of his
rubbers: Why didn't they do their duty?

Winter was here. From the shelter of his library window, he watched
the December wind flail the Hudson, the rain in sheets press the white-
tipped waters and vanish over the embankment like those crazy auto
racers when they missed a curve. Tonight it would snow; it was
already snowing upstate. But his room is warm. Like a child that
snuggles in its blankets, he felt ease creep upon him. —I'm old; why
not admit it? Sixty-three. At least I've made money. If I die, Greta
and Lucia will have enough and Jeff doesn't need— He stood, not
seeing the storm, the easy storm to cope with if one had warm rooms
and dry socks; feeling a less conquerable storm. . . .

He had stopped at the word "need": Jeff *needed*. Jonathan turned from the winter window, sat near his desk, lighted the lamp. Long ago, after much hesitation, he had written to Rebecca Lorne. Would she please come to his office? She took her time, then wrote she feared her work hours were too long: could he not write whatever he had to say? He replied that he would wait for her downtown, any afternoon she could come. When she came in, not offering her hand, taking the chair across his desk without swerving her eyes from his, her resemblance to her father pierced him: Evan was present again in his office.

"Miss Lorne, was your father Evan Cleeve?"

"Yes."

Her want of surprise did not surprise him. "I knew your father; he used to be my partner." He could not make out if her quiet was defensiveness or distaste. "You knew that too?"

"My mother must have mentioned your name. When I met you, it came back."

"He was my dearest friend. He died in my house." Irrational words: —I helped to kill him; he crowded them out with: "I tried to help your mother. She was entitled to a considerable fortune from your grandfather's estate. She wouldn't touch it."

Evidently she had come only to listen.

"I understand her motives, of course, and they do her credit. Your mother must be a remarkable woman."

"She's dead."

"I surmised as much. Then there's no reason why her motives should be shared by you."

"What are you driving at?"

"If a claim were made by you on the Grosvenor Cleeve estate, I feel reasonably sure the executors would gladly make a settlement."

"Why should you bother about this?"

He fought a stir of anger. "I hoped you'd understand. I'm speaking as a friend. Your father *was* my friend and I can't separate you—"

"I have nothing to do with my father."

He made himself be calm. "All the more reason from your standpoint why you should not continue your mother's attitude. You should be realistic about this. And impersonal. You're entitled to a good deal of money through your father. You can't avoid your physical descent from him. You can't avoid, by the way, having many of his traits. (I can see that.) Why not take what's yours?" She kept gazing at him as if she were aware, not of what he said but of a hidden action in him which his words falsely recorded. He continued: "I speak to you as a friend, I repeat. If you knew what your father means to me, you'd forgive me. You might even come to accept my friendship." He smiled. "But although I make my suggestion as a friend,"—what her eyes saw seemed ever more remote from what he was saying—"I *am* a lawyer and that means I will know how to help you. It will be extremely simple."

"I'm not interested, Mr. Hartt."

"You need not even appear. There'll be no publicity. I'll conduct the whole proceedings."

She kept gazing deeper than his words.

"Think about it, anyway," he made himself keep on smiling.

"Why do you insist?"

"I don't insist, Miss Lorne."

Now she smiled. "I can see where Jeff gets his stubbornness."

"He wishes you well, too."

"How do you know that?"

"Jeff is having a hard time."

"Has he anything to do with your writing me?"

"Of course not! He knows nothing about it. I don't think he guesses at the relation between us."

"So there's a relation between us?"

"You still believe, don't you, in independent human atoms?"

"It's all too sentimental for me."

"Only logical. You can't stamp out your bond with your father; nor my bond with him. That makes a kind of bond between you and me. And then there's Jeff; that complicates and strengthens it. . . ."

"I don't see it. I'd rather not talk of it."

"As you wish."

"I suppose you think you're being kind. From your standpoint, money *is* important." She had nothing more to say. But although the interview seemed to be over, she kept sitting there, imperturbably gazing.

"If you change your mind—"

"I won't change my mind."

"You're so absolutely sure?"

"Even if I was broke, even if I was starving . . . I never did starve. Mother saw to that."

Suddenly a child had spoken from her hardness. He said: "I know, dear. Your mother. Not your father. . . . Rebecca, I don't want to defend your father. It would be an impudence, after the way he made you suffer—"

"Mother suffered. Because she loved him. He just never meant a thing to me."

"Are you sure?"

"Jeff *is* like you! Always making simple matters complicated."

"You think your father was simple?"

"For me, he simply vanished."

"He's here now."

She shook her head indulgently, almost with affection. "You can't do it, Mr. Hartt. You can't complicate *my* life. I wouldn't touch the money, not for sentimental reasons like mother, but because it *would* complicate my life."

"You think *you're* simple?"

"What's the mystery, unless you make it?"

"You mean: unless you see it."

Now she was roused. "I can't bear people who always see more than there is to see. Always dark things, of course. Maybe it's true in Russia and wherever Ibsen came from. It's morbid. It's not American."

"Your father was not American?"

She got up; Jonathan felt she was enjoying herself: "I think my father was a spoiled rich man's son who drank too much and did something crooked in New York—probably with you if you were his partner, and had to clear out. I think he got involved with mother because he was weak and she was foolish. It's as simple as that."

"As simple as that, Rebecca?"

—As simple . . . simple? When she left, he had felt grateful that she had refused his offer. This also was not simple: it was as if she were forcing him to be what he had become, and not to be what he had been: the practical man advising her to take her due inheritance.

438

He had needed to show his gratitude. Holding her hand, he said: "Thanks."

"What for?"

"The young," he kept her hand and she did not withdraw it, "help the old to grow to be themselves. Thanks for that. Without you, the old would always manage to be young again."

"I don't know what you're talking about. Isn't it best to be young?"

He shook his head. "Best to be ignorant, arrogant, hurried and hard?" He said it so tenderly she was not hurt, and her hand in his was quiet.

—Simple? . . .

"Jonathan! What *are* you mumbling to yourself?" Jonathan clutched the book in his lap and looked up toward Greta smiling over him. Since Mrs. Lake, had her smile been different, as if she knew? as if what he had done had made her suffer, yet given her strength? Perhaps this was imagining. There was no way to be sure.

"I must have fallen asleep."

"With your eyes open? Dinner's ready."

As he ate the good soup: "You look tired, Jon. I hope getting wet hasn't made you catch cold."

—Coincidence? Why did it have to be Evan's girl who was lacerating his son's life? Coincidence? Why was wild Marius Schmitt the son of Frieda? It was fantastic. Fantasy meant nonsense. Coincidence meant nothing. The telephone rang. The ponderous old machine still hung in the pantry, and Jonathan still resisted talking in it. Greta came back to the table.

"It's Jeff. He wants to come over tonight to talk with you."

"Well? Let him."

She hesitated: "Couldn't you speak to him, Jon? If it's not important, couldn't you postpone it?"

"And why should I postpone it?"

"It's dreadful out—"

"And Jeff's made of sugar!"

"You needn't get so furious."

"If that boy of yours isn't a milksop, it's not your fault. Pamper, pamper!"

439

"All right. Stop it, dear!" She retreated through the door. And Jonathan, while he heard her tell her boy to be sure and wear his rubbers, drank his coffee and scrutinized his irrational outburst. Jeff too was coming . . . to join the company of fantastic presences? Jeff with Rebecca, Louella Lake and Evan, Marius and Frieda. . . .

Greta, again at table, said: "I'm worried about Jeff. And nobody pampers him. He's a sensitive boy and he works as hard as you ever did, and for months he's not been looking well. I've spoken with Corinna. Everyone sees it but you."

Without another word, Jonathan finished his coffee and went to his library, Greta to her chaise longue in the bedroom . . . to her new novel, Margaret Deland's *The Iron Woman,* which she knew would bore her like the last one.

—Coincidence. It has no meaning. Suppose Jeff tonight, on his way here, with the rain freezing underfoot, slips and is run over by a skidding auto? (They were plentiful now, and any fool could buy one and drive it.) Though their hearts broke, what meaning? A concatenation of unrelated events: Jeff's wish to speak with his father, clouds dropping rain on Manhattan and the cold freezing the rain, some idiot in an auto . . . nothing. —It won't happen; God forbid! The law of probability forbids: that's safer, Jonathan smiled to himself. By the same law of chance, sometimes coincidences happen. His old friend's daughter comes to New York and sits beside his son in the train. He is emotionally vulnerable. The encounter was chance, like that of an auto with a man. The nature of the auto, hard steel, collides with the nature of flesh: a wound follows. Evan's child and his own, the harsh and the soft, collide: a wound follows. It might have been another man, another girl. Or in other circumstances the same man and girl would have passed each other without collision. Coincidence has no meaning. And Marius? Jonathan's mind, functioning as when at work on a brief, proceeded to fit in the new factor. It fitted. There was only one New York; only one Radical Club, to which the not too numerous percipients of new ideas were drawn. So Jeff, Rebecca and Marius coincided at the Club. The final coincidence stemmed from a certain direction of interest in himself and Evan, making them friends; their interest in Frieda and in Rebecca's mother; a propensity of interests carried over to the children. —The sum total of your coincidence is *a convergence of propensities.* Jonathan enjoyed following a line of thought as other men enjoyed pool or poker. He leaned back in his chair (Jeff should be here by now); complacently surveyed his logical "machine" against the superstition of meaning in coincidences, and knew he had no faith in it.

What had he done? (He heard Evan's laughter against logic.) He had subtracted meaning from the strange by proving it was common; and what was this but to deny meaning to the common! Why this passion of his age to deny meaning to life as a whole . . . to deny the whole . . . to deny life? Evan in his shattered way had sought meaning; perhaps he, Jonathan, would yet learn that Evan had found it. If wonder inhered in the common as in the strange, there was no difference between them, and all his logic to extract the strange from the strange was based on a false premise. What if the commonness of wonder meant the commonness of meaning? His father had believed in meaning: that's what it was to believe in God; and from that premise his father used a logic strict as the logic of science which believed that nature has no "ends," which was to say no meaning! Either all was meaningless and dead, including the strange, or all was meaningful and alive, including the common. The wind and the rain compressed the room's silence; hushedly, the books swayed in their shelves. —There is meaning! Which is to say, there is God! Pascal had seen it! Because he was a man of science, he had seen it most clearly! Jonathan smiled at his complacent superiority over the Frenchman whom Jeff had brought (—also a coincidence?) from Paris. The world of sense was an abyss in which men lived desperately suspended; and reason lighted it! In the abyss itself, no power to overcome it. Modern knowledge lighted the abyss, as modern power raised its furies. Pascal prophesied the modern horror! and only meaning within man, meaning beyond the abyss, could tame it. Pascal had found that meaning in his "liberator"; we have lost it. And without it, what must the new century be? a nightmare of depths no longer mercifully dark but electrically glaring; no longer asleep but charged with modern power to rise and overwhelm us! Irrelevantly, Jonathan recalled the evening long years ago, when he had walked up Ninth Avenue toward his old home, fighting the new problem of Evan's disgrace; recalled the woman flung into the street from a saloon, who had made him think of Frieda. Of course, it had not been Frieda; therefore he was not responsible and until this moment had forgotten. Now he felt that his sense of freedom from responsibility because the woman was not Frieda, was as frightful as if it had been Frieda—was the abyss within and beneath him. —Jonathan, with eyes again young, looked up at Greta who came in followed by Jeff.

She sat in the straight chair near the door; sure of her closeness with her son, she was not jealous of his talking with his father. But if something was wrong . . . Jeff began to discuss a mere business matter: a client for whom he had already done a good deal of work wanted to retrench and was making trouble. If that was all, it could have waited and not dragged her boy from home on a wet night. But Greta said nothing: you had to allow the men to do as they wished, wait your chance, and perhaps undo. She got up, leaving the door open, and went back to her dull book. After a rumble of words, she heard Jonathan's slow step and the library door shut. She sighed. They had some secret!

Jonathan sat near the fire. "Bring your chair up. Your mother's worried about your catching a chill." They gazed at the cold blue gas flames rising irrelevant from the asbestos logs.

"These fake fireplaces," said Jeff, "are an abomination."

"Your uncle Philip used to say that, in the old house. Just the same, on a night like tonight, this would be a cold room—"

"I'd rather have it a bit cold."

"You're more of an artist than I."

"That's over. We're both businessmen, dad."

"Uncle Philip's not a bad businessman, himself. Raoul Mendis told me he's one of the best salesmen in the toy trade. He's a big boy and he loves animals. That helps."

Jeff smiled. "Once an animal fell in love with me. That ought to help."

His father was serious. "Tell me about it."

"It was the night I found Schmitt in the Club; you know, the night I learned that Rebecca had gone to Paris."

"Last summer?"

"I was so mad at the fellow's crudities in front of his cronies that I walked up Fifth Avenue, all the way from Washington Square, without knowing where I was or what I was doing. I guess hate drove me along, like the explosions in an internal combustion motor. Suddenly a little dog ran out and looked at me. He was a brown spaniel with huge rococo ears, like a bewigged gentleman at the court of Louis Fourteenth. He looked at me and that made me stop and grow aware of myself. I'd reached the Park! He was wagging his tail. Suddenly he jumped up, resting his front paws on me, and looked at me with eyes that seemed nothing but love. He recognized me, as if I was real! and he accepted me. . . . You'll laugh at me, dad."

"No, I won't."

"Suddenly, I felt healed. Of hate, I mean, and anger. There was something so easy about the puppy's attitude, I caught it. I was free of both Marius and Rebecca. I patted the dog's head; he sniffed at my hand, gave it a lick that was both recognition and a satisfactory taste, and ran off, wagging his stump of a tail. As if he were taking me along! You know, dad, nothing was ever right between Rebecca and me; even physically nothing was good. Now I seemed to know why. When I was close to her body, I was close to her conflict. You can't make love to a conflict . . . to a division. At least I can't. The embrace of passion, I learned, must be the most spiritual thing in all the world. That's why it went wrong with us." Jeff spoke into the fire, feeling his father, not daring to face him. "When Corinna came back from the mountains, I told her about Rebecca. You can guess how she took it."

"Corinna's a gallant woman."

"That's what brought Rebecca back. Beside Corinna, Rebecca's so weak, so *needy*." Now Jeff turned to his father and smiled. "The little dog's cure didn't last. And I never saw him again."

Full of his son, Jonathan saw his city hallucination-sharp as if he were detached from it. He saw the streets, the straight streets, the rigid houses: the cold rectangular hardness was a reaction of resistance to its mortal opposite, the swirling pressures . . . not straight, not hard . . . of men and women. There was a fury in them that could not issue; the streets of harsh houses, the laws, the customs and pursuits, kept the breath and the flesh inside! The city was frozen violence, and against it the nerves of the men and women were sore. . . .

Jeff passed nervous fingers through his hair; he was saying: "It's the

443

endless swing, up and down, that makes me dizzy. Sometimes I feel I can't stand it any longer. Sometimes I feel it would be better to fall off."

"Hold on!" said his father softly.

"I'm in a bad way, dad. I keep seeing Rebecca in Paris, and needing to be with her. But for what? To be free of her? I keep feeling, if I could get past the *break* in her, we'd both be healed. Healed of what? I need to find *her*. If she's alone, I need to find her. If Schmitt's there (he said he was going), I need to find her." His voice grew more quiet. "I told Corinna."

"You've told Corinna what?"

"That it's my business to find her, although I don't know why. Unfinished business of the worst kind, a builder's nightmare: where the foundations are wrong and have to be torn up, or the whole thing falls."

"What does Corinna say?"

"Corinna says: 'Go, if you have to go.'"

Jonathan mused for a long pause. "Perhaps she's right."

Jeff smiled. "To her, this is a sort of disease I've contracted and that must run its course. She's not afraid. She's certain I'll come back to health; and to her, she and I . . . our marriage . . . is health."

"Isn't it true?"

"The words don't make sense any more, dad. Health, disease, love —they've lost their meaning."

As Jeff looked from the gas flames toward his father, Jonathan saw in his son's eyes a bewilderment that hurt him, as if suddenly he felt a dark stone in, his own heart.

"I can't advise you, Jeff. I don't dare. I'm not as brave as Corinna."

Jeff stood up. His confession had been a steep climb, and here, sudden before him, was its destination. He said quietly: *"I* know I have to go."

Jonathan stood at his son's side and they looked down into the fire. "I'll go with you, Jeff, if you'll let me."

V

KNOWLEDGE

PARIS!, THE TRAIN DREW THEM THROUGH THE SUB-urbs: gray low buildings, slate-gray mansard roofs, soot-gray chimney pots and the sky gray. With a last pipe of the engine they subsided in the Gare du Nord, a cave of smoke and crowds strident, somehow blithe. Then the cab went down with them into the city. Pavements were wet, houses and sky were one wet color, but the city bloomed. Café terraces with men and women wreathed around the tables, streets of dancing, laughing, singing throngs, waved above them. It was, Jeff explained to his father, Mardi gras. They crossed boulevards that flashed and sparked like pistons, they followed a long empty street, the rue de Richelieu, that shut out revelry, and Jonathan felt its quiet to be the constant substance of the city. The long monumental building, Jeff whispered, was the Bibliothèque Nationale; little squares flared in trees and green grass; streets criss-crossed under lanterns that sealed house to dark afternoon. Again a gay thoroughfare, pulsant as a dynamo: modern shops, galleries, the Comédie Française (Jeff pointed); a swift tunnel and the immense calm measure of the Louvre. A bridge dealt them deftly over the Seine, and before the *rive gauche* closed them in, they breathed the ease of Paris on its river, in its hills, its church spires drawing heaven and the centuries together. Now they moved through mazed dark ·streets, the houses all in tune, modern dance jetting from eighteenth-century doors, folk electric in cafés within stone mellow and soft as candles. Jonathan kept insisting to himself: —Paris is real *today!* not history, not literature; men and women live here *now* and with success. He could not overcome the sense (though his mind shamed it) of a charade whose answers were his own American life. On the steamer, it had come to him: —If life has meaning, in most lives it is only latent. My destiny is to act out my meaning. His legal career had become merely a means of making money: was that implicit in his "noble" ambition—and his mother's? Evan's character had involved disgrace and death and Rebecca; were these implicit in what he had truly loved in Evan? Greta's distance,

447

the nearness of Frieda, Mrs. Lake, and Marius: how were they fulfilments of what he really wanted? And now this dubious journey to Paris? He struggled against the absurdity and there it was, real, so real it did not need belief. (What one needed to believe in was not real.) From the Gare du Nord to the Hotel Lutétia, Jeff told him, they had cut through the very heart of the great town. "Let's wash up quickly and go out. What a day to arrive in Paris!" Jeff's excitement momentarily made Rebecca remote.

The Boulevard Saint Michel throbbed wtih students and their girls, resilient, noisy, quaffing the city as if it were a family cup of wine. Clinging couples unashamed of their desire, youths four abreast jostling others, their dress careless and impromptu, they were children of the ancient stone cadences around them. Jonathan thought of New York's high houses that dwarfed and made men alien. . . . In the Luxembourg Gardens, lamplight was phosphorescent on the statues and spangled the damp trees. Jonathan saw the iron fence that defended the grace of bowered shrubs and of lovers, and a scene from his boyhood was with him: a man impaled through the throat on the spearpoint of an iron railing. That violence had been war—he had read hope in it! This violent gaiety was peace, yet somehow hopeless. The father looked at his son. They were strangers among these ripe and lovely streets, in this gay cynical resignation of revelers exploiting the Lenten fast ahead which few would honor. He wanted to take Jeff's hand and lead him back to the green raw world three thousand miles away.

The next morning, Jeff went to find Rebecca; Jonathan sat in the hotel lobby with his Paris edition of the *New York Herald* and his red Baedeker, bible of the tourist; and methodically planned his day. (He was going to leave Jeff alone, to be merely passive; but it was alien to his nature not to profit by his presence in Paris.) The old horse-drawn *sapins* were so delightfully cheap that he could ride around all day with a clear conscience; the sudden watery sun (he did not know how rare it was for Paris in the spring) washed the seething measured city. On the third afternoon (Jeff came back to sleep, worn and silent, revealing nothing except that Marius was in Paris), Jonathan drank his beer at a table of a café terrace, reading his first letter from home. Greta was well, so were Corinna and

448

the babies; Greta hoped her two big "boys" were enjoying their well-earned vacation. Did Jonathan know that Reuben was arriving in Paris and that Belinda was there? Jonathan and Jeff should see them, it would make them feel at home. Across from Jonathan was the church of Saint Germain des Près: those gray walls in their first centuries had stood in meadows, and Paris had crept up from its little island; and the walls' simple strength, pure act, seemed ready to outlast the confusion of shops, buses, modern buildings, commerce and vanity, that swarmed around them. A murmur moved from the direction of the "Boule' Mich'"; thickened and rose; at last Jonathan saw a tumult of students that now filled the Boulevard Saint Germain between the sidewalks. Their voices and placards shouted: *Vive Jaurès! Vive l'Internationale! Vive Anatole France! À bas le militarisme! À bas le service militaire de trois ans!* They came, their ranks irregular and shifting, youths loitering, running ahead, but serious. Soon they gorged the square before the church and the diagonal rue de Rennes, and their ranks became solid. A cordon of gendarmes stretched across the boulevard to block them; moved slowly forward against them; the students were pushed back but a number were sieved through the police line. The mass of demonstrators turned about. Now, at the end of the square where they had entered, another line of gendarmes moved slowly forward. Again the students were pushed back; again a number were filtered out and separated from the mass. Back and forth, under the church, the ever-lessening mass was squeezed between the two forward-moving lines of gendarmes and at each contact a number were sieved through; those remaining turned and were pushed against the other line where more were filtered out. Jonathan watched with amazement. The gendarmes did their work as expert craftsmen, their sticks raised but touching no one, with a minimum of effort. The students were angry, but even their anger was detached, part of the game; and the game continued, until the mass of students was sloughed off, the gendarmes gone, and the normal Paris crowd under the millenial church took the square back to itself.

Jonathan knew what the demonstration meant. France, feeling the threat of the saber-rattling Kaiser, had voted to increase its army by lengthening its national military service; and the students, who followed the great Socialist, Jaurès, and who read Zola, Anatole France,

449

Péguy, did not like it. They too, expressing hope, touched violence? There had been something frightening to Jonathan in the forbearance of the gendarmes: its motive not sympathy for the thought or flesh of the young men but a disdainful economy of effort, a mechanical skill more cruel than anger.

At last (the few days had seemed long and heavy) Jonathan was to have a chance to judge what was happening between Jeff and Rebecca: friends were coming to her place this evening, and he was invited. Rebecca lived in a spic-and-span apartment house on the new Boulevard Raspail. The automatic lift, tight as a closet, creaked with breathtaking hesitations up to the top story. Rebecca stood in the doorway, and again Jonathan was pierced by the fragile impatient palpitance of her face, sudden and separate on her body like a flower on a slender stem. Her eyes scarcely acknowledged him, as if too occupied by some continuous inner turmoil. The high-ceilinged room, bare of pictures and curtains, with two shrill lamps in parchment shades, and cannel coal burning in the hearth where Jeff and Marius stood, seemed naked and unrelated to Rebecca. There were a few other guests, among them Belinda, who had mysteriously changed into Hadassah Hartt, economist and Zionist, a squat forceful woman, and a short man deeply glowing, who appeared to be her friend and whose name was Baruch Brande. Jonathan was aware of himself: his bones brittle, his flesh without tension, yet his mind unsubdued and wonderfully free. Marius and Jeff were in an argument, which went on and on. "Swell," Marius jeered. "All you got to do is build beautiful homes and the folks who live in 'em will be beautiful." "I didn't say that! I said—" It was hard for Jonathan to follow the talk. Rebecca too seemed out of it. She sat deep in an armchair and smoked cigarettes, her green frock revealing both the gauntness and the rondures of her body, the too-bright lamp making her hair a copper helmet and her eyes pale fire. Jonathan sat next to her, but she was moved by no need to talk, the silence between them troubled him alone.

"Do you like your work here?" at last he said.

"Yes . . . It's all right."

"You're staying in Paris indefinitely?"

"Now I'm going to have a bit of a vacation."

"Where will you go?"

"We haven't quite decided."

"*We?*" he ventured.

She smiled and gestured with her head toward the two men still standing and arguing over the hearth. At that moment, Marius stopped his tirade; his face darkened as if his breath were suddenly cut off.

"What's wrong with him?" asked Jonathan. "He looks sick."

"He has those little spells. They don't last. You see—?" Schmitt was shouting again.

"Does he do anything about it? Does he see a doctor?"

"I don't think so."

"But perhaps he should. Perhaps it's his heart."

"He knows it's his heart. And *he* doesn't care—" as if to suggest: Why then should you or I?

"Rebecca, tell me. Just now, when you said 'We'—"

"Did you come here to spy on us?"

He was ready to attack her; then he realized that she was suffering, and that she needed to suffer. Anything he said would be fuel for her self-burning; Marius and Jeff were fuel for her conflict's need to feed itself.

"I'm going to leave," he got up and took her hand. "I'm not here to spy, my dear."

"Why then?"

"I don't know," his smile faded and he went toward the two men.

"I'm off too," Marius surprised him. "Got to work tonight."

They were alone in the tight little lift clicking its way down; they stood body to body. Marius was a head taller, sixty pounds heavier, and much of his weight was muscle. —So this strong fellow has a bad heart? thought Jonathan, and wished that Marius would die. —He has a good head; yes, this anarcho-syndicalism was not nonsense. Within the revelers of Mardi gras, within the gracious Louvre, and within the thin new towers of his own Manhattan, Jonathan knew, this moment in the car clicking downward, that catastrophe was coming. Because catastrophe was here! This fellow's theoretic violence, class war and general strike, was simply a use (as engineers use a waterfall) of the rising world potential. Schmitt was wrong about the reality of his ends, mythic and ideal (you can't make peace with war); but he was right about the motive-power: *violence!* —How do I know?

451

I wish the man were dead because stupidly (I know better) his being out of the way would simplify Jeff's problem. —I could kill him now! *(Deuxième étage.)* If I were as big as Marius and he as short as I, would I dare kill him? No doubt I want to. It would be a safe crime. No motive was visible. And no one in Rebecca's busily talking *garçonnière,* except Jeff, had seen them leave together. —I'd strangle him, I'd drop the elevator to the basement, pull him out (the *concierge* lives on the ground floor), ride up to the street and go home. *(Rez-de-chaussée.)* Jonathan was appalled at his own thoughts. —At this instant, my morality lies in my weakness? *The world has no such safeguard.* Then catastrophe is here. . . . They walked silently together to the street. —The fellow begets violence in others. That's a lie! He may arouse, he cannot beget. . . .

The Paris night was indolent, a lovely beast between warm and cold, sleeping and waking, satiety and hunger. Across the boulevard, a new apartment with florid balconies (pastry style, Jeff called it) rose above a large provision shop with fruits and vegetables behind shut glass doors; and a little below, the way Marius was turning, the mansions of the Boulevard Saint Germain lay in mist. Jonathan's hotel was in the opposite direction.

"How about a glass of something, Marius, before you go?"

At the boulevards' junction they entered a modest workers' café and went up to the *comptoir.* Behind the ponderous nickel-plated coffee machine stood the *patronne,* her red-veined mustachio'd face blooming above her stuffed magenta blouse. The bar was empty.

"Messieurs désirent?"

"Café black and a cognac," said Marius.

"Un bock, s'il vous plaît," said Jonathan. "Rebecca tells me you have heart attacks." Jonathan watched himself transfer his murderous impulse into sympathy—*and it worked.* Sincere advice was ready.

Marius swallowed his *petit verre.* "Is that what you wanted to talk to me about?" He slid the slender-stemmed glass toward the woman whose huge hand refilled it to the brim, precise, spilling no drop.

"Marius, I used to know your mother."

About to gulp his second drink, Marius lowered the glass.

"Aren't you interested, Marius? Do you mind my mentioning it? Your mother worked in our house when I was a boy. Until she was married. But it was more than that . . . Much more! I knew your father. I even knew you, when you were a baby."

The woman leaned her hard eyes toward them: "The broken glass, monsieur, that'll cost you one franc extra."

"Thanks for the drink," said Marius, who did not seem to hear her. He dropped the broken pieces of the glass on the counter and walked out. Jonathan saw that his hand was bleeding.

2

JONATHAN WALKED UP THE BOULEVARD TO THE hotel, but his mind went its own way. Why does he think of Belinda, now Hadassah, changed so violently from her girlhood and her father's shallow world, a woman now of roots? Then her friend was with him. He had spoken no word to him. Now Baruch Brande says: "I know you went down with Marius Schmitt, and you killed him." "Are you going to tell?" "Why should I? and whom should I tell? You've murdered before. But isn't it unreasonable to be offended that Schmitt hid his heart from you in the café—indeed you are offended!—when you'd just murdered him? You've always been proud of your murders, but though your modern principles approve, aren't you going a bit far to expect your victims to be thankful?" Jonathan sees Brande—the man glowed—more clear than the dim gray houses of the night. "Don't worry that you're a murderer," he says. "Who isn't, among us moderns with our pride that we're superior to our fathers, Jew or Christian? But do find out *whom* you have murdered: that'll be something new and hopeful in the world."

Jonathan opened the door into the hotel room, full of the hurt he had uncovered in Marius: a hurt more terribly his, because Marius would not share it. The room was muffled and too warm. A maid had turned down the two beds, their linen and red satin quilts gleaming against the single table lamp between them; curtains canopied in maroon brocade banished the windows, the carpet was thick, and the chairs floridly upholstered. As if afraid of shadows, he turned on all the lights: on the walls stood delicate pastels of the canals of Venice. It was an ingratiating room, more personal than those machines of comfort, the rooms of American hotels; but cloying as if its human touch were treacherous. He undressed quickly (he never waited for Jeff, if Jeff was late), opened a window slightly although the night was mild (the window worked like a door on adjustable rods), turned out all the lights, and sank in the warm bed.

He awoke cold. —I'm dreaming. He was encased in ice. Greta was there, but not close enough to warm him. The whole world was ice. He heard a violent hacking, it was Marius striking with an axe at the ice. He could not see Marius, but it was he, and the shattering blows were close to Jeff. Evan was on the side of Marius, and his mother was against him; Greta and Frieda and his father were warm and Rebecca was numb, not cold, not warm. Of course, he did not see them: —I'm lying in bed in the dark. But Jeff was in danger. If only Greta would warm him; then he might reach Jeff! Jeff was on the side of Marius; unlike Evan who did nothing, Jeff was directing Marius whose blows shattered the ice, but did not destroy it. And his son's flesh and the ice were intervolved! (It was all impossible, it was a dream, but the dread was real, and the danger.) They were all rigid in the ice: why did not Greta warm him? He struggled, unable to move, and touched pain: naked, pellucid ice. He raised his voice to warn Jeff, and it was soundless against ice. Suddenly the vibrance of his flesh, each nerve a throbbing wire frozen hard, became a question: *Who am I?* He was his son! The displacement of his entrails into Jeff's body was an unbearable anguish; the agony awoke him. He lay, still cold in bed, and heard the knocking on the window. The rod holding it open had loosened, the wind moved it. He was alone in the room. In his bare feet, still within the ice of his dream, Jonathan went to the window and closed it. His mind said: "The knocking of the window, that was the cause of my dream."

Again the voice of Brande: "That's a lie and you know it, whatever you *believe*. You murder your dream, you murder your roots (you call that reason and progress), you murder the spirit of your wife with 'standards' and your son with 'plans'." His voice fell to a whisper: "You murder yourself; and yet you wonder that your self rises up against you. . . ." Stubbornly, in bed again hearing the rain, Jonathan repeated: "It was the knocking of the window. You're overwrought. It was the knocking of the window." His reason soothed him to sleep.

He awoke late and at once turned to the bed beside him: Jeff was not there. He was warm, his nightshirt was damp with perspiration. He lay in his warmth, hungry for it, defending himself from the dream's distant ice-wall. Jeff must have stayed with Rebecca—what of it? He ordered breakfast in bed. The fragrant *croissants,* the hot *café au lait,* caressed his stomach and made it confident. But although his

455

body and mind were warm again, and the dream lost, the warmth had no depth. He read the news from home in the Paris *New York Herald*. Taft and Roosevelt—. He dressed and went down to the lobby, told the clerk at the desk he would soon be back, in case Jeff telephoned, and stepped out into Paris.

A cool sun with scudding clouds in a sharp sky seemed to mirror the streets still bright with the dawn's rain. He found himself in the Carrefour de la Croix Rouge where the rue du Cherche-Midi, the rue de Sèvres, the rue de Grenelle (he savored the names), came together. The food shops redolent of cheeses and fresh bread, the bars where men, lean, flexible and hard, already drank *vin blanc* tart as the day, the strepitous omnibuses, lush women at corners selling flowers from the Riviera, and the ancient rue du Dragon, handcarts in its gutters, housewives arguing from high dark windows, all came together at home under the sky. When he got back to their room, Jeff, still wearing his overcoat, stood in the light of the window, and his resemblance to his mother struck Jonathan like a revelation.

"I hope you didn't worry."

"No." The resemblance to Greta, since Jeff loved Rebecca, was increasing. What did this mean? That Greta was ever farther away, so that Jonathan saw the resemblance as a stranger sees it? or that the Greta in their son was truly growing?

"Rebecca wanted me to stay."

His father tried to be light. "This is Paris."

"It's not that. I mean, dad, it's not because this is Paris. I mean—"

"I understand. I'm sorry I said that. This is more serious."

What was the Greta in Jeff? What could there be of Greta in Jeff's tragic bondage to a woman incapable of giving? Deeper than the similarity of color in Jeff and his mother, deeper than the difference of eyes and mouth and nose and shape of head, was it a configuration of features through expression, as if Jeff were coming to resemble his mother because their lives, in a way yet unread, were one? And would he know the woman with whom he had lived for over thirty years only by the life he had begotten in her?

"I'm going away for a while, dad, if you don't mind being alone. Lent's a good time for Rebecca to have a vacation; a friend last night

456

—someone from where she works—offered her a house for a couple of weeks. On the Ile d'Oléron."

"Where is that?"

"Somewhere off the coast. I'm vague about it myself. Probably a bit of real old France; probably not a telephone or an auto on the island."

"So you and Rebecca are going there together?"

"It's pretty far south. We may find spring." He spoke too quickly, Jonathan thought; he was eluding something.

"And Rebecca will be cook?"

Jeff laughed too hurriedly. "No hut in France so humble it lacks a peasant woman in the neighborhood glad to add a few francs to the family stocking. I'd hate to count on Rebecca's cooking."

"This is serious, Jeff. I wanted a resolution, of course; so did Corinna. But now it's here . . . now Marius is out of the way—"

In the bitter smile that made Jeff's face look tender, Jonathan saw Greta suffering: "Who said anything of Marius' being out of the way? If he's out of the way, I don't know it."

"You're going with her! You're going to *live* with her?"

Jeff sank into a chair; then he got up, threw off his coat. Half turned away, he said as if to the wall: "Marius is coming."

"Do you know what you're saying? Do you know what you're doing? This time, Jeff, say no. If you go with the girl, you must insist that Marius stay out. That it's finished with Marius. Or you stay out."

Jeff was staring at his father.

"Don't you see," Jonathan went on, "don't you see the girl is playing with you? She's torturing you to torture herself."

The young man did not contradict, did not react; vacantly staring.

"Answer me, Jeff. Don't you know?"

Jeff moistened his lips with his tongue and slowly focused his eyes to his father's. "Whether she's torturing me, as you put it? I suppose so."

"And you're going to play her game?"

Jeff got up. "I thought you understood."

"Does that mean to submit? to let you go on, till your whole life falls to pieces? Don't impose too much on the endurance of Corinna; on the strength of your own family ties. You came here to settle this, not to drag it out."

At last, Jeff said: "I thought I understood why you understood. Why you came along. That woman of yours: she was playing a game too, and you forgave her. You never forgave uncle Reuben, because he stopped her."

"Jeff! with whom are you comparing Rebecca?"

"Why not?" Jeff smiled sternly. "Perhaps your woman was a swindler. She needed money and went after it. Where? In the man who cared for her. Rebecca needs pain and war. She goes after it in the man who cares for her."

Jonathan said nothing. Jeff went on: "A woman can love a man, and blackmail him, strip him, humiliate him, kill him. Isn't that what you learned? I thought that was what made you understand me and Rebecca."

Now it was the father who sank in his chair while Jeff stood over him.

Jonathan said: "Then you knew? you knew all along?"

"Rebecca," said Jeff, "happens not to be interested in money. What she wants is blood. Where does she take it? From a stranger? Of course not! Blood that loves her is what she wants; blood that perhaps she loves, after her fashion."

There was a long silence. Jeff placed a hand on his father's shoulder. "You'll let me go?"

Jonathan slowly swayed his head, without looking up from his chair. Then he met Jeff's eyes: "It should be pleasant on that island."

Jeff laughed. "The old house, I'm told, dates back to when Oléron belonged to England. The wine, I hear, is better than bordeaux."

Jeff packed his bag and went, Jonathan was alone. He was not idle. He wrote almost daily to his wife and sent long letters of instructions to his office, from which he received reports and documents by every boat. To Corinna he wrote that while Jeff was "traveling with friends" his letters home might be delayed, and not to worry. Assiduously, he read the continental editions of *The New York Herald* and London's *Daily Mail* and improved his French with papers ranging from the conservative *Le Temps* to the radical *L'Humanité*. He did not give up his wanderings about Paris, taking a different bus each time and getting off at hazard. (His rheumatism, strangely enough, despite the damp climate, troubled him scarcely at all.) He spent a few dull hours with a lawyer friend and others with a client who had found his address in the *Herald*. From Jeff came a letter chiefly describing the barnyard pigeons and rabbits before they went into the kitchen pot, and the peasant girl who cooked like an artist and was accumulating her *dot* (husband not yet selected) like a miser. Then Reuben sent a *petit bleu* inviting him to dinner.

Jonathan climbed on the *impériale* of an electric tram. The unwieldy vehicle lurched him on his high seat (it was cold and few passengers sat on the open roof) from the Boulevard Saint Germain with its stately monotone of mansions past the Gare d'Orsay, windy, glittering and hollow; over the Pont de Solférino spangled above the Seine, across the arcades noisy as bazaars of the noble rue de Rivoli, into the Place de la Concorde. Suddenly, a danger signal about Jeff possessed him. It filled the void of the great square, its emptiness surrounded by geometric grace was suddenly crowded with disaster. He realized he had thought little of Jeff, these days filled with busy trivialities; his unconsciousness had been a "concord" like this square which now Jeff brimmed and overflowed. —Jeff is in trouble! Through the early night the Champs Elysées (—Evan and Rebecca in Elysium!) rose to the Arc de Triomphe in a vast dimness; the tram swung suddenly with the Seine into the Cours la Reine, jolting him against the side of his seat, and he had a dual sense of the proud continental city and of his son in some unknown anguish: a double picture like those of the stereoscopes of his boyhood, in which each half gave depth to the other. Scarcely aware of what he did, he clambered down the twining stairs of the tram at the Place de l'Alma, followed a tree-bordered avenue toward the Place de l'Étoile, and entered the hotel lobby. He felt the inundation of his trouble: irrational worry or presentiment? He crossed the soft carpet toward the marble desk where the clerk waited; and found he did not know for whom to ask. Before the clerk could notice, he turned and sat in an armchair in view of the lift, a steel-lacework column that rose to the high ceiling. The car came down, discharged guests, took on others; came down again . . . and again. He waited for the name to come back, glad of the lobby's warmth after the chill of his ride which he felt only now. At last he saw him: the tall, white-haired American in a dinner coat, the hollow face, the arched brow: his brother Reuben.

459

"Jonathan! Why didn't you announce yourself? I knew you must be here. You're never late. Well, how are you?" He did not stop. "Belinda's dining with us. *She* is always late. Effect of those Polacks and Russian Jews she runs around with, I suppose. We'd better eat here. I meant to take you to Foyot or La Pérouse. Unfortunately, I must run off at nine. But I assure you we'd not have had a more excellent dinner. You'll see what the chef in this hotel can do. Our Ambassador wants to see me. 'Royal command,' you know, even if he is a Republican." He laughed at his own jest. "I suspect the State Department cabled him to sound me about China . . . There she is now. Who's that with her? By gad, she's brought one of her Russians! Well, he won't eat us, and we certainly won't eat him."

Belinda came across the lobby with Baruch Brande, and soon the four were at table. His sense of Jeff in trouble had been sudden; but whatever it was, the trouble itself had been a gradual rising, and now in its flood Jonathan felt relief. It was hard to grasp the reality of those he sat with. This Brande tended to merge with his fantasy of Brande, walking home from Marius with the bleeding hand; this Belinda continued to be apart from Reuben's daughter. The food was real enough, as was the solemnly obsequious *maître d'hôtel* and the haughty *sommelier* who selected the wine. And obvious in Reuben was his reinflation by the call to the Embassy. He kept talking about China.

". . . grand fellow, Yuan Shih K'ai, the new President, you know, of the new National Assembly. When I was there, he was Acting Viceroy of Chihli. Friend of the Dowager Empress and, what's more, of the Powers. He's a monarchist at heart; just the man, as I shall tell Washington, to be President of the Republic."

Belinda said: "Sun Yat Sen?"

"He's out, thank goodness. A firebrand . . . an unpractical dreamer."

Brande was listening with respectful attention, and yet detached as if he were dreaming. Both he and Belinda seemed remote from the table, and Reuben with his steady talk that was defensive seemed to be working hard to keep them so.

"When are you and Jeff going back?" he asked Jonathan. "Of course, the boats at this off-season are half empty, you can take your time about deciding. Except the new *Cosmopolis*. She'll be crowded. They say she's a wonder, and everyone wants to sail on her maiden trip. I'm booked. If it fits in with your schedule, Jon, let me know. I think I can get Demarest to find you a cabin. He's a business associate of mine now; that's what I was doing in London. A new automobile self-starter. I might be able to get you in on that, too, if you have a few idle thousands knocking about that you'd like to bring you twenty per cent. Cars in a few years will not be cranked. I'm as sure of that as I'm sure that John Hay's Open Door has started a century of peace and prosperity in China."

Brande smiled in a dream; his lips mumbled in his thick Russian accent: "Isn't that beautiful, when one American statesman can make four-hundred-million Orientals happy for a hundred years?"

"Well," said Reuben, vaguely disturbed, "I don't mean Hay alone; not even *us* alone. We've got to give some credit to the Japs. Splendid little fellows. Not everyone knows they had a lot to do with the abdication of the Manchu dynasty. They want the Open Door too, and they know they can't hold it single-handed. They're our best friends, the Japs, now they've got Korea and their fishery concessions. They're keen, faithful, progressive—the best servants in the world. Sun Yat Sen's party, the Kuomintang, may give a little trouble for a year or so, till the new President and the Canton generals clean 'em up, with us and Japan taking care of exports and imports. But after all, the Open Door *is* our idea."

Baruch Brande's Asiatic lips were thick but exquisitely subtle. They curled faintly. "Open doors," he smiled apologetically, "let in the flies."

"I agree, sir," Reuben said. "Democracies need safeguards. In Germany it's the army; in England it's the aristocracy. In China now with the Republic it'll be the ruling classes allied to foreign trade. Isn't the same thing happening in Russia? Aren't your landowners turning to industry and banking? If so, all will be well."

"The flies, Mr. Ambassador, are such little people. You can't buy 'em with gold . . . And they're hard to shoot down with cannon, especially when they get inside the house. Then if you shoot, you shoot your house down."

Reuben looked reproachfully at his daughter: —What kind of imbecile have you brought to dine with us? He looked at his watch.

461

"I'm afraid I must be leaving. Can't keep the Ambassador waiting. Especially since what I have to say will probably have to go by pouch to Washington."

"Uncle Jonathan," said Belinda, when the three were left sipping their coffee, "you don't look well. What do you hear of Jeff?"

There was something strange about this gentle Brande; even conventional lies were impossible before him. Jonathan said nothing to Belinda who seemed to understand and changed the subject. "Papa's like a big child, isn't he? I guess he never grew up. I guess in his growing-up time he was too busy making money to grow up."

"You can say that," said Jonathan, "about the whole modern world."

"There's always time," said Brande.

"You mean: it's never too late?" Jonathan was aroused.

"Not for the living." Brande looked at him, and Jonathan saw the quiet gray eyes rippling with humor, warmed by a deep sun.

In the street, Belinda said: "We must *rush;* we're terribly late," and asked the doorman to call a taxi.

"Never mind, dear," said Brande. "We'll look at the people when we arrive and see just what's happened."

"But the wrong thing may have happened already, if we're not there in time."

Brande, stepping into the cab after Belinda, touched Jonathan's arm: "So long as there is woman, there is hope."

Then Jonathan was walking in the luminous damp night of Paris, alone again with his fear for his son. There's always time; it's never too late . . . for the living; and the man's smile, and his touch on his arm, went with him. —What must I do? His impotence weighed heavy. How could he decide, when he knew nothing? when he had no way of knowing? He was an educated rational man, and he was utterly without *method* to pierce the fog of his emotions, to dissociate subjective fear from facts, to trace the roots, much less the effects, of his actions. Technics for everything except for living! except for the values that made life human! Was he responsible for Jeff's journey to Paris? for Jeff's dangerous journey to Oléron? How could he be responsible even for himself, moving blind through a blind world? Its clarities were falsehoods! that at least was clear. The proud new century, already more than a decade old, was cardboard: the democratic slogans, the Hague Peace Tribunal, the empires military and commercial, the new skyscrapers on lower Broadway—all cardboard! and behind their flimsiness lived hope which, to breathe, must break through, burn down. That was the disaster ahead, and it was integral with hope. But where was the method for hope's first step, lest it burn and break itself? The man Baruch Brande (his ugly face resembled Jonathan's image of a medieval monk) seemed to glow in a strength that must be method . . . method in life's madness. —What you need is a nucleus to start with, though it be no bigger than a point: a focus, a solid fulcrum for the leverage of action. And it must be in you. But you're in chaos. The focus, then, in you must also be beyond you. Beyond . . . beyond . . . how far beyond to reach solidity? Nothing less than the whole of life could make the viewpoint focus solid ground. He thought of his father's sense of a God within the humblest soul, within the humblest human behavior, and yet universal. That was a method for surety; and those who had lost it roamed the world, gained the whole world, from microcosm to astronomy, mastered the powers of sun and atom, and were still lost in a ravening jungle. The method to replace that old one could not be mechanics, whose principle was addition. Add a trillion shifting atoms of the world, combine, juggle, transmute them; still you have a trillion shifting atoms, no solid integer. The method must be beyond arithmetic—or calculus. Let a man somehow—not equate, not identify, but transmute and naturalize himself in that which was not he, and he could build: all else was to build confusion.

He had been walking a long time in this Paris. He knew because his clothes were damp, the streets, faces, endless ejaculations of electric lights, lay in his mind. He had an animal's sense of time and distance: organic, without words. He felt dimly the trail of his walking away from the Seine, away from the gracious rhetoric of the Tuileries and from the boulevards' swarming, into mazes of streets close-coiled like cells of a brain. A brain, this Paris, dark and yet lambent with feeling and with thinking. His own New York was no such curved matter: its angular streets were inorganic, outside the men and women who built them with the rigid deaths of their unicellular coral motions. The organicity of Paris sustained him. The dampness of his clothes, which

463

his mind told him was mere humid air, seemed the immersion in a living plasm. He walked without pain or fatigue. But this would lead him to no method! this was a dying into history! Was he not walking away from his need to know and to decide? away from himself?

He was in a fantastic quarter. Huge tin sheds loomed and glinted to the sky, their electric lights deepening the darkness. Immense bins were half-filled with tawny potatoes, with shrill green vegetables. Behind counters hung whole carcasses of beeves and muttons on bloody hooks and an odor of earth, of leafage, of blood, fought the night. A few men and women worked like dwarfs among the hills of carrots, tomatoes, turnips, beans, the deep mounds of slaughtered flesh. Thin lines of two-wheeled carts heavily converged on the sheds, the slow, ponderous horses knowing their way while the reins flapped on their backs and their drivers slept on the box. Jonathan knew of the great *Halles* of Paris. He must have walked for hours, these marts came to life past midnight: where had he come from? He found that he was hungry. His indolence was strong, tending toward some goal, but of the way beyond his hunger he had only a dim sense. He prodded with his mind; —where have I been? who am I? encountered pain and became humble: he wanted to eat, he was on his way: that was all he could know without hurting. Opposite a giant wall of sheds and bins was a row of lighted restaurants, and above one door an electric snail beckoned to a carpeted stair: a bright room with mostly empty tables, red leather banquettes along the walls beneath mirrors, smote his eyes used to the night. Feeling faint, he sat down and when the waiter stood over him with a long menu said: "Bring me something to eat; anything that's ready." Several unattached girls near the service bar eyed him; seeing the waiter puzzled, a tall one with a black mane of hair gathered at her neck, and a plump little one with porcelain-blue eyes, came over.

"You want to eat?" he asked.

"Bien sûr!" they both laughed and sat down.

The tall one said: "Anglais? I spik Eenglish."

"American." He saw the dark and the blond eyes gleam: he knew American to them meant money.

They ordered elaborately. When the waiter returned with a bottle of wine, they scolded him and sent it away; he came back with a different bottle, dusty and reclining in its basket.

464

"He's all damp!" the blond girl felt Jonathan's overcoat and pulled it off.

The tall one leaned down and touched his trousers under the table. "*Les pantalons aussi. Tout mouillés. Faut ôter ça—un peu plus tard.*"

"I'm afraid not," he said. "I have to go on a long journey."

"When?"

"Right away."

"*Où ça?*"

Without surprise, he heard himself: "*À l'Île d'Oléron.*"

The waiter brought snails, and they showed him how to draw them succulent from their shells. The little woman was maternal, the tall woman was obscene. But now, in their gestures and words, their traits became confused, each was a split element of one, and their separateness vanished: Jonathan thought of his wife, and longed for Greta who would give him food, draw off his wet clothes, take him to bed.

The two were angrily arguing: Where was l'Ile d'Oléron? The tall woman said it was in the Midi near Toulon. "*Idiote,*" said the other, "you're thinking of les Iles d'Hyères." "Well, where is it, you who know so much?" "Near Biarritz." The debate grew ugly. The doll-blue eyes were harder, the round face flushed about its paint; under her rouge the dark one paled. More food appeared and they forgot to eat.

They were two hostile elements that belonged together as one woman. Then he would have a name again, and be home with Greta. The wine and the fatigue of the long walk had drowned his name. These women would reveal their bodies if he wanted, but never ask his name. That was an intimacy beyond them. Unless they became one . . . became Greta.

"Anyway," the tall one suddenly turned from her argument, "wher, ever it is, you can't go today. You need to go to bed, chéri."

"You're very kind."

Heavy prosperous butchers and commission merchants leaned on their frail tables, some alone, some with girls, and eyed the little man and his two women with the indifference of comfortably feeding cattle.

"I'm an old man. Is it not so?"

Both girls protested: he was ripe . . . *mûr,* not old. They would not ask his name, not so long as they were split into two half women. If they were whole, he would have a name and be home.

"I'm an old man," he repeated. "I always sleep alone."

The plump one said: "You have no wife?"

"I killed her," he said without surprise.

The tall one laughed aloud. *"Tiens! C'est rigolo!* He's Bluebeard."

The plump little one was impressed. *"C'est chouette, ça."*

He opened the silk purse in which he kept his gold separate from his other money, and gave each of them a *louis d'or.*

"But do you really know," asked the maternal blonde, "where you're going?"

"Monsieur François!" called the other.

From behind the bar came the slim young *gérant:* a silken mustache and a transparently thin nose. He looked hard at the girls, saw the expensive basketed bottle, and bowed respectfully to Jonathan.

"Tell us, Monsieur François," said the tall woman. "Where the devil is l'Ile d'Oléron?"

He considered a moment. "Near La Rochelle."

"How do you get there?"

"Why . . . Gare d'Orléans, Quai d'Orsay. At La Rochelle, there's a steamer."

As if they had earned their *louis d'or,* the girls got up and walked toward a table where two meaty peasants with faces red as their hands and vests larded by large-linked silver chains had just sat down.

From the bow of the round little steamer, where he stood amid crates and tackle, the white wind and the morning in his eyes, the waves mildly spanking the hull, Jonathan saw the medieval stones of the harbor sea-gate glide past, its great chains hoisted, and ahead the islands of Ré and Oléron: long lazy bars to the Atlantic. The gamut of chance bringing him here was a trail that ran downhill. He had been lost, he had been unable even to recall the name of his hotel, but by chance he had plenty of money in his pocket; by chance he had reached the right station, boarded the right train, spent the night in a hotel where he learned of the right early morning boat. That was the first meaning of meaning: to act as part of it, at least for a while humbly to be lost in it. Now the mists were breaking: he knew who he was, he knew where he was going. No longer the dank city forest, the saturnalia of meats, legumes, lusts, in the *Halles:* the misty trail had turned into this sun and

466

bright water. The gray coast of Oléron became green; the island securely embraced him: fishing smacks gently heaving by the quay, stone pier steps grooved by generations of rough shoes, the square of sedate salt-weathered buildings, drab cafés, grim churches, wagons a-rumble on cobbles and the thick unhurried citizens. His hired cart followed a street that soon was a road in a flat field. A distant spire commanding a cluster of farms, the dunes on the west horizon dully reverberating the sea, vineyards gnarled like regiments of ancient fauns, gave him the long-breathed island. —*This is the village!* A street of single-storied dwellings (swallows in low volleys ahead of the horse), a square with a granite church, a bake shop, a cheese shop, a somber café and the brick-and-slate *Mairie,* then again the single street. —*This is the house!*

Rebecca opened the door; her face showed no surprise. Like an old refrain in a new music was her resemblance to her father, and the room into which she showed him: oak-paneled walls, bare rafters, canopied bed, was so mixed with what he knew that even strangeness was not strange. He was completely lucid, now, in a world completely strange.

"Where is Jeff?"

Now her face showed surprise. "I told you in my telegram."

"I received no telegram."

"Then how are you here? Is it in the papers?"

"Where is Jeff, Rebecca?"

"They've taken him away."

The trail was steep and narrow as it ended. "What do you mean? Where is Marius?"

"Marius is dead."

He took that in. It did not surprise him, but it was steep nonetheless. "What happened?"

For answer she opened a door in the rear and led him through a narrow chamber with an iron cot to a third room with a long table, shelves of dishes and copperware, and a fireplace. In the corner was another bed, and through the windows and open door Jonathan saw trees in bud and heard the cooing of pigeons. The house was solid, mellow, more enduring than they within it. Why was she showing it to him? Rebecca stood near the hearth and pointed to the iron rod on which a water kettle hung above the cold ashes: the rod protruded.

"When he fell," she said quietly, "this struck him. That, and his heart, killed him." She faced him again. "If you didn't get my telegram, and it wasn't in the papers, how did you know?" He was silent. "Did Jeff get in touch with you? He said he wouldn't. That's why I sent the wire—to your hotel."

"When did you send it?"

"What day is today?"

He began to feel the storm in her. She did not know the day—nor did he. Only the present was real, but it held all that was real.

"Can we sit down?" he asked.

She glanced at the hearth, and walked quickly back through the narrow chamber to the front room; she sat in a straight chair near the canopied bed and faced him.

"Now tell me," he said.

"I still don't see—"

"I had no word from anyone; not that I know of. Won't you begin at the beginning?"

"They were arguing as usual. When he came, I think both of us were glad. It hadn't gone any better between us. Marius drank too much. That's usual, too. It didn't make him any noisier than lots of times."

"Can't you remember when it was?"

"Amélie wasn't here. She cooks for us. It must have been Sunday. What is today?" When he said nothing, she went on: "We'd finished supper—. I don't even know what the quarrel was about. I never listen. Marius had found the little trapdoor under the floor of the room I showed you, where the wine's kept. He brought out two bottles of brandy."

"That's all?"

"That's all, Mr. Hartt. . . . He was standing in front of the fireplace, quite a bit in front, sideways, talking at Jeff like always. Suddenly Jeff, who was still at the table with me drinking tea, jumped up and lunged at him. I don't even know if he hit him. Marius dodged and lost his balance. He seemed to spin, then he went down."

"Go on, please."

"He didn't get up and his eyes were staring. Jeff bent over. Jeff was perfectly calm, like he always is after a burst of temper. They never

468

last longer than a second, not with Jeff. He said: 'I've killed him!' I
didn't believe it."

"What did you do, Rebecca?"

"I didn't believe it. I didn't do a thing. I guess I just sat there. Jeff
went over to the cupboard, and put on his coat and hat. I asked him
where he was going. To the police, he said. I said: Don't be a fool.
He'll come to."

"You didn't look for yourself? to see if you could help?"

"No," she spoke calmly, "I didn't. Jeff seemed sure. When I saw he
was really going, I said: Don't tell them, except that there's been an
accident. I won't say you struck him."

"And you, Rebecca? While Jeff was gone?"

"No," she said. "I did nothing."

"Marius lay there? and you sat at the table?"

She met his eyes and was silent.

"You hadn't finished your tea, perhaps?"

She smiled at his irony. "The tea was cold by then. Jeff came back
with two gendarmes. They took him away."

"They arrested Jeff?"

"They took Marius away. They told us two not to leave. In case we
were wanted. There was no excitement."

"What did Jeff tell them?"

"How should I know? He said nothing to me. He went to bed in
the little room; that's where Marius had slept. Jeff's bed was in the
farther room, where it happened. I guess neither of us slept much.
Next morning, the *juge d'instruction* came with a secretary; we were
questioned, each of us alone. I don't know what Jeff told them."

"What did you tell them, Rebecca?"

She had not moved on her stiff chair; she stared as she spoke, like a
child in recitation who is intent on the words, not on their meaning:
"I said Marius was an old friend who had come to visit us, a friend of
us both . . . I said he drank too much and had a bad heart . . . I said
the truth: that I wasn't paying attention . . . I said there'd been an
argument, that they often argued and got excited. It seemed best to
keep in the framework of the facts, so—whatever Jeff told them, our
stories would fit. I knew Jeff wouldn't lie. I just didn't know how
much he'd fill in. That was right, wasn't it?"

"That was right."

"When they arrested him, I told him I was going to telegraph to you. He got angry. He said: 'Don't you dare!' Then he said something strange: 'Don't let us spoil it!'"

"Yes; that was strange."

"He seemed to be behaving as if it hadn't been an accident; as if it *had* to happen and *he* had done it. I wonder if that's what he told them."

Jonathan kept his eyes on Rebecca.

"So I telegraphed you at any rate."

"When neither of you slept, you didn't speak to him? you didn't find out what he was feeling? you didn't fear what he might do?"

"It was only the next morning I suspected his crazy ideas."

"How do you know he didn't sleep?"

"I heard him. The iron cot creaks."

"Is that all you heard?"

She stared at him. At last, expressionless, she said: "I heard him cry."

"You didn't go to comfort him?"

"No, I didn't."

"You're a very old woman, Rebecca. Or is it that you're a child? You didn't think he might need help?"

"I can't help anyone," she looked away.

"You let Marius come."

"He wanted to come."

"You didn't want it?"

She turned to him again: "I don't want anything. I'm sorry if I got your son into trouble. I didn't want that."

"Are you sure, Rebecca?"

She met his eyes proudly; only her thin mouth trembled.

He said at last, when she kept silent: "I'm going to find Jeff now. I want to ask you one more question."

"Go ahead."

"That satisfies you: the idea that it was all an accident?"

"Yes, it does."

"You feel no responsibility in creating what made the accident possible?"

"Everything's an accident. My meeting Jeff was an accident."

470

"You liked Marius. Don't you feel sorry that he's dead?"

"Perhaps some day I will. Now I feel nothing. He had a good time, while it lasted."

"You're a demon, Rebecca. There was a demon in your father. It wasn't he. It's all of you."

"I don't blame you for being angry. I hope you can help Jeff."

"Perhaps at last *you*'ve helped him. Perhaps, when he lay alone out there, and you didn't come from the next room, he saw you as you really are. That would cure any man."

She smiled, receiving his hard words, and her eyes became open. He knew his words were blows of anger . . . unjust. He could not say, I'm sorry.

"What are you going to do, Rebecca?"

She caught the softening of his mood and her eyes again hardened and shut him out. She sat silent. . . .

Jonathan walked up the long street. Faces peered from windows; women, mostly in black, passing him seemed to peer at him also from within shut houses. The sun was gone, a wet wind drilled the dust into little whirling columns, the swallows still swung low announcing rain. He must see his son, of course; it should not be difficult. What then, if there was trouble? Telegraph Reuben? Get the Embassy in line? The American Consul in La Rochelle? A competent French barrister? "Don't let us spoil it" . . . Jeff's strange words. He understood them. No Reuben to repeat the indignities visited on Louella Lake. No Embassy. No French lawyer. . . . As Jonathan turned in the square to the *Mairie,* the first gust of rain touched his face; it felt good. —I'll spoil nothing, son.

Monsieur le Maire received Jonathan in a dusty room dominated by a plaster head of Voltaire on an old littered bookcase. His cool, quick eyes contradicted the creaking old man's body in the linen coat; his sensitive mouth contradicted the grenadier's mustache. Jeff had not been moved to Saint-Pierre, the *chef-lieu* of the island; Jeff in fact was in the basement, he hoped in comfort, and of course Monsieur 'artt could see his son. Jonathan was uncertain if the Mayor's courteous bow was benevolent or malicious.

Through the barred window of the dim low-ceilinged basement, Jonathan saw a segment of an iron rim and a few spokes that he knew

471

converged, out of sight, into the hub of a wheel of a big peasant cart that converged, he knew, into the street, into the village life, into the world. . . . He and his son were at the bottom of the process! this was where his ambitions and his gifts had brought them. What was the meaning? to be aware of the process? to know each man at each moment was at a bottom . . . not an end but a beginning? Rain pounded and bounded from the stone pavement, but Jonathan did not notice.

When Jeff came in, he seemed to his father tinglingly clean, as if washed by a hard cold water.

"Dad, you look tired."

"I had a good sleep last night in La Rochelle."

"Did you manage to see the town?"

"It was dark when I got there and dawn when I left."

There were two chairs in the room across a much-worn table. Father and son sat down and faced each other.

Jeff said, "I'm sorry about this."

"Of course. But I don't think you need worry about the legal end of it. It was clearly an accident. The autopsy'll prove that. What did you tell them?"

"I tried to tell the truth."

"Which truth?"

"I struck the first blow, the only blow. It took Schmitt by surprise."

"The provocation was in what he said, in his very presence. They can be made to see that."

"I suppose so."

"Don't make it harder for yourself. Not in this way."

"That's the devil of it! It's all too easy. There are so many ways of sliding out of life. Hard labor to keep one facing it would be a relief."

"You don't need a French prison to give you the hard labor."

"Dad," Jeff moved his hand tenderly toward him on the table, "whatever happens, let it come."

"If you're afraid I'm pulling strings—your uncle Reuben, that kind of thing, nothing of that. All I ask is, don't shut me out. We're in this together."

Jeff smiled. "The best night's sleep I've had in a long time was here. And it's not because the cot's a luxury."

472

"I understand."

"No wonder men love violence. It pays. Why won't they admit it?"

"Marius loved it, and admitted it. He asked for it."

"I know. It's terrifying how easily my conscience could accommodate itself, if I let it."

"I'm not worried about that."

"I'll miss Marius. In a way I guess I loved him. When I find myself feeling as I might if he'd been killed by some engine, that's when I'm worried."

"Wasn't he killed by his own engine?"

"It was mine, too. And I mustn't forget it. If I think less of that than of getting out of jail, I'm lost."

"But inviting the jail is also a danger, because it's an escape;—a violence others are responsible for."

"Don't try to pull me back where I was, dad. You're being subtle with your sympathy, but I see through you. I can't possibly go back, dad, without dying: and the sign of not slipping back is not to give a damn what happens to me next."

"All right. Leave it to me. And don't be afraid that you're going to have it easy."

"It's obscene! the way we can't help thinking of ourselves—and of our dear ones, of course, who are part of us. Not for a moment, here, have we thought of Marius."

"The French law won't do that for you. Your being here is an irrelevance; don't make it a pretext."

"I gave the *juge d'instruction* the best case I could against me."

"I don't blame you for that, and it's probably done no harm; it's shown them that you're honest. In France, thank God, the fact that you were with a woman who isn't your wife will not be material evidence. They can dissociate ideas in this country; they won't try to amend the morals of the world in solving the technical problem of whether you're criminally liable for what happened, man to man, with a rival. But you, Jeff, must be as clear-headed as the French police. You feel a profound moral responsibility; you take the blame for the violence and what resulted, accident or not. But don't ask the crude mechanics of the law to take over what you must do next. That's violence too; and too damn easy."

473

"You're a clever lawyer, dad. The only trouble is, I know why you're arguing. So what you say doesn't convince."

"You're wrong! You think all I want is to get you out of here. You're wrong, Jeff! I want to get you out of a vicious circle. You've been too passive all along: in your work, in your marriage, in your bondage to Rebecca, in your relation to Marius. Even your striking him was a submission to *him;* it's what he wanted. We've talked of the need of action in the world, in order that ideals should not stink. We've both loved Marius for his romantic sense of that. Don't you see that your going to a French jail, because of your bad conscience, would be just the opposite of action? that it would be—yes, don't smile—a mere continuance of your marriage, of your relation with Rebecca?"

Slowly and softly, several times, Jeff struck the table with his fist. "What do you want me to do?"

Jonathan smiled. "I used to have answers to that. When you were a boy, I knew just what I wanted you to do, and to be. My love for you is growing up."

Jeff rose, took a few steps in the bare room, sat again opposite his father: "You're right, partly—about my going to prison being an easy way out for my sense of guilt; about its having an appeal, as submission. But there's something else. They're investigating us all. And what are they finding? Schmitt was an Anarchist, an enemy both of the bourgeoisie and of 'respectable' labor. I'm a *diplômé* of the Beaux Arts, the son of a rich man, the nephew of an ex-Minister. The cards are stacked in my favor. It smells bad."

"It's hard to swallow. But it's as irrelevant as it would be to condemn you because you were the Anarchist and Marius had the good connections."

Jeff's hands on the table curled and his mouth puckered. For a moment he was a boy near crying. His head lifted again and his eyes again met his father's. "I repeat, you're a good lawyer, sir."

"Don't say that! I'm not here to get you out of trouble. I swear it, Jeff. I told you my love for you is growing up. I'm here to get you into trouble, into the heart of it!—into your own."

"I'm weak, dad. Maybe weak men need violence and prisons."

"All the power in the world is weak, when it's blind. Look at my life."

474

Jeff's hand went further across the table, and clasped his father's: "It's always easier to die."

"And there are many ways of dying." Suddenly Frieda Memel was in Jonathan's presence. It was her son that was dead. It was he, not so long ago, who had hoped for her son's death. Was he rejoicing now? Was he acting the noble man with his own son, because Frieda's son was out of the way? Oh, whom could he speak to, as Jeff spoke to him? He was alone. "Jeff," he whispered, "I'm going to leave you now to see the men upstairs. The Mayor said the *juge d'instruction* was coming. I leave you with a promise. I'll not be a clever lawyer. I'll try to be honest. I'll keep one thing in mind to help me: that I'm guiltier, far guiltier than you, toward Marius Schmitt. Don't ask me to explain. There's no time for it now. But it's true, and it will keep me at least humble. I know: it's easier to feel humble, and guilty, than to be honest." He smiled. "In fact, I'm sure I'll make a mess of it. I've been a good lawyer so long."

"Good-by, dad," said Jeff.

Rebecca was standing in the yard back of the house, when she saw Jonathan. The rain had roused the earth to a shrill vibrance and the sun stood again in a dry sky; her hair, heightened to the color of ripe wheat, her heavy green blouse clinging to her breasts, and her lean face and flanks, made her part of the day's contrast of sun and wet spring soil; she seemed desirable to Jonathan, for the first time he understood the hunger of his son, he saw her naked in his son's arms and his son's ecstasy and anguish stirred in his own veins.

She did not move; when he was close, she asked: "Did you see him?"

"I saw him. I saw the authorities, too."

"Why don't they let him go?"

"You want him back?"

"He'll not come back to me!"

So she knew she was alone. Jonathan felt compassion and it angered him.

"You think you have lost both your men?"

"Yes," she said.

"You'll find a couple of others."

475

She gazed at him patiently.

"There'll always be two," he said. "There'll always have to be two."

"Why do you say that?"

"There are two of you."

"Why do you need to hurt me?"

"You're right. That's what hurt does. It makes one need to hurt. On and on, forever."

She plucked a long stalk of grass and put it in her mouth, and again gazed at him.

"I'm sorry," he said, "that I hurt you."

The Mayor had stood up when Jonathan came in, but the pale young man who sat beside him, the *juge d'instruction,* had not risen; Jonathan's quickened sense had recognized his long head of a fanatic, his cold eyes of ambition. He had tried to keep his promise to Jeff: not to plead, not to be clever. He had revealed himself simple and a little confused; spoken of the generosity and noble purpose of the dead man, many of whose ideas, he said, came from the reading of French authors, and of the deep ethical responsibility felt by his son. He had asked no questions, and when he left he wondered bitterly if he had been more clever than cleverness, more persuasive than persuasion. Now Rebecca walked to the garden wall on which stood a row of pigeon houses. He followed her. In front of one opening a young pigeon lay dying, its feathers ruffled and bloody, its throat gashed.

"Who did that?" he asked.

"That's what happens when one of the babies walks into the wrong house."

Jonathan saw the filth in the cotes, the pigeons cooing in their own excrement. —And if a neighbor's child comes in, they kill it.

"The dove of peace—" he said.

"Did you think only humans—?"

"Yes," he whispered.

They walked to the corner where the rabbits lived. Rebecca pulled an armful of long grass, not caring that it soiled her blouse and skirt, opened the screen door and fed them. —This girl, he insisted to himself, this misery-making child of all my life! But he could not hate her, he wanted to talk to her as to himself and the silence with her did not

476

disturb him. They went into the house, and Amélie placed food on the table: a *ragoût* of rabbit in wine and herbs (—Yesterday, perhaps she fed it with her hands), an arm-long loaf of golden-crusted bread, a bottle of claret without label, that was suave and deep as the best bordeaux. Suddenly, quietly, she asked:

"Aren't you going to tell me what he said?"

"He feels morally responsible. He's told them so. He wants nothing done to escape whatever happens. But he won't try to be a martyr."

"And what did you do?"

"I promised to follow his wishes."

"Suppose it suits these people, for some political reason, to send Jeff to prison? Do you want that?"

"Jeff has a wife and two children, and a mother whom his disgrace would wound in ways I can't imagine. And he's my son. And I'm responsible for this. What do you think?"

"Did he speak of them?"

"You mean of his wife? No."

She hesitated and her voice softened. "Did he speak of me?"

"I don't think your name was mentioned."

Her voice hardened: "If you've done nothing to help him, I think you're crazy."

"I tried to do nothing."

She stared at him; tears gradually glazed her eyes that kept on staring. "Just to please him?"

"To respect him, Rebecca. He's worthy of it now."

—Now that he's free of me? her eyes told him, and she looked away.

The afternoon sun was warm. She placed a chair for him in the corner of the yard so sheltered a fig tree clung to the wall. She brought a shawl for his legs and feet, and he waited with a book in his lap while she vanished in the house. So focused was his waiting that he dozed, hypnotized by the strong light of it; and each time he awoke there was the same presence: his son and Rebecca. He recalled an old day-dream when Jeff was a baby: that Evan would marry and have a daughter who would marry Jeff: a new dynasty, the Hartts and Cleeves, for the new America. Well, here it was, his dream come true, in this irony, this distortion. But what he thought he saw as real, this sterile tragedy of Jeff and Rebecca, strangely seemed as unreal as the old day-dream.

When it grew damp, he went into the house. Amélie had gone; Rebecca placed tea and *fromage du curé* on the table. He did not ask, as they sat down together, how she had spent the afternoon; she looked younger, as if the pain suffusing her drawn face were childlike.

"I'm going for a little walk," she said when they had silently eaten. "Do you want to come?"

A few hundred yards brought them to the end of the squat gray houses; they followed the road through a calm field fading into sky. Another hamlet with two spires nestled on the horizon like a little boat with sails lowered. The road turned, the poplars hid the hamlet, they stood and were alone on a meadow gently heaving in green wheat, near a wood already slumbrous beneath a sky that was still day. Larks rose vertical almost from their feet and burst in the farthest air like pelted flowers. From the wood's sleep came the first nightingale.

"Oléron is beautiful," he said.

"At a distance? Like the pigeons?"

He answered her childlike pain: "The world is beautiful. Have you ever thought what that means? It means that it's ours. Beauty is our recognition that we belong in it."

"I'm alone," she contradicted.

The world was empty, and her pain filled it. The world was beautiful and her pain irradiated; he knew the destructive selfishness of this girl beside him, but her pain gave her dignity. He had a strange thought: —God accepts her pain and fills the world with it! The God in whom he did not believe . . . whom he was beginning to know. . . .

She was smiling again, lightly: "Jeff told us Oléron is about the size and shape of Manhattan. That's a funny idea. Two islands in the sea."

"So different," he said.

"Are they different?" She did not look at him, standing beside him while the birdsong wove a fierce frail counterpoint of day and night.

"Man has made them different."

"No," she contradicted again. "Remember the poor pigeon. Perhaps the only difference is that we see the city closer."

"Rebecca, that's a keen thought, and a horrible one. Perhaps to make it less horrible, we must see even more close."

478

He looked at her in this moment between day and evening, between sky and sea and earth, that was none of them: that was a wound within them, revealing a reality beyond them. He looked at the girl's body, exact in its limits of flesh. Yet within her so much more than she! her father and his son, her mother and Frieda's son and Frieda . . . and himself, too. . . .

Rebecca turned around. "We'd better get home before it's dark."

When they were back in the room that opened on the street, Rebecca lit a lamp on the table.

There was a soft knock on the door; Jeff came in.

3

THE IMMENSE SHIP WAITED IN THE FAILING TWI-light. As the tender neared, the hull seemed to expand, the seven decks diapered in lights beneath the four tilted funnels swelled with black human midges, but the ship against the sea stood separate and steadfast. Now, behind the flank looming high, the bow and stern vanished, the decks far overhead were lost, and the little boat that carried them and the hundreds of other passengers from Cherbourg was dwarfed with the waves under the ship's huge wall. They climbed halfway up on the stair that seemed treacherously based on water, and as they passed the iron door were swallowed, consciousness overborne, the waves and the night abolished, in the electric day of the *Cosmopolis* on her first arrogant voyage.

The cabin, aft of midship in C deck, had two beds, not berths, a writing desk, armchairs, pictures on the walls, and a curtained window instead of portholes: the identity with a room in a luxurious metropolitan hotel was perfect. Their baggage disposed, they went to the boat deck and watched the coast of Europe dwindle and darken while the seagulls wheeled, less flesh than wind and sea. Only when a bird caught a bit of the ship's garbage and settled on a wave did it become carnal; then it rose again to foam and motion.

Jeff said: "The ship's too big. You have to remind yourself you're at sea. The sea can't get in, not even here on deck."

His father said: "You can feel the vibration. That'll remind you."

"There's a slight list."

"Yes, on the port side. What causes it, Jeff?"

"Probably," Jeff spoke from his greater experience at sea, "there's more coal in the starboard bunkers. It'll even itself up long before we reach New York."

"Of course."

Jonathan woke early and, his son still sleeping, dressed silently so as not to disturb him. Except for the sailors swabbing, the wide, long upper promenade deck, glass-enclosed, was deserted. Briskly he walked his measured mile and the great vessel stood aloof above the ocean. Astern, the sun burned from circular clouds kindling the ship's milky, turbulent wake. The sea was calm; morning paled as it spread from the sun's violence, but the *Cosmopolis* lived its own calm. Jeff was right: the sea was too remote upon this mighty vessel. Jonathan swam in the warmed sea water of the tiled pool on F deck and returned to the cabin. Jeff was still asleep; his immobility seemed disturbed and fragile after the sun and the sea and the ship. There was a chaos in men, Jonathan reflected, and all the orders of nature and mechanics were outside it. Men longed to escape into the comfortable orders. But the chaos was within them. Law also was a comfortable order, in which he had believed; a web of external relations, touching no one's inward chaos, woven by a preponderant class to keep men in its bounds. Hobbes had said it best: law is for the security of *bodies,* individual and social. The greatest lawyer he knew, Justice Holmes, tacitly admitted it in his book, *Common Law*. "Here are the rules, break them and you get punished": —Rules of *convenience* in the literal sense of the coming together of age-old social practice. Good drains are needed in a livable house: what if the plumbers, on that premise, posed as priests and prophets? It was true that ethics, the justice of individuals, the rights of social change, were acknowledged, but how minorly! how filtered out by the sieves of precedent! The prime concern of the law was always to remain within the "frame of the law," although outside the human heart waited. Jonathan went down alone to breakfast. Was the law not becoming more humane? Less than two centuries ago, poor men still went to the gallows for a score of crimes against property; today, even the capital punishment for murder was challenged. An ethical advance? or the result of the heightened pressure of the masses as they became organized, hence stronger? Soon the masses would be strong enough to illegalize child labor, to pass eight-hour laws, to demand compensation for accidents, for old age, perhaps for unemployment. But power pressure was the antithesis of ethical motive whose signature was love and its free giving. What difference if the law was good? Ah! the difference was crucial! Suppose machine production, after organizing the masses and giving them power because it needed them, developed its automatic methods to the point where it needed them less? Then the power of the people might again fade; the good laws that had derived from that power might again recede: human life might grow cheap again —cheaper than when a man was hanged for picking pockets.

The dining saloon was half full; men and women in elegant déshabille sat at their tables and the stewards brought them the riches of the earth. Jonathan studied the bill of fare; literally, he could eat what he chose! hot-house strawberries and peaches in rich cream, fresh fish, chops and steaks, hams from Westphalia, bacon from Canada, a dozen blends of tea and coffee. The glass-arched ceiling loftily crowned the soft-carpeted saloon, absorbing in its silence the tinkle of silver and crystal, the obsequious footfall of servants. A great double stair converged upon the immense portraits of Britain's King and Queen, then flowed apart again into arcaded balconies with murals. An opposite balcony held a grand piano and music-stands for a large orchestra. —This is what success has brought me. It too was outside; the chaos that loved and counted on success could not reach it! He had made enough money not to have to travel in the steerage; he had the strange sense now that if he were eating porridge from a tin plate in the hold, the part of him that spoke . . . that was beginning to speak . . . would change no syllable. The dream of his career: to sit as judge on a high bench, had not come true; but he was strangely sure that this success would also have been irrelevant—like the steerage.

At lunch they were assigned to their table with Father Peters, an Anglican priest from Oxford, and Mr. and Mrs. Sunderland who, before the fish, had informed them that they had spent the winter . . . just to give Europe a try . . . in Nice and far preferred the customs and climate (to say nothing of the folks) of Pasadena; that their eldest boy, Percy, was a genius making good as a chemist in Wilmington, Delaware, that their second, Harvey, was doing very well with an advertising agency in Chicago, and that their youngest, Wilmer, would soon be the sharpest legal mind anywhere. As to their girl, Eda, her church activities in their old home town in Kansas were something to inspire Father Peters. The priest said: "I'm sure of it!" and meant it. With the roast beef, their table-mates knew that Mr. and Mrs. Sunderland were heavy partisans of National Prohibition, and that the discovery of oil on their old Kansas farm which they had sold for five-hundred-thousand dollars, was God's reward of virtue.

Jonathan and Jeff had the steward place their steamer chairs in a quiet corner of the sun deck, sheltered by a life boat in the lee of the mild breeze. It was wonderfully warm for April, so warm that the passengers played shuffleboard, deck golf and deck tennis. On the promenade decks, they clustered and boasted, or leaned on the railing and looked for porpoises and whales. The library, whose uniform red books seemed part of the padded furniture, was almost deserted. In the smoking room, there was more smoke than room; more din than smoke: here Reuben (who ate at the Captain's table) held forth with his business cronies. Jeff lay in his steamer chair with a book he did not read. He seemed hidden in a deep fatigue which his father respected. But Jonathan was restless and for hours wandered fore and aft through the decks. From the stern, he saw the mighty vessel stand in the sky, a steel permanence that a glimpse of the sea turned into a flashing rocket. From the bow, he watched her dip her nose into a perpetual titanic flower of foam. She still listed faintly to port; —perhaps it's the current, he surmised. Half buried in an armchair of the library he found Father Peters, a prayer book and Donne's *Sermons* in his lap and a volume of William Morris in his hand, which he waved, inviting Jonathan to join him.

"Doesn't the fresh air tempt you, sir?"

"Another of our many modern illusions: fresh air. Not that I don't appreciate its genesis. There was always so much of it about, no man needed to make a cult of it. Now, with our cities of coal-dust and coal-gas, there's not enough. If my place were in the steerage, now, I'd be longing for the promenade deck. Just because I couldn't have it," the blue eyes of the dark little priest twinkled, "my longing would be worthwhile."

"The man in the steerage: might not his hunger for fresh air and good food for himself and his children take shapes you don't approve of? anger, resentment, dishonesty?"

"It might and it does. In the steerage also a man needs Grace."

"Have you been down there?"

Father Peters jumped up. "Let's go together!"

. . . The high rails here kept the sea invisible, except for the gate on either side whose slim crossbars brought the pounding waters frighteningly close. Children romped too near; on rugs and tackle,

483

men and women played cards or chess, slept, nursed babies. The steerage deck was a well full of sky, a-throb with the screws, a-heave with
the slow huge rise and fall of the helm. A sailor ladled soup from
a caldron into tin cups.

"They have more of the sea," said Jonathan.

"They have more of one another, hence of themselves," said the
priest.

"Aren't we finding excuses for our guilt, because we're first class?"

"And why should we not? Who can forgive his brother that's obdur-
ate with himself? Who can love that hates himself?"

"Is that good Christian doctrine?"

"Aye, the best! But understand it. Neither can we forgive **our**
brother till we know how sore is our own need of forgiveness."

Jonathan thought of his son.

The priest went on: "Wanting all else, the sense of sin must draw
us all together. To the worst criminal, the world is one and related
to himself at least in his fear of it. 'Tis a beginning, though 'poor."

"Father Peters, what are you saying! Sophistically defending the
criminal rich? Isn't there something in your Testament about the rich
man getting to heaven less easily than a camel through the eye of a
needle?"

The little priest laughed. "If the Lord couldn't pass a camel
through a needle's eye, He'd scarce have the skill to create the camel."

"But the poor—"

" 'Tis as miraculous for them to look with compassion on the rich.
And that too must be in the beginning of Socialism."

"That too?"

"Love, Mr. Hartt. Love, which is the same as charity and begins
at home, no matter how humble or how rich. And guilt, which is the
same as knowing our share in every unhappy life, and which draws us
together at least in the fear that is a beginning of health."

An old Russian seated on a donkey engine began to play the accordion; children clustered and danced around him, laughing when the
ship's heave upset them.

Jonathan was silent and amazed, hearing in the priest's words again
the words of Baruch Brande; and in both the meaning that had moved

his son since Marius died. He looked at the faces of the men and women, drinking their soup. In some he read escape from what was past, in others hope for what might lie ahead: anger, sorrow, pain, and happiness, were more articulate among them, more flowing. He looked at the swift waves through the dangerous gate: one solid substance because they were flowing together. The steerage passengers were one solid substance! more important, more real, than the separate passengers on the promenade decks, because they flowed together. He remembered the mob of the New York streets, in whom long years ago —despite their menace, because of their oneness—he had read hope. He was beginning to understand. These poor were unified also: that made them real, and both a hope and a danger.

"May I ask you a personal question?"

"I pray you would," said the priest. "No other questions are worth much."

Jonathan needed to speak of Jeff; he did not know how. He said: "Are you a Socialist, father?"

The priest smiled. "I try to be one. On the true foundations of love and guilt which alone can save the sorely needed economic revolution. 'Tis not easy. Ah! 'tis not easy. May I ask *you* a question?"

The old Russian put aside his accordion, wiped his nose on his fingers, his fingers on his greasy cap, and hungrily drank his soup, while the little dancers waited. At last Jonathan said: "Yes."

"Why are you so worried about your son, Mr. Hartt?"

"I want to talk of it. But it's not my secret."

"I ask you for no facts. It's the truth I see under the facts."

"Perhaps more clearly than I."

"If so, not because my sight is better. But I have names for what I see. Can a man see anything for which he lacks a name? The modern world has thrown the old names overboard; with all its eyesight it's blind."

"Name it."

The priest leaned on a ventilator and primed his pipe. A young Irishman with a whiskey face and red-rimmed eyes began to play a fiddle. The children, German, Italian, Jewish, Slav, forsook the old accordion and flocked to the fiddle.

485

Father Peters got his pipe going, then he held it in his hand till it went out. He said: "Christ saw Hell, you recall, before He rose to the Father."

"*Your* Christ—"

"Your *man,*" he interrupted, smiled, and went on more softly: "Your son has been seeing Hell, the common modern Hell, the frozen Ninth Circle of Dante, the Hell of the traitors. 'Tis very wonderful to watch the young man thawing . . . thawing. That hurts, you know. The frozen ones don't feel it; that's why they choose it."

"Choose Hell?"

"Aye. Every man's in Hell by his own choice. He likes Hell; he'd have a worse time out of it, *he's* sure—or rather, his lusts are sure. Those who can name Hell and choose it are lost. Those who see it and cannot name it are soon lost. Those who see it and name it are saved and rise. They are very few." The priest stopped and listened to the Irish fiddler who played a jig with merry false notes. "Your son looks as if he's learned to name it. God bless him."

"What do you mean?"

"This frozen Hell your son's seen and named, and that most of us are in, numbs the sense of guilt. Any man who feels no guilt is in it. To feel no guilt in this world, you see, is to be a traitor. 'Tis the most popular, the most respectable part of Hell, I think. How the frozen ones love it! This ship I think is in it."

The first class smoking room—low cream-colored ceiling ribbed in oak beams, paneled walls with paintings of Britain's famous naval victories, leather-topped tables with brass nails—was solid with smoke and human noise, the guttural belly-rumble of practical men talking business and swapping smutty stories. Jonathan stood in the door, looking for a place to sit.

"Come and join us," he heard Reuben. A steward swiftly slid a chair into the group of four men around a table.

Murtry, the New York banker, said: "I took six hundred miles in today's pool. Don't mind telling you I got the tip from Cairns. He told me this morning they're pushing the ship for all it's worth."

"That means we dock Tuesday," said Reuben.

"Then I'm catchin' the night train," said Louden, the English promoter.

"You forget, old chap," said Sir Archibald Carvies, proprietor of a big London newspaper, "this ship has the Marconi wireless. When they learn in New York you're landing Tuesday, they'll be there Monday."

"I've fixed that," Louden's rugose face wrinkled in an unpleasant smile. "The man I want won't be in Pittsburgh Monday. And I didn't say I was takin' the train to Pittsburgh."

All the men laughed; Jonathan told the steward to bring him a cup of coffee.

"Why don't you all get together?" asked Reuben. "In the long run, wouldn't it be more money?"

"I'm no Marathon runner," said Louden, "my heat's the hundred yard dash."

"Louden's right," said Sir Archibald. "The pace is getting too fast for the long runs. That was all right in the coal age. The gasoline engine, the aeroplane, aren't built for keeps."

"We bankers have to think different," said Murtry.

"Whom do you think you're foolin'?" Louden's scowl was pleasanter than his smile. "We'd have fewer panics if you bankers contracted and expanded credit at a quicker pace. Quick as hell." He glanced at the electric bracket on the wall through the smoke; "Suppose the alternatin' current in those lights was slow, what'd happen? It'd blink us all blind."

Murtry said: "There'll always be some investments that only show in the long run. Take a ship like this one. If it wasn't going to be good for thirty years—"

"Sure!" interrupted Louden, "sure, in thirty years, there'll still be the holders of common stock that the old tub *Cosmopolis* helps pay their four per cent. Do you call that *business*? *You* know damn well, long before this boat starts actually earnin' money, the men who financed it will have written it off and be financin' bigger, faster ships to crowd the *Cosmopolis* out.

Jonathan broke a lump of sugar in half and dropped the half in his cup. Murtry's bland, blond face, benign as a baby's—he had not seen it for years, all the years since Murtry, then a crusading young economist, worked for the Civic Committee. He had come a long way in his "long run" from that crusading spirit. Jonathan wondered if Murtry remembered him. Feeling his silence conspicuous, he said:

"I'll settle for some of that safe common stock on the Cosmopolis. . . ."

They smiled at Jonathan. "She's safe enough," growled Louden. "Too damn safe, with her unsinkable double-skin hull. The truth is," he turned to the others, "a boat like this would be better business if she went down."

"So they'd have to build another?" Reuben nodded.

"To keep the credit moving? Banks, insurance companies, shipyards?" Murtry nodded.

Carvies said: "It would be all right if she could go down—without loss of public confidence."

"Or loss of life?" Jonathan smiled.

"Public confidence," Carvies ignored him, "is needed to keep the credit going."

"Yes," said Murtry. "If ships or factories could just disappear without scaring the public and freezing their money—"

"There's a problem for *you*, Sir Archibald," said Reuben.

"I think I know how it might be done." Jonathan sipped his coffee. For the first time, they really looked at him.

"War," said Jonathan.

"War?" They were not sure if the newcomer was pulling their legs.

"You gentlemen want industrial destruction on a large scale to speed up production—or rather the financing of it; without loss of public confidence. War's your answer. While it's on, there's no doubt of production *and* destruction. When it's over, the winner produces because he's won and must safeguard his winnings; the defeated starts producing as soon as he can because he's lost and must get his revenge. Isn't that what happened in France after 1870?"

They were a little uncomfortable, and Reuben a little ashamed: perhaps it had been a mistake to introduce his brother to these top men. Louden seemed angry, as if he were tempted by such sweet fantasy.

"Rot, sir!" he said. "You know as well as we do, war's out of the question. . . . I don't say border wars against inferior peoples—"

"What's this? what's this?" piped a high voice and they all looked

488

up at Hamilton Howland Sears, Sir Archibald's great American rival. Next to Sears, nearly as tall, stood a young woman, her superb body lashed in an informal dress of pure white wool.

"Won't you join us?" The men jumped up. The impeccable steward was already at hand with two more chairs around the table.

"Miss Daphne Comfort," Sears said, after the introductions, "has a great future in the motion pictures. I couldn't help overhearing you gentlemen. I wouldn't put war in the impossible class. After all," he chuckled, "*I* made one myself, not so many years ago."

"Spain was scarcely a great power," said Murtry.

Reuben added: "We were talking of war between the great civilized nations. Not some brawl in Africa or Asia."

Everyone nodded. Sears said: "What if one of the powers tried to take over one of our backward backyards—Mexico, for instance?"

"Europe wouldn't dare," Sir Archibald smiled.

"They've all got colonies enough," said Murtry.

"Does Germany think she has colonies enough?"

"She's making so damn much in trade," growled Louden, "she won't be that foolish."

"Well," said Sears. "How about us? Sooner or later, won't *we* have to take over Mexico?"

"With a ship or two and a regiment of marines?" said Carvies. "That's not what you'd call war." He turned gallantly to Miss Comfort. "What does the lady think?"

Her smile did not appear to move Miss Comfort's perfect features. "Do I have to think?" she said; and they all laughed.

Jonathan thought: —At this table sit three members of the old Civic Committee who were going to reform New York . . . Murtry and Sears and I . . . The thought was not agreeable. Sears was telling them about the new business in Hollywood, a town near Los Angeles.

"We're going to make pictures for the whole world. You ought to come and see it, Carvies. It's going to be news."

"Then why *are* you telling *me?*"

"I'm not only a newspaper man; I'm also an investor."

Under cover of the talk and the smoke, Jonathan slipped away. It was time to find Jeff. Looking for a stair to the sun deck (the vast ship's geography still confused him) he came to the great hall, larger than any hotel lobby. Innumerable chairs of innumerable shapes and stuffs and colors faced every way or clustered in small arbitrary groups that looked as if they might fly apart. The chairs were fat, comfortable, and so substantial that many would be hard to move. But there was a restless separateness about them; however close, they clashed and summed to chaos, and the glittering glass roof held them flimsily together. The few passengers were lost in them; overwhelmed in the chaos of hues and shapes, they appeared isolate, insulate from each other. —I must be seeing with Jeff's eyes! Jonathan knew what his son thought of the "bad taste" of the ship.

That evening, they again walked on the boat deck. It was considerably cooler than it had been the night before, and they had the open deck to themselves.

"You'd think," Jeff said, "it would get warmer as we go south."

"Any weather is possible almost anywhere. They say it is sometimes cool on the Amazon and hot in the Arctic."

They leaned on a rail between two lifeboats, dizzily high above the sea. The whole length of the ship tremored faintly in its immobility; the sea was a skin of tension, cool and exquisitely molded upon the curve of the earth.

"Jeff," said his father at last, "tell me if you know. Are you free?"

The young man held his silence; this was his father's first question since he had returned to the house in Oléron. At last: "You mean free from Rebecca?"

"Yes."

"Yes," he answered.

The wind was cold in their faces. Jonathan saw the sky, its blue blurred with stars; the sea had changed, it lay languid, its huge val vular swells stiffened as if freezing.

Jeff went on: "I'm free—and I'm closer."

Jonathan understood: no need to say it.

"You loved her father, didn't you, dad?"

"Not enough to help him."

"No one can help anyone."

"I don't believe it."

Jeff shivered and smiled. "It's cold! The universe is absolute zero. That's a pretty good argument, seems to me, against God. If you're

490

a pantheist, then most of your God is cold as absolute zero. If you're a deist, then your God who made the universe can't warm it."

"Except where He strikes man," Jonathan smiled too. "Then up goes the thermometer to ninety-eight degrees."

Jeff laughed. " 'Strikes' is good. Dad, do you believe in God?"

". . . I don't believe in belief."

"That's an evasion."

"Into reality," said the father. "Which reminds me: it's too cold here. You're not dressed for it. We'd better go down."

"Don't start nursing me, dad. Answer me."

"Knowledge is what is needed, Jeff. Not belief. Belief goes wrong!"

Next morning the sun blazed from a cold cloudless sky on the great heaving oval of the sea. Those of the fourteen-hundred passengers who came on deck spoke of the cold; from the steerage where it was always hot, they climbed the steep gangway and the cold smote them; on the promenade decks it made them gay and zestful. The wise stewards, recruited from older steamers, explained about the ice fields that the April sun pried loose, the fragments drifting south toward the ship lanes but never near enough to be seen. "Can't we see an iceberg?" The passengers were disappointed. It was Sunday; divine services in the great hall and the second class library were crowded. The luxurious, omnipotent ship speeding for a record to New York gave the worshippers much to be thankful for, but the pastors preaching humility sounded unreal, the hymns (especially the classic one: *For Those in Peril on the Sea*) sounded hollow. After prayers, fur coats and heavy sweaters bloomed on the wide decks; the passengers were impatient for lunch, for deck games again, for their drinks when smoking rooms and sun parlors were again open. The twenty-four hour run, posted at noon, was better than the day before; now they were sure to dock on Tuesday; the triumphal voyage, barely begun, was nearly over. Even the steerage shared the victory of the warm ship scything the sea, abolishing the cold. But subtly a pathos suffused the men and women: a regret that the victory of speed meant the defeat of time, the too swift death of the truce, between shore and shore, from land worries and land duties. There were sudden, illicit embraces in cabins and dark nooks, exchanges of secrets between sea friends who had been land strangers and would soon be strangers again, sea promises that the shore would erase.

It was too cold for his deck chair; Jeff sat with his father in the crowded Louis Quinze salon while the little orchestra played Offenbach and Délibes. The music, the creamy-gold walls, the hot-house flowers in cloisonnée boxes under the pale silk curtains, the stewards in knee breeches and silver buckles serving the French pastry and the aromatic tea from China, wove a vague self-erotic trance. From below came shreds of a vociferous "sing-song" arranged by a minister in the second class. *Onward Christian Soldiers* disturbed the plush first class music. Jeff smiled at his father:

"How we love ourselves! And in how many ways!"

Jonathan was in no hurry. The night before, true words between them had begun; they would go on . . . no hurry.

The Captain's dinner was put forward. (Monday, the first and second classes would be packing trunks, filling out U. S. Customs declarations.) Prohibition reigned even tonight at the Hartts' table; the priest who liked his burgundy, Jonathan and Jeff who preferred bordeaux, had respected the virtue of Mr. and Mrs. Sunderland which the Lord had so spectacularly rewarded. But all around them champagne corks punctuated, with the sparking of snappers, the rustle of elaborate paper hats, the strains of the orchestra, the chatter and the laughter. The climax was the dessert: each individual portion of ice cream was a model of the *S. S. Cosmopolis,* the hull chocolate, the decks vanilla, the ventilators and smoke stacks mocha and peppermint, the rigging spun sugar, the lifeboats marzipan. Mr. and Mrs. Sunderland, having consumed each course with zest, attacked this final dish with passion (both of them were tremendous eaters). Mr. Sunderland dismantled and devoured the superstructures first, Mrs. Sunderland gored the hull so that her ship toppled before it could melt. Father Peters smiled at them and said: "Save the lifeboats to the last."

The three men together wandered through the crowded public rooms, looking in vain for a place to drink their after-dinner coffee with cognac. In the great hall, a prima donna from La Scala sang Puccini. —How hard her voice, how soft the music! Both father and son were thinking of the superiority of Greta. In the second-class library, a missionary on his way home from India staged another sing-song of hymns of thanksgiving. From the well of the steerage, the accordion, the fiddle, the stamp of the dancers' feet, lifted the music of the Russian, Irish, and Jewish folk upward toward the priest, the lawyer, the young man who felt that he had murdered. They watched from the deck; simultaneously, they turned toward the sea, ghastly pale and smooth beyond the ship's incandescence. The stars stirred in a sky without moon.

Jonathan wanted to ask his son: —Jeff, are you ready for New York? The presence of the priest impeded him. But again, Father Peters seemed to answer his thought. He said:

"If men lived in the open air instead of in houses, the confessional might not have been invented."

Jonathan wondered at the little man's organic closeness to his mood —to all the world! It was true: the sea and sky drew him, the folk music (also of the open, unlike the hymns and the Puccini) urged him. Jeff's nervousness seemed vaguely rebellious.

"I think I'll turn in and read," he said. "Cabin's the only quiet place on the ship tonight."

The priest placed a hand on his arm. "Books may be noisy too."

"I know what you mean," smiled Jeff. "They can keep a man from thinking his own thoughts. I promise I won't read."

"Promise me nothing, my friend! I don't deserve it."

When Jonathan came in, the cabin was dark. "Put on the lights," Jeff said at once. "I'm not asleep." His father saw him propped high on the pillows, not the position in which he slept.

"Have you been reading?"

"No."

He seemed to his father to have been simply waiting. Jonathan undressed and got into bed. "Do you want to sleep?"

"No."

"Then my bed light won't disturb you. I'll read a little."

"Leave on all the lights."

Through the too-warm, muffled cabin they felt only the vibration of the engines, heightened this last day as the ship sped over the almost waveless sea. It was very still. Jonathan ached with the impotence of his love to communicate with his son. In all the years' communications with Jeff . . . with Greta . . . his will had entered. False communions.

493

Even in his friendship with Evan. This at least he had learned: to be still now, rather than let will enter. He thought of Frieda, of Louella Lake: there his will had not entered, yet there too disaster . . . Could love's strength irradiate simply by being? No! action was needed for the life of love; but action needed method, and he had no method. He put down his book and looked at his son. Jeff was looking at him, and their whole life was present in the cabin. He touched the margin of a truth: Action was given, it was one's life and destiny, one could not will it; but when life's action was accepted and loved, then will was needed, and was good, in order to enact it. When will became part of love's acceptance, then indeed the lives of all men, humble and great, were equal. He touched his fringe of a truth, he could not grasp it. He thought of Baruch Brande and of Father Peters, beneath whose differences, he knew, there was accord in this.

"The trip has been good, Jeff. Good. I'm sure."

Jeff answered: "Rebecca is terribly alone."

"Yes."

"It's as if I'd left her in hell."

"Yes."

"I suppose you'd say I must accept that too."

Jonathan felt: —Her solitude is in you, you have taken it. How this helps her, how this heals you, are mysteries I do not understand. But you will never again harm one another. Jonathan said nothing.

The engines were the silent cabin's breath. Suddenly they felt a heave delicate as the touch of the silken quilts on their beds; then a faint flurry, at once subsiding. Then the vibration, the ship's constant breathing, stopped.

"We've stopped," Jeff said.

Jonathan got out of bed, put on his bathrobe and slippers and went into the corridor. Two stewards were quietly talking near the exit.

"What's happened?" he asked. "We seem to have stopped."

"Nothing much, sir, I'm sure."

"Have you been on deck?"

"Mighty cold up there, sir," the steward smiled.

"Nothing to worry about, sir," said the other.

Jonathan went back to his cabin.

Jeff, now with a book in his hand, looked up: "We may have

494

snapped the blade of a propeller. That would explain the whirr, and our stopping. It'll slow us up, of course. There goes our record." He returned to his page.

Jonathan went back to bed. Stewards and passengers whispered in the passage. Jonathan got up again and began to dress.

"Where are you going, dad?"

"I'm not as experienced a sailor as you. I'm curious. I'm going to have a look."

"Dress warm."

"I'll be right back."

On the glass-enclosed promenade, a few men and women were peering through the windows. There was nothing to see. Jonathan climbed to the boat deck and stood on the rail between two lifeboats where he and Jeff had talked the night before. The sky was a spangle of stars, the sea was silent. A petty officer came up and drew the canvas covers from the boats. Jonathan wanted to speak to him; then he saw the phosphorescent foam where the ship's hull cut the water: they were moving again. He went down the gangway: there was something strange about its relation to his feet, its effect on his balance. He looked in at the smoking room.

"We're going again," said a man at the table nearest the door, snapping down a card.

"It *was* an iceberg," insisted the man standing opposite. "I tell you, I saw it off that deck." He pointed to starboard.

"Must have scraped off some of our new paint."

They all laughed. A man wearing a cap and overcoat came up. "We're the ones who did the scraping. The forward deck's full of ice."

They laughed at him.

"See this?" He showed a chunk of opaque ice. "Now do you believe .it?"

"Just what I need," said the first man, "for my highball."

"Don't do that," said his partner. "If it's really from an iceberg it's salt; it'll spoil your drink."

"Going to keep it as a memento?"

"How are you going to stop it from melting?"

"Say! if there's ice on the forward deck, how about a snowball match tomorrow before breakfast, instead of our medicine ball?"

495

"It's a date."

On deck, an elderly woman rushed toward Jonathan. "Why have we stopped in the middle of the ocean?"

"We're moving again."

"No."

"I assure you, madam, we're moving again. The sea is so calm—"

A young woman joined them. "Come to bed, mama. I've heard what it was. A man jumped overboard from the steerage. And they stopped the whole ship to save him!"

"How absurd!" exclaimed the old lady.

"Those poor people are always causing trouble," said the daughter, and Jonathan walked away.

On the steep stair from A to B deck, again he noted a subtle displacement of his balance. The steps with rubber corrugated treads braced in brass told nothing. But his feet did not rest flat on them, they must be tilting upward. What could that mean, except that the ship was tilting downward toward the bow? What could that mean? a load of ice on the deck? If they'd really scraped an iceberg, it was miles astern far out of sight by now. Probably they'd dock Wednesday, not Tuesday.

Jonathan felt too wide awake for sleep. He recalled a book he wanted. The library was deserted, but the steward stood at a desk making notes on a pad.

"Yes, sir?"

"Is it too late to draw a book?"

"It's after hours, sir. But I'll be glad to oblige you."

—For a bigger tip. "Do you know, steward, they say we scraped an iceberg."

"Indeed, sir? I hope we didn't 'arm it, sir." He laughed. "What was the book, sir?"

"*Governments and Parties in Continental Europe* by Abbott Lawrence Lowell."

The steward dubiously opened a glass case; found the red-bound volume.

"I suppose you don't have much demand for books like this?"

"No, sir. Most people, what they likes most is romance and murder. These 'eavy books kind o' steady the shelves, sir." He laughed again.

"Ballast?"

"You might put it that way, sir."

Jeff had turned off his bed lamp again and lay as he had been before, his eyes open. He asked no question of his father. About to say, "We seem to have scraped an iceberg," suddenly Jonathan recalled his dream in Paris. He said nothing; took off his clothes and got back into bed. His encounter with the law in France had made him realize how little he knew of democratic procedure in Europe, except England, of course. Britain's government was far more flexible than the rigid American system. Perhaps France, too? —We have more Hamilton than Jefferson. He had forgotten his dream, as he opened the volume. . . . Some one was pounding at doors; the noise and the voice came nearer. A fist struck at their cabin.

"All passengers on deck!" The voice was too quiet to awake a sound sleeper. "Put on your lifebelts."

Jeff sat up in bed. "What damned rot!"

Far away below, a hissing, a muffled roar.

"Do you hear that?" said Jonathan.

"They're letting off steam."

"We've stopped again."

"So we have to let off steam. You've heard it a thousand times when a locomotive stops at a station."

"This is no station, Jeff."

"I suppose there's *some* trouble. What good will it do to tack on those clumsy lifebelts and go up to freeze?"

Jonathan was still in bed. "We have to obey orders."

"I call it a damn nuisance."

Doors were opening as they passed down the corridor. Women appeared in furs over wrappers, men in overcoats and sweaters over pyjamas. Voices were gay and a little high; a lark even so late was still a lark. Through a shut door a voice urged, a voice replied: "Catch me leaving my warm blankets!" The lifebelts caused merriment. "How do you put 'em on?" "Ever been in an insane asylum? Just like a straitjacket." Behind a shut door, a woman shouted: "It won't open!" Two men heaved shoulders against it, the door held. A third reached for the fire axe on the wall and crashed a panel. A steward rushed up. "You might have called me, sir! You'll have to pay for this, sir!"

497

On the main stairs, winding from many corridors, slowly without heat the stream of men and women thickened and flowed upward. The dress and the mood were motley: some were petulant, some laughing, some patiently wearing belts, some without belts, none afraid . . . "This ship can't *sink*," a woman flung at an officer who was weaving down against the current. Those near her laughed, he made no answer. In the great hall, the lights blazed, the orchestra was playing. A mate stood at the head of the stair and sent his sharp voice down: "Ladies, aft when you reach boat deck; men forward." Women locked arms with their husbands to show they had no intention of obeying. A second officer came up to the first. "Tell 'em when they get there. Not now. You'll confuse 'em." The first nodded and ran out on deck.

Now the stair visibly sloped, the list to port was wide, the orchestra started *The Merry Widow*. Deep in the well of the stairs, Jonathan heard a rush of feet. He looked over the rail and at the very bottom in the ghastly glare of the electric lights and the tile walls saw the heads and stripped, soiled bodies of half a dozen stokers. The passengers rustled and pressed upward, but leaning for a moment on the rail he heard: "Get back! Back to your shovels!" The men vanished. He thought he had heard one word: "Water."

The cold night smote them, less real than the ship. Sailors busy at the uncovered lifeboats, bringing up supplies, cranking the davits, were a spectacle remote like the stars. There were few words, no thought that could prevail against the deck's solidity. A rushing hiss turned them all forward: a rocket pierced the sky, a second, a third. . . . Rockets meant danger, they knew, and the boats were swinging out above the sea, but only the deck was real.

An officer ran through them: "Women and children down one stair to A deck!"

Jonathan and Jeff moved aft. A gate barred a ladder from below, where the second class milled darkly in the lights. A woman's head appeared at the gate, another . . . a petty officer ran to them.

"We want to get to the boats."

"Sorry, madams. Second class has its own boats."

"Steerage is being let into our boats. They're full."

"Very sorry, madams."

Speechless, their eyes on him, they climbed down again.

498

All the boats were gone, the women were gone.

"How many boats are there?" Jonathan spoke aloud.

"Not enough by half," said Father Peters suddenly beside them.

"They won't be needed," said Jeff.

"Then why," asked Jonathan, "have boats at all?"

From below, they heard the press and scuffle of bodies, the creak of the craft, the sharp report of ropes tautened, the orders, the cries, as the boats loaded. "Women and children only!" "We're only half full. Don't lower." "Any more women?" "We'll sink if you get in." "Lower away." Suddenly to the deck, naked of boats, where Jonathan stood with his son, the sky and the sea came close and were real. —Death is real? The ship was solid still to Jonathan; if death was real it was because death was within him. His life had made this death: the dim stars, the cold smile of the sea, now told him this, but were not the cause of this death. —I must die! Not Jeff! Father Peters was gone. Jonathan took his son's arm; Jeff without question let himself be guided.

They went aft uphill, but the ship stood motionless and sure. The band below was playing, as soon as it finished one selection it began another. From boats already launched came the plash of oars, the creak of oarlocks clear in the vast silence. The ship, a huge being, kept its secret; the ship was more solid and more sure than the night that would pass, than the sea forever gliding into darkness, than the ship's wound, whatever it was. But the imperious sense within Jonathan was growing: this, not the casual disaster, was the sure thing and was death.

They passed men in groups watching the groaning davits from which the boats had been lowered; their ears and eyes were unavailing against the hard kernel of their belief that they were safe: the wireless had long since sent out calls for help, the *Cosmopolis* could never sink, must stand forever afloat. Against this fortress of belief, their seeing and hearing broke, dazed to numbness. The slope of the deck deepened.

Jonathan, clasping his son's arm tightly, closed his eyes. It would be easy to sleep. —Perhaps I am sleeping. Through his shut eyelids, he saw the great ship erect upon the sea, the boats upon the sea, the musicians somewhere playing a gay music. —Perhaps I am dreaming. Jeff was close and he must open his eyes. The deck was empty. They walked uphill toward the stern. Steerage passengers gushed toward them. "Where are the boats?" On one side, the bare deck seemed to skim the still distant water, on the other side it skimmed the stars. The steerage passengers saw there were no boats and poured down the gangway toward the promenade, mingling with the men of the first class. Jonathan groped with Jeff to the high side. Boats, some loaded to the gunwales, some half empty, waited on the water. The abyss down to the sea joined dizzily the abyss up to the stars. They climbed down to the promenade deck where the lights blazed and the music was loud. Here they saw boats still a-swing, agape from the rail because of the list. A woman leaped, and fell into the water; a man leaped, and they saw him folded into a boat that almost capsized with his added weight. In the distance, far forward, they saw the bow kneel in the sea as if the great ship were praying.

"Come up!" Jonathan pushed his son again to the stair.

"The boat deck's empty."

"We'll see."

Against a wooden bunker where the instruments for shuffleboard and other deck games were kept at night, Reuben was crouched, his black coat buttoned to his throat, his face and his gray hair pallid. With both hands he clutched the bunker against the tilt of the deck, and his eyes, as if separate from his face, stared at them.

"Come with us," said Jonathan.

Reuben shook his head.

"Come with us," Jonathan quietly repeated. "There may be some collapsible boats."

"I'm staying," said Reuben.

"You may die if you stay."

"Who said I wanted to live?" Reuben softly answered, and turned his face away.

Now Jonathan knew his brother. All his life he had despised him, they had had no common word. Now knowledge of the need of death joined them! he and the vain successful man who needed to die, were brothers. The stars suddenly made him cold. There were no clouds and no moon, but the stars were thin and sparse . . . were too flimsy to cover the cold of interstellar blackness. The stars' pale vibrance was the texture of Reuben's face. Jonathan clutched Jeff's arm as if it only could warm him.

The boat deck was utterly deserted, the abyss of the stars had frightened everyone away. Father and son climbed down again to the upper promenade, it too was desert, the trap of the glass enclosure had also frightened everyone away. They went down to the open second promenade deck: here the band played and played, here stood the crowd of all the classes, dark in the blazing lights.

Close huddled, each man stood alone; there were a few women close to their men who stood alone beside them; there were no children, all of them doubtless were in the boats with their mothers. The music did not touch these huddled men and women, nothing touched them: they were safe from the stars and they were safe from the sea—and safe from one another. A few stirred their lips in prayers; a few tried light remarks, their neighbors did not hear them. Jonathan's heart broke because he could not love them; he too was alone. If they touched him —they who were his world and generation, it was to contempt. A mean world it had been, building a continent, spanning the seas, without love, without light. And he had fought it meanly: loveless and lightless men, the reformers, and he had been no better. Who had been better? Not the leaders. Only they who were so alien to their generation they could not even fight it. The desperate ones! Evan . . . not Evan's sleek, successful father. Marius and Jeff who had killed him . . . not Jeff's father. There was hate in his heart. —I cannot bear to hate them, I cannot bear to hate myself! Jeff stood beside him.

"Come," said Jonathan, and clutched his son's arm.

"And where do you think we are going?"

Was there a plan in his wild search from deck to slanting deck? He did not know, but Jeff came along, Jeff was docile.

Hard uphill they went aft on the broad deck. If the hate was unbearable, a lesion, what difference did it make, with death there? It was worse than death, this want of love: it was darker, more permanent, more terrible than death; it cast a longer shadow.

They stared down at the steerage well directly below, where he and Father Peters had talked. It was deserted too: a doll, a guitar, a bundle of clothes, had rolled together against the foot of the stair on the low side, the gate in the rail where the children had dangerously played was open. Perhaps some mothers and children had stepped out from it into boats, perhaps others, barred from the cabin boats, had stepped from it into the sea; now it swung wide, held open by the ship's slope. Jonathan drew his arm around Jeff's waist and stepped down to the steerage well on the stair no longer steep; it was hard not to fall backward. A rumble, a cavernous roar, rose from below and all the lights went out. In the sudden black, the stars trilled; the water, now visible below the rails, glistened. The lights went on again. Then a crashing of wood on steel: engines or boilers had broken from their harness. The lights went out again. His arm still hard about Jeff's waist, Jonathan groped on the deck, crept to the open gate. In the now permanent dark, they heard the cries of passengers above. Then Jonathan, his senses tuned to the dark, heard the oars of a lifeboat. It was close, it was coming closer. Now he saw it, the long slender shade upon the water; he saw the men at the oars, the men and women huddled to the gunwales. A hoarse voice:

"One more! We can take one more!"

"Only one—or we sink!" screamed another.

He could not see the boat, it was too close and the rail beyond the gate too high. Now, straight under them, he saw it. Jonathan stanced his feet on the rail, his free hand clutched the gate, and with the other arm he hurled Jeff forward. Jeff seemed to fly and struck the water. Jonathan leaned over. Two men and a woman reached from the boat and gathered him. The others, co-ordinate like the muscles of a body, heaved to the opposite side, and as his son rose from the waters, the boat dipped dangerously in the swell that lipped the gunwales: Jeff fell inside on many arms, and the boat righted.

There were tears in Jonathan's eyes, and he found that he was laughing. He thought of Reuben. —You made it clear to me. The death is in us. He thought of his son. —Live! And his love, suffusing from his son to his brother, flooded himself and all his world.

It was easy to climb back up the stairs, flattened by the ship's deepening slope forward. He crept on all fours, like a child. —Like a child, he said to himself. His knees were not stiff. He saw his old body seated in their bedroom, his knees hurt, but Greta was there, kneeling, drawing off his shoes, putting on his slippers. Jeff would see his mother; Greta would hear Jeff's voice. He saw Greta, vivid as a bird, Greta

502

young as Jeff. At the stair's head, he tried to get up and nearly fell on his face; the deck fell dangerously forward . . . He must reach the others! He got down on his knees, clutching the rail, and rung by rung worked his way down through the dark. He must reach the others. Somewhere the band still played, but not gay music. They knew now; the band played a hymn. At last he saw them, those who had not leaped. Death was in them, but they were not strong enough, these builders of continents, to bring death forth to themselves. They stood passive before their works and their works must kill them! They stood against each other in the dark. Now they knew; now they were together. And he was with them at last, where he belonged. Jeff lived, and he could love them. Each of them was like his son who was a coward, as was he, as were they. Jeff in passive violence had killed; so had he, so had they. Each of them was doomed and in the saving of one whom they loved, was saved. He loved his son; now that he had saved him, he was free: free to love them who were all sons of guilt together; free to love himself.

He touched a hand on the rail. Clutching the hand, he gave up the rail and lifted himself, feeling in the steep slope of the ship the closeness of another body. Now he stood without support, wedged with them all. Warmth crept over him, and peace. The deck rose. A shudder like a sorrow shook the ship, and the deck rose. As he fell with the others, he saw the huge helm high among stars, and heard the welcoming waters.

The End

1940–1946